Seize
the
Power

Alexandra Larson

ISBN: 979-8-9874887-5-1 (paperback)
ISBN: 979-8-9874887-4-4 (e-book)

100% Author Written
Cover Design: Seventhstar Art

First Edition: October 2024

Author Note

A full character list along with pronunciation is available in the back of the book. Please note there are spoilers in the character list which are set off with a "SPOILER" alert.

This novel contains graphic descriptions of bodily wounds, gore, physical and psychological torture, threats of sexual assault, and violence. There are depictions of PTSD-induced panic attacks and nightmares. One minor discussion of infertility.

The sexually explicit content includes BDSM elements (all of which are consensual).

Read to the end for instructions on receiving a bonus chapter from Book One: *Ascend from the Shadows* in an alternate POV.

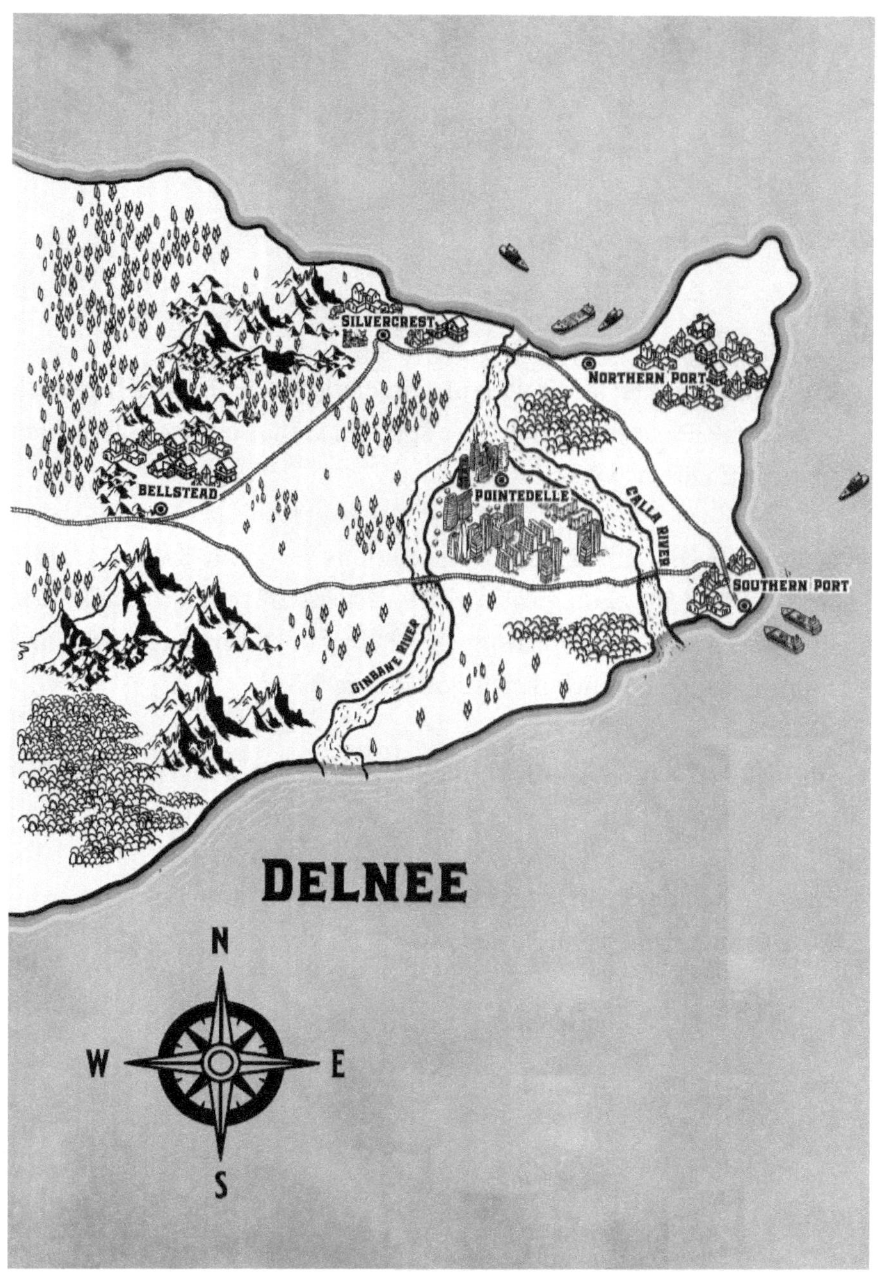

SILVERCREST
BELLSTEAD
POINTEDELLE
NORTHERN PORT
SOUTHERN PORT
CALLA RIVER
GINBANE RIVER
DELNEE
N
W
E
S

FAE PRISON
THE HOLLOW
MOLBRIDGE
WILLOW LAKE
PALAGUI CITY
PORT HAZELLE
MERBANY
CORAL BEACH

PALAGUI

Because thou hast the power & own'st the grace
To look through & behind this mask of me,
(Against which, years have beat thus blanchingly
With their rain!) and behold my Soul's true face…

{Excerpt from Sonnet XL}
Sonnets from the Portuguese
Elizabeth Barrett Browning

Recap: What Came Before

Amaya Mevson left her small-town life in Bellstead to earn a professional certification in the city of Pointedelle. On her first night, she was attacked by a draxis, a shadow demon creature, but saved by her soon-to-be best friend, Gwen Nueblots.

Gwen is a high priestess and the daughter of the captain of the high priestesses in the country of Delnee. High priestesses are one of the three fae types (high priestess, darkyra, and solisers). Gwen's family is part of the legacy high priestesses who were spared from eradication one hundred years ago when they pledged to only use their powers in military service for Delnee. Gwen revealed that the fae hadn't been wiped out, rather Delnee suppressed its citizens' fae powers and has been eliminating anyone who found out the truth. The draxis attack activated Amaya's fae high priestess power.

Gwen introduced Amaya to her high priestess friend Sloane Knight, and the three formed a fast friendship. Gwen and Sloane taught Amaya how to use her high priestess power.

Amaya was partnered with Rien Astora, the mayor's son, for her certification project. What started as a rocky relationship turned into a spicy duet as they worked together to help people who were about to get evicted from their homes.

As Amaya juggled high priestess training and working on her certification, more draxis kept popping up to interrupt her peace, along with the mysterious foreign ambassador and fae darkyra, Sebastian Renwick, who saved Amaya in one breath and threatened her and her friends' lives in the next.

Political alliances and backroom deals resulted in Sloane being kidnapped. After Amaya, Gwen, and Sebastian faced an enemy, Amaya realized she had both darkyra and high priestess powers.

In order to save Sloane, Amaya made a bargain with Sebastian to be his pretend fiancée in exchange for getting her safe passage to Palagui, where Sloane was being held.

In Palagui, Amaya waded through political uncertainty as she fought her attraction to Sebastian. The Queen of Palagui was ill, and her son, Xenos, was running the country in her stead. Except it was actually Sebastian running the country, since Xenos was more concerned with partying and females. Amaya teamed up with Gwen, Sebastian, Sebastian's soliser friend Nico, and a darkyra named Daria to break Sloane out of the research center.

Xenos was concerned about Amaya marrying into the royal family because, as a high priestess, she could challenge his claim to the crown. He demanded her powers be tested to determine if they were strong enough to sustain the crown. Amaya had to bind her darkyra powers so Xenos wouldn't find out that she had two powers. Xenos would be unable to sustain the crown as a male soliser, but he theorized he could if he also had high priest(ess) power.

The binding had side effects as Amaya's connection to her power was severed. Sebastian offered to help Amaya train her darkyra power so she could unbind them through the darkyra initiation process. She borrowed a part of his shadow because its presence helped her depression symptoms.

Sebastian revealed he was responsible for the deaths of his parental guardians and the disappearance of Adriana, the high priestess princess. Sebastian was intent on pushing away his feelings for Amaya to protect her, but that changed when Amaya proved she could control his shadow better than even he could.

After a steamy night out, Amaya and Sebastian were finally on the same page, and Sloane and Nico gave in to their feelings.

Amaya, Gwen, Sloane, Rien, and Daria fought a draxis in the city, but during the fight, Amaya recognized that the shadow tethering the draxis was Sebastian's shadow.

The Queen of Palagui told Amaya that Sebastian was her illegitimate son, conceived through a bargain with the Darkyra Deity.

Gwen's aunt, Caroline, convinced the girls that Sebastian needed to be stopped, but Amaya needed to go through darkyra initiation and unbind her powers if she wanted to defeat Sebastian. To unbind her powers, Amaya had to make a bargain with the Darkyra Deity. She promised to fulfill a task for the Deity on winter solstice.

The plan to corner Sebastian went awry when Amaya's own shadow stifled her attempt to kill him. Sebastian admitted that they were mates and they could not kill one another. He explained he was controlling the draxis to collect power for the dying queen, else Palagui's fae would lose their powers and the country would collapse.

Xenos interrupted Sebastian's explanations, but Amaya killed Xenos when his back was turned. Sebastian revealed he cannot accept the mating bond with her due to a bargain he made with the Darkyra Deity. Their reunion was cut short when Caroline demanded their arrests. Caroline's ward activated just as Amaya funneled Sebastian's power to sift them away. Within the astral field, a fire ball incapacitated Sebastian before they could escape. Daria betrayed Gwen by sifting her away in Amaya's time of need.

Nico broke his bargain with Sebastian by telling Sloane that she was his mate, not knowing that as they spoke, Amaya and Sebastian were being taken to the fae prison.

Chapter One picks up here.

Prologue

Sebastian – 112 years ago

Ice cubes rattled against the glass. My grip was so tight that tension radiated up my arm. I averted my eyes from the guests around the table. I needed to get it together. A royal dinner to celebrate Adriana's initiation was not the time to be losing control of my powers. My every action drew the eye of the courtiers, watching to see if I would shift into the devil right before their eyes.

Right now, I was barely keeping that from happening.

The ballroom was lavishly decorated for the celebration on the top floor of the forty-story building that held Palagui's court. The soft glow of the stringed lights around the outskirts of the room twinkled as the evening sky darkened the room through the floor-to-ceiling windows.

I took a deep breath, trying to control the power surging inside me.

Something was agitating my shadow. I should have taken more fae nettle before dinner to prevent this, but I'd upped my dosage so much over the last three months, I didn't want to embarrass my mother by being drowsy for this dinner. She already had enough reasons to be disappointed in me.

I could feel Adriana's concerned gaze and glanced up to the head of the table where she sat.

A female leaned over to whisper in Adriana's ear, but the courtier's eyes were on me as she smirked, as if she knew I was about to lose it.

The copper tang of blood filled my mouth, and I shuddered as the ghost of a memory flickered behind a screen I couldn't see through.

There was no holding back as the power swelled inside me. I made to push away, to murmur excuses and run to the hallway, but it wasn't just me shaking anymore.

Horrified, I looked around the room filled with widened eyes and shaking glasses. The ground trembled, and the building started swaying. Shadows spread through the room, swallowing the light in their cyclone.

Not again. Not like this.

I beelined to where Adriana and my mother were seated, but the crowd had started running and shrieking, trying to get away.

I pushed through them, my heart pounding. I needed to sift them to safety. That was what I did wrong the last time my power started the quake that killed my parents, that killed half of Merbany. Sifting away didn't take the wreckage with me. I'd saved myself and left them to die.

I wasn't going to make that mistake again.

People scrambled around me. The pit of darkness within my body threatened to erupt.

A sudden burst of power exploded through the ceiling, and shadows spread, blowing out the windows. Shards of glass scattered, and the sounds of the screaming courtiers filled the air.

My void eyes cut through the darkness, and I finally spot her. I sprinted to my mother lying on the ground. The shards of glass from the window stuck in her arms and blood dripped down her face.

A ring in my ears deafened me. She was speaking, but I couldn't hear what she was saying. She pointed franticly to the corner, and I realized she was telling me to find Adriana.

My gaze roamed over her quickly, but the cuts all seemed minor. She was a high priestess; she could heal herself once the glass shards were removed.

I ran to where she pointed to search for Adriana, but found no one.

I will find her, my shadow whispered. The humming built in my core as the shadows demanded their release. I clutched my temples.

This quake is your fault, I yelled at my shadow.

I grabbed my hair as the buzzing reverberated through my body. It was like being punched in the gut, and I fell to my knees, but that was when my shadow sensed her.

My shadow could always find her. He was drawn to whatever bond the Goddess weaved into our blood that made us family.

I jogged toward the windows. The tug of my power pulled me over the edge of the building. I didn't look back to the screaming courtiers. I needed to find Adriana. I sifted, following the guidance of my shadow.

Darkness as if in the depths of night, damp air, and chill pressed into me. I shivered from the familiarity of the Hollow's power.

My void eyes cut through the dark cave to make out my surroundings. Adriana laid on the stone ground, bound in shadows at the wrists and ankles.

Even though I knew she couldn't see, her face held no fear, only defiance, nostrils flared in anger as she glared.

The female courtier that had been whispering to Adriana laid dead on the ground beside her.

The Darkyra Deity stepped out of the shadows. Their thin, wraith-like body floated toward me. Behind them, a swirling black hole of emptiness formed that even my void eyes couldn't see through.

A portal.

"This is your chance," the Darkyra Deity said. "This is *our* chance. You will kill Adriana and take the crown, or I'll make sure she suffers for your disobedience."

I shook my head. "I can't hurt her," I pleaded with them, with my creator. Though half of my DNA came from them, I'd never consider them a parent.

They shook their head, brows turned inward in pity. "Darkness will reign, but it's your choice how painful this has to be for your sister."

Shadows, like knives, stabbed into my eyes, pouring into my mind and taking over my perception. Images filled my vision. Adriana with the queen's crown on her head, her angelic high priestess light trying to fight the darkness that surrounded her, but the power was too strong. Shadows overcame her, light dying in a wink, life draining from her eyes as her body was hollowed out, her skin yellowing and flaking until she was unrecognizable.

Her piercing cries, high-pitched and distorted, overtook my mind, until the shadows vanished and the hallucination lifted, leaving me staring down at my sister as tears streamed down her face.

"Bash," Adriana cried, tugging on her shadow bindings.

"Give yourself over to your shadow," the Deity said. "You need not be tortured by your emotions. Step into your full power and your soul will be severed from these pathetic feelings. Guilt and pain are for lesser creatures." They shook their head. "There will be none if you accept who you're meant to be."

The shadows floated around my shoulders, eager to please their creator, eager for me to give up my control, eager for destruction and death.

"Kill her," the Deity demanded with a blank face. They formed a shadow sword and handed it to me. Numbly, I grasped the hilt. Did I kill my sister to save her from suffering at the hand of an evil deity?

I lifted the sword.

Adriana blinked into the darkness, resigned to her fate. She nodded through her tears as if forgiving me for the betrayal before I'd even committed it.

My hand tightened around the hilt of the sword as my shadow coaxed my acceptance. His bloodlust pounded in my head. *Give over to me*, he said. *I'll make this so easy.*

I shoved my shadow and his wicked death promises away. This was Adriana. My sister. She was the only person who'd never looked at me with fear in her eyes. She was the only one who'd ever loved me and saw past the darkness that rotted me from the inside out. I couldn't do this. I'd kill myself before I'd harm her.

I crumbled to the ground, the shadow sword disappearing into mist, my knees bruising on the stone floor. "I can't do it. I won't do it. Take me instead. Just let her go."

The Darkyra Deity sighed. "You're my biggest disappointment. Your weakness has sentenced her to an eternity of agony."

"Bash!" Adriana screamed as the Deity flung her into the ripple of the portal. I lunged to grab her, but the portal disappeared, and with it, the tugging that had drawn me here snapped.

My shadow chanted insults and disgusted rage in my ears, and I shook my head harder, trying to control him, but stopped when I realized it was no use.

I hung my head, staring down at my hands but not seeing anything. *Please. Find her*, I begged my shadow. *If you and I are going to figure out how to work together, I need her back.*

My shadow and I fought constantly. His greed for power was overwhelming, but I'd promise to let him overpower me whenever he wanted if he brought Adriana home.

His answer was a low rumble. *She is gone.*

I slammed my fists into the cold stone, the Hollow shaking with the power erupting from my anguish.

The Darkyra Deity crossed the space and touched their cold hand to my shoulder. "Shadows will rise, and I will get what I want," they said before vanishing into the mist.

"No," I screamed into the void, into the darkness where the portal had been.

I tried to summon my power, to find a thread to follow, but the portal had closed. Adriana was gone. If my shadow hadn't confirmed it, that she was gone, I wouldn't have believed it.

You wouldn't feel this way if you let me out. Give me control, my shadow said, taunting me with the promise of freedom from my grief.

A murderous anger rumbled from my chest, but it broke into a sob as I collapsed onto the ground, running my hand along the spot where she'd been. I didn't deserve freedom from pain. I deserved to be ripped to shreds. I deserved to be tormented by her absence. I didn't even deserve the relief of death.

No, I said. *I'll never let you out. It's your fault I lost her. I'll never forgive you for this.*

I doubled down on my mental walls, locking my shadow in a prison stronger than I'd ever created.

I didn't know how long I'd laid there. Wishing with my entire being that I could have disappeared with her. That I could have disappeared instead of her.

When I had finally returned to court, only the top floor had been destroyed.

My mother stood, staring at the wreckage and the injured. Her eyes met mine and hardened when she realized Adriana wasn't by my side.

I walked toward her with my arm outstretched. "I'm so sor—"

But she didn't let me finish. She lifted the hem of her tattered dress and walked away.

Several hundred people had been killed from the windows shattering and the roof collapsing. The number of deaths I was responsible for was climbing, and I wasn't even an initiated darkyra yet.

Numbness overtook me as I realized I needed to bind my powers.

Adriana was gone.

These people were dead.

And it was all my shadow's fault.

It was all *my* fault.

Chapter One

Amaya

The cell I was locked in had no windows.

Four identical cement walls enclosed me. The buzz from the fluorescent light was whittling away at my sanity. Sporadic and uneven, the noise pierced my temples.

The tile on the floor must have been white at one point but was now dingy with permanent grime. The crevice where the wall met the floor had layers of dirt and debris caked in from decades of disregard, which also extended to the toilet in the corner.

Blood stained my dress. My blood, but also *his*. The pink gossamer was torn and burnt from the solisers who'd captured us. My neck felt hot and swollen, though I couldn't move to inspect my wounds with my arms cuffed behind my back.

I was stiff from being held in the same position. I tried to adjust, but there was no movement that eased the tension in my shoulders and neck, no position which gave me relief from the shooting pain in my muscles. My ankles were chained, the heavy metal tight around the tender, charred flesh.

How long had it been since Caroline betrayed us and demanded our arrests? Hours? Days? Weeks?

My high priestess light could have healed me, but there was only hollowness where my power used to reside.

A trickle of something dark seeped from under me, pooling.

I blinked. My hazy vision cleared enough to recognize it was my blood. I tried to stand but collapsed when a ripple of agony shredded through me, originating from my back. The skin was tight from burns. Whatever adrenaline had masked the full extent of the pain up until now failed me.

Tremors began in my core and shook my limbs. Cold, I was so cold. My pulse raced, no doubt making the blood loss worse.

Where was I? Was this hell? Was this torture my punishment for attempting to kill the person my power recognized as my mate?

"Sebastian?" I cried.

No one answered back.

I screamed his name. I screamed for the pain to stop. I screamed to drown out the whirring ring of the fluorescent light.

No one was coming. The pain continued. The light might have flickered, but it could have been my consciousness slipping away.

A vibration shook my leg. The image of a rat scurrying over me had me kicking my bare foot, and the chains around my ankles jangled.

The vibration didn't stop. I didn't bother to kick again. Didn't have the energy. The hum was comforting in a way. I let its presence lull me away from this place.

***

I woke. My body fully healed and unshackled. My dress in pristine condition.

Spreading my fingers and turning my palms, I inspected myself for wounds or scars but found no evidence of my burns.

When I stood, no pain lingered in my body. High priestess light and shadows pulsed within me, a renewed sense of power.

The fluorescent light ceased its buzz, and my room glowed with a soft, warm hue. The tiles had been washed, and everything sparkled.

A silver tray of food sat in the corner near the steel door. I sprang toward it. The bread was warm as I ripped into the crust with my teeth, swallowing around large chunks without chewing. I didn't know how long it'd been since I'd eaten, but I was ravenous. I gripped the cup of water with both hands and drank heartily to wash down the bread.

Except instead of the cool relief of water, the liquid I ingested burned my mouth like acid and blazed down my throat. I coughed and threw the cup across the floor. What I'd thought was water turned to black blood. The thick sludge splattered across the sparkling white floors and crawled up the walls, overtaking the lights.

The remaining bread in my hand turned to ash. The silver tray transformed into tiny bugs which scurried over me and through the room.

I flailed, trying to get away from the insects by crawling backward, but there were no walls. My void eyes faltered until utter darkness consumed me.

No walls. No ceilings. No floors.

No escape.

The immensity of the abyss crushed me. An endless void in all directions.

Tears clogged my throat as I opened my mouth to scream, but there was no sound.

Amaya. My name was chanted. *Amaya. Ah. Maya. Ah. Maya.*

I had no voice to answer it.

Chapter Two

Amaya

"Ah. Maya. Ah. Maya." A voice spoke in a taunting manner. "Time to wake up, prisoner."

Groggy and disoriented, I stirred. Shielding my eyes from the harsh light in my cell, I blinked away my clouded vision.

A guard crouched beside me. His face was round with a big, crooked nose, which seemed like it'd been in one too many fights, but that didn't concern me as much as his sleazy grin did.

Fear pulsed through me as he positioned himself in front of the door. Not that I could get out anyway, but mental alarm bells were ringing at the way he corralled me in.

Somehow reading my mind, he stood and took a step back, putting his hands up. "Easy there. You don't have to worry. I'm not like the other guards." His smile was far too delighted for me to believe that for a second, but he continued, "You can call me Kai."

"Get away from me," I said, but my voice was raspy and lacked the hostility I wanted to project.

He lowered his voice as if talking to a scared animal. "I brought you food. I know you must be hungry. You haven't eaten for days."

I only stared at him, grinding my teeth.

He reached into his pocket and slid a wrapped snack bar across the floor toward my feet.

My mouth salivated until I remembered what happened the last time I tried to eat. Eyes locked on the snack bar, I waited for it to turn into thousands of bugs.

"Come on now. You don't think I poisoned it, do you? It's wrapped. Snuck it in from the outside," he said. "I know you want to eat."

My gaze lifted to his face, and despite knowing better, I nodded.

"Good," he said. "I'm going to have to undo your cuffs then, unless you'd like me to feed you?" He laughed, taking a step forward and uncuffing my ankles. "Turn around and I'll undo the ones around your wrists."

I hesitated at first, but my hunger overruled my survival instincts, and I turned my wounded back toward him.

"Good," he said as he unsnapped the cuffs; the key rattled in the lock. His face was close to my shoulder. I could feel his breath on the wounds around my neck. "You know the other guards usually like to give the pretty prisoners an official welcome." His fingers were cold as they stroked down my arm and settled above the wounds on my wrists. "But I kept them all away from you. You should thank me."

The cuffs fell from my wrists, but I felt even more trapped. My shoulders slumped. Sharp tingling filled my muscles from the sudden return of blood flow.

Fight. I needed to fight. I wasn't going down this way, wasn't going to let him take what he was insinuating he wanted from me, but fear locked me in place. I bit my lip hard enough to taste blood, trying to summon my power, any power. It didn't even have to be fae power. I'd settle for some inner strength.

But my mind and my body were empty of both. Crippled by the empty void within me.

When I didn't respond, Kai's fingers dug into the burns on my wrists, and he pulled me up to my feet. I screamed as he jerked my shoulder hard enough it felt like it'd been dislodged. The wound on my back pulsed a hot agony through my body.

"I said, say thank you." His voice was hard, unyielding.

"Thank you!" Anything to get the pain to stop, to get his grip to loosen.

I wobbled on my feet, my legs unused to standing, and his hands turned gentle, steadying me

"Good. See?" Kai said. "I'm not anything like them. All I want is a little gratitude in return for my kindness."

I turned slowly, but kept my eyes lowered. A new sickness roiled in my stomach from the belittlement and humiliation of doing everything he asked without even being able to give him a snarky remark. I was pathetic, too weak, too beaten and broken by hunger and fear.

He put a finger under my chin and raised my face until I was looking up at him. "You'll learn to trust me or this isn't going to be very pleasant for you. There's no one else looking out for you."

I nodded because that seemed like the most appropriate response, and he put the snack bar into my hand. "Eat. I'll get you more if you behave when we go to the hose."

The hose? I didn't risk questioning him though, and instead scrambled to tear off the wrapping, devouring the bar in three quick bites. It barely satisfied the emptiness in my stomach.

"One more?" he asked and produced another.

I nodded eagerly, and he handed this one over as well, watching as I inhaled it.

"I have to put the cuffs back on your wrists to take you to the hose, but I brought gauze so they don't cut into your wounds," he said.

I clenched my hands into fists at my side, finding a spark of defiance at the thought of being re-cuffed.

His face fell into expressionlessness, and it was almost scarier than his razor-sharp smile. "Save your insolence for the other guards."

Maybe because he was offering to cover my wounds, I forced my fingers to unclench and did as I was bid, raising my hands.

"Good choice," he said and wrapped the worst of the wounds before refastening the cuffs. They no longer touched my skin, but from the red puckered marks on my inner elbows, I didn't think I needed the fae cuffs to block my power. They'd already pumped me full of the suppression. These cuffs were to underscore the futility of my resistance.

He pulled me toward the cell door. It buzzed opened for him, and with a tight hold on my arm, he dragged me into the hall.

The prison looked the same as my cell with cement walls and dingy tile. Numbered steel doors lined one side of the hall. Every ten cells were sectioned off into separate corridors and had a door between each that Kai unlocked with his handprint.

"I got you placed on the third floor because it's most convenient for me." He leaned in and whispered, "Less prying eyes down here if you know what I mean."

I swallowed, not knowing if that was good or bad.

"But," he continued with a flourish of his hand. "Most of the cells are ordered based on perceived strength of the prisoner's power. The most powerful at the top, furthest from the ground so they can't draw power from the darkness in the center of the world."

I stored that piece of information away, though I couldn't understand why Kai would tell me anything, why he'd feed me or do anything nice for me. My body tensed, bracing myself for the inevitability that this was all another hallucination.

"They've been trying to put you in general population," he said. "Can you believe that?" He hummed his disapproval, opening a door at the end of the corridor. "But you don't need to worry. You've got me keeping you safe. I won't let them put you with that riff-raff."

We stopped in front of an elevator, and I finally found the courage to ask, "What's the hose?"

"Oh, no need to fret. I'll make sure no one else is around." The elevator dinged, and he guided me into it. "The prison insists on not taking you to the med-room until we've hosed you down." He leaned in and winked. "Wouldn't want any contraband shadows on you."

If I don't leave now, they'll wash me away. I'll be back. I will always find you, a deep, familiar voice hummed through my head.

Sebastian? Was he here? Where was he? How could I hear him?

I looked around the elevator as if I'd find him standing beside me, and my gaze snagged on my feet. I stifled a gasp. Though I was standing still and the light above me was stationary, my shadow was bending while Kai's didn't move.

The elevator jerked and groaned as we ascended, and the fluorescent light buzzed with its shrill hum. My shadow ripped itself away from me. Or was it not my shadow at all?

Don't leave me, I pleaded.

I'll be back. I will always find you, it said, but it sounded like Sebastian's voice again.

A cold sweat broke out over my body as a nagging sensation tickled the back of my head. I wasn't remembering something. Like large pieces of my memory had been blocked or destroyed.

With a deep breath, I looked from the ground to Kai and finally summoned the nerve to ask, "What's the hose?"

Kai patted my arm. "You've lost a lot of blood. Shock can make you disoriented, but don't be afraid. I'm going to take care of you."

I nodded but furrowed my brow. My temples started aching as I strained to remember…something. Remember what, though?

Kai stared into my eyes with a toothy smile.

Don't worry. You can trust me. The words were in my brain, but I didn't know who said them.

Kai's lips hadn't moved at all.

Another hallucination?

Kai reached into his pocket and pulled out a hankey, wiping his nose as the elevator dinged and the doors opened.

Two guards stood on the other side and were about to move over to let us through when they did a double take at me.

"Taking her to the hose?" one asked. His lecherous gaze traced my body.

"Need help?" the other asked. His hand went to the buttons on his uniform and started undoing them. He flashed a strange tiny tattoo shown in the notch between his collarbones. A simple square with a diamond overlay.

I barely suppressed a shudder.

Kai grabbed my arm and positioned himself in front of me. "She's been marked for experiments. Pretty sure they're pumping her full of some kind of poison. I'm not risking my dick falling off, but if you want to, be my guest."

The guards curled their lips in disgust and gave us a wide berth. "Why do they always pick the hot ones for experiments?"

The other guard shook his head. "What a shame."

Kai dragged me past them. The two guards got into the elevator as we stopped outside a door labeled Contaminant Room.

"See?" he said. "I told you I'd protect you. Got to be extra careful with the ones who have that tattoo."

I had no idea what it meant.

We stepped inside a room with a drain in the middle of the floor. I shuffled forward, only then realizing I didn't have shoes, just thin sock-like slippers that slid on the slimy floor.

Kai positioned me over the drain and unlocked the cuffs at my wrists. "I'm sorry about having to do this, but it's the only way. Most guards would force you to take off your clothes, but"—he leaned forward, smiling—"I'm not like them."

My teeth began chattering as the air conditioning kicked on and my thin, ripped dress slipped off my shoulders.

His smile fell into a scowl. "What do you say?"

The burn of humiliation scalded me, catching light another flicker of rebellion. I wanted to scratch out his eyes, press my thumbs into the sockets until the soft gummy texture was shoved into the back of his head, but I had no strength. I closed my eyes before biting out the words he wanted to hear. "Thank you."

The sharp sting of a slap across my cheek had me stumbling back.

"That wasn't very convincing. It's almost like you're only saying it because you have to. Not because you want to," Kai said, his voice hard and face emotionless. "Want to try again?"

A sob threatened to escape, but I clamped it down. My legs wobbled, tremors shaking my entire body.

"Thank you, Kai," I said with as much gratitude as I could muster.

He harrumphed and turned toward a closet door at the far end of the room beside a flattened hose hanging on the wall.

The room was empty. There was nothing that I could use as a weapon. Unless I used the hose...to what? Strangle Kai? Then what? Run through the prison in a ripped dress and slipper socks, looking for an exit and hoping I didn't run into guards with that tattoo?

I had no power, no leverage, no hope.

Kai pulled on a white plastic jumpsuit from the closet, unwound the flat hose, and twisted the faucet, inflating the hose.

"This will work out better for you if you learn to respect me, but it's up to you how much you'd like to suffer," he said.

He flipped the plastic visor over his face and lifted the hose, pulling back the nozzle.

Water burst into me, but it wasn't pure water. There was something in it that made my body burn. Pain almost knocked me to my knees.

I groaned. Kai turned up the pressure and aimed the hose at my neck. The water shredded open the barely healed wounds.

I tried to block the stream, to cover my neck, but he only turned the pressure higher.

The water ran down my throat, my nose, into my lungs. I choked and coughed, while backing away, but there was nowhere to go as the water blared into me. I pressed myself into the corner of the room, but the stream didn't relent.

Kai was yelling something, but I couldn't hear over the sound of the water, over the sound of my own screams.

When the water ceased, I fell to the floor, curling up and squeezing my eyes shut.

Boots sloshed through puddles.

"Turn over," he said. "I need to get your back."

I shook my head. The burning water in my back wound would be unbearable.

Kai sighed. "I don't want to do this the hard way."

I didn't move. I couldn't move.

"Should I cuff you again? Do you want to be chained up?"

I couldn't make my muscles unlock.

A steel-toed boot slammed into my arm, then my stomach.

I shrieked, and my body jack-knifed, flipping onto my stomach to protect myself. Kai dug his boot into my shoulder, flattening me into the grimy tile.

My body wasn't listening to the demands of my brain to run, to hide, to fight.

Kai retreated across the room, and I tensed at the screech of the faucet, but there was no bracing myself against the stream of the hose.

Water blast into my back, shredding open my wound. I screamed as the flesh tore apart.

White spots flashed in my vision from the pain.

"If you continue to disobey me, you'll regret it," he said.

Despite his warning, a flash of instinct overpowered fear of his retribution.

I rolled and pushed on the heels of my hands, attempting to get up. To go where, I didn't know.

I blacked out before I could take my first step.

***

When I woke, I was lying on my stomach. I registered being on a medical bed, but I couldn't lift my head to look around the room. Couldn't move my arms or my legs.

"Hmm," a voice said, and I squinted to make out a figure in a lab coat standing near me. "Should have had this looked at when she first came in. It's going to be harder for me to clean now."

I winced as fingers inspected my back.

"The injections weren't taking on her," another voice answered. "Her body kept filtering them. We had to wait until her powers were sufficiently suppressed before moving her out of the cell."

"Hmm" was the only response.

The doctor crossed the room and searched in the cabinets. Satisfied, he sat down and scooted his chair toward me, rolling a tray of sharp instruments beside my face.

"I'll have to do this the old-fashioned way," the doctor said. "With fae power dying, I'm not wasting my healing power on a criminal."

He picked up a brown bottle, and I sucked in a breath as he poured a burning liquid over my back. It was enough of a diversion that I didn't see him pick up a scalpel, didn't even have a moment to prepare myself until the cold metal was slicing into my wound.

I couldn't hold in my scream.

"Can't you sedate her?"

"I've given her a sedation and paralyzing agent, but if the suppression doesn't work on her, I'm assuming the sedation isn't effective either. She isn't moving though, so that's good. There are ear plugs in the second drawer to the left."

The male grunted and crossed the room into my line of sight long enough for me to see he was in a guard uniform, but he wasn't Kai.

The doctor patted his pocket, put in earphones, and tapped around on his phone. I could hear the tinny sound of music playing in his earbuds between my anguished groans.

The doctor hummed a song to himself and continued to mutilate my back. I could feel every slice of the scalpel, every scrape along the tender, aching wound as he cut out the infection.

I prayed for the pain to take me away again, for the hunger and weakness to move me into the bliss of unconsciousness, but though my body was heavy and immovable, I didn't faint.

Every second that ticked by felt like an eternity. This *was* hell.

Until finally, the sharp, blaring agony of the doctor hacking away at my skin receded.

The soft press of a bandage covered my back, and the doctor tied a hospital gown at the nape of my neck.

"There we go," the doctor said. "Give her about thirty minutes and she'll be able to walk back to her room. I'll need to check her wounds every day until she's healed."

The guard grunted his acknowledgement.

The doctor threw his bloodied instruments on the tray and wheeled it out of the room.

Slowly, feeling prickled back, first my toes and fingers, then my arms and legs, and the numbness receded.

If I stayed completely still, maybe the guard wouldn't notice, and I could regain my strength and surprise attack him.

And then...? I didn't even have the sock-like slippers anymore.

My shoddy plan was foiled before I could see it through when the guard said, "You're twitching. You're good enough to walk. Let's go."

A hard grip on my arm pulled me up. Not all feeling had returned, and I wobbled. My limbs not cooperating.

The guard didn't care.

We left the med-room, and I tripped over myself as he dragged me down the hall. He mumbled something about taking the long way and going to the top floor, but I wasn't fully in my body, my mind still felt fractured.

As we entered the next corridor, tingling and popping flowed through me, different from the tingles of numbness. An ache throbbed in my chest, and my heart squeezed in desperation. I was filled with the memory of his touch, the smell of sandalwood, the sound of his voice, the sight of his blue eyes.

"Sebastian?"

A familiar flutter of power skated over my skin.

The guard's grip began to bruise. He huffed a laugh, completely oblivious to the presence of Sebastian's power. "You've really lost your mind, haven't you?"

I tried to resist as he yanked me down the hall, but my limbs weren't responding.

"Sebastian?" I yelled louder, frantic.

That was his power. I know it. I felt it. I'd recognize his power anywhere. I couldn't remember much, but I remembered he was *mine.*

The guard pressed me into the wall, his forearm against my neck. "Your mate is gone. You think we'd risk keeping him and his erratic shadow alive?"

My jaw quivered. I shook my head. He was lying. He had to be lying.

"He was practically dead the night he came in," the guard said. A sick amusement lit his eyes. He put his face close enough to mine that I could see the scar above his eyebrow.

I pressed my lips together, refusing to allow the tears to surface. "You're lying."

"You must be real proud of yourself for killing the Prince." Spittle flew onto my face. "But you're nothing but some kind of disgusting darkyra hybrid."

The guard pressed harder into my windpipe, and I coughed as he said, "Some guards think every prisoner is capable of reform. That our fire can purify you, burn away all of your evil darkness."

His lip curled in disgust. "Unfortunately for you I'd say you're beyond our help. Killing you would mean one less darkyra to infect our world with your shadows."

His hands curled around my throat, but I clawed at him and gathered enough control of my limbs to knee him in the groin.

He groaned. And as he bent over, I slammed the heel of my hand into his nose. The crack reverberated down my arm.

I didn't know how I did it. It'd been automatic. My muscles remembered what to do, even though my brain didn't.

"Fucking bitch," he said, one hand holding his nose, the other his crotch. "You're going to regret that."

I ran down the hall, only to skittered to a stop because the door to the next corridor was locked. Panic ratcheted my heartbeat higher.

The guard rushed toward me.

I had nowhere to run, nothing to fight with. I raised my hands to shield myself from his blow, but it never came. A wash of Sebastian's power blanketed the room in darkness for the span of a breath and lifted as if it had never been there.

I lowered my hands and peered down.

The guard laid unconscious at my feet.

The door on the other side of the hall beeped, and Kai came running.

"It's okay," he said and wrapped his arms around me, stepping over the guard. "I saved you from him. You're okay now."

He saved me?

I was breathing heavy. My back hurt; my chest was collapsing. I rested my head on his shoulder. "Thank you," I said automatically.

His fingers palmed the back of my head. "You're welcome, Maya," he said, soothing and calm. "He was a bad one. See?"

Kai turned, and we both looked at the guard. His clothes were rumpled and showed the tiny square tattoo with a diamond overlay at the junction of his collarbones.

"He said," I hiccupped, clinging tighter to Kai. "He said Sebastian is dead. That's not true, is it?"

Kai stopped stroking my hair and pulled back. "Sebastian is gone."

I shook my head, refusing to accept it. I felt his power. I felt him. He was here.

Kai's eyes narrowed. "Your mate is gone. You have no one except for me."

My hands clutched fistfuls of his shirt as my knees buckled.

"You did this," Kai said, shrugging. "I was there and saw everything. You pulled on his power as the wards came down, but when you tried to sift, he was hit. If you wouldn't have tried to kill him. If you wouldn't have betrayed him, Sebastian would be here right now."

"No. No. No." Denial was the only thing keeping me from tipping over into insanity.

"Say it," he yelled in my face, but I was confused and lost and my heart was breaking.

"You have to say it, to accept it, to move on. Repeat after me," he said. He grabbed my jaw and forced my gaze on him. "Say it with me. My mate is gone."

"My mate is gone," I said, tears filling my eyes as my body and mind accepted that fact.

"And it's all my fault," Kai said.

"And it's all my fault," I choked out. Tears broke the surface and trailed down my face. My body started falling, but Kai held me tighter.

"Shh," he murmured.

A tiny vibration rumbled along my arm from where it was wrapped around Kai's back. A shadow slithered up to rest over my chest. *You're safe. I have you. I'll always protect you.*

I whimpered, and Kai stroked my hair as I clung on to him. "I'm the only one you've got now," he said.

"I have no one except for you," I said. My chest inflated with breath; a strange relief filled me. The hum of a vibration settling near my chest was the only thing keeping me from complete emptiness and despair.

"That's right, Maya," he said. "That's right."

Chapter Three

Sebastian

I used to have a name.

It was on the tip of my tongue. The sense of who I am. The awareness of myself.

But I didn't think I liked who I was.

And I didn't think I would want to remember.

"Sebastian?"

My shoulders sank as I sighed. Her voice twirled around my spine, settling as a deep ache in my heart.

I didn't know who she called for, but maybe I could become that person.

The one she searched for.

The one she needed.

I'd be whoever she wanted me to be.

"Sebastian?" The beautiful voice screamed in fear.

Pain radiated through me as the shadows burnt through the poison in my blood. I thrashed against the restraints that held my arms above my head. Power twisted my insides, flooding me until it expanded outward in a desperate longing. An angry vengeance that would crush and kill any that dared to harm her.

The crunch of my bones cracking reverberated through the room.

Chapter Four

Amaya

Darkness surrounded me, suffocated me.

Dazed, I was stuck in a dark labyrinth within my mind. Trapped by the whispers of the shadows, coaxing me into further madness.

You have no one. You're alone, and it's all your fault. You should be ashamed of yourself for what you've done, for who you've hurt. The voice began as another's, but it had since morphed into my own.

The shadows haunted me with pieces of my memories. Of the dagger I held to his neck and plunged toward his heart. Of the moment the feel of his power disappeared. Of the world going in slow motion as he fell from my grasp, his incorporeal body vulnerable to the attack, which I had made possible.

Of the moment the ache in my chest—that constant gnawing pressure, which had been my companion for months, so gradual in its growth I'd hardly recognized it—all but vanished. It had stuttered, held like the gasp of a shocked inhale.

I was still holding my breath, still bracing for the impact, for the moment the ache in my heart snapped back into place.

That moment would never come.

He was gone. And I was alone.

The fragments of my memory were bitter company. I heard him in my head, felt the wisps of his power brush along my skin, the hum of his steady presence at my throat. His voice promised to save me, to protect me, but I shouted into the void for it to go away, to leave me in my pitiful existence, to stop tormenting me with promises of his return.

You can do this. Focus on my voice. You're strong enough to filter the poison. You're going to be okay. You're the strongest fae I know. His voice spoke to me, the warm-honey lilt so tender, so soothing. It made my grief unbearable.

"No!" My throat was sore as if I'd been screaming for a long time. "Leave me alone! Please," I cried. "Please just stop. It hurts." My pleas were broken with sobs until the voice receded, and its presence faded. For now.

Day after day, I was left to stare at the floor of my cell, until that is, the hallucinations returned, and the mental anguish began once again.

A shadow would enter my mind. I'd see myself climbing an infinite staircase, and after centuries, I'd finally ascend to the top, to the light, to the pulsating power that promised freedom. In the sky, the sun and the moon got to dance around the world, but as I looked down, my legs were chained to the ground. Darkness was bound here. Unable to leave, unable to escape. Forever locked away.

I fell to my knees and cursed the sun and the moon for their betrayal. The people I met had only distrust in their eyes. They refused to break my chains, so I spent the rest of eternity wandering alone, trapped in a world that was not my own.

When I roused from these nightmares, it took me hours to remember where I was, who I was, and what was happening to me.

And though I couldn't be sure, it felt like each day I was stuck further and further away, having to crawl myself out of the void.

Kai showed up each day to feed me. The food he brought was always much better than the slop the guards gave me.

From nowhere he produced a bowl of stew, biscuits, and an apple. He set the tray of food in front of me, and my mouth salivated, but I knew better than to reach out.

I looked up at Kai first and said, "Thank you." My gratitude was always genuine.

Pleasure lit his eyes. "You're welcome, Maya."

"Why do you keep calling me Maya?"

"That's your name."

"No." I shook my head. "It's not."

"What's your name, then?"

I opened my mouth, but closed it again when no answer came.

Kai's face softened. "Doesn't Maya sound right?"

It did in a strange way, so I gave a small nod.

"Your name is powerful," he said. "Maya means illusion. People look at you and see one thing, but I look at you and see so much more. Soon enough the whole world will see what I see."

He gestured to the bowl of stew and said, "Go ahead. Remember to eat slow or you'll get sick."

I did as he bid, and he didn't leave my cell, only watched as I ate as slow as possible despite my urge to devour it all at once.

When I finished eating, the tray and bowl disappeared into the shadows. This wasn't alarming. It hardly registered, like it had been erased from my mind as soon as it happened.

"Your nose is bleeding," I said, looking up at Kai.

He wiped at the dark trickle with his thumb. "No, it's not."

I furrowed my brow, confused. "What's not?"

He smiled. "I think you're ready."

"Ready for what?"

"To be remade."

***

The doctor came to check my wounds each day. I hated the doctor. He would always grumble when he inserted the syringe into my arm because my skin healed too fast and my body would reject it. Each time he'd resort to pulling out a scalpel and cutting a deep slice into my arm and injecting me under the skin. He'd sigh and glare at me as if I could control it.

Kai was nothing like him. Kai was nice to me. He kept me company, and whenever he was around, I didn't hallucinate.

Something about his presence helped me build back my memories. But it was difficult. Part of my mind was inaccessible, only disjointed pieces of memories bled through, and Kai would have to correct my perceptions.

I recalled images of a human I despised and his two soliser guards in the lobby of an apartment, the exhilaration racing through me as my power destroyed them. I had reveled in taking their lives.

"I...I was trying to save someone though," I said, furrowing my brow. But who?

"No, you wanted to kill them because it's in your nature to kill. Only the strong survive," Kai corrected.

"Oh," I said, nodding. "Okay." It made sense in a strange way. I *had* felt a rush of pleasure as they died.

I preferred my memories of killing to the other memories that replayed in my head. A collection of everything I'd ever done wrong looped continuously. Every misstep, every misspoken word.

Even what some may have perceived as successes were just masked failures. I'd gotten my professional certification, but I didn't earn it. It was all a lie.

Flashes of my mother's and father's faces flickered in my head.

"We're so proud of you and your success," they said. But the memory of their encouragements soured because I'd made them believe the lie. I wasn't successful. I was an imposter.

The only coherent story I could weave together about myself from my memories was one of constant failure and falling short.

Time passed, or I assumed it did, because I couldn't tell if it was day or night. I had no sense of the world existing outside of my cell, except when Kai would come and inform me of what was happening.

Fae power was disappearing because the Queen was dying. The council couldn't agree on a high priestess suitable for the crown since the female that was suggested wasn't a citizen.

"None of this would be happening if not for you," Kai reminded me.

The memory came flooding in as if a shadow had lifted from my mind.

A door was thrust open, and guards galloped in behind an angry female. She yelled for our arrests.

"I was there," Kai said. "I was part of the group that was sent to arrest Sebastian. We were told there'd be a girl, and she'd put up a fight, but that the wards would disable your powers and you'd be easy to take down." A hint of a smile played out on his lips. "You weren't easy."

Warm pride blossomed in my chest. "I wasn't?"

A wide grinned broke out over his face. "No. You started coming at us with a dagger, fighting and kicking and dodging fire balls." He chuckled. "Everyone was taken aback."

I bit my bottom lip, holding back my own grin as the memory played from where Kai's story left off. Slicing the dagger through the air. Cutting the guards down. I ducked left and right, lunging and kicking them off balance.

The memory ended, and I refocused on Kai.

"That's why I protect you," he said. "Because I need someone like you to help me."

"With what?"

He didn't say anything at first, his smile fading. A pit of dread formed in my stomach.

"Why are you asking so many questions?" he demanded.

I swallowed as my body tensed.

"I'll tell you when you're ready," he said. "But you're still weak and pathetic. It's your fault your mate was brutally murdered, and you think you can ask *me* questions?"

The memory slammed back into me, unrelenting as I tried to push it away.

Sebastian's shadows trickling toward me, but flickering out too fast as we emerged into the astral field. Fire replacing their cool caress. Flames burning my arm. Sebastian falling from my grasp. His body crashing to the ground.

The panic as I tried to wake him.

The utter desolation when I was captured, fire binding my limbs, unable to catch one last sight of him.

My last memory was of him dying.

Sebastian was dead.

Tears spilled down my face. I wasn't sure when they'd started, but as the memory ended, Kai scoffed. "Pitiful." He pulled out a hankey and coughed into it, loud and wet. "You need to try harder, Maya. How can you think this behavior is acceptable?"

His hands shook as he pushed the hankey back into his pocket and got up, disappearing from my cell in one blink.

I wrapped my arms around my knees, rocking myself as the tears continued to fall. My cries choked me, chest heaving in short breaths as I hyperventilated. A sharp pang stabbed me deep in my stomach.

I felt his presence again, the light vibration that usually preceded the hallucinations.

"No. No. No," I said. "Not again. Not again."

And that was when the shadows began their tricks.

Amaya, a voice said. *You're stronger than this. You can make it. Don't give up.*

I cried harder, digging my nails into the palm of my hand.

The voice kept going. *I never do anything right*, it said.

I killed my mate. It's all my fault.

How can you think this is acceptable? Do you know what you've cost me? This isn't good enough.

"I'm not good enough," I whispered, chanting it over and over, but it didn't feel like an admonishment anymore. It felt like an acceptance. I wasn't good enough. I'd never be good enough. I couldn't keep trying.

No, little warrior, the voice said. *Listen to me. Listen. You are perfect. You are strong. You can get through this.*

Listen to me, the voice said. *You aren't good enough.*

Listen to me, the voice said. *You killed your mate. It's all your fault.*

I curled into a ball on the ground. "I killed my mate. It's all my fault."

No. Sebastian is alive. I wouldn't be here if he was dead. I'm still here. You can feel me, the voice said. The warm hum coated my chest, blanketed me, eased the ache below my collarbone. *We're alive. Sebastian is alive. You have to stay alive too. You can't give up.*

"Sebastian is alive," I whispered. "Sebastian is alive."

The hum got louder, and I kept repeating the same three words, over and over and over again. Centering my mind, aligning every part of my being with the sentence.

Sebastian is alive.

I repeated the words as the hum continued, even when the sentence lost meaning, it was somehow the only thing I could cling to.

That was how Kai found me, murmuring to myself, or had he never left?

He jerked me up and slapped me. "You have no one. You're nothing. You're worthless. Pathetic. You'll never be good enough," Kai said, but his lips didn't move.

I flinched and rubbed my temples. "What?"

Kai was all the way across the cell near the door. How had he slapped me then? Unless he didn't?

He walked toward me and patted my cheek, eyebrows pulling together in sympathy. "Are you okay?" he asked.

"What did you say?" My voice was angrier than I intended it to be, and my eyes widened in fear, but he didn't move to strike me.

He cocked his head. "I didn't say anything."

My mate is dead. I killed him. It's all my fault.

I scrunched up my face and yanked on my hair.

It's a lie. Kai lies. Sebastian is alive. A hum filled my chest.

"Sebastian is alive," I repeated.

Kai tsked. "I'm disappointed in you, Maya. I thought you were better than this, but..." He started walking to the door.

I dropped my hands from my head, chest caving in. "No. No. Please," I said and crawled to him. I clung to his leg. "Please. I'm sorry. Don't leave." I didn't want to be alone. Alone with the shadows and the hallucinations.

He sighed. "Don't you want me to protect you?"

"Yes," I sobbed.

"Then say it with me. Sebastian is gone."

"Sebastian is gone," I said, my voice robotic.

He sat down on a stool that had appeared from nowhere, and I crumbled to the ground holding his ankle to keep him from leaving.

I killed my mate. They forced me to kill him.

"I killed my mate. They forced me to kill him," I repeated.

"Yes, they did," Kai said. "Doesn't that make you mad? That the guards and the doctors shoot you up with poisons and keep you caged like an animal? That you're only here because Caroline betrayed you?"

A shadow swept in, and the memory returned. The angry female with the guards, the one calling for our arrests, that was Caroline.

She'd hated me instantly. Her face had twisted in disgust when I reached out my hand to introduce myself. She'd refused to look in my eyes or acknowledge my existence unless it was to sneer at me.

How could I have been so stupid? Why would I have thought someone who blatantly despised me could be trusted?

Was the next image a memory or a wish? It didn't matter. I could feel it viscerally as if it was my current reality. The feel of my hands around her neck, squeezing her carotid artery while she struggled. Or perhaps I'd crush her trachea to watch for the moment she'd try to gasp and realize that she'd never breathe another lungful of air.

"I hate her," I said, wanting to spit, my vitriol was so intense.

She despised darkyras, afraid of the power our shadows could wield, and maybe she was right about me. I was a monster, but it wasn't my shadows that made me this way. I had to become this to survive.

The heat of rage burned through my veins. It hurt like I was burning through a foreign substance, but the hurt was good. The anger purified me.

"Good," Kai said, and his nose began bleeding. He touched his upper lip and started coughing. Standing, he pulled out his hankey and wiped his mouth of the black blood he'd expelled.

It triggered another memory. My brain produced this one without a shadow carrying it. A male shaking as he fought himself, coughing up black sludge.

"Jeremy," I whispered.

Kai put the hankey away and towered over me with narrowed eyes. "What did you say?" His voice was menacing.

There was no denying it, and lying would only make him angrier. "I had another memory," I said, quickly. "Jeremy tried to hurt me."

Kai exhaled a breath. "That's right. He did. You remember how he almost killed you?"

Jeremy's cold determination as he strapped me to the drop tower on top of the court building. The fear that froze me as I plummeted to my death.

He hated me as soon as he'd seen me. His hatred was different from Caroline's, more subtle and contained. Little insults and jabs thrown as he touched Sebastian while scoffing at me, trying to belittle our relationship.

I ground my teeth together. "Yes. I hate him too."

I imagined pummeling his face in, the satisfying crack of his nose breaking, the delicious pain in my knuckles knowing they'd beaten the smug look off his face. He would plead for me to stop, and I'd look at him just as expressionless as he had when he released the lever that sent me toward my death.

"You can't trust anyone, Maya. They all hate you. Hate what you are," Kai said. "Your soul is more dark than light. If you don't kill them, they'll kill you."

Slices of moments careened through me. The whispered gossip that surrounded Sebastian and me as we entered court. Their distrust and hatred evident in their hand gestures to ward off shadows. The disgust of everyone as they eyed him in the airport.

They didn't know what it was to feel true fear, but I'd show them.

Anger rumbled inside me. I looked up at Kai. "They're going to pay," I said. "I'm going to make them pay."

A sick pleasure filled Kai's eyes. "Who's going to pay, Maya?"

I gritted my teeth as rage flared through my body. "Everyone."

Chapter Five

Sebastian

Paralysis was a twisted kind of horror—to float in an awareness of being alive while being unable to move or to speak. When all my expressions of anger and grief were thwarted, the emotions became inescapable and festered within the shell of my body. My living corpse.

As time passed, pieces of me flaked off and fell away. My days were only darkness, but I didn't rue the lack of color. I'd forgotten what color was. I was erased; what was left of my consciousness, eviscerated.

A door slammed. I felt the rattle throughout my body. I couldn't see. My eyelids wouldn't open.

Footsteps grew closer. "You probably recognize me by a different name," a voice spoke. Their presence was familiar, but I couldn't place it. "But you can call me Kai."

They came close enough to jangle the chains that held my arms. The bite of the cuffs burned my wrists as my power tried to awaken. It stuttered under my skin.

"Everyone thought you were brain dead," Kai said. "But after that little shadow outburst and breaking both your wrists yanking the shackles off the wall..." A pause as cold fingers trailed along my shoulder, across my chest. "They're afraid of you now." Those fingers wrapped around my throat. Though my mind panicked, my body still didn't rouse, only the autonomic actions of my throat muscles worked as I gasped for breath.

And then the sensation was gone.

"Moving you to the UV room tomorrow," Kai said. They made a shivering, disgusted noise. "Terrible place."

Kai hummed. "You should be grateful for all I've done for you. I made sure the piece of your shadow she had didn't get washed away. Granted, it hasn't been strong enough to counteract the shadows I've been sending her as guides to reveal her true potential." They sighed. "Little bugger is persistent though. I'll give him that. Has seeped in a few times. I've only allowed it since it fuels her rage to remember you."

They paused as if waiting for my gratitude and exhaled heavily when I said nothing. "I even blocked the hall from the med-room to her cell so the guard would be forced to take her near you, bringing your pretty little mate close enough that you could sense her. To remind *you* of what you have to live for."

Mate.

A wave of peace washed over me. My power stirred, remembering.

"She's not weak like you are," Kai said. "If I killed her, you wouldn't avenge her death, you'd fall apart. Probably toss yourself off the nearest bridge." They tsked. "And then what? All my work and waiting would have been for nothing." A heavy sigh and it sounded like they were shaking their head. "I blame your mother. She was always touting self-sacrifice. It was convenient when I needed her to make a bargain, but if I'd known it was in the genes, I would have chosen someone else to birth you.

"But your little mate..." They hummed. "I told her you were gone, and she was sad at first, but now when I look into her eyes, the darkness has blotted out any lingering high priestess martyrdom. She'll destroy the world. Tear it down for vengeance."

If I could have smiled, I would have. She was so strong. She always fought for what she knew was right. She never backed down. My chest ached as I imagined her. As I watched the memories of her in my mind when she dug in her heels to protect her friends, to protect everyone around her.

"She's a true darkyra," Kai said. "More a darkyra than you've ever been, than you could ever be. She deserves better than you. Deserves a mate that can stand by her side. Deserves someone that doesn't cower from his own power."

The deep ache in my heart throbbed in recognition. I'd been alive over a century, and she had to teach me how to control my shadow. She wielded her power with ease, and I still struggled to contain him. She deserved a mate who was her equal, not one that would drag her down.

"I've remade her," Kai said. "Renamed her and made her stronger. It's your turn. You're damaged. You need to give yourself over to the part that is still functioning. The part of you that is strong enough to be your mate's equal. It's time to stop fighting yourself. It's time to accept your fate," they said. "You can't run from this anymore."

They were right.

She deserved better. She deserved the best.

I didn't like who I was anyway.

There would be no loss in giving up. No loss in becoming someone stronger for her. Someone better.

I could let the dying, weak part of me go.

She was beautiful darkness. I would step into the void if it would save her.

Finally, my shadow said. *Power is mine.*

And I faded away.

Chapter Six

Amaya

Buzz. Buzz. Buzz. Silence. Buzz.

The fluorescent light rung its hollow cry, driving me toward insanity, aided by the shadows that lived in the walls.

They crawled like vines, filling in the hollow depressions in the cement block. They dripped like blood and pooled on the floor in a perfectly symmetrical oval.

I crawled toward the puddle. It reflected a gaunt face in its shimmery pool, but that couldn't possibly be me. I touched my finger to its surface, and it jiggled, expanding outward and absorbing the reflection of my face. Engulfed it. Devoured it in its depths.

The shadows were angry. They seeped inside of me. Scratched my bones. Twisted my veins. They yelled and quaked with energy unable to detonate, squeezed my chest and stomach to enact their own sick revenge.

I understood their desire to hurt. I understood how it felt to be so deeply wounded that inflicting pain seemed like the cure, the salve, to the festering sores of unfairness.

This is for your own good. We hurt you to help you, they whispered. *We don't do this because we enjoy it. We do it to make you stronger.*

The shadows melted into the cracks of my mind. Nameless, faceless memories ravaged me. Moving so fast that I was only left with the imprint of emotions.

Fear ripping my spinal cord and stealing my structure, my strength.

Embarrassment over misspoken words and missteps blazing like an inferno on my cheeks.

Shame cutting up the center of my body with a serrated knife.

Grief so thick it choked.

Stop! I screamed.

Stop! the shadows mimicked and laughed.

They ignored my pleas and crawled inside me, attached to my organs and grew like bacteria, doubling, tripling, multiplying exponentially. Repeating the horrendous emotions until I fractured and splintered, unable to feel anything but their rage.

Trapped in this prison, in this cell, in my mind.

The heat of anger burned in my blood. I imagined obliterating every guard. Crushing their skulls. Dismembering them for keeping me here.

My mate was dead. I had nothing to live for. Which made me dangerous. Imagining terrorizing guards and burning the prison to the ground became my only escape from the shadows' mockeries. They didn't torment me when I was outlining how I'd suffocate a guard in his own blood.

And then I would laugh. I was only imprisoned because I betrayed Sebastian, thinking that I needed to save the world from *him*.

Such a stupid thought. It was *me* the world would need saving from.

It had always been me.

Soon I'd no longer need to endure this. I could feel it, could feel my power growing inside me. Each day my head was a little clearer from the anger purifying me and making my purpose shine in the distance.

Sebastian was dead.

And they were all going to pay for what they'd done.

Sebastian is alive, the darkness crooned like a demon lover, trying to loosen my grip on the already precarious hold I had on my sanity. I didn't want to slip into the murky expanse of hysteria again. Not when I'd finally clawed myself back from the all-consuming grief over his death.

I swatted at the shadow and pushed it away. It was another trick, testing my resolve, my strength, my determination.

I refused to believe the words, *Sebastian is alive*, even as they played like a lullaby in my brain, the lyrics becoming a melody sung to the rhythm of my heartbeat.

I'll avenge you, I vowed.

A shadow sighed, almost frustrated. *Very well. If that's what it takes for you to stay alive.*

I spent my days scheming, planning my revenge. I'd been interrupted from my latest murderous daydream—considering how hard it'd be to remove fingernails without a weapon—when my cell door swung open. The doctor and his guard entered.

"I know it's unplanned, but I was already in this wing for another prisoner," the doctor said, setting his bag down beside me.

The guard he brought was the one that tried to strangle me. The one Kai saved me from. I glared at him, but he only stared with indifference.

The doctor rifled through his bag and pulled out an unorganized heap of sharp medical instruments. Blood and gunk caked some of them. The used and unused tools touching one another with no concern for contamination.

This male wasn't a doctor. If his daily torture on my back wasn't proof enough of that, his disregard for keeping his tools clean proved he wasn't actually concerned with keeping people alive and healthy.

Maybe that was why my back wound wasn't healing.

"If she's being moved to general population," the doctor said. "I'll have to check her out soon anyway."

I blurted out before thinking, "Kai won't let you take me to general population."

The doctor furrowed his brow. "Who's Kai?"

"Uh," I scrambled for something to say, not wanting to get Kai in trouble for helping me. "Kai is the guard on this floor. He mentioned once that I wouldn't be moved to general population."

The guard crossed his arms. "There is no one named Kai in this prison."

Liar.

I smiled, showing my teeth as a feral rage filled me. When I got free, he'd be the first one I'd find. I'll slice his eyelids off and bleed him out by making deep cuts between the webbing of his fingers. Maybe I'd use the doctor's disgusting scalpels to do it.

The doctor sighed. "She's obviously got dissociative amnesia or post-traumatic stress hallucinations."

It struck me as hilarious that the doctor would be upset about the decline of my mental health when he was the one shooting me up with poison to suppress my memories and power.

I laughed, and when I started laughing, I couldn't stop. I clutched my torso, chuckling so hard my stomach hurt.

The doctor's eyes widened. "Add to that a possible psychotic break." He pulled out a tablet and started tapping around. "And no wonder. I've never seen anyone on this high of a dosage." He stared at me with a look of shock and disgust.

"You're the one giving them to her," the guard said.

The doctor shrugged. "The suppression is measured out by the team at the research center and sent in shipments with the prisoner's number on the label. I just administer it."

The doctor tapped on his tablet, and I stared at the scalpels sitting next to me. The doctor turned to the guard. "She can't be moved to general population with these symptoms. Do we have stronger cuffs? Then I can recommend notching down the dosage."

My hand crept to the left, inching closer to the heaps of medical instruments, and I forced my eyes to go blank, staring at a corner as if lost in my psychotic break.

"She's in the strongest cuffs we have," the guard said. "We could keep her in the UV room with the other one."

The doctor shook his head. "She has high priestess power. There's a chance she could draw energy from the moon if we move her to the top floor." The doctor started to turn back around. I swiped the scalpel lying nearest to my fingers and hid it underneath my thigh.

My heart was racing, sweat breaking out, but I forced my eyes to remain unfocused. I pulled my blanket from the other side of me and laid it over my thighs, shivering for effect.

The doctor shrugged and put the tablet aside. "We'll keep you alive, but no one said what condition you need to be in."

I clenched my jaw, fisting my hands to stop myself from picking up the scalpel and jamming it into his eye socket. He'd scream, and I'd grab two more and plunge one into each of his hands. That's the *condition* I'd leave him in.

I held back my murderous inclinations and pretended to be dazed. The doctor picked up a scalpel from his pile and gestured for me to spin around, knowing that my back hasn't healed, knowing he'd be scraping out infection once again, knowing that I had no pain killers, and simply expecting me to endure this torture day-in and day-out.

I turned, gingerly picking up my blanket while my fingers scooped up the scalpel from under my thigh and twisted until my back was to him. I set the blanket aside with the scalpel underneath and rearranged myself so he had full access to my back.

He peeled off the bandage, and I dug my fingernails into my hands and gritted my teeth as the blade cut into the tender flesh, but the pain hurt less this time.

I had a weapon.

I bit the edge of my lip to hold back my smile.

They'd all be screaming soon.

Reassuring myself it'd be one of the last times I had to go through this, I endured the doctor's torture.

The moment they left and my cell door closed, I lifted the blanket and picked up my new shiny toy.

"What's that?" Kai asked.

I startled, barely suppressing my shriek. I didn't know how he appeared since the door hadn't opened.

Slowly I turned, clutching the scalpel. He'd already seen me with it; there was no denying its existence.

I swallowed. "The doctor forgot it."

Kai's face held no emotion. "Is that so?"

I nodded my head shakily.

He held out his palm. "Hand it over."

My eyes darted to the scalpel and back to him.

He raised an eyebrow. "I'm the only one who's protected you," he said, soft. "You aren't thinking of hurting me, are you, Maya?"

I exhaled in sharp defeat. He was right. I couldn't hurt the only person who helped me.

With my eyes downcast, I handed it over.

The second it left my palm, he lunged at me. "You need me!" He pushed my body into the wall and held the scalpel at my throat. "You can't do this by yourself," he shouted. "You need me. You can't trust anyone except me. You think you're smart?" His lips curled. "You're nothing," he spit, eyes glaring at me. "You'd have no power if not for me. You'd have no hope without my help."

For all my anger and bluster, I couldn't drum up any for Kai. I felt myself retreating within.

"I know," I said, my voice was puny and small. I fought back tears, knowing they'd only make him angrier. "I'm nothing without you." The truth of it cut through my chest.

Kai grabbed my chin, his nails digging into my cheek. "Everyone betrayed you. Your friends betrayed you. They set you up to kill your mate and left you to rot in this prison. I'm the only one who cares for you. Look at everything I've done for you."

"I know," I whined out again. It took a second for his words to register, but then they hit me.

My blood froze. Something tickled the back of my head. Shadows lifted, and memories rearranged and came into focus.

"My friends betrayed me?" I said, and pressure released like a balloon popping.

"Your friends, Gwen and Sloane?" Kai said. "They set you up. Caroline is trying to make Gwen the queen, and you're going to rot here for the rest of your life. They don't care about you. They never have."

Gwen and Sloane. Their names glimmered in the distance like keys to the imprisoned parts of my mind.

Stop, a shadowed voice said. *Block Kai from your mind before you search for the memories.*

The words were whispered in my head so quickly I wasn't sure if I heard them, but part of me understood. I'd crafted this mental block before. With less than half a thought, it fell into place.

The memory poured in.

A brown-haired male putting out their hand in greeting to a pretty blonde-haired girl in a short flirty dress. "It's nice to meet you, Sloane," the male said.

Sloane gestured to another girl. Lean and toned, with flawless warm brown skin and black braids that went down her back. "This is

Gwen Nueblots," Sloane said. "We're Amaya's very best friends, and we're here to take her out."

A strange ease filled me. Healing light cleared the mental fog and cut through the lies and the confusion.

Gwen and Sloane were my best friends.

I looked up at Kai, eyes widening as the realization shook me. "My friends are out there?"

His eyes narrowed, and I realized I made a mistake.

"They don't care about me?" I revised.

Kai pressed his lips together. "That's right. They're out there, and they don't care that you're rotting away in here."

The ease continued to spread through my body. My shoulders sagged, and Kai smiled as if this was proof that I believed him.

It wasn't his truth I was accepting.

The memories whirled through my mind faster than my brain could catalog them, revealing what was always there, what had been shadowed until now, feelings of love and trust and loyalty for my two best friends.

My connection to Gwen and Sloane had been instantaneous. A settled surety that I never—not for one moment—doubted.

Truth and lies were jumbled in my head, but I was certain Gwen and Sloane cared for me. They loved me and I loved them.

Moments raced by in my mind's eye.

When Gwen and I sparred in the training room and I'd finally taken her down the first time, she'd smiled up at me from the ground, proud of my growing skills.

When Sloane and I sang and danced together.

When the three of us held each other while we cried, while we laughed, while we watched terrible tv shows.

We'd fought with each other sometimes, but at the end of the day, we'd always fight *for* one another.

Gwen had said, *I'm helping you because high priestesses have to stick together... The power in your blood is the same as mine. We're sisters.*

Sloane had said, *Best friends stick together, no matter their powers.*

A deeper bond than just being high priestesses. Deeper than being best friends. They were my sisters, my soulmates.

If they weren't here and they hadn't broken me out yet, it meant something was wrong. They were hurt or trapped or something terrible was happening. I needed to get out of here to save them.

Kai made a mistake. I could believe his prior lies, but this one had destroyed the credibility of everything he'd told me. I knew my friends would never betray me.

What else was he lying about?

"Sebastian is dead?" I asked. The hope was so tantalizing I couldn't keep it from my voice.

Kai slapped me, and blood filled my mouth as my teeth cut my inner cheek. "Your mate is gone," he seethed with narrowed eyes.

My head turned to the side from the impact. I grabbed my jaw to hide my smile behind my hand.

Kai was *lying*.

A focused vengeance filled me and honed in to my new goal. My friends needed me. Sebastian needed me. I didn't know where they were, but I'd find them. I'd find Sebastian. I'd find Gwen and Sloane.

I breathed in, filling my lungs with renewed purpose and hope. My core heated; power thrummed in my veins. A familiar hum vibrated through my body as if in relief, as if it too had been waiting for me to see the truth.

"My mate is gone," I repeated, knowing it would please Kai, even as a light filled me and burned through his lies.

Kai nodded, relieved. "You need me. I'm the only one you can trust."

"I need you," I parroted. "You're the only one I trust."

Kai exhaled. "Good. Good." He patted my cheek, and I winced from the bruise that was forming.

He laughed. "You had me worried there, but not much longer now. Just remember who protected you this whole time."

"You, Kai. You protect me," I said, speaking the language he'd taught me. The language he used to poison me.

Liar.

After he left my cell, I replayed the first memory, holding on to the one word which shattered all of Kai's carefully crafted deceptions.

We're Amaya's very best friends, Sloane had said.

Amaya. My name was Amaya. And Kai had been truthful about one thing: my name was powerful.

Because now I could end his illusions.

Chapter Seven

Sloane

"Oh no you don't," I mumbled under my breath and repositioned the computer on my lap, clicking the edit panel on the prison's administrator system. I changed "Randomize Meal Schedule" to "Normal Meal Schedule."

Double checking Amaya and Sebastian's profiles, I edited all of their inputs. Nico had finally cracked the firewall that blocked the research center and prison's network. We'd already adjusted their suppression injections to the lowest level, so they'd be ready when we broke them out.

A loud crash from the other end of the cabin stole my attention.

"Fuck." Nico's voice echoed down the hall.

"Babe?" I put the laptop on the coffee table and scurried toward the ruckus.

"I'm fine," Nico said. His curt tone had me halting outside the bathroom door. He laid sprawled out on the floor. The medicine cabinet and all of its contents scattered on top of him.

"What happened?" I pushed the cabinet off him and grabbed his arm. His shoulder-length auburn hair was sticking up everywhere from the fall.

"I'm fine. I don't need help," he grumbled but didn't push me away as he grabbed the edge of the counter and pulled himself up. I used all my strength to lift the other side of him.

Nico broke his bargain with Sebastian by telling me he was my mate, but he'd done it as Sebastian and Amaya were being taken to the prison, leaving him to deal with the consequences. His normally bright and cheerful hazel eyes betrayed the pain he was trying to hide.

"It's getting worse?" I whispered, but it was more a statement than a question.

He grabbed his side. "It's just a cramp. Caught me off guard. It's fading now." He pulled his hair into a bun at the back of his head.

I stared at the peeling plaster where the cabinet used to be. He'd obviously grabbed the cabinet to catch his fall.

A heavy sigh released, and he turned to me. "The Queen is dying. Palagui's power is fading, so the broken bargain's pain is fading too. I woke up and forgot I had any pain at all…" He swallowed. "But then it flared up out of nowhere."

Without fae power, the bargain had no magic to fuel it, but the broken bargain's pain reactivated Nico's old war injuries. Phantom pains that had no visible wound to heal.

I nodded. "Do you want fae nettle?"

He shook his head. If he ingested enough, it would dampen his power and the side effects of the broken bargain, but it also made him pass out for days.

He didn't like talking about his pain, but this was bigger than us, so I asked, "Is this bargain pain or old pain?"

He lifted up his shirt, gesturing to the brutal knotted scar on his torso. "Old pain."

I raised my palm. His marred skin seemed to pulsate. My high priestess healing couldn't fix scars this old, but sometimes the psychosomatics of the white light brought him relief.

"Don't," he said and pushed down his shirt.

I nodded once, not wanting to fight him on this, not again.

Nico didn't want me to waste the little healing power I had on him. *He had better ways of managing the pain*, he had said. Then he worked out all day to the point of exhaustion.

I bent down to pick up the contents of the medicine cabinet.

"Stop, Sloane," he said. "I'll get it."

"I can help."

"Stop. Seriously." The anger was back. It wasn't for me. He was in pain. He was angry that *he wasn't strong enough to fight through it*, but it still twisted me up inside.

My movements froze, and I left the pill bottles on the ground. "Fine," I said. "Breakfast is on the counter."

He grunted his acknowledgement and winced as he crouched to clean up.

I tiptoed to our bedroom in the back of the cabin and shut the door. Pressing my back into the wall, I covered my mouth with my hand to choke back my sob.

How did we get here?

The Nico on the other side of this wall was not the male that was declaring me as his mate a month ago.

Nico and I raced out of his father's office, only to watch soliser guards drag Amaya's and Sebastian's limp bodies out of the ballroom in chains. My power had expanded enough since I'd come to Palagui that I could feel they—through their power—were alive.

Nico grabbed my arm, hiding us around a corner. Xenos's dead and mangled body was carried out as Caroline watched with a satisfied gleam.

"Gwen?" I whispered.

Nico shook his head. "Caroline admitted she plans to make Gwen the queen. She won't hurt her, but the same can't be said of you, Sloane. She knows you'll fight to get Amaya out. We need to go into hiding."

It went against everything I was trained to do. High priestesses stick together, and more than that, Gwen and Amaya were my best friends. I couldn't leave them and hide. It didn't matter that Nico was my mate. My friends would always come first.

I tried to conjure up a plan to ditch Nico, but he obliterated my attempt when he collapsed against me with a pained moan.

"Nico?" I grabbed his arm and put a hand on his back.

He was breathing heavy through his teeth. "I broke the bargain with Sebastian by telling you we're mates."

I sucked in a breath. "Are you dying?"

He'd lied to me, bargained to keep the truth from me, but I didn't want him to die...

"No. I won't die. Just suffer."

"Why? Why did you make such a stupid bargain?" If he hadn't already been in pain, I would have hit him upside the head. Pressure built behind my eyes as the reality of the situation threatened to break me.

His posture relaxed, the pain seeming to have subsided for now. "I don't know if you've noticed, but I'm more an act-first-think-later kind of guy."

I snorted through my tears. He gave me a sad smile and wiped them away with his thumb.

"Sebastian knew, hell even I knew, I would end up blabbing to you, and you'd tell Amaya, and she'd figure out..."

I sighed. "They're mates too," I finished for him.

He nodded. "At first, I didn't want to tell you, anyway. You were going through enough after being kidnapped and held at the research center. I wanted us to get to know each other without the pressure of the mating bond. Making the bargain was a way to force myself to go slow." He shook his head. "But Bash kept dragging his feet and...well." He shrugged. "I couldn't go another day without telling you what you mean to me. Consequences be damned."

I swallowed, unable to find a response. The pulse of my heart throbbed, aching for him, for his touch.

And I knew. I couldn't leave him.

Finally, I asked, "Where are we going to hide then?"

He grabbed my hand. "I have a place."

I finished my silent sobbing and took a deep breath. Nico was what I needed when I was reeling from the aftermath of my kidnapping. I could be what he needed now, and he didn't want to be coddled.

I understood the sentiment. When Gwen and Amaya were giving me concerned looks after my kidnapping, Nico saw me, talked to me, flirted with me like a normal person. He was my distraction when I needed to get out of my head.

I fixed my makeup in the mirror, and went to the kitchen to pour myself coffee.

"Rien left a message on the site," Nico said, typing on the laptop at the dining room table.

Rien had texted me the day everything went down for an update, but I couldn't explain over the phone and risk someone from Delnee's government spying on our conversation, so Nico came up with a solution.

Apparently, Sebastian already had Nico set up an encrypted web-based portal that was tied to USB-sized authenticator keys so Sebastian could talk to Rashida Osman and Dr. Greg Henderson without the government spying.

Nico messaged Rashida to contact Rien and set him up with an authenticator key and instructions for the website. It worked out great because Rien and Amaya had worked with Rashida, so there was no need to convince him to trust her.

In the last few weeks, Rien told us our plan—to switch out the high priestess cuffs so his father, Harrison Astora, couldn't shackle the legacy families in Delnee—had worked.

Harrison was angry at first, assuming that Xenos had tricked him, but after word got out that Xenos died, Harrison lost interest in cuffing the high priestesses, at least for now.

I wandered over to the dining room table. A half-eaten plate of eggs sat beside the laptop, which was good because I think Nico skipped dinner last night and...

No. Stop.

No coddling.

I peeked over his shoulder to read Rien's message. *My dad hasn't made any moves on Palagui but is watching the change in power closely. Nothing else to report. Everything is quiet. How's Gwen? How's Amaya?*

I sighed.

"He asks the same questions every time," Nico grumbled and started writing him back. "Never cares about how Bash is doing though."

"He didn't date Bash," I countered. "In fact, Bash took his girl."

Nico turned to give me a playful eye roll. My heart soared. He must really not be in much pain today if he was joking like his old self.

"I didn't say he had to actually care," Nico said. "It's just common courtesy to ask. He knows he's locked up too."

I bit my lip. Rien not only didn't care that Sebastian was locked up, but he probably would have preferred he stayed that way, despite the fact that Nico and I had explained why Sebastian had to do what he'd done and how Caroline betrayed us.

As for Gwen, she was still missing, and as terrible as it was for Amaya and Sebastian to be in prison, at least I knew where they were. Caroline had told Gwen to go get stronger cuffs on the day of the engagement party and never returned.

Daria hadn't answered any of our calls either.

My hope was they were together, hiding somewhere from Caroline, who wanted to force Gwen to take the crown and make her queen of Palagui.

I sat beside Nico, staring blankly around the cabin. It was only four rooms, two bedrooms, a bathroom, and the open area of the kitchen, living, and dining room. These four rooms had become a bit like our own prison cell, though I couldn't complain when Sebastian and Amaya were going through something the prison system called "deconstruction" and "reorientation."

When I'd asked Nico what those terms meant, after hearing his explanation, I regretted asking.

"A fae's well-being and identity is drawn from our power expression," he said. "The prison suppresses our powers with injections like the research center does. Plus, there are several wards with different and changing origination points so even if a prisoner broke a ward in one area, they'd be powerless in another."

His eyes got a faraway look, body becoming rigid; a reaction I viscerally recognized. He was recalling from personal experience, not general knowledge.

"When we can't use our power, the body and mind rebel. The prison enacts a deconstruction procedure, which is a tearing apart of your sense of self." He swallowed and clenched his jaw before looking at me. "There is a physical torture process"—I scrunched up my face and pressed my hand to my mouth to stifle my reaction—"and a psychological element that strips away who you think you are."

Nico drew in a long breath before continuing, "Reorientation is the rebuilding process. An attempt to make prisoners moldable and docile."

"If both of their profiles say they are in reorientation, does that mean..." I couldn't verbalize the rest of the question. Were they not themselves anymore? Had they been broken?

Nico fidgeted and simply said, "It means that they are through the worst of it."

With great effort, he stood and wrapped his arms around my waist, pulling me into his embrace. It felt wrong to cry for them and find comfort in my mate's arms while I knew Sebastian and Amaya couldn't do the same.

"Amaya is strong," Nico said. "All three of you are made of tough stuff. She'll get through this."

He rubbed my back and held me tight. Tension released, and my shoulders slumped as my body took comfort in his heat, his scent, his touch.

"And Sebastian?" I asked in a small voice.

Nico's voice was thick with grief. "Bash is well-acquainted with psychological torture. There's nothing they could do to him that would be worse than what he's already gone through."

His answer was a hammer to my heart. A new wave of guilt washed over me. I'd done this to him. We had—Amaya and Gwen and I—planned to kill Sebastian for taking high priestesses' powers. Now Palagui's power was dying.

If the prison used power suppression as torture, we'd effectively sentenced an entire country to the same torture by taking away the only person who was keeping the Queen alive.

Despite Sebastian having saved me, having saved Amaya's life, we trusted Caroline because she was a high priestess and we believed we could only trust each other.

We'd been wrong, and Amaya and Sebastian were paying the price.

Nico and I bided our time, waiting for the Queen to die, hoping that Caroline wouldn't crown Gwen or another high priestess, because when fae power died, we could exploit the prison's defenses.

Nico got up, his chair screeching in the quiet of the cabin. He took his plate to the kitchen, but it clanged against the floor as he fell.

"Nico!" I sprung forward.

He made a frustrated, angry noise in the back of his throat and pushed himself into a seated position. He picked up the plate and threw it against the cupboard, shattering it.

I froze, staring at the broken ceramic.

His chest was heaving, face screwed up in anguish.

My heart was pounding, but I clenched my hands into fists to keep them from shaking. Tears came to my eyes, but I swallowed them back and navigated around the broken plate, numbly bending down and resting my hand on his shoulder.

"I can stand up on my own."

This time I couldn't stop the tears. I wasn't afraid of him or his anger. I wasn't even upset for his pain.

No. These were angry tears. I was sick of being pushed away.

"You're on the ground surrounded by shattered glass," I said. "I've seen you try to get up, and it isn't pretty or graceful, and if you fall again, you're going to cut yourself. I don't have enough power to be wasting on scrapes and cuts because you were too much of a bonehead to accept my help."

His eyes popped open, and he stared up at me. He was either too shocked at my outburst or too embarrassed to admit I was right because he let me help him to the couch without saying a word.

He winced as he sat back, and I fought the prickle of guilt that was working its way up, trying to twist my anger into shame for speaking to him so harshly.

I said I wasn't going to coddle him, right?

I crossed my arms over my chest and stood in front of the coffee table. He bent forward at the waist and held his head in his hands.

Nico was my mate, and there were going to be good and bad days in our relationship, but I couldn't keep pushing away my feelings to make him comfortable, so I said, "I know you're in pain, and I know you hate that you can't fight through it. I know you regret breaking the bargain—"

He looked up at me. "I don't."

I was silent, my anger deflating as my hands fell to my sides. "It's okay, I know it doesn't mean anything about us—"

He shook his head. "No, Sloane. No. Does this suck? Yes, but I haven't for one second regretted telling you. I regret not telling you sooner, but if I had to live with this pain for the rest of my life just to have you by my side, I'd do it again in a heartbeat."

My shoulders slumped. "Nico..."

"I'm sorry," he said. His handsome face pulled down into a frown. "I'm so sorry. You have every right to yell at me. I've been snapping and taking it out on you, and I shouldn't have broken that plate. I'm sorry if I scared you."

"I wasn't scared," I said softly. "I know you'd never hurt me."

He pressed his lips together and looked away. "Still. I'm sorry."

I went to sit by him on the couch. He rested his hand on his thigh, palm up.

My chest lightened at his silent invitation. He'd done that when I was lost to my kidnapping trauma. An offering of comfort, but no pressure, just him saying he was here, and I could choose if I was ready to accept it. I had been eager to touch him then, and that hadn't changed.

"I'm sorry for yelling at you," I said, interlacing my fingers with his.

He squeezed my hand. "You have nothing to apologize for. I want you to yell at me when I'm being a bonehead. I'm not usually like this. The person I was when I met you, happy and easy to live with, that's who I try to be. This person..." He sighed and shook his head. "This anger...I won't give in to it again. I promise you."

"You can be angry, Nico," I said. "I know you're hurting. I'm angry too. Everything sucks right now." I pressed my shoulder into his in a playful shove. "But maybe we figure out how to be angry and not break plates because of it."

He huffed a small laugh. "You're right. No more—" He stopped and turned to me, eyes brightening. "Actually...I have an idea." A wide grin broke out over his face as he pulled me up. "Can you go to our bedroom and get the wooden bat in the back closet?"

I narrowed my eyes but was fighting a smile because his joy and energy were infectious. He was impossible to be sad around, impossible to stay angry at when he was so buoyant.

I retrieved the bat and came out to see him holding a stack of plates. He tilted his head toward the door, and I followed him outside to the edge of the clearing.

My breath was visible in the cold morning. The forest around us was dead and barren, but Nico's excitement animated the lifelessness.

He put a plate on a stump and stood back, smiling with boyish glee. "Smash the shit out of it."

I grinned so wide it was almost painful. Gathering all my strength, I swung the bat over my head and brought it down with an angry yell. The plate shattered, pieces flying into the forest.

"Your war cry is hot," Nico said.

I threw him a flirty expression over my shoulder. "I want another."

He sat a plate on the stump, and I crushed it.

And another, and another, until I was breathing heavy, and the anger and frustration, the hopelessness of being unable to help Amaya and Sebastian, the guilt over Nico's pain, the fear of Gwen's disappearance, all of it moved through me.

"Good?" he asked.

I nodded and handed him the bat. He tossed it back and forth, twirling it around his wrist in a move that was far too sexy.

With a heavy swing, he brought the bat down and smashed several plates at once.

After a few swings, he stopped and turned to me with a vulnerable expression.

"I'm going to do better," he said. He came closer, letting the bat drop to the ground. "I'm new at this being in a relationship thing, let alone having a mate. I'm going to mess up, but I promise you I won't make the same mistake twice."

Tears filled my eyes, but I blinked them away, nodding.

He counted on one finger. "I learned never to make a bargain with Sebastian."

I snorted. "Yeah. Seriously."

He put out a second finger. "Don't smash plates inside when they can be smashed outside."

"A much better option," I agreed.

A third finger. "And don't refuse my mate's help when my pain flares up."

I fell into his arms. "That's all I want."

He cupped my jaw. "I'm not perfect, and I wish I could be a better mate for you—"

I shook my head, grabbing his forearms. "You are. You're perfect." I gave him a quick peck and pulled back. "And I learned that I need to bring up the things I'm worried about before I'm yelling at you and calling you mean names."

The corner of his mouth quirked up. "Don't worry. There's nothing you could say that would scare me away. I'm never leaving you." He kissed my nose. "Ever."

"I love you."

"I love you too." Nico barely got the words out as I planted my lips on his. The heat of his mouth, of his hands on my waist cut through the cold, warming me to the core. His tongue twined with mine, and I moaned as a molten lava pooled in my lower belly.

Out of breath, we broke apart, foreheads touching as he stared into my eyes. His breath tickled my cheek as he whispered in my ear, "Besides if you ever feel bad about yelling at me you could always apologize by making love to me until I'm one hundred percent sure you didn't mean it."

I pushed his shoulder. "Until you're *sure*? That sounds like a good way for you to get laid. You'd just tell me"—I used my male voice to mock him—"Hmm...nope still not sure. Think we need another round."

He laughed and made a fake shocked face. "What? No. I'd never do something like that." I rolled my eyes, and he bent at the waist and lifted me with his arms wrapped around my thighs. "What kind of male do you think I am?"

I squealed and held on to his shoulders as he spun me around until we were both dizzy. "A sex-obsessed kind of male," I teased back.

"Mmm. You might be right. But my obsession starts and ends with you," he said and spun me faster.

My giggling and our shouted teasing was making both of us out of breath again. When he finally lowered me, sliding my body down his, I thought I might be hallucinating from lack of oxygen as he said, "Accept the bond with me, Sloane."

"What?" The request was absurd. "No. The bond will increase our power and the broken bargain will worsen your pain."

He pressed his lips together, his eyes trailing along my face. "The Queen is going to die soon. I can feel it. The bargain's pain is almost nonexistent. If we're going to break Bash and Amaya out of prison, we need to do it soon." He cupped my face, thumbs stroking my cheekbones. "I don't want to go in there powerless. The mating bond isn't fueled by the queen's power. If we accept it, you and I will have power and the rest of the country won't."

I sucked in a breath. "You know this for sure?"

Nico nodded. "Bash and I have been researching the bond for a while now. The bond is an energy that is greater than the sum of its parts, when our life forces—our auras—are tied, as long as you and I are together, we'll always have power."

"But the broken bargain will have power to draw from too."

"I'd rather be in pain with power than powerless. The pain won't distract me from our mission. I've fought battles with gaping wounds before."

I swallowed.

"Plus, I could fly us in," he said. "We wouldn't have to drive across the country and take a boat to the island."

I sucked my lips into my mouth.

By fly us in, he didn't mean on a plane.

Nico had already told me I hadn't been hallucinating in the research center when I'd seen him as a dragon.

Because I was his mate, I could see what he was supposed to keep secret from the world: his true soliser form.

And since Nico was a shifter soliser, he could access his dragon form outside of initiation.

"But I thought shifting hurt?" I asked. He'd explained it involved burning away his body to morph, and it was even more painful to regrow back into a human.

"I don't care," he said.

No one knew why some solisers could shift, usually into flying creatures. Nico said it was theorized that all fae could shift at one point, that it was an evolutionary relic.

Darkyra used to be aquatic, drawing power from the depths of the ocean, and high priestesses used to be nocturnal, drawing power from the moon, but only solisers retained the ability to shift into other forms.

It made sense. Fae had evolved like all creatures over the millenniums of our existence. We'd once had pointed ears too, but we certainly didn't have those anymore.

I gave another weak protest. 'If people see you…"

Solisers weren't supposed to tell anyone they could shift. Those that did could be targeted for extermination. Nico had said wars had been won and lost because an enemy bumblebee or bird got close enough to see strategic plans.

The ability to shift was an almost extinct trait for that reason.

Nico kissed my nose. "This is important."

I nodded absentmindedly. Was I ready for this? To be bound to someone for the rest of my life?

Did I have a choice?

He was right. If we had even a smidge of power while the rest of the world didn't, we'd be at a huge advantage.

I took a deep breath and said, "Okay, if you're sure."

He raised his eyebrows, happiness lighting up his eyes. "Seriously? You...you want to do this?"

I grinned and nodded more vigorously. "Yes."

He made a whooping noise and picked me up again, spinning me around like a lunatic.

I held on to his shoulders, laughing as he carried me to our bedroom in the cabin.

Between giggling and kissing, I declared to myself and him, "I want to accept the bond with you."

And so we did.

Chapter Eight

Gwen

"Your slimy shadows must have blinded your mother cause that's the only way she'd ever love a face like yours!"

Okay, even I'll admit that insult was pretty weak, especially since the darkyra in question was objectively gorgeous, but after being tied to this Goddess-forsaken chair every night for the past four weeks, my creativity was running low.

Your shadow probably wishes it could sift away from you was a pretty good one, but it hadn't even gotten a reaction from Daria.

Though, I suppose, none of them had triggered a reaction from her. None, except on the first day, when she untied me to give me my first bathroom break, and I leaned over and whispered, "You're a dirty fucking traitor."

Then she finally deigned to look me in the eye. The rancid witch had the audacity to look like she was about to cry. Her jaw quivered and her hands shook until her void eyes flashed, and she shoved my shoulder toward the bathroom. I tripped over my feet but was smiling smugly the rest of the day.

"Gwen Nueblots!" Annabelle's scolding voice rattled down the basement stairs.

I sighed. "Sorry, Annabelle," I replied in a lackluster monotone.

Annabelle was muttering to herself under her breath—something about my lack of manners and knowing my momma didn't raise me that way—as she walked down the stairs with a tray of food and tea.

I watched her closely, holding my breath with each step. She was an old, frail lady, and every time she came down those stairs, I waited for her to wipe out.

And being tied to this Goddess-forsaken chair, I wouldn't be able to do anything but watch as she writhed in pain.

She made it down the stairs though, and I released my breath. Of course fucking Daria would make her poor nana be my jailor. She kidnapped me, was holding me hostage in her basement, but didn't have the courage to face me since that first day.

It was Annabelle who fed me and kept me company while we watched tv or she read the newspaper.

I was pretty sure that Annabelle was human. At first, when she untied me for bathroom breaks, she held out a taser. The message being, *Just because this basement is warded and you can't use your power, doesn't mean I won't fuck you up if you hurt me.*

But truth be told, after the second day of hanging with the old broad, I didn't think I could actually bring myself to hurt her even if freedom were on the line.

Daria probably knew that, counted on the fact that I wouldn't be able to lay a finger on her granny. She knew my weaknesses and used them against me. And I was the idiot who not only trusted her enough to let her in and show her those weaknesses but basically gave her a map of how to exploit them.

"Aunt Caroline! I got the cuffs!"

The guards that surrounded her were armed and ready to take Sebastian out.

Her face twisted into a scowl. "You weren't supposed to get back so quickly."

I furrowed my brows. Well, I ran like a wildcat, so...

Caroline grabbed my arm, yanking me toward the corner. "Gwen, I need you to listen carefully."

"What? Is Amaya okay?"

She looked up at the ceiling like she was praying to the Goddess for patience. I had no idea why my questions were annoying her, and frankly, I didn't care. Amaya and Sloane were my only priority.

"One hundred years ago," she started. "I saw the writing on the wall in Delnee before everyone else did, before even Evelynne, your mother, would believe me. The government was requiring fae to register their powers. I tried to convince the Society to act, but they ignored my warnings."

I shook my head. Why was she telling me this now?

"By the time I fled to Palagui to ask for help, it was too late. Darkness had spread through Delnee. Fae were vanquished, but by some grace of the Goddess, Evelynne and our family were able to make a deal.

"But that darkness is here, now, in Palagui, Gwen. It's happening again, and I have to stop it."

"No... No. The humans killed the fae in Delnee."

"Think about it." She pursed her lips, looking at me with pity. "How could humans have killed a country full of fae?" She raised her eyebrows but didn't wait for my reply. "They couldn't. Not without the shadow plague."

I held up my hands, shaking my head. "We were taught in school that the humans tricked the fae, weakened, and killed them. Only the legacy families were spared."

Caroline pinched the bridge of her nose. "I don't have time for a history lesson. Those stories were written by the people who won. The humans didn't kill a country of fae by themselves. I know it, but I don't have any proof. All I know is that it's going to happen again unless I stop it!"

My eyes widened, and I stepped back, icy dread curled down my spine. Caroline was intense, sure, I could be intense too, but she was talking crazy now. "What are you going to do?"

Her face deadened. "I'm going to do what needs to be done to prevent the shadows from rising. You and I are going to be the ones who save the high priestesses from extinction." With that, she marched to the ballroom door. The guards readied their weapons.

My palms started sweating. Something was wrong.

Caroline flung open the door and called for Amaya's and Sebastian's arrest before I could figure out what was happening. After that speech, I knew she had no intention of letting them live. "Accidents" happened in prisons all the time.

Chaos ensued. I tried to fight past the guards and toward my friend, but hands grabbed me around the waist. A familiar coolness engulfed me. I struggled and yelled obscenities at her, except it was too late.

Daria sifted us away.

I shoved her hard enough that she fell to the ground. I didn't know where she'd taken us, didn't care. I vaguely registered the smell of dampness and the light coming from a single bulb hanging by a string.

I jumped on top of her, throwing punches, but she was too fast, having already expected my attack and ducking before my fist could connect with her jaw.

Her legs wrapped around my waist, and she threw her weight, rolling until she was on top of me. She held down my wrists. Her shadows cinched around my waist, my neck, my ankles.

I shimmied and yanked at my hands, calling on my high priestess light.

The shine brightened in my upturned palms.

"The ward on this room is old and needs charged. You could break through it, but only if you use your light to blast me in the heart. And I know you aren't going to do that," she said, chest heaving out of breath.

I curled my lip and tightened my fists. Murderous rage filled me. I'd hurt her. I'd fucking kill her.

Except.

Her eyes were wild, and the chin-length strands of her black hair fell in her eyes as she hovered over me. She blew them out of her face and pressed harder into my wrists, quirking a brow. "Go ahead, Gwen. I dare you."

I swallowed and tried to summon the rage again. Amaya was being hurt, potentially killed. The heat of anger blew through me, and I wriggled with new energy trying to get out of her bind, but without the killing blow, I wasn't going to get loose.

And I couldn't do it.

Humiliation sapped energy from my movements.

I'd questioned Amaya's ability to kill Sebastian. I'd repeatedly asked her if she was sure she could do it, not because I distrusted her loyalty, but because I knew I'd never have been able to do it if it'd been Daria instead of Sebastian.

That lick of shame burned through me. I fell back to verbal sparring. "Is this what you wanted all along? To get rid of Amaya? Her power is too much of a threat to you, isn't it?" I taunted. "You're jealous of her. Or is it that you just like licking my aunt's boots?"

She gave me an infuriating smirk. "You're the one that blindly does whatever your aunt and mommy tell you to do. You bitch and moan about how she and the Society don't control you and then you bend over backward to do their bidding. If you're going to throw around insults, I'd hold up a mirror first."

She might as well have slapped me, at least that would have hurt less.

All of my brimming rage and instinct to fight died. I let her tie me up in that chair. Let her leave me in the dark, dank basement. Let her words echo in my head for the rest of the night.

She'd been right. I was an imposter. I thought my smart-ass remarks and little rebellions against my mother and the Society meant I wouldn't fall in line, that I wouldn't hesitate to do the right thing. I'd trained Amaya with her high priestess powers rather than turn her in. I disregarded Palaguian laws by breaking into records to research the disappearing high priestesses.

But those were miniscule, minor infractions.

Daria had seen through me. I'd confided in her, told her in a vulnerable moment that I was afraid I'd never truly be able to stand up to my mother.

And she threw my weakness back into my face.

I fucking hated her.

But she let Annabelle watch over me during the day, so at least I didn't have to stare at her stupid face.

Annabelle crossed the basement and set a tray of food and tea on the table before undoing the ties at my wrists.

My brown skin was deep red along my wrists were the ropes had dug in.

Annabelle tsked. "Sweetie, why didn't you tell me they were too tight? Oh dear, hold on, let me get you ointment."

She bustled off to the bathroom, rummaging around.

"You know if you let me out, I could heal myself," I said with a hopeful lilt.

Annabelle returned, picked up my hands from my lap, and started rubbing a sticky gel on my wrists. "Now you know I can't do that. Daria doesn't even know that I've been untying you during the day."

I should be angry at her, but I just couldn't muster it. Annabelle's face was withered and wrinkled, but her eyes were bright, and she had a sass that rivaled mine.

"Besides you're going free soon enough. The hurricane is going to hit downtown hard. They're recommending everyone evacuate."

"So Daria probably plans to leave me here to drown," I mumbled.

Annabelle made a disapproving noise and tapped at my plate. "More eating, less grumbling. The tea shoppe imported a new brand."

"Yes ma'am," I said and cleaned my plate while she tidied up in the basement.

It actually wasn't that bad down here. Yeah, it was a little musty, but a big rug covered the cold cement floor, making it less dungeon-like. There was a full bathroom in the corner, and a couch in the middle that sectioned off the living room area from the table where Annabelle and I ate. When all the lights were turned on, it was even kind of cozy.

And I had Annabelle's company to distract me from the fact I was sitting around while Amaya was in prison, and Sloane was...who the hell knows where.

I took a sip of the new green tea Annabelle had imported to her tea shoppe. It was good. Something more savory than I'd usually drink for breakfast, but good nonetheless.

Annabelle unfolded today's paper and hummed. "Your aunt is still looking for you." She slid the article over for me to read.

Councilmember Caroline Nueblots is asking all citizens to report to an anonymous tipline any information on the whereabout of her niece...

Aunt Caroline knew I wasn't strong enough to hold the crown's power, but she didn't care. For all her worry about high priestesses, she didn't care about us as individuals, only our supremacy over the other fae factions.

The fact that I'd likely die in a few decades—shrivel up like the current Queen of Palagui—didn't matter to her. By that point, she'd have another high priestess puppet lined up to use. That was obvious given she wasn't offering herself up as queen.

I pushed away the newspaper, but my eyes caught on the numerous articles about the hurricane.

Heavy rain and flash flooding is possible, accompanied by severe thunderstorms and damaging winds...

"Has it ever been this bad?"

"No," Annabelle said and sipped her tea. "We're going to watch Palagui be destroyed right before our eyes."

I swallowed. The deep sinking feeling that was spreading through my limbs wasn't fear for my life or even concern for the people who would most likely die.

I couldn't meet Annabelle's gaze as I asked, "This hurricane formed because the Queen is dying?"

"Most likely," she said. "Magic is a delicate ecosystem. Even the most minor disruption can create a ripple effect, and Queen Mari's passing will be anything but minor."

We did this.

Sloane, Amaya, and I caused this. Sebastian had been keeping the Queen alive by sacrificing high priestesses, and Caroline promised there would be a way to stop it, but her plan had been to sacrifice me instead. To give me the crown and let it siphon my life force, while she ruled through me from the sidelines. All in the name of saving the high priestesses from some supposed darkness.

"This is my fault," I whispered.

Annabelle put her hand on mine, misunderstanding what I'd meant. "No, dear, you wouldn't have been accepted as queen, even if you had the crown. Caroline was having a hard time convincing the council to approve a non-Palaguian citizen for the throne."

My head flinched back. "How do you know that?"

"Daria told me," she said simply.

"And how does she know that?" I asked, standing up, my voice raising. I had read the article that outlined the first thing Caroline did after getting rid of Sebastian was kick Daria—the only darkyra on the council—out.

Daria shouldn't have any knowledge of what the council was doing.

She shrugged. "Dear me…I guess I wasn't supposed to say anything." She went back to reading her paper, not looking sorry at all. "Let's just say Daria has connections."

I sat back down, rifling through my memories of the councilmembers and their interactions with Daria, but none stood out as particularly chummy.

"Why don't you go take a nap on the couch?" Annabelle said. "I have a feeling you're going to need your rest for tonight."

I didn't bother questioning what she'd meant. Annabelle spoke in codes, only telling me what she wanted me to know.

Whatever was going to happen tonight, I'd need to be mentally prepared.

I fell asleep quickly, having been exhausted by worrying, and the next thing I knew, a hand was on my shoulder shaking me.

"Gwen. Wake up."

It wasn't her voice that pulled me into consciousness. When she touched me, I sensed the shadows that lurked under her skin. They sang to me in a language I didn't know. Their calling dragged me from my slumber.

I lurched away from her, righting myself on the couch, and looked around the basement. "Where's Annabelle?"

Daria pressed her lips together, sitting on the coffee table in front of the couch. "She evacuated the city with her friends from the tea shoppe."

Normally, Daria had an annoyingly playful light in her hazel eyes, but that energy was nowhere to be found today.

"So you've come to tie me up?" I glared, trying to hide how unsettled I was that the echo of her shadow's song lingered in my mind. "Want to make sure I'm good and secure for when the hurricane drowns me?"

She heaved an exasperated breath. "I know you won't see it this way, but I've been keeping you safe."

"Yeah, I feel real safe tied up in your basement."

Her face fell into a bland look. "I know Nana was untying you. She's not as stealthy as she likes to pretend to be."

"Shucks, it must really suck when someone you trust does something to betray you. I couldn't possibly imagine what that's like..." I snapped my fingers and pointed at her. "Oh wait! I guess I can."

"If you'd let me explain—"

"I don't want your explanations."

Daria pressed her lips together. "Well, this room is still warded, and my shadows love a good tousle, so unless you'd like me to pin you again, you're going to sit there and listen."

I leaned forward, until our knees almost touched, until I was breathing the air that she exhaled, and curled my lip in disgust. "I'd rather fight than listen to a single lie come out of your mouth."

She quirked an eyebrow, challenge blooming in her eyes. "I figured you'd say that."

And she launched herself at me.

I interlocked our arms and threw her hands off, but her body was already moving in my direction and flattened me to the couch.

I kicked up and rolled onto the ground before she could get up, then crab crawled my way out from between the coffee table and couch.

As I pushed to stand, a shadow flung out and tripped me, my legs flying out from under me. I caught myself before I face-planted, but she threw her body on top of mine, legs on either side of my back.

Her shadows skated down the length of my arms, condensing around my wrists. She held them together at my back with one hand, the other pressed flat between my shoulder blades.

Kicking my legs was useless as shadows had already bound them.

I pressed my cheek to the ground to look back at her.

"You don't fight fair!" I yelled. "You're a cheater and a traitor! Why don't you unward the room and try to come at me."

Her mouth was at my ear, breath hot against my neck as she said, "Even unwarded this wouldn't be a fair fight. I've got fifty years of training and power on you."

I growled and started wiggling, trying to throw her off.

She just laughed "I think you're only still fighting because you like the feel of my shadows digging into your skin and me straddling you."

I froze, crinkling my nose in disgust. "I hate the feel of your slimy, freezing cold shadows as much as I hate the slimy darkyra they are attached to."

She pressed on my chest harder, squeezing air out of my lungs. "Mmm so I've heard. Apparently, those slimy shadows blinded my mother because how could she love someone as horrible as me?"

I smiled evilly.

Okay, it was a stupid insult, and I thought only Annabelle heard it, but Daria had too, and it'd upset her enough that she remembered it.

"Hilarious," she said, deadpan. "How did you figure out Annabelle fostered me? That my parents ditched me on the side of the road for exactly that reason?"

My smile died, and my muscles all went limp.

She used that as an opportunity to get off me and forced me into a seated position with my arms behind my back and ankles bound in shadows.

She sat across from me on the floor. Her eyebrows raised in faux shock. "Oh, you didn't know about that? Just a lucky guess?"

I couldn't look at her, couldn't explain why I was feeling bad for the person who put my friend in prison. "Daria..."

"No. Don't." When I glanced up, she was pressing on her thighs, steeling herself for what she was going to say. Her eyes swept to mine. "You don't owe me anything, and you can sit there and ignore me if you want, but for my own selfish guilt-ridden conscious I'm going to explain myself."

Despite the fact I could have probably done something immature like singing the alphabet at the top of my lungs, I sat in silence, curious as to how she would justify her actions.

"You were right," she started. "I *was* threatened by Amaya's power. Do you know how rare it is to have the ability to wield two powers? One in a billion." She shook her head. "And to not only have two powers but also have the capacity to control Sebastian's shadow? A shadow capable of killing an entire city? Fae with his amount of power come around once in a millennium, but it happened twice in the same generation? No one should have as much power as they do. Together they were able to freeze the fae guards at the research center…When they accept the mating bond, they'll be untouchable—"

I jolted back, shaking my head. "Mating bond?"

Daria shrugged. "I don't know for sure, but it'd surprise me more if they weren't mates. Power recognizes power."

Oh Goddess.

"Caroline and I never believed Amaya when she suddenly changed her mind about Sebastian, but I convinced Caroline that we could use it as an opportunity to get them both isolated and alone in a warded room."

"The whole thing was your idea!" Why did that make the betrayal worse?

"Yes." She looked down at her palms. "But Caroline said that she'd only arrest Amaya so there'd be an excuse to send her back to Delnee and keep her away from Sebastian. Though I don't think she actually planned on doing that, even before Amaya killed Xenos and gave Caroline the perfect excuse to keep her in prison for life.

"I was short-sighted." Her voice tightened into anger. "So stupid. So focused on eliminating the draxis, on preventing them from hurting more people, on getting my teams off the streets and not risking their lives fighting them." Her fists clenched as she brought them down to hit her legs. "I assumed Caroline and I were on the same page because she was the only other person on the council that cared about the draxis, about the disappearing high priestesses, but her concern wasn't for people's lives, it was because it was *high priestesses*, her delegation.

"I didn't question her long-term plans. She said that we would crown a new queen and rearrange the council's powers, that darkyra would finally be given the position they deserved…And I trusted her promises instead of seeing the truth in her actions. I didn't read between the lines. In her eyes, darkyra are the scum of the world and the only position we deserved to be in was powerless and locked away."

She took a breath and exhaled it out. "I sifted you out of that room to keep you from getting caught in the crossfire, but when Caroline started spouting plans that we'd never agreed to, I lied and told her you escaped. I needed time to think. My entire life has been bouncing from one crisis to the next, and I've never been good at planning for what happened after the most pressing crisis was averted.

"I'd been so upset that Sebastian was hurting people, that he pretended to care about the humans and the darkyra, but in the meantime, he was the one sending the draxis into the streets. I was so angry. I called him a traitor in my head so many times…"

Her jaw started to quiver. "And when you called me a traitor, it clicked. I was making the exact same choice that I was crucifying him for. Sacrificing one group of people to save another.

"And now? The Queen is going to pass away, the hurricane is going to hit, and thousands of people are going to die, but the council isn't doing anything to stop it."

Tears rolled down her face. "And the worst part is that the only person that would have fixed this—would have made sure there were evacuation procedures and buses and medical supplies at the ready—is locked in prison because of what *I* did." She pointed to her chest hard enough to bruise. "He was preventing all of this from happening, and I got him locked up."

She sniffed. "He should never forgive me, none of you should, but there you go. That's what I've done."

Heavy silence filled the space between us until her tear-filled eyes looked at me.

I dropped my gaze, unable to stomach the feelings rolling through me, the barrage of emotions from her, from me. She must have dropped the wards if I could sense her emotions.

"There's a supply van taking a shipment of saline to the Molbridge refugee area," she said. "Nico's got a cabin up there. I'd bet good money that's where Sloane is hiding. The van will be at Forty-Third and Albany Street in"—she looked at her watch—"twenty-five minutes. Takes about twenty to get there, so you should leave now."

Her shadows misted away from my wrists and ankles, and I stood, ready to flee from the tension between us. The air was thick with an impending storm, but it wasn't coming from the hurricane.

And I wasn't about to stick around for the downpour.

I crossed the basement toward the stairs, but paused on the first step.

"What are you going to do?" It was stupid to ask. She could drown in the hurricane for all I cared. Her sob story didn't matter to me. Amaya was still in prison.

Yet, I waited for her answer.

Daria shrugged one shoulder. "I'm going to do what I do best. Focus on the next crisis. There are humans and darkyra that need someone to get them to safety. I may not be on the council, but I can help get people out of here."

I stared at her a second longer, before jogging up the stairs and leaving her behind for good.

Despite the late hour, the streets were chaos. Cars packed to the brim inched forward in heavy traffic. The sound of horns in the air seemed like a collective cry of frustration.

I sprinted down the sidewalk toward Albany Street, dodging people on the way.

The medical supplies van was exactly where Daria had said it would be.

The male loading the back saw me and hollered, "Daria send you?"

"Yeah."

He tilted his head to the passenger seat. "Get in. We're late."

I slipped into the seat and buckled as the van driver pulled out.

The hours-long car ride was silent. My companion wasn't the talkative type, but that was fine because neither was I.

It was past midnight by the time we got to Molbridge.

The center of the town was already full of tents and makeshift buildings. The van driver and I silently unpacked the saline, before getting back in the van and heading off.

We drove deep into the forest. I hadn't seen darkness this thick and oppressive in a long time. There was no light pollution from the city out here.

The road turned from asphalt to gravel, and then from gravel to dirt.

"Daria gave you the address to this place?" I asked, starting to get serial killer vibes.

"Yeah," he said. "There somewhere else you wanted to go?"

"No." The driver had a small-build, so I was fairly confident I could take him out if I needed to. And maybe I was stupid to trust

Daria's contact, but then again, if she wanted me dead, she could have done it herself.

Driveways lined the road, leading up to camps and cabins of different sizes. After forty-five minutes, we stopped in front of a tiny log cabin.

"This is it," he said.

I threw open the door and was about to race away, but turned back. "Ah, thanks for the ride."

He shrugged. "No problem. I owed Daria a favor."

"You did?"

He nodded. "She got my delivery business approval when the solisers at the township office were trying to give me the runaround."

Interesting.

I closed the door, and he drove off, but I didn't bother to watch him go. I sprinted up the driveway toward the cabin. A soft yellow light glowed in the window.

I pounded on the door. "Sloane! Open the damn door!"

The pattering of running feet preceded the door being whipped open.

Sloane threw her arms around my neck. "Gwen! I'm so glad you're here!"

I hugged her tight, relief coursing through me. "Amaya?" I asked, pulling back.

Sloane shook her head, wiping her nose. "They're both still in prison, but I've been keeping an eye on them, and we've got a plan."

The tension in my shoulders eased marginally. "Good."

Sloane moved farther into the cabin, and I shut the door, following her into the living room area.

Nico was sprawled out, sleeping on the couch. His face was pale, dark circles under his eyes, and his skin was glistening with sweat.

Sloane went into the kitchen and turned on the faucet.

"He looks like shit," I said. "What's wrong with him?"

"Nice to see you too, Gwen," Nico managed to get out, but his voice cracked, and he clutched his stomach as if talking pained him.

Sloane sat a glass of water on the coffee table, kneeling beside him and interlacing her fingers with his.

I noticed that Sloane's face was blotchy like she'd been crying a lot longer than the two minutes I'd been here.

She brushed her fingers along his forehead. "He broke a bargain with Sebastian when he told me him and I are mates."

My jaw dropped. Them too?

But Sloane wasn't finished. "We accepted the bond so we would have power for the prison break, but..." She sniffed. "I think it's killing him."

Chapter Nine

Amaya

My name is Amaya Mevson.

I am a high priestess. I am a darkyra. I have two best friends. Sloane and Gwen need me to be strong. Sebastian is alive. He's in the prison somewhere. I'm going to break us out.

I paced up and down my tiny cell, repeating what I knew, over and over, trying to remind myself that the shadows lie.

The trouble was…the shadows' whispers felt like the truth. They would bombard me with emotions, crush me with their weight until the words were twisted in my head, making me forget again.

"My name is Amaya Mevson." *You don't know who you are,* the shadows said as anxiety collapsed my chest.

"I am a high priestess. I am a darkyra." *They all hate what you are.* Blistering shame ripped my insides to shreds.

"I have two best friends." *You have no one. No one actually likes you.* Misery made my legs tremble, my teeth chatter.

"Sloane and Gwen need me to be strong." *You're pathetic and worthless. You can't do anything right.* The shadows sent a long slow wave of resignation to numb me, accompanied by flashes of memories from all my past failures.

I took a deep breath, focusing on *my* words, not the past and not the despair.

"Sebastian is alive," I croaked out. *Your mate is gone, and it's all your fault.* A bubble of grief rose in my throat, and I gasped as a tiny sob escaped. I held my stomach with one hand, trying to protect myself from the sorrow.

"He's in the prison somewhere," I whispered. I closed my eyes and pictured him. Pictured his blue eyes and his infuriating smirk. The feel of being cuddled against him, my head on his chest, his arm wrapped around me as his fingers lazily stroked up and down my back.

"I'm going to break us out," I said, projecting strength and assurance. My words clawed into the demonic shadows until they scattered.

You can do this, little warrior.

I sighed as my mind quieted, leaving only Sebastian's shadow.

For now.

Can't you get them to stop? I asked. I'd finally cleared enough of the suppression in my blood to remember things. Like how Sebastian's shadow had been with me this whole time. It snuck away when Kai took me to the hose, but he returned when he sensed my distress and told Kai where I was when the guard was about to hurt me in the hall.

Kai had told me he'd saved me, but Sebastian's shadow told me that it wasn't Kai's power that emanated through the prison to knock the guard out.

Which meant Sebastian was being held near the med-room. He'd sensed my distress and sent his power to save me. I hoped that meant he was in better condition than me, if he'd been able to summon enough strength to bust through the wards.

Granted, that could also mean that they moved him to higher security after they realized what happened.

From what Kai told me—and I couldn't be sure if it was all truthful—fae power was dying which meant the wards around the prison were faltering. Prisoners were required to remain in fae cuffs at the wrists and ankles at all times, and the place was on lockdown.

I'm sorry, Sebastian's shadow said. *I don't have enough power to block the shadows. They're too strong. I've been trying to fight them off for weeks.*

They were too strong for me to block for long as well. It was one thing to construct a quick mental wall from Kai, but to sustain that barrier around my mind was proving difficult.

None of it made any sense though. If my powers were fading, how had I been able to filter the suppression?

I could only assume they'd lowered the amount of suppression they were injecting me with, because even with four fae cuffs, I'd been able to filter most of it out of my blood.

Why they'd do that, I didn't know.

The doctor had been concerned by the level of suppression I was on, but he also ended up shrugging off the condition I was in.

Maybe Kai was helping me? But why now? If he'd been able to alter my suppression, surely, he'd have told me. He would want to throw it in my face as another reason I should be grateful for his help.

Where are the shadows even coming from? I asked. Were the wards so weak that some prisoner's shadows decided to mess with me?

They feel familiar but also strange, Sebastian's shadow answered. *Kai is a darkyra but also not. I don't know how that's possible. He must be like you.*

I blinked and stopped my pacing. *Wait. These are Kai's shadows? They feel exactly like him.*

He was a soliser...wasn't he? I assumed all the guards were solisers based on their level of arrogance and hostility.

How can he use his shadows here? Shouldn't the wards block him?

If he's pretending to be a guard, he'd have access to the wards. He must have changed them to permit only his darkyra power, the shadow said.

How do you know he's pretending?

I don't, but for the short time I was with him while you were in the med-room, he did his best to walk in the opposite direction when other guards were around. He seemed to be sneaking.

The guard that accompanied the doctor had said there was no one in the prison named Kai.

So who was he?

And what did he want with me?

"Gah!" I flung my hands out. My memories were sporadic and sparse from the time I was under the heavy suppression. I was sure if I could remember everything Kai had told me, I could piece a theory for his motives.

Sebastian's shadow was here with me, but he didn't remember much because every time Kai was near me, the demonic shadows would attack him. There wasn't time to pay attention to the ramblings of my guard.

I paced with a renewed quickness to relieve my frustration. My mind was still so wobbly. Cognition slow and stuttered. Filtering the suppression and blocking the demonic shadows while wearing fae cuffs was taking its toll.

But if the shadows were Kai's, they would know I had enough power to block them. They would know I was talking to Sebastian's shadow. And if they were Kai's, as soon as he came into my cell, they'd have told him everything, but over the past few days, he hadn't acted any different.

So maybe they weren't his?

I sat on my thin mattress on the floor—a gift from Kai—and held my head in my hands.

As if I'd summoned him with all my thinking, the door opened with a beep, and Kai slipped in. He was smiling broadly. "Today is the day, Maya."

I stayed silent, waiting for the moment the shadows told Kai my secrets and he would explode with rage.

"Winter solstice," he said, annoyed when I didn't say anything. He rolled his eyes good-naturedly. "It's alright, I'll forgive you for forgetting. You don't have a calendar in here."

But if today was winter solstice...my bargain with Sebastian to be his pretend fiancée ended.

The fact that the bargain never, not once, itched or caused me pain should have been my first clue that even when I was planning to plunge a dagger in his heart and kill him...I was still pretending to be his.

No, not pretending. I had been his. I would always be his.

I had tried so hard to convince myself that I was a good person, that I could put my personal feelings aside to do what needed to be done.

It was laughable. I only needed to convince myself I was a good person because I knew deep down—I wasn't.

It just took me being thrown into prison and tortured for weeks to realize it.

And if it was winter solstice, I had another bargain tied to this day. The Darkyra Deity bargained to unbind my powers if I promised to complete a task for them. When I asked what the task was, they'd only said shadows were dying, and I'd restore our rightful place.

Even as a darkyra, that sounded pretty ominous.

But I'd accepted because I didn't have a choice if I wanted my power back. Sebastian didn't know the Deity would force me into a bargain when he'd suggested I bind my powers to hide them from Xenos. He had assumed the Deity forced him into a bargain when he unbound his powers one hundred years ago because he was their offspring and had refused to do their bidding.

His bargain...well, I didn't like thinking about it. He'd swore he would never bind himself to another, not through marriage and certainly not by accepting the mating bond.

We hadn't had time for him to explain why he'd taken that bargain before Caroline rushed in with her guards.

But he didn't need to explain. I knew him. His reason was clear. Sebastian bound his power to keep people safe from his shadow. When he went to the Deity to undo the binding, he had accepted their bargain because it would just act as another layer of protection between him and the people he loved. He'd have another reason to never let anyone get close.

That was until we found one another, and I showed him I was strong enough to control his shadow.

Before Caroline interrupted us, he had said he would give up his power, go back on his bargain with the Deity, just to accept the bond with me.

I would never let him do that...not after knowing firsthand the way it felt to be powerless.

Kai tapped his foot impatiently when I hadn't answered him.

"Sorry," I said, feigning sheepishness. "What did you say?" My dazed and confused act worked on the doctor, but I didn't think it was working on Kai.

He narrowed his eyes. "It's winter solstice. Don't you want to know when you'll get your three gifts?"

I forced myself to nod.

Reaching into his pocket, he produced a set of fae cuffs with chains and replaced the ones on my wrists. "I'm taking you to your first gift right now. How does a shower in the guard's bathroom sound?"

I sighed dreamily. "That sounds amazing."

Kai had done this for me before. Instead of forcing me into the communal area, where Kai said the guards watched the prisoners shower, he would sneak me into their locker room on the first floor of the prison.

I had never truly understood the value of privacy, soap, and hot water as much as I did after five weeks here.

My appreciation was genuine when I said, "Thank you, Kai."

He pulled me out of the cell. "See? This is what I mean. You understand gratitude," he said as we walked down the corridor to the elevator. "When I took him to the shower, all he did was stare at me. Wouldn't say a single word of thanks. I contemplated taking him back, but I figured he'd been burned enough." He laughed as if making some inside joke. "He'll understand gratitude by the end of the day."

I furrowed my brow. "He who?" I'd thought the suppression had been muddling what Kai said, but it was truly like he talked in riddles.

Unless he was talking about Sebastian. My heart raced, but Kai just shrugged. "There are a few prisoners I keep an eye on." He threw me an unimpressed look. "You think you deserve all my attention?"

I dropped my eyes. "No, Kai. I don't deserve your attention."

A shadow of despair crept in, and when I hung my head, I wasn't faking the feeling.

Kai wanted me to think Sebastian was gone. The only proof I had that Sebastian was alive was his shadow's steady presence, but in my worst moments, I convinced myself that wasn't enough. That maybe this piece of his shadow was the only thing left.

We walked into the guard's shower area. A Closed for Cleaning sign hung across the door.

Kai unlocked my cuffs, both my ankles and wrists, before handing me a set of fresh clothes and a towel. He leaned against the wall outside the stall as I walked in.

The hot water was bliss, and as I scrubbed, I tried to wash away my sadness. I needed to stay focused and alert. I needed to figure out what Kai was up to and how I could use it to my advantage.

He obviously needed me alive. And for all that his shadows had been torturing me, he did protect me. Maybe a part of him was trustworthy. He got me socks and shoes, snuck extra food into my room, and gave me a blanket and mattress. Most importantly, he'd kept all the guards away.

But why? What did he want? Was it because I had two powers and he wanted to research and study me like Xenos had?

I pumped shampoo into my hand and worked it into my hair, gingerly combing out the knots, thinking but not coming up with anything that explained his actions.

And though I could have stood there for hours, letting the scalding water work the kinks out of my body, I didn't want to push my luck and Kai's generous mood by taking too long.

I toweled off and slipped on fresh clothes before stepping out of the stall.

Kai held up a jacket.

"Is this my next gift?"

He shrugged. "Sort of." He held the shoulders of the jacket and put it on me like a child, including zipping it to my chin.

Something heavy and long lay inside the inner pocket, but before I could reach in to retrieve it, Kai tsked and fastened the cuffs around my wrists.

"Uh uh uhhh. Not yet," he said and yanked on the chain between my wrists to make me move.

But my ankles were uncuffed. Odd.

He made it clear that it wasn't a lapse in his memory when he winked as he dragged me into the hall.

The heavy object in my jacket felt to be the length of my torso, skinny at the top, wider on the bottom.

Distracted by trying to figure out what the object was, I didn't notice as we passed through several corridors until we halted in a hall with guards talking to one another at the end.

Kai grabbed my upper arm, and I winced. He dug his fingers in as he leaned in and whispered, "Don't you want to know what your third gift is?"

I fought the prickles of rage that wanted to tell him where to shove his supposed gifts, but instead I bit my lip and said, "You got me three gifts, but I didn't get you anything." Scared and desperate for his attention, that was how he liked me. He only enjoyed stoking my anger when it was directed at someone else.

Kai stopped us in the middle of the hall.

He chuckled. "No, you haven't, but you will."

Reaching under my arm, he unlocked my cuffs while keeping his eyes trained on the guards up ahead.

The cuffs loosened and fell to the ground with a *clang*.

My eyes widened. I looked from the cuffs to the matching bewildered expressions of the guards at the end of the hall.

Their faces turned from shock to anger, and they took two steps toward us before chaos broke out.

The edges of the walls rippled violently like heat waves on asphalt until they exploded with a burst.

The wards broke.

The guards faltered in their steps as hundreds of loud beeps echoed through the prison and every single door slid into the wall.

"Run," Kai said with a calm voice. He shoved me forward, but he didn't need to tell me twice.

I sprinted.

Pumping my arms and legs, I raced past the guards. The prisoners' slight delay from confusion evaporated, and they darted out of their cells and down the hall in every direction.

A siren started blaring.

The guards didn't know where to look, where to turn, their eyes darted around in panic, and several prisoners attacked them.

I dodged the fighting and made it to the next corridor where more guards wrestled with prisoners. Weak fire collars blazed on their necks.

But the guards couldn't fire collar us all, even their fire balls were puny. Fae power had decreased enough for the wards to have fallen, but depending on the level of suppression each prisoner had, they were probably still filtering it out of their blood.

Sure enough, by the time I made it to the next corridor, the playing field was leveled. Shadows snuffed out flames around the prisoners' necks. Some guards realized they were outnumbered and fled.

I weaved through the rush of prisoners and ducked as flames chased me until I made it to the stairwell.

Prisoners flooded down the steps. I attempted to fight my way up by holding on to the railing and yanking myself through the throng of bodies, but it was too much.

A blast of darkness flew over everyone. Screams and yells echoed, but I only sighed. His power fell over me like the soft pattering of rain. The darkness lifted slow at first like fog and dispersed.

Sebastian *was* alive.

I needed to get to the med-room. He was near there, but it was ten stories up, and I couldn't even make it to the second floor.

The elevator wouldn't be fast or safe enough.

I needed to sift, but I needed power.

If Sebastian had enough power that the whole prison could feel it, maybe I did too.

The suppression had been filtered from my blood in the time it took me to run to the stairwell. Even my wrists and neck healed without the fae cuffs. My back itched and tingled as my high priestess healing trickled through me without my conscious effort like stretching after a long hibernation.

I pressed my body against the wall and closed my eyes, searching for the thread of my power that dwelled within my core. Sebastian had always said I was the strongest fae he knew. I *had* to have enough power left to sift to him. I just had to.

There was no other option.

Shadows flowed through me, as natural as breathing, condensing so I could step into the astral field and sift to the med-room.

The floor was utter mayhem. These guards weren't running. They stood their ground and threw fire recklessly, unconcerned that the prison was burning.

Shouldn't there be sprinklers going off or something? But immediately I discarded that idea. The building was made out of concrete and cement, and the guards were solisers. They could extinguish flames. The only people who'd die in a fire were the prisoners.

Running past several guards locked in fights with prisoners, I unzipped my jacket and dug in the pocket, pulling out a small sheathed dagger.

Kai had given me a weapon.

A weapon he somehow knew I'd had training using.

I couldn't let myself dwell on how or why. Ripping the leather pouch off, I threw it aside and adjusted my grip. A zip of pleasure moved through me at the familiarity, at the strength the blade instilled in me.

I thrust my shadows out, snuffing flames to make a path toward the cells, but that drew the attention of the guards.

Three of them attacked at once. A fire ball flung toward my head, and I ducked. Flames blazed, licking my ankles with their heat.

But they'd picked the wrong prisoner.

We'll kill them, my shadow said, low and vicious. Pure delight filled me to hear her again. It ignited something dark buried deep inside.

Something bloodthirsty.

Kill. Kill. Kill, she encouraged.

I screamed something guttural and lunged at one guard, my hands around his throat. Shadows poured into his eyes, his nose, his mouth, and he clutched at his neck, choking.

The siren was still ringing in the background, but I tuned it out, if anything it was egging me on.

Destruction and devastation felt just at my fingertips.

A guard rushed at me, and he practically killed himself running into my dagger. Another guard tried to collar me with his flames, but my shadows easily extinguish them, just like I'd extinguish him.

I sprang forward, winding my arm back. *Crack*. My fists broke his nose making one of the sweetest sounds I'd ever heard.

My knuckles ached, but only for a second as my healing power restored me. A sick thrill bubbled up as I watched him struggle before my shadows encircled and suffocated him.

I jumped over their dead bodies and ran down toward the bend in the hall. Two guards appeared and caged me in, the blaze of fire in front of me, my back to the wall.

"You're the hybrid that killed our Prince," one said, casually walking toward me.

"It must be our lucky day," the other said. "We'll make you see the light."

"Oh no!" I said in a high-pitched girly voice. "Don't hurt me."

They both chuckled, and for all their talk about light, something dark resided in them both.

"You'll pay for what you've done," one of them said, and they both rushed toward me.

At the last second, I sunk my dagger into the abdomen of the guard to the right. My shadow collared him, his head yanking back as the momentum of his body kept moving.

Fire fought shadows, but I jerked my dagger up, cutting through the guard's stomach before pulling it out.

He gaped, clutching at his wound.

"You won't be hurting anyone anymore," I seethed.

He fell, and all my shadows blanketed the other guard in darkness, his flames unable to catch light. I stabbed him in the heart, blood spraying into my face.

I pulled down each of their collars, and they both had the tiny tattoo, a square with a diamond overlay. The strange marking that Kai told me I'd need to watch out for.

Whatever group they were a part of had a vendetta against me for killing Xenos.

Shadows snuffed the rest of the flames and revealed a final guard in the hall. He'd seen what I'd done.

I stalked toward him like the prey he was.

His eyes widened, backing away from me. I used a shadow to yank at his collar, pulling it down to see if he was a part of the group.

And sure enough, this guard was a bad male.

Now he was going to die.

He trembled when he saw my void eyes. "What are you?"

I tilted my head and smiled. "I'm the reason people are afraid of the dark."

Shadows poured into his ears, bursting his brain until blood trickled from his eyes, his nose, his mouth.

He fell to his knees and collapsed.

My decreasing morality may have concerned me in the past, but there was no remorse to be found anymore. No pity. No guilt. Nothing even close to it.

A sweet exhilaration raced through my veins as I watched him die.

This...this was *fun*.

My mind had quieted its anxious babble, my power honing in on its objective. I'd take actual danger over the threats produced by my imagination any day.

The moment Kai unlocked my cuffs, a calm calculation had washed over me as my priorities aligned.

Stay alive.

Find Sebastian.

Kill anyone who got in the way.

I looked to my left and right, waiting for the next guard, but the hall was empty.

I didn't waste time. Jogging down the corridors and shouting Sebastian's name, I paused to search inside each cell, but he wasn't here.

Most of this floor had emptied out, and I didn't run into prisoners or guards as I made the loop and ended up back in front of the med-room.

I put my hands on my hips and twisted left to right. *Where is he?* I asked Sebastian's shadow.

His power is near, but I don't know exactly. Follow the mating bond.

I furrowed my brow—about to ask how the hell to do that—when someone flew into me from behind and flattened me to the ground, knocking the wind out of me.

Trying to shove his heavy body off, I flailed and thrashed. My dagger was in my hand, but I couldn't swing it backward with his body blocking my movements.

I reached for my shadows, but could feel them weakening. They sputtered and slipped from my grasp.

The realization hit me as the guard grabbed the back of my head at the root of my hair and slammed my face into the ground.

Fae power was almost gone.

Chapter Ten

Amaya

My temples throbbed, and my vision spotted, but as I braced for another blow, the guard's movements stopped, and he collapsed on top of me. I rolled out from under his lifeless body. Sebastian's shadow floated back to my neck.

I'm sorry, he said. *I couldn't attack him until he was touching you. My strength is almost spent.*

It's okay, I said. A faint healing light tingled at my head and relieved the ache.

I pushed up. *How do I use the mating bond to find Sebastian?*

The bond lives within you both. It's attuned to one another even if your auras aren't fully braided yet, the shadow explained. *How do you think he found you every time you were in trouble with the draxis?*

I never thought about it, but it made sense.

The shadow continued, *That's how he knew you were in trouble outside the med-room, despite the suppression and the cuffs and the wards. He tapped into the power of your life forces.*

I wish you would have told me that before! Why didn't you instruct me to use the mating bond when I was being tortured in my cell?

Every time I tried to speak to you, you screamed for me to stop. The shadow sighed. *I couldn't fight back the shadows poisoning you long enough to explain anything. And I didn't mention it since then because with all the suppressions and wards, you were too far away from one another to tap into it. But now he's close.*

If that were true, why didn't Sebastian use the bond to sift us when Caroline's guards attacked?

An unaccepted mating bond is weak. It wouldn't have been enough power to sift both of you. You were already drawing on our shadows to sift us. We would have made it out if we were just mere seconds faster. If that fire ball had been just a hands-width off.

My eyebrows pulled together, and a sadness threatened to erupt. We could have made it out. If I hadn't told him not to take his cuffs off. If I had been quicker pulling on his power. If I hadn't trapped us both by trusting Caroline.

It was not your fault, the shadow said. *I don't blame you, and neither will he. Pull on the bond to find him.*

I couldn't let the what-ifs distract me. I backed up into a corner so no one could attack me from behind and closed my eyes. The hum of my power in my core was weak, I couldn't sense his essence there.

I brought him to mind and let the memory of his scent wrap around me. The feeling when I'd catch him staring and could sense his joy fizzing inside of me. As my panicked heart slowed and turned into a longing ache, I realized where his power dwelled.

I breathed into the pain below my collarbone, inside my heart, the pressure point that he'd massaged with his thumb. The one he promised would go away once we accepted the bond.

It was fragile and thready, the pulse of his power, but it tugged me toward the stairs. This far up the stairwell, there was no one to obstruct my path, but smoke from the fire below filled the space. I coughed and held my shirt over my mouth.

He had used our mating bond to find me in the mass of people in Daria's bar. It was why he'd said there was no where I could go that he wouldn't be able to find me.

It had seemed like a threat—one that had thrilled me nonetheless—but now I see, it'd been a promise.

His power in my heart tugged harder, and I sprinted the last few flights.

Kai had said the prison arranged its inmates by floor in order of their power.

Sebastian was the strongest darkyra in Palagui.

I should have known he'd be on the top floor.

I shoved open the door from the stairwell to the hallway.

No smoke or fire ravaged the place. There wasn't even evidence of a battle between guards and prisoners. No singe marks, no blood, nothing. This floor was pristine.

If it weren't for the blaring siren, I wouldn't have even known we were in the middle of a prison break.

I continued following the pull until I stood outside a door marked as the UV Room. Caution stickers hung all around it.

That couldn't be good.

I tried to open the door, but it wasn't budging like something was blocking it. I threw all my weight into it and it opened a sliver, but I shrunk back, blinded by a light brighter than the sun.

The sounds of fighting escaped from somewhere in the room as the door shut.

He was in there. I could feel it. He needed me.

I squinted my eyes and forced myself against the door with all my strength. My eyes burned. All I could see was white everywhere, but the door opened enough for me to slip in.

I blinked and blinked, retinas burning. My skin heated, cooking like a sunburn.

The reason for the door being blocked laid on the floor. The husk of a guard's body. He wore tinted goggles and reflective body suit.

I ripped the face mask off him and slid it on. It took several seconds for me to orient myself, but my vision cleared enough that

I could make out about twelve dead guards scattered throughout the room. Their bodies dehydrated like the power had been sucked out of them.

They'd all rushed here to control their deadliest prisoner, but his shadows had sucked out their life forces.

I moved from the entrance, and the door slammed behind me. Several guards' heads swung in my direction and charged.

My skin was baking, and the tiny bit of my healing power left tried to heal the burns, but I shut it down and contained it.

I had a feeling I'd need it soon. I ignored the pain and spread my stance as the first guard came at me.

He didn't see the dagger in my hand. Hadn't been expecting a prisoner to find a weapon. He fell as I plunged it into his stomach.

The others' steps faltered as their friend sunk to the floor. The blood of their comrade coated my blade.

How dare they touch what is mine! How dare they hurt him! my shadow yelled, but her voice was faint like she was far away.

Her rage, or my rage, clashed inside of me as the pounding of cymbals, an energy to hurt, maim, kill, kill, kill.

Make them pay, she demanded.

"Who's next?" A wicked grin filled my face as I cut the air with my dagger. It made a threatening *whoosh*, and something on my face must have made the guards realize what they were up against because it took a few seconds for one of them to attack.

He threw his weight into me, trying to get me off balance, but I used his size and shifted so his mass toppled over.

Another guard came toward my side, but I swung my arm out and stabbed him through his reflective suit.

His screams were glorious.

The feel of the skin-tearing, of blade sinking into muscle and ripping—it made for such a beautiful symphony overtop of the blaring siren.

All the titillating chaos may have made me a little cocky, or I had too much blood splattered on my face mask, because the next guard took me by surprised, coming at me from the side. He grabbed my right arm and slammed his leg into my stomach.

His stance was terrible though, and when I folded over from the impact, he fell with me until we were wrestling on the ground.

He pinned my arm, but wasn't in the right position to get my grip to loosen.

My training failed me in that moment, but pure unadulterated fury made up for my skill loss when I used all my strength and headbutted him while he was distracted as he reached for the dagger.

It didn't knock him off me, but stunned him enough he grabbed his chin, and I found enough leverage to kick my lower body free.

He still had my hand pinned, and it was risky, but I dropped the dagger.

The second he went for it, I bent my arm and hit him with my elbow, hard enough to knock off his goggles and slam into his eye.

He groaned and grabbed his face. I scrambled up, scooping my dagger off the floor as he pulled his hands away from his eye to find them covered in blood. The eye was bloodied and mangled and even if he recovered, I doubted he would see out of it again.

He screamed as pain overwhelmed him, and being such a *nice* person, I slit his throat to put him out of his misery. His body crumbled, and I turned.

There were only four guards left, all swarming a burned and brutalized male.

Before I could even launch myself at them, a wisp of his shadow whipped out and brought two guards to their knees.

Another shadow stabbed one of the guards in the chest and whipped back around to slice all of their necks.

Sebastian bent at the waist, his hands on his thighs, trying to catch his breath. He didn't see the last guard.

"To your right!" But I'm not sure he could hear me across the room with the siren still wailing.

I ran toward him as the last guard grabbed Sebastian by the throat. His fingers pressed into his neck.

Shadows teetered in the air, but they were too weak to push the guard off.

Jumping on the guard's back, I grabbed his chin and the top of his skull and jerked his head until his neck snapped.

I hopped down as the guard crumbled between us. Sebastian's eyes were squeezed closed.

Wow. He'd single-handedly taken down almost twenty guards literally with his eyes closed.

Shadows tried to gather, misting harmlessly over my skin. His hand swung out as if trying to fight me, but I easily grabbed his forearm to stop him.

The skin was blistered and broken, and I removed my hand so as not to harm him more.

All at once the siren cut out, though the ringing still echoed in my ears.

"Sebastian," I said. "It's me. You're safe. There are no more guards."

He didn't respond. His body swayed, arms grabbing on to me as he fell.

"Oomph." I tried to catch him, but he was too heavy and crushed me under his weight.

I took a deep breath and gathered my strength.

Standing, I scooped my hands under his arms, hoisting him up as much as I could, but mostly dragging him across the floor.

I had to set him down and use my back to prop open the door before pulling him out of the room.

I moved him until he was seated against the wall. My high priestess light leapt from my hands, reaching out to heal him before I even consciously tried, just like it had when I'd nicked him with the blade in the ballroom.

I hovered my hands over his head and his poor blistered face. His skin was so burnt and red, patches of it bubbled.

Tears streamed down my face. I didn't know how he'd survived this.

"Sebastian," I cried, but he didn't stir.

His face slowly healed, turning from blistering angry red, to pink, and back to his normal complexion. I dredged up the little bit of my healing power I had left, and it seeped inside of him until every inch of his exposed skin was healed.

I gingerly rested my hands over his pulse and sighed when I felt the faint but steady thump.

Pushing back the long pieces of black hair that fell over his forehead, I lifted one of his eyelids, but the whites of his eyes were bloodshot and veiny.

Sebastian was alive.

And I was going to get us out of here.

I repeated my mantras while biting my lip to hold back more tears. Sitting on my heels, I hovered more light over his head, his eyes, his entire body. This had to work.

"Please, Sebastian," I whispered. "I love you. Please wake up."

My healing light began to dull, turning gray as I pulled on the last bit that I had within me.

His skin was healed, the inside of his eyes looked better, and he had no external wounds, but still, he didn't wake.

I didn't have time for him to recover, and I couldn't carry him out. Without a lot more power, I couldn't sift us either. Panic threatened to take over, but I pushed it down.

He needed a jolt, something to wake him.

I gathered the piece of his shadow that had been with me, that had protected me more times than I could count, and held him in the palm of my hand.

"Time to go back where you belong, little guy," I whispered, hoping the shadow wouldn't fight me. I knew he didn't want to be within Sebastian because he kept such a tight leash on his power, but this was the only idea I had. Maybe the shadow could wake him.

To my surprise, the shadow didn't fight me or even argue when I pressed my hands to his chest and funneled the wisps back to their rightful place.

When I pulled my hand back, his presence—separate and distinct from my own power—was gone from my palms.

Sebastian sucked in a breath. His chest inflated, and his hand grabbed my left arm. Fury etched in his face. His void eyes stared with no recognition in them.

His other hand grabbed my right arm, and he looked to be gathering strength to throw me across the room.

"Sebastian!" I said, taking fistfuls of his shirt, trying to shake him from his stupor. "It's me."

I ignored his murderous squinting eyes, which seemed to be trying to puzzle out whether to attack or not, and threw my arms around his neck, hugging him tight. "It's Amaya."

He went utterly still as I buried my face in his neck, unconcerned I was covering him with my hair. He sighed heavily, cupping the back of my head as he brought his nose to my throat and inhaled.

"Mate," he said in the low deep voice of his power as he ran his lips along my neck. "My beautiful sweet darkness." His arms wrapped around me, and I sagged in relief.

"Sebastian," I cried. I felt all of my strength dissipating now that I was in his arms. "I'm so sorry. So so sorry. I don't know how you'll ever forgive me. I just love you. And I've missed you, and I'm so glad you're alive. That you're okay. I'm just so fucking sorry."

"Shhh," he said. His hands rubbed my back in a comforting rhythm. His voice was so deep it rumbled through me, settling something inside that was quaking with fear. "You have nothing to apologize for."

"I tried to kill you. It's my fault you've been tortured for weeks."

He snorted. "Come here," he said. "I need you closer." He lifted me so I was straddling him.

He rested his hands on my waist while I kept mine on his shoulders. His void eyes trailed along every inch of my face as if it was the first time he'd ever seen me.

He traced my bottom lip with his thumb. "I knew mates could not kill one another, but I pushed you to try, yes? Taunted you into it?"

I shook my head. "Yeah, but that doesn't excuse—"

He put a finger to my lips. "What if I told you, it was all just a sick and twisted form of foreplay?" His eyes heated, and his voice lowered even deeper. "I do so like to see you fight."

"Stop it. I'm serious."

"I'm serious as well." His face held no resentment, not even a hint of anger. "Perhaps it felt easier to push you into realizing the truth rather than having to admit my secrets and failings. Not a single part of me blames you."

"Okay, but...I also killed your brother." Sure, he was about to murder Sebastian, but he was still his brother.

"Ah. You did, did you?" He shrugged. "Well, that was a task I should have undertaken decades ago. I should be thanking you for saving me the hassle."

I couldn't help it. I giggled and playfully smacked his chest. "How can you be so okay with this?" I asked, half-sobbing, half-laughing.

He grabbed my hand and kissed my knuckles. "Because my mate is sitting on top of me, and there is nowhere else I'd rather be."

"Not even like somewhere that isn't a burning prison?"

He shrugged. "I want to be wherever you are."

My face scrunched up as more tears came, and I hugged him. "They told me you were dead."

While I sobbed into his chest, he just held me, letting the overwhelm of my emotions pour out. Relief and sadness, grief and happiness, and a million more emotions swarmed through me too fast to name.

He didn't rush me or pull away, only made hushed calming noises in his deep voice until I finally felt something release.

I took a shuddering breath. Maybe I did understand his sentiment. I didn't think I'd ever muster the desire to leave his embrace.

For an indeterminable amount of time, we held each other. His hands roamed over my back, and he inhaled deeply, breathing me in, memorizing the feeling of being together.

"You're really okay?" I asked.

"Now that I have you." His nose traced my ear, and I shivered. "Now that you're all mine, and we can be together without it having to be contained to stolen moments." His hands ran up the sides of my legs to my waist. "I've never been better."

I suppose in a way they were stolen moments. Our relationship had been "pretend," bound by a bargain up until today. I pulled back and kissed him, once, twice, and whispered on his lips, "Our bargain may be over, but I'm still yours. I'm all yours."

He made a deep male moan of satisfaction in the back of his throat and captured my mouth with his.

His kiss felt different. His lips not quite hesitant, but slow, relishing me as if I was a decadent dessert he had to savor because he might not get another taste.

I fell into the kiss, letting him take control of the pace.

The shape and feel of his mouth was so familiar, so right, along with the way he tugged my body even closer like we could mesh into one person if we tried hard enough.

His hands squeezed and caressed my thighs, my waist, my ass, and when he nipped at my bottom lip, I moaned. I wanted his teeth biting into my lip, into my neck, into every inch of my skin.

When his tongue swept through my mouth, heat pooled low in my stomach. A pulse of power thrummed in my chest, energized by our touch, making my heart throb.

I pulled back, pressing one hand to my heart and the other to his. He knew right away what I was doing, and his fingers swept under mine on my chest and massaged in circles to soothe the ache.

"You promise you're okay? Nothing hurts?" I inspected his body, looking for bruises or wounds I'd missed.

His hair was longer. The sides, which were usually shorn close to his head, had grown out, and the long portion at the top had become unruly and stuck to his forehead with blood. The black ink of his darkyra tattoos on his neck and arms stood out more under the harsh fluorescent lights.

"I promise. I'm completely healed." His eyes were hooded and full of lust.

He must have been feeling alright then.

But images flashed in my mind: his burnt skin, the guards hurting him, the one that had gotten close enough to strangle him. A renewed rage began simmering under the surface.

His hand came to cup my jaw and pulled me back from the memories. "Shall we find ourselves an exit?" he asked.

I sighed and tilted my head into his hand.

He was healed. We were safe.

And...I had a dagger.

This would be our only chance, my shadow taunted.

I bit my bottom lip. "There's something I want to get before we leave," I said, staring into Sebastian's void eyes which were locked on my mouth.

"What's that?" he asked, maybe a little distracted.

"Revenge."

His gaze darted back to mine. The corners of his eyes crinkled as a slow smile spread across his face.

Chapter Eleven

Sebastian

My mate was so fucking beautiful with vengeance in her eyes.

I couldn't take my gaze off her. I wanted to catalog the way her hips moved as she sauntered through the burning prison, to sear into my memory the sound of her laugh as she slid her dagger over another guard's throat, to imprint the sight of her smile into the backs of my eyelids when she grabbed my hand to find more guards to torture.

Most of all, I wished I could memorize the way her eyes heated when she watched my shadows. She wasn't afraid or cautious of their devious intent. She seemed to hunger for their violence, for my violence.

It was beyond thrilling. Absolutely intoxicating.

The fact that *he* had locked me out and tried to keep me away from her all this time made me bristle.

But he'd never be a problem again. She was *mine*. All mine.

And if her proclivity for wickedness rivaled my own, perhaps she'd take in stride the news of my other half's demise. I was still here. Her mate was still alive. Perhaps…

Or I'd lose her forever.

I refused to consider that outcome.

Patience. Patience was what I needed. Once we escaped the prison and found safety, a moment to breathe, I'd figure out how to tell her.

There was just the little problem of my memories. While I was in control of our body, I had episodic amnesia. I could easily access procedures and knowledge, general facts. I certainly remembered moments I'd been able to sneak past his blocks, but I was missing *his* personal experiences.

Maybe she wouldn't notice. I didn't like lying to her, but I could blame it on the suppression until we were out of harm's way.

Amaya interlaced our fingers. "Come on." She tugged me through the corridor to the ground floor. "This is the last floor."

"I doubt any guards remain," I said, snuffing out the flames as I'd done for each level. I loved destruction, but fire was unpredictable and could become uncontrollable.

I detested the uncontrollable.

She pushed her bottom lip out in a pout. I wanted to sink my teeth into that plush lip. But to appease her appetite for murder, I hastened my steps.

The Queen hadn't died yet. I'd know it, feel it in my bones if she had, and given Amaya and I were the strongest fae in Palagui, that meant when we combined our shadows and pulled on the mating bond, we had a bit of power while the rest of the country didn't.

And we were using it viciously.

As luck would have it, a guard stumbled dazedly into the hall. Fear widened his eyes when he saw us. As he tried to run, my shadow caught him by the throat. Only one of us could use our shadows at a time, but Amaya preferred more hands-on methods anyway.

She was so breathtaking. I was quickly becoming addicted to watching her lethal skill with a dagger.

I used a shadow to tug at the guard's collar. My mate had some honor code. If the guards had a tattoo at their suprasternal notch, we'd kill them, but unless the guard attacked us, we simply locked them in a cell. Her only explanation was that they were the bad ones.

And this one had the tattoo.

"Do you want him?" she asked sweetly.

I considered the guard. Weeks of imprisonment and torture while inside this body—along with my consciousness being held captive in a tiny box in the back of our mind for a century—would be a solid justification to take out my anger on this guard.

I imagined every guard I killed had Xenos's face. My half-brother and childhood tormentor, the artist of the masterpiece that is my scarred back. The male who, despite our hatred, my other half obediently served for decades to save the Queen.

The Queen, not my mother, because though *he* begged for any ounce of attention and affection from her, I'd certainly never understood the urge. That female had abandoned me, and when that didn't work and she was forced to raise me, she'd avoided me and kept me away from Adriana, my half-sister and the only person who didn't see me as a monster. The Queen left me to deal with the consequences of her bargain all my life. So as far as I was concerned, she was no mother to me.

All of these resentments were more motivation than I usually required to lash out, but I'd killed several guards on the way down, and I loved the sparks of pleasure in Amaya's eyes when she took her revenge.

"I want to watch you do it." I grabbed the back of her neck and pulled her close, nipping at her earlobe. "Show me how you make them beg for their lives," I purred.

Her brown eyes went molten, desire hooding them. She planted a quick kiss to my lips and wiggled in excitement.

Goddess, she was so adorable.

I knew she'd thrive in hell, had known it the second shadows filled her eyes at that rooftop lounge in Delnee.

She spooled our shadows toward the guard, letting them creep toward him threateningly.

He shook his head as his eyes darted between us. "Stop! Don't!"

More shadows appeared.

The guard ran toward the door. My beautiful wicked mate let him get through the threshold and around the corner before the sound of his body falling to the floor echoed in the empty hall. Her shadows dragged him by the ankle slowly back toward us.

"No, no, no," the guard kept saying. He scratched his nails in the cement floor, trying to find purchase.

A faint smile curved her lips as she watched his pointless attempts to escape until he was lying below us.

"Please don't kill me," he said.

I pursed my lips. "This one was far too easy for you." He was already begging for his life, and we hadn't even gotten started.

She shrugged. "It's our scary eyes," she said, gesturing to her void eyes. "They do all the work."

The guard continued, "Please. I have a family. A wife and two kids. They just started preschool. This is just my job. Please don't kill me. I won't tell anyone what you did."

She tilted her head. "What I did?"

He swallowed. Regret flashed in his eyes.

"What do you think she did?" I asked.

He trembled.

Amaya crouched down and held her dagger at his throat. "What did I do?"

His jaw was quivering, but he said, "All the exits have been sealed shut with shadows. The doors. The windows. The guards said you two started the prison break."

I furrowed my brows. "If the doors had been sealed, there would be thousands of prisoners in here?"

"They only sealed after the prisoners escaped. Backup was called, but they've been busy trying to capture the prisoners, so no one has tried to make contact with you about the hostages. The only reason I took this job was to make extra cash for my kids. Please don't kill me. I swear—"

"Where are the guards hiding on this floor?" Amaya interrupted his sob story.

"I...I..."

"Where?" I demanded, growing irritated at his insolence.

He swallowed again. "They're in the front office. Locked themselves in."

She straightened. "Alright, then."

Her shadows dispersed, and the guard looked up with wide eyes. "Thank you. Than—" His gratitude was cut off by a gurgling noise as Amaya ran her dagger across his throat.

I blinked, taken aback.

Even I hadn't expected that.

Something cold shot through me, a pang of something from the center of my chest deep into my stomach.

I'd never felt *that* before.

Her face was blank, and her void eyes vacant as she caught me staring. "What?"

I shrugged. "Nothing. I just thought you'd let him go."

She pressed her lips together and wiped the dagger clean of his blood on the guard's shirt. "Because he had a wife and kids? None of the guards cared that I had friends or family. Why should I care about theirs?"

I opened my mouth and shut it, following her brisk steps down the hall.

Why was I questioning this? Something felt off. My stomach began churning. None of this made any sense. We'd been killing the guards without much thought up until now and…Oh Goddess save me.

Is this fucking guilt?

That was why my stomach felt sick and my chest hurt? Since I was fully in control of this body, I'd have to deal with these irrational emotions now?

Amaya found the front office and jiggled the door handle, but it was locked. She looked back and raised an eyebrow at me. "I'm not the same girl I was before, Sebastian."

Maybe that was good. Maybe she'd handle the truth about me better than I thought. "I'm not the same either."

She gave me a sad smile and squeezed my hand once before sending shadows into the door lock until it burst.

Shoving the door open, her eyes darted around the small room. One of the guards ran at us with a chair over his head.

I flicked my fingers, and a shadow disintegrated the chair from his hands. He froze.

Really what did he expect to accomplish with that?

He was obviously not intelligent. He had a scar above his eyebrow. No doubt from other ill-thought-out plans.

Amaya grabbed him by the shirt, dagger at his throat, pushing him backward until she slammed him against the wall. He tried to swing his arms to hit her, but she blocked his attempts.

I just watched. She was more than capable of handling him by herself.

"Hmm," she said. "I don't think this one is capable of reform. I'd be doing the world a favor if I…' She dug the tip of the dagger into the right side of his chest, slashing down and across to his left ribs, and repeated the action to make a deep X in his chest.

He screamed and tried to stanch the blood. The others in the room didn't move to help him.

Amaya's eyes scanned each person and landed on one male cowering in the corner. He wore a lab coat like a doctor.

She made an angry noise in her throat and ran at him. I thought to stab him because she held her dagger in the air, but she grabbed him by the shirt, forced his arm to lie on the desk, rose her dagger, and staked him through his hand.

The male screamed. He tried to pull the dagger out of the desk with his freehand, but it was too deep.

"Hmm," I said. "Creative."

Amaya gave me a devious grin.

The other guards weren't even trying to fight us and stood in the corner blubbering.

She passed a disinterested eye over them, pulled down each shirt to check for their tattoos, and killed them with her shadows.

"I really don't think there are any left now," I said over the screaming. We had to have killed or locked up every guard in the prison.

She took a deep breath, held it, and then exhaled. Her shoulders relaxed. "That's okay. I feel better now." She nodded to herself. "I feel done."

The doctor and first guard were still screaming from their wounds.

Amaya rolled her eyes. "Okay. Almost done."

Her shadows encircled the guard with a scar across his eyebrow and entered his ears. They twisted his brain until blood poured from his nose and eyes. He collapsed to the ground, choking on his own blood.

Then she sauntered over to the doctor. "Honestly, why all the screaming? I certainly wasn't this loud when you cut into my back every fucking day," she muttered.

She yanked her dagger from his hand and slit his throat, but she must have purposefully not cut deep enough for his death to be quick, because he gasped and stumbled back.

His blood sprayed and splattered both her and me, but I barely noticed as my mind took in her words.

"He harmed you?" I asked, staring at his body as it twitched and fought his inevitable death. A rumbling rage grew inside me.

She shrugged. "My wounds kept getting reinfected, but instead of healing me, he cut the infection out...every day."

My fists clenched. He gave one final spasm and slumped over. I wanted to bring him back to life and kill him slower. Maybe keep him alive and cut into him like he'd done to her for weeks on end.

She let the dagger clatter on the desk and squeezed my arm. "It's okay. It's over now. I'm not letting these people or this place have a second more of my life by thinking of them. I've purged them from this world and from my mind."

I could almost see it. The way she shadowed the memory. Smothered it in darkness and stored it somewhere far away.

And I would know, I was very familiar with the process.

She may be over it, but I wasn't. "Let me see," I demanded.

She hesitated.

"Please," I asked, softening my voice.

She sighed and turned, pulling her shirt up just over her shoulders.

I gathered her hair and pushed it aside. Her back was destroyed. The skin was healed, but scarred with uneven divots. Her back was even worse than mine, and looked more similar to my inner wrists from the way the fae cuffs burned when my power flared. Her power must have been trying to heal her, and been thwarted over and over by the suppression.

I take it back. I didn't want to torture the doctor for weeks. I'd keep him on the edge of death for years, centuries, as pay back for this. Then I'd find him in the afterlife and torture him there too.

How dare he touch her?

How dare he hurt my sweet, perfect Amaya?

I forced down the sick need to claw out his throat and his eyes with my bare hands. I would rip apart his chest, crack open his ribs, and annihilate his organs. No logic or sense in the deed just destruction that would burn hotter and become more depraved with each soft entrail I destroyed.

But carnage like that would scare even this new vicious side of my mate, and she'd still have to live with the evidence on her back of my inability to keep her safe.

It'd been *my* duty to shield her from all harm.

That thought shifted my need to rip and tear into a desire for self-mutilation. My heart twisted, and I felt as though I was being shredded. The heat and tension of anger turned into a crippling helplessness, which threatened to bring me to my knees. I was defenseless against its brutality as it spiked through me. Couldn't find the separation between myself and this body's physical response.

I ran the back of my hand along her spine over the marred skin. "I should have protected you." I could barely get the words out. Something felt like it was lodged in my throat. The backs of my eyes burned, and my entire body shook. "I didn't protect you. This never should have happened. You shouldn't have been here. It's my fault. It was my idea to bring you to Palagui."

I suggested to my other half that we would be better off taking her with us than leaving her in Delnee. She'd unsettled us enough that I was able to slip through his shields, and it was only too easy to convince him. He wanted to be around her as much as I did.

"I made you a promise in Delnee that I'd never let anyone take you to jail, and I let you down," I said.

She turned, letting her shirt fall back into place. Frustration pulled her brows together. "No. Stop it. You didn't let me down. I asked you to bring me to Palagui. Nothing that happened here was your fault. The piece of your shadow you gave me protected me as much as he could. That one"—she pointed to the guard with the scar above his eyebrow—"tried to kill me outside the med-room, and your power saved me. I didn't know it was you then, but your shadow told me. You did protect me." She grabbed my hands and pressed my palms to her face. "Don't you dare blame yourself. Please, Sebastian. I don't blame you."

I held her fragile, small head between my hands. My mind was overtaken by the terrible sensations in my body and started offering me thoughts from a foreign voice. *You don't deserve her. You're going to hurt her. You'll only make her life worse. Look what you've already done.*

Her fingers brushed under my eyes, and when they pulled back, they glistened with moisture.

Moisture, I realized, which was my tears.

Goddess save me. What was happening to me? I'm a shadow consciousness, I didn't cry. I didn't have *feelings*. I never cried, even after the first time I took over his body and…

I shook my head. I wasn't going there. Not now. Not ever.

This body was producing reactions I didn't know how to control, affecting me in ways it never had before.

Turning away, I put my hands on my hips and stared at the ceiling, waiting for these atrocious sensations to pass.

Amaya slipped under my arm, nuzzled her head into my chest, and wrapped both of her arms around my waist.

When I focused hard enough, I could sever the *feelings* by pushing them away as I did certain memories.

I sighed when they finally dissipated and looked down at her.

She smiled and said in the low husky voice of her power, "You look really sexy with our enemies' blood all over your face."

The heat in her eyes and the way her mouth pulled into a taunting little smirk had my mind shutting off and my body turning on.

Now this was a physical sensation I was used to experiencing.

"Do I?" I gripped her chin and smeared the blood on her cheeks with my thumb.

She nodded.

"So do you. Does getting revenge arouse you, little warrior?"

She sunk her teeth into her bottom lip, trying to be innocent. With a solemn nod, she feigned a repentant expression. "I've been a bad girl, haven't I?"

I groaned, and my eyes threatened to roll back into my head. "What am I going to do with you?" I lifted her in one arm and used the other to sweep the top of the desk clear before setting her down.

"I don't know," she said with a little shrug.

"Should I punish you?"

She widened her eyes and shook her head vigorously. "Please no."

I smiled because no wasn't our safe word.

Planting both of my hands on the desk, I leaned over until my mouth was at her ear. "If you promise to be good, I won't punish you."

Her fingers found their way under my shirt and spread across my stomach while I traced my nose along the curve of her ear.

"I can't. I can't promise to be good," she said, a moan escaping as I sucked on her earlobe.

"Hmm," I said. My hands trailed over her hips, her waist and up to cup her breasts through her shirt. I squeezed, enjoying their soft weight and the way she arched into my hands as I thumbed her nipples. "Then I'm afraid I'll have to punish you until you learn your lesson."

She only moaned in response. I tugged off her shirt and tossed it aside.

I had memories of her naked body because *he* had been distracted by her and I'd been able to sneak past his defensive. But as my eyes darted down to her perfect breasts, they were caught on the skin of her neck. It was lightly scarred, nothing like her back, but enough to see that there had been infected wounds here too. I pressed my lips to the junction of her neck and shoulder, making a slow half circle of kisses. I'd have a similar scar on my neck. We'd have them on our wrists and ankles as well.

How could I have let this happen?

You don't deserve her.

Our game fell to pieces as the reminders of my unsuitability to be her mate, of all the pain I caused her, welled up.

I wasn't used to emotions, and I wasn't used to blocking them either. She sensed the shift within me again.

She grabbed the longer portion of my hair and tilted my head back with a sharp tug.

"Maybe I should punish you," she said, smirking. "You've been just as naughty as I have."

All thoughts scattered and vanished as she trailed kisses down my neck, sucking and nibbling.

I grasped her hips, pulling her to the edge of the desk. The heat of her body pressed into mine. Her hand slid down the back of my head to my neck, and my eyes lowered.

I wanted to savor her but wasn't sure I had the control. All of this, being with her, was so much better when it wasn't secondhand. It was like I'd been living behind a glass wall, and now the experience was so full, so overwhelming, so intense. Our bond was vibrating with the anticipation. It ached from our separation.

"What exactly did you have in mind?" I asked as the backs of my fingers stroked up and down the sides of her waist.

Her hand smoothed down my chest and tugged on the bottom of my shirt. I pulled it over my head, tossing it with hers.

"I'm in control now," she said. A single finger traced the swirled pattern of my darkyra tattoos on my chest.

I raised an eyebrow. "Are you?" I didn't remember ever playing this role before, but then again, there was absolutely no one in the world I would willingly submit to except her.

She hopped off the desk, pushing me until my back hit the door. "You're not going to speak. You're not going to move. You won't even think for yourself. Unless I allow it. You'll do everything I say. Understand?"

The husky voice of her power went straight to my dick. "Uh huh," I said. She knew what I needed. She wasn't going to let me get lost in my head and distracted by my thoughts.

Being confined for centuries might have made some resistant to her demand for control, but I was relieved.

I'd be whoever she wanted me to be.

And right now, my dark goddess required a willing supplicant.

Even weakened, our shadows thrummed their approval.

She flattened her palm over the bulge in my pants and squeezed a touch too hard, making me grunt. "Use your words," she said.

My body went languid even as my stomach clenched. I smiled. This was going to be fun. "I understand. I'll do whatever you say."

She pushed onto her tiptoes, held my jaw, and turned it to the side to whisper in my ear, "And you won't come until I allow it either."

I groaned. "Yes ma'am."

She tugged at my pants until I pushed them off. I kept my hands at my side, following her rules if only because I wanted to see what she'd do next.

Amaya stood back, eyes trailing up and down my body until they rested at my cock, already hard and jutting up, reaching for her.

Her voice was smoky in the way that told me her power was influencing her when she said, "Look how hard you are. Is this all for me?"

"Yes," I said. "You're so fucking gorgeous. I want you so much."

"Hmm," she said, gazing at my body. I remembered our first night at the beach house when I stripped her naked and stared at her, completely overwhelmed by her beauty.

I smirked. Not being able to resist breaking the rules, I asked, "Do you like what you see?"

Her eyes found mine, the desire in them answering the question for her. "You only speak when spoken to."

I licked my lips. "Yes ma'am."

I used that as an opportunity to gaze upon her as well. The dark ink of her tattoos twisted around her arms, flaring on top of her shoulders. Her torso was an expanse of pale skin, except for the hint of ink escaping the band of her pants and swirling around her hip bones.

The air between us sparked, charged with a wanton danger, which made my body react. Every nerve was on alert, and yet, she wasn't touching me with anything but her piercing gaze.

The longer she forced me to stand in silence, the more the need built, to the point the mating bond screamed out from the ache.

She blinked and stepped forward, stunned, putting her hands on my chest to steady herself. "Did you feel that?"

"It's the bond," I said, unable to stop myself from resting my hands on her hips. I stroked my fingers along the sweet little dip of her back above the swell of her ass.

"No touching." She swatted at my arms and grabbed my wrists, pressing them to the door. She looked up at me through her eyelashes. "You can send me your feelings down the bond?"

My cock pressed into her belly, and she let my wrists go to run her hands up my forearms and biceps to my shoulders and over my chest.

"Uh..." I was distracted by her touch, my fingers spreading and fisting in the fight between following her rules or grabbing her and fucking her against the door.

My voice was strained. "Only really intense feelings since we haven't accepted the bond. Like when you're in danger or... Do you recall the time in my bedroom? When you rocked those sexy hips on my thigh until you came?" I'd been there and remembered it vividly.

She nodded and inched back to slide her hands down my stomach, my hips, my legs, not touching the part of me that was aching for her.

"Then you disappeared for weeks. Yeah, I remember," she said dryly.

I ignored that comment because I didn't have access to the memories of anything that happened after. "You said you felt my shadow orgasm."

"Yeah," she said, a little breathy. We were both watching as her finger skimmed the underside of my cock.

She was making it increasingly hard to focus. "It wasn't my shadow you felt. Or it wasn't just my shadow. It was the bond. Your aura's boundaries fell, and our shadows intertwined. It opened the connection between us."

She rewarded me by wrapping her hand around my length, just under the head. "And you got some of my powers?"

My eyes fluttered shut at the feel of her hand tight around me. I released a strangled breath from the sensation and nodded, but then realized that wasn't right. "Well, not quite. My powers expanded through accessing yours. It's not that I took from you."

"Oh." She gave me one slow stroke.

My stomach clenched, and my arms ached from the tension it took to keep them at my side.

She didn't stroke me again, so I said, "And your powers also expand through accessing my shadow when my aura is vulnerable."

"Meaning when I make you come?"

"Yes," I hissed the word as she pumped me once, twice.

"I see." Unbidden, my hips bucked up into her fist. Stilling me with a press of her hand on my stomach, she asked, "So every time we orgasm, our powers increase?"

Her thumb teased up over the head, and I barely got out, "Uh huh." Pleasure zapped up my spine, holding myself back was starting to become impossible. The urgent need to touch her, the incessant craving to be inside her, was locking up all of my muscles.

"And when we accept the bond, we'll be unstoppable?" she asked as she spread the precome along my shaft to slick her grip.

"Unstoppable," I agreed. Her pace quickened and lost its teasing edge. I watched her breasts bounce as she worked me. Her pretty nipples were hard and begging for my mouth.

With quick jerks and twists around the head, my core clenched as she brought me close.

"I'm going to—" The words were hardly out of my mouth before her hand was gone.

My head fell back against the door with a hard thud. "Fuck."

When I opened my eyes and looked down at her, she smirked. "I didn't say you could come yet."

My eyebrows pulled down and something like a whimper came out. "Amaya."

She pressed soft little kisses on my chest, along my collarbone, and over my heart.

"You are a wicked female," I said.

She smiled. "I'm *your* wicked female."

This beguiling creature knew just what to say to make my heart soar and my cock hard.

She restarted her punishing pace, suspending me not once, not twice, but three times.

My abs were clenching, my entire body shaking with the need for release. I bit into my fist to stop myself from tossing her onto the floor and sheathing myself inside her.

After the third time, the delicious torment of the stalled orgasms had me growling in frustration. "Fuck, please," I all but snarled. "Amaya. Please."

Her hand tickled up my chest, and I looked longingly into her eyes. "Please let me touch you," I said, softer. "I need to fuck you. Please."

Her face was positively smug when she said slowly, enunciating every word, "You're so pretty when you beg."

My eyes narrowed because those words were familiar.

Very familiar.

She walked backward to the desk, curling a finger in a gesture to follow. My body listened to her command without any input from me.

Then I remembered, I had said that to her on the floor of my bedroom, after she'd asked me to take her home when I was seconds away from killing Jeremy. She'd redistributed the anger into passion, and both *he* and I lost ourselves in her touch.

"Have you been waiting to use those words on me?" I asked.

She pushed down her pants and kicked them aside, hopping onto the desk. "Maybe," she said with a bright smile.

"Is that what you want, little warrior?" I stalked the rest of the way to her, put my hands on either side of her hips, and brought my mouth close enough to hover over her neck, knowing she'd feel my breath as I whispered, "Would you like me to beg on my knees for you? Worship your pretty little pussy with my tongue?"

Her eyes hooded. "Yes."

"I would have thought you knew by now."

"Knew what?"

"That this is my favorite place to be," I said and dropped to my knees, running my hands up the backs of her calves.

It was all making sense now. Her shadow was influencing her, so of course this is where she'd want me.

The last time she'd been under her influence, Amaya had walked out of the Hollow after initiation, hunger in her eyes, desperate for me. For *me*, not *him*. And he knew it. He knew she and her shadow wanted me but refused to let me take control, and instead, pacified her by getting on his knees to prove his devotion, while I did my best to take the edge off her shadow's demand to fulfill the bond.

But that didn't matter anymore because he was gone. And she was all mine.

"Do you want a taste?" she asked and leaned back on the desk, propped up on her forearms.

"Yes," I said. "Fuck yes, I do."

She parted her thighs, and at the sight of her legs spread for me, I felt precome leak from my tip.

The scent of her arousal filled my nose. I couldn't wait for further instruction. I stroked my thumb through her folds once, so hot and wet, and then dove in, licking until her taste coated my tongue. I was desperate to memorize it. Part of me was still waiting for the moment I'd be jerked back into my prison in his head.

My arms escaped my conscious mind, and I snaked them under her thighs, dragging her closer and pressing them down. I kept her wholly bared to me. She didn't protest the use of my hands despite it breaking the rules.

I flicked my tongue over her clit, circling just the way she liked. She moaned, and satisfaction swelled in my chest that I could elicit such a sweet sound.

After licking gently around the nub, I plunged my tongue inside, lapping up the taste of her. Her body jerked and melted, caught between resistance and giving in.

I wanted to be slow, to tease and build her up like she'd done for me, but a single taste made me ravenous.

"That feels so good," she said, throwing her head back. One hand threaded in my hair. "More. I need more."

I grabbed her breast with one hand and used the other to dip two fingers inside while my tongue kept a steady rhythm on her clit. Her walls gripped me in a way that made my cock jealous.

I angled my fingers up, up, up and...there...found the spot that made the cadence of her breath increase into short little gasps.

When I started sucking on her clit, her legs began shaking. I squeezed her breast, then pinched the nipple.

She writhed under my touch, and an animalistic, possessive need filled me.

She was mine. Mine. Mine.

The pulse of our bond intensified, quivering, until she sucked in a strangled breath, and her little tremors grew into a hard spasming orgasm.

I licked her through it, not letting up until I felt her pleasure sweep over me through the bond like an echo.

My cock throbbed with the ghost of an orgasm without a release.

I pressed my head to her thigh and held her calves as the sensation crested and fell away.

She sighed, spent and relaxed, and stroked my hair, her nails digging across my scalp, sending shivers down my spine.

After a moment, she sat up.

I peeked up at her from where my head rested on her lap.

"I'm going to fuck you now," she said and scooched off the desk, pushing me to lean back on my heels as she straddled me.

Wrapping her arms around my neck, she pressed her mouth to mine.

I held her jaw with both of my hands and nipped at her lips. Her hips rocked in my lap, her wetness dripping onto the base of my cock.

When our tongues met, I felt something settle inside of me. Something that had been vacant and empty and searching was now found. She kissed me with an intensity that enslaved. This female had all of me.

My hands fell from her jaw, brushed over her shoulders, and caressed the underside of her breasts. The denied orgasms kept my body taut, but more than that was the overwhelming need to protect her, the desire to wrap her in my arms and shield her from everyone. I wanted to shadow us from the world and make sure nothing ever happened to her again.

She broke the kiss by lifting her hips and angling my cock at her entrance. She slid down, slow, achingly slow. A sharp pleasured breath escaped us both when she took all of me. The tight, wet heat of her core sucked me in. It was such utter bliss I thought my eyes might go cross.

"Sebastian." She whined my name and made a sound that made me feel like I was flying. "Do you feel that?"

I couldn't answer her, only crushed her mouth to mine, grabbing her hips and making her rock on top of me. Her tongue tangled with mine.

She gasped. "It feels like…it's like…Fuck," she said, voice strained.

Heaven. It felt like heaven.

I knew I would never make it there. But I didn't need to wonder what it'd be like.

This was it.

Divine. Bliss. Home.

All words too pale to describe what touching her, feeling her, being inside her felt like.

"It's the bond," I choked out. "We've been apart too long. It wants… It's trying to entice us to…"

Her eyes flashed in understanding, but then something like worry filled them.

"I don't want to accept the bond," she said. "I don't want you to lose your power by breaking your bargain."

"It's okay. I know. Not like this," I assured her. We'd never be able to accept the bond. If the Darkyra Deity took my power, I'd cease to exist. Another thing I couldn't tell her yet.

And even if we could accept the bond, I certainly wouldn't want to do it on a prison floor.

"I love you," she said, soft as if trying to ease the rejection. She brought me back in for a kiss.

"I love you too," I said against her lips.

The craving to accept the bond was powerful though, especially as her shadow beckoned me. *Need you. Make me yours. Need you to make me yours.*

I pulled back, sucking in a breath.

Amaya's eyes filled with concern as I tried to shake her shadow's whispers from my head.

Amaya didn't know her shadow talked to me. I didn't think *he* knew either. The few times they were lost in each other, us shadows had been magnetized as the bond tried to snap into place. It couldn't without their consent, but it didn't stop the shadows' instincts to try.

"We just need a rearrangement," I said. And I needed a moment to calm her shadow.

I curled a hand around her waist, lifted her up enough to put my legs out, and spun around to lean my back against the desk. I bunched up our discarded clothes on either side so Amaya's knees wouldn't hurt and lightly strummed the bond to get her shadow's attention.

You are mine. You're all fucking mine, I told her.

I made the wisps of my shadow squeeze hers tight, sending a fierce possessive darkness through the bond to soothe her.

Her shadow trembled, and then I felt her relax. She liked to fight, liked to pin me, but only because she needed a shadow strong enough to match her ferocity. Her shadow needed my dominance and assurance to feel safe while our bond was insecure.

Amaya's eyes closed, probably feeling the effects of her shadow's satisfaction. She blinked and looked down at the clothes I'd stuffed under her knees.

"You're so thoughtful," she said.

"Your pleasure is my only priority."

"You just don't want me to not let you come again."

"I'll die if you don't."

"Mmm, but you're my mate, I can't kill you," she said.

Her hands came to my shoulders, and she ground down onto me, rubbing her clit into my pelvic bone.

I moaned as she clenched around me, and revised my statement, "I will have blue balls for the rest of my life if you don't."

She laughed and started bouncing on my cock. "Well, I wouldn't want that."

My hands cupped her soft breasts, pinching the nipples, knowing she liked a little bit of pain.

Leaning forward, I sucked on one, and then the other until she moaned my name and scratched her fingernails into my shoulders.

"You ride me so good, baby," I said. The faster she went, the closer I came, but I didn't want to do this alone. I grabbed her hip to steady my hand and flicked my thumb over her clit, circling and teasing the little bud.

"Yes…" The word was wrenched from her mouth as her body convulsed. "Come inside me, Sebastian," she said between ragged breaths.

Her inner walls squeezed me, and I clutched both hips, thrusting up into her. The promise of bliss tantalizingly close.

"Need you. Need you," she cried, shuddering as she came. Distantly, I registered that was similar to what her shadow had said.

But I was gone, lost in her, before I could give it much thought as I tipped over the edge.

I squeezed my eyes closed, throwing my head back as ripples of ecstasy tore through my body. The remnants of our shadows brightened our darkyra tattoos, and the faintest flash of light blinked as her high priestess power flickered. I groaned as my release emptied inside her.

She shivered in my arms as the pulse of our bond climaxed in a sharp aftershock.

An uneven breath filled my lungs, and I sighed it out, resting my head on her shoulder.

She stroked the back of my neck over the places that would have little crescent imprints of her fingernails.

I wrapped my arms around her waist so all of her body pressed into mine and buried my head into her neck.

Please don't leave me. Goddess, please, don't leave me. Everyone always leaves me. My thoughts floated between us. I hadn't intended to share them with her, but the urgency that was erupting through me, along with the lowered boundaries of our auras, hadn't allowed for my thoughts to be masked and hidden away.

I'll never leave you, Sebastian. I love you. All of you. Forever, she responded in my head as her arms tightened around me.

And, for a brief moment, I indulged, resting in her embrace, and lying to myself that she'd feel the same even after she knew the truth.

Chapter Twelve

Amaya

Since the moment I met Sebastian, my body reacted to him, to his power, unlike it had for any other. I felt his shadow, felt his emotions, felt the pull of our powers' desire to unite, and had written it off because there was no explanation, no words to describe it.

Having a name for the unexplainable made it impossible to ignore; it sharpened and clarified the sensations.

The mating bond had always been there, pulsating under the surface, influencing my feelings, my actions, my thoughts.

I could never unknow it.

Could never unknow him.

And paradoxically, despite the faint pulse of our unaccepted bond making me want to trace the shape of his soul with my shadows, I still felt like he was keeping me in the dark.

Maybe if we accepted the bond, I would understand why his body was rigid against mine.

Although, perhaps that wasn't fair. Even mates deserved a corner of their mind that was only theirs.

When I had told him I wasn't the same girl, he had said he wasn't the same either. After the traumas we've been through during the past few weeks, I couldn't ask him to reveal the parts of his mind he needed to keep hidden, the parts maybe he was hiding from himself.

The irreconcilable truth was I wanted to give him his privacy as much as I wanted to crawl inside him and tune my heartbeat to his.

We redressed in silence. I cleaned off the blade of my dagger and sheathed it inside my jacket before we exited the prison office.

I searched for the right words to ask if he was okay, but it seemed so asinine.

Of course he wasn't. Nothing about this situation was okay.

The high of reuniting with him and the adrenaline of exacting our revenge had ended with me using his desire, my desire, as a way to escape our new reality.

And if I was being honest, I didn't want to voice my concerns because they would be turned around on me, and the same fragile stability that I felt within him was only holding on by a thread within me.

We walked to the doors, lost in our own thoughts because neither of us remembered what the guard had said until we stood at the exit.

An impenetrable shadow darkened the entire threshold.

"Who would have enough power to shadow the entire prison? We barely had enough to kill the guards," Sebastian said.

He put his hand to the darkness, and it snapped back.

Enough of my bloodlust, and regular lust, had cleared that I was able to put things in perspective.

"Kai," I said flatly.

Sebastian furrowed his brows. "Kai?"

A single shadow inched out of the wall, crawling down the hall and around the corner.

"Come on," I said, following the shadow's trail like breadcrumbs. "There's one more guard we need to attend to."

"Amaya," Sebastian said in a low warning tone. "This feels like a trap."

"It most certainly is, but the only way out is through."

The shadow disappeared as we walked past, extending into a back corridor of the prison.

Sebastian grabbed my hand as we followed. "There's something about this shadow that feels familiar, but it's like I can't—" He abruptly stopped and cleared his throat.

Was he embarrassed? After all the suppression they pumped us both with, there was no shame in not remembering.

I squeezed his hand. "Kai is a guard. Or he's pretending to be one." I still didn't know his motives, but I had a feeling I was about to find out.

"Ah," he said.

"Kai knew about the prison break," I continued to explain. "I bet he planned it. He uncuffed me and gave me the dagger. He's sort of been helping me..." I didn't want to get into everything Kai had done. It was too confusing to explain, and after how Sebastian reacted to my back, I wasn't ready to wade through both of our feelings on it.

"This guard must have been in my cell," Sebastian said, but his tone didn't reveal how Kai had treated him. "That must be why his shadow feels familiar."

So Kai *did* know Sebastian was alive. I knew he'd been lying. He wanted to make sure I thought I had no one but him to rely on.

Sebastian's grip tightened around my hand. "If this one guard has enough power to shadow a prison..."

"He doesn't want us dead," I said. "He wouldn't have planned a prison break and given me a dagger if he did. He could have slit both our throats at any time."

Sebastian pursed his lips. His eyes kept searching the ground unseeingly as if trying to rifle through memories.

A similar worry had been nagging at the back of my head, but I'd been trying to piece together fragments of my memory for days, and it hadn't worked. I needed to see this through.

The shadow trail disappeared at a cell door. We peered into the small window at the top. The cell was full of shadows. They dissipated to reveal a male tied to a chair.

"Is that Jeremy?" I asked.

His face was gaunt, his brown hair disheveled. No longer the pristine male that had insulted and belittled me.

Seeing him flipped a switch inside me like a sleeper cell had been lying in wait. My knees shook as the fear from the night he tried to kill me flooded my body. I wasn't in the prison anymore. I was strapped to the ride, helpless to stop myself from being crushed at the bottom.

I yanked on the handle, and shadows unlocked the door. He was going to die for making me feel so powerless.

Sebastian grabbed my arm, jolting me from the memory. "We can't go in there."

I blinked and reoriented myself. My rage simmered. "We have to. He has to pay for trying to kill me."

Sebastian clenched his jaw. His eyes slid to the window and then back to mine. He nodded once. "Very well."

I strode into the cell and stood in front of Jeremy with my hands on my hips.

Jeremy lifted his head as if coming out of a stupor. "Oh Goddess," he said. "You really have come to kill me."

In my memory, he'd stared at me, so cold, so expressionless as he released the lever. I painted the same look on my face.

Unzipping my jacket, I pulled the dagger out. "I'm not going to kill you," I lied, tilting my head. "I want to ask you a few questions."

I dragged the tip of the dagger along his throat. "But if I don't get answers, I can't promise my grip won't..." I scratched just the slightest bit to draw blood. "...slip."

"Amaya," Sebastian said, his voice hard.

I turned. His expression was not hungry for blood like he'd been when we murdered the guards. He was trying to remain impassive, but there was too much tension in his body, his fists clenched, jaw tight.

His void eyes were cold as he stared at Jeremy, but something passed over him. Not quite pain, but certainly not the eagerness for terror that had accompanied our revenge spree.

Was he…did he…

A blistering, white-hot jealousy gripped me.

Sebastian didn't want me to torture Jeremy because he…he still had feelings for him?

Jeremy flinched as I glared at him. His jaw quivered, and his eyes darted back to Sebastian. "I really did love you," Jeremy whispered. "Please just kill me before they get to me."

"Who?" I demanded. "Who tied you here? Who forced you to try to kill me?"

Memories were imperfect. They could become fractured and damaged, but the night Jeremy tried to kill me, he wasn't himself. He'd been coughing up black sludge, pulling at his hair, fighting an inner battle.

Kai had done the same.

Jeremy's eyes stayed locked on Sebastian as tears fell from his eyes. "I was possessed."

"Possessed?" I asked. Sebastian had told me darkyras couldn't possess people.

Jeremy's eyebrows pulled inward. He didn't look at me, only spoke to Sebastian. "A couple months after we ended things between us…I made a bargain. A trade." His throat worked. "To take away my heartbreak, I'd have to cause another."

Confusion scrunched up my forehead, and I turned to Sebastian, who'd gone still, eyes wide.

Jeremy had made a *bargain*.

The answer hit me as soon as Sebastian said, "The Darkyra Deity possessed you."

It wasn't a question.

"I'm so sorry," Jeremy said, trying to fight his binds. "I'm sorry. If I knew it would be you that they would force me to hurt, I never would have...I never thought...I just wanted the pain to end. I'm sor—"

His words were cut off as his skin was leached of color. It turned ashy and flaked off.

I stumbled back as his body hollowed and desiccated. His fingernails turned black. The skin knitted together, hands and arms becoming unrecognizable, morphing into a spindly tentacle.

"Happy winter solstice, Maya."

Kai appeared from the darkness and smiled. "Now you see what happens if you break a bargain with me." With a single blink, shadows filled their eyes.

Kai.

The Dar*kyra* Deity.

Sebastian reacted quicker than I did. He crossed the room, standing between me and Kai. His arm outstretched to keep me back.

"Come now," Kai said with a wave of their hand. "No need for all this hostility."

Sebastian radiated rage and growled, "You'll stay away from her."

Kai rolled their eyes. "So territorial, you fae males are. How do you even stand it, Maya?"

"My name is Amaya," I said over Sebastian's arm. "Not Maya."

Kai chuckled. "You are what I made you to be."

The Jeremy draxis made a hissing noise that, though menacing, I could now recognize as pain.

"Turn Jeremy back," I demanded.

"Can't," Kai said. "He broke his bargain. These are the consequences."

"What do you want?" I asked, not bothering to keep the harsh bite from my words.

"Goodness, Maya," Kai said. "How about a little gratitude? I used all of the limited power I have to pave the path for you and your mate to break out of prison. I even gave you one of your enemies on a silver platter." He waved a hand at Jeremy and looked at Sebastian. "You wouldn't believe all the ways she pictured killing him. She's got quite the imagination. Though I've always found people pleasers have the deepest well of rage."

Kai was about to see a demonstration of that rage.

"At the very least you could thank me for turning off that incessant siren," Kai said in a huff. "This body's ears are still ringing from it."

"That's what you want?" I stepped out from behind Sebastian. "Us to thank you? Fine. Thanks. Now let us leave."

"Not until you complete your bargain." They looked at their wrist, even though there was no watch. "You've got six hours until winter solstice is over. You would have had more time, but you were a little preoccupied in the office."

What did you bargain to do? Sebastian's question popped into my head.

Complete a task on winter solstice.

He grimaced. *We're going to have to talk about your bargain making skills after we get out of this.*

Nothing about this was funny, so it really underscored how close to insanity I was that I had to fight the urge to laugh.

"Tell us her task, and we'll finish this," Sebastian said.

Kai smiled. "It's the same task I created you to complete."

Sebastian clenched his hands into fists. "You want her to take the crown."

"Precisely."

"If that was your plan, why did you have Jeremy try to kill me?" I asked.

Kai sighed. "Because I needed your relationship to progress if I was going to see a darkyra take the crown and claim the throne."

I shook my head, confused.

"Don't you see?" Kai stepped closer. "I've been helping you. If I would have left it up to him, he'd still be lying to you about your relationship." Kai's eyes widened, and they put a hand to their mouth, feigning shock. "Oh, I certainly hope he isn't lying to you about anything else. That'd be tragic, wouldn't it?"

"She's not taking the crown," Sebastian said.

"Then your mate will die. Gosh, what a price your loved ones have to pay to be around you. Ex-boyfriend is a draxis. Sister is gone. Mother is near her end. Everyone who loves you comes to an early demise, don't they?" Kai shook their head. "What a shame. I tried to help you with our bargain. I made it clear that you couldn't bind yourself to another. And yet, you still managed to hurt people."

Sebastian was shaking with tension, but we weren't going to get out of this by falling for Kai's emotional manipulations.

"You weren't trying to help him," I said. "You were trying to isolate him. Just like you tried to do to me by telling me he was dead."

Kai's eyes were cold as they glanced at me. "I do all of this to teach you both how your world works. You cannot rely upon anyone. You'll come to see this after a few decades as queen."

"Why?" I asked. "Why do you want me to take the crown? You're a deity. Why do you care who's in charge of Palagui?"

Kai's lip curled. "Because my siblings think they're superior to me! Think they're so much better because shadows in this country are cuffed and chained. I'm putting an end to it. *You* are putting an end to it."

"This is all for some sibling rivalry?" I asked, incredulous.

"It's a matter of life or death. The inability to live freely, to our full potential..." Kai's eyes slid to Jeremy. "We might as well all be husks."

"Palagui won't accept Amaya as queen. She's not a citizen," Sebastian said. "And she has no claim to the throne…"

Kai grinned. "Not alone she doesn't."

"Why don't you force someone else into your bargains," I said. "An actual citizen of Palagui maybe. Just leave us alone."

"Force?" Kai chuckled. "I only make bargains with people who seek them out. They enter into their bargains willingly. Just like you did. Like you both did. I cannot be held responsible for your regret."

Bullshit. I didn't have much of a choice. It was bind my powers or Xenos would kill me. Then, it was accept Kai's bargain or be powerless.

"Alright. We'll do it," Sebastian said.

My jaw dropped. We *will*?

Kai's grin widened. "Of course you will."

"You'll negate both of our bargains," Sebastian said. "Amaya and I will marry. She'll take the crown, and I'll claim the throne. Palagui will accept her once she's married into the royal family. You get a darkyra with the crown and the throne."

"And," Kai said and crossed their arms. "You'll do it tonight, or I'll kill her and make you immortal so you'll be forced to live with the consequences of your disobedience for all of eternity."

Sebastian's eyes slid to me, waiting for my reaction.

I bit my lip.

"You do realize that I could wait the six hours that are left on our original bargain and watch as it takes your life," Kai said.

We both have to agree to this, Sebastian said in my mind.

I…I don't want to be queen.

"You know I can hear you, right?" Kai rolled their eyes. "You can lie to him, and you can lie to yourself, but you can't lie to me. You do want to be queen, Maya. I was in your mind. I've seen every one of your sick little killing fantasies. Seen the desire brimming within you to take control. To right the wrongs of the world"—they threw their arm around in a mockery—"You have more power than most, and yet, you insist on squandering it. The crown will make everyone see what I already know. You can free the world from their shackles."

I chewed on my lip.

"Power will give you freedom," Kai continued. "You'll decide how history is written. I'd think being born in Delnee and not knowing you were fae your whole life would have made you learn that lesson early on. Narratives are written by the ones with the most power. Are you going to be written out of existence or…do you want the pen?"

I swallowed as the tingles of temptation sparkled somewhere inside me.

Kai's voice filled my mind. *This is what you've always wanted. What you've both been searching for. Power. Control. Freedom. You'll protect the broken. Punish the guilty. You'll never have to hide who you are or deny yourself what you want.*

Slowly their words morphed from coercive and manipulative to…enticing.

I didn't believe Kai actually cared about what Sebastian and I wanted, but at least with this deal we would be alive.

If I took the crown, it'd shorten my lifespan, but with my fae power I already had a lifespan far exceeding what I thought I would as a human.

And what was the alternative?

I refused and Kai killed me. Sebastian would be crushed. He'd already lost so many people in his life. I wasn't just making a decision for me; it'd be for him too.

And really, after what I'd done—after trying to kill Sebastian— didn't I owe it to him to prove that I loved him? That I'd sacrifice the end years of my life as penance for attempting to take his? He'd never ask it of me, but it felt justified in a twisted sense.

And if Sebastian's bargain was negated, we could accept the mating bond without risking his power.

I'd made this bargain, and these were the consequences. At least this way, we would get Kai out of our lives.

More than that, Palagui saw the two of us as criminals. Even if we somehow escaped Kai's bargain, escaped the prison, we would have to go into hiding.

This was a solution to all our problems.

I don't see any other way out of this, Sebastian said in my head, despite knowing Kai could hear us. It was still a comfort to feel his voice rumble through me. *At least this way, we'll be together.*

I swallowed and took a deep breath. "You'll add one condition to the bargain."

Kai raised an eyebrow. "Quite arrogant to think you have any power here, but that trait will serve you well as you rule." They waved a hand. "Proceed."

"You agree not to use your powers to mess with our lives or our friends lives ever again," I said. "And if you do…" My mind spun trying to think of a consequence. How did one punish a deity? "If you break the bargain, you'll not make another with anyone for the next thousand years!"

Sebastian grabbed my hand and squeezed. It felt like approval for my addition. I'd finally learned my lesson about making bargains.

Kai drew in a deep breath and shook their head, looking to the ceiling with annoyance like they were dealing with children. "Fine. I negate the bargain I made with Sebastian to disallow him to bind himself to another. I negate the bargain I made with Maya to finish a task on winter solstice. In their stead, they agree to marry. She will take the crown and not transfer it to another for as long as she lives. He will claim the throne. They'll do this by midnight tonight, or she will die, and he will turn into an immortal."

Kai smirked and added condescendingly, "And I promise not to use my powers on you or your friends at the risk of losing my ability to make bargains for the next thousand years."

Sebastian stared at the wall, eyes going back and forth as if trying to find loopholes. After a minute, he looked at me and nodded.

"I accept," we said in unison.

A surge of electricity zapped through the air. Shadows darkened our veins, and our darkyra tattoos pulsed along our arms. I sucked in a breath as the magic of the bargain shot through me, sharp and hot, like the crack of a whip.

Kai looked on, nonplussed.

The sensation receded as our new bargain fell into place.

Rain battered the prison, hard enough to be heard from inside the cement walls. A foreboding wind whirled. Dread prickled up my spine. When I woke up this morning, I was a prisoner, but by the end of the night, I'd have a crown and a *husband*.

Having a mate was certainly more permanent than a spouse, but possibly because I grew up thinking I was human, getting married somehow seemed more official.

Unfortunately, coercion tainted the intimacy of our impending nuptials.

Do you want to be married to me? I asked Sebastian. Anxiety filled me.

I want to be yours in all ways.

Before I could respond, the thudding of people running and frantic voices echoed from down the hall.

Kai clasped their hands. "And just in time! Our witnesses have arrived."

Chapter Thirteen

Sebastian

Amaya had once said she wanted a winter wedding.

It'd only been an attempt to distract Xenos in a council meeting when he was questioning the validity of our pretend relationship, but my other half had thought about what she'd said.

Often.

He had daydreamed about it so vividly his defenses would melt away, and I'd quietly watch as he pictured our mate in an elegant wedding dress, holding a bouquet of pink flowers, smiling with love in her eyes as snow fell delicately around us.

He had thought about their winter wedding as he wrote his proposal, as he rehearsed it until it was perfect. A tiny hope had bubbled up that maybe, just maybe, if he got the phrasing right, she would hear in his words that none of their fake relationship was pretend for him. She'd realize the depths of his feelings and would have more bravery than he did to name them. She'd tell him she loved him, and he'd tell her they were mates, and she'd jump into his arms in excitement.

His yearning would be so great, his imagining so wonderful, that I would forget to hide my presence. He would recognize that I'd slipped through his defenses and berate me. I was the reason he would never have her as a mate. The reason he had made his bargain and would never live out his wedding fantasy. The reason he couldn't get close to her without risking her getting hurt. All because of his evil shadow.

He never trusted me when I promised I would never harm her. Hadn't believed me when I told him that I was just as devoted to her shadow as he was to her.

He would leave me with one image before he'd slam me back into the prison in his mind: Our beautiful mate in her elegant wedding dress sprawled in an unnatural position, being drained of her powers as our shadows took her life.

If my other half were alive, he would be furious *I* was living his dream of marrying her.

Do you want to be married to me? There was no mistaking her anxiety as she asked the question.

I want to be yours in all ways, I assured her.

But her anxiety wasn't quelled.

My heart plummeted. She wasn't anxious of rejection, rather she was anxious because she was being forced to marry me.

I tried to rationalize that no one would want to be compelled into a marriage, but that logic didn't hold up since I held no resentment over this part of the bargain.

Perhaps I was shielding him. He would have surely buckled from the pain of her reluctance.

Once again, I was the consciousness that would witness his worst nightmares and hold the memories so he wouldn't need to endure the agony.

Of course she doesn't want you, the foreign voice said.

A memory flashed. Her face angry and tear-stained as she said, "Every single bad thing that's happened in my life is because of you."

You think changing the bargain so you can accept the bond with her will solve anything? The voice taunted. *She won't accept you when she finds out the truth. You're responsible for everything bad in her life.*

The sound of commotion jarred me out of my self-pity.

Kai clasped their hands. "And just in time! Our witnesses have arrived."

Two fae females skittered into the cell, daggers strapped to their thighs. Their eyes were wide, but joy replaced their fear when they saw Amaya.

I racked my brain, scanning through *his* memories, trying to place them. Amaya's friends…high priestesses…but what were their names?

"Another reason to be grateful, Maya," Kai said. "I made sure your friends were able to get here, though I hadn't anticipated the storm would be this bad."

Amaya ignored Kai and ran into her friends' embrace as a fae male shuffled into the room. His gait favored one side. I almost didn't recognize him until he exhaled in relief, smiling as he saw me.

Nico.

This was not good.

I fought down a grimace and tried to imagine how my other half would greet his friend. *I* wanted to throttle Nico, but that would make my current predicament very obvious.

I was spared from my fumbling when Kai snapped their fingers and shadows created a see-through boundary, separating Amaya and me from our friends.

"You can have your little reunion later. We're having a wedding now," Kai said.

Amaya touched the shadow boundary.

"Ow." She yanked her hand back.

I grabbed her hand to inspect the damage, but there was none visible.

"Unless you want to lose your fingers to frostbite, I suggest not touching it," Kai said.

I held her cold fingers between my hands until warmth returned.

Kai snapped again, and shadows swirled. Their magic surrounded us as fabric rustled and smoothed over my skin.

My clothes transformed into a black tux. Amaya's were replaced by a deep-purple, almost black, lace wedding dress.

My heart sunk as she slid her hands along the length of her torso. She would always be beautiful to me, but the snug dress only emphasized how thin she'd gotten. Her collarbones jutted out, and her cheekbones were too sharp. I didn't notice it when we were naked. She had been so vibrant and alive that it didn't register.

But none of this was right.

She was too thin. She was unhappy.

I needed to take her home. Feed her until she was plump, not let her leave my bed, erase her bad memories, shadow us so we could slip away from this world.

You don't deserve her.

Amaya's eyebrows pulled inward. Her gaze darted from her friends' panicked expressions, to Jeremy's draxis body still tied to the chair, then to me.

She didn't look at me with love in her eyes, only resignation.

It was a knife to the heart.

She forced a smile, grabbed my hand, and turned to Kai. "Let's get this over with."

And those words twisted the knife.

Chapter Fourteen

Amaya

Kai recited the vows, but when Sebastian didn't respond, they tapped their foot impatiently. "Well?"

Sebastian's eyes were unfocused. He was lost somewhere in his head. Neither of us wanted a forced wedding in a prison cell.

"Sebastian?" I gave his hand a light shake.

"Hmm?" he said, staring down at me.

"Kai said the vows. You have to say I do."

They weren't the darkyra vows Nico had recited in Sebastian's townhouse. The beautiful ones about partnership and standing by each other as we surrendered to the void, but I couldn't expect romance when there was a clock counting down to midnight.

Sebastian's face was unreadable as he said, "I do."

Kai asked in a bored tone, "Do you take this male as your magically bound partner for all eternity?"

I searched Sebastian's dejected face. In his fake proposal at court, he'd asked if I'd descend into the darkness with him. Our time in this prison had been nothing but darkness, but with this bargain, we were going to crawl ourselves out. Together.

I gave one final look at Gwen and Sloane behind the boundary. They watched us as if at a funeral not a wedding.

My voice was small. "I do."

"Then by the darkness vested in me, I seal your marriage binding for all eternity," Kai said in a rush.

Magic prickled like static through me, congregating on the fourth finger of my left hand, inking a small band below the knuckle. I guess that was why fae didn't bother with rings. They had magical tattoos.

I waited for Sebastian to lean down and kiss me, but that seemed another frivolous gesture we were going to skip for the sake of time because he only stared impassively as the tattoo was etched into his skin. He curled his hand into a loose fist and dropped it to his side.

Kai dropped the boundary, and I ran to Sloane and Gwen, squeezing them to me.

"Are you okay?" The question came from all three of us as we all searched one another for wounds.

"I'm fine," I said. "We made a bargain. It's a long story, but I have to claim the crown, and he has to claim the throne."

"Amaya," Gwen said. "The crown is going to drain your life. You saw Queen Mari."

"It was either that or die at midnight," I said, shaking my head. "It's going to be okay. We're all going to get out of this alive." I projected a confidence I didn't feel, but somehow comforting my friends felt easier than letting the reality of my situation sink in.

"We need to get to the Queen, to the palace," Sebastian said. His void eyes still shone, and the deep tenor of his power spoke. I'm not sure why they didn't recede, but maybe he felt he might need his power at any moment.

"We took a boat to the island after driving through Molbridge's forests, but we should hurry because the ocean is rough with the hurricane coming," Nico said.

"Hurricane?" I squeaked. "You came here on a boat in a hurricane? What were you thinking?"

Sloane gave a half smile. "We were thinking no better time for a prison break, but seems you two already had that part under control."

"The hurricane is hitting the southern coast," Gwen said. "The water is choppy up here from the storm, but we weren't sailing through the worst of it."

"And plan A didn't work," Nico said. "Sloane and I accepted the mating bond, hoping that it would give us power, since the Queen dying shouldn't have affected it…but I guess our research was wrong."

I blinked, hung up on the part about Sloane and Nico being mates.

"The palace should be safe from the worst of the hurricane too. What with the ridges north of Merbany protecting it," Nico added and winced as he held his side.

"Are you okay?" I asked. "Are you hurt?"

"It's the broken bargain with Sebastian," Sloane explained. "Can you please negate it already?"

Everyone turned and looked expectantly at my new husband.

He cleared his throat and said, "I negate our bargain."

Nico narrowed his eyes. "You know that isn't good enough. You have to say what bargain you're negating."

Sebastian squinted as if he was trying to remember.

I pressed my lips together, pushing down the sympathy that I knew he wouldn't want. The suppression must have affected his memory even worse than mine.

Crossing back to him, I held his hand.

The stuff they gave us here affected our memories. Remind him, I sent the thought to Nico.

Nico's mouth pulled down into a pitying look, which was exactly what I was trying to avoid by not saying it aloud. "Seriously, dude. Sloane and I accepted the mating bond, so the whole *don't tell Sloane about the mating bond* is really a moot point."

Sebastian nodded once. "I negate our bargain to keep your silence about the mating bond."

Nico's shoulders slumped, and he exhaled a sharp breath. "Never again," he said with a wincing smile. "I'm never getting into a bargain with you again."

"I'm sorry I got sent to prison to be tortured for weeks. That must have been terribly inconvenient for you," Sebastian said, deadpan.

Nico's eyebrows pulled inward, Gwen's mouth fell open, and Sloane sucked in a breath.

"You were tortured?" Gwen asked.

Sloane looked like she was going to cry.

Kai chose that moment to clear their throat. "If you're done chitchatting, you've got five and a half hours until midnight, so...if you ask nicely, I'll sift you to the palace."

They were a deity, so despite the rest of us having no power or very little, theirs wasn't affected.

I scrubbed a hand down my face. "Will you please sift us to the palace, Kai?"

They smiled. "Of course, Maya."

I bristled at the name, but my gaze landed on Jeremy. His draxis tentacles were fighting the binds around what would have been his wrists. "Should we take Jeremy?" It felt wrong to leave him.

Sebastian shook his head. "He's safest here. In this cell, he won't hurt anyone or himself. We'll come back for him."

When things were settled, we would take him to the research center until we could figure out how to heal him.

Kai's shadows filled the room, and quicker than I'd ever sifted before, we were in the Queen's bedroom inside the palace.

The Queen laid in her bed. A heart machine's beep echoed in the room, almost completely drown out by the rain thudding the windows.

As we approached, the faint beeping of her heartbeats seemed to get further and further apart.

Her body was gaunt, skin sunken and hollowed so every bone in her face stood out.

The sound of footsteps approaching and retreating came from outside the door.

"I'd hurry this along," Kai said. "The council and over half the court are downstairs in the great room."

They took out a handkerchief and wiped black sludge from their nose and from under their eyes, and I realized why. Every time Kai used their power in a body that wasn't theirs, the body broke down.

"Why?" I asked. "And how do you know that?"

"I've told you several times I'd take care of you, Maya," Kai said. "I've been keeping a close watch on your enemies. The council and the court are here to witness the coronation of the new queen. And since they couldn't do it at court because downtown is flooding and the Queen's condition is unstable, Caroline gathered them here."

Sebastian placed a hand on the small of my back, and we walked to the side of the Queen's bed.

I gathered one of her withered hands in mine. She stirred, and her eyes opened.

"My son, you've been away for so long," she said, a slight crack in her voice.

Sebastian pursed his lips. "Amaya and I have married."

Her throat worked, and her eyes went unfocused, but she lifted my hand and peered at the inked band on my finger.

Her smile was soft. "I knew you would."

"We've come to claim the crown and the throne," Sebastian said.

"Good. And Xenos…"

"He's not going to get in the way" was the only explanation Sebastian gave.

The Queen nodded. Her other hand came to cover mine. "You'll take good care of my baby?" she asked me.

I didn't hesitate and squeezed her hand. "Sebastian is my family. I take care of my family above all else."

Gwen and Sloane were my family too. A bond of sisters before we had even known one another. And Nico was Sloane's mate and more Sebastian's brother than his own brother had been. These people were my family. Nothing would stop me from protecting them. They were my priority.

The Queen blinked. "Ah yes, well, him too."

My face fell, and I shrunk back a little. Her baby wasn't Sebastian? I glanced at him, but he remained unaffected by her cruel words. She meant the crown and the country?

When I visited her weeks ago, she had pulled me aside and said she felt guilty for how she treated Sebastian when he was a child. That she regretted foisting him off on distant family members and keeping him away from Adriana, but was that all just an impending death regret?

Even after everything Sebastian had done to keep her alive, she was more concerned about me taking care of the country than her child?

Maybe she was. She raised Adriana to give her the crown. The very thing that would suck her life away. She had expected her daughter to make the same sacrifice she did.

Sickness roiled in my stomach. She'd been so nice to me the last time I was here. Was her excitement because I was a high priestess marrying into her family? Was I just someone to sacrifice to keep her country alive?

Her breathing slowed, and her chest rattled.

I shook my head. This was unfair to think. The Queen was dying. I couldn't judge her for one thing she said when she might not be in her right mind.

A loud wind howled outside the window, and the rain beat harder on the glass.

"The deities are displeased with Palagui. Your continued disobedience will draw their ire,' Kai said. Black blood trickled from their ears, but they didn't wipe it away.

"You started this hurricane? Then stop it!" I said.

Kai seethed, "The sun has abandoned you, and the moon controls the tides, yet you blame me for this storm? Look outside, Maya!"

I looked out the window. Shadows covered the windows, protecting the palace from the heaviest of the rain and winds.

"I am the only deity that is currently on your side," Kai said. "Darkness is all that you have left. Now transfer the crown before it gets worse. I promise you do not want to deal with their wrath."

Kai was a liar and a manipulator, but I didn't think they were lying about that.

"Queen Mari," I said. "I'm ready to rule Palagui."

Her eyes had closed, but she opened them and nodded. She raised her hands to the crown on her head. It was a tarnished gold with several black diamonds around one large black diamond in the center.

With a deep breath, she seemed to be gathering all her strength. Her voice came out clear as she hovered the crown over my head. "The crown represents the responsibility and the privilege of sacrifice to the people of Palagui. A mother is the leader of the family, the silent organizer, the untiring strength, the scaffolding that holds every fear, every injustice, every emotion of her children and metabolizes them to allow her family to prosper." She lowered the crown, resting it on my head and whispered, "Remember that every citizen is your child. The family you've promised to protect has grown considerably."

My final thought as Amaya Mevson, high priestess and darkyra, daughter to Nevaeh and Victoria Mevson, citizen of Delnee, best friend to Sloane Knight and Gwen Nueblots, wife to Sebastian Renwick—was that Queen Mari seemed fully lucid.

She had known exactly what she was saying.

Magic filled me, and I swayed, feeling woozy.

My eyes landed on Kai as they winked at me. "See you soon, Maya."

Shadows encased them, and they vanished as my eyes rolled back. I collapsed into a strong pair of arms.

Chapter Fifteen

Amaya

I had drowned like this before.

The nightmares that plagued me after I bound my powers at the Hollow were preparation for this moment.

Kai had always known I'd end up here.

I was caught in the waves. My body tossed and tumbled, and I couldn't figure out which way was up. Each time I kicked my legs and fought to the surface to suck in a breath, another wave would crash into me. My nose and lungs burned as I took in water.

Tentacles wrapped around my ankles and pulled me below the tumult of the waves. I opened my eyes but couldn't make out anything except a foggy abyss.

I kicked and flailed, fighting as the darkness pulled me under. The pain of not breathing grew, and against my own will, my mouth opened to suck in air, only to be flooded with cold water.

Panic and desperation gripped me. The instinct to get air overcame any other thought. I thrashed, trying to swim, but there was no up.

A pressure surrounded me, collapsing me, crushing me. I gasped, inhaling another swallow of water.

I was choking, asphyxiating, drowning.

There were no brilliant colors or bright lights, no peace, when I died. Just an all-consuming fear, until there was nothing.

I became bodiless. An entity without shape or form. Floating amongst a void. Not within water or air or clouds but expansive nothingness. There was no pain.

There was no sound, not even an echo.

And within that silence, something waited, watched. Judging if I was worthy.

I had the sense that I failed their test.

Cleared of the panic of dying, I could remember Sebastian had told me the fairy tale of the creation of the fae. The deities were sucked into a lake and punished for fighting as they drowned.

What would my punishment be?

Water rushed around me as I was hauled upward. The pain of drowning returned as I was dragged to land.

I coughed and coughed, expelling black water. My lungs ached, and my throat stung. For what felt like hours, I heaved until finally I could suck in a lungful of air.

Slumping over, my hazy vision cleared. A vast wasteland spread in all directions. No sky and no end in sight.

"Are you quite finished?" Kai had shed the body of the guard they'd been possessing in favor of their usual androgynous, wraith-like body. Their ears were sharp and pointed, almost as long as their head. Clawed fingers tapped on their crossed arms.

I stood, and vertigo almost took me back down.

"Where am I?" I asked.

My clothes were soaked and plastered to my skin. I'd lost my shoes, and cold mud slipped between my toes. The water of the lake lapped gently along the shore as a chilled breeze blew. No storm, no crashing waves.

"When the queen places the crown upon another's head with the intent to transfer the power, the crown opens a portal between the worlds. We're nowhere and everywhere," Kai said and then mumbled something like, "Since they can't come to your world."

"Why? Who?" I asked, but Kai ignored me and yanked me along. They were always talking in riddles.

I pushed my hair off my face and felt no crown on my head. Maybe that was why the thing in the lake found me unworthy. Two minutes as queen and I'd already lost the crown.

"Why am I here?" I demanded.

"To tie your life force to the crown," Kai said, full of annoyance.

The vertigo didn't dissipate. Something about the expansive emptiness made me queasy. I had no landmarks to set my bearings.

"Come on, Maya. Keep up," Kai said, and I hurried to follow them, not wanting to be left in this wasteland of nothingness, nor wanting to go back in the water with the thing that didn't find me worthy.

Kai leaned over and whispered, "By the way, we should probably pretend we don't know each other. It'll be easier that way."

"Easier for who?"

Kai smiled. "For everyone, Maya. My siblings are already going to be in a bad mood because Palagui took so long to crown another queen."

"The Sun God and the Moon Goddess?" I asked, eyes wide.

Kai pursed their lips. "Luna and Saul have quite the temper, but believe it or not, Luna is the worst of the two. Strange, since you'd guess it'd be Saul, what with the fire and all."

"What would they have done if the Queen died without passing on the crown?"

Kai shrugged. "Magic would have ravaged your country, terrorized your people, until a new queen was selected. It would have been brutal. But look at you, saving everyone."

We continued to walk in the darkness, no end point in sight. "Why do they care if Palagui's citizens have fae power?"

Kai pinched the bridge of their nose. "Because Maya, haven't you been paying attention? The crown connects to Palagui's power. My siblings want me and our shadows to be as powerless as possible."

Kai stopped, and I halted beside them. Their voice filled my head. *The question is would you rather be a servant to the light or the ruler of the dark? Will you light yourself on fire to keep others warm?*

I blinked, and they were gone.

White orbs circled me until my vision was blinded. A moment passed, and the intensity of the orb's light eased, revealing three figures sitting in their thrones in a huge room made of shining silver.

Taller than the forty-story court building, the deities squinted down at me.

To the left, a male with horns protruding from his head. His dark skin was covered with gold body armor. His face had a sharp nose, pointed chin, and long feathered eyebrows. Though his body was large and thick, like he'd been drawn with a heavy hand, he had an otherworldly grace as he tilted his head and considered me.

In the middle, a female with white glowing eyes as big as two full moons. The black of her hair was set off by the translucence of her skin. Her blue veins wrapped around her body only disrupted by a flowing silver dress that billowed around her as if there was a constant breeze.

Kai sat to the right with a bored, petulant expression. They'd donned a long black tunic over tight, shiny leather pants.

I lowered my gaze as sickness pitted my stomach from staring up at them.

No more than a few feet away, a smaller pedestal stood. The crown that I'd thought I lost rested on a pillow. It looked different. The gold was no longer tarnished, and the diamonds were no longer black but clear and shimmering.

"There is an otherness about her I don't like," the Sun God said. His voice boomed, deep enough to shake me. "She's a halfing. I detest spoiled blood. I thought this world didn't have that?"

"They must be interbreeding between one another and the humans as well because she's puny and weak," the dainty voice of the Moon Goddess responded.

"I'm not!" I wanted to say, but when I opened my mouth, I couldn't form words, only made strange squeaking noises. Magic had taken my speech.

"You say that every generation, Luna," the Sun God said.

"That's because every generation is weaker," Luna said, full of contempt. "And look at her! She's uninitiated. This will not do, Saul."

Saul hummed.

Magically muted, I couldn't plead my case. I looked at Kai, begging with my eyes for them to come to my aid, but they said nothing. Their face unreadable. They didn't want their siblings to know they wanted me to have the crown.

A sharp crack of pain split through my body, and an invisible hand pressed me down until I was kneeling before them with my forehead on the ground.

"Well," Saul said. "We could take her life force."

"Why would you do that?" Kai spoke for the first time. "It'd burn through the power too quickly."

"Then they'll send another," Luna said, indifferent. "There will be a plague, weather events, and destruction until the point gets across that we're unsatisfied. In the meantime, we'll suck out her life force, and it can dwell inside the crown until a worthy servant is sent. This one is simply not good enough."

Kai, Luna, and Saul started bickering and yelling over top of one another.

Not good enough? Not *good* enough? I wasn't good enough for their damned crown?

My jaw clenched, and my hands tightened into fists.

Why was that everyone's assumption about me? I wasn't good enough in Delnee for my certification project. I wasn't good enough for Sebastian, according to Palagui's courtiers. Everyone judged my high priestess powers as weak.

The constant mantra of not being good enough played in my mind, no matter how many times I thought I mastered it.

I would finally find my voice, my power, only for a new situation to beat me back down and make me question my worth.

Because you aren't listening, my shadow said. *You forget me, but I'm always here.* The words came out faint and strained. I wasn't sure how I heard her at all.

I sucked in a deep breath, fanning the heat of my anger in my core, stoking the shadows to life, trying to tune in to the power that dwelled within me.

They aren't going to give us the crown, my shadow said, voice becoming clearer, stronger, as I focused on her.

My shadow had always been speaking to me, through me, even when I thought she was gone. She was my voice of strength. She fortified my inner defenses. She was my wickedness and my scaffolding.

A deep wellspring of power filled my core, and my breathing came easier as shadows burst through my veins.

The deities were distracted with their squabbles, and the heaviness pressing me to the ground was lifting. I pushed myself up onto my hands and knees.

They aren't going to let us leave here alive, my shadow said.

I wouldn't forget my power again. I would only need to listen to her and drown out all the other voices in my head.

Blood dripped from my nose and fell onto the mirrored silver floor. My distorted reflection stared back. Clothes soaked, hair damp, blood smeared across my gaunt face.

I should have seen someone about to collapse.

I'd been tortured for weeks, drowned in a mystical lake, and coerced into being a pawn for a deity's game. But as the shadows rose within me, there was no defeat in my void eyes.

I was a girl in an industry that demeaned females. A high priestess in a country that despised the fae. A darkyra in a world that was afraid of the shadows. I would always be the outsider. A threat to the status quo.

No one was going to give me power.

If I wanted it—I was going to have to take it.

"Fuck it," I murmured, and before the deities could stop me, I lunged for the pedestal, snatched the crown, and slid the cold metal over my head.

Frost filled my blood as the ground rumbled under my feet. The crown was dry ice, burning a ring around my head.

I screamed and fell to my knees, trying to rip the crown off, but it was burnt into my skull. My skin lit up with high priestess healing. Shadows burst around me in a frantic attempt to keep my body from tearing itself apart.

I vaguely registered Saul say, "Huh. Guess we'll see if she's strong enough after all."

"Just end her already," Luna said. "Her screeching is hurting my ears."

My mouth was sewn shut, lips melted together by fire, and I couldn't even form a single syllable of anguish.

"Better?" Saul asked.

I was going to die. I'd never been so certain of anything in my life. The next few moments passed with an eternity between them as the crown's power split me in two.

I caught a glimpse of Kai before my entire body crumbled to the floor. They weren't smiling, but there was a gleam in their dark eyes.

I thrashed as an unimaginable pain twisted my organs inside out. My body was trying to escape itself. Fire and ice seared my skin as sharp shooting pain stabbed my core.

"Your disrespect won't be forgotten, girl," Luna said. And I was flung into the portal in the lake.

Breathe, my shadow said. *Breathe through the pain.*

I couldn't. I tried to gulp air and swallowed water instead, falling further into the black abyss of the lake.

The pain continued as the burn of drowning combined with the agony of the crown's power.

A ripple of light flickered above me. The surface of the water. Some self-preservation instinct had me kicking upward.

I swam hard but didn't get far. The water was thick like cream.

White light filled my vision, and I sat up, gasping for air, back in the Queen's bedroom, sitting on the couch.

I curled over, dry heaving as my body tried to expel water that wasn't there. A hand came to rub my back.

"You're here. You're safe. I've got you," a deep shadowed voice said.

I gagged again, but the feeling was starting to settle. My body's clenching eased.

My stomach cramped from a dark foreignness which seemed to reside within me, but my breathing started to slow.

Sparkling black shadows brushed my hair from my face, and I fell back onto his chest. He sat behind me, holding me between his legs. His shadow encased my body and vibrated on my skin with a calming, soothing hum I felt deep in my core. He kept murmuring that I was safe, that he had me, that I was here with him.

I twisted enough to peer up at his perfect face and crystal blue eyes. His beauty only spoiled by the worried crease in his brow.

"You were gone so long. I was afraid I'd lost you," he said. He kissed my forehead. "But I knew you were strong enough, little warrior."

His fingers stroked down the side of my face, across my shoulders, and down my arms.

"Your mom?" I croaked.

"The Queen has passed."

"I'm so sorry, Sebastian." I pressed my hand over his heart.

"It was a long time coming."

His form became hazy, and my head felt heavy. I blinked and blinked to clear the fog, but as I refocused on him, I thought it strange that his void eyes stared back almost like I'd hallucinated them having been blue at all.

"How do you feel?" Sebastian asked.

I pushed myself up, taking stock. "Slightly woozy, but it's passing."

Gwen and Sloane ran in from the attached on-suite. Sloane handed me a glass of water, and Gwen lifted a washcloth to blot sweat off my face.

"I'll do it," Sebastian said, his voice sharp with a *do not test me* tone.

Gwen curled her lip and glared at him as Sloane looked warily between them. With a hand on her arm, Sloane took the cloth from Gwen and gave it to Sebastian.

There was a weird tension that I couldn't make out. A nurse—Louisa I recognized—was quietly unhooking equipment from Sebastian's mother and taking care of her body.

Sebastian ran the wet cloth over my face. His voice was gentle once more as he explained, "Louisa has not informed the guards of the Queen's passing yet, so Caroline and the council do not know, but I don't expect that to buy us much more time," Sebastian said. "Nico is assessing the situation."

I glanced around at the room and noticed three dead guards slumped over against the wall.

The body that Kai had possessed was desiccated in the corner. Whatever life force that had been inside was gone. His possession must have lasted too long.

A thick cloud of shadows hovered around us, which meant fae power was back. I touched my forehead and felt the metal crown encircling it.

I was the queen.

It hadn't sunk in. None of this could be real.

The door opened, and Nico slipped inside. "Caroline isn't here, apparently everyone is waiting for her. She's held up from the storm. The general consensus is that she could be here any minute, but that they've been saying that for hours."

Sebastian's eyes didn't leave my face. "And the guards?"

Nico's lips flattened into a thin line as he glanced at the dead guards in the corner. "Two at the entrance to the great room and three at the front exit, but it's a skeleton staff due to the hurricane."

"No one has noticed their powers have returned?" Sebastian asked.

"No, half of them are getting blitzed, and the other half are panicking about the storm."

Sebastian set the cloth aside. His thumb on my chin tilted my gaze from Nico to him. "I know you feel weak, but there isn't much time until midnight, and I must claim the throne."

I took a deep breath, but my unsteadiness had been subsiding since I'd woken up. "Will the court and council recognize you as the Queen's son?" It's not like the Queen could tell everyone from beyond the grave.

"She all but said the words to claim me when she approved of our engagement at court," Sebastian said. "That ritual is only for the royal lineage. That's why the courtiers were upset by it. Xenos didn't care because a marriage binding between me and a weak high priestess guaranteed I'd never take the throne from him."

But Xenos didn't know I wasn't weak. I never had been. My darkyra power was strong enough that Sebastian's powers recognized me as his equal, his mate.

How I could be equal to him—a demi-god and the offspring of Kai and Queen Mari—I had no idea.

But I also didn't care.

All that mattered to me was that he was *mine*.

"How exactly do you claim the throne?" I asked.

A dangerous smirk tugged at his lips. "Just let me handle that part. Are you well enough to walk?"

I nodded, and he helped me to stand.

The crown dug into my forehead, and I took it off to inspect it. The gold was no longer tarnished, and the diamonds were clear, not black, just as I'd seen on the pedestal in front of the deities. The crown must change along with the queen's life force as the years pass.

I resituated the crown on my head. "Alright, I'm ready." My deep-purple lace dress was in pristine condition, and my hair wasn't perfect, but it wasn't plastered to my face either. My body hadn't been in the place between the worlds.

"The throne must be claimed before midnight or Amaya will die," Sebastian said. "Therefore, I expect everyone's cooperation when we enter. *Everyone*." His eyes narrowed at Nico, who only crossed his arms over his chest and shrugged. "This is for Amaya's sake." Sebastian's gaze swung to Sloane and Gwen. They both looked like they were holding their tongues, but they nodded anyway.

I furrowed my brows. "Why are you being so mean to them?"

Sebastian grabbed my hand with a harsh grip. His voice low and angry as he said, "I will be *mean* to anyone who gets in the way of me claiming the throne. I refuse to lose you."

My mouth parted, and confusion creased my forehead. "Sebastian—"

But he was already tugging me out of the bedroom and down the hall at a fast clip. Our friends trailed behind us, and when I glanced back, they gave me concerned looks but tried to hide them with forced smiles.

What happened while I was out? I sent the thought to both Gwen and Sloane, but Sloane shook her head and forced another smile. Gwen frowned and stared at the back of Sebastian's head.

Alright. This was weird, but with fae power back I could feel their emotions again. They weren't afraid, just a muted yellow anxiety, a wariness. Maybe Sebastian snapped at them when I passed out, and they were anxious about what we're about to do. Couldn't blame them for that.

People lined the halls and spilled out of rooms on the main floor, but no one noticed us as we stood at the threshold of the great room.

It was as big as the ballroom at court with several chandeliers hanging from the ceiling and pockets of fireplaces and seating set up along the wall. At the front of the room, a small dais was set up with a throne, not unlike the one at court.

Two guards leaned against the wall, looking bored, but they startled to attention when shadows encircled their necks. Their choking noises silenced the cacophony of talking in the great room.

Sebastian's shadows lifted the guards until their feet couldn't touch the ground and floated them into the center of the room.

Gasps turned into shrieks, but everyone remained frozen, watching as the guards clawed at the shadows at their necks.

Sebastian! You're killing them!

They're bad ones, Amaya. They're all bad ones.

He hadn't checked their chest for the markings, but he must have known they had them, so I didn't stop him.

The bloodlust that had pumped through my veins in the prison was still bubbling in the background, but it wasn't quite the potent zing of satisfaction it had been. I wanted revenge on the guards at the prison. Not these guards.

It took an excruciatingly long time for the guards to die. The shadows dropped their bodies, and they tumbled to the ground.

The shadows spread through the crowd and darkened the room.

People screamed and tried to fight to get past one another, but more shadows blocked the windows and exits.

"Why are you running?" Sebastian said. His words boomed through the room, enhanced by the shadows. There was a glee in his voice that seemed out of place. "Haven't you all gathered to crown our new queen?"

The crowd froze. Shadows hovered at eye level, making it clear that if anyone tried to fight, they would lash out.

A few people ran their thumbs over their foreheads. An ancient gesture to ward oneself against darkyra mind control. But since darkyras couldn't actually control people's minds, it was just a blatant insult.

"I appreciate your patience and weathering the hurricane to witness our coronation," Sebastian said with a wild look in his eyes. "Where's the council?"

At first no one moved, until one male pushed through the crowd and stood in front of us.

"Hugo," Sebastian said with a taunt in his voice.

"What the hell are you doing, Sebastian? Who do you think you are killing guards and terrorizing everyone?"

A sly smile spread across Sebastian's face as he stalked closer to Hugo. Hugo stepped back, but then he clenched his fists and puffed out his chest, trying to hold his ground.

"Who do I think I am?" Sebastian's left eyebrow rose. He continued toward the front of the room, a swagger in his step as the crowd parted for him. People flinched as he came near.

He climbed up on the dais and asked again, voice louder, deeper, "Who am *I*?" His deep menacing laugh bellowed through the room.

Something animated him, a manic darkness unleashed.

"Oh shit," Nico whispered.

"I'm so glad you asked," Sebastian said, putting a hand on his chest as he strutted across the dais. "I am Sebastian Renwick-Laurent. Darkyra son to the late Queen Mari. And the only living heir to Palagui's throne."

He lowered his chin and pierced the crowd with his gaze.

The corners of his mouth curled up. His voice became sweet as honey. "I am the King of Darkness," he said as he reached his arms out on either side of him, and shadows flooded the room.

A collective gasp echoed around us. So taken aback by his display, I hardly noticed when he sifted me.

The shadows cleared and revealed us. Wide, fearful eyes stared up at me, at us, at my crown as I stood next to him on the dais.

"And as you no doubt have come to realize, fae power has returned to Palagui because she"—Sebastian gestured to me—"is our new crowned queen."

The weight of the crown suddenly felt heavy on my head.

"All will bow to Queen Amaya," Sebastian growled.

"We will never bow to the darkness!" Hugo shouted.

A wicked grin filled Sebastian's face. "Those who do not kneel to the darkness will find themselves as servants to the dark unknown of the afterlife."

Shadows snapped out and twisted Hugo's neck. His body fell to the ground.

Someone screamed.

"Anyone else?" Sebastian asked.

A beat passed before the stunned crowd scrambled to the ground, fighting one another for the space to press their foreheads to the floor.

Sebastian...what are you doing? I recognized it was hypocritical to be unnerved. I was the one who stole the crown from the deities. But something was off about this.

Claiming the throne, he said. *Making sure the world knows your name. Making sure no one will ever hurt us or any darkyra again.*

I...I don't think...

Sebastian grasped my hand, and he guided me to the throne. Too dumbstruck to fight or protest, I followed his lead and sat on the throne with my back stiff and straight.

"A new era has begun," Sebastian said, standing by my side. "Darkyra will no longer be confined. We, the children of darkness, will reside in our rightful place as rulers of Palagui."

Yellow sour anxiety blanketed the room, interspersed with the spice of anger, of hatred.

Sebastian looked out over the crowd with his void eyes as shadows floated over everyone, waiting for the moment someone stepped out of line.

Gwen and Sloane stood with shocked faces at the entrance of the room. Nico beside them, rubbing his jaw as if coming to the same conclusion I was.

The three of them had noticed his odd behavior, his callous treatment, while I'd been passed out. Sebastian's void eyes hadn't receded, and his memories were more fragmented than mine. All the little ways he acted different, spoke different, that I'd ignored or attributed to the trauma of the prison.

He'd called himself the *King of Darkness* for Goddess's sake.

A clock struck midnight; its twelve chimes resounded through the room. I gazed up at my new husband—as my awareness filled with his chai-spiced vengeance—and realized I didn't know which part of Sebastian I had married.

Chapter Sixteen

Sebastian

I'd thought she died in my arms. I'd thought I lost her.

The moment she'd put the crown on, she fell, and I barely moved quick enough to catch her. When her heart had stopped and the bond went silent, I almost collapsed along with her.

Sloane and Gwen's screaming had caused the guards outside to burst into the bedroom, but my shadows disabled them without my gaze leaving my mate. I'd carried her to the couch and nestled her between my legs. Her head had lolled to the side, and I'd carefully positioned it on my chest so I could stroke her hair.

I hadn't been able to feel her shadows under her skin. Her body was limp. She was dead. She was gone. I was seconds away from losing it, but then it hit me.

If my shadows were back at full strength, the crown's power was funneling through her life force, which meant she *had* a life force even if it wasn't within this body.

The girls continued screaming, and Nico was trying to tell me something, but I couldn't focus with all the ruckus they were making.

"Unless all three of you want to die, you'll shut the fuck up and stay away," I had bellowed, and my shadows covered Amaya and me. I twisted the guards' necks in the corner to prove I wasn't joking.

I could not lose her. I would not lose her. No one would take her from me.

I began rocking us, making the soft, soothing noises that had always calmed her when she was in distress. I didn't know if she could hear me; maybe I was only doing it to comfort myself. Her body may have felt dead, but Kai wasn't here. If she'd died, Kai would be upset over their plan not working.

Wherever her consciousness disappeared, it could be a timeless place like the Hollow. She could wake up and reanimate her body without any repercussions.

Minutes turned to hours. Distracted by trying to keep my impending sorrow at bay, by trying to control the overwhelm of emotions within this body, I hadn't noticed him until it was too late.

When her heart started beating again and the bond vibrated with life, she'd fluttered her eyes open.

I wasn't sure if I'd been in control when my mouth said, "You were gone so long. I was afraid I'd lost you."

But as if he'd only been a phantom in my imagination, his consciousness faded out, leaving my mate in my arms where she belonged, and my head blissfully empty of my doppelganger like he'd never been there at all.

If her death was the only thing that was strong enough to arouse him from his eternal sleep, I'd just make sure she never came close to death again. A task I'd already vowed to undertake.

One could say I took my anger and fear over almost losing her out on the guards and the councilmember I killed.

Or one could say it was a justified response. A demonstration of my commitment to my new resolution.

No one would hurt her when I was here to protect her.

No one would even get close enough to breathe my mate's air while I was in control of this body.

Chapter Seventeen

Amaya

"Councilmembers rise," Sebastian commanded the crowd in the great room from the dais.

Four people rose to their feet, their heads bowed. The entire room held a collective breath, the silence stilted and tense. Sour fear and spicy anger swirled in the room. I blocked the sick concoction.

"Tomorrow at noon we'll meet in the blue room. If you wish to step down due to the regime change, you may do so after appointing your replacement," Sebastian said. "But if you come tomorrow, you will be serving Queen Amaya, and I'll expect your diligence and respect." The shadows pulsated in the air, underscoring his threat. "Is Hugo's second in the room?"

Someone rose from kneeling. I squinted and made out a female with long straight blonde hair. "Leva Lussier, your majesty," she said, barely above a whisper. "I'm ready to represent region two of Palagui City and serve Queen Amaya." She bowed at the waist.

"Thank you, Leva," Sebastian said. "Please inform the councilmembers not here tonight that if they don't show up tomorrow for the meeting, they will be replaced."

Leva bowed in acknowledgement.

"A funeral service for the late Queen will be held tomorrow evening at dusk in this room. I expect all to be in attendance," he said.

The shadows swept forward. Hair and clothes rustled as if caught in the stormy winds outside.

"You may all rise," Sebastian said. Slowly each person stood. Their faces ranged from placid to fearful. I couldn't see any that dared to show outright anger, though I knew they were feeling it.

Sebastian held out a hand, and I placed my palm in it. He led me down the dais and through the crowd. His shadows surrounded us from all directions, thick enough to protect, but not so thick that the crowd's gazes couldn't follow us until we were at the entrance beside our friends. The shadows encased the five of us, and we sifted away.

When the shadows cleared, I barely cared where we'd sifted to. I yanked my hand from Sebastian's and whirled around. "What the hell was that?"

Sebastian only sighed and ran a hand through his hair.

Nico's arms were crossed over his chest. "I'd like to know the answer to that question as well."

Sloane and Gwen subtly shifted beside me as if they'd need to protect me from this version of Sebastian.

"Have you lost your mind?" I asked and threw my hands up and looked around to see where we'd landed.

A small room with wood-paneled walls and an open concept kitchen and living area in front of a fireplace. It was too dark to see outside, and the only sound was rain pelting the roof. "Where are we?"

"Nico's cabin," Sloane supplied.

"There was no way we could stay at the palace tonight. There'd be at least three assassination attempts before morning," Sebastian said.

I rubbed my tired eyes. "I know you are his shadow. We aren't in danger anymore, so please let my Sebastian out." My voice lost its force. I was too tired to do this. I wanted a shower and to sleep for the next three months. I couldn't do the latter. A few hours would have to suffice.

Sebastian snorted. "Your Sebastian?"

Nico huffed and stomped away down the hall.

"Yes," I said. "Look I get it, okay? You took over when he was distracted, and after everything we went through, he hasn't been able to fight you back, but I'm asking you to let him out now. I need him. I need the Sebastian that doesn't kill people all willy-nilly."

His void eyes deadened. "You had no such qualms when we murdered half of the guards in the prison."

I blew out a breath. My irritation was rising. "That was self-defense."

Sebastian rolled his eyes. "Maybe the first ten or so could be called self-defense, but the rest were for revenge. Don't you recall, my sweet mate? I wanted to leave, and you wanted to sweep through each floor of the prison and torture and brutally murder everyone. Now I certainly didn't request for your shadow to be locked away nor did I stop you. I've only ever done exactly as you've asked!"

"I did not ask for you to hang those guards by your shadows while the entire court watched. I didn't ask you to kill that councilmember. I didn't ask you to terrorize everyone in the palace!"

"Those people are loyal to Xenos. They were given their positions as courtiers because he favored them. They wouldn't have responded to anything less than me asserting dominance." Sebastian put a hand on his hip. "As much as you might have preferred us to walk in and ask them nicely to bow to a darkyra queen and king, they would have revolted right then and there. Fuck, Hugo tried to, but now they know the consequences if they disobey."

"You sound like Kai," I seethed.

Sebastian's face was appalled. "I am nothing like them."

"Forcing submission?" My anger took over, and I started talking with my hands. "Consequences for disobedience? That doesn't inspire loyalty, it inspires terror."

"What do you think the solisers and high priestesses have been doing to us for centuries?"

"So that's why you were so quick to bargain with Kai! Put the crown on my head, marry me, and then you'd get to be king. You get all the power you've been denied your whole life. Power to kill everyone you don't like!"

He narrowed his eyes. His voice low and scathing. "You truly think me so evil and ruthless as to sacrifice your life by bargaining for the crown just so I could gain power?"

I crossed my arms over my chest. A memory rose of the video Sloane had shown me at court during our engagement party. Sebastian—with his shadow controlling his body—had smiled with wicked glee as he took the high priestesses' powers.

My Sebastian had to take their powers to keep the Queen alive, to keep Palagui from losing power, but he didn't *enjoy* it.

His shadow certainly did.

"You love power. It doesn't matter who you hurt to get it," I said.

He shook his head and sighed. Such disappointment and grief was etched in his face that my arms unthreaded and fell to my side.

This was the expression of betrayal I'd expected to see when I tried to kill him. But what grieved him most wasn't that I'd try to plunge a dagger into his heart, it was that I didn't trust his motives.

If his shadow cared about me more than he cared about power, I just needed to make him see how important Sebastian was to me.

"Please. Please, let Sebastian out." I made my voice sweet and pressed my palms together in a pleading gesture. "I promise I'll talk to him. I'll ask him to not push you away. You know I've been influencing him to trust you more. It might take some time, but I'll keep trying. I just need him right now."

He curled his lip in disgust, staring up at the ceiling with one hand on his hip.

"Let him out!" I demanded. My hands clenched into fists, and I fought the urge to shake him until the shadow backed down.

Sebastian's eyes fell to mine. With no emotion, he said, "There is no him to let out. There is only me."

My heart stuttered. My mind slow to comprehend. I was tired and traumatized and hungry, and I couldn't grasp his words. "What...What do you mean?"

Sebastian pressed his tongue into his upper lip before saying, "The Sebastian that you call 'yours' is gone. The consciousness that you so desperately want cannot animate this body any longer."

The ground shifted underneath me. Grief and hopelessness and agony unsteadied me. It was hearing Kai say Sebastian was gone all over again. A wave of lightheadedness washed over me. I reached out and clutched Gwen's arm as my knees almost buckled. "He's dead?"

Sebastian flung out his arms. "I am right here."

I shook my head, squeezing Gwen's arm in a death grip.

He blew out a breath through his nose, shaking his head, his smile dejected. "I am the one who protected you when he couldn't. I am the one that has been at your side for weeks. I am the one you married. I am your mate."

"You...you aren't. He's..." I wrapped an arm around my stomach as my body caved in on itself. He's gone. Sebastian is dead. My mate is dead, even as his body stands before me.

I wrung my hands. "Did you...did you kill him?"

His face hardened. "The attack within the astral field damaged our psyche. He couldn't recover, but I did. I'm here. The only thing gone is the weakest part of me."

"He wasn't...he wasn't weak." Oh Goddess. If the astral field attack killed him...Then *I* killed Sebastian.

It was my plan that put us in that room as Caroline's wards came down. It was me pulling on his power to sift us as the fire ball hit him. I put my head in my hands, tears flooding my eyes. "I did this. I killed my mate."

"You did not kill your mate. I am not dead!"

A loud zapping noise filled the air, and Sebastian collapsed to the ground as Nico stood over him with a black handheld electric shocking device.

"Nico!" Sloane said.

I rushed to Sebastian and fell to my knees, grabbing his hand.

Mate. Save mate. Protect mate, my shadow chanted.

"What did you do?" I asked, anger replacing my sadness as I glared at Nico. "You hurt him. You hurt my mate."

I lunged at Nico's legs, wrapping my arms around them. He toppled over. I crawled across the floor and pulled my fist back to pummel him, but someone caught my arm. "How dare you fucking touch him!" I screamed and flailed, trying to fight off the arms holding me back. "Don't ever fucking touch him."

"Amaya! Stop!"

I didn't hear them. I didn't care. No one was going to hurt my mate.

I kicked and flung my body around and broke from Gwen and Sloane's grasp as my shadows burst from me and encircled Nico.

Mine. Mine. Protect what's mine.

"I will kill you!" I threw myself into the shadows, wanting to kill the person who hurt my mate with my bare hands.

"Amaya. Sebastian needs you," someone said.

I froze. My shadows halted in the air as my attention went back to Sebastian. I crawled toward him. His body twitched, and he groaned. I let my shadows cover him, and his breathing steadied when I held his hand.

"Are we going to have to deal with both of them trying to kill us anytime the other is hurt?" Gwen asked. "She was worse than he was."

I didn't register what they were saying, didn't care. I was wholly focused on Sebastian, and when Nico came closer, I growled at him. "Stay away."

Nico put his hands up in surrender. "Shadow Bash does this sometimes," he said. "He takes over and tries to pretend he is Sebastian, until eventually I figure out his game. He always claims that he's the only one, but then I shock him unconscious, and it gives our Sebastian enough time to fight his way back."

I put his head on my lap and stroked back his hair from his eyes. I didn't want anyone to hurt him. I wanted Sebastian back, but after everything we went through, after how brutalized we both were in the prison, this seemed too cruel. I took a ragged breath, and my anger shifted once more.

This time my tears had no end.

There was murmuring behind me, and Nico bent down. "I'm not going to hurt him, but I want to move him to the couch. Will you let me do that?"

I bit my lip but nodded and let Nico scoop him up and lay him on the couch. His gentleness made my guilt rise.

"I'm sorry, Nico," I said. "I know you were trying to help. Did I hurt you?"

"You didn't hurt me. Everything's okay, Amaya," he said. "I should have told you what I was doing, but I had to catch him off guard for it to work."

My shadow throbbed in an angry discordant rhythm, but Nico wouldn't hurt him if he'd had any other choice.

Sloane pulled over a chair, but I was already climbing on the couch and sitting behind Sebastian, putting his body in between my legs like he'd done with me in the Queen's bedroom. I ran my hands through his hair while his head rested on my chest.

I didn't know how long it would take. Maybe all night. Maybe days, but nothing mattered. I wasn't leaving this spot until he opened his eyes.

I must have dozed off because I woke to the sensation of being moved. "No. No. I need him. Don't take me from him," I said, groggy.

"It's alright. I'm here," Sebastian said. "I'm not going anywhere."

He had positioned me so we were lying on our sides, face-to-face. The living room was dark. The others must have gone to bed.

"Sebastian?" I reached out to stroke his face, but his eyes were closed.

He sighed and opened his eyes. Only shadows stared back. "I'm still not who you want me to be.'

My jaw quivered, and the little bit of hope I had washed away as I cried into my hands. "He's dead. He's dead." I kept repeating in between sobbing.

"Amaya," he said, rubbing my arm. "He's not dead. We aren't dead."

"You said he was gone."

"I don't feel him, but if I were to give up control of this body and only dwelled in the portion of his brain I'd been relegated to for the past century, this body wouldn't die. It would just sleep...a lifeless sleep."

I sniffed and lowered my hands. "So it's like he's in a coma?"

He gave me a half-shrug, crestfallen.

"People wake up from comas," I said, my voice lightening. Maybe the pain and trauma of the prison, of the UV room, had been too much. His psyche needed more time to heal from the damage done in the astral field. "I could heal him? Heal him until he wakes up."

Sebastian shook his head. "High priestesses can't heal the mind."

More sobs rose in my throat, but he just needed time. Time to heal. Time to wake up.

"Perhaps..." he started, but stopped.

"What?" I asked, my hands clutching into his shirt. "Perhaps what?"

He shrugged and stared into my eyes. "Perhaps you'll need to shock him awake. Like you woke me in the prison by returning the piece of my shadow. The stun weapon didn't work, but maybe..."

"Maybe what?" I asked. "Tell me."

"Maybe if you accepted the bond with me, it would wake him," he said. His eyes were wide with hope.

Accepting the bond will strengthen us both, my shadow added.

I bristled. Both shadows were on board with accepting the bond, not because it would bring him back, but because they wanted more power.

"How dare you!" I said, pushing away from him and scrambling up from the couch. "You try to make me feel guilty for assuming you made the bargain for power, and the first thing you do is try to convince me to accept the bond? You're nothing like him. He wouldn't try to manipulate me."

Sebastian swung his legs off the couch and stood, glaring. "Wouldn't he? Wasn't your entire relationship one long manipulation? Your friend was kidnapped, and he manipulated you into a fake relationship. Your fake relationship put you at risk, so he had you bind your powers so he could be around you without either of our shadows growing stronger. He lied to you, repeatedly. I have not." He tapped a hand on his chest. "You and I can have the relationship you crave. Partners. Mates. Without any of the history of his deceptions."

"You kept this secret from me," I said.

His face softened into something like pleading. "It's not like we've had even a single moment to catch our breaths. Would you have liked me to tell you before or after we made a bargain with a shadow deity to take the crown? Or maybe while we were trying to break out of prison? When would have been the right time to tell you? You'd have been angry with me or sad or both, all of which would have put us at a disadvantage when we were trying to get out of there alive."

I gritted my teeth. "How about you could have told me in the prison office? We'd caught our breath enough to fuck on the floor," I said, crossing my arms.

He tilted his chin down to give me an exasperated look. "Neither he nor I would have had the mental fortitude to choose to forgo an intimate encounter with you over a conversation that would surely leave you upset."

I huffed. "Well, it would have been the right thing to do!"

He flung a hand out. "Now that he's gone, you're rewriting the past! His moral compass was no more straight than mine is, or need I remind you that he chose to fuck you at the beach house even after you asked him to tell you the truth. He could have told you that you were mates or about the draxis, but he didn't, so it's a bit hypocritical to get upset about my decisions when they were the same as his!"

I scowled because he kind of had a point. My Sebastian had put off a lot of important conversations with me in the past. He might also have a point that telling me half of my mate was dead while trying to escape a prison might not have been the best timing.

But my irritation had me refusing to back down. "You just should have told me!" I stomped my foot like a child throwing a tantrum. I was so exhausted. I'd lost the ability to control my emotions or think logically.

Sebastian took a deep breath and let it out slow. "If we accept the bond, you'll feel me, you'll know me. You cannot lie to your bonded." His voice was so sweet, trying to tempt me. He reached out a hand and cupped my jaw. "This will be a partnership, Amaya."

I slapped his hand down. "I should accept the bond with you so you're forced to never lie to me? Really? How about I should be able to trust my *husband* to not lie to me without a magical bond?"

He tried to take a step closer to me, his hand in the air to touch me again, but I retreated back.

"I will not be accepting the bond with this side of you," I said, my words sharp enough to cut.

His hand dropped, and anger flared in his eyes. "You've lied to me as well, *wife*. You told me you would love all of me in that prison, so I suppose neither of us can trust a word the other says."

I gritted my teeth, trying to fight the impulse to apologize and take everything back and soothe the hurt my words had created.

Just because the shadow loved me enough to keep me alive, didn't mean I could trust him to make the right decisions. I couldn't rule a country when the person I relied on would kill anyone that posed a problem. That wasn't the leader I wanted to be.

Our arguing must have woken everyone because a hand wrapped around my arm from behind. Gwen and Sloane stood beside me. With their comfort close, my defenses melted.

"It didn't work?" Nico asked. His voice was as lost and sad as I felt. "It always worked before."

"Would you like to shock me again?" Sebastian asked, arms out wide in invitation. "Perhaps stun me this time until my heart stops? Or I could walk into the astral field and you can throw a fireball at me. Maybe this time it'll kill me, and you'll be rid of the evil shadow for good."

No. Goddess no.

Despair collapsed my chest, and I rounded into Sloane's shoulder, clutching her, and started bawling so hard it was difficult to breathe. I choked on my tears, unable to take a breath to expel the desolation settling into me.

This wasn't how it was supposed to go.

I was going to save him. Save us. We were going to have a life together.

And he was dead. I'd killed him.

"Amaya," Sebastian's voice softened, but Sloane said, "I think that's enough for tonight."

She wrapped her hand around my back, and she and Gwen guided me down the hall.

"Let's just get you a shower and get you comfy. You two just need to cool off, okay?" Gwen said.

I was walked into a bathroom. Gwen set out towels.

"We're going to get you clothes and something to eat," Sloane said, and they both started for the door.

The bathroom was dark and small. Adrenaline started racing at the thought of being in this room by myself.

I reached out for Gwen's arm. "Don't leave me. I can't...I can't be alone. They kept me all alone for weeks. Please."

Gwen's eyes widened, but she nodded. "Sloane will make you food, and I'll sit right here." She gestured to the vanity and hopped onto it.

I sighed, and the fear dissipated as I took off the crown and set it on the counter. I undressed in the shower, not wanting Gwen to see the state of my back. The heat of the water should have been a relief, but I was numb.

"Talk to me," I said over the sound of the stream.

"Well, Sloane and Nico have been keeping in contact with Rien," Gwen said. "He says Delnee is watching Palagui's power transfer closely. When Harrison heard about the hurricane, Rien mentioned sending emergency relief assistance, but Harrison said it wasn't their responsibility."

I scrubbed my hair. This felt better. A country in crisis was a problem to distract from the opening cavern in my heart.

"How much does Rien know?"

"He knows you both were in prison, and we told him our prison break plan and about Daria kidnapping me. The only thing he doesn't know is about...well, the mate situation," Gwen said.

"Daria kidnapped you?" I asked. "I remember her sifting you away, but I didn't think she'd betray us. I thought she was protecting you."

Gwen spent the rest of my shower catching me up on what happened with her and Daria. She kept her retelling of the story to the basics, and in typical Gwen fashion, refused to divulge her emotions on the matter.

She handed me sleep clothes when I got out of the shower, and we went to a bedroom in the back of the cabin.

Gwen sat behind me on the bed and started combing my hair when Sloane came back with a smorgasbord of food.

"I got a bit of everything," Sloane said. "Wasn't sure what you'd be hungry for."

"I've eaten almost nothing but hard bread for weeks. This is all going to be the best thing I've ever tasted." I tried to make it sound light, like a joke, but sadness filled her eyes.

"I'm okay," I said and squeezed her hand. I didn't want to go into it, not when I felt so close to breaking down, so I said, "Do you think Daria will come to the council meeting?"

If she did, what should we do with her? Can we trust her knowing she betrayed us to Caroline but regrets it?

Gwen was hesitant to believe her, but I didn't think the Daria I'd gotten to know was bad. She was just confused about whom to trust, and given what we did to Sebastian, who were we to judge?

Gwen huffed. "Daria is a coward. She isn't going to show."

"And your aunt?"

"I hope she comes so I can personally choke her," Gwen said.

She'd already told me what Caroline had done while I was in the prison. She'd accomplished very little given she couldn't find Gwen or someone else she could control to be queen. The entire council was a disorganized mess and didn't respond appropriately to prepare Palagui for the hurricane.

Sloane and Gwen took turns telling me about the prison break. Nico had hacked into the prison's administrator system, and a lot of what I attributed to Kai's kindness had been Sloane's doing.

I didn't tell them anything about what happened while I was there. They didn't need to feel guilty, and I didn't want to relive it. I wanted to leave those five weeks in the past.

Nico, Sloane, and Gwen had felt fae power dying and drove across Palagui and then took a boat off the coast to get to the prison.

"So Nico's boat is probably swept out to sea by now," I said.

"That is literally the least of our problems," Sloane said.

"I know…I just feel bad."

"Don't," Gwen said. "It was a shitty boat anyway."

And something about hearing Gwen's snobbishness was so normal and familiar that I started laughing which prompted them to laugh along with me.

We giggled for so long, gasping for breath, tears coming in an unhinged hysterical release, at some point I forgot what we were laughing about.

I grabbed my best friends' hands. "I'm so fucking sorry for getting you both into this. If you didn't offer to train my high priestess powers in Delnee, none of this would have happened."

"None of this is your fault," Gwen said, shoving me with her shoulder.

"We should have listened to you when you kept standing up for Sebastian," Sloane said. "None of this would have happened if we would have listened."

"And it's my fault we trusted my aunt," Gwen said. "I was so blind, looking everywhere for danger except the one place it was staring me in the face."

I sighed. "Alright, so the consensus is all three of us suck?"

Gwen snorted. "Yep, but maybe if they taught spy skills in high priestess training, we'd have been better off."

I laughed, and they told me the happier pieces of their stories from the last few weeks.

"It's been unbearable being the third wheel to a mated couple," Gwen said. "Now I'm going to be the fifth wheel." She threw a piece of popcorn at Sloane. "We're one big dysfunctional family, just like you always wanted."

Sloane threw the same kernel, and it *plinked* Gwen's head. "I wanted a big family. Not the dysfunctional part."

I bit my lip. "What does accepting the mating bond feel like?"

"Basically," Gwen said. "They walk around all day with lovesick expressions and completely ignore me when I talk in favor of just staring at one another."

"Okay, that happened one time," Sloane said, wrinkling her nose but smiling. "It feels odd, honestly. It's like I don't know where he ends and where I begin. It does take some getting used to. I think it'll be better now that the broken bargain isn't feeding off his power."

"Do you think I'm a terrible person for not accepting the bond?" I asked quietly. "He said that it was kind of like Sebastian is in a coma, which means I think I need to wait for him to wake up. He always said his shadow was a separate entity, so would he think it's cheating or betraying him if I acted like everything was normal?"

"I don't know. Didn't Daria say that shadows weren't separate?" Sloane asked.

"But just because that is some people's experience of their shadow, doesn't mean that it's Sebastian's," Gwen countered. "He's obviously different than most darkyras."

"True," Sloane said. "And there's a reason the mating bond needs to be consented to by both parties. You get a choice."

I chewed on my lip but didn't say anything. I wanted to do the right thing by Sebastian. I just didn't know what that was.

His shadow always protected and comforted me, but I was still incensed by his attempts to manipulate me into accepting the bond.

"I mean this part of Sebastian killed those guards ruthlessly," Sloane said. "I get that he claims he was trying to show dominance, but I couldn't picture our Sebastian doing that. He was more a silent behind-the-scenes plotter, not a straight-up homicidal lunatic."

"I don't know..." Gwen said. She pulled at the threads on the blanket. "I know this sounds crazy, but I kind of get it. We tried to kill him, and the shadow part of him knew all along. Then he's tortured in the prison because his mate betrayed him? I guess I can kind of understand becoming a little homicidal."

Sloane and I gaped at her.

Gwen rolled her eyes. "I'm capable of seeing my mistakes and changing my mind. Why are you both staring at me like that?" She made a disgruntled expression. "All I'm saying is we were wrong about Sebastian. Maybe we shouldn't jump to conclusions about his shadow?"

I sighed. Exhaustion weighed down my eyes, and with a full stomach, I was having trouble staying awake, let alone debating shadow consciousness.

Gwen, Sloane, and I crawled into bed together under the cool, crisp sheets. The softness of the bed and pillows was almost too much after having slept on a thin mattress for weeks.

I should have fallen to sleep right away. I was safe and cuddled beside my two best friends, their limbs intertwined with mine.

Rather than being comforted by their nearness, I tossed and turned. A vague sense of unease haunted me. It felt dangerous to close my eyes like I needed to be hyper vigilant in case Kai's shadows were going to come for me or the doctor or the guards.

The only thing that soothed me enough to finally fall asleep was imagining the guard's fear when I took their lives, the crunch of their bones and the snap of their necks. The feel of my power as it coursed through me like a promise. It said: I could protect myself. It said: no one would ever hurt me again.

It said: kill or be killed.

I turned to my side and looked at the crown I'd moved to the nightstand after my shower. It gleamed, catching the reflection of the moonlight from the window.

As I dozed off—visions of murder comforting my fears—I wondered if my vivid revenge imaginings made me a powerful queen who would stop at nothing to protect her people…or a queen who had already let her power corrupt her.

Maybe I had only been projecting my own brutal anger on Sebastian's shadow because—like I'd thought before—it was me the world should be afraid of, not him.

Chapter Eighteen

Amaya

A sinking horror plummeted me from one reality into another. Vines of darkness wrapped around my torso, whispering that I was more dark than light. My sensory perception distorted until my brain could only interpret its own fucked-up projection as reality. Every nerve screamed an emergency signal.

Kill them all before they kill you.

A violent pain erupted in my chest, something searching, straining, reaching out. Hunger for violence gathered in my gut.

I awoke with a start. My hands in fists and body primed for an offensive attack. Panic seized me, convincing me for a terrible moment that I was back in prison.

The sound of dishes clinking and cabinets thudding rearranged my perspective.

I sat in a soft bed, wrapped in a blanket. The pale morning sun brightened the dark wood-paneled walls.

I squeezed my hands into fists, clenching and releasing my muscles to signal to my body I was safe, but the fringes of the nightmare lingered. Taking a deep breath, I focused on the low murmur of talking and the whine of pipes from the shower until the creeping dread finally receded.

The sweet smell of baked goods drifted from the kitchen, making my stomach rumble, so I slipped out of bed and padded down the hall.

Nico was at the dining room table, typing on a laptop, and Sloane had her head perched on his shoulder. She giggled at something he said, and he turned to kiss her temple.

They were so freaking cute.

"Isn't it disgusting? Do you see what you left me to deal with?" Gwen said, but her tone was light. She stepped from the kitchen and handed me a mug of coffee.

I inhaled the scent, letting the nutty earthy aroma fill my nostrils. "This smells amazing."

"Sloane made a big breakfast," she said. "I'll make you a plate."

"Thank you." Walking to the dining room table, I sat across from Nico. "What are you working on?"

Sloane wrinkled her nose. "We messaged Rien about everything that happened yesterday. You being queen and married to Sebastian..."

Great. That'll be a fun message for him to read.

Nico shut the laptop and pushed it aside. "I've been reading news reports of the hurricane. It made landfall last night and hit south of Palagui City and the western portion of Merbany but lost strength quickly and was only considered a heavy storm by the time it hit downtown."

I nodded. "Does Palagui have a disaster team?"

"We do," a deep voice responded from behind me. I turned, and my jaw dropped as Sebastian strode out in nothing but his underwear.

He'd always been lean, but he'd lost weight in the prison. The dark vines of his tattoos along his neck, chest, arms, and legs stood out on the unhealthy pale of his skin. Guilt wormed its way into my heart. I'd had him naked on the prison floor and didn't notice how much of a toll being there had taken.

And yet, he was still so devastatingly beautiful, it hurt to look at him. His face was perfection, strong jaw and cheekbones like the sharp angles and dark lines of a painting. The way the longer portion of his black hair swooped in his eyes made my fingers twitch to push it back.

My eyes traced the veins along his forearms, up the swell of his biceps, and down his chest to where the V of his stomach disappeared into his tight black underwear. When I realized I was practically salivating, I sputtered an indignant, "Where are your clothes?"

Sloane and Gwen stared at him with wide eyes. Something hot crept up my neck, and my shadow buzzed with agitation.

They shouldn't be staring at him. He's ours, my shadow said. *Stake your claim on him so they know they cannot have him.*

I pressed my fingers into my eyes. *They are staring in horror not lust. Cool it*, I told her.

She scoffed, and her energy heightened, trying to burst free, trying to touch him.

With a steadying breath, I tried to take my own advice and not throw myself on top of him.

He pulled out a seat and sat beside me, ignoring my question. My body leaned closer to him, pulled in by his magnetism. His eyes searched me. Shadows rose and fell under my skin in accordance with the path his eyes took along my body until they settled at my bare thighs. My sleep shirt only long enough to cover the most important bits.

Remove our clothes so he forgets all others, my shadow said.

Her lewd suggestion distracted me enough that when he put his hand on my leg and tingles cascaded through my body, I jolted. A poof of my shadows broke free before misting away.

I pushed his hand from my thigh but could feel every inch of space between us, alive with a static energy.

Was this another manipulation tactic? He thought he could distract me with lust and work up my shadow, and then I'd fling myself on top of him and accept the bond.

I hated how out-of-control he made me feel.

I clenched my fists and scooted my chair over.

Sebastian's face pinched in annoyance, but he didn't try to touch me again. "My clothes are in the wash," he said. "I can't exactly borrow Nico's. He's at least three of me."

"You could have sifted to the townhouse and back," I said.

"I cannot leave you," he said and plucked a few pieces of fruit off my plate. His eyes fluttered closed as he savored a strawberry like he'd never tasted it before in his life.

Maybe this side of him hadn't.

"It'd have taken two minutes," I said, being petty and moving my plate out of his reach because I didn't like how his sigh of pleasure was making me wish he was savoring me instead.

Sebastian shrugged. "I can't be that far away from you." He scooted his chair until it was flush with mine and wound his arm around me to get another piece of fruit.

I made an exasperated noise in the back of my throat. *My* Sebastian wasn't so pushy, and he certainly didn't walk around almost naked. He was prim and proper and controlled...except when his shadow was involved.

I recalled a memory of us on his balcony. Our bodies inches apart, both of us teasing and taunting one another. He'd told me he liked to push me just to watch me fight back, but was that him or his shadow?

I needed to parse how much of the male I knew was influenced by his shadow and how much of his shadow was still him. Once I understood the distinction between the two of them—if there was one—then I could figure out the appropriate way to act around him.

At least until my Sebastian woke up. With any luck, it'd be a few days of rest and food, and he'd be back to normal.

"To finish answering your question," he said. "The council should have declared a national emergency which would have allowed PEM to allocate resources for evacuation and coordinate the disaster response."

Nico eyed Sebastian suspiciously, his arms crossed over his chest. "The council hasn't done shit. Caroline refused to declare an emergency until the new queen was crowned. It was her way of forcing the council to go along with what she wanted."

Sebastian's arm brushed against mine, and wisps of my shadows escaped, following his hand as he stole a piece of toast from my plate. My shadows sprung back, leaving me with a faint residual of his essence.

We need to take care of him. Hand feed him to make sure he regains his strength, my shadow said.

I gritted my teeth and pushed my plate toward him. That was the best my shadow was going to get because I was absolutely *not* hand feeding him.

"What's PEM?" I asked, trying to focus on the topic and not my shadow's hum of disapproval.

"Palagui Emergency Management," Sebastian said.

"How can you remember that?" I asked. "You were struggling to remember things yesterday."

"I have mild episodic amnesia," he said. "I can remember facts and recall knowledge. I can remember names and faces if I search my memory for them. The personal experiences and sensations he's had while I was locked away are harder to find, but it's getting easier to locate them the longer I'm in control. I stayed up all night sorting through his memories to come up with a plan."

"You have a plan?" I asked. Tension I hadn't known I was holding released.

Of course he does. He'll always take care of us, my shadow said.

He nodded. "I'll take care of the council meeting today." His words oddly similar to my shadow's. Could he hear her goading me to take my clothes off and feed him from my hand?

A blush rose to my cheeks.

"I know you think I'm an evil shadow only concerned with power." His void eyes met my gaze, and he took the most obscene bite of pineapple I'd ever seen. My lips parted, and I had to fight every single fiber of my being to not lean over and lick off the juice that glistened on his lips.

"But rest assured," he continued. "There needs to be a country left to rule if I wish to have power over it."

My eyes snapped back to his, and he winked. His boyish grin made my stomach flip.

"This is such bullshit. Whatever his plan is, it will only destroy Palagui," Nico said.

Sebastian shook his head. "Trust me, I do not intend—"

"Trust you?" Nico said. "I've had to deal with you fucking up his life every single time you were in control." He slammed a fist on the table and flung out his hand. "You'd take his body, fuck everyone in the vicinity, drink until you were obliterated, and ingest every drug you were offered. And when I'd finally track you down at whatever strip club, bar, or hospital you ended up at, his body and his reputation were trashed. What makes you think I'd trust you?"

"That was before," Sebastian said.

"Before?"

"Before he disappeared. I have no incentive to rebel anymore. How can you blame me for taking advantage of the little freedom I was able to wrestle away from him?"

"How? How!" Nico shot up from his chair. The legs screeched against the floor. "Pretty fucking easily. Because I'm the one who had to watch as he tore himself apart with guilt over what you did." His voice cracked. "You're a fucking monster, so yeah, I do blame you."

"I'm the monster?"—Sebastian gestured at himself and then to Nico—"You are the one that electrocutes me every time you see me!"

"Because there's no other way to get him back!" Nico's chest rose and fell in an unsteady rhythm. The spice of his anger became overpowered with a bitter grief.

He turned to walk away, but doubled back, leaning over the table to point in Sebastian's face. "I tried to vouch for you," he said in a low voice. "I told him you wouldn't hurt Amaya. I told him to loosen up on you, but I never would have told him to give up control. You don't care about anything but your own power and freedom."

"That's not true—"

Nico snorted. "Yeah, because you care about Amaya, too? You care about her because your mating instincts tell you that you can increase your power through the bond. That's not enough. It doesn't make me trust you."

Nico straightened and stormed off. A door slammed, and Sloane trailed after him. Gwen gave me wide eyes and picked up her mug of coffee and made herself scarce.

I sensed the shift in Sebastian, felt the shadows under his skin reacting to Nico's anger. His mood grew darker until the connection between us was shunted.

My emotions warred within me, but sympathy won over them all.

"He's just grieving," I whispered. "We're all trying to figure out—"

"And what of my grief?" Sebastian said. "You truly care more for his pain than you do mine?"

"That's not true," I said cautiously. "I know you're hurting too. Your mother died last night, and there's been so many changes—"

Sebastian scoffed. "My mother? You mean the Queen. The female who abandoned me and kept me locked in a basement until Adriana found me?" He shook his head. "Yes, I'm real heartbroken over losing her."

My eyes widened. "She...She locked you up?"

He stared at the table. "She didn't know what else to do with me after the quake in Merbany. I was a child trapped in little more than a dungeon. After we lost Adriana, *he* locked me away once again."

I'd been imprisoned for a few weeks, but I couldn't imagine being a child, a child who lost their parents, who was scared and lonely and blaming themselves for an entire town's destruction.

"I'm so sorry. I didn't...I didn't know." I didn't need my shadow's encouragement this time to reach out and rest my hand on his arm. "He never shared that with me," I said. "He seemed to love his mother. He'd been protecting her all these years. I didn't know the Queen treated him so terribly."

Although I had started to wonder based on our last interaction with her.

Sebastian picked up my fork and pushed food around but didn't eat anything. "That's because the part of me that loved her was weak and pathetic and would have done anything to get affection from her."

It wasn't weak or pathetic to want his mother's love, but I didn't think me saying so would change his mind.

The shadow's hatred was the other side of the coin. One part of him did anything he could for her acceptance, and the other part of him distanced himself so as not to feel her rejection.

I took a deep breath and whispered, "You're both so similar and yet so different."

His eyes swung to mine but held no emotion. "That's because I've experienced the horrible things he didn't have the courage to."

I swallowed. Sebastian had told me he gave control to his shadow to take the high priestesses powers because he couldn't stomach doing it himself.

Sebastian gathered both of my hands. His eyes wide, pleading. "This is what I meant. I'm stronger than him. It was foolish of me to think that I could simply step into his place. If you can't accept that I'm *your* Sebastian, fine, but I will be a better mate to you than he ever could. I'll do whatever you want to get you to accept the bond with me."

I stiffened and pulled my hands back.

I wasn't going to accept the bond if that meant betraying one part of Sebastian for his shadow. Everything he'd just told me only underscored that they were separate entities, and I couldn't discount Sebastian's experience of his own body and his own power.

I needed to tread carefully.

"How do I know that everything you do isn't just a ploy to get more power from the bond?" I asked.

He huffed. "So what if it was? We'd both be more powerful. We'd both be able to protect ourselves from anyone and anything that ever tried to harm us. Why does wanting that power make me bad?"

"Because you used your power last night to kill people," I said.

"So did you!"

"That was different!"

"Is it?"

"Did you look for their tattoo?" I asked. "Did you know for sure they were bad?"

He pressed his lips together but didn't answer.

"Exactly," I said. "You could have roughed them up. Hell, your shadows could've just held them, and everyone would have been scared. You didn't need to kill them. I may have killed people, may have even enjoyed it, but I drew a line at innocent people. You don't have a line, and that's why we can't trust you."

"I have a line," he whispered. "I would have let the guard you killed go. The one that begged for his life because he had a family? You slaughtered him, but I wouldn't have. Just because we have different lines, doesn't mean yours is any better than mine."

He pushed out of his chair and walked into the living room, leaving me stunned.

I had slaughtered that guard. I hadn't given a second thought to his family because it didn't matter to me, but it had to Sebastian.

I worried my lip. To me, those tattoos meant they were bad people, but did I know that for sure? What if it was just a group of people and some bad apples made me believe they were all bad? Kai had poisoned my mind, and I'd blindly believed.

Which was more evidence I was not any better than—in fact, maybe even worse than—Sebastian's shadow.

He returned from the living area and tossed three notebooks on the table.

"What are these?" I asked.

"Notes. Plans. Outlines. Draft policies," he said. "I'd have more information if I had my laptop, but this is what I could remember. You don't trust me to accept the bond? Fine, but I've devoted my life to Palagui. At first because the Queen demanded it, then because I wanted the country to thrive for Adriana's return, and now because…well, trying to protect this country is all I've ever known, shadow or not."

He turned and disappeared down the hall as I stared at the notebooks. He reemerged dressed in his freshly washed clothes and opened the front door. A cold gust of wind swept in and died as he exited the cabin.

I sighed. My shadow whined as whatever aura of magic Sebastian emitted dispersed. I ignored her suggestion to follow him and flipped open one of the notebooks.

Page after page of his elegant handwriting. It started with basic facts about the country, organizational charts, lists of the councilmembers and other governmental officials.

The information moved to the emergency management protocols and scenario planning dependent on the extent of the damage from the hurricane. He drafted policies and wrote lists of funds Palagui had on reserve.

He theorized which councilmembers would give us the most trouble and the best ways to handle their disagreements. While *killing them all and electing new ones* did feature on the list, it was only one of twenty different solutions, almost like he had to think about the worst possible situation and work his way backward.

Diligent. Precise. Thorough.

A trait the shadow had in common with my Sebastian.

These plans were far too detailed for it all to be an act or a ploy.

Guilt festered in my belly. I gathered up the notebooks and tiptoed down the hall. Knocking on the door to the bedroom Nico slept in last night, I waited until Sloane appeared. I handed her the notebooks. "Unless Nico is going to coach me on how to rule a country, we need to hear Sebastian out."

Sloane bit her lip and nodded, taking the notebooks and closing the door.

I grabbed a jacket from Gwen, who was eating breakfast in our bedroom. "Family meeting in ten," I said, not waiting for her response.

Pulling the jacket on, I made my way outside, preparing myself for a trek to find Sebastian, but I should have known he wouldn't go far.

He sat on the top step of the porch, posture immaculate, staring down the driveway as his shadows curled around his shoulders.

I put my hands in my pockets and asked, "If I didn't find out about his...being in a coma," I said. "Would you have let me accept the bond with you, without telling me the truth?"

He inhaled slowly. His breath became visible in the cold air as he exhaled. "You aren't going to like my answer."

That was a yes.

But I was strangely comforted. He was being honest with me despite it not getting him what he wanted.

I crossed the porch, wood creaking under my feet, and sat on the top stair beside him. My shadow hummed happily as the shadows around his shoulders drifted over and clung to me. "Truce?"

He didn't answer, only continued to stare out at the barren forest surrounding the cabin.

"Palagui needs a queen and king united," I said.

He turned and met my gaze. "And what do you need?"

I needed to eat and sleep for two weeks straight. I needed peace and quiet and to be shed of my new responsibilities. But most importantly, I needed Sebastian back, whole and unfragmented.

But he couldn't give me any of that.

I shrugged one shoulder, my eyes on the horizon as the sun rose. "Time," I said.

Time for Palagui to heal. Time for my body and mind to recover from the prison. Time for Sebastian to come back to me.

We sat there for a few minutes, our sides pressed together, shoulder to thigh.

I released the hold I had on my power, and our shadows danced together in the cold morning air. For the first time since he'd held me in the prison office, a contentment washed over me. My body's pains, my mind's torments, my heart's aches—all vanished.

Footsteps from the other side of the door reminded me I'd called a family meeting. Palagui needed us to focus on rebuilding from the hurricane and undoing the terror that Xenos enacted. We didn't have time for our interpersonal drama.

"Come on," I said, and we walked inside.

Gwen, Sloane, and Nico sat around the dining room table, and though Nico's arms were crossed, his spicy anger had faded.

I inclined my head to Sebastian. "Tell us what we need to know."

He flipped to a page in a notebook, sliding it across for us to read.

"There are seven councilmembers," Sebastian said. "One for each fae faction, so Caroline, Gerald and Daria. And four for the major regions of Palagui: Micah, Leva, Erik, and Vince."

Sebastian flipped to another page with a seating chart of the council meetings. "While a clean slate would be easiest and within our rights as a new regime, these people were elected into their positions, and the citizens wouldn't take it well if we removed them."

"They were strong-armed into accepting Caroline's plan," Nico said. "She convinced them crowning a new queen would be in the best interest of their constituents and threatened my father and Micah when they protested both of your imprisonments."

Sebastian nodded. "I figured as much."

He pointed to a sketched map of Palagui and circled Palagui City. "Erik Barbeau represents region one of Palagui City and after last night Leva Lussier represents region two. Hugo never brought Leva to a council meeting so I can't speak to her personality. I know you didn't approve of my methods, but Hugo would have been our biggest worry on the council. He was a soliser elitist and wasn't afraid to show it."

"So he got along with Caroline?" I asked.

Gwen scrunched up her face and made a so-so gesture with her hand. "They tolerated one another. They hated darkyra enough to align on most things but fought against each other for their own faction's benefit."

"Erik is...he's a wildcard," Sebastian continued. "He's been in politics for a long time and is well versed in spinning stories to his favor, but he doesn't have a solid track record of siding with one group over another. Daria always considered him her swing vote."

Sebastian pointed his pen to Merbany. "Then there is Vince Kane, who you probably remember from the meetings."

"The soliser that was always a dick to Daria?" I asked.

Sebastian nodded. "I don't know their history. They both needled one another."

Gwen rolled her eyes. "Daria always said to never take anything Vince says seriously. That he's a schoolyard bully who's only mean because he's insecure."

"Vince was close to Xenos," Sebastian said. "But I think he's more worried about his own personal position of power than inclined to lead a revolution against the crown. He campaigns on being self-made, coming from a humble background and working his way through the ranks."

I rolled my eyes. "Meaning he probably had a rich father that got him to where he is."

Sebastian shrugged. "Probably. He represents Merbany, which is the wealthiest area of Palagui."

He moved his pen north and circled everything above the mountain ridges north of Palagui city. "Then there's Micah Bensen, a high priest, who represents Molbridge and the outlying areas. He's fair and decent. He's made what used to be a little rural village into a thriving suburban town."

"And the humans don't have a councilmember?" Sloane asked.

"No, they don't," Sebastian said. "Darkyras only received a representative a decade ago. At first, Daria didn't want the position, didn't want to be involved in politics, but something changed her mind last election. She won by a landslide."

The admiration in his voice was unexpected. "Aren't you angry with Daria? For..." I couldn't finish the sentence.

"For being a dirty traitor?" Gwen said.

I winced. All three of us were technically dirty traitors. We'd all been conned into Caroline's plot to kill Sebastian.

He sighed. "I'm angry with her because her actions got my mate sent to prison, but if you're asking if I'm upset about what she did to me?" He shook his head. "I don't blame any of you. I only blame myself."

My stomach clenched so hard it felt as though the wind was knocked out of me. That response was very Sebastian. Not at all the vengeful, swaggering shadow of last night.

Maybe they weren't so different after all.

Chapter Nineteen

Amaya

"We're sorry, Sebastian," Gwen said, clasping her hands in front of her on the table. "For, you know, trying to kill you."

Sloane stared down at her palms, even Nico's posture loosened, his arms no longer crossed at his chest.

Gwen took a deep breath and continued, "I know nothing excuses it, but I did think I was protecting people. I should have listened to Amaya when she defended you. I shouldn't have trusted my aunt. I can't tell you how sorry I am."

Sebastian blinked several times. Gwen had said she changed her mind about him, but I hadn't expected her to apologize so sincerely.

"I'm sorry too," Sloane whispered, tears in her eyes. "We were so stupid. Amaya tried to tell us, tried to stick up for you, but we thought she couldn't see the truth. It was us who were blind."

"I...I, uh, there's really nothing to forgive," Sebastian said. "I don't blame you, but thank you."

There was an awkward silence as no one said anything or even looked at one another. Nico seemed conflicted, flickering between guilt and anger and grief.

Sebastian cleared his throat. "And I should also apologize for, uh, threatening to kill you all yesterday. I momentarily thought Amaya was dead. So, uh, sorry."

Gwen snorted, breaking the tension, and leaned back in her chair. "You know, you're right," she said. "That wasn't cool. I guess that means we're even now, right?"

Sebastian smiled, and the brief flash of his sweet happiness made my chest lighten.

"Yeah, Gwen," he said. "We're even."

The next few hours were spent strategizing for the council meeting. Gwen agreed to fill in her aunt's place as the high priestess representative until we could hold a vote.

By lunch time, we had a tentative plan, but I needed to sift to the townhouse to get clothes appropriate for a queen before the meeting.

"I'm coming with you," Sebastian had said after I yelled down the hall to ask if anyone needed anything while I was there.

I put a hand on my hip. "Thought you didn't need to sift to the townhouse cause you were *washing your clothes.*"

"The point was I wasn't leaving your side. It had nothing to do with my clothes."

"Alright. Fine."

I sifted, and the sparks of Sebastian's magic trailed behind me.

After grabbing an outfit for Gwen, I pulled out my favorite black dress from the closet. I wore it on the first day I went to the Hastings Building to get my certification. It was my go-to for stressful situations since it made me feel confident and capable.

I flung the dress on the bed, and as I turned to gather my makeup from the bathroom, I caught Sebastian smirking.

"What?"

He raised an eyebrow. "Nothing." He fingered the fabric of my dress. "I just like this one."

I furrowed my brow. "I thought you didn't have his memories without searching for them?"

"I don't, but I have memories of his memories. There were moments I could slip through his head unnoticed, and the first thing I'd do is rifle through his mind for images of you so I had something to keep me company when he inevitably locked me up again."

My face softened. That was sweet.

But just because they had similar taste in my outfits wasn't proof enough that they were the same.

"I don't think we should tell anyone about the"—I waved a hand down the length of him—"new you."

"And how will you explain my eyes? I can't change them."

I sighed, grabbing my makeup from the bathroom counter and bringing it into the bedroom to lay out on the dresser. It made sense his void eyes wouldn't go away. When our shadows were influencing us, they overtook our eyes.

"Well, I don't think anyone will question them. They'll all be too scared of you," I said.

He shrugged, and then flopped down on the bed, his legs hanging off the side. "Alright."

"But you'll have to, you know, act more like him."

"Very well. Tell me when my actions depart from his and I'll modify my behavior," he said, closing his eyes.

I crossed my arms. "Well...for one, he wouldn't walk around in his underwear in front of Sloane and Gwen."

He peeked an eye open. "Were you jealous? I don't know why you would be. Sloane only has eyes for Nico, and I'm obviously not Gwen's type."

I huffed. "I was *not* jealous. It was just weird. He'd never do that."

"Right." He drew out the word and stretched out on the bed, resting the palms of his hands under his head. His body pulled taut. He hadn't buttoned up his shirt entirely, and the tattoos along his neck and spiraling down his chest teased me. It'd be so easy to climb on top of him, straddle him, and trace his tattoos with my tongue.

We had time before the meeting, plenty of time to feel his hands on me, feel his shadows against my skin, feel his hard length inside me. Maybe...

"Okay," he said. "What else wouldn't he do?"

"Uh," I said, snapping out of my trance. I couldn't even blame my shadow for egging me on this time. "Well, he wouldn't kill people like you did last night. I know you said you had a different line, but the other Sebastian wouldn't have hurt anyone without a good reason."

"I had a good reason."

"Okay, a better reason than *needing to assert my dominance*." I used air-quotes.

He inhaled and exhaled a long breath through his nose. "Fine. I will refrain from murdering anyone unless they attack."

"Okay," I said, feeling a little more satisfied. I turned to sort through my makeup and put what I was taking into my cosmetic bag. "Good."

"So no killing people and wear clothes at all times..." He snorted. "No wonder why he was so uptight. He never had any fun."

"He wasn't uptight," I said, playfully lobbing a tube of mascara at him.

His shadow stopped it right before it smacked him. He laughed and started tossing the tube between his hands.

"How did you do that?" I asked. "You did that in the UV room too. Used your shadows with your eyes closed."

He tossed the mascara back to me, and I caught it. "I don't need to see," he said. "I can sense with my shadows."

"Huh," I said, eyeing the mascara thoughtfully.

"Did he not do that either?" He exhaled heavily. "Goddess, I don't know if I can pull off pretending to be the most boring version of myself."

I rolled my eyes, but a smile was tugging on my lips as I zipped my bag. "You know what? Just do whatever you want."

If anyone got suspicious about his behavior, we would blame it on being tortured in the prison.

"Anything?" His eyes popped open, and he gave me a dangerous smirk.

"Except kill people!"

He smiled and sat up. A shadow swept out, corralling me toward him. He grabbed my hips and pulled me between his legs.

I'm not sure why I let him, but it was like my body had a mind of its own.

"I know, little warrior," he said and leaned forward until his lips were at my ear. His breath caused a shiver to skate through me. "I just like getting you all worked up."

My body melted under his touch. The aura of his shadows hung thick around him, making me sway, and for a brief moment, I floated in a peaceful nowhere, an unreality.

Until the comfort turned overwhelming in its ability to obliterate my sense of reason.

I pushed his hands off my hips. "Don't...Don't do that." The words came out weak and tinny. I took an unsteady step back.

"Do what?" he asked, his teasing tone shifted to concern.

"T-touch me," I stuttered.

"Amaya—"

"No," I said, holding my elbows as a strange trembling took over my body. "I...just...I can't. You said it yourself. You aren't him."

This wasn't right. None of this was right. Sebastian was in a coma. He thought his shadow was a separate entity. I couldn't flirt with his shadow, couldn't fantasize about him, couldn't enjoy his touch. It was wrong. Maybe it wasn't cheating *technically*, but it felt like a betrayal. I wasn't going to betray Sebastian. I couldn't. Not again.

He wasn't dead. He was coming back. He'd heal. He'd wake up. Everything would be fine. I just needed time.

My Sebastian was coming back.

A crease formed between his eyebrows as he pressed his lips together.

I tried to fill my lungs with air, but a tight band constricted my chest. "I want to trust you, okay?" I whispered, staring at the ground. "I want to, but I need you to prove that I can."

I needed him to not push me into the mating bond or emotionally manipulate me. I needed to see he wasn't the shadow that Sebastian was afraid he'd be if he had free rein in his body.

"Okay," he said. "Okay, Amaya. I'm sorry." His voice was gentle, remorseful.

I glanced up and wished I hadn't. The hurt in his eyes gutted me. I didn't want to have to choose between hurting my Sebastian or hurting his shadow.

I'd already hurt them both too much.

A dark pit opened up inside of me, swallowing all my feelings until I was left numb and confused.

"Let's go get Nico's stuff," I said.

While he went downstairs to get his laptop, I grabbed my dress, Gwen's outfit, and my makeup bag before going to Nico's apartment over the garage to grab him clothes.

After we sifted back to the cabin, we went our separate ways, though I could feel his eyes on my back as I went to get ready.

My shadow grumbled, hating to be parted from him even by a few walls.

Luckily, my two best friends thoroughly distracted me for the next thirty minutes arguing about what hairstyle went best with a crown.

"Queen Mari always wore hers in a bun," Gwen said, gathering my hair in her hand and flinging it atop my head.

Sloane swatted her hands away and brushed the length of my brown hair over both shoulders. "Yeah, but she was old. Amaya's hair is long and pretty, it'd be a shame to hide it."

Gwen made a contemplative face in the mirror and shrugged. "Yeah. Plus, if your hair is pulled back, the crown might make your ears look big."

"Hey!" I pushed her shoulder. "I do not have big ears."

Sloane giggled.

Gwen smiled. "I didn't say you *had* big ears, but that the crown might make them look that way." She plugged in the curling iron I'd brought from the townhouse.

"You suck," I said.

Sloane and I did our makeup while Gwen curled my hair.

As the finishing touch, I put the crown on.

The three of us looked in the mirror, all staring at the shining gold diadem with its glimmering diamonds.

I bit my lip. "Can I do this?"

"Well, if you *royally* fuck it up, we'll be right beside you," Gwen said.

I elbowed her, and we laughed at her terrible pun.

Sloane wrapped both her arms around me and rested her head on my shoulder. "Best friends stick together, you know."

Despite the anxiety roiling in my stomach, I smiled.

I wasn't alone.

Chapter Twenty

Amaya

The metal of the crown dug into my head. I smoothed out my dress to wipe away the sweat on my palms as we stood outside the double doors of the meeting room.

Ready? Sebastian asked in my head.

As I'll ever be.

Sebastian opened both doors, and the din of the councilmember's conversation halted as their gazes swiveled to us.

A moment passed, but Sebastian didn't move into the room, only stood in the doorway, almost expectantly.

"Your queen has arrived," he said, his voice harsh. "It's disrespectful not to bow. Though given she saved all of Palagui from a powerless existence, I'd think you'd be kissing the ground she walked on." Shadows swirled around his shoulders as a promise of violence for noncompliance.

I modulated my facial expressions as I yelled in his head, *Is this necessary? They all kneeled last night.*

My protest was too late. Everyone shook off their shock and scrambled to push their chairs back. They lowered to their knees and bowed their heads.

The council knows it's protocol to bow or kneel before the queen. It's disrespectful not to. We can't tolerate that, not now, not ever.

He walked behind me as I went to the head of the table.

I need to earn their respect, I protested.

He pulled out my chair and motioned for me to sit. When I didn't, he pursed his lips. *No, Amaya. You already earned it the moment you put that crown on your head. The moment you gave up your body to allow every fae in this nation to access their power. You know what it is to live without it. It's no life. You've given life to every citizen of Palagui. They can bow to show their respect and appreciation for your sacrifice.*

I blinked once and took a seat.

This wasn't him gunning for power for power's sake. He was right. Everyone had always bowed when Queen Mari was in the room. If they didn't for me, and I did nothing about it, they would know they could walk all over me.

Even Gwen and Sloane had kneeled and lowered their heads at the entrance of the room.

Remember you promised not to kill anyone, I felt compelled to remind him.

He pushed in my chair. *I recall my vow. I will not kill anyone unless they attack. I serve you, my queen. I'll do anything you ask.* He fell to a knee, bowing his head along with the rest of them.

I took a breath and released it as quietly as I could. "You may rise," I said with as much authority as I could muster.

Each person rose with lowered eyes and sat. In some coordinated dance, the two councilmembers on my right and left vacated their seats, and Sloane and Gwen replaced them. Their eyes were on Sebastian as he walked to the other side of the table. He must have spoken in their heads.

Sebastian began the meeting. "I don't think I need to remind you that the new queen reserves the right to remove the past regime's councilmembers and request a new vote. However, Queen Amaya, in her mercy and grace, has decided to retain the councilmembers seated here today."

I scanned the councilmembers. No surprise that Daria and Caroline weren't here. We'd need to hold a vote to find replacements for them.

No one made a sound, but all their eyes were trained on Sebastian as he continued, "Therefore, before we begin, each councilmember will pledge their fealty and renew their bargains to their constituents."

A dramatic male groan broke the silence. "Do we really have time for formalities? Merbany has been destroyed," Vince said. His head whipped to me. "We're going to do the whole song and dance when we should be discussing how to rebuild?"

Vince's face was pinched. He had a long, rounded nose and avian-like features, and even when he turned to look at me, his light brown, perfectly coiffed hair didn't move a single strand.

Sebastian wasn't flustered by Vince's outburst and only gave him a stern look. "The quicker you pledge your loyalty," he said. "The quicker we can get to the productive portion of our meeting."

Vince grumbled, but to my surprise, he was the first to rise. He angled his body toward me and placed a hand over his heart. His smile was practically a sneer as he said, "I, Vince Kane, renew my bargain to commit myself to the best interests of Merbany, and I pledge my loyalty to the Queen and King of Darkness."

My eyes cut to Sebastian, who was watching Vince with sharp eyes.

Are you happy? We sound like comic book villains, I said to Sebastian.

He smirked. *I like it.*

I fought an eye roll. *Of course you do.*

Palagui is lost right now, he said. *They need a Queen of Darkness with a heart of light to lead them through the shadows of the wreckage.*

My jaw slackened, and a shiver ran through me at the immensity of his words, but I caught myself before displaying any outward reaction and forced my gaze to the next councilmember. I focused on memorizing each of their names, faces, and regions.

Keeping my eyes on the councilmembers, I asked, *If every councilmember is bound to help their constituents, how was it possible that Caroline's bargain wasn't broken when she refused to declare a national emergency?*

Fae magic is about intentions, Sebastian responded. *If Caroline truly believed what she was doing was in the best interest of the high priestesses, the bargain wouldn't affect her. It only really stops the councilmembers from making decisions that they know would harm their people. From Caroline's perspective, her bargain is to the high priestesses of Palagui, not the rest of us.*

I thought about how the bargain I made with Sebastian to be his pretend fiancée had never given me any inclination that I was breaking it, despite the fact I'd been planning his murder.

I'd never intended to not be his pretend fiancée, so I never experienced the itching and pain associated with a broken bargain.

After the last councilmember finished their pledges, Vince cleared his throat, and his beady eyes stared pointedly behind me.

I furrowed my brow and turned.

A person was perched in a tiny chair, typing furiously on a laptop.

"Blake," Vince snapped.

Blake startled, and clumsily stood, setting the laptop aside before saying, "I, Blake Fletcher, uh, am just the secretary and have no bargain to renew, but pledge my loyalty to the Queen and King of Darkness."

"Thank you, Blake," I said as gentle as I could to hopefully make up for Vince's rudeness.

"I contacted a darkyra friend to sift me to Blake's house and bring them here," Leva whispered. Her small stature seemed to collapse in on itself as we all turned to look at her. "I figured if you wanted all the councilmembers here, you'd also want the council's secretary."

"Thank you for your thoroughness, Leva," I said. She gave me a shy smile and looked away. I inclined my head to Blake. "And thank you for coming on such short notice, Blake. Next council meeting, you'll have a chair at the table. I'm afraid this one was abruptly thrown together."

They blinked and bowed their head. "Thank you, uh, your majesty." Blushing furiously, they returned to their seat.

I turned back to the councilmembers, but before I could speak, Vince said, "They didn't do it." He pointed his chin to Gwen and Sloane's direction. "Or ginger over here," he said, throwing a thumb at Nico.

Nico only rolled his eyes, but I was insulted for him.

I glowered. "My privy council has already proved their loyalty, but thank you for the concern, Vince."

Vince slouched in his chair, not like he'd been cowed but more like a petulant child. "You praised Leva for thoroughness. I was just doing the same, your majesty. Since our fealty is important enough to waste time on when my city is disintegrating by the second."

Sebastian stared blankly at Vince. He would step in if I asked him to, but though he had created our agenda for the meeting, Sebastian insisted I lead it, so the councilmembers recognized I was in charge.

Vince had been a troublemaker even when Xenos ruled, but I wasn't going to let him undermine my authority.

I steepled my hands. "Well Vince, why don't you start our meeting by updating us on what you've done to help Merbany to prepare for the hurricane? Oh, and"—I leaned over to Blake—"Blake, can you please make sure to record everything that Vince has done for his people. I want to make sure that these meeting minutes are a *thorough* reflection of the councilmembers' actions so the citizens know exactly who they can thank for their current situations."

"Yes, your majesty," Blake said, their fingers poised over the keyboard.

Vince pressed his tongue into his top lip. "Well, I haven't been able to do much since Caroline kneecapped us."

Erik cleared his throat. "Caroline wouldn't let us declare a national emergency. She used it as leverage to get us to approve her choice for queen."

Erik was broad-shouldered but on the short side. There was a tightness around his mouth that spoke of a life spent with pursed lips.

I rested my chin on my steepled hands. "You're telling me you've done nothing to help your people in the last few weeks?"

Vince sneered. "You mean you want to know what we did while you and Sebastian were imprisoned for killing Xenos and murdering high priestesses?" Vince said, all wide-eyed innocence. "Blake, make sure you get that in the meeting minutes, too. I can repeat it if you need." He started speaking slower. "Imprisoned. For. Killing. Xenos. And—"

I raised a hand, and a shadow flicked out, covering Vince's mouth and nose. I didn't want to use my power in these meetings. I specifically asked Sebastian not to hover his shadows around the room as a threat, but I wasn't going to stand for Vince's bullying.

I let the room sit in silence as Vince glared at me. He tried to burn through my shadows, but without any intake of air, they couldn't light. I just smiled at him and waited.

His eyes grew panicked as the seconds ticked by, darting around the room when no one moved to help him.

He pushed back in his chair to get up, but he was already swaying with wooziness from lack of air.

Finally, he tapped the table three times.

"I suggest you not speak ill of your queen or king again, or I'll make sure you're not around to speak at all," I said before waving my fingers. The shadows misted away as he gasped for breath.

"A public release will go out today that the Queen and King of Palagui were wrongly imprisoned," I said. "I killed Prince Xenos in self-defense as he was about to stab his brother, Sebastian Renwick, in the heart with a dagger."

The only sound was the click-clack of typing. I let the silence expand as I looked each councilmember in the eye before continuing, "Sebastian Renwick did not kill any high priestesses. This was an egregious lie created by Caroline Nueblots in order to undermine his authority on the council and delegitimize his claim to the throne."

It was technically true. He hadn't *killed* them.

"Alright, fine," Vince said. "Then where are the missing high priestesses?"

"Wow, a soliser caring about a high priestess. That's a first," Gwen said, echoing the statement he'd made to Daria in our first council meeting.

Vince narrowed his eyes but ignored Gwen's comment, adding "Yes, and speaking of fae faction sympathizers, where the hell is Daria?"

"Why are you so concerned?" Gwen asked. "You miss her putting your balls in a vice?"

Vince leaned back and smirked. "Actually, I loved when she fondled my—"

Gwen shot up, her chair hitting the wall behind her, but she seemed to catch herself before jumping across the table and strangling him. The spice of her anger and hatred choked me in its intensity.

"That's enough," I said. My shadows rose under my skin, and the tattoos along my arms blinked. "New council rule. If you say anything about anyone that could even vaguely be considered sexual harassment, you'll lose your seat. Understand?"

"She started it," Vince mumbled.

She sort of did, but I didn't acknowledge that.

Sebastian cleared his throat. "The missing high priestesses aren't missing. They're being held at the research center due to a contagion. That information was not public knowledge, which is why there was a misunderstanding. Our best scientists are working to find a cure, and I'm confident they'll be healed and released without the public ever needing to know."

Calling the high priestesses' condition of being a draxis a contagion was as close to the truth as we could get. We needed to gather the rest of the draxis from Palagui and Delnee, along with Jeremy from the prison, and keep them at the research center until we could go through the portal to get Adriana to heal them.

"I may have people in Molbridge that can help with that," Micah said. He had a strong, comforting voice. He was the oldest of everyone in the room with graying stripes in his brown hair. "We have a clinic that specializes in alternate healing modalities."

Sebastian nodded at Micah. "We can discuss after the meeting."

He'd have to politely decline Micah's suggestions. I doubted the clinic's healing modalities worked on draxis, though my vision in the Hollow did make it seem as if they could be healed.

We just had to figure out how.

"Leva," Sebastian said. "Did you inform Caroline and Daria of this meeting?"

"Yes sir," she said in a small voice. A sour anxiety hung around her. First day jitters, I decided. "I left voicemails and emailed every councilmember as you requested last night. I had my friend sift me to their houses, but they weren't home."

Leva really was thorough. It was hypocritical to be glad that Sebastian killed Hugo, but with her as his replacement, I was.

"As of today," Sebastian began. "Daria and Caroline are no longer councilmembers. Which means anything discussed in our meetings that is not already public knowledge cannot be shared with them.

Gwen will fill in for Caroline until we hold a vote to elect new representatives."

"If either of them contact you, please inform us," I added.

"And if you don't, you'll be guilty of aiding and abetting a criminal fleeing prosecution," Sebastian said.

"You're arresting Daria?" Vince asked, his voice hard.

I narrowed my eyes. Why *was* he so worried about her? Maybe he thought if we arrested Daria and Caroline, we'd go back on our word and get rid of the councilmembers too? Sebastian did say Vince was only ever concerned about his personal power and position.

"Daria will not—nor will any of you—be tried for assisting or becoming an accessory after the fact of Caroline's treason. We know she put you under duress," Sebastian said. "But Caroline will be found and punished for her crimes."

Gwen had told me her aunt had lived in Delnee before the fae-human war one hundred years ago. She had experience in running and hiding, but karma would catch her eventually.

"Let's move on," I said. "I'd like an update on each region's status."

The councilmembers discussed how the hurricane affected the areas they represented and what their current priorities were.

The hurricane flooded western Merbany and damaged the southern portion of Palagui City, but Coral Beach and the rest of Palagui City wasn't in its the direct path. There was minor exterior damage in those areas due to winds, but repair work could begin as early as tomorrow since the worst of the rain would ease by tonight. The areas north of the mountain ranges, including Molbridge, only experienced heavy rainfall.

Power was only out in the worst hit areas, but damage to the circuits in one electrical hub could spread if the emergency breakers didn't hold.

Despite Caroline not letting the councilmembers declare a national emergency, they had actually been able to do a great deal.

Micah opened Molbridge up for any displaced citizen. He and his team organized several charities and businesses to run shelters in their university dormitories and arena. As long as food, water, and medicine could be brought in, he was confident that Molbridge could handle the influx of people.

Erik made deals with private transportation companies to get as many buses of people from downtown Palagui City to Molbridge as they could before the hurricane hit. "Hugo helped," he had added, throwing a contemptuous look at Sebastian, who ignored him.

Gerald and Vince managed to pull funds together for Merbany. It hadn't been much, but it got a few thousand people out and funded the supplies for the first responder teams to help those who hadn't been able to evacuate in time. Vince opened up a stadium as a shelter for the people who couldn't get to Molbridge.

My first official act as queen was to declare a national emergency, which allowed PEM to get pallets of saline, food, and water into the shelters in Molbridge and Merbany; begin repair to the downed electrical stations; and reassign all guards from patrol duty to search-and-rescue teams.

"No," Vince interrupted. "We need to keep the guards where they are. Businesses near the stadium shelter have been calling me concerned that there's going to be looting and anarchy with all the people in-and-out of the area."

"It's more important to find trapped people than it is to protect businesses," Gwen said.

Vince threw his hands up. "There's going to be backlash." He turned to me. "These are important, wealthy solisers."

I frowned. "I don't care if they're wealthy or if they're solisers. People are more important than property."

Vince ran a hand down his face. "You aren't hearing me! These are the people you want on your side. The people who own the news stations and the media. The people who can swing popular opinion. If you piss them off you may be queen, but no one will support you."

I met Sebastian's gaze.

He might have a point, he said.

Or he's trying to save his own ass so he doesn't get voted out?

Possibly, but I've never had the best reputation in the country, he said. *It never mattered, because I was too valuable to Xenos, but now...*

I sighed and leaned back in my chair.

"Amaya and I will go to Merbany and assess the situation," Sebastian said diplomatically.

The meeting wound down from there. Everyone had their tasks and needed to confer with their teams to start organizing people.

My temples throbbed from a tension headache. It had been forming all day, but with my focus on our issues, my mind hadn't registered it.

My power felt like it was short-circuiting, and my body was on the edge of exhaustion. Sebastian didn't seem much better.

As the councilmembers left the meeting room, Micah pulled him aside. Sebastian held himself with his usual straight posture and regal grace, but he looked even paler than he had this morning.

If it weren't for his void eyes, I'd have completely forgotten that his shadow was in control. The meeting went better than I could have hoped for. Other than Vince's little tantrums, the other councilmembers hadn't treated Sebastian or me with disdain.

I remembered noticing at my first council meeting how everyone had looked to Sebastian as the de facto leader, despite Xenos taking credit for his ideas and decisions. It seemed that respect hadn't diminished.

After Sebastian finished his conversation with Micah, he turned to me. "I need to speak to the staff about the funeral preparation."

His voice hadn't wavered, but I fought the urge to reach out and hug him. Whether or not he wanted to admit he was affected by his mother's death, he needed my support.

I nodded. "I'll be here."

It would be a slippery slope if I touched him.

I'd have to support him in other ways. Staying beside him, bringing him food, stepping in when people without genuine sympathy tried to pull him into conversations.

As he sifted from the room, the thin string of our connection wavered. Something in my gut nagged me, a vague uneasiness, but I couldn't put my finger on its origin.

Gwen, Sloane, and Nico wandered out to stretch their legs after Sebastian left, which meant I finally had a moment to myself.

Or so I thought.

"Your majesty."

I didn't bother stifling my groan. "What do you want, Vince?"

"Just a word."

I eyed him as he smiled with his arms behind his back and swaggered toward me.

There was something about him that set me on edge, and it wasn't just me who felt it. Everyone seemed to almost unconsciously curve and bend around him as if his very essence repelled them.

"Are you going to be a problem?" I asked.

He projected an innocent expression. "Of course not. I'm bound to protect the people of Merbany."

I rubbed my eyes. "Don't think I've forgotten what you said to Daria when she brought up dissolving the law that forbids darkyra gatherings."

He tapped his finger on his chin. "I don't seem to recall that."

"You said when darkyra gather, crime rises," I said. "Your opinion of us isn't very high, and given most of your constituents are solisers, it's not instilling me with much confidence that you'll do what's best for every citizen. Including the darkyra."

"Why," he said, a hand on his chest. "I couldn't see myself ever saying such a thing."

I leveled him with a stern expression. "I'm not tolerating any discrimination along fae faction lines, so this is your final warning."

His faux smile fell, and he narrowed his eyes. "I'm not Hugo. You can't get rid of me without losing control of this country." He put a hand on the table and leaned over, lowering his voice. "The bloodiest part of a rise to power isn't overthrowing the old government, it's securing your reign once the enemy is gone. The crown may be on your head, but the people are not behind you. You need me. You need the council just as much as the council needs you."

I curled my lip. "Is that a threat?"

He straightened and ran both his hands down his torso to smooth out his suit jacket. "Of course not. We're bound to the best interests of our regions, and it's in Merbany's best interest that you wear the crown and give our people power for centuries to come."

He turned and walked to the door before I could come up with a retort.

As he left, he said over his shoulder, "Long live the queen."

Chapter Twenty-One

Sebastian

My new sweater—the one my parents bought me for my eleventh birthday—was ruined. The checkered pattern had been distorted by the splatter of blood. A coppery smell invaded my senses.

My mom trembled as the darkness held a blade against her neck. Tears smeared her makeup down her face.

I looked to her for guidance, for answers, but her eyes remained on my father's unconscious body as she repeated over and over, "Please. Please let us go."

I wanted to say "Mama, tell me what to do" but terror clogged the words in my throat.

"Do it like I showed you," the darkness said.

I shook my head.

"This is the only way. This is how you become who you were made to be. Do it or your mother will die."

She finally looked at me then, but still, she didn't tell me what to do. She was frozen in their grip, which was when the realization settled over me.

I'd been too young to find out my parents didn't have all the answers, that they wouldn't be able to keep me safe. Too young to hold all the fear and pain and guilt over the consequences of my actions.

My mom wasn't strong enough to give me permission to do as they asked. She hadn't been strong enough to fight the darkness.

But I was eleven now. I could be strong for her. I could save her.

When my shadow took over, I felt my face slacken, completely expressionless.

The fear ended.

The pain stopped.

I turned from my mom. Her desperate pleading became the backdrop to my act.

I crouched on the ground, held the handle of the blade with both hands, raised it above my head, and stabbed my father in the heart.

His blood sprayed into my face and soaked my hands.

Not a single thought filled my mind as I pulled the knife out and let it clatter to the ground. I'd been blissfully abandoned by guilt or pain or sorrow.

My mother's pleas shifted into shrieks of grief but were cut off by gurgling. I whipped around in time to watch as the darkness slit her throat and she fell.

"There's your first lesson," the darkness said. "Never trust anyone's word. Make bargains, not promises."

A tornado of my power engulfed me, my house, my town, as my entire world shattered.

✳✳✳

I gasped awake.

Shadows coated my room in a thick abyss. I let them hover, hoping their freedom would ease my racing heart.

I looked at my hands expecting to see blood caked along the nail beds and stained into my fingerprints, but they were clean.

Over a hundred years passing hadn't dulled the vividness of the memory. My body could still conjure the horrifying details of the things I'd done while in control of it.

I tried to remember the last time I had this nightmare, but it'd been decades since I let myself fall asleep sober.

Nico had wanted to know why I sought out any and every substance I could when I took control of our body.

Well, it was more about avoidance than it'd been about wanting to feel alive and free.

I'd successfully avoided sleep last night by staying up to sort through his memories for the council meeting.

And since I'd never fully fallen asleep in the prison, I hadn't had to experience the nightmares then either. Now the physical torture of the UV room seemed preferable over this mental anguish.

The bottle of scotch on the bar cart in the corner of the room looked tantalizing, but given how sick I already was, I resisted its allure.

Sweat made my clothes cling to my body, so I stripped and walked into the bathroom to shower the remnants of my nightmare away.

My void eyes saw through the darkness, and my shadows drifted around me, but I didn't worry about them escaping. Nico and I had only spoken once after the council meeting. I'd asked him to charge the wards on my bedroom, and though surprised, he'd done so before we went to bed.

There would've been no way in hell my shadows wouldn't have seeped out and found Amaya if he hadn't. Not with the way our bond was disintegrating.

But she didn't want me to touch her, and she wouldn't appreciate my shadows reaching for her either.

I wasn't going to lose the opportunity to gain her trust. She said I wasn't him, so I had to prove I could be better.

She'd been testing me last night at the funeral, standing close enough for my power to sense her, but not close enough for our auras to align. I couldn't hear her shadow without touching her, but by the way she fidgeted the entire time, I knew her power was begging to get closer. Yet she remained steadfast.

I'd been miserable but hadn't wavered.

I would pass every single one of her trust tests, no matter how painful.

The funeral's perfunctory rituals and speeches had taken hours. Maybe that was another reason the nightmare had resurfaced. Putting the Queen to rest had reminded me of the real mother I'd lost.

After we'd sifted back to the townhouse, I wanted nothing more than to curl up next to my mate and fall asleep, but she wouldn't permit that, and I wasn't done reckoning with my past.

"I'm going to transport Jeremy to the research center," I had told Amaya.

"I'll come with you," she said.

I shook my head. "Stay here. Don't leave the townhouse"

"I thought you couldn't be far away from me," she huffed with a hand on her hip.

"I want you to be safe. You are safest here within the wards."

"I can handle a single draxis, let me help—"

"No," I snapped. "I need to dc this alone."

Her eyebrows pulled together, and she frowned, but didn't follow me as I sifted.

Jeremy was my responsibility.

Hardening myself to my memories and emotions, I'd sifted to the prison. The mating bond tugged. Its threads frayed like yarn being sawed away little by little.

Jeremy had been exactly where we'd left him. He didn't stir as I untied him from the chair, picked him up, and took him to the research center. He was put in a room with a steady stream of electrical power pumped through a metal conductor to keep him from deteriorating.

He would be safe here until spring equinox when I brought Adriana home. She'd heal him. She'd heal all the high priestesses like she'd done when we were sixteen and I'd accidentally turned our trainer into a draxis.

It'd taken three days, but she restored him. When I asked her how she did it, if it was part of her high priestess healing power, she'd only shrugged and said, "Must be."

But no other high priestesses had been able to recreate it, so she must have been using a power special to only her.

I didn't question it further at the time because I was just grateful that she'd fixed my mistake, and my shame prevented me from speaking of it again.

The shower water turned cold, breaking me from my thoughts.

I considered going back to sleep, but I didn't want to risk another nightmare, so after replacing my sweat-soaked bed sheets, I trudged downstairs.

The mating bond was more damaged than it should have been because I didn't sense Amaya's presence before I saw her sitting at the dining room table.

She stared in her bowl of breakfast grains and didn't glance up.

Another test then. Could I leave her alone? Respect her wishes and not engage her in conversation or come near her?

My shoulders caved in, but I'd pass this test too. Devastated with her indifference, I shuffled into the kitchen.

Sloane stirred something on the stove and whispered to Nico. They shared a worried glance with one another as I walked in.

The synchronicity of their movements grated me. They were only in sync because their mating bond attuned them.

I wanted that.

But I wasn't *him*.

"Breakfast?" Sloane asked.

I nodded, and she handed me a bowl.

"Thank you," I said, my voice hoarse and raspy like I was sick.

I guess I was. I'd read last night from the anatomy book that Amaya and I would develop bond sickness if we didn't touch and stayed too far from one another.

I'd thought I would have time to pass her tests and gain her trust before it got bad enough to be noticeable, but our bond had been severely taxed in the past six months. We were together and separated too many times, our powers bound or suppressed, and our bodies weakened by our time in the prison.

These were the side effects.

I went to the dining room and pulled out the chair furthest from my mate to sit and eat.

She'd been annoyed with me yesterday for eating from her plate, but after she devoured me with her eyes when I walked out, I'd hoped teasing her would loosen her up and prove to her that I was still part of the person she fell in love with.

But my attempts only further underscored the ways I wasn't *him*.

She seemed intent to ignore me today, but it was impossible to not gaze upon her.

Her hair was messy from sleep and her clothes were askew. Even her shadow must have been tired because I couldn't feel any power eddying around her.

She had to be feeling the effects of the bond sickness, but obviously her trust tests were more important than being hollowed from the inside out.

You won't pass the tests. She doesn't want you. She never will. You're nothing but a burden to her, the voice in my head confirmed. I didn't have the energy to disagree.

We ate in silence. Two halves of a whole that were too broken to slot together anymore.

"What the hell is wrong with you two?" Gwen asked, startling both of us.

Amaya recovered and shrugged. "Tired. Didn't sleep well last night."

I wondered if she had nightmares as well. I wondered if I was even allowed to ask.

Nico and Sloane joined Gwen as she sat at the table.

"Maybe you should take the day off," Sloane said. "You both need to rest and recover. PEM is handling the day-to-day disaster relief, and the council knows what they need to do. One day won't matter in the long run."

"No," we said in unison and then stared at each other.

The corner of my lip inched up. Maybe we were in sync.

But any hope of that was dashed when Amaya averted her eyes as if my gaze had scalded her.

"I just need coffee," Amaya said with forced cheer. "Then I'll be good as new."

I snorted. "Yeah, coffee will fix it," I said, unable to contain my derision.

Her nostrils flared, but she kept her gaze on her bowl. "Why are you being so sarcastic?"

I glared. "Because coffee isn't going to cure bond anemia."

Her eyes darted up, settling on me. Finally.

"What are you talking about?" she asked, brows furrowed.

I pursed my lips. "Your trust tests. Like you haven't noticed it's gotten worse since you told me to stop touching you yesterday."

I'd suffer through the sickness for her, but the very least she could do is not play dumb about it.

"I...I don't know what you're talking about," she said.

I narrowed my eyes, but her confusion seemed genuine. If she didn't know, maybe she hadn't been purposefully testing me. If she didn't know it was making us sick, she wouldn't know we needed to touch and be near one another. Maybe the sickness had muddled my mind.

I straightened in my seat as a lightness filled me. "We should sleep together to make sure our auras—"

"What the fuck!" She shook the table as she shoved her chair back to stand.

I put my hands up in surrender. I hadn't tried to touch her, so why was she jumping away? I was on the other side of the room for Goddess's sake.

"Our bond is sick," I said slowly. "We lived together for weeks, and binding your powers put it in a stasis for a while, but then we reactivated it every time we were together. The suppression in the prison weakened it, and now we're close enough the bond knows what it needs is nearby, but it isn't being fulfilled so it's deteriorating."

She wrinkled her nose in disgust and clenched her hands into fists. "I thought mating bonds were a choice? How is making me sick until I accept it a choice?"

I grimaced. "It is a choice. You can choose not to accept the bond, but you need to stay away from your mate so the wound can heal, so to speak. Being near one another keeps ripping it open."

Her head shook in incredulity. "So what? I have to move out? Then we'll be fine?"

I shuddered at the thought. "If we lived in separate places and never crossed paths, yes, it would eventually stop hurting."

This was it. This was the moment I lost her. I wouldn't even have the chance to pass her trust tests because she wants to leave me.

She made a squawking noise. "So...so...what? Mates that don't want to be together can't work together or like go to the same grocery store?"

I shrugged, dropping my gaze as the sickening pit in my stomach from her rejection grew. Pushing my breakfast around the bowl with my spoon, I said, "Mates that don't want to be together don't live together, sleep together, and *then* decide not to be together. If we never got involved to begin with, it wouldn't affect us like this."

"Okay," Sloane said gently. "So if you guys hold hands or like sit closer, would that fix it?"

"I...I can't!" Amaya said. "It's cheating!"

Cheating? On her trust tests? Really?

"Ten minutes of hand holding isn't cheating," Sloane said. "Especially if it's what you need to make you healthy. You know he wouldn't want you to be in pain."

"It may help," I said. "But ten minutes isn't long enough. We need to sleep together."

"I am not *sleeping* with you," she said. "How dare you even suggest that!"

Her emphasis on the word sparked my realization that she'd misunderstood my meaning, but it didn't remove the sting of her disgust.

I dropped my spoon and it rattled in my bowl. "Sleep as in literal *sleep*, Amaya. Our astral fields want to merge, but we can appease them through prolonged physical proximity."

Her face fell, and her shoulders loosened. "Oh," she said. "I thought you meant..."

I shook my head, staring at the ceiling with a humorless smile on my face. "I can handle the bond sickness if it proves to you that you can trust me, but the symptoms are going to get worse. Eight to ten hours of sleeping next to one another should at least let us be functional and wouldn't involve direct contact."

Nico and Sloane hadn't needed to worry about this. They had been together almost constantly before they accepted the bond.

Amaya and I, however...Our bodies, our powers were put under too much stress in the last few weeks. Just one day of not touching was breaking us apart.

Sighing, I said, "Unless you'd like me to move to the beach house. It'd be challenging to run the country without being in the same room, but I suppose we could alternate which days we were in court. You could use an office on the other side—"

"I don't want that," she interrupted, her voice quiet. She sat back in her chair and rubbed her temples.

She didn't want to leave me, but she didn't want to be with me either. No matter what she decided, she'd only be forced into it by the bond sickness. I deflated. I couldn't even be angry. An empty cavern opened within me.

I sifted to my bedroom and picked up the book on my nightstand and returned, sliding the book across the table to her.

Her eyes met mine, full of defeat as her body drooped.

"Since you can't trust me, you can read about it for yourself," I said and sifted back to my bedroom before she could reply.

I didn't have it in me to witness her despair when she realized she was stuck with me. I couldn't listen to her lament about how everything would be alright if only I were *him*.

Numbness greeted me as I opened the sliding glass door to the balcony and stepped into the cold, letting the icy bluster freeze my emotions.

I pulled out one of the chairs from the outside closet and slumped into it. My mate was either going to leave me or only tolerate my presence to avoid getting sick.

I didn't know which was worse.

My throat thickened, and I covered my eyes with one hand. The cold wasn't enough to keep me from flinching as another strand of our bond snapped.

Chapter Twenty-Two

Amaya

I am a terrible person.

The residuals of his magic dissipated slowly as he sifted, almost like the tendrils of his shadow wanted to linger in the room with me. My tongue was coated with his bitter sadness, overpowering any trace of his vanilla affection. I laid my head on the table and tried not to cry.

"Amaya," Sloane said in a soft tone that was going to tip me into all-out bawling.

It was Nico who unleashed the torrent.

"Sebastian wouldn't want you to feel like this," Nico said. "I...I know I thought Shadow Bash was untrustworthy because of his past, but after the council meeting yesterday...I mean he isn't acting out."

I lifted my head to look at Nico. The acidic brine of his regret burned my throat.

He frowned. "If it weren't for his eyes, I wouldn't have even known Shadow Bash was in control. He handled the council, the funeral, everything exactly like he would have before."

Nico's voice strained. "He'd want you to be happy, and he'd kill me if he knew I sat off to the side and watched you wither away because you thought being with his shadow was cheating on him. He and his shadow had a bad relationship because he was afraid of his shadow's outbursts, not because he inherently hated him. You aren't betraying him."

I scrunched up my face, but the tears broke through anyway.

"How would you feel if you died and your shadow took over?" Gwen asked. "Would you be mad at Sebastian for being with her?"

"You don't understand," I said between hiccupping sobs. "It's not the same."

My shadow wasn't a separate part of me.

She was me. I was her.

I didn't want to hurt Sebastian or his shadow, but if he woke up from his coma and learned I'd spent that time touching, kissing, being with his shadow like nothing was wrong, he would be hurt.

Sure, he would understand because he literally understood why I tried to kill him. I couldn't do anything wrong in his eyes. But that didn't mean deep down he wouldn't feel horrible. He would think I didn't wait for him. That I just moved on and didn't care that he was in a coma.

But I was hurting his shadow by rejecting him. I knew it, could feel it. I could barely look at him this morning because the depth of his pain was carving me out.

If that wasn't enough, I was also hurting him physically because our bond was sick.

I was an awful person, an awful, terrible mate.

And I didn't know what to do.

Pushing out of my chair, I grabbed the book he left on the table.

"I'm"—sniff—"just going to get ready," I said, my voice weak. I sifted to my room before anyone could say anything.

Tears flowed freely as I walked around the room, trying to distract myself by setting out my clothes for the day.

My chest stuttered, sucking in breaths and clenching as the memory of his pain moved through me.

I brought my clothes into the bathroom and laid them out next to the sink, resting the crown atop the pile. My head throbbed. The headache from yesterday hadn't gone away and was ratcheting higher from the pressure of my tears.

I twisted the shower on, forcing myself through my daily routine, but my eye caught on the fourth finger of my left hand, the inked band representing our marriage.

I couldn't feign normalcy while my emotions were taking every drop of my energy to suppress.

I shut the water off, grabbed the book Sebastian left on the table, and sat at the tiny desk in the corner of my room.

It wasn't that I didn't believe him, but I wanted to understand what was happening to us.

Maybe this book held the answers I needed. At the very least, I'd understand the extent of the damage I was inflicting.

I flipped through the pages. It was a basic anatomy book, most of the chapters were something I'd have studied in a college elective course, except for one chapter devoted to "the exchange of magical biology."

The pages were softer in this chapter, like he'd read them multiple times. He'd underlined some paragraphs, and knowing what I knew now, the formal words made more sense than they had when I read them months ago while snooping in his room with Gwen.

There were two sentences underlined on the first page. "The series of muscle contractions leads to a loss of energetic boundaries. The boundaries can be breached through touch, which results in an exchange of magical biology. Once energy is shared, it's incapable of destroying itself or its energetic match."

I translated that into normal people speech. Orgasming lowered energetic boundaries, and we shared powers by touching. After we shared powers, we became unable to kill one another.

To think that if I hadn't slept with him before I tried to stab him in the heart...he would be dead.

Tears welled up, but I blinked them away and scanned the chapter for the bond sickness.

"Auric Bond Anemia (ABA) is a condition that can develop if the energetic boundaries (auras) have been repeatedly broken down, but the bond has not fully engaged. The exchange of magical biology becomes unstable within each of the energetic pair without bond acceptance."

I snorted snottily. Unstable. Yeah, I was unstable alright.

"Symptoms include the following: exhaustion, depression, anxiety, irritability, muscle aches, headaches, insomnia, fatigue, dizziness, chest pain, loss of appetite, problems concentrating or thinking, and decreased magical abilities."

My stomach churned. Sebastian deserved a better mate than me. He deserved someone that didn't try to kill him and then literally give him a health condition.

Nausea wasn't on the list, but that was probably more a side effect of being a terrible person than the bond sickness.

I scanned the rest of the page until I found the treatment heading. "Auric Bond Anemia will disappear once the mating bond has engaged. This is the recommended course of treatment. If the mating bond cannot be engaged, permanent separation of the energetic pair is the only sustainable long-term solution. The bond will break down over an indefinite time. The process is emotionally and physically taxing to the energetic pair, but no reports of death due to bond dissolvement have been reported."

My jaw quivered, and tears fell onto the page, bubbling the paper. I didn't want our bond to dissolve. I loved him. He loved me. We just needed time. This wasn't fair.

I flipped to the next page. "Though not a permanent solution, the pair can delay bond engagement and lessen the symptoms of ABA by stabilizing the exchanged magical biology. The auric field of each individual will relax, putting less strain on the insecure bond, through repeated and prolonged exposure to the aura of its energetic match. The most effective exposure would be regular climax and integration of magical biology of both partners, but touch and physical proximity of the auric fields can also delay symptoms albeit less effectively."

I reread the paragraph several times trying to translate the formal medical wording into something I understood. To stabilize, we needed to be close enough for our auras to touch or physically touch one another or climax together.

I put the book aside to rub my eyes. If this was simply a matter of changing sleeping arrangements, there'd be no problem.

The issue was I didn't trust myself to be around him. Last night at the funeral, I couldn't focus on what was going on because I was holding myself back from touching him, holding him, pulling him into an empty room and fucking his pain away.

Little did I know, I would have *literally* been fucking his pain away.

I opened the drawer of the desk and pulled out a pen and a sheet of paper. I needed to organize my thoughts.

All of this came down to whether or not Sebastian and his shadow were two separate entities or if they were one person.

What made up a person?

Their instincts, their personality, their memories, their judgment, and how they acted all combined to create who they were.

I drew a line down the page, and wrote blue-eyed Sebastian on one side, void-eyed Sebastian on the other.

With blue eyes, he saved me from the draxis at the Welcome Ball. He saved Gwen and me from the solisers and Silas. He brought me to Palagui to save Sloane. He saved me from Xenos. He saved me from Jeremy.

But each of those times he also had, at least briefly, void eyes when he called upon his power. I put an X under his column to indicate they were the same.

Under void-eyed Sebastian, I wrote "impulsive." He killed the guards in the prison, killed Hugo and the guards in the palace, and admitted he would have lied to get me to accept the bond.

But when I thought about it, blue-eyed Sebastian also had his impulsive moments. He got worked up when Delilah touched me in court. He lashed out at Xenos when he suggested scarring me. He lied to me for months about the draxis and the mating bond. I put an X under blue-eyed Sebastian to indicate his impulsivity was similar to void-eyed Sebastian.

Then I wrote every trait that could describe blue-eyed Sebastian.

He was meticulous and a control freak. Tidy to an almost pathological degree.

Smart and competent. The way he solved problems in council meetings and took care of issues was really hot.

He was a workaholic, which made sense since he'd made it his responsibility to keep Palagui running for his mother and Adriana's return.

He was sweet and thoughtful, but he also challenged me, like when he helped me train my darkyra powers after I'd bound them.

He protected me without making me feel weak or helpless. A partner not a savior.

Most of all he cares so fiercely for people, for the citizens of Palagui, for his family. He protected everyone around him, even if that meant protecting them from himself. He loved so selflessly he'd tear himself apart if he thought it'd help.

When his mother was sick and needed power, he got it for her, even though it meant dissociating from himself to get it. He'd denied himself the opportunity to pursue his mate because he thought his shadow might hurt me. He let everyone in Palagui believe he was a scary shadow wielder while trying his best to keep the entire country from falling apart.

And today, he said he thought I was testing him when I asked him to prove that I could trust him.

Of course he would assume I was purposefully making him suffer. That was what everyone in his life expected him to do.

With a deep breath, I leaned back and read over all the traits in blue-eyed Sebastian's column.

I didn't need to finish the list.

Sebastian, no matter his eye color, with his shadow or not, was all of these things, all the time.

The only difference was the way I perceived his actions depending on who I thought was in control.

I assumed he wanted me to accept the bond because he wanted power, but shadow or not, there was only one thing Sebastian ever wanted.

Acceptance. Love. To know he wasn't alone.

And I denied him repeatedly and made him think he would need to walk through fire, tear himself apart, to prove he was trustworthy.

My jaw quivered, and fresh tears followed the already wet paths down my face.

In light of all of this, everything made sense.

Sebastian experienced his shadow as a separate entity. That separation gave him mental distance. A way to divorce himself from the parts of him that he'd been told his whole life were bad.

If he made his shadow the enemy, then all he had to do was prove he wasn't him.

His shadow said he experienced things that the other parts of Sebastian didn't. They had separate memories because he dissociated from his trauma.

His power had killed an entire town when he was eleven. Of course he would want to distance himself from that.

The separation between them was a coping mechanism.

He wasn't two people.

I inhaled deeply as a surety zapped through me, twisted around my spine, and settled in my core.

My shadow and I weren't separate. It wasn't like she didn't exist before my powers activated. I still had gut instincts and impulses. I still had a voice in my head that just knew things. I still had the calmness that settled over me in chaos. I just hadn't had the words to name it before I activated my powers. I didn't have the ability to tap into it on command.

But I hadn't been less of myself.

I was her. She was me.

If Sebastian couldn't tap into all the parts of himself due to the trauma from the prison or the damage to his psyche from the attack in the astral field—that didn't make him less of himself.

It just meant he needed time to heal. He needed my support. He needed to know he was safe and worthy of love just the way he was.

And if I turned out to be completely wrong about this, Sebastian would forgive me.

I would tell him I loved him, all of him, even the parts of himself that he hated. And hopefully, that would be enough to soothe any inkling of perceived betrayal.

With the shadow drama, I'd gotten confused about who I was supposed to be loyal to, but it was arbitrary.

His shadow was him. He was his shadow.

And I was going to love him unconditionally for the rest of my life. I would stand by him no matter what. Just as he would for me.

I've been saying this, my shadow said. *When are you going to start listening to me?*

When you start explaining yourself, I replied.

What I know can't be explained. It is just known.

I rolled my eyes. Maybe one day I'd figure out how to blindly trust my gut instincts, but for now, I needed to look at all the evidence and make a rational decision.

Shouldn't I get some credit though? It's only been a day and a half. At least it didn't take me months to finally listen to you this time. That's progress.

She harrumphed, but there was a twinge of relief mixed with it that I was going to take as reluctant approval.

My head still ached, and my body was still sore, but I felt lighter as the clarity swept through me.

The rasp of a knock on my open door turned me in my seat. Sebastian peered around the door hesitantly. "Can I come in?"

I crumbled the list I'd written, and without taking my eyes off him, I tossed it in the trash.

"Yeah, I was just coming to talk to you." I got up and pushed my chair under the desk. "I'm so sorry."

His face darkened. A burnt bitter taste filled my mouth. Hopelessness.

"I know. It's alright," he said. "I understand. You feel you have no choice—"

I cut him off by racing across the room and wrapping my arms around his torso. "I'm so sorry. I love you. I wasn't testing you. I would never purposefully hurt you like that. I'm sorry."

He stiffened. "I...uh, what?"

Pressing my face into his chest, I breathed in his spicy, sweet sandalwood scent and felt my entire body relax like I was coming home. "I'm sorry for hurting you. I thought I was cheating on you by being with this part of you, but I was just confused. I'm so sorry."

"You...aren't leaving me?"

I squeezed harder and looked up at him, shaking my head. "No. Never. I'm never ever going to leave you. It hadn't even crossed my mind as an option." I put both of my hands on his face and widened my eyes. "Do you hear me? I'm never leaving you. Ever. You're stuck with me forever."

He blinked and opened his mouth but no words came out. His cheeks were cold like he'd been outside, his nose slightly red, and his eyes were a little bloodshot, but he was so beautiful.

"I don't want to accept the bond," I said, stroking my thumbs along his cheekbones. "Not yet. Not until you're better, until all parts of you are here, until we are both settled, but I'm not going to hold back anymore, and I'm not going anywhere."

We'd waited this long to accept the bond, and after everything we went through, I wanted us to be healthy and happy and whole. Our wedding had already been forced on us. When we accepted the bond, I wanted it to be special, to be something we both chose because we loved each other, not because we had to do it.

His brows furrowed, and his mouth was still parted. The burnt bitter hopelessness hadn't faded.

I would just have to show him, so I interlaced our hands and tugged him toward the bed.

He shook his head. "Amaya, I don't think we should—"

"We have an hour until we need to get ready. If we cuddle, it'll help the bond, right?" I said, my face hurting from how wide I was smiling. I hopped on the bed, crawled to the middle, and patted the spot beside me.

"Uh, yeah. Right," he said and climbed on the bed.

When he laid down, I threw my leg over his and wrapped myself around him, holding on like a barnacle. He gradually relaxed, his arm under my head and his hand resting on my shoulder. I smooshed my face into his side, practically in his armpit, and breathed him in.

"Goddess, you smell so good," I said, sighing.

What had I been thinking? I was so stupid. I can't believe I denied myself this. My mind went fuzzy, just full of him, of his scent, of the warmth of his touch.

My shadows seeped out, and I barely noticed until they wrapped around us, cocooned us in their embrace.

"Amaya," he said, his voice strained. "Is this...? Are you...?"

He seemed to be having trouble thinking, but honestly so was I.

I rolled on top of him so my entire body was flattening his. I wished I could crawl inside him, just press into him hard enough that he surrounded me.

Maybe his shadows heard my unspoken plea, because they came out to join mine and hovered around us.

I rested my head on his shoulder, letting my nose trail up and down his neck. His palms made a journey along my back, pressing me even harder into him. The ache in my heart softened from a blinding pain to a subtle twinge.

Nothing else mattered. Everything honed and focused into this moment.

My mate. My mate. My mate.

The person I was a match for. The person the universe made for me to find, to love, to hold. Never again was I going to forget it. He could murder everyone in the world in cold blood and I didn't care.

It was just him and I.

I'd die for him. I'd burn the world for him.

My love for him was so intense. My heart felt like it was going to burst. I wanted him. Needed him.

Our bodies pressed together and his hands on my back sparked a physical need to match the one in my heart. I wanted his skin on mine. A heat spread through me, molten desire pooling in my core.

Unbidden, I started rubbing myself against him, grinding into his groin.

"Amaya, I don't think we should do that," he said, but his voice was anything but convincing. The spice of his cinnamon lust filled my awareness.

"Why not?" I asked and nipped at his ear. "I want you."

"Because it's the bond. It's not…It's just your power."

I thought back to after my initiation, and how he didn't want to fuck me just because my shadow wanted it. He needed to know that I wasn't under the influence, that my need for him was real. I could respect that, but he'd still helped me out after my initiation.

"Okay, we won't fuck," I said and sat up to undo his belt. "There's plenty of other stuff we can do."

"No," he said, grabbing my hands in both of his.

I pouted.

"I just…Just let me hold you, okay?" he said. His eyes were sad, and I hated seeing it.

He needed a different kind of love, and it was my turn to prove to him that he could trust me, trust me to love him.

"Alright," I said. "Can we touch bellies though?"

A confused, reluctant smile spread across his face. "What?"

I lifted my shirt to below my bra and bunched his up too, and laid against him so our stomachs were touching skin-to-skin.

I exhaled a long sigh. The peace and pleasure rippling through me was almost as good as an orgasm. Almost.

He huffed a laugh and wrapped his arms around me. "Yeah," he hummed. "We can touch bellies. I like this."

His hands rested on my lower back, and we stayed like that for a long time, breathing together.

My eyes closed, and I might have drifted off, but it wasn't a deep sleep, just a pleasant floating.

"Why did you come in here anyway?" I asked after we'd laid there a while, and my head cleared from the fog of want. It became a softer pull, still there, but no longer blinding in its insistence.

He shifted under me. "I came to apologize for how I acted downstairs. I'm sorry for being so harsh with you. I should have realized you wouldn't know about bond anemia, but I was confused and for some reason convinced that you did know."

I lifted my head and kissed both of his cheeks. "You don't have to apologize. You didn't do anything wrong. I was being an idiot. And the book said the sickness can make us disoriented so you can't blame yourself for that either."

"You were not being an idiot."

"I am absolutely a dumb, stupid idiot for forcing us to stay away from each other. I'm so sorry."

"No. Don't say that about yourself," he said and squeezed me tight. "You're perfect."

We were interrupted by a feminine squeak at the door. "Sorry," Sloane said, putting a hand on her eyes. "I really didn't think I would walk in on this."

"We're clothed, Sloane," I said and reluctantly rolled off Sebastian and sat on the bed.

She peeked through her fingers and smiled. "I wanted to check on you. You said last night you wanted to be early to the meeting this morning."

I glanced at the clock. We'd been lying here longer than I thought. "Oh, okay. I just need to get dressed."

It felt uncomfortable moving away from Sebastian, not painful exactly, but like the sensation of pulling tape from your skin.

I walked toward the bathroom as he got up. "Wait," I said. "Stay."

He nodded. "I won't leave the room."

I did my best to change and do my hair and makeup as quick as possible.

I situated the crown on my head before returning to the bedroom. My headache lingered, but the happy endorphins flooding my body were making it manageable.

When I walked back into the bedroom, Sebastian was tidying my bed, pulling the covers until the creases we'd made disappeared.

"You're a neat freak," I said, interlacing my fingers with his. The tattoos on our fourth fingers lined up.

He grimaced. "I know."

His eyes were still sad, so I leaned up and gave him a peck on the cheek. "I like it though."

I liked everything about him. I loved him.

His smile didn't meet his eyes, but he squeezed my hand once, and we sifted downstairs to take our friends to court.

Chapter Twenty-Three

Amaya

The brunt of the hurricane didn't hit the CBD. With only some exterior damage and debris from the high winds, most of the city would be reopened by the end of the week. A structural engineer had already inspected the court building and approved it for reentry.

To help heal the bond, Sebastian took the seat next to me, which even before the council meeting started, proved to be distracting.

He'd opened his laptop and was scrolling through some documents when I leaned over to see what he was reviewing.

Purchase orders or something. I was going to ask questions—really I was—but my knees pressed into the side of his leg, and our heads were only inches apart. I put a hand on his forearm, stroking his skin without my conscious control. Spicy cinnamon and vanilla affection filled my mouth, and an electric adrenaline buzzed through me.

He stopped scrolling, and we both watched as I traced a finger along a vein that protruded from his middle finger and twisted down over his wrist. I pictured his hands: his long fingers gripping me, tensing as he grabbed my hips when I straddled him. I imagined biting the hard muscle of his shoulder, sinking my teeth in, and marking my claim along his collarbone and up his neck.

His breathing grew shallow. The tattoos along his arms darkened as shadows rose under his skin. Our eyes met, his searching my face.

I didn't know if he found whatever he was looking for because Sloane diverted my attention. "We heard back from Rien this morning."

"Oh," I said, forcing myself to drop my hand from his arm. How was I supposed to get through the meeting if all I wanted to do was jump him?

"What'd he say?"

"He said he wasn't surprised that you were queen, and it's about damn time they got someone good in charge."

I snorted. "You told him Sebastian and I are married?"

"Yeah, but he didn't comment on that part."

"Well, that was a surprisingly upbeat response. Did he say how the rest of Delnee was handling it?"

"Apparently, the president and vice president are eager to meet the Queen and King and will be extending a formal invitation."

"How kind of them," I said, deadpan.

"Rien thinks that Harrison has officially given up on cuffing the legacy high priestesses, so that's good," Sloane continued.

Nico shook his head. "I still can't believe Harrison made a side deal with Xenos for those cuffs. Xenos couldn't even be bothered to remember to go to council meetings most days, let alone make side deals."

Sebastian pursed his lips. "It doesn't make sense, but clearly Xenos saw some personal advantage in Delnee losing their high priestesses."

"To invade?" Gwen asked.

Sebastian tapped his fingers on the desk. "I don't think so. He just didn't care about that stuff. He wasn't interested in world domination."

"Didn't Rien mention that it wasn't Xenos who met with him to give him the cuffs, just a random person? It must not have been a huge priority for him if he had someone else do it," Gwen said.

"Speaking of, where did those fae cuffs ever end up?" I asked. "The ones Rien switched out for the less powerful versions?"

"Last time I saw them they were at Caroline's house on the night of the engagement party," Gwen said. "They were gone when I checked her place for clues of where she went. Her place was cleared out."

I sighed.

"We'll know if they turn up," Gwen said. "They were unique. Silver cuffs with black numbers etched on the side. I guess Harrison planned to keep track of the legacy high priestesses like prisoners."

Great. I guess we could only hope Daria ended up with them and not Caroline. Or even better, they just fell into the ocean somewhere.

"Well," I said. "At least we have Rien in Delnee to watch for Harrison's next moves, and we can focus on rebuilding Palagui."

"Speaking of wayward parents, I called my mom last night," Gwen said. "Haven't spoken to her since I escaped Daria's basement, but figured she'd want to know I was alive." She rolled her eyes. "Imagine my surprise when I call and say, *hey, I'm not dead, just wanted to let you know your sister betrayed me and my friends and tried to force me to rule Palagui,* and she had the gall to start asking me all these questions about my childhood as if testing that it's really me calling." She flung her hands up. "Can you believe that? No one could pull off pretending to be me!"

I laughed. "Did you convince her?"

"Yeah," she said. "I answered her stupid questions, and she seemed satisfied. Caroline told her she was hiding me for my own protection."

"And you told her that was a blatant lie?" Sloane asked.

"Yeah. She was horrified by what Caroline had planned to do. She said if Caroline contacts her, she'd tell me, but I'm not going to tell her anything important. I...I don't think she had any idea of what Caroline was capable of, but I also know the only people I can trust are sitting in this room."

"Do you think I should be worried about my parents?" I asked. "If Harrison found out who I really was, he could use them as leverage against us."

"No one except Rien and the people in this room know you aren't Amaya Rhodes," Nico said.

I bit my lip. Caroline knew our engagement was fake, but she didn't know I faked my name.

As far as anyone else knew Amaya Mevson was living in Pointedelle and working with Dr. Henderson. There was nothing to tie us together. Even Gwen's mother only knew my first name.

I didn't particularly want to uproot my parents lives if I didn't have to. I should call them later today. They still thought I was working in Pointedelle, and though we were close, it wasn't all that strange to go a month without talking due to our busy schedules.

"They're probably safest where they are for now," Sebastian said. "If anything changes, we'll get them to Rashida's safe house."

I furrowed my brow. "Her safe house?"

Leva entered the room before Sebastian could explain. She sat quietly in her chair, gave us a trepid smile, and then averted her eyes. Her sour yellow anxiety wasn't as strong today.

I should ask Sloane to take her to lunch and make sure she was settling into her position. Given all the bullshit I used to deal with as an anxious female surrounded by blustering males, I didn't want her timid personality to get her crushed or overlooked. If I asked Leva to lunch, I'm afraid she'd be too intimidated by my position to speak freely.

I rearranged the crown on my head as the metal dug into the grooves on the sides of my head. The low-level headache I'd been ignoring flared into full force as the councilmembers took their seats and I started the meeting.

The electrical grid in western Merbany was down, and the engineers informed us they needed to import specialized equipment to fix it. In the meantime, they were focusing on shoring up the other substations and downed power lines.

Our public relations team released an official announcement that a vote would be held in one month for new high priestess and darkyra representatives.

We had almost finished the meeting without any drama when Gerald spoke up. "I should warn everyone I've been receiving messages from SoCo."

I squinted my eyes. "SoCo?"

"Soliser Coalition," he said. "They're a..."

"An elitist gang," Nico said and crossed his arms.

Vince rolled his eyes. "Don't mix the bad with the good. The Soliser Coalition is a reputable organization that has been slandered by a bunch of disgruntled lowlifes."

"What are the messages?" Sebastian asked.

Gerald sighed. "Anonymous letters have been mailed to my office. Juvenile stuff, misspelled words with sticker letters and pictures of graffiti drawings with their logo." He turned to me and explained, "They aren't classified as terrorists or domestic extremists because the legitimate group disavows any illegal act that is undertaken in their name."

"You're making them sound like an organized crime syndicate," Vince said. "The ones making problems are bored teenagers who have twenty bucks to blow on spray paint."

Gerald shrugged. "I know. Normally, I wouldn't have brought it up, but given the nature of the threats..."

"What is the nature of the threats?" Sebastian asked.

Gerald pulled up his phone and flipped it around to show us an image.

Give up the crown or we'll take it back with your head still attached.

"If they knew how uncomfortable the thing was, they wouldn't want it," I muttered.

Sebastian was not amused. His hands clenched into fists, and shadows billowed from him, blanketing the room in darkness.

Grabbing Gerald's phone, I zoomed into the bottom of the picture to make out the symbol in the signature line.

A square with a diamond overlay.

Returning the phone to Gerald, I caressed Sebastian's arm until his shadows receded.

Vince leaned over the table and rudely snatched the phone from Gerald, but even his face paled as he read the threat.

"I've seen that symbol," I said. "Some of the prison guards had it tattooed on their chests."

I turned to Sebastian. "Did you know what the tattoo meant?"

He shook his head. "I've never been told about SoCo."

Gerald looked sheepish. "There was nothing to tell, just juvenile pranks. The security force has never mentioned them to me as a significant problem. They've never made threats to the crown before."

Of course not. Xenos was in charge.

Which is why the prison guards with that tattoo had a vendetta against me for killing Xenos.

"And how do you know so much about them?" I asked Vince.

He winced. "SoCo funded my first campaign," he said. "The actual SoCo, not the SoCo gang. After I realized that they were tangentially associated with crime, I cut ties and have had no contact since."

"A hate group funded your campaign?" Nico asked, incredulous.

Vince massaged his temples. "Not the group who does shit like this. The social club that holds fundraisers and sponsors raffles and has a few club-only bars. I didn't have connections when I first ran for representative, and when they approached me to fund my campaign, I didn't look too hard. I was just grateful, okay?"

I turned to Gerald. "Do we have any reason to believe they can back up these threats? Have they ever done anything other than spray paint their symbol?"

Gerald shook his head. "Like Vince said, it's mostly teenage antics. Breaking into empty buildings, getting busted with alcohol and drugs, graffitiing buildings and parks and bridges."

I rubbed my eyes but nodded. "Keep me updated if any more threats come in. Contact the security force and tell them that if they receive any word on SoCo activity, they'll call us right away. I want to be in the loop on this. Even the juvenile teenage stuff."

I dismissed the councilmembers, and by the time everyone left, my head was throbbing.

I yanked the crown off, ripping a few hairs in the process, and flung it. The metal rattled against the table.

"I hate wearing that thing."

"Why don't you go home and rest? I can handle Merbany on my own," Sebastian whispered.

I shook my head and reached out to hold his hand. "We have to be together for the bond to heal."

His smile was tight, but he acquiesced.

Chapter Twenty-Four

Sebastian

I watched Amaya rub her temples, wishing I could do something to ease her headache. The bond sickness was affecting her more than me.

Your presence in her life brings her nothing but pain and misery.

"I've reached out to palace security to have them reassign the Queen's fae warders to you." I made a mental note to check that we weren't employing any SoCo members.

Amaya furrowed her brows.

"Body guards," I clarified.

She narrowed her eyes, but the expression was replaced by a wince. "I have the crown's power," she said and dug her thumb into the place below her collarbone. "I don't need body guards."

"Yes, well"—I leaned over and gripped her shoulder, replacing her hand with mine and massaging the area over her heart—"Even the queen can't be aware at all times. They'll make sure you're protected from surprise magical attacks."

She sighed, fluttering her eyes shut and melting into my touch. "I've never heard of fae warders?"

"Xenos only used them when he left court since most of the places he went were warded." Or so he thought. There were obviously guards that Caroline or Daria had bribed to change the wards in the ballroom. An issue I already had trusted security advisors looking into. "The Queen didn't need many since she never left the palace, and the palace has multiple wards."

I didn't insist on body guards for Amaya when she first came to Palagui because she mostly stayed in the townhouse or with me and Nico, plus no one other than Xenos was a threat. The courtiers only cared about her presence as gossip fodder.

I reconsidered it after Jeremy tried to kill her, but with all of Gwen's comments alluding to me spying on them...insisting they be trailed by fae warders seemed like a bad idea. And Jeremy seemed like an isolated event.

But she was queen now. Everyone in Palagui had a vested interest in her life. For good or bad.

"I thought wards were difficult to put into place?" she asked. "So how does their magic work? Is it like when I block Gwen's empathy power from reading me?"

"Yes, except fae warders can do that without needing to concentrate. It's a natural expression of their power like your empathy. They can also cast and charge location-dependent wards much quicker than the rest of us."

"Are they darkyra?"

"Any fae can manifest a warding ability."

"Won't it be obvious to whoever wants to attack me if I have a shimmering ward?" Amaya asked. "They'll take out my warder first?"

I sighed. She wasn't going to like this answer. "Depending on the skill level of the warder, the ward can be made invisible...but even so, if your warders fall that gives you a couple seconds to sift away."

She opened her eyes. "They're decoys."

"Yes."

"No. Nope," she said. "Not happening."

She leaned forward and started massaging my heart too. I tried to pay attention to what we were talking about and not the zing of pleasure that her fingers over my heart created.

I needed her to understand how necessary this was.

Together, we were the most powerful fae in Palagui, but we also had targets on our backs.

"Can we compromise?" I asked.

"I'm listening," she said tentatively. She was leaning forward close enough that her knees slotted between mine. Her light citrus scent was tantalizingly close, making my mouth water for a taste of her.

"The townhouse and our offices are all warded to only allow our powers," I said. "But if you leave those three places, can you promise to take either me or the warders?"

She tilted her head and considered.

"I want to keep you safe," I added, letting her feel the extent of my worry and hoping she would take pity on me.

I couldn't lose her. I couldn't bear the thought of living in a world without her.

She took a deep breath and exhaled it out. "Alright," she said. "But you need them too."

"Fine," I said. "If I go anywhere that isn't our house or my office or with you, I'll bring a warder."

"Two warders."

"Two warders," I conceded. Whatever made her agree.

She smiled and stood up. "So am I allowed to use the restroom alone or do I need to wait for you to accompany me?"

I tapped my fingers on my thigh. Court employees hadn't all returned yet, so there wouldn't be too many people around but...

"Oh come on, Sebastian!" she said, throwing her hands up. "I was kidding. No one is going to assassinate me here!"

The words "partner not savior" flashed in my mind.

I sighed. "Fine, but don't go anywhere else. I need to grab some paperwork from my office before we go to Merbany."

She rolled her eyes but leaned down to kiss my forehead. "And don't you go anywhere else either, you hear me?"

My skin tingled from the brief contact of her lips, and I smiled despite myself. "Yes ma'am."

I followed Amaya down the hall, and when I turned the opposite direction toward my office, I tried to rationalize the anxiety that increased the further away she went as coming from the mating bond.

Nico stopped me along the way. "Can I talk to you?"

I nodded, and we entered my office. I rounded the desk, grabbing a few folders from the file cabinets.

When Nico closed the door with a click, I tensed.

He was going to yell at me for being untrustworthy. Or he was going to accuse me of making the bond sick on purpose. Or something else equally untrue and insulting.

Resigned, I sat in the chair behind my desk.

He rubbed a hand over his mouth and paced the length of my office.

"Fuck," he muttered and stopped abruptly. "You know, in the hundred years we've known each other, I don't think we've ever apologized to one another for anything."

I narrowed my eyes. He wanted me to apologize to him?

"We never really fight." He shrugged. "The one time we did, we ignored it after."

I pursed my lips. The memory effortlessly floated to the front of my mind. It'd been the year Adriana disappeared, and Nico decided to enlist in the military.

I didn't want him to go. He didn't want to watch me live as a shell of myself with my powers bound.

Neither of us relented.

He left. I coped. And our friendship ended.

I didn't see him or even know if he was alive for decades.

Then one day, I opened my door to find my best friend offering me a bottle of scotch.

Shock had bolted through me, and I'd mutely shook my head as he asked if my tastes had changed since the last time we hung out.

We poured the liquor, turned on a sports game, and sat beside one another like no time had passed at all. Halfway through the bottle, he said he needed a place to stay, and with eagerness, I told him he could stay with me.

I'd been so relieved that he was alive. That he wanted to be in my life. I didn't care about the fight. He moved into the apartment above my garage, and I got my best friend back.

I flinched inwardly and revised the thought: I mean *he* got his best friend back. *I* certainly didn't care.

But the longer I was in our body, the more seamlessly I was starting to remember.

Like *his* memories were becoming my own.

"The thing is," Nico said, wringing his hands. "I'm sorry."

My head reeled back. "What?'

"I'm sorry for electrocuting you." He cringed. "I'm sorry for accusing you of being untrustworthy. I know you won't believe me, but I thought I had to get him back."

I frowned. None of this made any sense. It must have been some kind of trick or test.

Except I had no clue how to pass.

"I've spent the last day and a half thinking that my best friend was dead," he said. "And this morning, I realized it's wrong for me to treat you like this."

I shook my head, too flabbergasted for words.

"The moments he let you out, when he stepped into his power, I could see it on his face, the relief. That's why I encouraged him to let up on you. I told him you wouldn't hurt Amaya, but he was afraid."

Nico shook his head. "I don't know if he's in a coma, or what, but I see now that you aren't not him." He tilted his head and scrunched up his forehead, thinking, but nodded to himself. "Sounds funny to say, but that's what I meant. You aren't not him. And I'm sorry, and I'm here for you. I'm your best friend if you'll let me be."

I gaped and finally stuttered, "I—I don't know what to say."

He rounded the desk and clapped a hand on my shoulder. "That's okay, buddy. I wouldn't have expected anything else."

"Okay," I said, extending the sound of the word.

He smiled. "We're all coming to Merbany with you, right?"

"Yes, I believe so."

"Great," Nico said. "I'll go find Sloane and Gwen."

"Okay."

He left the office, and I stared at my desk, stunned.

Nothing about this day was making any sense. First Amaya apologizing, now Nico.

If it weren't for what I found while Amaya was changing before we'd left for court, I might have started to believe they were accepting me, but as it stood, I had no idea what their motivations were.

I pulled Amaya's list from my pocket and smoothed out the crinkles on the edge of the desk.

Her full accounting of all the ways I wasn't *him*.

Blue-eyed Sebastian had positive traits and memories, while my column only listed all the times I'd been "impulsive."

Some of his positive behaviors I could emulate. Working long hours came natural to me since I was much better at drafting policies than I was with interpersonal issues.

Tidiness wasn't an issue either. Being unable to leave a room spotless was the reason I'd noticed this crumpled list beside the trashcan instead of in it. I'd been about to toss it when I caught sight of my name. When she came out of the bathroom, I shoved the list in my pocket and pretended to have been fixing the bedspread.

Working, tidiness, solving problems, those I could manage. The problem came with the traits at the bottom of the list: sweet, thoughtful, caring, selflessly loving.

I killed my parents. I took pleasure from taking the high priestesses' powers and turning them into draxis. I enjoyed killing Hugo and those guards. I'd done so many terrible things all so *he* didn't have to live with the memories.

She hadn't finished filling in my traits, hadn't needed to. It was obvious. I was impulsive, vindictive, and selfish.

And I'd never be who she wanted.

This list reminded her of all the reasons she loved *him,* and why she'd endure being with me to pacify the bond until he woke up from his "coma." She wouldn't accept the bond until he was back, but she'd touch me and hold me and say she loved me while she waited for him to return.

I should be grateful.

I should be rejoicing.

I should be smiling and holding her hand and kissing her like I'd dreamt of doing.

But anything she did with me was tainted by my bitterness because she was only biding time until *he* came back.

And when he didn't?

How long would she wait? A year? Two years? Ten? What then? She'd leave me and find someone who didn't *kill people willy-nilly*.

"Guess what." Amaya strolled into my office. "I managed to not get assassinated during my walk down the hallway."

I rolled my eyes. "Glad to hear it, smart-ass." As stealthily as I could, I folded the list and put it in my pocket. Gathering my paperwork and files, I put them inside my laptop bag and crossed the office toward her. She held my hand, like it was the most natural thing in the world, and we walked down the hall to where Sloane, Gwen, and Nico were waiting.

Vince stood to the side, scowling with his arms crossed. "We're ready?"

Amaya nodded cooly.

"Rosalind and Second Street." Vince jutted his chin at me as if I were his taxi driver.

I grunted my acknowledgement and sifted us to Merbany.

The stadium was located at the highest point of the city and was one of the newest facilities in Merbany. It'd been upgraded to handle the huge influx of sports fans that poured in and out during the season.

But in the years since it was built, I'd never seen this many people waiting outside.

They huddled together, sitting on the ground or on flattened cardboard boxes, waiting in a line that didn't appear to be moving. Hundreds of people seemed to have given up waiting and set up camp outside the building.

"We can't sift in," Vince said, pushing through people near the entrance. "We warded it so darkyra wouldn't skip the line."

Amaya and I glanced at one another, but the enormity of the situation—of the amount of displaced people—had muted me.

Vince spoke with a guard, and he waved us through. Angry shouts followed us as we made our way toward the turnstiles.

"The Queen of Palagui needs in," the guard said, pushing people out of the way.

I cringed as the crowd's boos turned into a flurry of surprise.

Tension ratcheted up, and my shadow buzzed under my skin with the desire to cover Amaya, to shield her, but I retained control and refused to do anything she might deem impulsive.

The first thing I was going to do when I got back to court was insist the palace security's fae warders arrived at court tomorrow morning.

Maybe I'd have them follow us anytime we were in public, even if I was with her. Extra security couldn't hurt.

Most people outside the stadium just stared. A few ran their thumbs over their foreheads. The archaic and offensive gesture to signal they were protecting themselves from darkyra mind control.

A female at the front of the line held a child to her hip. She stepped back to let us through and gave Amaya a once over. "You're the queen?" she scoffed.

"Yes," Amaya said but didn't engage more than that. I placed my hand on her back and angled her away from the crowd.

"I never thought I'd see the day," the female said, hiking her child farther up her hip. "Palagui ruled by darkness. Everyone under your control." She tapped her temple. "Not me though, I've been training. You can't get in this noggin."

Neither Amaya nor I commented. There'd be nothing we could say to change her opinion.

We pushed through the turnstiles and entered the stadium.

The roar of talking greeted us.

Sporadic groups of people hung around the main concourse, but Vince explained the system was to corral people around the stadium, collecting blankets, cots, food, and visiting the medical areas, before funneling them onto the field. The lines at each station were moving at a decent pace, so it didn't make sense why the line at the entrance was as long as it was.

We walked across the concourse and toward the center to look out over the inclined stadium seats.

The field was crammed with people. Cots were lined up in organized rows, but the aisleways were congested with chairs and people sitting on the ground. The stadium boards were lit up with emergency announcements instead of game scores.

My shadows were agitated by the overwhelming bustle, on edge with the amount of people and the sense of fear in the air.

I ripped my eyes away from the field as two males approached us with outstretched hands.

"Leon Navarro," the first introduced himself with a firm grip. His stature was as large as Nico's, and his polite smile deepened the wrinkles on his face. "Stadium manager."

"Avery Wright," the second male said. He was smaller than Leon, but he smiled brighter and clasped the other side of my hand as we shook. "Shelter coordinator."

"I've been working with Leon and Avery to keep things as under control as possible," Vince said.

The males exchanged handshakes and introductions with the rest of our group.

"Is there somewhere private we can speak?" I asked.

The noise was at a decibel that wouldn't be conducive to hushed discussions.

Leon led us down the main concourse, passed the medical area stations and along a portion of the stadium that was unused. We stood in an alcove beside a food stand with shuttered rolling doors.

The noise from the field floated up, echoing from the capped stadium roof, but there weren't people around to overhear our conversation.

"We're here to help," Amaya said. "I'm sure you're in contact with PEM as well, but if there are supplies you need, food, volunteers, let us know so we can figure out how to get them to you."

Leon nodded. "We're good on food right now. As soon as Vince contacted us when the storm was predicted, we got our regular caterer to treat it like a sporting event."

"We did have a problem in the beginning," Avery said. "With people hoarding food, but we set up a ticketing system which helped."

"Any other issues?" I asked.

"There have been operational issues," Avery said.

Leon stiffened.

Amaya's eyes narrowed. "I see. And are these issues why the lines outside are so long?"

"The line is long because it takes time to check everyone in. We give them a wrist bracelet, a cot, a food number," Leon said. "It takes a while to get everyone settled."

"The line is long because the background checks take five to twenty minutes each," Avery said, exasperated.

Leon glared at Avery.

Vince pinched the bridge of his nose.

Amaya leveled him with a glare. "And why are there background checks at a shelter?"

Vince looked at her blandly. "What do you expect? Would you want your ten-year-old daughter to sleep next to a criminal?"

"The background checks will be discontinued," Amaya said. "With how many guards I've seen on our short walk so far, I don't see why we need them."

Leon opened his mouth, but his eyes cut to Vince, who gave him a single head shake, and he closed it.

"I agree," Avery said. "Thank you, your majesty. I can let the guards at the entrance know immediately."

"Very good," Amaya said. "Sloane will go with you to determine if there are any guards you can spare for the rescue efforts."

I want to split these two up, get them away from Vince, and see if we get different answers, she sent the thought to me, but I assumed she sent it to Nico, Gwen, and Sloane as well.

"Leon, would you mind showing Gwen the rest of the facilities? We'll catch up in a moment. I'd like to have a word with Vince," Amaya said.

Leon gave a sharp nod and walked with Gwen down the concourse.

Anxiety hung thick around us.

Whether it was from the remnants of the minor confrontation outside the stadium or the magnitude of the loss all of these people were enduring—I didn't know. I wasn't even sure if anyone else could feel it. My heart was racing as if I was under threat, but it made no sense. I was fine. I was better than fine compared to everyone in this stadium.

Amaya turned to Vince, but I suddenly couldn't hear what she was saying.

Across the hall, a boy struggled to carry an opened cot while his father lugged suitcases and bags of belongings behind him.

They'd obviously gotten lost because there wasn't anything down this way, and frustration wrinkled the father's forehead. The boy shuffled behind, sweat beading on his face.

The cot fell from the boy's grip and scraped along the floor. I made a move to help but stopped in my tracks. My body went rigid, sensing something my mind hadn't realized yet.

The father spun back, raising his voice, "I told you not to carry it like that! Do it like I showed you," he said. His anger bounced off the metal walls.

My breathing quickened as my hands started shaking, and a cold sweat broke out over my body.

"I can't," the boy said, in tears, as he pressed and pulled the legs of the cot.

All sound and outside inputs faded as my mind narrowed. The tang of coppery blood filled my nose. Helplessness curdled in my stomach. I was shrinking, becoming smaller.

"Forget it!" the father yelled. "I'll do it myself."

The boy ran down the hall, and the father dropped all his bags and started kicking the cot. "Nothing but a stupid. Worthless. Piece of—"

If I had a heartbeat of time to think—to pause and process—I wouldn't have reacted as I did. However, my mind snapped, and I was no longer standing in a stadium in Merbany.

I was in the living room of my parent's house, trembling as darkness blotted out the sunshine from the windows.

An erratic explosion of my shadows coursed through the corridor, and I did nothing to halt their detonation. They lashed out and wrapped around the male with malicious intent. Sickening bloodlust consumed me. A viciousness, a rage, fueled my shadows as they squeezed the power from him.

When the shadows cleared, a draxis stood in the father's place.

My stomach plummeted.

With an out-of-body awareness, I turned around. Amaya's eyes widened. Horror played out on Vince's face. Nico muttered a curse.

I continued shrinking. I became smaller until I was eleven years old again, standing, staring at my mother because I didn't know what to do, how to fix it, how to save her, how to save myself.

"Nico," Amaya said, her voice calm, steady. Her eyes glued to the creature behind me that I couldn't look at. If I didn't see it, it didn't exist. I hadn't done this. Hadn't hurt someone again. "Capture it," she said. "Do not kill it."

Nico sprinted down the empty hall. The crackle of fire filled the air.

High-pitched female wails pierced my ears as I looked at my palms. Blood. There was blood everywhere. So much blood. It made my shirt stick to my chest. Slimy and thick, it coated my shaking hands.

Amaya stepped in front of me and held my bloody hands in her grip. "You're going to sift Nico to the research center. Can you do that for me?"

A weak, pathetic sound escaped as I opened my mouth. My heart pounded so hard I could feel its pulse in my temples. Fragments of memories whirled through my mind, leaving me frozen in place. Stuck in an endless terror.

My mind was fraying. I was coming apart at the seams. I was lost and afraid and helpless all over again, wandering around in the dark.

"I...I didn't. I'm sorry," I croaked. "I didn't mean..." Worthless, pitiful pleas that wouldn't change what I'd done. Didn't fix the mess I created. I couldn't look at her. Couldn't bear to see her hatred, her disgust.

Small parts of me chipped away, and I began disintegrating. My shadows. Where were my shadows? I was alone. I couldn't control them. They weren't mine. I wasn't me. I didn't do this.

The ground was quaking under my feet. Everything was falling apart around me, crumbling. I was crumbling.

What had I done?

Small hands came to my face and tilted my head until my gaze settled on her. I blinked repeatedly until she was the only thing I could see. Amaya nodded her head slowly. "I know, baby," she said. "You're okay. It's okay."

I sucked in a breath as her shadows surrounded me in a warm embrace.

"Everything's going to be okay," she said as her thumbs stroked my cheekbones, and I sighed a shaky breath out.

Her shadows knitted me back together, and the ground stopped shaking—or it never had begun. There was no blood on my hands. No female screaming.

She kept my entire world from falling apart.

"You're okay," she said. "Everything's going to be okay. I'm going to fix this, but I need you to do this for me. Can you sift?"

I swallowed. My shadows were here. They hadn't left. I wasn't alone. Amaya was here and I wasn't alone.

I focused on condensing the shadows around me and nodded.

"Okay good," she said. "I need you to sift Nico and the draxis to the research center. Then you go home and wait for me. Can you do that?"

"Yes," I whispered. Clear steps. Her calm instructions focused my mind. I could do as she asked. I would do anything she asked.

She released me. My mind emptied of everything except the tasks she'd given me.

As I ran down the empty hall to where Nico had cornered the draxis in a vacant alcove, some part of me heard Vince chuckle. "Well. This changes things, doesn't it?"

Chapter Twenty-Five

Amaya

I fixed my facial expression into a stern neutrality and walked back toward Vince.

He huffed a laugh. "Well. This changes things, doesn't it?"

The mating bond tugged like a rope around my heart, squeezing as Sebastian sifted away. I scanned the corridor, but no one else was around. The only witness I needed to worry about was Vince.

"I don't know what you find funny," I said. "I'm going to have your silence one way or another. It's just a matter of whether or not it'll be permanent."

Vince smirked, but brought his fingers to his lips, miming a zipping gesture, and raised an eyebrow.

I let a beat pass, cycling through my options. Maybe Sebastian and I could wipe his memory like Gwen had taught me to do to humans? If Sebastian and I could freeze a fae, maybe we could wipe a fae's mind.

It would be risky though, and that was assuming Sebastian was able to access the full extent of his powers. He wasn't exactly in the best headspace, and the longer we waited, the harder it was to take a memory. I didn't even know if we had the power to do it.

If only I'd figured out how to use my shadows to shift emotions...but even that wouldn't help. Gwen was able to notch emotions down, but not change them entirely, and neither of us would be able to change Vince's emotions enough to make him into a decent person.

I had to do something though. If the public found out Sebastian created the draxis, it wouldn't just be SoCo calling for my head. Everyone in Palagui would want us dead, and I'd slaughter anyone who tried to hurt my mate.

Vince had to go.

His eyes narrowed as my decision played out over my face.

"You can't get rid of me," he said, a bravado in his voice that was only grating my nerves and confirming my decision. "I have every single soliser in Merbany backing me up. Everyone was already on edge after Sebastian killed Hugo, and if the public sees a pattern of soliser councilmembers being killed, they're going to revolt. Merbany has already expressed concerns about the safety of my life. I've informed them there is nothing to worry about. That our new queen and king are fair and decent, and that Hugo was erratic and going to hurt people. The courtiers are all too scared to say otherwise, but if I end up dead, I know several who will speak up to tell the truth of what happened." He shrugged. "Maybe a few even have a video of the events that transpired."

Hugo had been a one-off, but who knows, maybe his death had been the impetus for SoCo to start making their threats. If Vince has as much sway as he says he does, it could be disastrous.

Could I make Vince's death look like an accident somehow?

I glanced around. The corridor had started to fill up with people who would be witnesses if I killed him here. The influx of people must have been from Avery discontinuing the background checks.

Vince continued, "Gerald might be the soliser representative, but he's only kept his position because the old guard has their traditions. *I* am the one the solisers listen to. *I* am the one they trust. You think there's a few disgruntled solisers in SoCo making threats now? If I mysteriously die, you'll have every soliser in Merbany after your crown. You need me to keep everyone under control."

I frowned, but the angry female outside the stadium was fresh in my mind. There seemed to be a lot of upset people in Palagui, and I didn't need to give them more reason to hate us.

"What do you want?" I bit out.

"Keep the guards assigned to their current positions instead of the search-and-rescue teams. You and I both don't want the soliser businesspeople at our throats."

"Blackmailing the queen and king is a dangerous game, Vince."

He shook his head. "Not as dangerous as the game you're playing. You'll lose everything when the public finds out Sebastian created the draxis. That those missing high priestesses are the shadow creatures lurking our streets."

My eyes widened before I could hide the reaction.

"I can put two and two together. They're taking the draxis to the research center, and that's where the missing high priestesses are being treated for a so-called contagion." He snorted. "Sebastian is the contagion."

Blistering anger surged, and I snapped, grabbing his shirt and pushing him into an alcove that barely hid us from view. "Watch your fucking mouth."

He coughed as my shadows squeezed his throat. "Or what? Will you make me into a draxis too?"

"I'll string you up by your fingernails and make you wish you were dead," I said.

"Then you'll be left with a country on the brink of a civil war. The public turned against you. Merbany won't follow a darkyra queen. Not without me to assure them you are on our side," Vince said, his voice strangled by my shadows.

I curled my lip and released him. He sucked in a gasp of air. "You tell our secret, it'll break your fealty bargain to us."

Vince straightened and fixed his clothes. "I love Merbany and care so deeply about my constituents that I would go through the pain of a broken bargain for them. Besides after word gets out that the King is responsible for making the draxis, it'd only be a matter of time until you were overthrown and a new queen was crowned. My bargain with you dissolves when the crown is no longer on your head."

Fucking bastard.

He put his hands in his pockets. "This doesn't have to be hard, your majesty. We both want the same thing: a strong and stable country."

I gritted my teeth, bristling. My only viable option was to allow Vince to blackmail us.

He tilted his head down the hall. "I think I'll find my own ride home. You've got a lot to deal with on the domestic front."

I watched him saunter down the hall and out of sight before letting myself collapse against the wall. Sixty seconds. I had sixty seconds to panic before reeling it back in.

I put an arm over my stomach and tried to take a breath, but it was stunted, the air flow blocked by the emotions welling up.

The sixty seconds passed, and I'd found little relief, but Sebastian needed me, and I told him I would fix this. Vince wouldn't tell anyone what he saw. Blackmailing us was too valuable.

I readjusted my posture and held my head high as I marched down the hall to find Gwen and Sloane.

We needed to get home. Regroup and reassess.

Sebastian was freaking out. The icy terror that emanated from him when he turned that male into a draxis was unlike anything I'd ever sensed from someone.

It almost brought me to my knees, and I'd only experienced it secondhand. There were no words to describe the way his emotions flooded me. They called out for help, and my mind and body reacted to his panic by sending me into my calm, calculating state.

We hadn't accepted the mating bond, but in so many ways, I was already attuned to him. He needed me, and instinct steered my words and actions to become what he needed. Everything dropped away as I honed into the situation, prioritizing without conscious effort.

That heightened clarity, almost a placid adrenaline, kept me walking until I found Gwen and Sloane, and made our excuses to Leon and Avery, assuring them we'd be in touch.

My friends read the unspoken words in my eyes that there was a problem as we sifted home.

"What happened?" Gwen demanded as we rematerialized in the dining room.

I ignored her and sprinted to the kitchen, then to the living room, looking for him, but my heart was still aching, so he wasn't back yet.

I almost sifted to the research center to find him, but Gwen grabbed my arm.

"Tell us what's going on," she said.

"Sebastian made someone into a draxis."

Sloane sucked in a breath.

"It wasn't like what you think," I started, but black sparkling light shimmered in front of us, and Sebastian and Nico stepped out of the shadows.

I released an exhale, crossing the room toward him. "There you are."

"Were you under attack?" Gwen asked.

"No," Sebastian said, his voice dead, shoulders hunched.

I grabbed his hand, but he didn't look at me, only stared at the ground.

"Then why?" Gwen asked.

"It was an accident," I said, trying to catch Sebastian's eye, but his gaze didn't move from the floor.

This was nothing like the night at the palace. This was different.

"We're going upstairs," I said, sifting us to his room before anyone could say anything to make him feel worse.

They didn't understand and were just making assumptions based on the last time Sebastian lashed out.

Nico could fill them in.

"Come on," I said and pulled him toward the bed. His movements were robotic, but he sat on the edge of the bed.

I got on my knees in front of him and held his hands. I wanted him to look at me—actually look at me—but his eyes were distant and unseeing. "What do you need? What can I do?"

His lips barely moved as he said, "Leave. You shouldn't be near me."

"Okay, anything else but that."

He went mute and frozen. His body tensed.

I swallowed and stood up. He was lost in his head. Lost in whatever trauma he had relived to make him lose control of his shadows.

"How about a shower?" I asked. "We'll get you comfy, and we can watch a movie in bed."

He didn't answer, so I slowly started unbuttoning his shirt. When he didn't stop me, I continued down the length of his buttons and carefully undid the cuffs of his sleeves before slipping the shirt over his shoulders.

"Amaya." The pain in his voice didn't match the lifelessness in his eyes. "You need to leave. You were right not to trust me. I'll hurt you."

"You won't," I said, kneeling to remove his shoes and socks. "You can't. You're my mate, remember?"

"As I've demonstrated today, there are ways to hurt you that won't kill you," he said, monotone.

"You aren't going to scare me away, Sebastian," I said, standing. "It never worked before, and it isn't going to work now. I love you, and I'm never going to leave you."

A flash of anger narrowed his eyes. "You don't love *me*." His eyes went distant again, losing all heat. "And there's no reason you should."

Confusion furrowed my brow. I tried to grab his arm, but acidic disgust stung the back of my throat. A shame so pungent it overwhelmed me long enough to delay my reaction as he disappeared into the bathroom.

I took a deep breath, waiting a moment for the feeling to fade.

The hiss of the shower turning on cleared the rest of the sensation, and I went back into action. We weren't going anywhere for the rest of the day, so I sifted to my room to gather my clothes, phone charger, and laptop.

I deposited them on the nightstand and changed my outfit, before going into his closet and picking out comfy clothes for him.

Then I sat on the bed and waited.

And waited.

And waited.

I'd been anxiously tapping my knee for thirty minutes before it got to be too much. The shower was still running, but the water had to be cold by now. I knocked on the door and called his name, but heard nothing.

The door was unlocked, so I slowly opened it.

"If you don't answer, I'm coming in," I warned. What if he's hurt? What if he sifted away after starting the shower?

There was still no answer. I tiptoed in. The steam rushed out of the bathroom as I entered.

"Sebastian?" I said and pulled the shower curtain back. Visions of him hurt overrode any respect for his privacy.

The water beat down on him. His forehead pressed to the shower wall, leaning over as if he'd been standing there, unable to move this entire time.

"Okay," I said and reached over to shut the water off. He didn't react. I grabbed a towel and wrapped it around his shoulders. "Come on." I slung an arm around his waist to pull him out.

He complied, and I finished drying him off as quickly as possible before dragging him into the bedroom.

I offered him his clothes, and numbly, he dressed.

He seemed to need further prompting to get in bed, so I lifted the blankets and pushed his shoulder as gently as I could until he climbed in, lying on his back, staring at the ceiling.

I joined him on the other side and pulled the blankets over us.

He shuddered when I pressed my face into the side of his shoulder.

"You're making everything worse," he said. "Why are you doing this to me?" His voice was so small and broken it made my heart crack.

"Doing what?"

"Touching me."

"I'm trying to take care of you," I whispered. "I love you."

He rolled, turning his back to me and curling up on the edge of the bed as far away as possible. "Don't bother. I'll never be who you want me to be."

My jaw quivered, but I kept my hands to myself. "You're already exactly who I want. Exactly who I need."

He didn't answer, and though I wanted to respect his boundaries, every part of me, my shadow included, was screaming to give him comfort, something to make his pain ease.

I swallowed and whispered, "I understand you feel like you shouldn't be around me. That you want to protect me, even if that means protecting me from yourself. But I'm okay, and I'm safe, even if you lose control. I've already proved I can wield and redirect your power." I let that sink in before saying, "I'd like to put my arm around you because I want you to know, to feel, that you aren't alone."

I worried my bottom lip, waiting for the rejection.

He thinks he's weak, my shadow said. *Rephrase it so it sounds like it's for our benefit.*

I sighed. "It's for me really. I...my shadow is going crazy right now, needing to touch you, and I won't if you don't want me to...but I really need it."

There was a prickle of guilt because while that was true, I was manipulating him even if I thought it was for a good reason.

He took a ragged inhale, but said in a hoarse voice, "Okay."

I shimmied myself closer, slowly, until my arm wrapped around his torso, hand flat on his chest, and curled my body around his.

My shadow relaxed and filled my body with ease. I tried to infuse that comfort, that peace, into the shadows trickling around my shoulders, cocooning both of us.

His shadows didn't come out to meet mine, but that was okay. He was wary of his power.

I pressed a kiss to the top knob of his spine and flattened my face into the curve of his back.

The sigh that escaped him seemed involuntary as it traveled through his body.

The intensity of his emotions faded, and eventually, despite the chaos of the day, his breathing deepened and sleep overtook him.

I stayed awake as long as I could, watching the rise and fall of his torso, but being pressed to him was loosening the aches from the bond sickness, and I relaxed into sleep.

***

We'd slept through the rest of the day and into the night curled up together, limbs intertwined.

When I woke, his shadows were floating peacefully next to mine. His dreams must have been mercifully benign because I felt no emotions emanating from him.

My stomach grumbled—we'd missed dinner—so I snuck out of bed and into the kitchen.

Gwen, Sloane, and Nico were drinking coffee, leaning against the island counter as I entered. Their sympathetic eyes greeted me.

"How are you? How's Sebastian?" Gwen asked.

"I'm okay. Sebastian is…" I ran my tongue over my teeth. "Not great."

Nico shook his head, radiating a sour yellow anxiety. "The last time I saw him like that…"

"When was that?" I asked, pouring myself a cup of coffee.

He scratched the back of his neck. "He was like sixteen, maybe? We were training with Adriana's instructor outside the palace. The guy was a total dick, but the Queen hired him because he was supposedly one of the best. We were practicing some technique, but Bash wasn't getting it, and the guy went off on him. Bash, well, he…"

"Turned him into a draxis?" I finished after he trailed off.

"He didn't mean to," Nico said. "Immediately he started spiraling out. Adriana and I caught the draxis but had no idea what to do with it, so we put it in the basement of the palace. Bash was a wreck for days until Adriana told him she'd healed the draxis."

"He told me she could do that," I said. "That the portal to her world will open on spring equinox, and he's going to go get her."

"Yeah," Nico said. "That's what he's been banking on for years. The only way I think he could justify taking people's power was because he thought Adriana could fix them."

"But how?" Gwen asked.

Nico shrugged. "I don't know. She never said. Just three days later she told us she'd healed him and paid him to disappear so he didn't tell anyone what happened."

Nico ran a hand down his mouth. "We never saw the instructor again, and the secret never got out. I always kind of wondered…"

"What?" I prompted after he didn't seem inclined to finish.

Nico met my gaze. "If maybe she killed him and told us she healed him so Bash wouldn't beat himself up."

I had to close my eyes to stop the rush of tears. "So there might not be a way to heal them at all?"

"I don't know. His whole plan to go into the portal and find Adriana." Nico shook his head. "It's dangerous, but the hope that he could bring her back was the only thing he had to live for until he met you."

I cringed. His words were like a physical blow with the way they slammed into me.

Silence expanded as the hopelessness of the situation became apparent.

"But what about your vision in the Hollow?" Sloane asked, turning to me. "You could heal the draxis."

"Yeah," I said. "But there was a lot of that vision I didn't understand. I thought it told me I couldn't kill Sebastian because I wasn't emotionally strong enough to do it, and that wasn't true. Who knows what the vision actually meant?"

"If you can heal them, it isn't any normal high priestess healing," Nico said. "Sebastian had the research scientists trying that for decades."

I rubbed my temples as the beginnings of a tension headache flared up.

Gwen sighed. "That's a problem for another day," she said. "We're going to take things one step at a time. The three of us are going to the council meeting this morning, and we'll get the guards reassigned in Merbany to the search-and-rescue team—"

"No," I interrupted. "Vince is blackmailing us."

"He has no proof," Gwen said. "What about the fealty bargain?"

I shook my head and explained everything Vince told me. They were horrified by his threats but unsurprised that he delivered them.

"I should probably come to the council meeting to keep an eye on him," I said, but it was the last thing I wanted to do. I couldn't leave Sebastian, and he was in no state to go anywhere.

Everyone shook their head.

"We've got it under control. We'll keep Vince in line," Gwen said. "You haven't had a second to breathe since breaking out of the prison."

Food and sleep and no responsibilities sounded lovely, but this wouldn't be a fun vacation or even a restful sick day.

I worried my bottom lip. "I just…I don't know what to say to him. He's in so much pain, and I don't think I can fix it."

"You don't have to fix it," Nico said. "You just have to be there."

I thought about how Nico let Sloane experience whatever she was feeling after her kidnapping without pushing her to talk about it.

"Okay. You're right. Thank you."

We ate breakfast together, and I ran down what Sebastian and I planned to do today at the council meeting. After finishing, I gave each of them a hug and sifted back upstairs.

To my surprise, Sebastian was awake, his back to me as he stared out the balcony window.

"Hey you're up—" He turned to me. My eyes fell to the bottle of scotch in his hand.

"I thought you finally listened to me and left," he said, his voice emotionless.

"Nope. Just went downstairs."

He pressed his lips into a flat line.

"Are you hungry? I can go get you breakfast."

"No," he said and threw back his head as he took a hefty slug from the bottle.

"Just thirsty then, huh?" I tried to joke, but his vacant eyes had my smile faltering.

I'd never seen him drunk before and couldn't tell how much of the sway in his body was from alcohol or the aftereffects of yesterday.

"Why don't you come back to bed?" I asked, climbing on top of the covers. "Sloane, Gwen, and Nico are handling stuff at court today, so we can just hang." He stared at me blankly. "And it'll heal up the bond too."

His knuckles whitened as his grip tightened around the neck of the bottle. A spicy anger filled my awareness. "Right. Got to do it for our mystical, magical ball and chain," he said and staggered to the bed.

I squinted my eyes but didn't respond as hurt churned in my stomach.

"You wanna fuck for the bond too?" he said, his pronunciation impaired by the alcohol. "I can close my eyes so you can forget which part of me is in control."

I gaped, momentarily at a loss for words.

He sprawled out on the bed, taking another swallow of the bottle. "Or I can fuck you from behind so you don't have to see me. I know you like it like that. I was there that night. I was there every night, so at least I'll behave exactly like him in bed since I can't be like him in any other way."

Shock morphed into outrage at his crass remarks, and I pressed my lips into a sneer. "Oh, okay. I get it," I said, my hands flying around as my anger rose. "Changing tactics, are we? You can't scare me with warnings of hurting me, so you'll pretend to be cruel until you push me away?"

"It's not pretend," he slurred. "I'm an evil shadow. I'm cruel."

"Your words are cruel, but that isn't who you are." I yanked the bottle from his grip as he put the opening to his lips, and slammed it down on the nightstand before turning back to him.

He glared. "You don't know me."

"You're my mate and my husband, of course I know you." I hopped up onto my knees and faced him. "But it seems you don't know me, or else you're forgetting, but I don't back down when you push me."

His eye twitched.

I waved a hand. "Go ahead. Keep it up. You got me angry to snap me out of my depression. I'll fight back to get you out of yours. I'll do whatever it takes. I'll destroy the world for you if that'll make you feel better."

He shook his head. "You were such a good person before you met me. Before I corrupted and ruined you."

I leaned forward and got into his face. "Uh, uh. No fucking way." I stabbed a finger into his chest. "Don't you dare reduce me to a weak, pathetic little girl that can be molded and manipulated. I may have been her before I was taken to the prison, but I will never be her again."

His jaw dropped. He blinked several times.

His shoulders fell, and I could practically see the fight leaving his body.

He pushed up into a seated position, his face sobering.

A long, tense moment passed until he finally said, "I wasn't...I didn't mean to imply that you're weak."

I sighed. My anger deflating. I didn't blame him for lashing out. I did it too when I was hurting.

"I know you didn't," I said. "You just want to use my choices as another weapon to beat yourself up with, but I'm not going to let you get away with it."

"You aren't—and never have been—weak, Amaya," he said, full of conviction.

"I was. I used to be," I said. "I let Gwen and Sloane convince me you were bad. That Caroline and Daria knew more about the person you are than I did. I didn't listen to my heart...to my shadow."

Was it wrong to want to kill Vince to keep him quiet? To lie to the council and the country about the draxis? Morally speaking, yes. But as my time in the prison taught me, as Kai had always been telling me, I was more dark than light.

I'd do whatever it took to protect Sebastian. To protect my family.

"Our shadows aren't always right, or react appropriately, but they are only trying to protect us," I said.

That was what happened yesterday with him. I was sure of it.

Silence filled the space between us. The spice of his anger shifted to bitter sadness.

He swallowed. "I'm sorry. I shouldn't have said those things. I don't want to be cruel to you. I don't want to hurt you."

"I know you don't," I said, fighting the urge to reach out since he hadn't wanted my touch yesterday. "It's okay."

He pressed his fingers into his eyes. "It's like the more I don't want something to happen, the more likely it is to transpire. Sometimes I can't tell if I'm in the present or the past. How can it be that"—he took a ragged breath—"I'm finally in control of my body, but I've lost control of my mind? I get stuck reliving the same moments over and over to the point that I recreate them."

I clutched my hands around my torso, wishing I could comfort him in some way. "That's what happened yesterday? You got stuck?"

He nodded.

After what Nico explained this morning, this wasn't the first time.

"A part of you recognized a threat and reacted. Your trauma responses don't make you a bad person," I said.

"Sometimes I like doing it. That's what makes me a bad person," he snarled. "I like the feeling of taking power from people. The freedom, the power, the control, all rushing through me. It's fucking exhilarating."

"I liked killing those guards," I said. "I liked feeling powerful. Sometimes I relive those memories to fall asleep at night."

"It isn't the same. You were only protecting yourself."

I pursed my lips. "As you've reminded me before, it may have started that way, but it wasn't all self-defense." It was also revenge.

I turned to him, getting closer until my knees pressed to the side of his thigh, but he refused to look at me. "Sebastian, you've been locked up in a tiny piece of your mind with no power, no control, no freedom. It's like you've been holding your breath for a century, so of course a lungful of air feels good. That doesn't mean you are bad. It means you've had bad things happen to you."

He clenched his jaw.

"In fact," I continued. "I think what happened yesterday is proof of how good you are. You spared one part of yourself the agony of remembering all these years. The only reason he shut you away was because he couldn't control what was happening to him, not because you're bad. If he focused his anger on you, it meant he wouldn't have to hate himself."

Silence filled the room for several moments.

Sebastian stared up at the ceiling, blinking several times until he finally whispered, "But I hate me." The agony in his words cut deep, the taste of vinegar in a wound. "And I don't know how to stop."

My chest hitched as I fought to suppress a whimper. Waves of helplessness crashed into me through him.

I knew that feeling of self-hatred intimately, battled with it my entire life. I had believed I was never good enough, and my mind performed intricate acts of self-deception in order to convince me that all I needed to do was work harder, reach this goal, then this one, and then I would finally be worthy.

Except achievement never provided the relief that was promised.

It was the same for him. Leading Palagui, saving his mother, saving his sister. He'd undertaken all of these impossible goals in an effort to prove to himself that he wasn't the evil shadow the world made him out to be.

The irony was my feelings of inferiority only began to dissolve when I listened to my shadow, felt into her power, *my* power, but Sebastian couldn't integrate with himself in that way. Not with parts of him lost or asleep or...gone.

I didn't know how to help him or what to say, so I did what Nico suggested and closed the distance between us.

He tensed when I wrapped my arms around him, but the stiffness eased, and in the next moment, he turned toward me, resting his chin on my shoulder and embracing me back.

He took a deep, uneven breath.

"I love you so much," I whispered into his neck because even if it didn't fix anything, maybe if he heard it enough, he would start to believe it.

And maybe, if I tried really hard, I could love him enough for the both of us.

Chapter Twenty-Six

Amaya

An omnipresent sense of foreboding followed us through the next three months.

Sebastian's trauma had no resolution, and I could see the specter of dread haunting him each day from the tension in his shoulders and the vacant look in his eyes.

We didn't discuss what happened again, except when I asked him if he could explain what had caused his flashback. If we knew what triggered it, maybe we could avoid it.

But he hadn't been able to speak about the incident. He became inarticulate, mouth moving, opening and closing, reaching for words he couldn't find. His body became stuck in a strained position, holding a hand over his chest, clenching and unclenching his fingers.

There were layers to his emotions that permeated my senses. A thick shield of numbness barricaded the intense and inexplicable feelings underneath. There was no taste, no color, only a stomach-dropping sensation of the ground disappearing from under my feet. A frozen panic and helplessness, all wrapped up inside the shame of subjugation from something that was not tangible and had no end.

It was horrifying to feel secondhand, and I had no desire to send him back to that place by asking again.

I assumed it was a flashback to the quake that killed his parents in Merbany. Hopefully, it'd only been brought on that day due to the combination of stress and exhaustion from the bond sickness.

I initially protested when he said he wanted to collect the draxis that were still in Palagui.

It made sense to do so—it would protect them and others—but I was concerned about it triggering his memories.

But he insisted. So we went together after work and transported the draxis to the research center.

Other than a tense silence, he had no outward reactions.

I'd asked him why he was able to create draxis but other darkyras couldn't. He assumed he inherited it from Kai. The power to create a draxis was similar to the power all fae had to borrow and pull on another's powers, it's just Sebastian could drain someone while the rest of us were only capable of borrowing a tiny slice when that person allowed it.

After he answered, I changed the subject rather than continue to pick at his wounds with my curiosity.

Sebastian had lived with his trauma for a century—his shadow had held it apart from his consciousness—but it always lurked under the surface, and he coped with the trauma in the same way he had in the past.

By distracting himself with work.

Each day was another test to find solutions to impossible problems. There was no policy, no law, no amount of emergency funding, that could have fixed everything that was wrong in Palagui or even put it back into the position it had been before the hurricane.

Three weeks after the hurricane, the shelter in Merbany had been vacated. Citizens were transferred into short-term rentals in Molbridge or Palagui City, and we worked on diverting funds into interest-free loans to businesses and housing assistance to individuals.

Debris removal had finished, and buildings were repaired or demolished, but our biggest drain on our capital was the construction delays in western Merbany due to the power outages. The electrical engineers were still waiting on imports of specialized equipment. Crews couldn't build new houses without electricity, which meant citizens had to stay in provisional housing that Palagui's government funded. There was nothing we could do except wait for the shipments to come in.

We estimated we could continue this level of public funding for a few months, but each day that passed without the imports was another day closer to Palagui running out of money.

We weren't bringing in money either. The hurricane knocked out several of the factories that manufactured most of Palagui's exports, putting our balance sheet into the red.

Sebastian had reached out to the international monetary fund for aid the first week after the hurricane, but our short-term promissory notes were coming due soon, and while we could transfer them into longer term loans, the IMF wasn't going to be fooled for long if we didn't start paying back what we borrowed.

Palagui was a small country, and other than some metal reserves, we didn't have natural resources to entice other countries to invest in our reconstruction.

Sebastian spent decades as an ambassador trying to forge alliances, but Palagui's friendship with Delnee—a country of fae suppressors—angered the rest of the world.

Delnee was our closest ally. Our only ally.

And turning our backs on Delnee would mean angering a country that could have warships on our shores in two days with no guarantee of allegiance from anyone else.

We couldn't risk it, especially since public relations within our own country was tenuous at best.

Vince was using his leverage on us to make sure that soliser companies were awarded the rebuilding contracts so he could curry favor from the prominent businesspeople in his region.

To top that off, the changes I wanted to make—removing the laws against humans and darkyras and setting up grants and positions to help counteract the pervasive discrimination—were all shot down by the councilmembers.

I was the queen and could do what I wanted, but given how much turmoil the country was in, it was thought best to focus on getting Palagui up and running before making huge changes.

It bothered me, but I understood their reasoning. People were trying to get back on their feet, and Sebastian and I had enough policies and budgets to look through without adding more to our plate.

There'd been one issue I'd been steadfast about enacting as soon as possible though, and I couldn't have been convinced otherwise, despite the fact it was the most unpopular thing I'd done as queen so far.

Our swift action after the hurricane gave us an initial boost in popularity, but I lost what respect I'd gained after announcing that a human representative would be added to the council. The media spun outrageous stories about horses being the next group to get a council seat, given horses had more physical power than humans did.

Insane media coverage seemed to become the new normal as every decision we made—and my very existence—was spun as being bad for Palagui. Money given to shelters was reported as money being taken from taxpayers. A report on the decline in children's health was also my fault because *clearly* it was due to fae power being funneled through a darkyra queen.

Though I couldn't see how I was contributing to that, I did wonder if the public could see through me.

That they hated me, not from darkyra discrimination, but because they could see the color of my soul as well as Kai could.

That they knew what I dreamt of at night. The sick pleasure I took from my memories of killing the prison guards.

Could they see on my face the way I imagined my shadows strangling the worst of the instigating newscasters, especially the ones on Fire News Five?

Maybe they had every reason to distrust a darkyra queen.

Most days, I didn't let myself linger on those thoughts, rather I tried to ignore the media and focus on what I could control.

The vote for the new high priestess representative got pushed back because the High Priestess Society wanted more time for candidates to develop their platforms, so Gwen continued acting as temporary liaison.

Darkyras and humans didn't have societies, but if the high priestesses needed more time to organize candidates, they probably did too, so we pushed all of the council votes to the spring.

It was like the promise of spring held all of our hopes within it. I wasn't sure a time after spring equinox even existed, because my thoughts of the future begun and ended on that day.

The portal would open. Adriana would come home. The draxis would be healed, and Sebastian could finally find peace.

And though I worked, joked with my friends, and called my parents from encrypted phone numbers, it was like I wasn't really living life.

In some ways, I understood what Sebastian meant when he said he didn't know if he was living in the past or the present. I felt as though I wasn't living in the present at all, just waiting for the day in the future where all our problems would be solved.

Then I could finally relax.

I could finally live without fear.

I could fall asleep without having to comfort myself with images of torturing those who hurt me.

I would finally be able to accept the bond with my mate. And the ache in my heart, and the one between my thighs, would end its ceaseless throbbing.

The bond sickness never got as bad as it had. I still got headaches, but attributed those to stress.

And while sleeping next to Sebastian helped the worst of the symptoms, it didn't curb my desire.

Some nights I swear I could feel his shadows chasing me in my dreams, but when I woke, it would only be mine that were hovering around us. Like even in sleep, he didn't trust himself to relax his hold on his power.

And while he wouldn't rebuff me if I held his hand or touched him, he rarely initiated himself.

Once in a while, he would catch me pressing into the pain in my heart, and he would reach out and massage the ache away.

Though it always returned the second his fingers left my skin.

There were moments that insecurity convinced me he was avoiding me, moments my shadow would scream out that we were losing him, but logic told me he wasn't avoiding me. He was avoiding himself and the thoughts of self-hatred that being near me prompted.

I spent many nights trying to stay awake until he came to bed, thinking about how he'd said I didn't love *him*, that he could never be like the other parts of him.

I couldn't figure out how to convince him that wasn't true, so I tried to be what Nico had been for Sloane. A constant presence, waiting, but not pushing. We were physically recovered from the prison. Our scars had shrunk and could only be seen up close. Our bodies filled out, no longer a sickly gaunt, but there was still a darkness in Sebastian's eyes that had nothing to do with his shadows.

In time, he would see I wasn't going anywhere. That we were better together.

I just hoped I had the strength to wait.

Wait for him to work through his trauma and come back to me. Wait for the portal to open to save Adriana. Wait for construction equipment to arrive to rebuild Palagui. Wait for the country to accept my *radical* ideas for equality.

And so weeks passed, waiting, as I continued to live for a day in the future that I wasn't sure would ever come.

Chapter Twenty-Seven

Amaya

A slow methodical thump began somewhere behind me. Footsteps, a heartbeat, the rhythmic breathing of something dangerous stalking me.

My heart rate climbed as excitement mixed with a hint of fear.

I ran. Running and running, running forever. I ran into a dark haze of shadows. They swept along me, clinging to me. They tightened around my wrists and ankles and dragged me back to slow my escape.

I fought their restraint halfheartedly.

We both knew I was faking.

We both knew the fire in my belly was stoked when we played this game.

I struggled against the shadows, but my thrashing was thwarted, and the edge of fear magnified as I realized how strong their grip was, how easily they could overpower me.

Breath tickled the back of my ear, and shadows fluttered around me, veiling my vision, blurring everything into a sparkling black haze, which twisted around my head like sheer fabric. Around and around and around.

The shadows chilled my spine as they traced a freezing path down my neck, my shoulder, along each ridge of my spine, over my hips, down my thighs.

My nipples hardened and peaked, but I tried to suppress my shiver.

A deep male chuckle filled the air as I attempted to fight my body's reaction.

The flash of familiar hands, a glimpse of a naked back, a bare shoulder, emerged in the distance. Recognition and desire flared within me.

I clawed the shadows, ripped at them like I was tearing down curtains that kept me away from him.

I yanked at them as he walked away, quicker now, until I was free.

I ran. Each step, each patter of my footfall, took me closer.

He'll be mine. Mine. All mine.

Except the faster I ran, the faster the shadows reemerged, taking me further and further from him. The ground disappeared from under my feet and took the breath from my lungs.

Shock became anger, and anger became tearful frustration. The darkness thickened until I was blind.

Arms grasped me around the waist from behind, and a hand covered my mouth as I tried to scream.

"Shhh," he whispered. My body sagged against him from the resonance of his voice. "Is this what you want?"

The hand on my mouth fell away, the backs of his fingers caressed my jaw, my neck, in a soft barely-there touch. My legs shook in anticipation as his fingers traced the valley between my breasts, over my stomach, to the button of my pants.

He fingered the metal button, pressing it into the hole. I could feel the parting of the teeth of the zipper, slow, impossibly slow, the metal releasing bit-by-bit.

The fabric didn't need to be removed. His hand was there now, inside my underwear, cupping me where I was warm and wet and aching. I ground my pelvis into the palm of his hand, impatient for more.

"Desperate for it, aren't you?" he said as his nose ran along the shell of my ear. "Are you going to take your pleasure like this? The

orgasm will wash through you so quick, and I'll be gone. You'll be left with nothing."

I whimpered.

"Spread your legs," he ordered.

His middle finger broke away and stroked my folds with a feather-light touch, teasing and testing. "How long do you think I can keep you on the edge?"

Teeth nibbled my neck. "Can I keep you for eternity? Will you stay here at the edge and be mine forever?" The words elongated, like a request that had no hope of ever being granted, but wrapped in a desperation that forced the words to be spoken aloud anyway.

I was at a loss, confused, but safe. Held in the stasis state of a dream where words and sentences didn't make sense, but I could feel the intentions behind them.

A tap on my clit. A tap, tap, tap. A finger slick with my arousal spread open my folds, dipping inside just a knuckle before retreating. My chest heaved, and my legs shook from standing and holding myself upright. He gave me no comfort, no relief, no release.

My body gyrated against his hand. His fingers, too slow, too soft, too far away from where I needed them, almost like they weren't there at all, the ghost of a sensation.

He was speaking now, whispering words into my ear. Dirty, filthy, wicked words spinning around, melting into a moan that rocked me from the inside out, full of need and desire and unspoken promises.

The heat and the need continued to gather like fire carving its way through a forest, incinerating anything in its path, dangerous to be near, deadly to be within, and impossible to escape.

My pulse quickened as the thumping behind me increased, the heightening of danger, the darkness hunting me like prey. It was coming closer now. Lips kissed and sucked along my shoulder. Teeth bit on the flesh of my neck, sinking into the vulnerable skin.

His hard consonants turned into soft syllables that rolled on and on like thunder in a valley, an echo of darkness, of love, of desire.

"Need you. Make me yours. Need you to make me yours," I said. They were the only words I had been able to form as every nerve ending held taut, ready and willing to be shattered from his touch.

I begged for my destruction, but his answer was lost to the sound of a long agonized groan. Every emotion compacted into a strange dark language, refracting from the inside out, painting the shadows in rainbow sparkles.

Until the final touch broke me.

The shadows, like the cracks of ice, fractured. Small at first until the fissures spread, plunging me into a freezing darkness, all-consuming, all-encompassing.

I cried as the pathetic orgasm rolled through my body, little jerking motions of my hips that gave no pleasure. A pained moan escaped my lips. Tears gathered in my eyes from the frustration.

I was shaking.

No. I was being shook. By a hand on my shoulder.

I woke to soft light chasing away the darkness. Sweat clung to my forehead and pooled in my lower back.

"Hey. Hey," he said. His voice was softer than it had been in my dream. "It's okay. It was a nightmare. You're safe."

I blinked and sat up. My eyes adjusted to take in the bedroom.

Sebastian was rubbing my arm with one hand and pushing my hair that was plastered to my forehead away with the other.

"You're okay. It's safe," he repeated.

"A nightmare?" I asked, disoriented.

He frowned but kept stroking my hair. "I get them too."

I blinked at him. "You get nightmares?" He had never woken me up with one. I had no idea.

He sighed. "Well, only when I fall asleep at my desk. I don't get them when I'm with you."

"Oh." The bedsheets were damp with my sweat, and I pushed them away, tossing my legs over the edge of the bed.

"Do you want to talk about it?"

"No." Shame heated my cheeks. I couldn't explain that I woke up screaming and moaning not from memories of torture, but overpowering lust for him. After the physical and psychological torture that we endured in the prison, of course he would think it was a nightmare. It was weirder that I hadn't had one since...well, since the last night I slept alone.

Being next to each other had kept the nightmares at bay, and I hadn't even realized.

"I'm going to shower," I said, making my escape before he could scent my arousal or sense my deception.

He inhaled a ragged breath. "Okay."

I closed the bathroom door, leaned against it, and slid to the floor. The muscles of my abdomen ached. With my head in my hands, I fought the urge to cry. It was stupid, embarrassing, and pitiful. Sebastian had actual nightmares, reliving painful memories that haunted him, while I fell asleep beside him conjuring illicit dreams about his shadows and his hands.

That I could blame the unfulfilled mating bond for my imaginings did nothing to relieve my guilt.

One thing was for sure: I wasn't going to be able to keep this up much longer.

I didn't have the severe symptoms from the bond sickness anymore, but I was going stir-crazy, and not just from the gap between me and Sebastian, but everything, all the things I was in a holding pattern for.

I was constantly tense, waiting for a future date to arrive. I wasn't going to make it to spring equinox without changing something.

I pushed up off the floor and got into the shower.

As I stood under the stream, pieces of my sex dream floated behind my eyes, but they rearranged themselves into something my mind hadn't been able to comprehend while I was sleeping.

I'd been running from the shadows, trapped in them, and only when I clawed my way through, did I get what I wanted.

Maybe the dream was a vision like in the Hollow. Maybe I couldn't keep biding my time, trapped in this waiting period. I needed to take action. To do something.

Anything.

The shadows beckoned me forward in the Hollow too. Some innate part of me came to life. Maybe the dream was part of my shadow's knowing, visions of what she couldn't articulate.

She was silent in my head lately, only speaking up to encourage me to be near my mate, touch him, feed him, care for him. The distance he put between us was wearing her thin.

There wasn't much I could do. I couldn't make the imports of equipment come faster. I couldn't prevent Palagui from losing money or make the portal open. I couldn't do much of anything other than my day-to-day duties.

But my vision in the Hollow kept playing over in my head as the water in the shower went cold. I had hovered my hands over the faces of Sloane, Gwen, and myself as draxis and healed them.

Maybe *I* could heal the draxis. They were shadow creatures, and I was a darkyra. The draxis were husks of their former bodies, and I had high priestess healing. The draxis lost their power, and I had the power of the crown.

If anyone in this world could figure it out, it was the girl with the crown, right?

I turned off the water and got out of the shower, feeling clearer in my purpose and already less stifled. Healing the draxis was a goal I could focus my attention on, and if I could do it, Sebastian would have one less reason to hate himself.

The lamp on the nightstand was still on when I made my way back into the bedroom. Sebastian was sitting with his back against the headboard, staring at a book on his lap, though he didn't seem to be reading it.

"Feel better?" he asked, setting the book aside.

I nodded, lifting the blanket and slipping into bed.

He'd changed the sheets for me. Goddess, he was so sweet. It made my heart ache, my bones ache.

He clicked off the lamp, plunging the room into darkness. The bed rustled as he settled in.

"Sebastian?"

"Hmm?"

I swallowed. "I'd like to go to the research center and try to heal Jeremy."

With my void eyes, I could see he was staring at the ceiling. "The scientists have been trying to reverse engineer the process for decades..."

"I know," I said. "But I was able to filter the poison from Sloane's blood by combining my powers. Maybe I can do something they haven't been able to?"

He sighed and didn't respond for a long time, but I didn't detect any overwhelming emotions.

"Okay," he finally said. "But I need to come with you. I don't want you to be alone with him. It's too dangerous."

"Because you want to keep me safe?" It was a stupid question. He'd hired fae warders for me. Obviously, he wanted to keep me safe. But knowing he loved me and hearing it from his lips were two different things.

He turned on his side, his void eyes meeting mine. "Yes. To keep you safe."

I gave him a small smile. Not exactly a declaration of love, but more verbal affection than I'd gotten in months. Bunching up my pillow, I closed my eyes and hunkered down.

"Hey." His voice came gentle as a shadow in the night.

I opened my eyes, and he stared back.

"I could hold you if you want,' he said. "Maybe it would keep the nightmares away."

A yellow sour anxiety accompanied the offer. I wasn't sure if he was still worried he would hurt me or if it was for some other reason.

Guilt over my lie made my stomach clench. He was only offering because he thought I was scared, but there was no way I'd be able to pass up the opportunity to be in his arms.

"Okay."

He laid on his back, and I crawled over to him, resting my cheek on his chest, my hand over his heart.

His fingers stroked along my face, temple to jaw, lulling me to sleep. Every part of my body relaxed. My shadow sighed and unfurled the tension she'd been holding.

He didn't say anything, but when he was holding me, he didn't need to. I could feel the intention even in the absence of language. His heartbeat under my hand thumped out the words I wanted to hear.

Th-thump. *Love.*

Th-thump. *Mate.*

Th-thump. *Mine.*

Chapter Twenty-Eight

Sebastian

I gave up resisting.

My plan to work and distract myself to the point of exhaustion backfired. It shredded my will to stop myself from touching her. In the middle of the night, her cries spurred an instinctual reaction within me. A necessity that I was powerless to defy.

Touch. Mark. Claim. Protect.

It was shameful how her moans of terror aroused me, but I blamed my body's response on the fact I'd been resisting her for far too long. I wanted her naked skin on mine, her hands on my cock, her arousal on my tongue, her breaths panting in my ear, but I compromised by offering to hold her under the false pretense that maybe my touch would soothe her subconscious.

It was a paltry substitute for what I really wanted.

I wasn't withholding to make us miserable. It was just that each time my skin pressed to hers, each time her shadow cried out for me, the voice in my head reminded me I wasn't the person she wanted me to be.

I tucked Amaya's list in my shirt pocket every day. It would burn its folded square mark over my chest until I became the Sebastian she outlined on her note.

I needed to save Adriana, heal the draxis, rebuild Palagui, and fix my broken mind.

Only then would I deserve her. Only then would I be worthy of her touch and the bond between us.

And yet, I was—and have always been—a selfish bastard.

In the stillness of the night, as her breathing evened out and her shadow clung to me like a second skin, I admitted to myself I would never be *him*.

The truth was there was no strength of will I could summon to stay away from her any longer.

Amaya didn't have another nightmare, but she let me use it as an excuse to pull her into my arms every night.

I gave up trying to put distance between us. We had breakfast together in the kitchen and ate lunch together at court. She made silly excuses to see me in my office during the day, and I always found a way to touch her, brushing against her as we passed in the hall or resting my hand on her thigh during council meetings.

Hope grew in her eyes each day, but she didn't ask me about the flashbacks or force me to discuss my past for which I was grateful because I couldn't find the words to explain it. Even if I could describe the moment my life altered course, retelling my memory wouldn't bring me relief, it would only transfer some of my grief and helplessness to my confidant.

And I couldn't do that to someone, much less my mate.

So I twisted reason and logic to convince myself that I was only indulging in her touch to help the mating bond and prevent her nightmares.

I still feared another flashback occurring, and when I was around other people, I remained hypervigilant as if that alone could prevent it. It was exhausting to be constantly on guard for something that could happen at any moment, but I had no other choice.

The weeks passed, and despite no longer burying myself in work in an attempt to distract myself, there was no end to what needed done. Amaya had said she wanted to see if she could heal Jeremy, but we hadn't had a single free day to do so.

Nico had returned to teaching after taking a short sabbatical to help us manage Palagui.

The High Priestess Society was consuming more of Gwen's time than would have been ideal as they tried to keep their organization running while finding candidates for the representative position.

Sloane helped me and Amaya with our numerous administrative tasks, approving new budgets and finding funding from our dwindling reserves to ensure citizens didn't go hungry or homeless.

Our main issue remained that our electrical engineers hadn't received their equipment imports. Our suppliers indicated they'd been sent, but we'd never received them, and not only were we wasting money reordering things that weren't being delivered, the time wasted waiting was an expense Palagui couldn't keep footing for much longer.

Needing to get to the bottom of the situation, I sifted to talk to the port manager in person about what was happening.

"I've spoken with companies in three different countries," I said to Jenai, the port manager. "They claim they've shipped the equipment, and those shipments were accepted by Palagui. These countries have no reason to lie. We've been trading with them for decades."

If it wasn't against international policy to sift into a foreign country without getting proper approvals and going through customs, I would have been knocking on their doors demanding answers.

Hell, I would have tried to sift the equipment to Palagui myself, but since the equipment was too large to fit on an airplane, I wouldn't have been able to sift it across the ocean either.

Jenai handed over a record of our port logs and shook her head. "One lost shipment is bad luck. Three lost shipments is foul play.

Someone must be intercepting the ships and accepting the equipment by pretending to be us."

I rubbed my forehead, flipping through the documents.

Palagui's topography made an eastern port impossible, meaning all ships from the east had to go around the southernmost tip and cut north in order to sail into our port.

Based on maps drawn up hundreds of years ago, the waters between Palagui and Delnee were not bisected evenly down the middle, and for boats to get into our port, they sometimes had to cut into Delnee waters to make the turn.

We had a good relationship with Delnee because we were the only country that would continue to deal with them after they suppressed their fae population, so it had never been a problem that our imports technically crossed into their waters.

But if Delnee thought we were weak—thought the power transfer and the hurricane were opportunities to exploit us—all they would have to do is pretend to be us, flag the ships down in the middle of the ocean, tell their captains there was a problem with our port due to the hurricane, and steal our goods in the middle of open water.

We bought most of our naval resources from Delnee itself, meaning our ships would look similar. They would need to forge some paperwork to prove they were authorized to receive the shipment, but that'd be easy enough.

And without those goods, we couldn't rebuild. We would keep hemorrhaging money until the IMF cut us off. When population unrest spread—already primed by the hatred of a darkyra queen and king—Delnee could overthrow us.

"I think you might be right, Jenai," I said, shaking her hand after gathering the paperwork she gave me. "I'll take care of it."

I sifted to court. I needed to get back before Amaya found out I left unaccompanied by fae warders.

Luckily, she wasn't waiting in my office with a stern expression. She had several television appearances she needed to make this afternoon and was likely preparing for those with Blake and our public relations team.

I sank into my office chair.

Before I accused our only ally nation of sabotage, I needed proof. I needed to get ahold of the captains of the ships sent by the three countries we ordered from. I needed to get someone in our naval force to spy on Delnee waters.

I started dialing from my office phone to authorize another shipment of equipment when there was an impatient knock on my door, and someone swung it open without waiting for an invitation.

"You aren't busy, are you?" Gwen said. She crossed into my office and plopped in the seat across from my desk before I could reply.

"Not at all," I said dryly and returned the phone to its base.

"Good," she said, either not hearing my sarcasm or, more likely, ignoring it. "The Society is up my ass about everything lately! Can we move up the vote so I can stop getting five phone calls a day about every little thing? I swear they act like no high priestess in Palagui can even blink without my permission to do so."

I leaned back in my chair, trying to catch up to what she was talking about and how it concerned me.

She continued, "Yesterday I got a call from the event coordinator because she asked me what color theme I wanted for the annual gala. I gave her the first color to pop into my head, and she spent the next two hours explaining to me why that color wouldn't work." She slumped down in the chair. "I'm exhausted. If I wanted to plan parties, I would have married a rich old guy. I'm a high priestess for Goddess's sake. I have actual issues to attend to, like vetting the people running for representative."

I squinted my eyes at her, and when her rant seemed to be over, I leaned forward. "Not that I don't sympathize with you,

Gwen, but why are you telling me this? Why don't you go ask Amaya or Sloane for advice?"

Or literally anyone other than me since almost every conversation I've ever had with you has either ended in insult or threat of bodily harm.

Gwen pursed her lips. "Because they're not helpful. Do you want to know their response to me laying out my issue? The first thing out of both of their mouths was *well, what color* did *you pick*?" She threw her hands up in exasperation. "And then *they* spent two hours telling me why my random color choice was terrible."

Despite myself, the corners of my lips twitched into a smile. I could see Amaya and Sloane doing that.

"And you know…" She waved a hand in my direction as if I could interpret her hand movements as words. "You're…you know."

I narrowed my eyes. "I'm what?"

"You know. You're good with people, diplomatic and whatever. You always find compromise in the council meetings. If everyone doesn't leave happy, they're all at least equally peeved because they didn't get exactly what they wanted."

My eyes widened. I'd been taken aback when she apologized for planning my murder and getting me sent to prison, but the shock that she was complimenting me left me speechless.

She wiggled her fingers and gestured to me. "Not including the whole scary void eyes, fear my shadows, King of Darkness schtick." Gwen shrugged. "Mostly good with people."

I shook my head. A compliment with a qualifier was still a compliment.

Blinking away my surprise, I paused long enough to consider her issue. "I'm assuming if the event coordinator spent two hours discussing color choice, the problem isn't incompetence, but the lack of authority to make decisions without your approval?"

"Right," she said. "I mean, she's great. Seems to know what she's doing, but every time I tell her to just pick a color, she gets all worked up." She sighed. "And I know I can be blunt, which probably isn't helping. Aunt Caroline had this poor girl strung out because she micromanaged everything and snapped when the littlest detail wasn't right. I think because I'm not all sunshine and rainbows, she thinks I'm going to snap at her too."

I leaned back in my chair, thinking it through. "Why don't you tell her that for every decision she needs you to make, you'd like her to preselect three options she believes will be suitable. Then you can pick one. It's still time consuming, but it will help her gain confidence in your relationship, and you'll know she already likes the three options without having to go into every detail."

"That's perfect," she said, slapping the desk and standing. "See? This is the advice I needed. Not an hours long discussion about how every shade of green clashes with Palagui's high priestess uniforms." She pointed a finger at me. "Your wife has strong opinions on the color green, just so you know."

I huffed a breath through my nose. "I'm not sure what I'd ever do with that information, but I appreciate you telling me."

"You're welcome!" she said over her shoulder as she walked out of my office.

I was still shaking my head, simultaneously confused and amused by the conversation when she popped back in.

"Hey?"

"Yes?"

"Thanks," she said and genuinely smiled, giving me a glimpse of the person behind all the snark and insults.

I nodded, unable to help smiling back. "Anytime, Gwen."

She clapped her hand on the doorframe and whirled away, disappearing down the hall.

After she left, I replayed her compliment in my head.

I'd never thought of myself as being good with people. Killing an entire city of people by starting a quake meant I was usually met with looks of contempt or fear from people who knew who I was.

And while sometimes I could get away with anonymity in dark bars and clubs, finding it easy to convince strangers to be my bedmates said more about my appearance than my people skills.

Maybe I couldn't take credit for the compliment. Gwen didn't say which council meetings she based her observations on. They were probably the council meetings *he* attended, not me.

Although, I was the one who came up with a solution for her.

Could it be we shared that trait? That we were mostly good with people, diplomatic, and adept at finding compromises?

Amaya's note listed competent at work as one of *his* traits. If Gwen could see it in me, maybe she could too.

Maybe there was hope I could be who she needed after all.

***

Amaya had her elbows on her desk, massaging her temples on a rainy day in late winter. She'd removed the crown as soon as she walked in. Her headaches were getting more severe, and though she claimed it was stress, I couldn't help but worry it was the bond. I had no physical symptoms, but maybe since she was a high priestess, she was more sensitive to the bond than I was.

We'd become inseparable at this point. She even moved her desk into my office so we didn't have to walk down the hall to see each other.

I was afraid being near one another and touching on a regular basis wasn't enough anymore. We hadn't had sex since the night in the prison, but I couldn't figure out how to bring up my concerns without sounding like I was asking to fuck her.

And though we were in a better place, and she might not resent me for asking, her anger and rejection when she thought I was suggesting sex to heal the bond a few months ago prevented me from discussing it now.

If she wanted to do more than cuddle and hold hands, she would have made a move. I tried my best to hide my lustful thoughts when she walked into a room or when she pressed her body to mine late at night, but I knew she could feel how badly I wanted her.

And though I could hear her shadow's demands for intimacy, I knew better than anyone what shadows would do to get what they wanted...I mean we, what *we* shadows would do.

"I just...hate this waiting," Amaya said, interrupting my thoughts. "I feel like we aren't making progress in anything."

"I know," I said. "But we're running a country. Things are slow. With the scale of everything we do, it takes time."

She sighed. "I'm just in a complaining mood today. I don't want to do this speech."

I rolled my chair around my desk and beside hers. She smiled, peeking up from her hands as I interlaced my fingers with hers. The black banded tattoo on our fourth fingers lined up perfectly, making my longing for her intensify.

"You're going to do great," I said in a low voice and squeezed her hand. "You're a good public speaker, and I would know because I've seen it."

"You weren't even paying attention at my cert presentation. I recall you scowling the whole time."

"Silas was saying nasty things in his head, and the fact that my only outward reaction was a scowl is a testament to my self-control."

She laughed and shook her head.

"It's a recorded speech. If you mess up, you can do a retake."

"I know you're right," she said, grudgingly.

"Do you want me to come?"

"No. I'll be more nervous if people are watching."

I shook my head. "I would do it for you if I could."

"I know you would." She smiled. "But your scary eyes don't turn people on like they do me."

Our public perception was bad enough without the citizens watching their king with void eyes deliver a speech.

I shrugged a shoulder and grinned. "I don't know....maybe it would help. There are people in Palagui with darkyra fetishes just like you."

"Hey! It's not a fetish!"

"Isn't it?" I liked teasing her far too much. I just wished our flirting turned into something more.

You should be grateful she can stand to be around you at all, the foreign voice said.

My smile died a little.

"It's not a fetish," she said and leaned close enough that our noses almost touched. "Because only my husband's void eyes get me going."

A dual warmth of affection and desire simmered inside me. "That's good to hear, wife."

We stared at each other for a moment. A piece of her hair had gotten loose from her bun, and I tucked it behind her ear. My fingers lingered, tracing the shell of her ear and down the side of her neck. She shivered. A possessive surge overcame me as I reveled in how my touch made her body react, made her shadows pulse under her skin. She was no longer gaunt from the time we spent in prison. Her face and cheeks filled out, her body supple and delectable.

When her coffee-brown eyes darkened, my gaze flickered to her lips, and she inched ever so closer—

My office phone rang.

I sighed, disappointment washing over me. "That's Dr. Henderson. Nico set up a one-time encrypted call for us to discuss the portal. If I don't take it, Nico will chew me out for making him set up another."

She nodded, and I wondered if it was wishful thinking that she seemed to be disappointed by the interruption as well.

Don't be ridiculous. She doesn't want you. It's her shadow influencing her. You'll never be who she really wants.

I shut the voice away, forcing it into a tiny box in my mind.

"I have to go anyway," she said. "They want me in the studio early for hair and makeup."

Her shadows gathered as I moved my chair back to my desk.

"Your fae warders are at the studio?" I asked.

She gave me placating eyes. "Yeah, they already texted that they arrived."

As she sifted away, I called out, "You'll do great."

I spent the next several hours on the phone with Dr. Henderson, discussing his portal research.

I had gathered decades of data by going in and out of the portal and tracking the stars, the sun, and planets in order to try to figure out where Adriana went. It wasn't until I shared that information with Dr. Henderson—who had an expertise in pattern recognition and a strong interest in all things magical—that we could start to predict the portal's destinations.

Dr. Henderson calculated when the portal would reopen to the world Adriana was in, and he spent the last several years trying to predict attributes about the world I was going to walk into.

While we talked, I scrolled on my computer through the calculations he sent through our encrypted server. Page after page of information and predictions.

When we finally hung up, I had more questions than answers.

For each prediction there was a confidence score, but none of the predictions could ever be one hundred percent accurate. I had to decide if I trusted the eighty percent confidence interval that the world would be a rainforest or the forty-five percent confidence interval that it would be a tundra.

How was I going to pack for this? Prepare myself? I could sense Adriana because we were family, but there was a limit to my range. Who knew how big this world was?

Dr. Henderson predicted that the portal would open once at dawn for five minutes, close, and open again at dusk for three minutes. There was a solar eclipse happening on Adriana's world, meaning the moon on our planet and the moon on hers would align twice.

Based on the trajectory of the planets, Dr. Henderson calculated twelve hours in our world would be equivalent to a day and a half in Adriana's world.

Someone knocked on my door, and I didn't look up when I said, "Come in."

I'd been so focused on waiting for the portal to open that I hadn't truly considered how difficult it would be to go to a strange alien world and try to find someone who'd arrived a hundred years earlier, and do it in less than twelve hours, our time. That's not even considering if any of his calculations were even slightly off...

"Is this a good time?" Sloane asked.

"Yeah. It's fine." I waved to the chair and was admittedly still distracted when she sat down.

"I spoke with Micah about the housing assistance program. They've been having trouble finding properties because the homes have to go through an inspection process before they're approved for subsidized housing. Normally that'd be a good thing—to make sure there aren't slumlords—but in this case, I think you'd agree it's better to get people in a house, any house, than have them on the street?"

"Sounds reasonable."

"I drafted this policy for a temporary waiver of inspections for six months. Hopefully, by that point, people will be back in their own homes."

"You need my signature then?" I asked and printed out the most important predictions Dr. Henderson had sent me.

"Uh, no," Sloane said, shifting in her seat. "Not technically. I already ran it by the housing program's director, and since it's temporary, it doesn't require your approval, but I wanted to make sure you were okay with it."

"Sounds good to me," I said and gathered the pages from the printer. "You know you don't have to run this stuff by me? I mean, if you need another set of eyes on something, I'm more than happy to help, but if something needs done, I know you'll make the best decision you can. I trust you."

I bent down to retrieve my laptop bag and slid the papers inside.

A distressed gasp yanked my gaze up. Sloane started crying into her hands, her chest heaving as a violent sob racked her whole body.

"Sloane?" I leaned over the desk. "Hey, what's wrong? Is it the policy? Because I can look over it if you want me to—"

She sniffed. "No, it's not the policy. It's just you. It's just...Goddess." She removed her hands from her face, eyes bloodshot and red. "I'm so sorry, Sebastian. I know I already apologized, and maybe I shouldn't be bringing it up again, but I feel terrible about what we did. And you..."

She waved her hands around. Why was it all three of these girls communicated in hand signals that I couldn't decipher?

"You saying you trust me," she said between broken sobs. "And I know you meant it about the job, but the fact that you can trust me at all is...I don't deserve it."

I rounded the desk and sat in the chair beside hers. "Hey. Okay. Wait," I said, putting my hand on her shoulder.

"I'm so sorry." She buried her head in her hands again and cried harder.

I rubbed my hand up and down her arm. "I know, Sloane. It's really okay. I'm okay."

"And now I'm blubbering at you, and you have to comfort me when I'm the one who hurt you."

"Hey," I said. "It's alright. Really. While I hope you don't try to kill me again, you never have to doubt that I'm glad Amaya has friends who are as loyal and protective as you and Gwen are."

My poor attempt at a joke earned me a huffed breath.

"I hold nothing against you," I said, reaching over my desk to grab her a tissue. "And I trust you to make the best decisions for Palagui because I know the lengths you'll go to in order to do the right thing."

She sniffed and wiped her nose, her sobs having calmed down.

With wide, earnest eyes, she looked at me and said, "That loyalty and protection extends to you too, Sebastian. Amaya claimed you as family. And so have I. I'll do whatever the right thing is to protect you just as I would for her."

I blinked rapidly as unexpected emotion rose in my throat, and I had to swallow hard.

The corner of Sloane's mouth twitched up. "And Gwen will too. If you haven't figured out, her love language is whatever the opposite of words of affirmation are."

I snorted. "Insults? Threats?"

"I prefer to think of them as loving jabs," Sloane said.

"Oh, okay sure," I said, smiling.

"If you haven't noticed she's softened in the last few months. I mean, she only calls Nico a fire breather like once a week now, and I can't remember the last time she said something rude about your shadows."

"She did sort of compliment my people skills the other day."

"See?" She laughed. "That was basically as good as an invitation to winter solstice dinner. We're one big family now."

I didn't know how to feel about that. It'd been a long time since anyone other than Nico had had my back. It almost didn't feel real.

"You okay?" I asked, unable to find a response to her declaration.

"Yeah. Sorry for the outburst."

"You never have to apologize for having feelings. Not to me. Not to anyone."

"You're a really good guy. I'm glad that you're Amaya's mate."

I shrugged because denying I was good didn't feel right in this moment.

Shadows congregated in the middle of the room, and Amaya stepped from the astral field already mid-sentence. "So that was a clusterfuck—" Her face fell into panic as she spotted Sloane's blotchy face. "Oh Goddess. What's wrong?"

"Nothing. Nothing," Sloane said, waving her hand. "Sebastian and I were bonding."

Amaya's eyes darted to mine, concern knitting her brows together.

I gave her a minute nod to signal everything was okay. She must have sensed our feelings because she wrapped her arms around Sloane and hugged her.

Amaya pulled back to ask, "Does this mean I have to go bond with Nico now? Cause I could see him making me watch sports or challenging me to a contest of who can eat the most hot peppers or something. And I really don't think I can handle either of those things."

Sloane and I laughed.

"I can confirm," I said. "He would do both of those things, and I wouldn't get into any kind of contest with him involving spicy food. I swear I don't know how he hasn't burnt off his taste buds."

"Maybe he has, and that's why he wants everything to be so spicy," Amaya said.

"Actually," Sloane said. "I know a bonding activity we all can do, but we'll have to sacrifice some plates."

Amaya's eyes brightened, and she wiggled her fingers together like an evil villain. "Oh boy. Sounds violent. Count me in. You're okay with losing some plates right, Sebastian?"

I shrugged with my palms up. "What are a few plates if it makes my mate and my sister-in-law happy?"

Sloane beamed at me as I figured claiming her as family would.

I leaned back and watched them talk and joke with each other, lounging amongst the buoyant feeling their joyful energy brought to the room.

A soft peace fell over me, but the flash of contentment was fleeting. Almost as if happiness was so strange an occurrence in this body, it could only be accompanied by a sinking feeling of knowing it wouldn't last.

It was these moments that I most felt as though I was two people. The one experiencing the moment and the one observing.

I could mimic the facial movements of a smile and the contraction of my stomach as breath left my lungs in a chorus of happiness, but the experience of laughter was not as rich when you were watching it from afar. The sum of the parts was a pitiful rendition of the emotion, and the experience itself would always be tainted by the very act of observation.

But being an observer was a necessity. I had to remain removed. A safe distance between me and everyone around me. I was dangerous. My flashbacks were dangerous. If I didn't remain aware of myself at all times, I would hurt someone.

And it'd never been as clear to me as it was then, how my decision to separate myself into pieces, to protect myself from the pain of remembering, had robbed both *him* and me of an embodied life.

Chapter Twenty-Nine

Amaya

Midway through sifting to the research center the thought cropped up that trying to heal Jeremy might do more harm than good. Sebastian hadn't had another flashback, but what if this triggered one?

It felt too late to back out now. It was rare that we had a full day free of work responsibilities, and if I told him I changed my mind, he would be suspicious since this had been my idea.

The thing was, I sensed, my shadow sensed, even though he hadn't had another flashback, he wasn't quite better.

We spent the day together, and we cuddled at night, but something was off. There were brief moments when I was sure he wanted to kiss me, moments I could taste his cinnamon lust, but then, he would shut down and hold me at arm's length.

On top of that, he was constantly tense. More than his usual strict, controlled self. I couldn't ask him about it since I wanted to give him space and not pressure him to talk.

It was ridiculous to think his behavior had anything to do with me, but insecurities liked to invade my rational thoughts.

He's going to leave us, my shadow had said. *We have no way to keep him. We need to accept the bond.*

That's ridiculous. He's not going to leave. We're married. Our fourth fingers literally have an inked tattoo of our binding.

Doesn't count. It was forced, my shadow said.

The marriage doesn't matter. We're mates whether or not we've accepted the bond yet. He won't leave because he loves me.

Can't remember the last time he said so.

Neither could I.

I made a promise to listen to my shadow's instincts, but gut reactions could still be wrong or interpretations off. My shadow sensed that Sebastian wasn't completely open to me, but that was only because he was dealing with his trauma. It didn't mean he was going to leave.

He was my mate. Our powers bound us together. He wouldn't leave me. He couldn't.

Distracted by worrying, I barely paid attention to our walk through the research center. We were led to the basement where the scientists held the draxis.

Entering the observation lobby, we peered through the glass into Jeremy's room. He'd been strapped down to the table.

The scientist informed us that they only fed the draxis enough to keep them from deteriorating, but not enough for them to be active so they wouldn't break out.

I tried not to think about how that tactic sounded familiar to the one that was used in the prison.

Jeremy laid motionless on the table. The bones of his face protruded, outlining his skull. His fingers were crusted together with black pus, making the individual digits indistinguishable. The draxis bones were malleable, jellified. The arm appeared like one wiggly tentacle. What should have been his wrist and forearm hung limply over the edge of the table.

He had no clothes, but all traces of body parts were melted. No knees or elbows, no groin, no fingernails. His ears were gone. He was a person-shaped skeletal blob. A shadow creature.

Without fae power or electricity, Jeremy didn't produce any of the shadow mist that the draxis outside the research center had.

It hit me, staring into that room, how reckless I'd been in the prison. Seeing a creature that used to be a person tied to a table put in perspective what my actions could have wrought. I'd almost tortured and killed Jeremy, seeking revenge on him for a sin he wasn't at fault for committing, all in order to feel in control of my life. Driven by an entitlement to revenge that Kai stoked while my mind was weak from the suppression.

Was I a bad person?

I'd told Rien once that narcissists didn't worry about becoming narcissists…Evil queens mad with power probably didn't care about the darkness of their souls either.

I certainly hadn't. Not until right this moment, staring the reality of my irresponsibility in the face.

What was worse was I still couldn't drum up any regret for what I'd done.

Only guilt that I didn't feel guilty for it at all.

I shook my head to end that line of thinking. Moral crises—or lack thereof—could wait.

"I'm going in," I said.

Sebastian nodded and followed me into Jeremy's room.

My senses went on high alert as I walked toward the table. His body was emaciated, and there was a faint stench of rot that I'd never noticed around a draxis before.

His skin was flaking away, body disintegrating without his power. I could only hope whatever parts of his mind were alive were blissfully ignorant of what was happening to him.

I held my palms over his body, and high priestess light trickled down over him.

The power flowed through me in a constant stream. I moved my hands over his head, down his torso, spreading out the healing, but nothing happened.

My visions in the Hollow made it seem so easy. I healed the draxis in thirty seconds. The skin knitted back together and the person underneath emerged.

But as five minutes, then ten passed, the stupid hope I had been holding shattered.

Sebastian stood, watching with a quiet intensity.

My arms ached from my position at the twenty-minute mark. "Can you get me a chair?" I asked. "This might take a while."

I would stay here all day. Drain my power if I had to. Even if only one tiny piece of him was healed, it would be worth it.

Sebastian went to the door, pressed a buzzer button, and spoke the request into the intercom.

Someone came to the door and brought in two chairs.

We sat down beside one another, and I said, "I'm going to try to intermix my shadows into the healing, filtering like I did for Sloane."

Sebastian nodded. "You want my help?"

I shrugged. "Couldn't hurt."

Actually, it might even help Sebastian too. It'd only been when Sloane and I started using our powers that our mental and emotional healing began. Maybe it would be beneficial for him as well as Jeremy.

I need to heal him, I told my shadow.

There is nothing to filter, she said. *And no part of him is wounded.*

I worried my lip at her dismissiveness. This had to work. I kept her disheartening comments to myself and interlaced my fingers with Sebastian's. Our joined palms rested on his lap, and his free hand hovered over Jeremy's body, letting shadows trickle out.

I shivered in pleasure as his shadows mixed with mine. My cheeks heated because I remembered how good it felt to feel his power flowing through me, even stronger than when I'd done it for Sloane since our auras had several opportunities to attune since then.

I hadn't had this open of a connection to him in weeks. I sensed his regret underneath so many layers of numbness that I wasn't even sure if he was aware of feeling it.

"What are you thinking about?" I asked in a gentle voice. Nico was a much stronger person than me because this whole *giving him space and not asking him to talk* went against all my instincts.

He scrunched up his face. "You don't want to know."

"Um, that makes me want to know even more," I said, eyebrows raising.

He smiled ruefully and shook his head. "I'm thinking about the day Jeremy broke up with me."

"Oh." I wasn't expecting that.

"He gave me an ultimatum. He wanted commitment or we were over. And I couldn't give him that commitment because of the bargain, but I was too ashamed to explain." He sighed. "If I would have told him, he would have been warned away from making his own bargain, and this would have never happened to him."

"This is not your fault, Sebastian."

"My other half bound our power because he was scared of me, but he had to make that bargain to get his power back."

The shadows falling from his hand stuttered and stopped.

"I've been so angry," he continued. "It was easier to hate *him* as much as he hated me. Resent him for locking me away. But by blocking those memories and trying to prevent pain, it only made everything worse."

I turned toward him, taking his hands in mine. "You were trying to protect yourself the best way you knew how. You have to forgive yourself."

"I can't," he said, staring at our interlocked hands on his lap.

"Okay," I said. "Well, can you forgive your eleven-year-old self? That little boy didn't know how to handle his powers. What happened was not his fault."

His nostrils flared, and his eyes darted to mine. "You don't know what happened that day."

I shook my head. "I don't need to know because I know the person you are now. And I can guess at the boy you were. It doesn't matter what you've done. I will love you without conditions or exceptions."

He pulled his hands from mine. "How can you say that? How am I supposed to believe it? It doesn't feel true. It doesn't feel possible."

And it wouldn't.

How could I possibly convince him it was the truth when four months ago I tried to kill him? When three months ago I made him feel inferior to the other parts of himself. When all his life people have feared and hated him.

I had hope in time my actions would prove my love, but there was one thing I could give him to help him see the truth of it right now. I was sure of his love because I could feel it, could taste it on my tongue.

Maybe I could give him that too.

I ran my hands over his arms, up to the sides of his neck, cupping his jaw and stroking my thumbs over his face. Leaning forward, I pressed my forehead to his. "Can I try something?"

His hands rested on the outside of my thighs, and he nodded against me. Eyes already fluttering shut.

I closed my eyes and dropped into my body to feel into the ache in my heart, where our mating bond lived. Its threads were cut and reknotted from the constant turmoil between us, but I chose to think that made it stronger. That the scar tissue thickened rather than weakened its integrity. I tapped into the unconditional love that dwelled in my heart and imbued my shadows with that feeling, using them as a vehicle to transport that sensation to him.

I recalled the moment that he first professed his love. I only knew it in hindsight. The moment my body, my heart, recognized what was between us, even if my mind didn't. The engagement ritual that I had thought was fake, but every fiber of my being knew was true. The perfect symphony of every taste, every emotion, the very essence of life and love wrapped up in one moment. I left the imprint of that memory within a shadow and sent it to him.

He sucked in a breath, and I opened my eyes. The tattoos along his neck blinked as my shadows sunk into his skin. His face slackened. All tension melted from his body. Euphoria etched in his features.

"Amaya," he said, thick with longing. He gripped my wrists, holding me to him.

"Does that feel true?" I asked.

He nodded.

I smiled. Warmth effused from my heart. It was by pure chance that I noticed movement out of the corner of my eye.

I gasped. "Sebastian."

He startled, looking at the twitching tentacle arm.

Maybe something was finally working, but I didn't know if I'd be able to continue healing him today. A dull pounding had already begun in my temples.

Jeremy didn't move again.

"It took Adriana three days to do it," Sebastian said, having sensed my disappointment.

My shoulder slumped. The metal of the crown dug into my skull, exasperating the tension headache. I took it off, set it on my lap, and massaged my temples.

The ache didn't fade. It spread throughout my head and down my neck.

"Are you okay?" His voice sounded distant.

My senses dulled. A pulse throbbed behind my eyes, and it felt like the muscles and veins that held my eyes into their sockets were bursting with pressure.

"Mmmhmm," I lied. "Just a little headache."

"You've been getting those a lot lately."

"The crown is too tight," I whispered. The sound of our voices was too loud and pierced my eardrums.

"Let's go home. We can try again another day," Sebastian said.

I opened my eyes, but my stomach dropped, and I became woozy and lightheaded.

"I—"

Jeremy's void eyes opened. The lower part of his tentacle arm wrapped around my wrist. I yanked myself back. My chair toppled over. The crown clattered to the ground.

Already weakened, my vision dotted as power was siphoned out of me. I attempted to sift, but summoning the power from my core only drained it faster.

Sebastian was yelling instructions I couldn't make out. His shadows pried the tentacle from my wrist, and his arm wrapped around my waist, dragging me out of reach.

Sebastian's shadows gathered to sift us, but I screamed, "No! The crown." If Jeremy drained the crown, all of Palagui would be powerless.

As if he understood my words, the tentacles gave up reaching for me and waved through the air, landing directly on the crown.

It was over. I'd sentenced us all to a powerless life.

The tentacle touched the metal, and a hiss of smoke curled up. He pulled away, making a screeching whine of pain.

Sebastian plunged the room into darkness. My void eyes shifted, and I lunged for the crown as he picked me up by the waist and sifted us into the observation lobby.

I was lowered to the ground, but his hands remained on my waist to steady me as the room spun.

His eyes searched me frantically. "Are you okay?"

My white healing light was blinking and fizzling in my palms, betraying how weak my powers were. The burn around my wrist from the tentacle arm stung and was a pale red, not fully healed.

"I'm okay."

Fury filled his eyes. "You aren't okay. I can see the burn."

"What happened? How did he wake up?" I tried to distract him with questions.

The pursing of his lips told me he saw through my distraction attempt, but we both turned to look through the glass as Sebastian's shadows misted away.

"We weren't healing him. We were feeding him our power," he said. His anger was palatable.

"What's he doing now?"

Jeremy was flinging his tentacle arms around, a long black tongue hung from his mouth. Carrying on almost like he was dancing in a drug-fueled state.

"Feeding on my shadows," Sebastian said. "I needed to distract him so we could get away."

"But why did the crown burn him? Does it have protection properties? Like only the queen can touch it or something?"

Another wave of lightheadedness hit me, and I leaned into Sebastian.

"Not that I know of. I have memories of both Adriana and I trying it on as children. I've seen nurses and maids pick it up. I know my mother used to have it cleaned by a jeweler."

My body was relaxing, melting. Sebastian stepped forward, and I rested my forehead on his chest. "Next time we go—"

"There will be no next time," he said, voice firm. His hands were rubbing up and down my back, making me so relaxed that it took a second to process his words.

I stiffened. "We have to keep trying."

"No. We aren't healing him at the expense of your health."

I shook my head—about to say that I was fine—but he cut me off. "You are risking the country, every fae's power, when you put yourself in harm's way. I know your own life doesn't matter much to you, but think about the citizens." He gave me a sad smile. "Think about your mate. What would you unleash upon the world if I had no reason to be on my best behavior?"

I rolled my eyes. "You were running the country self-sacrificially before I came. You would do the same if I couldn't."

His silence and emotionless eyes startled me.

"Sebastian"—I yanked on his shirt—"Promise me you'll run the country and find a new queen. Promise me if I..." I took a deep breath. "If I can't do it, promise me you will." I looked back and forth between his eyes. "Please."

His gaze followed his thumb as it traced along my face. "Promise me you won't purposefully put yourself in harm's way."

I sucked my bottom lip into my mouth. He was right, and as much as I wanted to save Jeremy, I had a nation's worth of people to think about. With great reluctance, I closed my eyes. "I promise."

He wrapped his arms around me, and I burrowed my nose into his chest, letting his spicy, sweet sandalwood scent envelop me.

"I promise I'll run the country to the best of my abilities if you aren't there to do it."

I clung to him tighter. "Thank you."

A twinge of sour anxiety emanated from him, and I chose to believe that it was from imagining life without me and not because he was lying.

"We're done for the day," he said. "I'm taking you home. We can come up with a new plan after you've slept."

"Hold on—"

He scooped me up and sifted us to our bedroom. My headache vanished into a faint echo of what it'd been.

"Wow," I said, sitting up after he laid me on the bed. "I think he was drawing on my powers the whole time. My headache is almost gone. Do you feel different?"

He thought for a minute, but shook his head. "No, but I didn't have any pain to begin with."

I flung my legs over the bed about to get up and use the rest of the day to get caught up on work, but Sebastian blocked me. "No. You aren't moving. You aren't doing anything at all. If he was draining your powers, you need to sleep."

"I'm not tired."

"I don't care."

I narrowed my eyes. "You're being overprotective. I feel fine now that I'm not in the room with him."

"Lie down, Amaya."

"I need to check my email, and we're supposed to go over that proposal—"

"Rest. Now," he said, crossing his arms over his chest.

"Jeez. Fine. Okay. At least let me brush my teeth and change my clothes."

I squeaked as my legs were lifted, and I was bridal carried into the bathroom and set down on the vanity.

"This is a little overkill," I said, but my admonishment was undercut by my smile. I kind of liked him doting on me.

He opened the vanity drawer, took out my toothbrush, and spread the toothpaste on the bristles.

"Okay, extremely overkill now. I can most definitely squeeze my own toothpaste."

He ignored me and ran the brush under the faucet. I reached out to take the prepared toothbrush from him, but he swatted my hand down.

"Open," he said in a flat, stern tone.

I gave him an incredulous look. "My hands work just fine."

He shook his head. "You almost passed out. I'm not risking you overexerting yourself."

I lunged for the toothbrush, but he held it up over his head and raised an eyebrow. "Be a good girl and open your mouth."

My smile died, and I swallowed. A flicker of heat in my core sparked to life. I searched his face for any indication that this was flirting, but all I found was a serious expression.

I crossed my arms over my chest. "No. You can't make me. I'm fully capable of brushing my own—Urgh."

My sentence was interrupted by his hand gripping the bottom of my jaw, thumb and fingers pressing into my cheeks until they breached the opening between my top and bottom teeth. He hadn't needed to push hard because the surprise from his rough treatment caught me off guard.

My hands flew up, intending to push him away, but instead squeezed the toned muscles of his forearms.

"Open up, little warrior," he said. His eyes hooded as he stared at my parted lips.

I obeyed, opening my mouth wide. My body became pliant to his every demand despite my initial protesting.

There was absolutely nothing sexy about imagining someone brushing my teeth, and yet, the intense concentration on his face as he gripped my chin and angled my head just how he wanted it was making my breaths come quicker.

I didn't know if it was the feeling of being completely taken care of or the suggestive nature of the way the brush moved in and out of my mouth that was making my stomach clench in anticipation. My brain began to fog; all thoughts jumbled and lost. There was only him, his scent, his touch.

I tried to hide my panting as he scrubbed my teeth, but it didn't matter, because he dutifully ignored it.

My legs parted, and he stepped closer between them. Somehow even the feel of his hips on my inner knees was erotic.

I moved to rest my hands on his chest. His grip on my jaw loosened, and I opened wider, tilting my chin and looking at him with half-closed eyes.

I traced his cheekbones and jawline with my gaze, then along his perfectly straight nose. Even with his shadows blacking out his eyes, I had no trouble reading his expressions. The tightening around the edges of his eyes when he was frustrated or the way the corners raised when he was happy or lowered when he was sad.

The messy swoop of his black hair fell over one eye. I so rarely saw it unkempt, like everything else in his life, he liked to keep his appearance impossibly perfect.

But he didn't even have to try. He was always perfect to me. Always so fucking beautiful. Maybe that's why I liked seeing him messy. It felt special to be given a glimpse of him that the rest of the world didn't see.

He finished brushing my teeth, set the brush down, and gathered all of my hair in his fist. "Spit," he said, gesturing with his chin to the sink.

I did as he commanded and rinsed my mouth out with water before returning to my upright position.

He didn't release his grip on my hair, just stared at me, his eyes traveling along my face.

Kiss me, I tried to convey with my body.

His grip on my hair tightened, pulling my hair to tilt my head toward his. When he leaned forward and his free hand cupped my jaw, I thought maybe he'd heard my desperate silent plea, but his thumb only brushed along the corner of my mouth.

"Missed a spot," he said, but his thumb didn't leave my mouth after wiping away the toothpaste. It settled in a back-and-forth motion over my lower lip.

His shadows seeped out from his shoulders in a thin mist that fluttered along my arms, making my skin pebble with goosebumps.

My hand found his belt, and one finger slipped under the waistband of his pants to tug him closer.

I knew he could feel my heavy breathing on his thumb. There was no way he couldn't tell how aroused I was, but instead of kissing me, he lifted me up off the vanity, holding under my thighs.

I clung to his neck and wrapped my legs around his waist. His eyes didn't leave mine as he returned me to the bed. The heat of lust dissolved into an overwhelmingly sweet affection. I laid on the pillows as he planted his hands on either side of my shoulders and leaned over to kiss my forehead.

When he pulled back, I grabbed a fistful of his shirt to halt his retreat. "Stay."

"Where do you want me?" he asked, looking to the right and left of my body as if I was only asking to cuddle.

It wasn't coy or sexy, but the art of seduction went out the window when I realized he wasn't going to take my hints. I'd been giving him space, waiting for him to come to me, but I couldn't wait any longer. I hungered for him, starved for what only he could give me.

With absolutely no finesse, I grabbed the wrist of his right hand and shoved it down my pants. "I want you here."

His eyes widened, but as his fingers met my wetness, his eyelids lowered. "Oh," he breathed.

He gathered the slickness of my arousal dripping from my entrance and circled my clit in a torturously slow pattern.

I arched my back and spread my legs, wishing more than anything that I was naked and bared before him. The hollow relief of my dreams was making me wanton for any pleasure he would give me.

"Look at you," he said, eyes trailing down my body. "I've never seen anything more perfect in my life."

I whimpered, closing my eyes, letting the sweetness of his praise pour over me.

"I want you," I said. "I want you so bad."

He plunged a finger into my core, and I sucked in a breath. "You want *me*? Amaya? Me?" He added a second finger, and I clenched around him, moaning my desire.

"Who do you want?" he asked. The anger in his voice shifted into desperation. "Tell me who it is you want. Tell me how to be him. Tell me what I'm supposed to do."

"You. You," I said. "I want you. This part of you. Every part of you. Please." I met his desperation with that of my own as the orgasm built too quick. I rocked my hips into his hand. The move so reminiscent of my dream that tears sprung from my eyes. I couldn't be sure if this was real or not.

The heel of his hand brushed my clit as his fingers curled inside of me, thrumming the inner pleasure point that had my breath becoming shallow and my mind centering in on how close, close, very close I was, but despite my body being tensed and taut, I couldn't get there.

"No," I said. "No. No. No." It was painful, being so close and knowing I'd never feel relief.

Too much time passed.

I had this sense I couldn't get there. That I wouldn't orgasm. That I should tell him to stop.

I'd been in a constant state of arousal for months, but something held me back, something was missing. It felt so good, but I couldn't—

"Please," I cried out, not even sure what I was begging for. "I'm sorry I'm taking so long. I can't—" My body arched, but still held back. All my muscles clenched to the point of pain.

"Shhh," he said. "There's no rush. There's nowhere else I need to be, nowhere else I want to be. I'll do this all night long if you let me."

His fingers didn't ease up on their pace, even though they had to be cramping from the awkward angle.

"Don't leave me," I said, but the words were distorted by my cries of frustration.

"It's okay," he whispered into my ear. "I'm never leaving. I promise."

He pressed his lips to my neck, teeth notching into the skin and sucking. Marking me. Claiming me.

And that was it. That was what burst the tension apart, and my body started quaking with the hardest orgasm of my life. It all shattered. The fear that this was a dream. That I would come and he would disappear into the mist of my imagination.

On and on and on, the orgasm wrecked my body as the pleasure turned to pain to pleasure and back again. My thoughts scrambled into nothingness. My mouth was moving, but the words I was saying didn't register until the intensity faded.

"Don't leave me," I said. I'd been saying. I'd been screaming and crying with the way my voice was rasping.

"My sweet mate," he said, pained. "I'm not leaving. I won't ever leave you."

New tears fell, following the well-trodden path of the old. "Doesn't feel true."

I sobbed, admitting what I'd sensed and hadn't been able to speak aloud. He was beside me each day. He touched and held me, but it felt like at any moment he'd leave. Something inside of me had been reduced to an insecure, little girl. I hated being so scared and needy, but I couldn't stop.

He climbed on top of me, pressing all of his delicious weight onto me. The tears stopped as my body recognized the press of him, grounding me.

He leaned back enough to stare into my eyes. My heart stuttered as the vanilla of his affection and the cinnamon of his lust slammed into me and shifted all at once into the perfect harmony of all tastes, of all feelings, of unconditional love.

"Does that feel true?" he whispered.

I shut my eyes but nodded and dug my nails into his shoulder.

"These last few months I've been reassessing a century's worth of decisions and experiences," he said as his lips traced up and down my jaw. "But the one thing that I never have to question is how much I love you, how much I need you in my life. I'll never leave you."

"Promise?"

"I promise."

His mouth found mine, kissing me in earnest, sealing his intention, and I let the tender brush of his lips against mine soothe my insecurities and worries. Nothing mattered when his mouth was on mine, when his tongue twisted and twined with mine.

He laid on top of me, crushing me into the bed, trapping my body with his forearms on either side of me, trapping my mouth with his plundering tongue, trapping my heart with his claim on me.

When he let me up for air, my head was spinning with want, cinnamon lust thick on my tongue and spicy-sweet in my nose.

With a soft, gentle touch, he undressed me. Hands unhurried, caressing every inch of my skin as each article of clothing was removed and tossed aside, as if memorizing every detail of my body.

He rose for a brief moment, his clothes joining mine on the floor, and I missed the weight of him, but when he lowered himself back on top of me and I felt the full expanse of his naked skin on mine, my eyes rolled back into my head.

The hard tip of his cock stroked up and down my entrance, gathering my arousal. I quivered in anticipation, but he didn't tease me. The heady desire rocketing through me was mirrored in the spice of his lust.

He sunk deep inside me, connecting our bodies and eliciting the completion of something more than desire, more than lust. A fulfillment of a promise that had been made at the beginning of the world.

He took his time, pumping into me at a slow rhythm, letting me luxuriate in his nearness without fear that he'd disappear and vanish from underneath my fingertips.

"You feel so good." He sighed into the skin of my shoulder. "Goddess, I've missed you."

"Missed you. Need you," I managed to get out.

I wrapped my legs around his waist and rocked my hips up to meet each thrust, not chasing the orgasm this time, just letting the pleasure build, elongating the moment together. My hands ran down his back, along the hard muscle contracting as he moved inside me.

A reuniting.

There was no past. No future.

Just now. Just us.

"Shhh," he said, peppering my face with kisses. I was whimpering again, but I didn't know when I started or why. Bliss was filling all of my limbs, but some inner part of me was trembling.

"You're mine. You're all fucking mine," he whispered, sweet but forceful. A claiming that unfurled the scared part of me. It freed whatever piece of my mind that had been distracted with fear. The moments expanded into an eternity. My sensitivity heightened, every touch was extraordinary, every inch of his skin on mine was exploding with tingles, every thrust felt better than the last, magnified and mirrored.

The pleasure was blinding.

"Sebastian?"

"Hmm," he murmured into my skin, the sound turning into a deep masculine moan that I could feel in the arches of my feet.

Mine. Mine. Mine.

"I...feel...." Words. I couldn't find them. My chest ached. There were words. My mouth was making the letters. The letters, the sounds, the consonants that would end the fear once and for all. The ones that would tie me to him forever. "You...and me."

"I know," he said. "It's the bond. It's just the bond."

He started breathing heavier, winded though we were moving slow. Sweat broke out over our skin; our muscles tensed from holding back the feelings erupting between us.

He pushed up, shaking his head. And I got the sense it wasn't the orgasm he was holding off, but the bond's insistence for completion.

Grabbing my hips, his fingers dug into my flesh. "I can't..." he trailed off. Face contorting into pain or pleasure or both.

"Fuck me, Sebastian," I said. "Fuck me hard." I needed it. Maybe it was the bond. Maybe it was my shadow, but I needed his hands to squeeze me so tight they'd brand me, claim me.

His biceps flexed, holding my hips and fucking me just like I'd asked. His shadows only needed to flick the hard throb of my clit once, twice, before my body seized up in an orgasm that left me gasping and tingling throughout its entirety.

A deep noise was caught in his throat as he tried to hold back, but his entire body shuddered as his release filled me. He fell forward in three angled jolts, catching himself each time only to tip further until he was pressed to me once again. His body aligned with mine, his elbows planted below my shoulders, his head hanging, his breaths panting in my ear.

The reverberation of his orgasm vibrated through me, leaving me satiated for the first time in a while.

We stayed like that for a long time. His cock softening inside me. I was too boneless to move, too out of my mind to want to. I closed my eyes and just listened as our breath returned to a normal pace.

When he finally rolled onto his back, I felt the absence of him viscerally. A whine escaped, but he wrapped me up in his arms, cradling me tight, erasing any doubts.

I hated feeling so weak and needy. The strong independent woman I wanted to be was nowhere to be found.

Vulnerability isn't weakness, my shadow chided. *Wanting affection doesn't make us needy.*

I sighed, too tired to disagree or argue with her, too deliriously happy to be in Sebastian's arms. I nuzzled my head into the juncture of his shoulder and his neck, breathing in his scent and the pleasant musk of his sweat.

"I love you," I said, planting my hand over his heart. I inched up a bit to look in his eyes. "*You*. This part of you. The shadow. The power. Every part that you think is bad. Every part that I know is good. I love *you*."

His eyes glistened, but he blinked away the emotion. He squeezed me to him, and I hoped the pressure alone would disintegrate us both into one another.

"Amaya." His tongue caressed my name, and I could have sworn his voice shifted an octave out of the deeper tenor of his power, but

I must have misheard it because his shadow spoke through him as he said, "I love you so much."

This time it wasn't just his heart, but the mating bond itself that pulsed the rhythm of our love.

Neither of us had to ask if it was true.

There was nothing in the entire world that could have felt truer.

Chapter Thirty

Sebastian

Amaya had sensed the distance I'd been keeping between myself and everyone around me due to my fear of my flashbacks.

She'd been distraught over the thought of me leaving her, which I would have found entirely unbelievable, except she'd sent me her emotions, her love, and I felt the truth of it like a balm to my soul.

She loved me.

Me.

Even the foreign disgruntled voice in my head couldn't come up with anything to accuse me of once we'd felt that.

Somehow Amaya had found it in her heart to look past my inadequacies and accept the damaged pieces that dwelled within my body. I vowed to spend the rest of my life trying to live up to the version she outlined on her list. That's what she deserved.

I wouldn't leave her—couldn't—even before I knew the depths of her feelings, but especially now. I needed to figure out how to control my power once and for all.

I had tried to corral the memories, and *he* suppressed them along with me for a century, but going back to a fragmented self was not an option.

I tried to avoid, to distract, to exhaust my mind and body so I'd have no energy to relive the pain, but that wasn't sustainable in the long term.

I was out of ideas and out of options. Which meant I'd have to ask for help from the one person I loathed to prostrate myself before.

I cleared my throat as I walked into the kitchen.

Nico glanced up. "Hey," he said and went back to aligning globs of dough on a cookie sheet. His shoulder-length auburn hair was pulled back into a bun like it usually was when he was baking. "What's up?"

I shifted left and right. "Where's Sloane?" I asked, hoping his mate wouldn't be around to overhear my request.

"The girls are outside training," Nico said. "Gwen's been on their ass about slacking on practice." He pitched his voice in a mockery of Gwen's. "Just cause you have a crown doesn't mean you're infallible and just because you have the fire breather doesn't mean you can play damsel in distress."

I nodded, tilting my head to the side. "Sounds like her."

Nico rolled his eyes, but it was good-natured. The fact that Gwen's "loving jabs" never landed with him only seemed to make her try harder.

"Are you taking to heart Gwen's digs about you moving out?" I asked, trying to stick to casual conversation while I got up the nerve to ask what I really wanted to.

Nico scoffed. "No." He paused and considered something. "I mean if Sloane wanted to..." He shrugged. "You know, whatever. I don't know. We'll see what happens. You know I don't like plans."

No, he didn't. Didn't like anything that involved planning for further in the future than what he was doing that weekend. He was sometimes too easygoing. Just doing whatever promised the most fun.

Which is why this might be idiotic, but I didn't know where else to turn. I pulled out the stool on the opposite side of the island counter and interlaced my fingers in front of me. "I need your help."

He didn't look up from his task. "With what?"

Taking a deep breath, I said, "I need to figure out how to control my power. To control my…episodes. I can't suppress my memories anymore, and distracting and exhausting myself isn't working. Short of a lobotomy, I'm not sure what to do."

I forced myself to meet his eyes as he set his spatula down and crossed his arms over his chest. "And you're coming to me?"

Nodding once, I said, "Amaya has enough on her plate. I can't keep burdening her with my issues. I need to fix me for her."

Nico shook his head. "Won't work. You gotta fix you for you."

"Fine. For me. I want to fix me for me."

He tilted his head and was quiet long enough that I began to give up on the idea. To admit my weakness to the person who had no qualms electrocuting me every time I was in control of this body and then expect him to help me was foolish.

My memories were mixing and meshing with *his.* To the point I'd started feeling like the time Nico spent with *him* had been spent with me as well.

That we were one and the same.

And I'd stupidly assumed that Nico had meant what he'd said about friendship. He'd obviously only been trying to smooth the discordant energy in our group. That didn't mean he wanted to bear my burdens.

"Actually, forget I said anything." I pushed away from the counter and made to get off the stool.

"Hell no," Nico said. "Sit your ass back down."

I bristled at his command but sat. He really was my only hope.

"I'll help you, but Amaya will need to be a part of this."

I sighed. "I don't see why that's necessary—"

"Of course you wouldn't. You've been trying to go it alone your entire life. The only reason I'm still around is because I don't take your moody-ass bullshit." Nico pushed the mixing bowl of dough aside and leaned his elbows on the counter. "If you want to do this, you're going to have to accept our help. All of our help."

I pressed my lips together and looked through the sliding glass door. Every so often a burst of white light shot across the back yard.

I exhaled heavily. "*All* of us?"

Nico smiled wide. "Yes, even Gwen."

I put my face in my hands and rubbed my eyes. "I'm already regretting this."

Nico huffed a laugh. "No you aren't. You need this. And I'm glad you asked me because I've been trying to figure out a way to broach the subject that wouldn't send you spiraling out."

Lifting my head, I narrowed my eyes. "Broach what?"

"You look like shit, dude," Nico said, matter-of-factly. He'd gone back to spooning out his dough.

"Wow. Thanks," I said.

"You look like what I saw in the mirror when I came back. Like what the guys in my unit looked like. Like you've got one foot in the past, and I don't know, but can guess, when you lose control of your powers, you aren't actually here anymore."

I froze. My muscles locked up. I wanted help, but I didn't know if I could survive dredging up my memories. If his plan involved me confessing my sins, I wasn't going to make it.

He kept his eyes on his task, and I saw now it was because he knew I was uncomfortable. He averted his gaze while speaking to me because he'd experienced this. Had been around people who'd experienced this.

"I've tried to bring this up before," he said. "Several times really, but I suppose this part of you wouldn't remember that. He hadn't hit rock bottom yet. Wasn't ready." He picked up the cookie sheet and turned to put it in the oven. After setting the timer, he looked at me. "The fact that you came to me at all means you're ready. You're stronger than him. He couldn't admit when he needed help. He wouldn't let me in. Wouldn't even let Amaya in." He shrugged. "He might have gotten there eventually, but I know you're strong enough to move past this."

I only stared at him, at a loss for words. I'd blustered about telling them I was stronger than the other half of me, but I didn't think I'd ever hear someone agree. I didn't think I even truly believed it.

Nico let me stew in silence until he brought out another cookie sheet and started over his process. "There's a program in Molbridge. It's got a long waiting list, but I signed up for a slot the day after we brought Sloane home, thinking she'd need help to get over the kidnapping, but she doesn't need it as much anymore, and she agreed with me when I mentioned giving the slot to you. I've been putting off telling you because I knew you'd shut me down."

"What is it?" I asked. My heart pounded. I knew this would be hard. I didn't expect an easy fix, but my hands were still sweating.

"It's a kind of group ritual therapy."

"Therapy?" I asked blandly. I searched my memories and found vague references he'd mentioned before. I shook my head. "I don't want to talk about what happened."

He hummed. "You don't have to. It's not therapy like you think. You don't ever have to talk about what happened. The ritual is performed by the healing facilitators, but it works best if there are people participating in the ritual who are energetically aligned to one another. The five of us all live together, so our magic is naturally attuned."

Before I had the chance to insist on details, the sliding glass door opened, and the girls walked in, sweaty and hair askew, but smiling and obviously full of exercise endorphins.

As soon as she walked over the threshold, Amaya's eyes found me and brightened.

Her brown hair was in a messy, loose bun on top of her head. My eyes traced the curves of her body outlined by her tight workout clothes. The sports bra highlighted the mounds of her breasts, and her skintight leggings made my fingers itched to squeeze the swell of her hips, turn her around, and palm her perfect ass.

"Hi," she said, smiling and crossing the room.

I opened my arm and pulled her to my side, resting my hand at a respectful place on her waist, instead of where I really wanted it.

I shouldn't tempt myself.

"Probably shouldn't touch me. I'm sweaty," she said.

"I don't care," I said and pressed a kiss to her forehead, licking the salt of her sweat from my lips and enjoying how well she fit next to me.

My entire being eased when she was in my arms. My broken pieces felt less sharp and painful.

"What are you guys making?" Sloane asked, peeking into the mixing bowl.

"Goddess save me," Gwen mumbled with a mouth full of cookie. She snatched another one from where they cooled on the metal racks. "These are actually good." She waved the cookie in the air, and I tried not to cringe at the crumbs flying everywhere.

Nico scoffed. "Of course they are. And if you would have waited before helping yourself, they would have been iced."

Gwen stuck her tongue out at Nico, and he returned the gesture in kind.

Children. They were both children.

Amaya rested her head on my shoulder. "Were you helping him?" she asked, her voice low, making it feel like we were the only ones in the room.

"I was more observer than participant."

"And thank the Goddess for that," Nico said. "He'd mix up the baking soda and baking powder."

Amaya and Sloane laughed.

I wasn't amused and rolled my eyes. "No. I wouldn't." I may not enjoy cooking, but I wasn't completely inept.

"I don't get the joke," Gwen said. "What's the difference?"

All eyes landed on her as we tried to decide if she was serious, but when her expression didn't change, we all burst into laughter.

She glared at us and pinched some of the sprinkles and flung them at us across the kitchen.

"Oh, it's on!" Sloane said, but I spoiled whatever she had in mind. My shadow zipped out, closed the lid on the sprinkles, and slid the container to the other side of the counter.

"Uh uh. No food fights in my kitchen," I said.

"You're so boring," Gwen complained. "I don't know what Amaya sees in you."

Amaya took a step back and gave me a once over. She smiled with a mischievous glint in her eyes. "It's the tattoos," she said. "I've got a weakness for guys with tats." She winked, and I grinned, snatching her by the waist and pulling her in between my legs.

"Is that so?" I whispered, nuzzling my nose against her ear. "I do recall mention of tongues and licking in regards to my tattoos. When will you be making good on those promises?"

"You guys are gross," Gwen said. "It's burning my eyes."

"I think it's cute," Sloane said.

Amaya and I turned to our friends, who were watching us.

"I don't like an audience," I grumbled into her neck.

Amaya giggled. "Oh, I remember. You're not an exhibitionist," she whispered. "Your kinks are more of the bondage variety."

"What good are shadows if not for pinning my beautiful female to the bed and never letting her go?"

She pulled back to look at me. Her eyes heated, and she bit her lip seductively. I couldn't resist the temptation any longer and lowered my hands from their respectful position on her waist to rest at the swell of her backside.

"I'd like to remind you," Nico said. "That though this is *your kitchen*. I'm the one who cooks here, and I'd prefer if you didn't fuck where I painstakingly cook your meals."

Amaya shrugged, glancing at him. "Well counter sex never appealed to me before but now that I know I *shouldn't* do it…"

Goddess. I loved my little brat.

"We're going upstairs," I said. "Amaya and I have paperwork to go over."

"Paperwork? Is that what we're calling it?" Sloane asked.

"That appointment we talked about is next week," Nico said as my shadows gathered. Amaya threw her arms around my neck, pressing her chest to mine.

I nodded my acknowledgement, but my mind was elsewhere, planning on taking my bratty mate to our bed. If the desire in her eyes was any indication, it wouldn't be too difficult to convince her the rest of the day would be best spent not leaving our room.

Chapter Thirty-One

Sebastian

The therapy ritual could not have been scheduled at a worse time. All week Amaya and I were busy at work, putting out fire after fire.

The port manager indicated the captain of the ship that sent the first delivery of electrical equipment was due to dock at our port this afternoon. I sent our naval fleet out to keep an eye on the waters near the Delnee border to make sure this ship actually made it in today.

I wanted to be there to question the captain about the last shipment and see that the equipment made it to Merbany, but those plans were in jeopardy when Nico texted me.

Nico: Appointment is at noon.

I clenched one of my hands into a fist under my desk. I couldn't take a half day. Not today.

Maybe this whole therapy ritual was unnecessary. I hadn't had another episode or nightmare. Maybe I was cured. Maybe it was a fluke at the stadium shelter.

Or maybe you haven't been triggered yet, the voice in my head said.

Still, the urge to cancel, to push it off and claim I was too busy was making my thumb hover over my phone, hesitating over my response.

Nico: You can't save the world if you can't save yourself. Whatever you are in the middle of can wait a few hours.

I stared at the screen, rereading the words over and over, trying to convince myself they were false.

Nico: Adriana wouldn't want you to live like this.

Nico: Amaya needs you. Palagui needs you.

A minute passed, and another text buzzed in.

Nico: I need you. I can handle you being a moody bastard, but you aren't any fun to mess with when you're two seconds away from collapsing from exhaustion or staring into space with dead eyes.

Sebastian: What makes you think I want your harassment to continue?

Nico: Because I've been doing it for decades and you haven't kicked me out of the apartment so you must secretly like it.

I chuckled, shaking my head.

I guess I did like him being a pain in my ass.

Nico wasn't typically so...insistent. He usually let things slide, but the fact that he was pushing this so hard, must mean it was really important to him.

Taking a deep breath, I typed out my reply. I stared at the words a long time before hitting send.

Sebastian: I'm coming. I'll get the girls and be there.

Nico: No need. We're already here. Just waiting on you.

I clicked the screen of my phone off. A feeling of warmth filled my chest, but it was immediately replaced with shame.

If I was stronger, I wouldn't need them to be there for me. If I was a better male, a better mate, I wouldn't need to burden them with my problems.

But I wasn't, and the only way I'd change into a person that deserved Amaya as his mate, deserved Nico as his friend, deserved Gwen and Sloane as part of his family, was if I sucked it up and did this.

I sifted to the healing center in Molbridge.

The waiting area was set up with chairs on the outskirts of the room. The spot between Amaya and Nico was empty.

I made my way to the spot they'd saved for me, unable to meet their eyes, but I was saved from the awkwardness when a female with a clipboard came into the room and called Sloane's name.

Everyone stood, and we all walked toward her.

"Actually," Nico said. "I called last week about switching the recipient."

The female looked down at her clipboard and shrugged. "That's fine. This paperwork must be old. The facilitator will get all the correct info when you start." She smiled. "My name is Addie. Follow me."

Amaya saddled up beside me, her hand slipping into mine as we walked down the hall. The waiting room made the healing center look like a doctor's office, but as we walked down the hall, the smell of incense and the sound of gentle music floated around, making it seem more like a massage studio. We followed the female down two flights of stairs and into a large room.

Three walls were painted in comforting beiges and greens. The furthest wall was made up of natural rock and had a soft trickle of water pooling into the floor. It was dark but cozy with small, soft glowing lights hanging from the ceiling.

The middle of the room was made up of big cushiony chairs arranged in a circle.

A female in a burgundy scrub-like outfit greeted us. "I'm Karina. I'll be guiding your ritual today. Who's our recipient?"

I reached out my hand to introduce myself. "Sebastian Renwick. Thank you for meeting with us."

She smiled and cupped my hand in both of hers. "It's my pleasure."

Addie gasped, and we turned to her. With wide eyes, she asked, "You're the king?" Her gaze darted to Amaya. "And the queen?"

I nodded.

Addie's eyes were wide with shock and excitement. "My girlfriend is going to flip that I got to meet you. You're like our aspirational power couple. Literally we swooned over the videos of the engagement ritual at court. We were so excited for the royal wedding, like the flowers, the dress. I guess the hurricane probably ruined that, but like we were so pumped. Are you going to hold a royal wedding later? Or—"

"Addie," Karina scolded. "The next client intake probably needs completed."

Addie blushed and clutched her clipboard to her chest. "Right. Yes, of course. Sorry." She retreated from the room.

"I'm sorry about her," Karina said. "She's new."

"It's really okay," I assured her. I didn't think I'd ever encountered anyone who was starstruck to see me, but I suppose our public relations team was working up the power couple angle.

"If your friends don't mind setting themselves up in the circle," Karina said. "I'd like to ask you a few questions before we begin."

Everyone went to sit in the middle of the room, while Karina gestured to the chairs near the door, and we sat.

"Would you allow me to place my hands on your shoulders to sense into the areas that need attention?"

I took a deep breath and sighed it out, before nodding.

She rested her hands on my shoulders and closed her eyes. I watched her face for changes in her expression, bracing myself for the moment she'd feel the evil shadow of my soul, the broken pieces of my mind, but she was a professional and made no outward reaction. She removed her hands and placed them in her lap.

"You've been carrying a lot of pain for a very long time," she said. "But I felt nothing inside of you that we haven't been able to heal before."

I jolted back, shocked. "With all due respect, how is that possible? High priestesses heal physical ailments. I've never heard of these kinds of treatments."

"This is a new type of healing in Palagui," she said. "But it's based on ancient rituals that were performed thousands and thousands of years ago. My parents were ship captains, and I grew up visiting and learning from different countries and cultures." I must have not seemed convinced because she laughed. "It's okay to be skeptical. That won't affect the efficacy."

"Okay."

"You may experience intense emotional reactions, but that is to be expected. If at any time anything feels like too much, you can tell me and we'll stop. Sound good?"

"If...if this doesn't work..." I couldn't quite form the question.

Karina put her hand on my forearm. "If this doesn't work, there are several other techniques we can employ. Our center was built on top of a magical crossroads. I'll call upon the power of the sun, moon, and darkness to help conr.ect—"

"Not the deities," I said, alarmed.

She shook her head. "Not the deities, but where even *their* magic originates in the natural world. We've also performed healing rituals from within the Hollow for especially tricky cases since being near the source of power can help reestablish your connection. If even that doesn't work, we have options. Just try to have an open mind, okay?"

I nodded.

"Let's get started."

Everyone, except Nico, looked a little wary as I entered the circle and sat in the chair at the top. Amaya squeezed my hand. She sat to my left, and Nico to my right. Sloane beside him, and Gwen beside Amaya.

Karina explained, "The process I'll guide you through will induce a sort of waking REM sleep. The power of your friends will create a container of safety so you can revisit traumatic memories. My power will nudge different parts of your brain waves to help encourage integration of the memory."

She asked everyone's name and their relation to me. Nico and Amaya's answers were obvious. Sloane claimed me as her brother and friend. Gwen narrowed her eyes at me when she was asked and smiled. "Well, I guess technically he's my boss."

We all chuckled, and it helped break the nervous tension.

Gwen shrugged. "But he's my brother and friend, too."

It was still shocking to hear both of Amaya's friends claiming me as family. A confusing sensation rocked my body. Something like longing for their love, but also fear and anxiety from the sense I'd inevitably let them down. I'd already let one sister down.

"You can keep your eyes open or closed for the duration," Karina said. "This process connects each of you to the power within yourselves, each other, and the natural world. If anyone at any point feels overwhelmed, speak up, and we'll slow down. This works best if everyone is as comfortable as possible."

Karina stepped onto a stool behind my chair. "My hands will be hovering over your head. You may feel heat or tingling, but that's normal."

"Okay," I said, my voice almost a whisper.

For a long time, nothing seemed to happen, and I only noticed how tense I'd been when my shoulders started to relax, jaw releasing, face softening. Finally, I sensed the warmth of magic on my head, seeping into me.

"When you feel my magic, try your best not to fight it." Karina's tone changed into a soft whisper, as if coaxing a scared animal. "Your body has spent a long time protecting itself, but you're safe here, and your friends and I would like to help you, but you'll have to let us in as best as you can."

I didn't respond. Didn't know if I could.

Something like rivulets of magical water poured down, finding creases and depressions in my mind, flowing through me. I let it, but the magic increased velocity and became more probing, pressing, searching. I could feel myself start to panic.

"Amaya?" Karina said. There was the rustling of movement, but my eyelids were too heavy to open. My heart was pounding harder and I tried to control it.

"Your mate is going to touch your left arm now, Sebastian," Karina said. "Go ahead dear. A gentle but firm grip."

Amaya's tiny hand grabbed my forearm below the elbow. I inhaled in three parts. Her magic replaced the fear and tension. The panic ebbed away.

It felt so good. So right. Like I slipped into a warm, milky bath made up of her liquified energy. She was equal parts strong and soft. Like falling into a cloud of foamy shadows secured by a scaffolding of steel. The sensation of tears rose.

"How does that feel, Sebastian?" Karina asked.

"Good," I said, but the word was slurred by the peace filling me.

Karina's magic increased, the cold trickle of a burbling brook. With Amaya's warmth and safety, I let it wash over me.

It was slow, like the opening of a lid with rusted hinges. Karina's magic creaked and groaned, but finally the magic pried me apart.

"That's good," Karina said.

It didn't feel good though, it felt terrifying. I tensed, but it was already too late. My delicate, vulnerable bits were exposed to the world that I tried so hard to protect myself from.

"Focus on Amaya's magic," Karina instructed.

I concentrated on her sparkling light within the shadows. She was a contradiction. A high priestess and a darkyra. Warm light and cool darkness. Soft and strong.

I exhaled, long and slow. My soft vulnerable parts felt safe being held by my mate's magic.

"Okay," Karina said. "Nico is going to touch your right arm."

I didn't tense this time. Innately, I knew Amaya would protect me from getting hurt, and that Nico would too.

A much larger, rougher hand grabbed my forearm. His magic felt different as it coursed through me. Heat, of course, melting me into a puddle of relaxation, but intertwined with a boundless joy. The sense of gratitude for life that came from taking pleasure in mundane activities because at one point, you thought you'd never experience them again.

"Gwen is going to hold Amaya's hand and Sloane is going to hold Nico's. Are you still feeling alright?"

"Yes," I said softly.

A fainter magic passed through me, impossibly sweet, but it was soon followed by another magic that was puckering and sour, though not unpleasant. The two magics were like candy melting on my tongue.

"Gwen and Sloane are going to hold hands to complete the chain," Karina said, and a second energy zapped through me, clearing and shaking the last little bits of tension I hadn't noticed I had in my hands and my stomach.

I didn't think I'd ever felt so relaxed, so empty of thoughts. Not since I'd been a child. Memories I hadn't had in over a century flickered in my mind. At the beach outside my parent's house. Playing in the waves. Helping my mother bury my father in sand while he slept.

And other memories too. Adriana and I finding the hidden hollow cavity at the base of an old oak tree, and the plans we made to run away from the palace and live there together.

"I wish Adriana were here," I said. It was a wistful sadness, not overwhelming and soul crushing as it was when I usually thought about her.

"Me too," Nico said. He squeezed my arm, and I felt the ache of his own sadness within his magic. The same longing. The same sensation of missing a limb without her.

"Alright," Karina said. "I'm going to ask you questions to help guide you through a memory. You can answer silently in your head, and if at any time I'm going too fast or you'd like to take a break, you let me know. Does that sound good?"

"Yes," I said, though my nerves kicked up at the thought of what I was about to be asked. It was tempered by the pulse of magic, of love and peace, that flowed through me from my friends.

"While I'm using my magic to comb through any snarls," she said. "I'd like you to bring to mind a painful experience you'd like to work through. Take your time and let it come to the surface."

My breathing became heavier, my body anticipating the pain before the images even began.

The smell of blood. The sound of screams. I tensed, muscles freezing. My hands clutched the handle of a knife.

"On a scale of one to ten, how intense does this memory feel?" Karina asked.

"Ten," I croaked, but I wasn't sure if I spoke aloud because my entire body was stuck.

The top of my skull heated, and my arms were prickling with magic where two hands were holding on to me, grounding me.

"Take a deep breath," a voice said from far away.

I inhaled, but my lungs didn't fill completely.

"There are heavy, dense parts within you that are blocking my magic. Are there parts of your body that feel frozen?"

"Yes," I whispered. My hands were tight, locked. The core of my power felt like a heavy ball of lead, trapped and trying to burst.

"Take a deep breath and imagine air flowing into those areas, not needing to open them fully, just give them a little space."

I tried, but the action didn't help release the feeling. Karina suggested different visualizations. Imagining sunlight shining on the tense areas, or moonlight, or darkness wrapping around the hurt.

Nothing made a difference until she suggested allowing Amaya's magic to hold the tension. My body must have twitched in response because she suggested I allow Nico's, Gwen's, and Sloane's magic to wrap around the places inside me that needed to be held. Their magic blanketed the small, scared child inside me. It melted my frozen muscles.

The part of me shivering with fear warmed and stilled.

It went on for what felt like hours. Karina asked me questions, asked me to visualize different memories.

My body tingled in weird localized places. My hands and my chest and my right thigh.

Images I hadn't seen in my flashbacks came floating to the surface. The feel of the ground rumbling as my power exploded into a cyclone around me. The second I saw my mother's dead, unseeing eyes. The way I scratched at my hands until the skin tore, trying to clean my hands of my father's blood.

The moment I sifted away. The moment I knew I was entirely alone, and that unless I diverted the energy and the memories inside me, I'd die under their weight. I ripped myself apart and still knew no matter what I did, I'd never be safe again.

Except Karina was saying, "You're safe." And something wiggled in my brain. I wasn't reliving the memory but remembering it as the past. I wasn't there now.

I was forced to kill my father. I watched as my mother's throat was slit. My grief had caused my power to erupt and tear apart my house and all of Merbany, but that happened a long time ago.

I was in a room in Molbridge. I was in a circle with my friends around me.

And now there were two energies, presences, standing in the middle of the circle.

"Please forgive me for not protecting you," my mother said.

"We're so sorry we couldn't keep you safe," my father said.

"It's my fault you're dead," I said, but it wasn't me speaking. It was the small part of me. The little boy in the ruined shirt.

"No. It's not," they said, and their magic wrapped around the boy, hugged him and released him from blame.

From an outside point of view, I saw there was nothing that boy could have done differently. He was afraid and hurt and upset.

My heart split down the middle for all of his suffering. For all the denial of love and acceptance that would continue for the rest of his life.

Amaya had encouraged me to forgive the eleven-year-old boy, but that was no longer necessary because like my parents said, there was nothing to forgive. He wasn't to blame.

"How does the memory feel for you now on a scale of one to ten?" Karina asked.

I stared at the ground. Thinking of the dagger. Of the blood on my hands. Of my dead parent's bodies.

There was sadness, but a level of remove to the memory. It hurt, but my heartbeat wasn't rapid; my breathing was normal. There was no panic, only grief.

"Four," I answered.

Karina led us through a closing ceremony. Each person's magic gradually receded. She grounded our energy and pulled away.

We sat in silence for a few minutes, getting our bearings from the ritual.

"You may feel sleepy or energized after these treatments," Karina said. "Both are normal. Try to get a good night's sleep and drink plenty of water. If you decide you'd like another session, we recommend waiting at least a week in between to allow the power to settle. In the meantime, I recommend to everyone that you use and stretch your power to its full capacity for at least sixty minutes, three times per week. Healing comes from the movement of energy."

She checked in with each of us to make sure our magic was disconnected and fully embodied.

I thanked her for her guidance, and she indicated if any of us needed to speak privately, she'd be in her office.

A pleasant tiredness and the residual of peaceful magic simmered under my skin.

Sloane had a relaxed smile and bright eyes. Gwen's gaze was trained on the ground, reflective. Nico's knees were bouncing. His fidgeting kicked up to a higher degree than normal.

Amaya, though, seemed upset. Her mouth was pinched, hiding worry.

I interlaced our fingers. *Are you okay?*

She nodded too quickly. Her eyes darted around our circle and back to me before giving a tiny shake of her head. *I think I need to talk to Karina. Will you come with me?*

"I have some follow-up questions," I said, making our excuse. For whatever reason Amaya didn't want the others to know what was going on.

"Sure. Take your time," Nico said.

Addie had come back into the room to check if we needed anything, and Sloane had animatedly started asking her questions about her job and what she does at the center.

Amaya and I went down the hall to Karina's office. After knocking, we went inside and sat in the chairs opposite hers.

"How can I help?" Karina asked.

Amaya worried her lip. "I think there's something wrong with my magic."

"What makes you think that?"

She interlaced her fingers, clenching her hands in her lap. "I saw a shadow during one of the visualizations. It wasn't my shadow. And it wasn't Sebastian's. It wasn't even, uh, Kai's shadow."

"Kai?" Karina asked.

"Uh," Amaya scratched her head. "Kai tortured me in prison with their shadow."

She nodded, not flinching at all. "I see."

"But this was a really bad shadow," Amaya said. "Like the magic was thick and dense and evil. It was like…" She made a gesture with her hands over her torso. "It was like feeding on me."

Karina didn't appear concerned. "We put our participants into a REM-like sleep and hallucinations are common."

"A hallucination? It wasn't real?" Amaya asked. "It wasn't…It wasn't coming from the crown?"

I furrowed my brow at her, and Karina mirrored my expression before shaking her head. "The crown is more of a funnel than a siphon. The way I understand it, the energy from the sun, moon, and darkness of the natural world is drawn to the crown, funneled through you to the people of Palagui. It's the amount of power that is drawn into you that eventually breaks down the body. If anything, it's the opposite of being fed on."

"But if that was true," Amaya said. "Why does the queen have to have a certain amount of power? If she's only a funnel even the weakest fae could be a funnel."

Karina tilted her head. "Well, being a funnel, having that much energy drawn into your body is taxing. The queen needs to have a significant amount of power for her body to handle being a vessel. Plus, the stronger the high priestess power, the more naturally her body will heal any damage done over the course of her life. A fae with weak powers could be a funnel, but their body wouldn't be equipped to endure the onslaught of constant energy."

Amaya sat back but seemed unconvinced. Karina explained the crown how I'd always understood it, so I wasn't sure why Amaya believed otherwise.

What aren't you saying? I asked.

She stared down at her hands. *The deities didn't exactly grant me the crown…I stole it. They said I was too weak. They were going to kill me and send more natural disasters to Palagui until you sent a stronger high priestess.*

Rage bloomed to life at the thought that I'd almost lost her. I clenched my hands into fists. *You didn't tell me this.*

Her eyes met mine, and she pressed her lips together. *It didn't seem important.*

I raised my eyebrows. *Stealing the crown and angering the deities didn't seem important?*

She sighed. *I stole the crown, but they let me get away with it. If they wanted to stop me, they could have. The thing that I can't figure out is if the deities don't care about my life or my lifespan, why do they care if a powerful high priestess holds the crown or a weak one?*

I shook my head, coming up blank.

She continued, *And Kai's reasoning about wanting a darkyra to have the crown so shadows are more powerful doesn't make sense. Solisers are the most politically powerful group in Palagui and there hasn't been a soliser queen. Something isn't adding up.*

Karina cleared her throat, no doubt knowing that we'd been having a conversation in our heads by the fact we were staring at one another in silence. "I wouldn't worry about it. Perhaps you were affected more by the ritual because the magic between the two of you is strong."

Mating bond strong.

Amaya put on a fake smile. "You're probably right. Thank you for the session."

Karina smiled back. "I'm glad it helped. If you'd like another, either of you, just call. There is no waiting list for the Queen and King of Palagui."

We said our goodbyes, but stopped outside the room we'd left our friends in.

Amaya opened her bag to look at the crown inside. She wasn't wearing it for the ritual, probably hoping we wouldn't be recognized, but as we both stared at it, the peaks of the metal seemed sharper, the gold glint, biting. It could have been my imagination, but the diamonds seemed to have darkened from their clear crystal shine.

"Did your mother get headaches when her body started deteriorating?" she asked.

I shook my head. "She never complained of them. It was her memory that went and that was when we knew something was wrong." But what if I hadn't been paying attention? What if she had symptoms and didn't complain? "I never would have suggested you take the crown if I knew it would feed on you. I mean, it shortens a fae's life span, but you're so powerful. More powerful than my mother, so I assumed it wouldn't affect you as bad. She lived for 241 years, almost a full life."

Amaya threaded her fingers with mine. "Don't you dare blame yourself. We don't even know if this has anything to do with the crown."

"Maybe we should ask Kai? Do you think they'd tell us the truth?"

Amaya snorted. "All Kai does is lie."

"We'll figure it out. I'm not going to let a fucked-up piece of metal or even the deities take you away from me."

"I know." She touched my face. "Sorry for hijacking your ritual. You don't have to tell me anything, but do you feel better?"

I rested my palm over her hand. "I do."

She grinned. "Good. I could feel your magic inside me."

"Yeah?"

Her eyes got a wicked gleam. "Felt real good. But there's something else of yours that feels even better inside me."

I chuckled. How she could make dirty jokes while standing in a trauma healing center, having made the discovery that an evil shadow might be feeding on her, was beyond me. "That was a terrible come on."

"I know, but you liked it."

I did.

Chapter Thirty-Two

Amaya

I saw darkness feasting on my soul during the healing ritual. A shadow monster smiled at me with sharp, jagged teeth. Blackened guts and entrails, the remnants of my life force, hung from its mouth.

But I wasn't afraid.

"You asked for this," it said. "Your soul is more dark than light."

I had thought I saw something evil feeding on my power during the ritual, but what if I had only seen the truth of who I was? What if trying to find an outside source for the darkness inside of me was an excuse to not claim responsibility for what I had become?

For what I had always been.

More dark than light.

The moment I stole the crown's power, a foreignness seemed to take up residence within me. But what if it had always been there? Lurking in the background. And the crown had just been what allowed it to come out.

I enjoyed having the power to kill. I reveled in the exhilaration of enacting my revenge.

I took Kai's bargain and stole the crown from the deities, not only to save my own life, but because the thought of ruling—of having power—thrilled me.

My first impulse had been to lie and buy off Vince's silence. Actually, no. My first impulse had been to kill him. My second impulse was to buy his silence, to lie to the world and cover up the draxis.

Killing. Stealing. Lying.

I hid behind excuses. I killed Silas to protect myself. I killed those guards in self-defense. I killed the other guards because Kai poisoned my mind. I lied to protect my mate. I stole power to right injustices.

More lies. I liked killing. Lying was my second instinct after murder. I wanted power.

I had been able to ignore the nagging in the back of my head until now. There were too many other issues that warranted my attention. I could ignore the little voice that wondered why I hadn't had any traumatic flashbacks to the prison. Why killing Silas, killing Xenos, killing the guards, had never churned my belly with guilt. Why the torture I endured in the prison didn't haunt my dreams. Why the only nightmare I had of that time wasn't full of terror, but adrenaline that accompanied inciting violence.

Was this who'd I'd always been? Or is this who I had to become to survive?

The ritual hadn't only prompted my own inner reckoning. Everyone seemed changed by the experience. Sebastian had started to smile more, and his emotions were no longer blunted. He didn't hold himself back from me or anyone else. I no longer sensed the vague undercurrent of sour unease emanating from him.

Nico was full of energy, even more than usual. His sweet, buttery joy filled the house.

Gwen started going to a tea shoppe downtown, which was strange, but she was coming home with a lilac-colored serenity each time, so neither Sloane or I teased her about it.

As for Sloane, she hadn't been able to stop talking about the healing ritual. She was fascinated by the process, so much so that she'd gotten Addie's number and had been texting her regularly to find out more about her job.

"And did you know there have been dozens of new matings in a single month? It's insane. Addie says they're theorizing that when fae power went down, people's life forces kicked into a higher gear trying to make up for the loss," Sloane said over breakfast. The pink, cotton candy of her excitement was overpowering the fruit I was eating.

"You're really into this stuff, Sloane," I said. "Maybe you should work there."

"I already have a job," she said dismissively.

"Yeah." I shrugged. "But what about your fresh start? Construction has finally started in Merbany, so it's only a matter of time until things are back to normal." The shipments that had been held up for months finally came in.

"I couldn't. I'm not a medical professional. I'd have to go back to school," she said.

"So?"

She shifted in her chair and faint sour anxiety drifted into my awareness. "So that's years of my life and what if I get out and don't like it? What if I change my mind?"

She'd said once that she never got to choose her job in the High Priestess Society. That she wanted freedom to choose her path, but maybe fear of that freedom was holding her back.

"Maybe if we reached out to Karina, she'd set up an internship," I said. "You don't have to make any commitments. If you don't like it, no big deal. What could it hurt?"

"It'd be good for the queen and king to know more of these statistics too," Sebastian said. "If there are more matings, more power activations, and the like. It's important we know how our citizens are doing."

Sloane chewed on her lip and blew into her coffee mug to cool it down. Her anxiety faded to a pale yellow, and she nodded slowly. "Okay. Yeah," she said. "A week or so to gather information wouldn't have to turn into anything permanent."

I took a sip of my coffee to hide my smile.

Gwen plopped down into the chair beside mine and stole a few grapes off my plate. "My mother called. Again," she said, annoyed. "It's like she woke up and decided she'd pretend that she's a devoting and concerned mother who misses me."

"Maybe it's not pretend," I said. "You haven't seen her in months. She probably does miss you."

Gwen rolled her eyes. "Uh huh, sure." Gwen and her mother had an odd relationship. They could bond over High Priestess Society details, but when it came to affection, Gwen's emotional distance and suspicion of all people seemed to be genetic.

She glanced at Sebastian. "What do you know about the fae war in Delnee?"

"Admittedly not much," he said. "Delnee keeps the specifics of what happened under wraps. You already know the official story."

"Yeah," Gwen said. "The humans rendered the fae powerless, then killed them all, except the legacy families who surrendered and pledged allegiance to the humans. The government came up with a substance that would suppress fae power and put it into the water supply to prevent people with fae genes from activating their powers."

"My human history classes taught me all that, save the fae power suppression part," I said and put down the piece of toast I was nibbling on. "Wait, they couldn't have killed every fae in Delnee because somewhere in my family tree there was fae magic. And if they'd killed all of the fae, why would they need to suppress anyone's powers?"

"They killed every *known* fae in Delnee," Gwen said. "Fae children without activated powers are indistinguishable from human children. If their powers never activated, they'd still have the fae genes."

"But how has it stayed a secret?" I asked. "If my great-great grandmother was fae, why doesn't anyone in my family know?"

"Would you want to tell your children a secret that could get them killed for knowing?" Gwen asked.

I shrugged since I'd been put at risk for *not* knowing.

Sebastian nodded. "I don't remember all the details from one hundred years ago because it was a year or so after Adriana disappeared and I wasn't in a great place, but we felt a ripple in our power from the death of so many fae. It happened so fast, and no one knew why or how. Delnee wasn't going to answer questions about their methods and risk undoing whatever it was they'd done. Another reason most countries don't trust them."

"The reason I'm asking," Gwen started. "Is that Aunt Caroline mentioned that I didn't know the full story of our past. She claimed to have known the humans were going to kill the fae, but no one would listen to her. By the time she returned to Delnee, *the shadow plague* as she called it, had already taken hold. I don't trust a word she said, but my mother called me last night and asked me to come back to Delnee. She said that there were things about the past I needed to know."

"That's eerily similar," I said. "Do you think Caroline has gotten to your mom?"

Gwen shook her head. "I don't think so. I mean, she was horrified about what Aunt Caroline had done. I don't think she'd forgive her, let alone start listening to her conspiracy theories."

"Do you want to go back to Delnee?"

She sighed. "Not really, but I think I have to."

After today's council meeting, Gwen would be free to go wherever she wanted because the votes for the new high priestess, darkyra, and human representatives had been tallied last night. We didn't know the results yet, but the High Priestess Society and the joint human-darkyra commission had contacted the new representatives, and we'd meet them this morning.

Sebastian and I would also need to make a trip to Delnee soon. We needed to collect the rest of the draxis and get them to the research center.

Also, he wanted to speak to Harrison and Delnee leadership to get a sense if they'd been sabotaging our imports.

He hadn't been able to get conclusive evidence from the captain last week. The Palaguian naval force went into open waters and escorted the captain and the specialized equipment into our port without incident.

Sebastian's theories were confirmed after interviewing the captain about the prior shipments. Someone had impersonated our naval force and forged documents.

But that didn't necessarily point to Delnee's interference. It could have been anyone in Palagui or even someone from Delnee who was working alone.

Sloane and I wrote to Rien over the encrypted server to ask him to look into the missing shipments or any information about Delnee sabotaging Palagui's imports.

He hadn't found anything yet, but said he would keep digging.

***

"Good morning, Blake," I said, fast-walking down the hall toward the war room.

"Good morning, your majesty," they said, keeping up with me, tablet in hand. "Packed day today."

"Oh, good. Being queen was starting to get boring." I gave them a smile because it was our little joke. We were never *not* busy.

I had offered Blake a position as my administrative assistant, and they'd eagerly accepted since humans had previously been barred from working at a higher level in the government. They could type notes and blend into the background, but Goddess forbid a fae have to actually talk to, or rely on, a human.

Blake dreamt about going into public relations, so I put them in charge of liaising with the PR team, and from there, their duties kept expanding, helping me in other ways. As soon as a position opened up in PR though, I was going to move them to that department.

"Starting out with good news," Blake said. "I checked in with the security force and the detective in charge of the SoCo threat. They said there have been no reports of suspicious activity."

"Good." I took a sip of my coffee, trying not to spill any while walking.

"The public relations team would like to set up another interview and requested that the King also be in it," they said. "The PR guys want it to be a fluff piece. You talking about your marriage and what it's like to have two powers—"

"You're kidding me."

Addie wasn't the only one that was interested in our love life. It seemed being queen meant ruling the country *and* being expected to flaunt my life like a reality tv star. I'd turned down these fluff pieces every time they were brought to me.

It was disconcerting how the collective mental image of me that the PR team was trying to form resembled nothing of the person I thought I was.

Not that I even knew who I actually was anyway. A darkyra and a high priestess. That's all I knew for sure.

Gwen and I had been training my high priestess power to see if my empathetic powers could be used like hers to notch up or down emotions, but so far, I'd been unsuccessful.

"You can already sift, fight with shadows, heal people, compel humans, and you're an empath. Do you really need another power?" Gwen had asked.

No. I didn't. My high priestess power was weak, and it was unlikely that I would develop any additional power even after high priestess initiation.

But that was okay with me. I didn't want this particular one. The power to change people's emotions was an ethical minefield I should probably avoid. Although, I couldn't deny I wished I could make the public like me.

"Don't worry," Blake said. "I already told the PR team no."

"Thank you. Anything else?"

"We were sent the names of the new representatives this morning. For the humans, Aurelio Gustav from Palagui City. He/him pronouns, twenty-four years old, graduated summa cum laude from Palagui University."

I nodded, trying to commit that information to memory. I rounded the corner of the hall as Blake said, "The high priestess representative is—"

"Delilah," I finished, staring at the female standing beside my mate outside the war room.

"Uh, yes, Delilah Pembroke, ninety-seven years old, she/her pronouns, former lawyer for Bayter and Pew, worked several decades in an urban policy and planning think tank, and first female to be named president of the economic institute of foreign affairs."

Ah. Fuck me. She was gorgeous, cruel, my mate's ex, *and* had already worked my dream job.

A shot of anxiety zapped me, but it was fleeting. I was the Queen of Palagui. I wasn't intimidated by anyone.

Blake followed me down the hall and disappeared into the war room as I stood outside the door with Sebastian and Delilah.

"Delilah," I said with a nod.

"Your majesty," she answered in feigned deference. She wore a pristine business suit and navy-blue heels, impeccably styled. Her black hair was curled in big rings, and she looked effortlessly professional and beautiful.

"Delilah is replacing Gwen," Sebastian said. His tone curt.

"Blake informed me," I said and turned to her. "Congratulations on your new position."

She smiled, saccharine sweet. "It certainly is nice to be recognized as qualified to lead my people, having *earned* their respect." Her eyes flickered to my crown, making her insult clear. I hadn't risen through the ranks to become queen. I stole the power that the crown afforded me.

Eviscerate her, my shadow said.

I kept my face neutral, letting the silence hang in the air before saying, "In a world like ours, where females are hardly ever recognized for their leadership nor given the respect they deserve, I have to agree with you. It *is* nice you were recognized. Your job history is certainly one of the most accomplished of everyone in the war room, and I look forward to working together and hearing what you have to contribute."

Her smile died, and her bottom lip parted from the top.

"If you wouldn't mind," I said, gentle but firm. "I need to discuss something with my mate before we get started." I grabbed Sebastian's arm and tilted my head, smiling at her.

Delilah remained frozen another beat, and then blinked away her surprise and opened the door to the council meeting, leaving without a word.

Sebastian raised an eyebrow. "Rendered her speechless and didn't even have to threaten her with your shadows. Impressive."

"I like to keep everyone on their toes."

Sebastian shook his head, the corner of his mouth quirking up. "What did you need to talk to me about?"

"Oh nothing," I said. "I just wanted to remind her that you're *mine*."

My shadow hummed her approval.

Sebastian smirked. "So possessive."

I winked at him as I pulled open the door and strode inside. Everyone stood and bowed until Sebastian and I took our places at the head of the room, and I bid them to sit.

"Aurelio Gustav is our new human representative," I said. "Welcome." I inclined my head to the new male face at the table. He looked even younger than twenty-four, closer to sixteen with a round face and big green eyes. His blonde, almost white hair was very curly. It bounced softly as he nodded to return my greeting.

"Are you even old enough to drive? Did you need a work permit to get elected?" Vince said.

I glared, ready to jump in and defend Aurelio. He was only two years younger than me, but his baby face and innocent eyes would make him a prime target for Vince's antagonism. Let alone the fact he was a human surrounded by fae.

"Oh, I'm legal," Aurelio said, leaning forward and staring Vince down from across the table. "But I know it becomes difficult to estimate younger people's ages as you get older. What with your eyesight going and all. If you'd like, I could send you a recommendation for an optometrist that specializes in geriatric cases."

"You little—"

I cleared my throat, interrupting whatever Vince had been about to say. "Can I please move on with my meeting? Or would you like to finish that sentence and Merbany can hold a representative vote next month?"

Vince glowered at Aurelio, who only smiled back. I already liked him if he could put Vince in his place.

"Delilah Pembroke was voted as representative for the high priestesses, and she'll be taking over for Gwen. Gwen will remain as one of the members of my privy council," I said. "And the darkyra representative is…"

I trailed off because Blake hadn't finished telling me who was voted in, and as I looked around the room, no new faces stood out.

Blake cleared their throat. "Uh, so, there were four candidates on the darkyra ballot, but a write-in won."

I furrowed my brow. "Who?"

"Daria Reeves."

The entire room sat in silent confusion.

Vince snorted. He rubbed his forehead with his fingers. "Only Daria could win an election while hiding in the shadows. A darkyra through and through."

"But how?" I asked. "She hasn't been here for months, and she was still voted in?"

Blake shrugged. "The commission said that even in her absence she was the best representative for the darkyra. She's who the people want."

"Alright," I said. "I guess we hold the seat open for Daria's return. Did the commission mention if they were in contact with her?"

"They wouldn't say," Blake answered.

Daria was somehow inspiring loyalty without any public appearance. I glanced at Gwen who stared unseeingly at the table.

The council meeting continued. Aurelio and Delilah swore fealty and bound themselves to their faction's best interest.

Sebastian explained that human bargains only worked if they were bargaining with a fae. Basically, the fae's magic bound the bargain to the human's life force. It was effectively the same outcome.

The councilmembers went around the room with their usual updates.

"You need to officially approve Rosen Construction as the contractors for the sites in Merbany," Erik said.

It was a simple word: Approved.

And yet, I couldn't say it.

This was another soliser company that Vince was forcing on me, and I'd grown tired of giving in to his demands.

I'd been debating if I should call his bluff on his threats. Over the last few months, I watched Vince's decisions and actions. He only cared about himself and his personal power, so I had the inkling that he was far too selfish to expose our secret. He'd have to deal with the pain of a broken bargain, revolting solisers, and the disruption of another potential regime change. It was all too risky for him.

"Actually," I said, flipping through the stack of paperwork in front of me. "The contract approval goes to A&L Construction." They had a faster turnaround time and cheaper cost than the soliser company.

"What?" Erik said, sitting up. "That wasn't what Vince and I discussed with you earlier."

"I changed my mind." My tone was bland.

"You sure about that?" Vince asked.

I blinked and cut my gaze to him. "Yes."

I couldn't shoot down every one of his requests because he'd have nothing to lose then, but I was done letting him get everything he wanted.

Vince had no evidence Sebastian turned the high priestesses into draxis. And if he scrounged some up, we would take care of it, but I really didn't think he'd risk the broken bargain.

Erik huffed and stood up. "How is what you're doing any different from what Xenos did? You're putting the darkyra above the solisers, giving them advantages over everyone else. You do realize that queens mad with power don't think they're doing anything wrong."

I refused to let him see that his words phased me at all. "Sit down. My decision is final."

Erik pursed his lips and looked at Vince. His forehead was wrinkled in an angry grimace, but he didn't say anything. After a moment, Erik sat back down.

"Moving on," I said. "I've made a decision that will be a major change for Palagui. We're repealing all of the darkyra and human laws currently on the books."

We'd been focused on hurricane relief in the last few months, but the rebuilding had begun, and I wasn't putting it off any longer. The first day of the new human representative's term seemed as good a day as any.

Gerald cleared his throat. "I thought we weren't going to do that all at once?"

"I've changed my mind."

"A lot of that going on today," Vince mumbled.

"Queen Amaya," Gerald said. "I know you intend to change social and cultural patterns here in Palagui, and I've always been a supporter of darkyra rights, but..." He paused and winced. "Honestly, it's a bad idea. There could be riots."

"The laws should be rolled back one at a time," Erik said. "Wrapped up underneath a bunch of more interesting policies. These changes should be addenda items so the public and the media aren't looking at what you're doing."

"No," I said. "I'm not hiding, and I'm not going to be intimidated. The laws will be removed, and new ones written that criminalize fae faction discrimination and human-fae discrimination."

"Palagui has a new queen," Sebastian said. "People expect changes. The hurricane disrupted normal routines, and we're taking advantage of that disruption."

"For every outspoken person on the news, there are five people who will silently celebrate," Micah said. "But I wonder what the PR plan is for this? Because though those outspoken people are the minority, they will be a problem. I think"—he looked around the room—"all the councilmembers agree that this is long overdue, but it needs to be done with caution."

I interlaced my fingers and nodded. My eyes caught on the way Leva was shifting awkwardly in her seat. "Leva, do you have these concerns as well?"

Her face turned bright red, and she stammered a little. I instantly felt bad that I'd called her out. I only wanted to make sure she knew it was safe to voice her opinion.

Since Sloane's lunch with Leva, her shyness had been getting better. She gave her region updates without her voice trembling anymore.

"Well…uh, I do think darkyra and humans should have rights," Leva said. Her eyes landed on Vince, and he scowled at her while rubbing his temples in aggravation. She spoke the next sentence so quickly the words ran together. "But-it-is-very-sudden-maybe-we-should-wait."

She clasped her hands together on top of the table and kept her gaze down.

I nodded slowly. "Okay. Thank you for your input. I hear all of your concerns, really, I do. But whether we do this one at a time or all at once, there will be upset people. Creating the human representative position was a good test. There was negativity in the media, but there were no riots or public outcry. I think it's time. The darkyra and humans have been waiting long enough."

I tried to catch Leva's eye, but settled with looking at Micah. "To address your concerns, I'll make sure that our PR team has a full plan outlined, and ask them to prep each of you so you're ready to handle any potential backlash."

There was nothing left to say, so I ended the meeting, and the councilmembers exited the room. I expected Vince to stay behind and threaten me with exposing us for creating the draxis or go off about repealing the laws, but he was the first one out the door.

Sebastian, Gwen, and I were the only ones left in the room when I stood and walked to the window that overlooked the city.

"How bad do you think it'll get?" I asked.

The city's pollution had all but gone away in the few months I'd been queen. The magic had settled, but the country wasn't healthy. Not really. Not underneath.

"Hard to say," Sebastian answered. "There were riots after the darkyra were given representation, but like you said, there haven't been any protests about the humans. I think Micah is right. Most people think humans and darkyra should have equal rights, despite what the media likes to say."

"And Vince?" Gwen asked.

"I'm going to tell the PR team to be ready for the possibility that draxis rumors could be spread about us, and that they are just backlash to the changes," I said. "Vince doesn't have any evidence, if he did, he would be waving it in our faces to prove it."

"I'm not as concerned about Vince as I am about our budget," Sebastian said. "Riots about the changes in the laws will eventually cool down, but if we start bouncing checks, there's going to be a lot of angry people at our doorstep."

"We need more loans?" I asked.

"More loans, better terms, relief in general," Sebastian said. "The IMF said they're done helping, and if we don't start paying, we're going to have to start privatizing and selling governmental assets. The mines in the north. The fishing rights in the south. They'll systematically chunk Palagui off and sell us to the open market."

"Almost like giving us these shitty loans was exactly the plan the whole time?" Gwen said.

Sebastian frowned. "We had no other choice."

"How long until we're bankrupt?" I asked.

Sebastian ran a hand through his hair. "If we don't start cutting spending drastically, we have two months. Three months tops."

We needed money. And fast. If it hadn't been for all the delays in rebuilding, we'd be in a better position. People would be back in their homes, and we wouldn't be funding their temporary housing. The hurricane relief took out a huge chunk of our reserves, but it's the continual drain that has been the most problematic.

And if Sebastian's theory about Delnee intercepting our imports was true, that was exactly what they wanted to happen. The IMF wasn't going to give us more money, and we didn't have a strong enough relationship with any other country to ask for a loan from them.

Delnee was Palagui's strongest ally.

I turned and looked at Gwen and Sebastian. "What if we go to Delnee. Ask them for a loan. And if they say no..." I shrugged one shoulder. "We make it so they can't say no."

Gwen narrowed her eyes. "How?"

Sebastian sighed. "You want to compel the president to give us money? That breaks about fifty international laws."

"Yeah, well, it's not like Delnee is on good terms with anyone," I said. "What country is going to come to their aid if they start complaining about Palagui compelling them? Plus, they deserve it. Harrison kidnapped Sloane. They're probably messing with our imports, and they were going to cuff their high priestesses."

I was aware how *mad queen* this was sounding and I didn't care.

"The leadership wears protection rubies for any meeting with the fae, and Evelynne and the rest of the legacy high priestesses will be there to make sure there's no fae compulsion," Sebastian said.

"Pretty sure that's half of my mother's job. Being babysitter for fae meetings," Gwen said.

"That's why you're coming with me," I said, smiling. "You're going to convince your mother to work with us. Sebastian and I will relieve the president of his protection rubies, and Delnee will pay for what they've done."

I clasped my hands behind my back and turned to look out over the city. At least Palagui would benefit from my darkened morality.

Chapter Thirty-Three

Amaya

Pointedelle hadn't changed. But I had.

The city—which used to intimidate me with its bustle and excite me with the promise of legitimacy—had faded away.

The miles of concrete, the towering pillars, the dark and dirty alleys, no longer held the power to terrorize me. I'd seen, been through, far worse than anything the streets or the people in them could inflict on me.

We flew into Delnee since we couldn't have leadership knowing we were capable of sifting across the ocean. Sebastian followed all of the proper protocols, submitted the travel permits, and requested a meeting with the president.

Gwen returned separately as her flight had been set up by her mother.

Sloane stayed behind because we technically weren't sure if Harrison ever withdrew her deportation order. Gwen would straighten it out with her mother while she was here. Also, Karina had agreed to start Sloane's internship at the healing center. She and Nico were staying in Molbridge for a week, which worked out well because Nico's school was on spring break.

During this trip, I'd be Amaya Renwick. She'd grown up in Palagui her entire life and married Sebastian Renwick. She had nothing in common with Amaya Mevson. The girl that had grown up in Delnee and thought the fae had been eradicated. That girl had been partnered with Rien Astora, had gotten her certification, and stayed in the city to work with Dr. Henderson as far as anyone in this country was concerned.

Keeping my lives separate would be imperative as I didn't want to bring attention to my parents.

Sebastian and I would limit our sifting to absolute emergencies as Delnee's High Priestess Society had a surveillance team—the one that Sloane had been a part of—who could detect the use of magic used on city streets. Building-to-building sifting had never gotten Sebastian in trouble, but it may have been because the surveillance team was more concerned with draxis activity than a lone fae ambassador. They still had the capability of detecting magical usage if given the proper incentive.

"The night Nico burnt down that bar," Sebastian had explained on the plane. "The owner knew someone who pulled the magical surveillance records that showed there was fae power used. If it hadn't been for Rashida, I'm pretty sure Delnee would have tried to execute him."

"Seriously? That's extreme."

"It wasn't just about the bar. They didn't want knowledge of the fae to get out."

"So that's how you met Rashida?"

Sebastian nodded. "She's the best lawyer in Pointedelle. Argued that technically there'd been four fae permitted to travel in Delnee that night, and since they couldn't prove who it was using the fae power, nor that it was fae power that started the fire, the case was dropped. Delnee suspended Nico's travel permits, but that was the worst of it."

"How did she know about fae power?"

"She comes from a powerful political family in Delnee."

"Huh," I said. "So how did you meet Dr. Henderson?"

Sebastian made a face. "Well, Delilah introduced us."

My jaw dropped. "How did she know him?"

"Dr. Henderson came to Palagui early in his career to research our fae archives when Delnee and Palagui had a sort of exchange program. Delilah was in charge of the archives he'd been working on and was supposed to wipe his memory before sending him home, but as you know, it didn't take."

"Yeah, he told me he was a high priest."

"Delilah told me to reach out to him when I was struggling to research the portal. Then last summer when I needed an excuse for an extended stay in Pointedelle, he got me on the cert panel."

"So we have Delilah and Dr. Henderson to thank for us getting together?"

He chuckled. "I guess we do."

"Why did you need an extended stay last summer?"

His face fell. "The Queen was getting worse. Xenos didn't want more draxis in Palagui, so we increased the amount we were shipping to Delnee, but I needed to be here to tie them down, and we couldn't do it all at once or someone would have caught on."

I nodded and changed the subject, hoping the bitter grief of his guilt would dissipate, but it hadn't for long.

Sebastian, Gwen, and I spent the first night in Delnee driving around the streets of Pointedelle and transporting draxis to a shipping container at Delnee's port.

All of the draxis in Delnee were on their way to the research center by the end of the night.

I'd been worried it would make Sebastian regress from the progress he'd made since the ritual. His aura was full of guilt, carrying a pain that he tried to hide, but was obvious in the tension in his shoulders. He'd been wearing sunglasses all day—to hide his void eyes—but he'd taken them off tonight, no longer hiding his bleak expression.

Gwen had returned to her apartment, and to keep up appearances, Sebastian and I stayed in a hotel near the capitol.

We showered and worked on our laptops, but as my eyelids started drooping and I crawled into bed, I broke the silence.

"Are you okay?" I asked, afraid the question would prompt a complete shutdown. That he would rebuild the wall we had broken down.

He closed his laptop and turned to face me from where he was sitting at the tiny desk by the TV.

"I don't think I'd say I'm okay," he answered cryptically.

I worried my lip.

He sighed and got up, climbing under the blankets with me. "Even if we turn all the draxis back, there were so many that were killed. So many people they killed to collect their power."

There was nothing I could say. Nothing to change the past or make him feel better.

But, at least, he didn't shut me out.

"I know," I said, reaching for him. He accepted my touch, and we held each other until we both fell asleep.

***

It killed me to be only a train ride away from my parents and not be able to see them. We talked regularly on the phone, and though they sometimes questioned why my phone number came in with strange area codes, they always bought my excuse that I was working on confidential governmental projects.

It wasn't *totally* a lie.

They were safer not knowing or being attached to me in any way.

We weren't scheduled to meet Harrison until tomorrow, so we were driving to Rashida's office, where Rien suggested we meet.

Gwen was spending the day with her mother, trying to feel out if we could get her to work with us at the meeting tomorrow or if we would need a different tactic.

Rien hadn't been able to find any conclusive evidence that Delnee was responsible for sabotaging our imports, but he told us that there were *developments* since we'd last talked.

Sebastian was quiet all morning, but he'd been on his laptop, trying to make sure everything was in place for the end of the week when the announcements of the law repeals went out.

I stared out the window as we drove through the city. Spring hadn't been kind to Pointedelle. While Palagui had been warming, and the first green of tulips were poking out of the ground, Pointedelle was in the middle of their melt. The gray slush of snow and the de-icer they used on the sidewalks was piled in the corners. It might have been the weather and everyone's bundle up clothes, but the people here looked...different from the people in Palagui.

It was hard to put my finger on it. The clothes were different and no one wore cuffs on their wrists, but it was something more than style.

People walked different, carried themselves different. As if everyone in Pointedelle was uncomfortable in their bodies. They all wore pinched expressions. They shifted their weight when they walked and hunched their shoulders. Their strides were quicker like everyone was in a hurry to get somewhere.

No matter their skin color, they all seemed pale and a little sickly. Had it always been this way?

I pushed my awareness toward a few of the people on the sidewalks. Sebastian had taught me how to read a human's mind so that we would have an extra advantage for our meeting. We could also read the minds of fae who didn't activate their powers because their minds weren't protected with magic.

Most people's minds were a whirlwind of thoughts. Worries and past grievances. Everyone was stuck somewhere far away, either in the future or the past.

I didn't blame them. I'd been stuck in the existential in-between too, but this was different. It was like they were all blocked, stagnant, and stuck.

"Is everyone…" I turned my attention to Sebastian. "Are the humans here different from the ones in Palagui?"

He furrowed his brows.

"Like everyone seems kinda…mentally constipated."

"Ah," he said. "That's how you can tell the humans from the fae. The most uptight ones aren't humans."

"We can tell the difference?"

"Sometimes. It's not foolproof. The suppression they give people isn't without side effects. Our bodies were born to express power. If it can't, you get a country with chronic pain, autoimmune diseases, and general malaise."

How has no one put together what was happening? Though, I guess, it was an unfair question. I certainly hadn't known what was happening to me.

Didn't know the reason I couldn't control my emotions was because I hadn't tapped into the power inside me.

How many un-activated darkyras had depression, a void where their power should be? How many un-activated solisers had unexplainable anger, a fire that had no release?

The problem was never us. It was that our true selves had been muzzled.

That lovely thought was rolling around in my brain when we pulled up to Rashida's office. I hiked the stairs of the converted townhouse and walked into what would have been the living room, but had been set up as the reception area.

The secretary, Christine, rose from her seat as we walked in. "He's upstairs. Come with me," she said instead of a greeting.

I glanced back at Sebastian, who only shrugged, and we followed her up the stairs.

She put her hand on a doorknob and spun around. "Try to get him to eat something. I don't think he's been out of this room in two days."

I frowned, but before I could respond, she knocked on the door. The sound of rushing footsteps boomed from the other side of the door until it swung open.

"Finally," Rien said. He grabbed my wrist and yanked me inside.

His collared shirt was crumpled and wrinkled, the buttons haphazardly done. His hair had grown out again, a messy, greasy mop atop his head like he'd been pulling at it.

Sebastian squeezed in behind me, and the door shut with a soft click. The room was a tiny studio. A kitchenette in the corner with a mini fridge and microwave. A dining table with a single chair in the center, and the bed and a dresser made up the rest of the room.

I recalled Rashida having said that she'd converted the upstairs into studios that her clients could use while she was working on their cases.

"Do you live here?" I asked.

"No," Rien said. "Uh, sorta. I guess. Technically I'm living in the condo my dad owns, but I needed a place that wasn't bugged."

He was walking around the table with some kind of purpose—though I couldn't figure out what it was—moving piles of papers from one place to another.

"What do you mean bugged?"

He rubbed his eyes and pulled at his collar. "Well, my dad is vice president, so I have body guards that follow me everywhere. I'm pretty sure my phone and laptop are bugged." He pulled out a tablet from the side table by the bed. "Keep the one we communicate on in a separate place, just in case. That's why I haven't been able to tell you what I found in the last few days. The new bodyguards I got were getting wise to my hiding spots. Had to stay over at Justin's place, sneak out the window, and call a taxi to get here."

I looked around the rest of the apartment. It was a mess. The bed had a single sheet crumpled in the middle. Take-out containers of half-eaten food and piles of paper everywhere. I turned to Sebastian, who'd donned a neutral expression, but his eyes were roaming the room, taking it all in.

"Rien, what is going on?"

"He's psychotic. He's going to take over everything. We don't stand a chance, don't you see?" His eyes were wide and crazed.

I put my hands up. "Okay. Why don't you sit down, huh? When's the last time you slept or ate?" Or showered, but I didn't say that aloud. "Christine said you haven't come out for two days?"

Rien scoffed. "Oh, she's exaggerating. She likes to mother me. It's only been..." He looked at his wrist, but he wasn't wearing a watch. "Like...well, I guess. I don't know."

I reached out for his shoulder, wanting to guide him to the dining room chair, but he shook his head, muttering to himself. "I'm fine. Fine." He shrugged off my touch and turned back to the table, pointing. "This is what you should care about. This is our problem."

I licked my lips and walked over to the table, but it was just stacks of papers, emails, and memos. Nothing I could see making any sense. I didn't understand whatever chaotic organization he had.

I had no doubt Harrison was up to something, but the frenzied look in Rien's eye was more concerning at the moment.

Sebastian went to the other side of the table and picked up a piece of paper.

"Don't touch that!" Rien leaned over and snatched it from his hand.

My eyes widened.

Rien gently put the paper back in the spot it had been. "I looked into our imports and exports like you asked. I didn't find anything that talked about Palagui's supplies, but the more I dug, the more I found all these orders for equipment."

He handed me one page with an almost gingerly touch.

I scanned the memo, but it might as well have been in a different language. A list of words ten to fifteen letters long. "I don't know what any of this is."

"It's the chemical compounds needed to make the fae suppression," Rien said. "My dad is going to invade Palagui and suppress everyone's powers."

I swallowed. "Okay…" I said, my heart racing as my mind tried to follow these threads. "How do you know he's planning to use it on Palagui? Maybe he was ordering more suppression for Delnee?"

"You don't believe me," Rien said. His voice deadened.

"No, Rien. It's not that," I said. "I just don't understand—"

Rien made a frustrated noise in the back of his throat. He snatched the paper from my hand and started waving it in my face.

"Has your shadow boyfriend completely brainwashed you? Don't you get it? While you've been playing faerie queen, war is brewing over here. Everything is going to shit!"

Rien slapped his open palm on the table, causing some of the pages to flutter to the ground, but he ignored the destruction of his strange organization and grabbed my shoulders. Wide eyes stared into mine. I winced as his fingers dug into my skin and he shook me. "We're all going to be under his thumb—"

Shadows wrapped around both of his wrists and pulled his fingers back.

"Get your hands off my wife," Sebastian growled as shadows pressed Rien to the wall. He sifted in front of me, blocking me from Rien.

The shadows fell away from Rien, and he stepped toe-to-toe with Sebastian.

"Not really a fair fight is it," Rien spit out. He outstretched his arms to either side. "If you want to hit me, use your goddess damned fists and not your devil shadows."

Sebastian huffed a breath. "You think this is a fight?" His voice flattened into a sadistic calm. "If I thought for a single second you'd hurt Amaya, I wouldn't have to fight you. I'd snap your neck before you could take your next breath."

I stepped from behind him to stand between them and put a hand on Sebastian's arm. The spice of anger from both males swirled around the room.

He lowered his chin, staring down at Rien. "But see, I wouldn't even get the pleasure of killing you because if you were going to hurt her, she'd be the one to do it. I've watched her kill males twice your size, severed their spinal cords with her *devil* shadows. Just. Like. That." He snapped his fingers. "But make no mistake, if you grab her again, touch her at all, I can't promise I'll have the self-control to hold myself back."

"Sebastian," I said. *He isn't himself. He wasn't trying to hurt me.*

I know he wasn't. Doesn't mean he gets a pass to touch you. I could hear the fury in his voice even in my head. *I won't stand by and watch him grab you like that. I saw you flinch.*

I took a deep breath and released it slow through pursed lips.

"Rien," I whispered. "Why don't you go shower and everyone can cool off? I'll order food, and after you eat something, you can explain what all this means."

Rien sighed. His glare faded into a deep tiredness as his shoulders sunk. "Fine."

He shuffled across the room and disappeared into the bathroom. I called to order food from the restaurant we'd always ordered from when we worked on our certification project.

Sebastian and I rifled through the emails on the table while we waited, but neither of us could figure out why Rien considered one chemical order as proof of war brewing.

"Even if Delnee made the suppression and somehow got into Palagui, it's not like that would make the fae lose their powers. It'd only prevent children from activating theirs, right?" I asked, sitting on Rien's bed so I could read the papers he'd laid out on the nightstand.

"One would assume." Sebastian scanned another paper and set it aside. "I've never wished I knew how Delnee tricked the fae into giving up their powers as much as I did now."

"If it was as easy as ordering chemicals, they'd have done it a long time ago." I picked up a set of emails. All of them with a single sentence subject line: Shipment detour completed.

"Sebastian," I said. "What dates were the imports expected to be delivered to Palagui?"

He pulled out his phone, looked up his records, and read out the dates. Every single one of these emails was within a few days of when our deliveries should have been completed.

The emails came from different senders. Each a string of nonsense letters and numbers, but they were all sent to one person.

I handed the emails to Sebastian. He flipped to the end of the stack.

"Harrison Astora," he said, shaking his head. "I knew Delnee was behind this, but I still didn't actually believe they'd do it."

My phone buzzed with a text that our food delivery was here. Sebastian handed me the stack of papers and went downstairs to grab our order.

I snapped a picture of the emails with my phone and put them back where I'd found them.

The bathroom door opened, and Rien walked out from the steam with just a towel wrapped around his waist.

I averted my eyes, but the room was small, and the bed was basically against the dresser. I inched as far back as I could as he opened the drawers and pulled out his clothes.

"I'm really sorry, Amaya," he said. "I didn't mean to get up in your face like that. I think I overdid it with the caffeine."

I glanced up at him. Water ran down his chest in rivulets. The heat of the shower radiated off his skin.

A faint blue guilt radiated from him. And something else. An emotion I did not want to be feeling from him.

Where he stood, he blocked any attempt I could have made at a casual escape since I'd have to climb over the bed and the side with all the papers.

I tried to smile, but it might have been a grimace, and waved a hand like this wasn't incredibly awkward. "It's alright. I understand this is all stressful."

The door opened, startling us and making it look like we'd been caught doing something.

Sebastian's expression didn't change. His eyes flickered between me and Rien. He deposited the food on top of the mini fridge as it was the only flat surface that didn't have papers atop it.

Rien stepped away from the dresser and back into the bathroom to get dressed. Sebastian still had his back to me. I got off the bed and crossed the room to stand over the mini fridge next to him.

You're playing it very cool, I said to him in his head. *If I walked in on Delilah or Jeremy in a towel and talking to you, I don't think they'd have a head anymore.*

I've had a century of experience denying myself what I really want.

I put my hand on his forearm, and he met my eye. There was a speck of blue in his eyes which were usually completely black. I blinked, and it was gone.

He wants you back, Sebastian said.

I put my hand on his chest over his heart. *He can't have me. I'm yours. I'm your wife. I'm your mate. And your mine.*

He sighed. His void eyes staring down at me.

Stop reading his mind. You'll make yourself crazy.

I know, he said, making a scrunched-up face.

Rien reemerged, and I handed him the takeout while scarfing one of the vegetable pastries for myself. I went to the other side of the room as Rien sat at the table to eat. He took off the lid to the plastic bowl. "You remembered?"

His eyes cut to mine, and I blushed for some reason. "Of course," I said. "You never changed the order."

He smiled, and my insides twinged. The heat of embarrassment grew in my chest as his happiness filled my awareness, way happier than takeout should make him.

Sebastian leaned against the wall near the door, arms crossed and silent. His jaw ticked, but he had his emotions on lockdown because I didn't feel a thing.

I have your lunch orders memorized too, I said. *I know exactly what you like to get from the four places downtown you rotate through.*

Sebastian's eyes softened from their intense glare at the side of Rien's face as they looked at me. *I'd have yours memorized, but you always get something different.*

Life's too short to repeat.

He smirked. *Life's too short to chance getting food you don't like.*

Fair enough, I said.

I busied myself reading the last pile of papers that were lying on the dresser while waiting for Rien to finish eating, but my eyes snagged on a word.

"Rien, what is this email from the military coordinator?" I asked.

He wiped his mouth with a napkin and put the bowl aside. "That's what I've been trying to tell you."

He shuffled some papers on the table and handed a pile to Sebastian as he said, "I was looking into Delnee's imports and exports like you asked. I told my father I received a tip that there were companies that were exporting black market products, so he gave me access to the server that has import and export approvals and the port logs. I found an email exchange between a Delnee company and our military coordinator. It was an official governmental request to cease exports of their main product."

Sebastian glanced up from the emails. "Their main product being?"

"Weaponry," Rien answered.

He ran across the room to the table and pulled out a thick bound stack of papers. "The company is publicly traded, and if the government was asking them to cease exports, their stock price should have gone down, right?"

He handed me the annual report with several tabbed pages. "But it didn't. The report shows they're still producing and selling weapons, so either they're lying or..."

"Or someone is buying them in Delnee," I finished.

"Exactly, so I started going through the military reports that circulate through the capitol. It's top-secret enough that the public doesn't know, but nothing that a presidential aide couldn't get a hold of, and you know what I found?"

I couldn't tell if he was kind of having fun explaining all this. "What?" I asked.

"The western border has been thinned. They called the troops in, but the reports didn't say where they went," he said and ran back over to the bed and handed me a notebook.

He'd scribbled notes on it, fragments of words and sentences. "I don't exactly have a good relationship with the human military coordinator, but I spoke to Evelynne, uh, Gwen's mom, even if she only handles the high priestesses, I thought maybe she'd have insight since she technically is in charge of the Department of Defense. I casually mentioned it was weird that the western border troops had been sent home, and she corrected me, said that they weren't sent home, they'd been repositioned to the naval force. She only knew this because the high priestesses had to move their annual training at the military base by the port."

I set the notebook down and sat on the bed as my mind raced trying to figure out other plausible reasons for these things to occur.

Rien was getting worked up again, the crazy look in his eyes returning. "I'd initially thought it was good that my father stopped discussing cuffing the high priestesses. That he'd dropped it, but what if he'd only dropped it because he found a reason to need the high priestesses again?"

"Stockpiling weapons, moving forces from the western base into naval training, no longer gunning for the high priestesses..." I ticked each thing off.

"And we've all but confirmed Harrison was responsible for intercepting our imports," Sebastian said.

"You did?" Rien asked.

"It was a vague email that's probably why you missed it, but they corresponded to the timeline of our missing imports."

Rien nodded. "None of these things individually mean much, but when you put them together..."

The world tilted under my feet. "Delnee is preparing for war."

Chapter Thirty-Four

Amaya

My mind couldn't wrap around the idea of war. It was this abstract concept that was reserved for history class and documentaries with monotone droning male voices.

There was nothing I could have learned in school, no college class I could have taken, certainly no certification I could have earned, to prepare me for the crushing weight of responsibility that landed on my shoulders.

The rest of the evening Rien went over the emails and information that he'd acquired. Sebastian and I took pictures and made notes on our phones, but unfortunately there wasn't an email with the subject line: War Against Palagui Strategy.

We had pieces of the puzzle but were missing the edges and couldn't find a place to start. Every email and document was important, and yet none of them were without context.

Palagui didn't have the weaponry that Delnee had amassed. We certainly didn't have a weapons factory.

Any fae wars were usually fought using fae power, and while there was always the chance that power could be negated with cuffs, the soldiers were also trained in hand-to-hand combat, close proximity fighting like Gwen had trained me in.

Palagui's military forces were sent abroad throughout the years on skirmishes here and there, as Nico had been, but there hadn't been war on Palaguian land in several hundred years.

Our only saving grace was that our naval force was strong. Being on an island meant that most of our domestic military personnel was concentrated on protecting us from attacks on the sea. If Delnee wanted to attack, they'd have to get here by water, and our forces wouldn't let that happen.

Sebastian and I left Rashida's office before Rien did to make sure no one saw us together. Rien was convinced his body guards thought he was at Justin's house, but we couldn't be too careful.

"We need to take my parents with us," I said to Sebastian on the way back to the hotel. "If there is going to be war, there's a chance that someone could dig deeper into my past."

He shook his head. "I'm not strong enough to sift someone across the ocean with me, and it'd take at least a day for Nico to make fake identification for one person, two for two. Plus, if we're being watched, it'd be better if we didn't leave with them."

"They can't stay here."

"I'll get Nico to set up an encrypted call with them tonight. You'll explain the situation, and I'll ask Rashida if they can stay in one of her safe houses until we can figure out how to get them out of the country without drawing suspicion."

"You mentioned that before. Why does Rashida have safe houses?"

Sebastian was already texting on his phone. "She had a lot of high-profile cases as a defense lawyer. Honestly, I think we have a don't-ask-don't-tell kind of relationship. She's into a lot of things I don't question."

I nodded distractedly.

The only people who knew Amaya Mevson went to Palagui are Gwen, Sloane, Nico, and Sebastian. And Dr. Henderson because he's lying about my research position.

Caroline only knew that Amaya Rhodes was from Delnee. She never knew my real last name.

Evelynne, Gwen's mother, knows that Gwen and Sloane are friends with an Amaya from Delnee that went to Palagui, but Gwen said she never told her my last name.

Xenos and the councilmembers knew Amaya Rhodes was from Delnee and came to Palagui to marry Sebastian.

The airline records would have recorded an Amaya Rhodes with a Palaguian address flew to Palagui from Delnee last fall. If someone looked into it, they'd see that Amaya Rhodes didn't have flight records coming into Delnee, which might make someone question where I appeared from, but it still didn't connect me to Amaya Mevson.

The only thing that connected Amaya Mevson to Amaya Rhodes was Rien. Caroline knew Rien was friends with us and part of our plans. She knew Rien was Harrison's son. If we were being followed, or Rien was being followed, the three of us meeting at Rashida's office would raise suspicion.

It'd be a leap, but not an impossible conclusion, to figure out how we were all connected. We all had something to do with the certification program.

Amaya was a common first name in both Palagui and Delnee, which would slow down the search, but would it be slow enough to get my parents into a safe house?

Unless it was already too late, and they were being watched.

I wanted so bad to sift to them right now. Sift them to the airport and put them on a plane to Palagui and get them out of here.

But we had no fake identification for them. The high priestesses in the airport wouldn't let them on a plane.

Sebastian squeezed my hand. "Rashida is going to send a private detective to your parents and escort them to the port in Silvercrest. They'll get on a Palaguian trading ship that leaves tomorrow night. It takes about seven days to get from Silvercrest to Port Hazelle in a ship of that size." He turned and held my hand in both of his. "Your parents will be in Palagui by next week. They'll be on our ship and safe by tomorrow."

I swallowed, trying to use the information to slow down my heart rate.

"How will the private detective get them from Bellstead to Silvercrest without travel permits?" I asked.

"This guy is experienced in smuggling situations," Sebastian said. "It won't be a problem."

Tears pricked behind my eyes, but I nodded. "Okay."

One week. One week and I would see my parents.

Something clicked in my head, and I pulled out my phone calendar to confirm. "Sebastian, the portal opens next week."

He pursed his lips. "I know."

For as much time as I spent thinking about that day, we still hadn't talked about it. It'd always felt so far away, something I was counting down for, but couldn't believe would actually ever come.

"According to Dr. Henderson's calculations, the portal opens at dawn on spring equinox for five minutes and will reopen at dusk for three minutes," he said.

"It won't stay open the whole day?" I asked, panicked.

"No. The way the sun moves in our world and the recipient world makes the portal window pretty short. It's some complicated calculation that has to do with the trajectory of the speed of light and physics of when the planets tilt into certain positions on their axis. To be honest, I don't understand it, but Dr. Henderson does, and his predictions have been mostly correct in the tests we've done over the years."

My brain hung on the words *mostly correct.*

I shook my head. "So you have twelve hours to search the entire world for Adriana?"

"Twelve hours in our time, but that's roughly equivalent to one and a half days in Adriana's. I'll bring a watch to track the time. Because Adriana and I are related, I can sense when she's nearby. I'll sift around the world until I get a read on where she is…"

I worried my lip. "I should come with you. You don't know if the world is dangerous or not and—"

"No."

"Sebastian—"

"No. Amaya. No. You aren't coming. You can't. You have to stay on this world. Who knows what would happen if you went into the portal with the crown tied to Palagui's citizens. At the very least, the citizens would lose their power, and if that started another natural disaster…"

"You need help. Someone to have your back. Maybe Nico could—"

"No. This is…I have to do this myself."

I wanted to beg him not to go. What if he missed the portal back? What if he got hurt? What if Adriana was already dead? Or what if she was alive and had been spending all this time imprisoned on a hellish world?

If I asked him to stay, he would. I knew he would, but what kind of mate and wife would I be if I asked him to choose me over his sister?

I let the conversation drop. There was nothing more to say. On spring equinox, my parents would arrive in Palagui and Sebastian would go into the portal.

I couldn't let myself dwell on the possibility he might not come back or I wouldn't be able to function.

When we got back to the hotel, I spent the next hour rehearsing what to say to my parents to convince them I hadn't lost my mind after telling them they had to pack and run for their lives because their daughter was a faerie queen ruling over another country.

When I finally got ahold of them, I spent most of the conversation apologizing over and over.

Not because they were being forced to uproot their lives and leave everything and everyone they ever knew.

Not even because I'd been lying to them for the last year about what I'd been doing.

No. None of that was all too upsetting after the initial shock wore off.

What had actually bothered them—and required my repeated apologies—was that I'd gotten married...and hadn't told them.

***

Our strategy for the meeting with the president and vice president had to change. We were no longer going in with the hope that they'd give us a loan as a show of Delnee and Palagui's allyship.

We were going to compel them to give us the money.

Then we were going to compel them to tell us their plans of attack.

The Queen of Darkness was going to this meeting, and she was not leaving without money and answers.

As this was a diplomatic meeting, we were meeting Doyle Helman and Harrison Astora in the executive office at the capitol.

Gwen convinced her mother, Evelynne, that she could trust us, so Sebastian and I went to her office before the meeting on the pretense that Evelynne had to do a fae sweep down to make sure we weren't carrying magical items that could affect humans, such as gems that carry magical currents or metal that could be used to disarm the legacy high priestesses.

As the door to Evelynne's office closed, we took a seat beside Gwen.

"I'm deeply sorry for what my sister did," Evelynne said, skipping greetings and introductions entirely.

She had brown skin and appeared to wear little makeup, but like Gwen, she didn't need it. Her brown eyes had dark eyelashes as if born with natural mascara, and her angular face was outlined by thick, curly black hair that stopped just below her collarbones.

Evelynne sighed. "She's always been an intense individual, but I never suspected she'd go as far as she did. I'm very sorry for what you both had to go through."

"You haven't heard from her?" Sebastian asked.

She only shook her head.

Gwen mentioned last night that the things her mother had wanted to tell her about the past weren't military related at all. Evelynne didn't know what Caroline had been talking about with her "shadow plague." She just wanted to share her family history and "bond" with her daughter. Gwen had visibly shuddered when she said that word.

How much do we tell her? I asked Sebastian.

She and the legacy families have the most to lose if Palagui goes to war. They'll be on the frontlines. I think we should tell her everything if we want her help to prevent it.

I nodded.

Sebastian leaned in, took off his sunglasses, and told Evelynne about Harrison's war preparations.

She listened, expressionless. Didn't even flinch at Sebastian's void eyes.

After he finished, she stared behind us at the door, contemplating.

"Harrison still hasn't revoked Sloane's deportation order," she said. "He doesn't even try to hide that he would prefer there were no fae in Delnee at all."

"It doesn't surprise me," I said. "He's trying to get rid of you. I mean the deal he made with Xenos for the fae cuffs alone should be proof of that."

The boxes of silver cuffs that could negate fae powers were still missing, but at least they hadn't ended up on the wrists of the legacy high priestesses.

"What's your plan for this meeting?" Evelynne asked.

I glanced at Sebastian and took a deep breath, knowing that this was going to be the hardest sell, given what everyone thought of darkyras and brainwashing.

"I'm going to compel answers out of them. Compel them to stop whatever actions they have in place against Palagui," I said.

Evelynne only nodded. "You'll compel Harrison to revoke Sloane's deportation as well?"

"Of course. And anything else you need."

***

Evelynne led us to the president's office in the executive wing of the capitol. Unlike the court in Palagui, no ancient statues stared down at us as we walked through, rather painted pictures of past presidents lined the walls.

I was wearing my crown today. The gem in the center glinted under the fluorescent lights. My business attire had a far more regal tone with ruffles and lace, but I averted my eyes as I passed any surface with a reflection.

I didn't recognize myself. Nothing I said or did or wore seemed to fit into my self-perception. I'd changed so much I didn't know who I was anymore.

I wasn't Amaya Mevson, anxious and naïve, fighting to make sure people didn't lose their homes, fighting for equality between people.

I wasn't Amaya Rhodes, depressed and powerless, and too scared to follow her heart, her shadow, even after she'd learned better.

I wasn't Amaya Renwick, the persona that the media created for me. A nobody who didn't earn her crown.

I wasn't the Queen of Darkness, whose rage hummed under her skin as illicit killing fantasies soothed her to sleep at night.

I wasn't any of those personas, not entirely. Kai had tried to rename me too. Tried to make me into someone they wanted me to be. And maybe they'd been right.

I was Maya, the illusion. I didn't know who I was because I put on different outfits and attitudes depending on the situation and who was around.

It made me feel as though my steps were wobbly, in heels too high, shoes too tight.

But I'd only need to hide my teetering in the shoes of the Queen of Darkness for the rest of this meeting.

Once we were home and settled, once my parents were safe and Sebastian was back from the portal, then I could take a deep breath and reorient my internal compass to who I really was.

Whoever that girl ended up being.

Evelynne opened the double doors to the presidential office. Doyle and Harrison stood, both of their gazes swinging to us.

A large floor-to-ceiling window brightened the room from behind Doyle, who stood at his desk. Gold garnishes outlined the trim of the room. The plaster of the walls was molded into intricate shapes, and dark mahogany furniture filled the room.

It was all very...masculine.

A masculinity that was ostentatious in the way only human men who had something they needed to compensate for could be.

"Mr. President. Mr. Vice President," Evelynne said. "The Queen and King of Palagui," she introduced us with a wave of her hand.

Both her and Gwen promptly walked to the outer edge of the room near the doors, standing guard to watch over the proceedings.

The president had thin white hair, age spots, and a face that drooped with wrinkles. He put on a big smile as he walked out from behind his desk toward us.

"Call me Doyle," he said, shaking Sebastian's hand before turning to me. "Nice to meet you, little lady."

Dealing with darkyra discrimination was bad enough, but I'd forgotten how irritating misogyny could be. Palagui didn't have much going for it in the way of progressive views, but certainly no one called the queen "little lady."

I bit my tongue, but didn't return his smile, uncaring if my expression made him uncomfortable.

Doyle barely noticed. "Well, Harrison is going to take real good care of you. I have a one o'clock tee time, but it was so great to meet you."

He walked around us and disappeared out the door without another word. Honestly, it didn't surprise me that the president was a puppet. I didn't know how Harrison had jumped from mayor of Pointedelle to vice president last year, but I'm sure the puppet masters were behind it.

Harrison grinned. "Sebastian. Amaya. Sit, please." He waved a hand to the couches perpendicular to the desk.

"It's Queen Amaya," Sebastian said.

Harrison's smile tightened. "My apologies. Queen Amaya, won't you take a seat?"

Sebastian and I sat on the couch to the right of the room.

"You don't have to wear those in here if you don't want to," Harrison said in a friendly tone, tapping the side of his eye while looking at Sebastian.

Sebastian pulled off the sunglasses and folded them into his breast pocket. "It's nice to see you again, Harrison. You've improved your position mightily since I last saw you."

Sebastian spread his arms across the back of the couch and crossed his leg over his knee at the ankle. We'd agreed he would lead the conversation with Harrison to see how he played his cards before we made our move.

"I could say the same to you." Harrison smirked. "You've even acquired yourself a wife. I'd say you've made out better than I have." He went to the hutch behind the couch that faced us. "Have you been to your beachfront property this year?"

"No, not this winter. Too much work to find time to sneak away," Sebastian said, tapping his fingers, looking around the room. "How about you?"

Harrison poured drinks from a decanter of amber liquid with his back to us as he talked about his latest vacation.

I smoothed out my skirt and sat at the edge of the couch cushion with my back erect. I couldn't lounge like Sebastian since my legs weren't long enough for my feet to remain on the floor if I tried.

Sebastian sensed my unease because he leaned forward, so my posture wouldn't look as awkward.

Harrison came over and handed him a drink. He placed his own drink down on a table opposite us. "Sorry. I don't have any wine for your wife. Would she like water?"

He didn't even look at me. His question directed to Sebastian like I was a child, and he was asking my parents for permission to give me a juice box.

Sebastian's voice was icy. "I don't speak for the Queen. Maybe you could ask her."

Harrison's face pinched as his eyes shifted to me. "Apologies. What can I get you?"

"I'll have the same. Thank you," I said, not bothering to hide my disdain for his actions.

Harrison turned back to the hutch. "You'll have to forgive me. My wife died over twenty years ago. I'm unaccustomed to the new trends with women."

I couldn't help but roll my eyes and look at Gwen near the door.

She curled her lip and rolled her eyes back.

"Our condolences for your wife," Sebastian said.

"And mine for your mother. She was a great queen." Harrison handed me the drink, but his hand didn't release when I grabbed the glass. He leaned in. "Quite a legacy you have to live up to. Must be overwhelming for someone like you."

He released the glass and went to the opposite couch. I schooled my features as he lounged back, arms wide, legs spread.

"Excuse me?" Sebastian said. The pulse of his shadows flickered, and he didn't bother to hide his power simmering with anger.

Harrison looked unperturbed. I pressed my awareness toward him and sensed the ruby medallion he wore. A kind of empty void resting at his chest.

"I meant no disrespect," Harrison said. "It's just when we looked into your wife, there wasn't much we could find out about her. Seemed to have lived a very average life in Palagui, and yet, she became one of the most important people in your country. I'd say, out of all of us, her position has improved the most."

"You're admitting to spying on the royal family?" Sebastian asked.

Harrison shrugged. "Spying is a bit of a stretch. I'd call it keeping tabs. I'm sure you do the same. Know thy friends and all that."

Sebastian gave a cruel smile. "I believe the saying is *know thy enemy.*"

Harrison smirked.

They both stared at one another, having some sort of showdown, but I couldn't tell who was winning.

Harrison put his drink down with a loud *clink*. "Things are a bit...delicate in your country right now, aren't they? I know transfers of power can be tricky."

I didn't hide my eye roll this time. I couldn't stand it, the posturing, the subtle belittlement.

"We know you stole our imports," I said. "That you tried to prevent our rebuilding efforts. I'm sure the international naval association would love to hear about your theft."

"I don't know what you are talking about," he said.

"No?" I said, smiling sweetly. "That's interesting because we have proof you forged our documentation and the testimony of three captains."

I was bluffing, since all our evidence was circumstantial at best, but I wanted to see if he'd admit it, if I could work him up enough to let something slip.

Harrison snorted. "Do you think I'm going to be intimidated by a little girl playing dress up?" He raised an eyebrow. "Here's some advice from someone who has been leading since you were in diapers: keep your mouth shut. I'd hate for our countries to get into a spat because you couldn't control your emotions."

I curled my lip in disgust. "Here's some advice from someone who has more power in their pinky finger than you do in your entire country: I'm counting on you not being intimidated by me."

I stood and downed my drink in one swallow. "Male pride and hubris have been—and always will be—the reason wars are started. Female sense and intuition will be why they don't escalate to mutually assured destruction.'

Walking to the hutch with my empty glass, I said, "This is what's going to happen." I poured myself a refill. "You're going to return all of the equipment you stole."

I came back around and stood at the front of the room, leaning on the president's desk. "And you're going to send Palagui a relief package to make up for the time we spent waiting."

He scoffed. "What makes you think I'm going to do that? You have no power here, little girl."

I smiled and walked to his side of the couch. His eyes narrowed, but he wouldn't run or flinch because that would mean he'd be admitting to being afraid of a *little girl*.

He did make a fatal error though, and glanced at Evelynne, who was making a show of walking over. Her high priestess light came alive in her palm.

When his gaze was distracted, I yanked at the chain around his neck. It melted easily under my light. Some of my power was sucked into the ruby medallion, but I had destroyed one of these before.

Harrison flinched back. His gaze ricocheting between me and Evelynne. I saw the moment he realized he was betrayed in the widening of the whites of his eyes.

Without the ruby, his fear radiated into my awareness. His sour, yellow terror tasted delicious on my tongue.

Evelynne halted at the couch, crossing her arms. My shadows gripped him around the neck.

"You haven't been alive long enough to see a queen in her full power," I said. "Fuck with me and my people, and I will show you what I'm capable of." Shadows descended upon the red ruby, shattering it. "And you'll never see it coming."

His hands started shaking. A shot of blissed-out adrenaline coursed through me as my power reveled in his reactions.

Sebastian's shadows joined mine, hovering over Harrison's head. He nodded when he had a firm hold on his mind.

"Do you know who I am? Where my family is?" I asked.

"No," Harrison answered, robotic. "But I have a team trying to find your information."

"How are you going to attack Palagui?"

"Our naval fleet will attack from the south," Harrison said.

"When?"

"Within the next month."

"How did you know which ships to steal our equipment from?"

"We looked for the largest cargo ships with foreign emblems on them."

I clenched my hands into fists and stepped away from Harrison. "Log on to the computer," I commanded him.

Harrison walked like a zombie to the desk, sat, and clicked around on the computer.

I stood behind him watching. "Tell your military commander to pull back your troops and cancel all plans to attack Palagui. And email whoever is hiding our equipment and tell them to put it on a boat to Palagui today."

He clicked around and typed the message without really looking at the screen. He sent the emails.

"Login to your budget system and approve from your slush fund a transfer to Palagui for the highest sum that is allowed without legislative approval," I said, crossing my arms over my chest.

He moved a couple million to our accounts. Not nearly enough to pay all of our loans, but enough to buy us more time to get back up and running.

"Delete Sloane Knight's deportation order," I said.

He leaned forward and typed on the laptop. Clicking around different software systems.

After a few minutes, Evelynne pulled out her phone. "It's done."

Evelynne asked me to get him to approve some transfers of high priestesses. There was a budget approval she needed and other administrative tasks Harrison was using to keep control of her.

After I finished directing him through those, I walked to the other side of the desk and leaned over, trying to look in his eye, but his gaze was unseeing.

"You don't want to cuff the legacy high priestesses," I said. "You think Evelynne is an excellent and skilled leader. You don't want to attack Palagui because we're strong and will destroy your country if you do."

"That's not how this works," Sebastian said. "I can't influence the mind like that. I can only compel actions. Darkyra can't actually brainwash people."

I shrugged. Upset for once that that rumor wasn't true.

"Anything else?" I asked Evelynne.

She shook her head.

We twist his neck until his eyes pop out of their sockets and shove them down his throat, my shadow offered.

Not today.

I used a shadow to isolate the memory that was currently being created in Harrison's head and smashed it. Unfortunately, he wouldn't remember my bad ass speech, but we got what we came for and couldn't push our luck.

We walked out of the office, leaving Harrison with a bad headache. He might be a little peeved that the Queen and King of Palagui canceled their meeting with him, but he wouldn't know what we'd truly done until we were out of the country.

He would figure out what happened soon enough when the troops were moved and money was transferred.

Evelynne had a high priestess catch up with the president and erase his memory of meeting us. She took care of all security videos as well.

Evelynne and Gwen walked us to the back entrance, and we drove back to the hotel. Gwen went home to pack and would be on the next flight to Palagui tonight.

Sebastian blocked his emotions, and with his sunglasses back on, I couldn't read him. Neither of us said anything on the car ride, but I could barely sit still. My legs were bouncing as energy coursed through me.

We held our composure until we stepped into our hotel room. He yanked off his sunglasses and threw them on the floor. One hand wrapped around my waist, and the other cupped the back of my head as he pressed me into the door. His lips were crushed to mine.

A surprised squeal escaped, but lowered into a moan as his tongue found its way into my mouth.

I knotted my fingers into his hair and slanted my mouth against his, my legs wrapping around his waist. Shadows flowed from my wrists, my shoulders, and intertwined with his.

"You were fucking amazing," he gasped between kisses. "I don't know if I've ever seen something so hot in my whole life."

"And you're quite old," I teased.

He nipped at my bottom lip. "Only by human standards."

His lips pressed kisses along my jaw, down my neck. He pulled at my shirt until my shoulder was bared to him. He sucked at the skin until I was sure there'd be a mark.

"Was it hotter than when I had the blood of our enemies on my face?" I asked, my shadow asked

He groaned. "That was really hot too. I love watching you destroy people. With words, with your power, with just one look. I could watch it all day long."

Our mouths devoured one another until finally we pulled apart, gasping for breath.

"I'd like to fuck you, but our flight leaves in forty minutes, and we don't want to be around when Harrison figures out what we did."

I gave a sad smile and ran my hands through his hair. "Thank you."

"For what?" he asked. His hands kneaded the flesh of my hips.

"For supporting me. For knowing when to stand up for me and when to let me stand up for myself. For having my back."

He kissed me. "Thank you," he whispered. "For seeing good in me even when I can't."

I pulled him back in. Our kiss slower now, languid. When the cinnamon of his lust started burning the back of my throat, I pulled back with a disappointed sigh.

"Let's go home," he said.

Relief replaced the disappointment. Home was my friends. Home was the townhouse. Home was him. The promise of that sense of safety, of that warm blanket of relaxation, left me speechless. I could only nod in agreement.

Chapter Thirty-Five

Amaya

"I miss you, but I'm glad you're getting to spend time with your grandmother," Nico said into his phone as he walked by me in the kitchen. His broken puppy dog eyes and bitter sadness contrasted with his feigned upbeat tone. He didn't glance at me as he left out the backdoor.

My heart twisted for him. After Sloane completed her internship at the Molbridge healing center, she'd gone to Delnee since her deportation order was finally rescinded. It was the first time they'd been parted since accepting the bond.

At her mother's request, Gwen had decided to stay in Delnee a little longer. Despite her initial grumbling, I think she liked her mother's sudden affections.

"There's been no sign that Harrison suspects what we did," Gwen had told me last night on the phone. Rien had already confirmed that the troops had been reassigned, and it seemed, for now, we'd avoided a confrontation. "My mother and Harrison actually seem very chummy."

"That's good," I said, shoving the paperwork on my desk to the side. I liked to think it was due to my compulsion, even if Sebastian said that wasn't how our powers worked. "The money we took must have been so small that it won't be questioned until someone does the year-end books."

The infusion of money from Delnee helped us pay off our most pressing loans, and with the threat of frost fully behind us, construction ramped up in Merbany. Our stolen equipment had been returned, and we were able to get a partial refund on the stuff we no longer needed.

"How's our blackmailer doing?" Gwen asked.

"Quiet. No new intimidation attempts." Just like I'd thought, Vince's threats were hollow. No rumors about Sebastian creating the draxis had popped up. "I approved one of his proposals that Micah co-wrote with him, so that probably helped. He's been a little distracted at council meetings lately. Always the first one to leave."

Gwen snorted. "Maybe he's finally come to terms with the fact that everyone hates being around him."

"Maybe." I flipped through a proposal Aurelio and Leva wrote together. They seemed to be settling into their roles, and the last council meeting had been less tense and hostile.

"And you don't need me to come back early?" Gwen asked. "No riots or protests?"

There hadn't been any backlash from repealing the darkyra and human laws. Oh sure, the media had a field day with spinning their hatred, but the PR team's polls indicated that most people agreed with the repeals, and Sebastian and I's approval ratings got an infinitesimal bump, even though those same polls also said people were scared of us.

"We're good, Gwen. There's actually a darkyra-human festival to celebrate in a few days." It would be the first official gathering since the law was repealed that forbid more than ten darkyra to gather in one place. It would be an all-day carnival event with rides and food stands.

I asked my next question in a tentative cadence. "But maybe you want to come home...in case Daria decides the festival is the right venue for her reappearance?"

I could see Gwen's pursed lips in my head. "I'll pass."

She quickly wrapped up our call after that.

Things were going well, and it was like Sebastian and I were living within a sugar-crafted glass bubble. Everything was sweet, but fragile.

We purposefully avoided all discussions of the portal.

We both knew that he had to do it. We both knew I didn't want him to go, but that I wouldn't stop him.

We talked about spring equinox as if the most important thing happening was my parents' arrival. Neither of us risked shattering our peaceful domestic bliss by discussing the fact that he could come back from that strange world without Adriana and without a way to heal the draxis.

Before Sloane left for Delnee, she'd given me the binder of meticulous notes she'd taken during her week at the healing center. She outlined each ritual in detail and every discussion she had with the healers. One of the things that repeatedly came up was that patients typically needed several sessions in order to heal.

Karina had called Sebastian—I'm pretty sure he only told me the details of the call because I'd been in the room when he answered—and asked if he wanted to schedule another session.

He'd declined because he felt good and didn't have any symptoms, but I convinced him to call back and schedule one for the day after the portal. Sloane and Gwen would be back from Delnee by then, and if everything turned out for the best, Adriana could join too.

If she didn't...Well, it'd be good that the appointment was already scheduled.

Sebastian did seem genuinely better though. His aura was sweet and light with happiness and affection. We talked about the future. About buying a house for my parents. About what to do with the palace since neither of us wanted to live there. About what to do with the top floor of court, which no one had stepped into since the engagement party. He'd asked me whether I wanted to live in the townhouse or buy a property somewhere else.

I didn't, but it was nice of him to ask. I loved the townhouse, and I liked being near the city, but not in the hustle.

We even planned a vacation at the end of summer to the beach house.

We were living like an actual married couple. Not a queen and king. Not the most powerful fae in Palagui. Just a guy and a girl who got to think about what they were going to do with their lives in the future tense.

Maybe I'd been enticed by hope for the future, or overcome by the lust that was an omnipresent part of my life, or persuaded by my shadow's whispered fears about him going into the portal, but one evening while we were getting ready for bed, I blurted out, "Do you want to accept the bond tonight?"

There was no reason to wait anymore. He was whole. As whole as any of us really were.

He'd been standing at the end of the bed, taking off his shirt. His gaze faraway, probably thinking about whatever policy we needed to approve tomorrow, and I was distracted by his long fingers unbuttoning his shirt, slowly revealing a thin strip of his torso a little at a time. Honestly, it was probably the strip tease that had me asking before thinking.

His fingers paused their task. He opened his mouth, and closed it, then furrowed his brow. "Tonight?"

Shocked and confused wasn't exactly the reaction I was hoping for. A *fuck yes and the shucking off the rest of his clothes* was more what I had in mind, but once the idea settled in my brain, it didn't seem that crazy.

"Yeah. Why not?"

He got flustered. "Don't you want a mating ceremony or to redo our wedding? Your parents will be here. We could plan one for this winter."

It was my turned to be confused.

I squinted my eyes. "For PR?"

Sebastian hadn't ever seemed that concerned with our image. He cringed every time I told him about the fluff pieces the team had wanted us to do, but I guess a big royal wedding *would* make people like us better.

He shook his head. "I was thinking something small and private, but if you wanted to go big, that's good with me too."

I shrugged. "I don't really care about all that..."

He made a facial expression I couldn't decipher. Eyes narrowing, face scrunching up, and then he went blank. He blocked his emotions too which made me even more confused.

I thought about how he said this winter, as if he already had a plan in mind. "Do *you* want a mating ceremony or wedding?"

He shrugged, and didn't meet my gaze as he disappeared into the walk-in closet.

Oh. My. Goddess.

I slumped against the headboard.

Sebastian wanted to marry me.

I mean he was already married to me, but he wanted something that wasn't a hasty marriage binding in a prison cell while our lives were being threatened.

My heart melted, and a grin so wide it hurt my cheeks broke out.

I climbed off the bed and went into the closet.

He was turned away from me as he rifled through a dresser drawer. I couldn't help but appreciate the delicious curve of his shoulders and the toned muscles of his back. The scars that marred the skin along his spine from Xenos's cruelty were faint and only served as further proof of his goodness.

He'd told me the story of their origin. It'd been just an average day when he was a teenager. Xenos had been humiliated at a council meeting by the Queen when she'd reminded him in front of everyone that Adriana would rule in a few years, not him. Xenos couldn't take his anger out on the Queen or Adriana, but he could take it out on his half-brother, who according to Xenos, only received more of their mother's attention because Sebastian followed Adriana around like a guard dog.

Xenos told him his life wasn't any more important to their mother than his was. That if Sebastian wanted to be Adriana's shield, he'd take the beating she deserved.

Xenos burned him and threatened that if he went to a healer, he'd burn Adriana next. Sebastian didn't think he would actually go through with it, but wouldn't have been able to live with himself if he did, so the burns remained as Xenos's reminder of his place in the world.

My mate was so good. I can't believe I ever doubted it. He'd endured so much brutality and still loved so deeply.

If he wanted an official ceremony, I wanted one too.

I wanted to declare my love to him, to promise my loyalty and devotion to him, in front of our friends and family. I'd do it in front of the entire world if he wanted. He deserved people who loved as fiercely as he did, and I wanted to make an official vow that I would spend the rest of my life trying to be the mate he deserved.

I crossed into the closet and pressed my face into the curve of his back, wrapping my arms around his chest. "I want a mating ceremony *and* a wedding," I whispered.

"Yeah?" He laid a hand over mine which was resting on his heart.

I nodded into his back and hugged him tighter. "Yeah."

I asked Blake the next day to find us a wedding planner, and accepted the incessant lust that demanded we fulfill the bond as part of life.

Funny enough, my shadow's reminders that Sebastian would leave us if we didn't accept the bond had all but stopped since then.

Like she understood someone who held on to the idea of a winter wedding because you mentioned it one time in passing wasn't going to leave.

I wouldn't say I was *content* to wait, but I was willing to hold off and do it the right way.

That didn't mean it wasn't sometimes impossible to sleep. The only thing worse than not being near Sebastian, was being right beside him. During the day, I could distract myself with tasks and plans so I didn't register how horny I'd become until I was staring at the veins in his forearms as he pointed to a map in a council meeting. His shirt cuffs were rolled up, and I couldn't stop staring at his big hands and long fingers.

You're making everyone uncomfortable with your scary eyes, Sebastian would tease me, and I'd blink away the shadows and refocus on our meeting.

He wasn't immune either. I had woken up more than once from dreams of his shadows chasing me with the taste of his cinnamon lust on my tongue.

Tonight, there was a frantic edge to our chase. I ran, but my body was fraying around the edges. The cord that tied him to me tugged, aching and straining to capture and consume.

My heartbeat stuttered. The pattern discordant like an emergency signal calling out and trying to summon him. Finally, his darkness encased me and caught me in its snare. The cord of our bond sagged.

My shadow hummed. She reached out, and I knew her claws had sunk into him when he grunted at the force with which she dragged him to me, trying to bind us physically if not spiritually.

One of his arms had found his way under my neck, the other over my waist, winding around me, clutching me. In the haze of sleep, I registered rustling behind me, his lips on my neck, on my ear.

Without waking or opening my eyes, I tilted my head, wanting more, wanting closer. Wanting his hands that were playing with the hem of my shirt to find their way to my skin.

"Amaya," he whispered and flattened his hand on my stomach, pressing my back to his chest. The smell of spicy, sweet sandalwood enveloped me.

"Hmm?" I murmured, still partially asleep. I wrapped my arm behind me and grabbed at the back of his head, threading my fingers through his hair.

He curled his body around me, pressing his hardness into my ass. "I want to be inside you." His breath tickled my ear and sent shivers down my spine.

"Mmm." I reveled in his warmth, in the way his voice spoke to each and every one of my cells and bade them to calm, to ease, to attune to him. "Okay."

"Okay?" he asked. His voice a mixture of surprise and relief. His hand trailed higher, stroking the undersides of my breasts.

"Yes," I said but kept my eyes closed. Reality and dreamland were melding. Some part of me was nervous to make any sudden movement, else I'd truly awaken and find he had disappeared. That his hands, his lips, his body were gone.

A thick tension mounted inside me, and the familiar ache of unfulfilled need fired up in my belly when he didn't do anything other than stroke my stomach and caress the valley between my breasts.

Impatience overtook the fear that this was a dream, and I took the initiative to hook my fingers into the sides of my underwear and shove them off my hips, kicking them the rest of the way down and losing them under the blankets.

To my relief, he followed my lead and shimmied his own pants off. The heat of his naked body seeped in through my thin shirt. He spread his hand over my bare hip and pressed his cock between the flesh of my ass.

He dragged his fingertips over the curve of my hip and dipped them into the hollow impression that my hip bone made as it became the swell of my thigh.

I stayed still, eyes scrunched shut, enjoying the sensation of him touching me, teasing me in this sleepy middle of the night haze.

His fingers parted me to find my clit, to circle slow and easy. He was in no rush. Content to give me a languid pleasure that slowly stoked the heat pooling in my lower belly.

"Mmm," I murmured and opened my legs, throwing the top one over his hip to give him more room to touch me.

He nipped at my ear and sucked on the lobe. The sensation pulled a taut line down my body as if his tongue and teeth were playing the same string that was strummed by his fingers stroking my clit.

"That feels so good," I said on a single hushed breath.

His fingers explored lower, stroking my entrance, finding me slick with need. I was already swollen and ready for him when he finally plunged two fingers inside.

"What a good girl," he said. "So wet for me." His hot breath teased my ear.

Unbidden, I started bucking my hips as he pumped his fingers in and out in a slow, methodical rhythm. The heel of his hand rubbed against my clit, but his pace made it clear he was in no hurry to give me what I was writhing for.

He nibbled on my shoulder, my back, kissing and licking and biting. I opened my thighs wider, needing him deeper, needing his very soul to be inside mine.

If I hadn't been so keyed up, I would have been embarrassed by the obscene sounds of my wetness and how my arousal was coating his hand.

My breaths came faster as I gasped for air, but his fingers halted and retreated.

Desperate, I grabbed his elbow to keep him where I needed him. His chest rose and fell behind me in heavy breaths.

He ground his hips into my ass, and I released him as his intent became clear. His hard cock slipped through my parted legs. I reached down to guide him into me, and he angled my hips so he slid in easily.

A sharp hiss whistled through his teeth as he filled me.

My dreams could never compare to the reality of this. Imagination never truly mimicked the feel, the pleasure, the bliss of him inside me.

He thrust all the way in until he bottomed out. His hips pressed into my ass, his chest flat against my back, his face nuzzled into my neck.

He didn't move only murmured, "That's it. You're perfect. Stay just like that."

I exhaled a ragged breath, stomach tightening in anticipation as his hand came to my lower belly. His fingers spread across my mound, middle finger almost close enough to my pulsing nub of need, but not quite there.

He didn't move at all.

Only a moment passed before I started rotating my hips, searching for friction, for movement.

"More," I panted, feeling wanton and depraved and unashamed of both.

And...he still didn't move.

I wiggled harder, whimpering as he nipped my ear.

"Shh, baby. Go back to sleep. It's early," he whispered and laid his head on the pillow behind mine.

"What?" I asked, suddenly a lot more awake. His cock twitched inside me, but he didn't *do* anything.

I tried pressing back, pressing forward, anything. But his hand and his shadows held me tighter, held me immobile against him, completely restricting my movements.

"I just wanted to be inside you," he said. His voice gravelly with the roughness of sleep. The deep commanding tone raked my insides. "You'll keep it warm for me, won't you? You'll be so good for me and hold still and go back to sleep, right baby?"

I turned my head and moaned into my pillow. No. Maybe I *was* dreaming. This was exactly the explicit drawn-out kind of torture that had haunted me at night.

I couldn't do this. I needed him to move. Something about having him hard and thick and hot inside me, his hands on me, everything I wanted, yet still not enough, was driving my impossible need even higher.

My chest heaved like I'd been running for hours, but he didn't let any of the rest of my body move an inch.

The tingly need low in my stomach grew more insistent. The anticipation increased my arousal and made my wetness feel like it was spilling out of me and down my leg.

My clit felt hot and needy, and I shifted my thighs, but he gave me no relief. I could feel him pulsating inside me, could feel the micromovements of his hips, and the way he dug his nose into my back when I clenched down on him.

As much as this was taunting me, it was teasing him too. This was a game of chicken. Which one of us would break and give in?

His hand on my lower stomach felt like it was searing me, branding me. His breath on my ear remained heavy but steady.

Unless...unless was it possible he could actually go to sleep like this?

That he truly just wanted to use my body to warm his cock?

My teeth dug into my lip. The thought made me even wetter.

Shivering and shaking, my muscles tightened, further and further like a wind-up doll that couldn't wind anymore.

My clit felt like it was begging for his fingers to just move one inch lower. If he touched me, I'd go off instantly.

I wanted to cry as the frustration mounted. I wanted to scream, but my mouth could do nothing but whimper and whine.

My pussy clenched around him, fluttering, and I heard it then, the hitch in his breath.

He wasn't going to sleep. Oh no. This was definitely a game.

When I felt his heart beating faster against my back, I knew exactly how I was going to win.

Since I couldn't move, I used my shadow to grab the wrist of his hand that was resting on my stomach and positioned it under my shirt, over my breast, forcing him to cup the aching flesh.

"You're not being very good," he said. "I'm trying to sleep." His voice was thick with desire, betraying the lie in his words.

"I just need you to keep it warm for me," I said, repeating his line and not being able to keep the smile from my voice.

Two could play at this game.

He groaned into my neck and squeezed my breast. "You're going to sleep now?"

"Yes," I said, but it was broken by a soft moan as his thumb tweaked my nipple.

I clenched down on him unable to help myself and shimmied my ass back. He made a noise in the back of his throat.

"Good," he said. "You need your sleep."

I needed something right now, and it most certainly wasn't sleep. I wasn't going to last much longer. But neither was he. His hips made the slightest of movements, inching back and thrusting in again as if he couldn't help himself. I was so wet, and he slid back in so smooth.

His hand moved to the other breast and played with it until that nipple too was hard from his ministrations.

The angle of him hit my inner walls, just right, so right, but without steady movement, I couldn't get there.

"Sebastian," I moaned. Frustrated tears formed in my eyes.

He pulled back halfway and pressed back in. "You're going to make me fuck you, aren't you?" he growled. "You need to be fucked don't you, baby?"

My answer was accompanied by a relieved exhale. "Yes. Yes. Yes."

His hips pulled back until he almost slipped out of me, and he slammed back in.

I gasped. It felt so good the breath was stolen from my lungs and replaced with the sharp coldness of the shadows that surrounded us.

I usually needed stimulation to my clit to get off. I'd never felt so close to orgasm without it, but our game or the bond had edged me to the cusp of oblivion.

He grabbed my waist for leverage, but we weren't in the best position to go any faster as we laid on our sides. The slow pulses were driving me insane. My legs started quivering.

His shadows released me and moved to caress my thighs and my breasts and my neck with the softest and coolest touch, intimate and sweet.

He pressed his face into my back and nipped my shoulder, my neck.

I tilted my head to give him more space, wanting him to mark every inch of me with his teeth. As he sucked love bites into my neck, I reached behind to grab him. He ground into me. The sharp press of his hip bones bit into my ass.

"This is so much better than my dreams," I mumbled.

He paused, panting. "Your dreams?"

"That night I woke you up with a nightmare? It wasn't a nightmare. I never have nightmares when you're next to me."

I'd won our game, and I wasn't going to put up with him stopping, so I pulled away to spin around and face him. Hooking my leg on his hip, I pushed his shoulder to make it clear I wanted to be on top.

He complied, and I threw my head back as I sunk down on top of him.

His hands latched on to the swell of my hips, squeezing the flesh hard enough to bruise.

"You didn't have a nightmare?" he asked. The realization dawned on him with a hard swallow of his throat. His eyes squeezed shut as

I bounced on top of him, hitting a perfect rhythm. "You were moaning and whimpering because you needed my cock?"

"Yes. When you assumed it was a nightmare, I didn't know how to tell you it wasn't. Didn't want to pressure you…"

His shadows swept my hair back off my face, gathering it behind me. "Is this what you imagined? Fucking me? Taking what's yours?"

"Yes," I hissed. "Mine. Mine. Mine."

"All yours, baby." He groaned as I picked up my pace.

My thighs burned, but I liked the heat, liked that I was working for it, earning it.

"You take me. So. Fucking. Good," he said, thrusting upward on each word. His shadows swirled around my throbbing clit in slow, methodical circles. One and two and three, winding and winding and winding until—

Light burst from my hands, the tattoos along my arms blinked, and my shadows trembled around me as my body convulsed from the bright, blinding pleasure. My hips stuttered, becoming uneven, and I lost the rhythm as my muscles tightened and I curled forward. Sebastian gripped me tight and fucked up into me.

"That's a good girl. Fuck. There you go," he said.

His thumb brushed along my clit, just the softest pressure, on the edge of too much, elongating the delicious wave of my orgasm. I careened into the oblivion I'd been flirting with, trembling and shaking as I clenched around him.

"Ah, fuck." His body hardened, and his eyes squeezed shut as his own pleasure played out over his face. He shuddered, and I felt the pulse of his orgasm inside of me. His thrusts slowed, becoming jerkier as his face slackened.

I went boneless, falling onto him, nuzzling my face into the crook of his neck. Our shadows sighed in relief, vibrating in time, syncing our heartbeats, finding harmony once again.

Only the sound of our heavy breathing filled the room as we came down from the high.

Even after I recovered my ability to move, I didn't shift from my position atop him, and he made no indication that he wanted me to. I wanted—no needed—to feel every inch of his skin against every inch of mine. His fingertips traced up and down my back as our hearts slowed.

He kissed my neck over the tender spots he'd bitten and sucked. I wondered idly if he was appreciating his work, delighting in the visual proof of his claiming.

I'd heal the hickeys before anyone could see them, but I liked getting them as much as he liked giving them.

Shadows wrapped around us, thick and heavy like a weighted blanket. They were drunk on the bliss as much as we were. Squishing us and crushing me to him as if they alone could imprint the very essence of our beings on to the inside of our skin.

"I love you," I whispered.

"I love you too." He tilted his head to find my mouth. His kiss, soft and reverent.

I cupped his jaw and deepened our kiss. We'd missed this step because of our little game. Cinnamon lust shifted into sweet vanilla affection.

I leaned back and pushed the long strands of his black hair from his face.

He was sedated and relaxed. A weird sense of pride shot through me that I'd given him those feelings.

He opened his eyes as I ran my thumb over his cheekbone. Then I noticed it. I had to blink and squint my eyes to see if I was seeing things.

His eyes widened with worry at my expression. "What's wrong?"

I sat up and leaned over toward the nightstand to turn on the lamp. My void eyes could see in the dark, but I needed to know for sure what I was seeing.

I put my hands on his face and looked into his eyes.

The shadows receded. The usual darkness faded, and the whites of his eyes shown through. Ice-blue eyes that I hadn't seen in months stared back at me.

"Your eyes." I said, glancing back and forth between them.

He tensed and rolled out from under me, getting out of bed and hurrying to the bathroom. I followed behind, hastily pulling on my underwear.

He leaned over the vanity, as if getting closer to the mirror would change what he saw, and pulled down the skin under his eyes.

Sour and bitter, anxiety and fear and sadness whirled within him.

"Hey," I said and grabbed his arm so he'd stop pulling at his eyelids. "It's okay. Everything's okay."

He swallowed and squeezed his eyes shut. Tension radiated from him.

I didn't understand what was happening, but obviously neither did he, so asking questions wasn't going to help. He didn't seem exactly like the old Sebastian, but he also no longer seemed like the shadow that had married me in the prison. He was both people or neither. Maybe who he really was?

After spending the last few months feeling like I was someone different in every situation, I knew how useless it was to try to figure out where the line between each of our selves was.

Sebastian reopened his eyes.

Only darkness stared back at me.

His jaw clenched, and I knew he was waiting for my reaction. Maybe waiting for my disappointment because he still didn't believe I could love his shadow self as much as his other self.

I only interlaced my fingers with his and lifted his hand to my mouth to kiss the knuckles. "Come back to bed."

The tightness around his eyes smoothed, and he sighed, relaxing marginally and letting me tug him into the bedroom.

I curled up around him and imbued my shadows with the depth of my love. I didn't care which Sebastian I got. Shadow or not. It didn't matter to me. He was mine. All mine. Every part of him.

424

Chapter Thirty-Six

Amaya

"Does this dress say *I'm the queen so you should respect me, but there's no reason to fear me consuming the souls of your children*?"

Sebastian scratched the back of his neck and stared at the dress for about two seconds before he said, "Uh. Well, you already know I like the black one best."

I groaned and waved him off. "You're no help. A dress that makes my butt look good is not going to instill the public's confidence in me."

"Couldn't hurt," Sebastian said, lighthearted.

"Argh. I wish Sloane and Gwen were here."

"When will they be back?" Sebastian asked.

"Tomorrow evening," I said and purposefully averted my eyes back to the dresses hanging in the closet. Their plane lands tomorrow, and I'll be picking them up at the airport while my mate was on a strange world searching for his lost sister.

My parents will be here, but he'll be gone, and I'll have to put on a brave face and act like it isn't affecting me.

Like there isn't a possibility that he may never come back.

I sighed, refocusing on the task at hand.

"You'll look amazing in anything you wear," Sebastian offered.

I gave him a wan smile. "Thanks." I pulled out one of my more modest dresses and paired it with a blazer.

Sebastian was already dressed for the darkyra-human festival. Males had it so easy. Only needed a collared shirt, tie, and suit jacket, and they'd look professional and hot.

Well, at least, Sebastian always did.

This was actually the first event he was attending with me because it was being held outside, and the PR team said it wouldn't look weird if he gave his speech with sunglasses on.

Plus, the whole event was to celebrate the darkyra laws being repealed which meant that his void eyes wouldn't be out of place surrounded by other darkyras showing off their powers.

I'd casually mentioned this morning that maybe he wouldn't even need to wear the sunglasses, trying to be subtle about the fact his eyes shifted to blue last night.

He made a dismissive comment about wanting to wear them anyway, and since his eyes hadn't so much as flickered all morning, I took that as confirmation that he wasn't exactly in control of the shift.

He was so shaken up last night, I didn't want to trudge up hard feelings when he was leaving tomorrow. We scheduled a healing ritual for the day after the portal, and hopefully that would help him navigate the internal war he was having with himself.

After getting dressed, I put the crown on my head.

Except this wasn't the actual crown. I'd had one of the jewelers in the city make me an identical-looking crown, but had it shaped to my head so hopefully I wouldn't get as many headaches.

The official crown was locked away in a safe, and since the power was already tied to my life force, there was no reason I had to wear it.

Sebastian walked behind me, and rested his hands on my hips. "You look perfect," he said, staring at me in the bathroom mirror.

"Thanks." I smiled and grabbed his hand.

We sifted to the entrance of the festival. A member of our PR team and our fae warders were waiting to escort us in. Several guards manned the entrance, and a ward outlined the edge of the park where the festival was being held.

As the first event the Queen and King would attend together, not to mention a celebration of fae and human equality, we spared no expense on security, but that hadn't stop Vince's words from prickling me at the last council meeting.

He'd sneered when I reminded everyone of the date of the festival. "You really think it's a good idea for the darkyra and humans to flaunt their new rights like this?" Vince had asked. "It's going to upset the solisers."

I clenched my jaw. While there hadn't been anymore SoCo threats, that didn't mean there weren't upset people in Palagui. We weren't naïve. There was always the possibility that a disgruntled soliser could come and try to ruin everyone's day, but we'd planned for it, and I refused to cancel out of fear or intimidation.

"This is an important day," I said. "We hired properly vetted guards. It will be fine."

Vince sighed. "And you and Sebastian are going to go to this darkyra rave too? And you'll both be there all day?"

I glared at him, not understanding what he was getting at. "It's not a rave. It's a festival. There's going to be funnel cakes and face paint. Not drugs and EDM."

Vince shrugged. "Sketchy club music seemed more the darkyra style." He narrowed his eyes. "But you're sure you'll be there all day? You won't be at court, you know like, doing your actual jobs?"

I rolled my eyes. "Yes, Vince. We won't be in court that day, but don't worry, I'll look at your budget proposals before the next council meeting."

Vince pursed his lips but nodded once, seemingly satisfied with my answer.

I shook my head. I wouldn't let his negativity ruin the celebratory mood of the day.

Our fae warders trailed behind us as Sebastian and I walked through the festival to the stage where we'd give our speeches, but even with the crown on my head, very few people glanced at us.

They were all too busy taking in the lights and the sounds of merriment. Children ran around, zig-zagging this way and that, balloons tied to their wrists and the smear of powdered sugar on their faces. The sun shined unseasonably hot for spring, but a light breeze kept everything cool and spread the delicate floral smell of blooming trees through the park.

The general aura of everyone around us was pleasant pastels. Yellow happiness, pink joy, purple excitement, all wrapped in the budding green of the spring leaves.

Booths of festival games had been repurposed for the event. Instead of winning a prize by aiming a water gun, people shot their shadows into tiny little holes. Skee ball could be played traditionally for the humans or enhanced with shadows to help the angle of the balls. And ring toss...well, it looked like ring toss was just ring toss.

I leaned over to Sebastian as we passed a merry-go-round. "I know the festival is supposed to be darkyra themed, but there is just something wrong about black cotton candy."

He laughed. "I don't know. I can kind of see it. Shadows are light and floaty like cotton candy."

"Yeah. I get the imagery, but it's just"—I made a shivering disgusted noise—"wrong."

He tilted his chin down and pushed his sunglasses lower on his nose to look out over the top of them at me. "You just aren't in the darkyra spirit."

I opened my mouth to respond, but his face went serious. He flung out his hand. A shadow raced past.

I turned.

Sebastian's shadow held a boy in mid-air, hovering above a puddle of mud he almost wiped out into.

The shadow set him back on the ground.

The little boy grinned. "That was so cool!" he screamed and sprinted away, shouting that he could fly.

What I assumed to be his mother waved a grateful hand to us. Her void eyes flickered away, and she chased after the boy, calling out his name in an exasperated tone.

"I don't think I could handle that," I said as we walked to the back of the stage. The rest of our team was here, setting up the equipment.

"Flying children?" he asked. We sat in the chairs that were off to the side. I'd learned from my first speech that everything went better if I stayed out of the way until it was my turn to talk.

"Children in general," I said. "I'll be the best aunt ever though to Sloane and Nico's seven kids."

He raised his eyebrows and put the sunglasses on top of his head. Shadows filled his eyes. "Seven?"

I shrugged. "Just a guess. Sloane said she wanted a big family."

"I'm going to have to build an addition to the garage apartment."

I chuckled. "Maybe we should move out there, and they can take the townhouse."

He nodded. "You're right. That'd be very selfless of us."

"And we can sift to the beach house when the kids start crying."

"Also an excellent idea."

"So," I said, picking lint that wasn't there off my dress. "You're okay with that then?"

"Living in the garage apartment?"

"Not having kids," I corrected.

He shrugged. "I never really considered having children as an option, what with my bargain to never get into a commitment with anyone, but it never bothered me that I wouldn't." I could feel his eyes on me but kept mine trained on my suddenly very linty dress. "I'd figure out how to wrap my head around being a father if you wanted them, but it's not a problem that you don't either."

I continued to fidget.

"Unless…" Sebastian started. His body turned to mine, and he forced me to meet his gaze with a finger on my chin. "You only don't want them because you think you can't have them. I said it before, but the tester was not qualified to determine whether you're infertile. And even if you were, or I was, we could figure something out if you wanted to have a family."

I interlaced my fingers with his. "I already have a family, and it's not missing anything as far as I'm concerned, except a dozen nieces and nephews. I just didn't want me not wanting them to have ruined your hopes for the future."

"Does Nico know his seven kids just turned into a dozen?" Sebastian grinned. His eyes crinkled around the edges. That bright, brilliant, genuine smile of his never failed to make my entire being feel like I was floating.

I snorted my laugh.

His eyes turned serious, and one blink later the shadows had disappeared. The sincerity of his blue irises pierced me.

"You being in my life means my future could never be ruined." He kissed the back of my hand. "You know I'd do anything you wanted and be happy for it. All you have to do is ask."

My smile faltered, but he didn't see it because someone had called his name to get prepped to go on stage.

When he turned for a final check by the PR person, his void eyes had reappeared, and the person fluffing his suit jacket put his sunglasses back into position.

I knew he would do anything for me.

But I couldn't ask him to do the one thing I wanted: Stay.

***

Aurelio spoke first. A speech about human equality and the history of partnership between darkyra and humans.

I couldn't listen to Sebastian's speech because, at that point, I was starting to sweat for my turn. I'd done over a dozen of these, but they hadn't gotten any easier.

I walked out onto the stage after Sebastian introduced me. The crowd was restless, but I attributed that to the fact a popular band was slotted to play after us and they were anxious to get on with it.

My speech was short and sweet, and boring. Darkyra pride and human equality and Palagui being the best country ever. The usual patriotic stuff.

I'm pretty sure it went well enough, but I could never tell. I blacked out most of it. My nerves made it impossible for me to register the crowd's emotions over my own racing heart.

Sebastian and I were supposed to stay after to meet people and shake hands for positive publicity, but after the adrenaline of speaking wore off, I was exhausted.

And even though the fake crown wasn't digging into my head like the real one did, I still developed a terrible headache.

I made my excuses to the PR guys—who were mildly annoyed with my change in plans, but they were always annoyed at me for something—and told Sebastian I'd meet him at home after I picked up some paperwork that Blake had left on my desk this morning.

I wasn't planning to go into court tomorrow. No way in hell I'd be able to act like it was a normal day knowing Sebastian was gone and might never come back. So a "work" from home day it was going to be.

Sebastian insisted he come with me. We told our fae warders they could go enjoy the festival since we wouldn't be in public anymore and sifted to the office.

The file folder I needed was piled atop my usual stack. As I leaned over the desk to grab it, the blare of the fire alarm went off.

I cringed and held my hands over my ears. The painful screech and bleating worsened the pounding in my temples.

Bright white lights flashed in the hall.

"What's happening?" I asked. One too many fire drills in school made me passive to the outburst. It was likely someone bumped the alarm or there was an unopened email in my inbox about a scheduled drill.

Sebastian walked to the door. He looked left and right down the hall, and then turned and shrugged.

Blake sprinted past the open door and came to a skidding halt as they saw us.

"Your majesties," they said, out of breath, clutching the door frame to keep from falling over. "You have to get out of here."

"What floor is the fire?" Sebastian asked.

They shook their head. "I don't know. All of them."

"What's happening?" I asked.

"They said over the intercom." Blake tried to take a deep breath, but started wheezing a bit. "They were going to burn the place down if they didn't get it."

"Get what? Who said this?" Sebastian asked.

"Blake, do you have asthma? Do you have an inhaler?" I crossed the room. "I'll sift you out and—"

"No!" they said, backing up. "I mean, yes." Another wheeze. "I do, but you have to help everyone in the conference room. They jammed our cell phones and disconnected the internet and phone lines. Someone in the security office sounded the active shooter drill. Everyone on each floor will be barricaded in room five. I hoped there would be a darkyra"—wheeze—"But none strong enough to—"

"Okay," I said. The eerie calculating calmness came over me. I couldn't feel my headache or a single pain in my body. Priorities and plans arranged into place.

I grabbed Blake under the shoulders to keep them from collapsing. "We're going to the conference room. Sebastian and I can sift people. Everyone's going to get out safe."

Sebastian moved to take my place and lifted Blake into his arms. I followed him down the hall to the conference room.

Frightened eyes and startled gasps greeted us as we opened the door. Three fae in the front of the group extinguished the fire in their palms when they saw us.

They'd been guarding the rest of the group. They'd been expecting to die fighting, not from a fire.

What the hell was going on?

I shouted instructions over the fire alarm, and everyone gathered in groups of five. We sifted in and out three times until everyone in the conference room was safely out of the building and standing in one of the parklets three block south of court.

I commanded a few people to call the security force, firefighters, and ambulances.

Blake was on the ground, wheezing, and couldn't speak anymore. Their complexion was a disturbing, pasty blue.

I didn't know if they'd make it until an ambulance came, so before I could get more information, I sifted back inside.

Sebastian was on my trail, and without needing to explain, we started tossing Blake's office, looking through the desk drawers, their bag, and coat pockets for an inhaler.

Found it, Sebastian said in my head as he opened the last drawer on the right of the desk. He tossed it to me. *Go. I'm going to the next floor to get people out.*

I sifted back to the parklet.

Two people were sitting beside Blake on the grass, trying to calm them. I kneeled and handed over the inhaler.

Blake breathed in the medicine a few times, and the color in their face started to return to normal.

"Blake is the first one to get checked out by the paramedics, you hear me?" I said to the two closest people. They both nodded.

I gathered my shadows and almost sifted away before Blake got out a broken, "It's SoCo."

"How do you know?"

"They came over the intercom. They said they wanted the crown and would burn the building down if they didn't get it," Blake managed to say before needing to suck on the inhaler again.

It was the backlash we'd been waiting for. The moment we hoped wouldn't come.

SoCo had waited until we started to believe we could move toward equality without violent consequences.

But like a dormant virus. Their hatred was too engrained to have expected they would accept change without retribution.

A determined rage tightened in my gut. I stepped into the astral field and focused on the mating bond and sifted to Sebastian.

He'd cleared two floors, and I helped him clear the third while relaying in his head what Blake had told me.

Do you think we could freeze them? I asked Sebastian, thinking of the two fae we froze outside the research center.

He grimaced. *If it was only a couple people, we probably could, but a whole mob of fae? We aren't powerful enough for that, even together.*

We sifted back and forth from court to the parklet more times than I could count. Time ticked away. It felt like there were more than forty stories with how many times we sifted in and out.

In between sifting trips, Blake gave us quick updates about the situation.

Someone in court had saved hundreds of lives because they'd initiated the active shooter lockdown, giving everyone a chance to shelter in one room and sealing the fire doors in the stairwells to keep the flames from spreading.

We were lucky that it was the day before the weekend, so court was mostly empty.

The fire was concentrated on the first floor, and though the firefighters had arrived, they couldn't get into the building because fireballs were being thrown into the street when anyone got close to the entrance.

We sifted to the chief of the security force to see what Sebastian and I could do about the mob on the first floor.

A group of paramedics, firefighters, and guards stood on the outskirts of a blockade around the entrance of the building. Interspersed with media and camera crews.

"They have human hostages," the chief of the security force said. "We called in the negotiator, and they allowed us to send in a handheld transceiver to set up communication with the leaders, but so far they just keep repeating their demand for the crown."

I pulled Sebastian a couple steps away from everyone. "I need to go in. We'll make a trade. The hostages for me."

"Absolutely not," Sebastian said.

"They want the crown." I pointed to my head. "This is a fake. I'll exchange the crown for the hostages and get out before they realize."

"They're going to throw fire balls first and exchange hostages never," Sebastian said. "There has to be some other way."

He walked back toward the group of guards staking out the entrance.

I followed him. "I'll sift in. Toss the crown. Scoop up the hostages. Sift out. Done."

"Not going to work," the chief said, overhearing my plan.

Apparently, the security force ran a power sensor scan, which showed there were at least one hundred fae inside the building and a small ward in one of the back rooms with approximately five humans. The team had been able to detect the origination point, making it simple to deactivate the ward, but it was *inside* the building.

A team was working on casting a ward around the first floor to negate the solisers' powers, but it took time to set up, and the downward force of a fae ward activation was known to cause heart attacks in humans. Which was probably why the solisers took the humans hostage in the first place, knowing we wouldn't risk their lives by activating the ward to negate the solisers' powers.

The security force couldn't place the ward until the hostages were out.

But they couldn't get them out without activating the ward.

Sebastian and I were the only ones strong enough to sift five people at once.

"We sift in," I said to him. "You take down the ward, and we'll get the hostages out."

Or we could sift in. Kill them all. And then, save the hostages, my shadow suggested.

It was an appealing option, but we needed to do this properly. The right thing to do was save the hostages and let the authorities handle bringing the rioting solisers to justice through the proper channels.

This wasn't like the prison. This was about saving people, not violence and vengeance.

Sebastian put one hand on his hip and the other rubbed his forehead for a moment, and then he nodded. "Alright."

We informed the chief of our plan. The negotiator tried one last tactic and informed the solisers that the queen was going to relinquish the crown in exchange for the hostages, but we wanted the hostages first.

A tense few minutes passed as we waited.

The staticky response came in five minutes later. "We'll release the hostages to the Queen in person when she hands over the crown, and for every minute you make us wait, we'll execute one of the hostages."

The negotiator waved a hand. "It's a bluff. They're bluffing, but this is good. They're talking—"

The entrance door opened, and a charred body was tossed into the street. It tumbled and rolled over and over until it stopped a few feet from where we stood.

I gasped.

The eyes and eyelids had been melted. Revulsion churned in my stomach. All the skin was blackened, except the bright red oozing areas that peeled off from where the body had scraped along the asphalt road.

Paramedics ran toward the person; a darkyra and a soliser guarded them as they lifted the body onto a stretcher.

The person let out a low agonized moan that would live in my memory for the rest of my life.

I covered my mouth with my hand as tears welled behind my eyes. They were alive. I didn't know if that was better or worse than being dead.

I blinked away my tears and turned to Sebastian, whose eyebrows were drawn together in horror.

SoCo wasn't bluffing.

Interlacing my fingers with Sebastian, I said to the chief, "We're going in."

He didn't stop us this time.

We sifted into the hall that looked into the lobby, and peered in at a hundred solisers packed together like they were at a concert, blocking the door to the backroom.

If Sebastian and I sifted over there, we would have a hundred fire balls thrown at our backs. If he could focus on disabling the ward, instead of wasting his power on fighting through fire, he could get it down and sift the hostages out in less than a minute.

The solisers were chanting something, but the only thing I could hear was the blood rushing in my head.

The air was thick with smoke, and my throat burned with the spice of anger. My eyes started to water with the need to cough.

They want the crown, I said. *I'll distract them. You unward the backroom and sift the hostages out.*

His nostrils flared and his eyes turned sharp. *No!*

I never learned how to take down a ward and now doesn't seem like the best time for a lesson. I pleaded with my eyes. *If we start killing everyone, you and I would get out alive, but they'll start slaughtering the hostages before we can get to them.*

The hostages were powerless, and as SoCo promised, another person was going to be killed any second now.

He pressed his lips together, but he knew as well as I did, we didn't have time for a better plan.

Without wasting another moment, his shadows gathered, and he sifted.

I just needed to distract them.

I sifted to stand on the lobby reception desk. All I needed to do was keep their eyes away from Sebastian as he broke the wards.

Holding my arms out, I took my time coating the ceiling with shadows to create my diversion.

They thickened slow at first, then took over the expanse of the room. Chanting turned into confused yelling as shadows dripped down onto the solisers' heads.

My shadows toyed with their prey. Wisps of darkness caressed their faces with the threat of sharp claws. One by one the solisers' attention locked in on me.

That's right, I thought to myself. *Look over here. Not over there. Over here at the shadows, not at the darkyra breaking your ward.*

Sebastian disappeared into the backroom. He'd only need a few more seconds to sift the hostages out.

"I am the Queen of Palagui," I said. "You will extinguish your flames, or I shall do it for you."

One of them shouted a slur.

Another called out what they planned to do to my body before they cut off my head.

Cheers followed.

A fire ball was flung toward me. I lifted my hand to stop it, but shadows overtook the room.

They weren't my shadows.

Chapter Thirty-Seven

"This is Bob Salner for Fire News Five. The only channel in Palagui with a recording of the live stream from last night's attack. Viewer discretion is advised for the next clip we're about to show."

A fuzzy phone video jiggled left and right.

It finally focused on a group of male solisers outfitted in black. Their faces partially covered by bandanas. Fire was burning bright in their palms as they listened to their leader outline a plan to restore Palagui to the light.

Their fists of fire were raised in the air. Cheers erupted as flames caught around the outskirts of the room.

A chant started in the background, mumbled at first behind the cloth on the protesters' faces until the steady drumbeat of words became clearer when their excitement reached a fever pitch.

"Down with the Queen of Darkness."

"Down with the Queen of Darkness."

"Down with the Queen of Darkness."

Except something was growing, hanging down from the ceiling. A black mold, creeping and crawling. No wait. Not mold.

A shadow.

A shadow that expanded until it covered the entire ceiling.

The chant turned into hollering as the shadows trickled down.

"I am the Queen of Palagui. You will extinguish your flames or I shall do it for you."

The phone was dropped, and the only thing that could be heard was the clatter as it hit the ground.

Luckily, it landed on its side as the solisers started to cheer once more.

The screen went white with a burst of light, but it cleared in time to record the confusion and fear that replaced the excitement on the solisers' faces.

Shadows crawled down their necks, down their spines. Panicked, the solisers tried to run, but couldn't escape. They screamed.

The shadows latched on to their vertebrae and entered their minds.

The solisers were no longer screaming.

With a *whoosh* of darkness, shadows blotted out the orange in their eyes.

They didn't stop there.

The shadows squeezed and wrang out the life essence from every soliser on the screen.

Shadow creatures took their place. Shriveled bodies, black pus, flaking skin.

With an echoing *crack,* a hundred necks snapped at once.

And then they fell.

Darkness overtook the screen as the video ended.

"Horrible," the newscaster said. "To think that this could happen to a group of peaceful protesters, light bringers, is despicable. How do you feel as a darkyra watching this?"

The newscaster handed a microphone to a female on the street.

She shook her head. "It gives all darkyra a bad name. To think that this whole time the draxis were created by the Queen? The darkyra people cannot create draxis." She looked into the camera. "I don't know what she is, but she isn't a darkyra, and I won't follow someone like her. She's not my queen."

The newscast cut to a different person. "I'm a human," a young male said. "And at first, I was excited about the laws being repealed. I thought we finally had a queen on our side, but after watching this?" He stared into the camera. "I felt so much safer when Xenos was in charge. A soliser with reputability. A soliser we could trust. If the Queen does this to her citizens, there's no saving any of us."

Palaguian citizens weren't ready for a darkyra queen.

That much was clear.

And with this video, they had a rally cry that all fae—and even humans—could get behind.

Down with the Queen of Darkness.

Chapter Thirty-Eight

Sebastian

What had I done?

Instinct took over.

But I didn't lose control.

I didn't.

I didn't fucking lose control!

I did what I was born to do. I protected my mate as every fiber of my being was made to do.

I took their power.

They didn't deserve it anyway. Not after what they said. After what they threatened to do to her...

I killed them all. And I'd do it again.

I *didn't* lose control.

The voice that was no longer foreign in my head. The one I tried to convince myself had died. The one that was refusing to be shut away any longer.

That voice whispered, *Yes you did*.

Chapter Thirty-Nine

Amaya

Exhaustion fought with adrenaline as I tried to close my eyes and sleep, but I only tossed and turned under scratchy bedsheets that were not my own.

Sebastian had sifted all of the hostages to safety, and only the burn victim was badly injured. He, James Endlouer, was a soliser that was in the wrong place at the wrong time and had tried to fight the SoCo members who'd threatened to burn one of the human hostages. That act of bravery might have cost him his life. He was in intensive care, but the doctors couldn't give a prognosis due to the extent of the burns.

After Sebastian retrieved the hostages, and we sifted out, the entire first floor blew up. Early reports are saying it was due to a malfunction of the sprinkler system, which apparently allowed the fire to spread to a gas pipe.

There was nothing left to the first floor.

It burned late into the night before the soliser firefighters got it under control, which in one way was a saving grace. No one would find out what Sebastian had done.

I didn't blame him, but it was better that their desiccated bodies could be explained by the explosion.

The darkyra-human festival was shut down when the organizers heard of the attacks happening only a few miles away. I was just grateful they decided to attack court and not a festival full of children.

But the darkyra and humans weren't their targets.

It was me. It was the crown.

While court was under attack, another faction of SoCo tried to undertake a raid of the palace, but the wards had kept them at bay until more guards were called in.

SoCo didn't seem to know we lived at Sebastian's townhouse, but out of an abundance of caution, Sebastian, Nico and I rented the house Nico and Sloane stayed at in Molbridge during her internship at the healing center.

I took the crown from its place in the safe and have been wearing it despite how bad my headaches were. I was too afraid that SoCo would somehow find it, no matter where I hid it.

It was only after being threatened that I realized how desperately I wanted to hold on to the power the crown gave me. I wasn't going to give it up or back down.

I sent a message to Gwen and Sloane over our encrypted server and told them to delay their trip by a few days. We hadn't had any airport bomb threats, but I was scared about what SoCo might have planned.

I knew they'd try again if we didn't stop them.

It was past midnight by the time I sent the message though, so I didn't hear back from them before I went to bed.

We were all shaken.

Nico, especially, was panicky because Sloane was in another country. Sebastian and I could see he'd been going crazy without her. Every time I saw him—which wasn't much because he spent all his free time in the basement gym working out—he looked frazzled.

Sebastian suggested that Nico fake his identification and get around the ban on his travel permits, but Nico didn't want to make things harder on us given all the political turmoil we had with Delnee.

And since they were texting and talking over security-encrypted phones every day, he "had no reason to be worried" and "didn't want to smother Sloane by being overprotective when she had enough on her plate."

Sloane's grandmother wasn't taking her decision to permanently live in Palagui very well, and Sloane was upset because she didn't want to disappoint her only living family member.

But after what happened at court, I think Nico was regretting the decision *not* to be overprotective.

When I'd slipped into bed in the rental house, I hoped sleep would take me quickly, but something buzzed inside me and refused to be quelled.

I turned to my side and stared at Sebastian's face resting on his pillow.

It'd been on the tip of my tongue to ask him if he had another flashback, if killing the solisers was an accident, but from the hollow look in his eyes after we sifted out…I think I knew the answer.

There wasn't much we could say to comfort each other, but he didn't push me away. I didn't know how I would have functioned if he'd disappeared inside himself less than twelve hours before he left through the portal.

Every part of me tensed at the thought of what could happen at sunrise. I could lose Sebastian. He might never come back.

And there wasn't a damn thing I could do to prevent it.

I traced the slope of his nose with my eyes, along his cheekbones until they were hidden under the long swoop of his dark hair.

I couldn't ask him to stay.

It was so selfish. And I'd been the selfish one in our relationship from the beginning.

But Goddess, did I want to.

I wanted to beg him to stay with me. To not go. I wanted to wrap my body around his and somehow weigh him down so he couldn't leave.

His eyelashes fluttered, and his eyes opened. I wasn't even surprised that blue shone through.

"Can't sleep?" he whispered.

I shook my head.

"Me either."

He scooted closer and wrapped an arm around my torso, twisting his legs with mine, holding me tight against his body. I was covered by him, and it wasn't enough. The ache in my heart throbbed.

I'm not sure we ever truly fell asleep, suspended in restless resignation and anticipatory grief.

Dawn came too soon.

We only parted for ten minutes so I could shower, but it felt like I'd wasted ten minutes I should have been with him.

It was still dark outside. Sunrise wasn't for another hour. I almost rounded the corner into the main living area, but Nico's stern voice halted my steps.

"Don't do this. You're risking everything for the remote chance that you'll find her. It's been a hundred years, Bash. Over 150 years, if Dr. Henderson's research is right about how time moves on that planet."

"I'll find her," Sebastian said. "She's family. She's blood."

"This is so fucking stupid. Don't throw your life away. I'm begging you."

"Nico, I have to save her."

I peeked my head around the corner.

"You have a mate now," Nico said. He stood on the other side of the counter from Sebastian with his back to me. "If you won't stay for me, then for Goddess's sake stay for her. After what happened yesterday? You're going to leave her to deal with that alone?"

Sebastian shook his head. He was wiping down the countertop. "I'll be back tonight—"

"And what if you aren't?"

"I will."

"If you go through that portal, you might never come back. Just like Adriana," Nico said.

Sebastian clenched his jaw. His gaze focused on running the dishrag over the same spot. "I have to do this *for* Adriana. I have to bring her back. I have to fix what I did. How can you even ask me not to save my sister?"

"She was practically my little sister too," Nico said. "Somehow you always forget that I lost her as well, that it kills me that we don't know where she is. I've had to watch you hurt yourself for decades from the grief, and now, I have to lose you too after all of this?"

Sebastian halted his cleaning and glared at Nico. "Right, because trying to get yourself killed in military service was a much better way to deal with it."

The muscles in Nico's back tensed. "My dad convinced me to enlist—"

"And since you always *go with the flow* and do whatever everyone else wants, you did exactly as he told you." Sebastian tossed the rag on the counter. "But he didn't tell you to sign up for the most risky missions. You chose to do that, and for years I thought you were dead. I thought I lost you too."

Nico crossed his arms. "You abandoned me first. You're the one who bound your powers and numbed yourself with drugs and alcohol. Do you know how hard it was to be friends with someone who was self-destructing? How much work and effort it still takes to this day to deal with your bullshit and stick around when all you do is push me away?"

Sebastian threw his hands out to both sides. "No one asked you to stick around!"

"Adriana did!"

If the words were meant as a blow, they'd hit their mark. Shock jolted Sebastian's head back, and his arms fell to his sides as he retreated a step.

"What?" he whispered. I couldn't tell if it was anger or sadness that hushed his words.

Nico clenched both of his hands into fists. "Adriana made me promise that if she wasn't around, I'd take care of you... It was before her initiation. She knew she was going to take the crown soon, and I think she knew that it'd eventually take her life. She made me promise...and I broke that promise because I was so pissed that she was gone, but when I came back..."

Nico walked to the counter again. "Don't you get it? Don't you see? She always knew she'd die before you. She knew you'd have trouble letting her go. She wouldn't want you to do this. Please, Bash."

Sebastian's eyes narrowed and remained fixed on something beyond Nico. "She didn't die. She's lost. And I'm going to find her."

Nico sighed, and his shoulders slumped as if his last hope had been dashed and the weight of disappointment was crushing him.

"But..." Sebastian inhaled and grabbed the edge of the counter. His eyes focused back on to Nico. "If I can't..." He exhaled. "If I don't come back with her tonight, I'll stop. Okay? I'll let her go. But I have to try."

Nico shook his head for a long moment until he threw a dismissive hand and turned and stormed out of the house. All of the walls shook with his anger as he slammed the door behind him.

Sebastian closed his eyes, devastation etched on his features.

I crept out from the hallway and into the kitchen.

He didn't open his eyes. "How much of that did you hear?"

"Pretty much all of it." I halted at the other side of the counter from him. I wanted to hug him, hold him, but something in me told me to tread lightly.

"We don't fight. We never fight," Sebastian said, staring at the counter.

"It's a stressful time for everyone."

"I think I preferred it when he was electrocuting me."

I huffed out a breath and rounded the counter and leaned my hip on the cabinets so I was facing him. "He just loves you. He wouldn't have said those things if he didn't."

Sebastian rubbed his forehead with his hand. "Do you think I shouldn't go?"

"I can't make that decision for you."

"I don't want you to think that if I go it means I don't love you enough to stay," he said. Almost unconsciously, he started rubbing below his collarbone, where the throb of our unaccepted mating bond lived in his heart and mine.

"No," I said as emphatically as possible. I replaced his hand with mine and rubbed circles, knowing that his touch on my heart did more to soothe the ache than my own fingers ever could. "I don't think that at all. You're kind and selfless and caring, and I know you love me. And I know you love Adriana, and I want you to do what you need to. I'm going to support you no matter what."

I wanted to be like Nico. Wanted to beg him to stay, but Nico didn't realize that Sebastian would carry the guilt of this decision for the rest of his life.

If he made this choice based on Nico's pleas or mine, if he didn't decide for himself, he'd carry with him the possibility of going in another hundred years. He'd live his life waiting for the day he could go back and find his sister.

Sebastian's eyebrows pulled together. His eyes darted between both of mine, and I had a moment of déjà vu back to our engagement ritual when I told him I'd follow him into the dark. He searched my face, looking for answers to a question he couldn't articulate.

I knew now the question he was trying to puzzle out.

He wanted to know if it was true. If I meant what I said.

I had then. And I do now.

I sent him my shadows, filled with the full depth of my unconditional love for him. No matter his decision. There was nothing in the world that would make me stop loving him.

He closed his eyes and let the wave of it wash over him. I buried my face into his chest, and his arms wrapped around me.

We stood in the kitchen for a long time, but also not long enough, because when his phone alarm went off, my heart sank into my stomach.

It was time.

He pulled the phone out of his pocket and swiped the alarm off.

There was so much pain in his eyes as he met my gaze. "I have to save her." He said it like an apology.

I forced a smile and grabbed his arm and squeezed. "I know."

This was okay. I could be strong for him. I could handle this.

At least, if I kept telling myself that, maybe it would become true.

Sebastian grabbed the backpack full of supplies, and together, we sifted to the Hollow.

A thick fog curled low in the meadow outside the Hollow. The pale morning sun glistened off the dew that clung to the budding trees. Spring equinox brought a day of equal light and darkness. A fragile blossoming hope for better days.

The bright green of new plant life emerged from under the dead rotting leaves of autumn to brave the cold, somehow trusting that warm weather and sunshine were on their way.

Sebastian and I walked hand-in-hand through the darkness of the cave, venturing farther inside than I ever remember having gone before.

We weren't worried about Kai showing up since they'd bargain to not use their magic against us.

The cave became narrower the longer we walked. Only the sound of water dripping from deep within the cave kept us company.

The walls and floors and ceilings felt alive, pulsating as if they too were preparing for the thinning of the wards between our worlds. I could almost feel it. The way the wards would scrape along one another, shearing and rubbing away until they became thin enough for the portal to appear.

The air became colder, sharp enough to pierce my lungs as I inhaled.

A ripple of light within the darkness flickered ahead like a heatwave off asphalt on a scorching day. Spider webs of sparkling light glittered in an oval, swallowing the path of the cave in a void.

The tear in the wards between our worlds.

Sebastian squeezed my hand as we came to a stop a few paces away from the portal. He dropped the backpack from his shoulder and turned to me.

Cupping either side of my jaw with both his hands, he angled my face up to his. When his lips brushed mine, a heavy pit of dread formed in my stomach. His touch was careful and tender as his thumbs caressed my cheekbones.

I ran my hands up his torso and grabbed the back of his neck, holding him to me like I longed to do, like I never intended to release him, and for that moment, I didn't.

I angled my head and pressed into his mouth harder, deepening our kiss until the heat of its smolder threatened to burn us both. I ignored the way my body had started trembling.

His vanilla affection tasted thick and heavy and far too much like a final goodbye. I couldn't stop the tears from escaping the corners of my eyes.

He pulled back but didn't release me. "Tell me not to go."

"Sebastian…" I choked out.

His eyes pleaded with me. "Tell me you want me to stay."

From behind him, I thought I saw the portal shrinking, speeding up my already racing heart with a sickening urgency as time ticked away.

I tried to blink my tears back but more replaced them. "You know I can't tell you that." I clutched fistfuls of his shirt. "I'm not making this a choice between your mate and your sister. I was in that position, and betraying you will haunt me for the rest of my life. I'm not going to ask you to stay." I forced my hands to release the fabric of his shirt. "I'm just asking that you come back."

His eyes trailed over my face as if trying one last time to commit me to memory. "I'm coming back. I promise you." He pressed his lips to my forehead once before leaning down and pulling the backpack over his shoulder.

As he walked toward the portal, my heart felt like it was stretching out of my chest, trying to grab him. He was only a step away when he turned back. His face contorted in agony.

Maybe I should just tell him to stay. Wouldn't having a Sebastian who resented me be better than no Sebastian at all?

The portal receded. The shimmering of its lights became duller. Our worlds were so dissimilar that only a few minutes of alignment were possible.

No. I couldn't be that selfish. He had been planning this day for a century. He was coming back with his sister. I couldn't let myself dwell on any other alternatives.

I forced a smile, dredging up a false cheer to attempt to say something bland like *good luck* or *see you tonight*.

Except Sebastian's eyes turned sharp, focusing behind me as the feel of a cold hand gripped my neck.

"She may not ask you to pick between your mate and your sister. But I will," Kai said.

I grabbed at their hands, trying to pry their fingers off. The shimmering darkness of the portal faded.

"Go, Sebastian! Go," I said, gathering my shadows. "I can take them. They bargained not to use their magic to interfere."

"I'm not using my magic, am I?" Kai said. "Just my natural strength as an immortal." They tightened their grip around my neck, and I choked. My shadows bounced off them harmlessly as if Kai was impenetrable.

Sebastian's eyes were wide. He dropped the backpack and put his hands in the air in surrender. "Stop. I choose her, okay? Please don't hurt her. I'll do what you want."

"They won't hurt me. They want me to have the crown," I said, but my words came out strangled. "Just go!"

"Interesting theory," Kai said. He shook me hard enough it felt like my brain was rattling against my skull. "You ready to test it?"

"Release her," Sebastian said. His hands were still up in surrender, and he walked toward us, away from the portal. "I choose Amaya. Okay? I pick her. Please. Let her go."

The portal flickered. The last of the glimmering lights condensed and shuttered like the flash of a camera.

"Hmm," Kai said. I felt them shrug. "Okay."

Kai pushed me with the brute strength of an immortal deity across the length of the cave, past Sebastian's outstretched arms.

And into the portal just as it closed.

Chapter Forty

Gwen

"My mother is starting to freak me out," I said to Sloane, taking a sip of sparkling wine. "I swear to the Goddess she hugged me this morning for like five minutes."

This might have been normal for anyone else's parent, but my mother didn't even hug me when I was a child and had a nightmare. All I got was a pat on the head and locked in my room.

"Seriously?" Sloane raised her eyebrows and took a sip from her flute. She and I carved out a spot in the corner by the bar at the latest High Priestess Society gala. Swanky dresses and shimmering jewels surrounded us.

I nodded. "I don't know if it's because of your kidnapping or what, but she's always watching me with this concerned expression. Like am I dying and no one's bothered to tell me?"

Sloane giggled. "Maybe it's because Caroline betrayed us? She's reevaluating her life, figuring out who's really important to her?"

"Maybe..." The suggestion had merit. Every time I tried to talk to my mother about Caroline, she shut me down. I questioned where she could be hiding and all I got was, *what's more important is that you're here and safe. I don't want you leaving to search for her. I should have never sent you to Palagui.*

I told her I was going back soon, but she pretended like she didn't hear me.

I wasn't looking forward to the day I left. I didn't know how I was going to stand up to her if she tried to guilt me into staying.

Again.

Every night we had dinner together, she would tell me about her day and ask me about my life, listening to my answers with such rapt attention, you'd have thought she was going to be tested on it later.

She even let her shield down.

My mother *never* let her emotional shield down.

Not with me. Not with anyone.

I didn't know why she wanted me to feel her love. Not when in the past twenty-five years of my life, she'd trained me to keep my emotions guarded. Had modeled that restraint for me since my power activated when I was seven.

It was beyond weird.

Because, for brief moments, I had started to *enjoy* her company and attention. But I knew better than anyone that emotions turned on a dime, and I wasn't sure I truly trusted my mother's sudden love for me.

Even though I desperately wanted to.

There was just no way it could last. She'd go back to being more concerned about the Society and her position as captain once the novelty of my presence wore off.

I was so ready to go back to Palagui, but Sloane, Rien, and I received a message from Amaya late last night about a minor skirmish at court. She was vague in the details but mentioned we shouldn't come back for a few days until the air cleared.

We messaged back that we received her suggestion.

And in direct defiance of Amaya's wishes, I told my mother I was leaving right away. She convinced me to wait until after this gala.

Something was going on in Palagui, and with Sebastian leaving through the portal, Amaya was going to need back up.

Sloane was still undecided about what she wanted to do.

"My grandmother is just as bad as your mother. I feel bad about leaving. She keeps telling me that she forced the Society to leave my position open in the surveillance office." Sloane wrinkled her nose. "And she thinks I'm lying about having a soliser mate, that I'm just confused because *young love* can be intense."

I snorted. "Maybe she's right and you can ditch the fire breather?"

Sloane gently shouldered me. "You don't have a mate, so you wouldn't understand, but I promise you, it's very real."

I rolled my eyes and downed the rest of my drink. "Uh huh."

She sighed. "But if anything, being here has made me more confused. For the first time in my life, I have endless job options, endless life options, and I'm paralyzed. I don't know what the right choice is."

Sloane enjoyed her internship at the Molbridge healing center, but it brought up more questions than answers about her future.

As a legacy high priestess in Delnee, there were two options after initiation: either you'd be a field agent working abroad or you'd work in the Department of Defense.

I shrugged. "It makes sense that you're confused." She furrowed her brows, so I elaborated, "The Society screwed us up. They told us we could have potatoes or bread for dinner. Then we bust out of Delnee and find out there is a whole damn buffet out there! It makes sense you're going to gorge yourself. You're going to try things and see if you like them, and eventually, you'll find your favorite food, but you can't beat yourself up for not picking the perfect meal on the first go around."

"I...I don't know. And what about Nico? I'll feel bad if I ask him to uproot the life that he's been living for decades on some whim I have when I don't even know if it'll pan out."

She lifted her empty flute and smiled sweetly at the bartender, who jumped up to get us refills.

After the bartender refilled our drinks and walked away, I turned to her. "Look Sloane, obviously Nico and I aren't exactly besties, but even I can see that the guy is in love with you. If you told him you were joining the circus, he'd learn to swallow a sword for you. It doesn't matter. Pick something, try it out, change your mind and do something else, but no matter where you live, or what job you do, or what's happening in your life, you'll be able to count on him to be there…" I threw back the rest of my drink and mumbled, "…to love you."

Nico wasn't going to disappear into the shadows on Sloane. And that was more than most of us could expect.

Sloane gaped at me.

"What?" I asked, irritated.

She closed her mouth and jutted her head back. "Nothing. I'm just shocked to hear relationship advice from the queen of commitment issues."

"Fine. Don't listen to me. I don't care." I scanned the expanse of the ballroom, looking out over all the ritzy people schmoozing.

She grabbed my hand and shook my arm until I looked at her again. I tried to give her an annoyed look, but it was ruined by my smile peeking through.

"You're right," she conceded.

"I know. I'm always right," I said. "Remember when I told you Sebastian was behind the draxis attacks? That he was a demi-god bent on stealing fae powers?" I mimed scoring at a ball game and said, "Called it."

She giggled.

"There you are!" My mother's shoulders slackened in relief as she click-clacked her heels toward us. "I've been searching everywhere for you."

"We've been right here the whole time," I said.

"Well, come on. I need to speak to you both privately."

I furrowed my brow. "Right now?"

"Yes."

I narrowed my eyes, shooting Sloane a look. She only shrugged.

We followed my mother through the ballroom and down the hall to one of the smaller dining rooms.

She held the door open for us and squeezed my forearm affectionately as I passed.

I tried not to shrink away. It was just so freaking weird.

The room was empty, save for a large dining room table in the middle and someone standing with their back to us looking out the window.

I put my glass on the table down, about to turn to my mother, but the male spun around.

"Rien!" Sloane said. "What are you doing here?"

He turned around with a puzzled expression and held up a piece of paper with a note scrawled on it. "Didn't you want to talk to me?"

"No, I did."

Sloane and I spun around at the sound of Caroline's voice.

"Shut the door, Evelynne," she commanded.

My mother shut the door and clicked the lock.

"You can make this easy or hard, but before you choose, I'd like to remind you that your friend is human and wouldn't survive an injury like you would," Caroline said.

"Mother!" I said. "I told you she betrayed us."

Her eyebrows pulled together in concern. "I'm so sorry I sent you to Palagui, Gwen. I didn't think for a second that they'd brainwash you right under our noses, but now that you're back, we can't let the darkyra infiltrate the Society. Caroline knows how to get the shadows out of your head. You just have to cooperate."

My jaw dropped. "She's lying to you. There are no shadows in my head. I'm not brainwashed!"

"I watched that shadow queen brainwash Harrison," she said. "I wouldn't have believed it if she hadn't done it right in front of me. I know you don't understand, but that's because you're sick, honey."

"You saw her influence his actions," I said. "Neither she nor Sebastian could change his mind about something. You know that."

She put a hand on her hip, radiating disappointment. "I thought if we got you and Sloane away from them, their influence on your actions would wear off, but you're as determined as ever to do their bidding. I know you're confused, but we're going to fix you."

I swallowed. "How? How exactly are you going to fix me?"

"The only way to kill the shadows in your brain is to kill the shadow wielders themselves," Caroline said.

My mother hadn't believed us when we told her what had truly happened. She'd been working with Caroline all along.

I knew I shouldn't have trusted my mother's new affections.

"What does Rien have to do with this?" Sloane asked.

I backed up to use my body as a shield for Rien.

Caroline tilted her head. "I've been watching him, and he knows too much. He'll act as my insurance to make sure Harrison keeps his promises."

"Amaya will know something is wrong when we don't come back," Sloane said. Her voice was strong. A heat radiated from her, anger rolling off in waves. "Whatever you have planned won't work. She and Sebastian are more powerful than all of the high priestesses in the Society combined."

"Oh, don't worry," Caroline said. "We'll make sure the shadow queen doesn't notice your absence until I want her to. Her and her mate's reign of darkness is about to come to an end."

Chapter Forty-One

Sebastian

I lunged after Amaya toward the portal. My hand brushed her ankle, but I didn't careen into an unknown world. I smashed into the rocky ground.

The heels of my hands were bleeding. The knees of my pants torn. I registered none of it.

Scrambling up, I turned, but the ripple of the portal had vanished.

Time froze. My mind hadn't quite caught up to what was happening, but my body knew. The mating bond tugged harder than I'd ever felt. Like claws had slashed my chest and were trying to rip my heart out.

No. No. No. This was not happening.

Pacing the cave tunnel, I searched the darkness for even the smallest ripple. All I needed was a tiny fragment of the portal, and I would tear it back open.

I waved my hands through the air, used my shadows to sense the denser quality of the portal's broken wards.

But there was nothing.

I dropped to my knees.

I lost her. Just like I'd lost Adriana. My breathing came quicker, chest expanding and contracting without taking in any air.

"Well, that was anticlimactic," Kai said, almost petulant.

With wide eyes, I turned to stare at them. My grief was replaced with anger as I got up. "Why! Why would you do that? We've given you everything you wanted. You said you'd stay out of our lives. You had a darkyra on the throne, and now she's gone." My voice broke on the last word.

Kai sighed out a breath, annoyed or disappointed, as if they'd been waiting for something to happen and it hadn't. "Who said I've gotten everything I wanted?"

My hands clenched into fists, and a rage the likes of which I'd never experience catapulted me forward. I ran, fists raised, shadows slashing through the air, seeking vengeance.

Kai didn't even blink. My shadows harmlessly bounced off their body. They moved at an unnatural speed. Their hand came up to catch my fist before it landed. "Yes. Lash out at a being that cannot be wounded and cannot die. That will certainly solve the problem." They twisted my hand and flung me to the ground.

I couldn't feel any pain, but I was covered in rocks and sand, all of it mixing with blood. I didn't care about being hurt. Didn't care if it was pointless. I wanted my knuckles to connect with their face. I might have spent most of my time in an office, preferring to fight my battles with strategic plans, or shadows if necessary, but since I trained with Nico, I could hold my own in a fight.

I hopped back up and threw myself toward Kai again. They sifted to the other side of the cave. "While I do think this reaction is interesting, given last time you collapsed into a pathetic, whiny child, I'm not interested in playing."

They sifted in front of me, holding me to the cave wall with their unnatural strength. I was still fighting, every muscle tensed and pressing against them. I knew I couldn't win. I knew I'd never kill a deity, but it didn't stop me from wanting to try.

Kai shrugged. "We'll just have to hope she comes back tonight."

I halted in my struggle. "We?" Rage made my vision narrow. "We! You did this. You sent her there. Why did you do it if you're hoping she comes back?"

They shrugged. "Wanted to see what would happen."

With that, they vanished, and I fell. Kai disappeared into whatever pit of hell they resided in.

I collapsed, pressing my forehead to the ground. My anger faded into grief. The pain of the mating bond squeezed and twisted, and I let myself disappear into it.

Not again. Not like this.

Amaya didn't have the backpack. She didn't have the food and water and camping supplies. She didn't have the extra clothes and the protections and the weapons. She had nothing. She was in a strange world for the next day and a half on their timeframe, and she'd go hungry and thirsty and be alone and vulnerable, trying to fend off whatever creatures or terrors that world held.

She was strong, but she wasn't invincible. She wasn't prepared. She wouldn't be coming back.

I'd lost her. Sentenced her to a terrible death. I'd killed her.

Just like I'd done to my sister.

I could barely live with myself knowing what I'd done to Adriana. I couldn't breathe, hadn't been able to take a deep breath for years after she disappeared into the portal. Not until I'd made my plan to get her back.

But I wouldn't survive without Amaya. I didn't deserve to. My heart agreed, each panging ache from the bond squeezed like a noose.

Alone. Again.

And I didn't deserve anything different. I shouldn't have come here. I shouldn't have risked my life with my mate for the small chance that I could find my sister. I should have accepted that I killed Adriana and accepted that I killed the high priestesses by turning them into draxis. I should have accepted that I was a terrible person.

Amaya. My sweet, perfect mate was gone. Gone. Gone.

Shock stunted my emotions. I stood and mechanically walked through the darkness of the Hollow, but instead of sifting home—I didn't have a home anymore, not without her—I kept walking.

One foot in front of the other, aimless and empty, I trekked through the meadow and into the forest.

My eyes fixed on nothing at all. I saw nothing. Heard nothing. Felt nothing. Numbness shackled my emotions.

The paper with Amaya's list chafed the skin over my heart in my breast pocket. The proof of my inadequacies. The proof I had never deserved her. The proof that I had been stupid to ever think I could.

I lied to Nico and Amaya this morning. I told them both I was going into the portal to save Adriana, to get her back.

Of course, I wanted my sister back.

But I also *needed* her to come back. I needed her to fix my mistakes. To heal the draxis I'd created. I'd lost control of my power again when I'd killed those solisers. I wasn't ever going to be fixed. I needed Adriana to right my wrongs. I needed her to save me as much as I wanted to save her.

I wasn't selfless or caring or kind.

I was selfish.

I would never be the mate Amaya deserved.

Time passed. Or it didn't. At some point, I tripped over a root and didn't get up. I rolled onto my back and stared at the gray sky through the bare, lifeless tree branches.

I'd been here before. Wandered these forests. Alone and lost.

The memory came back as a visceral gut punch. I'd killed my father, watched my mother's throat be slit. My power had erupted all around me with an agony that overwhelmed my eleven-year-old body. The shadow cyclone destroyed everything. The house. The neighborhood. The city.

I'd sifted in hopes to take the destruction with me, but the power had already picked up too much momentum. A life of its own.

I made the decision then to fractalize myself. To cut up the pieces, shrinking each of the emotions, each of the memories, until they could be stored away and ignored.

And here I was a hundred years later, no more capable than an eleven-year-old boy.

Except this time there was no possibility of separation from what I'd done.

I'd felt it in the last few weeks. Seen it happen in the mirror each day the shadows in my eyes lessened. Each time a memory was unveiled from somewhere deep within. Each time I felt myself integrating, being stitched back up.

I thought I could handle it, thought the healing ritual had worked to make me whole.

But I wasn't a shadow and I wasn't a fae.

I wasn't the person I'd been when I met Amaya. I wasn't the shadow she broke out of that prison either. I was a combination of everything I hated. I wasn't whole. I was a conglomeration of broken and damaged pieces.

A boy who killed his parents.

A brother who'd been too weak to save his sister.

A darkyra who stole high priestess powers.

A murderer. A monster.

A king without his queen.

A mate without his bonded.

I can't remember how I was found in the woods that day a hundred years ago, but I do remember the guards grabbing me, holding me down, cuffing me. I hadn't resisted.

When I saw their flames, I'd only thought, *Finally. They'll kill me and put me out of my misery.*

But the world is cruel, and I was only taken to the castle. Locked in a warded basement. Left to live with a dark vacant spot in my memory. To not know why I felt empty and hollow.

Later, they told me what I'd done. That I'd killed my parents and everyone in Merbany with my power outburst. That I was locked away for my own protection. For the country's protection.

At least I didn't remember doing it.

I remembered now. I remembered everything I'd ever done. As a shadow. As a fae. There was no hiding from myself anymore.

Rain splattered my face as I stared up at the gray sky. The droplets were sharp. My body shivered, but it was a dissociated experience as my clothes became soaked with freezing rain.

My pocket buzzed, and with a habitual slowness, I answered the call with a flat, "Hello?"

"Bash." Nico sighed in relief. "I'm so sorry. I'm so glad you decided not to go. I'm so sorry. I shouldn't have said that shit this morning. When I couldn't get ahold of Amaya, I've just been panicking for the last few hours. Sick to my stomach, thinking that could have been the last thing I said to you. But I'm so glad you didn't go. Adriana wouldn't—"

"Nico," I said. My voice cracked.

"What?"

The words could barely leave my lips, could barely get past the thick emotion in my throat. "Amaya's gone."

The silence from the other end of the call expanded.

The branches of the trees shook as a breeze whirled through them, but they weren't as bare as I'd initially thought. Tiny green buds sprouted from the limbs. Proof of life in a lifeless expanse.

I sent my shadows above me and clipped every single one of the buds off until they fell to the ground. *Plink. Plink. Plink.*

There didn't deserve to be hope for new life in a world that didn't have Amaya in it.

I waited for Nico's anger, for the fury he'd displayed this morning when he told me what a stupid idea this was.

I was ready. Ready for his rage. I welcomed it. I needed it. The punishment of his disappointment.

But his voice was soft, almost pleading, when he said, "Come home, Bash. Just come home."

Grief had weakened my will, and I had no reason to fight nor the wherewithal to make a decision for myself, so I sifted to the townhouse.

Nico was in the living room, still holding the phone to his ear, when I stepped out of the shadows. He must have spent the morning driving home from Merbany. He always did like to drive when he needed to think.

Nico pocketed the device and crossed the room. His arms wrapped around me, but I didn't move, only let his body heat seep into my skin.

"She's not gone," he said. "She's coming back. This isn't like last time. We've got another shot at this. The portal will open. She's coming back and bringing Adriana with her."

I pushed out of his embrace. "You don't know that."

Anger flashed in his eyes. "That was your plan, wasn't it?"

I turned from him and walked to the front window, staring out at the rain puddling in the road. The early morning light was bleak and desolate.

"I'm sorry," I said. "You were right. I shouldn't have gone."

Nico sighed.

He didn't ask what happened, which was good because I didn't think I would be able to put it into words.

I pulled out Amaya's list and rubbed the paper between my fingers. I didn't need to unfold it to know what it said. I had it memorized. The paper was worn and the edges were fraying from the fumbling I did with it every day.

Nico stepped beside me and held out a hand.

I glanced at his palm and gingerly gave him the folded page. I didn't have any fight left in me or any reason to hide. He knew, just as Amaya did, that I'd never been worthy. Neither blue-eyed nor void-eyed.

He unfolded it and quietly read.

"I wanted to be that person for her. Wanted to fix what I'd done…"

He blew out a breath and returned the folded page. "You gotta forgive yourself, buddy."

"I'm not going to condone what I've done," I said. My voice harsh. "Adriana probably suffered and died. All those high priestesses. I took their lives—"

Nico shook his head. "I'm just as much responsible for what happened to the high priestesses as you are."

I scoffed. "Hardly. You didn't take their powers."

"No," he said. "I gave you the rubies to transport their powers and created the monitoring equipment. Without me, you would have never been able to keep the queen alive. I did this too. Would you sentence me to endure even a fraction of the punishment you've been putting yourself through?"

I swallowed and clenched my jaw.

"We made choices," he continued. "Fucked up choices and we have to own that. We hurt people and took away their lives, but we didn't have any other choice at the time."

I shook my head. His words didn't penetrate the shame that had wrapped around me for almost my entire life.

He clapped a hand on my back and pushed my shoulder, steering me into the kitchen, and positioning me in front of the counter.

My gaze was unfocused until he slid a bowl toward me.

He measured out the flour, yeast, and salt. "You know I've killed people, right?"

I sighed. "It's not the same. In war, you either kill or be killed. You didn't have a choice."

He pointed to the dry ingredients until I picked each up and put them in the bowl.

"I did though," Nico said. He handed me a wooden spoon. "I could have not joined the military. I could have deserted. I could have just not killed."

I combined the dry ingredients. "It's still not the same."

"Isn't it?" Nico measured out water and olive oil. "You were in a political war, trying to keep the most people alive. You were doing what you had to. You had other choices, but none of them were as good as the one you took."

"I was selfish," I said and stirred in the water, then the olive oil. "I was trying to keep my mother alive long enough to bring Adriana back."

"So the Queen is your mother again?" he asked.

I opened my mouth and closed it. When had that changed? At some point my shadow's anger had melded with the part of me who would always love his birth mother despite our complex relationship.

Nico only nodded despite my nonanswer. He took the bowl from me when my stirring didn't quite meet his expectations. "Your mother, the Queen, the female who sent you away when she didn't want to deal with the consequences of her bargain. Who locked you away when she was forced to actually be responsible for her child. Who taught you not to trust your powers."

He put the bowl aside and sprinkled flour on the counter. "The mother who refused to acknowledge that you were hers until she realized that you were her only hope to pass on the crown."

I clenched my jaw.

Nico scooped the dough out of the bowl and plopped it on the flour. "And you call it selfish that you were trying to save that mother?"

"She was trying her best," I conceded. She never hid that the country was the most important thing to her, and I didn't mind coming in third after Palagui and Adriana. I was grateful that she tolerated me at all.

"And so were you," Nico said. He kneaded the dough a few times and then motioned for me to take over.

I worked my hands into the ball. "What's your point?"

"My point is," Nico said. "We're all trying our best."

I squeezed the dough and pressed into it, rolling it on top of itself and repeating. My movements became harsher and angrier the longer I did it.

"When Adriana disappeared," Nico said. "My whole life felt out of control. I was already angry at the world, and I was in a lot of legal trouble from getting into fights. My dad said he'd get the charges dropped if I enlisted in the military."

"You could have told me," I said, halting my kneading and staring at him. "The Queen would have made the charges disappear. You didn't have to go."

Nico shrugged. "I think I knew that, but..." He sighed. "I was lost and having some direction, any direction, felt better than nothing. I felt like I couldn't keep Adriana's promise of taking care of you because you wouldn't unbind your powers. I told myself I *had* to enlist in the military, that this was where my life was taking me."

I went back to aggressively kneading my dough. He repeated his process and stirred the dry ingredients in another bowl.

"I looked for you," I whispered.

"What?"

Swallowing, I focused on my dough and didn't meet his gaze. "When your father told me that they couldn't find you. That..." I took a deep breath. "That you'd been taken prisoner. I applied for flight exemptions, and when I got to the continent, I sifted as close as I could get to the prisoner camps." I shook my head. "Our military was pissed I was there, just sifting around, but I found someone who was there the day you were taken, they told me you were probably dead."

"Bash, you shouldn't have—"

"I know," I said. "But I couldn't not look for you. I couldn't not try."

Nico and I didn't talk about our feelings like this. We didn't talk about our pasts.

After a long silence, he sighed. "When I got back, I was worse than I'd been before. Angry at everything at the best of times, numb at the worst. When my friend asked me to be in his healing ritual, I did it, and eventually agreed to do my own. It finally clicked when the facilitator walked us through a forgiveness meditation."

He sprinkled the flour on the counter and started kneading his dough. "I pictured every single one of the people I'd killed in battle, and told them I was sorry for killing them even though I knew I'd do it again to survive. We were all just doing what we could to survive. I even pictured you and asked for your forgiveness for taking my anger out on you. I pictured Adriana and asked her for forgiveness for not keeping my promise to take care of you."

"I'm sorry, Nico," I said, squeezing the dough between my fingers. "For what I said this morning. I know you lost her too. When I was an idiot teenager, I didn't think anyone could feel as bad as I did, but I should have realized at some point that you were hurting. I was so focused on my own pain, and then I was so focused on researching the portal and trying to wrestle control over my life, I didn't see what you were going through."

He patted his dough into a ball, put it in a bowl, and stored it in the fridge. "It's my fault too. You didn't know I was hurting because I didn't tell you. I didn't want to own up to it. Just wanted to *go with the flow* and pretend everything was fine."

I winced. "I guess there's a middle ground between controlling everything and letting everything happen to you. You and I just need to find it."

In that way, Nico and I were the exact opposite. Maybe that's what made our friendship work all these years.

"I hear you."

I put my dough in the bowl and handed it to him, but he didn't put it in the fridge with his own.

He pressed the lever for the garbage can with his foot and dumped the dough into the bin.

I furrowed my brows. "Why'd you do that?"

"You beat the living shit out of it. No one wants to eat that."

"Well, you didn't tell me to stop."

He shrugged. "You looked like you needed it."

I pressed my lips together. I guess he was kind of right.

But aggressively kneading dough didn't make me feel any better about Amaya being gone.

"She'll be back," Nico said, reading my mind. "Dr. Henderson's calculations were correct this morning. There's no reason to think they wouldn't be correct this evening."

"She doesn't have any of the supplies."

"She's resourceful. She has her powers to protect her, and it's only a day and a half on that planet. She'll be okay."

I closed my eyes. I wanted so badly to believe him, but I was so afraid that it made my heart hurt.

I opened my eyes as the realization hit me.

My heart hurt.

The bond would have dissolved if she'd died.

So as long as my heart hurt, our mating bond was intact, which meant she was alive. I pressed my hand into the pain below my collarbone.

She would come back. She had to. And if she didn't step through that portal as soon as it opened, I'd go in and find her myself.

I didn't care what was on the other side. Didn't care if I'd be trapped there.

My phone chirped with a calendar notification, but when I pulled it out, it wasn't for me. Amaya and I had synced calendars, and her reminder that she had a meeting with Blake to go over damage control from the attack yesterday came through.

And worse, right under that was a reminder that her parents were set to dock this afternoon.

"Fuck," I said and ran a hand through my hair. At Nico's questioning glance I showed him the phone.

"It's fine," he said. "I'll pick Amaya's parents up at port and you go talk to Blake. I'll keep them busy until you're done."

I pursed my lips. "And when they ask where she is?"

He squinted his eyes and puckered his lips. "Yeah...You're going to owe me for this one."

I rubbed my forehead and put my other hand on my hip. "If I sift to Blake, maybe we'll have enough time to go over everything..."

"Wait. You sifted here."

"Yeah," I said, listing out the things I needed to do at court. The engineer would need to be called in to see if the damage to the first floor affected the structural integrity of the building, and I'd need to call the security force chief and see if they had any leads on the whereabouts of SoCo—

"You sifted," Nico said. "And I still have powers. Palagui still has powers, but Amaya and the crown aren't on this world. How is that possible?"

I furrowed my brows. "I...I don't know. We had powers as soon as she put the crown on and was sent to the place between the worlds where the deities bound it to her life force. I guess it doesn't matter what world she is on? Since the crown is tied to her."

Another sign that she was alive. We wouldn't have powers if she didn't have a life force.

It made it easier to think, having tangible evidence that she was alive. I'd see Amaya in twelve hours no matter what. I'd be with her in this world or the next.

"I'll go pick up her parents and tell them she's busy running the country," Nico said. "You go make a game plan with Blake and meet us back here when you're done."

I sighed but nodded. It was our best option. Her parents didn't need to worry any more than necessary about her.

"But before you go, you need to sift us somewhere first," Nico said.

"Where?" I asked, distractedly.

"The research center."

***

"I don't know about this…"

"Just trust me."

Reluctantly, I pushed open the door to one of the draxis containment rooms. Three draxis were strapped down to a table.

"They can't even hear me," I whispered, which was weird because if they couldn't hear me, why was I whispering?

"You don't know that. Maybe they can understand everything we're saying," Nico said. "But even if they can't, think of it like practice, for when you apologize to them after they're healed."

I sighed. This was going to be a huge waste of time. Apologizing to shadow creatures—who, even when they weren't being held in what amounted to an artificial coma, weren't capable of complex thought or reasoning—felt pointless.

Nico talked like the draxis would be healed any day now, but unless Amaya found Adriana, which was unlikely because she couldn't sense her like I could, how would we heal them?

I had a list of things I needed to do at court, but Nico wanted me to do this, and I did owe him. I owed him for far more than just picking up Amaya's parents.

I stared at the hollow face of one of the draxis and started to explain what I'd done to them and why.

Oddly, once I got going, the words came pouring out. I told them how sorry I was for the pain I'd caused and how I wished I could give them their life back. That I'd give them my power if I could.

I told them about the Queen, about her condition, and about watching her deteriorate. I explained how I split myself into two people in order to take their powers because I couldn't handle hurting them. I told them about my shadow, about how it wasn't the first time I'd dissociated to deal with painful experiences. About how my shadow only enjoyed taking their power because those were the only moments I let him free.

I tried to outline the reasons I felt like I had no choice, but always ending with an acknowledgement that none of my reasons excused what I'd done.

It never got easier as I went through my story over and over again in each draxis containment room, but something shifted. Almost as if by speaking out loud my impossible circumstances, I could see it for what it was.

A situation with painful consequences no matter my choices.

In the final room, I said for the last time, "I'm sorry for the pain I've caused you. I took your power to save my mother, to save Palagui, but it wasn't an easy decision, and it wasn't fair." I steadied my gaze on each of their faces. "I'm so sorry. I'm sorry that you're hurting because of me."

I couldn't bring myself to end with a promise that I'd heal them, that I'd fix what I'd done, because even if we figured out how to return their power, there would never be any fixing the years of their lives I'd taken.

I let the weight of that, the uncomfortable guilt I'd been carrying, settle within me. I wasn't relieved of it. I didn't think I'd ever be.

But I saw it now, felt where it dwelled within me, and could acknowledge that there was no avoiding it.

The weight didn't lighten, but it did feel like I'd shifted its load so I could better carry on.

Nico was waiting outside the door and pushed off the wall when I came out. "There is one more left," he said, walking with purposeful strides down the hall.

"There is?" I'd thought we'd gotten them all, but maybe I missed one.

He grabbed my shoulders and shoved me toward a door.

"Nico, this is a bathroom," I said as I was pushed in.

"Yep." He wheeled me around and clapped me on the back as I stood in front of the mirror.

"Ha. Ha," I said. "Very funny." I made to leave, but he blocked me with crossed arms over his chest.

"I'm serious. You recite the exact same thing you said to them into that mirror," he said. "Go ahead. I'll be in the hall."

I clenched my jaw and refused to look in the mirror.

He spun around, pushing the door with his back and gave me a stern pointer finger. "I will know if you don't do it, so don't try to pull one over on me."

I rolled my eyes and waved him away as he left.

With a sigh, I glanced up at the mirror and away again. The door to the bathroom shut with a soft click, and I took a few deep breaths, unable to raise my eyes, unable to say the words I'd already said multiple times.

I could wait a few minutes and walk out of here, and Nico would never know the difference, but some part of me was buzzing with anticipation, and I knew then who needed my forgiveness, my acknowledgement.

I raised my gaze to the mirror. No shadows darkened my eyes. I couldn't say for sure when my void eyes receded for good, but I saw myself in the mirror each morning and night, saw that I wasn't the same person that I had been.

I blinked once and let the shadows fill my eyes. The darkness was another mirrored reflection, like a carnival mirror maze that seemed to go on forever. I was looking further and further into my own soul.

I took a deep breath and breathed out, "I'm sor—" but the words got stuck.

I forced myself not to look away even as tears pricked the backs of my eyes. Tightening my grip on the sink, I leaned forward, staring harder into the void, into the soul of my shadow, my own life force.

"I'm sorry for the pain that I've caused you." The words were drawn out, interspersed by emotion bubbling to the surface. "I took your power to save my mother and to save Palagui." I took another breath because this apology still held true even if it'd been meant for the high priestesses who I'd turned into draxis. It had been exactly what I'd done to myself—took my shadow's power, stifled it—in an attempt to save people. "It wasn't an easy decision, and it wasn't fair that it happened to you."

I squeezed the sink harder as tears broke over my eyelids. "I'm sorry," I whispered, my jaw quivering. "I'm so sorry. I'm sorry that you are hurting because of me."

It was only by seeing the suffering within the infinity mirror of my void eyes that I could see the recursive pain I was stuck within.

The loop of self-hatred seemed inevitable, seemed pre-ordained, but until I could see there was a person who was on the receiving end of all the self-harm, I couldn't justify stopping.

In asking for forgiveness and retelling what happened, I'd finally been able to step back and see the story from outside myself. Just like the healing ritual had helped me see the memory as something that happened in the past.

And it crystallized the truth of my reality in my mind.

All of the pain in my life had come from Kai. They forced me to kill my father. They slit my mother's throat. They stole Adriana. They tried to do the same to Amaya.

But while my pain came from Kai, all of my suffering had come from me.

I split myself into two because I couldn't handle the grief and guilt from my parents' death. I bound my powers because I was afraid of my outbursts. I didn't tell Amaya the truth about us, or about the draxis, because I thought I wasn't worthy of her.

Kai did terrible things to me.

But *I* also did terrible things to me.

I repeated the apology again, this time under my breath, fighting the thoughts in my head about how self-indulgent and egotistical the practice of forgiving myself was, but the relief of emotional release was too bittersweet to engage in that line of thinking.

Again and again, I repeated the apology, until the words *I'm sorry* became easier to say, easier to accept.

My grip on the sink loosened, and I released a deep breath.

I didn't see a monster staring back at me in the mirror anymore.

My shadow sighed. A knot of tension that I'd been holding for over a century released.

I wasn't afraid anymore.

Finally, my shadow said. *Power is ours.*

The barest of smiles tugged on my lips. I turned from the mirror, seeing my century of self-hatred for the ploy it really was: a distraction.

As long as I was too busy fighting myself, I wouldn't see the true problem, wouldn't have access to my true power, but no longer.

"Power is ours," I confirmed, not bothering to reign in the shadows that were dancing in joy around my shoulders and fingertips.

I didn't have it in me to quell their excitement.

We were one. I was whole in a way I hadn't been for my entire adult life. Which was good since I was going to need all the fortitude I could muster for what came next.

My phone trilled with the pings of several incoming text messages. It buzzed with an incoming call just as Nico slammed open the bathroom door with a panicked expression.

"There's a video," he said.

Chapter Forty-Two

Amaya

Power fizzled over my skin as I was flung through the portal. The magic between our worlds was abrasive along my skin like sandpaper.

I careened through the air, toppling over myself. My stomach dropped. I couldn't get my bearings.

A high-pitched whirl whooshed in my ears. Even my void eyes couldn't see through this darkness. Everywhere and nowhere, all at once. A place that was no place. Endless space and nothingness that continued forever.

I gasped for breath, but there was no air.

But before the panic could set in, I was spit out.

I somersaulted onto solid ground. The wind was knocked out of me from the impact.

When I finally stopped rolling, the tumbling had bent my neck in a funny position, and my entire body splayed out awkwardly.

I hissed a breath as dizziness overtook me.

My thoughts slowed. I felt a presence before my mind could register a threat. In slow motion, I turned my head even though I was still plastered to the ground.

"I made a landing pad, but you kind of overshot it," a weird sounding voice said.

I blinked and blinked, trying to make sense of the voice, but there was a thick pink fog clinging to everything.

"What?" I asked, but it came out gurgled like, "Whaargh?"

Hands came to mine, lifting and pulling me into a seated position. My body ached, but it'd been muted and dulled by a hazy muzzle.

The hands left my skin, and a finger pointed to my left.

My gaze followed the pointed finger, turning so slowly that infinity could have passed. The hand gestured to an area that had been built up with soft-looking leaves and a bed of moss.

"Your landing pad," the voice said. "I guess I should have taken eagerness into consideration."

With sluggish movements, I took in my surroundings.

The world was a vibrant jungle with heavy vines. A chorus of alien insects, the rustling of leaves, and the trickle of a faraway water source created the backdrop. A howl sounded behind me that my brain labeled as a monkey. An alien monkey, I guess.

The air was humid, wet and hot, so thick it felt difficult to expand my chest to my lung's full capacity. Heaviness dragged me down but not unpleasantly. It was a comforting press of powers like the air was alive with magic. It made my eyelids heavy. Made my breathing slow. Drunk on the air. High on the pure peace of a sweet magic.

I was situated in an opening lined with a border of ferns and undergrowth. Vibrant flowers dotted the space and dripped a thick golden sap that reminded me of honey.

"Well," the oddly accented voice said. "You're not who I was expecting." The words were hesitant like someone unaccustomed to using the language.

Everything sparkled and demanded my attention, seducing me into a state of bliss. A kaleidoscope of color in every direction. I could have stared at one flower, one leaf, one blade of grass for the rest of my life and not gotten bored, but I dragged my gaze away from the brilliant landscape and took in the sight of the female sitting before me.

Gracefully, she raised us to our feet.

And I couldn't stop staring.

The light condensed around her like an angel. Her white-blonde hair was braided into one thick braid down her back. Everything about her was delicate. Tiny upturned nose, sharp defined cheekbones, big beautiful blue eyes, almost purple. An angel or what I used to think faeries looked like before I knew I was fae. If she'd had gossamer wings, I wouldn't have been surprised.

The sparkles in the air clung to her heavily. Her skin shimmered with golden sparks as the light filtered in through the treetops above.

"Wow," I said, my words slow. My mouth felt full of cotton, but I found no reason to care, no reason for fear. Maybe I died, and this was the afterlife.

Her hand caressed my jaw with a cool touch, tilting my face to look into my eyes. "I think you're intoxicated," she said. "The magic is quite potent here."

"Are you the Goddess?" I asked. "Am I dead?"

The Goddess of the afterlife. The mother of our world. She would look like this.

I guess I died.

But I found none of the fear or even loss within me that would have accompanied such a statement any other day, only fascination and acceptance. My heart was full, and bliss overtook any sadness. There was longing, but no grief. There was only love, so much love. It floated in the air around me, palatable.

"No," she said, her voice sweet and angelic. "You aren't dead. And I'm not the Goddess. You've come through the portal. My name is Adriana. What's yours?"

"Adriana?" I breathed out and clutched her arms. "I found you. We found you."

I squeezed her arms, though my muscles were having a hard time firing, soft and languid as I was.

"You've found me. Have you been looking long?"

"Sebastian has been looking for you." My words were coming faster, but slurring, and the more I tried to focus on forming my lips into sentences, the harder it became.

"He's been searching for a way to get you back since the day you were taken," I said, or I think I did, but my eyes were so heavy, and my body was falling.

I only heard her sigh. "That's what I was afraid of."

And then I passed out.

My dreams were circular but threadless.

I was spiraling, touching ground, only to leave it once more in flight. There was a demand within it, that I must pay attention, but the meaning slipped from my fingers.

When I woke, the world was orange and red from behind my eyelids. Softness under me, around me. I was reluctant to leave its embrace.

I stretched and felt no pain anywhere. Well, almost anywhere.

I rubbed at my collarbone. The deep ache from the stretched-out mating bond squeezed my heart.

"Sit up slowly and we'll get this tea into you."

I obeyed, blinking my eyes open to see I was in a tent. Red fabric surrounded me, and I sat in a bed of feathers.

Adriana walked into the tent from the fire pit. She held a cup of liquid to my mouth, and I sipped it. My eyes never leaving hers.

She didn't have purple eyes in the picture album. I wondered why she did here.

She looked much older than Sebastian. There were laugh lines on her face, but they added to her beauty. She looked mature and wise, like someone who walked with a light step, but laughed with her full body. The magic wasn't as thick around her as it was outside the tent, but still her skin glimmered, tiny pieces of magic clung to her as if she bathed in glitter.

"You're so beautiful," I whispered in awe as she wrapped both of my hands around the cup until I gripped it for myself.

She pressed her lips together, fighting a smile. "Thank you. You still haven't told me your name."

"Amaya."

She repeated my name in her odd accent, sounding like she laced magic with each syllable.

"Drink the rest of that tea," she said. "And then we can talk."

"Okay."

I drained the cup to the dregs and took a deep breath as my mind started to clear. The golden sparkles in the air dimmed, and I became woozy.

"Oh," I said.

"Breathe through it," she whispered.

"What did you give me?" Maybe I shouldn't have ingested something from another planet without even asking what it was.

"The magic in the forest is potent," Adriana explained. "The tea dampens the effects, though you'll need to drink more in a few hours if you want to keep your wits about you."

I rubbed my eyes as the dizziness faded, and my brain finally caught up to where I was. "I'm pretty sure Sebastian assumed this world was hell, but all this planet does is get you high."

She huffed a laugh. "Well, the forest has been known to cause people to peel their own skin off, so I think the difference between heaven and hell is a perspective shift away."

I shook my head still staring at her, even though I couldn't blame a magical high for my rudeness. "I can't believe you're alive. That you're fine," I said. "This was too easy."

I'd thought Sebastian would have to search frantically in the short time he had on this world to find her, but she was just sitting here.

It dawned on me.

"You knew. You were waiting for Sebastian." I remembered the landing pad she'd made.

She nodded and sat in front of me with crossed legs, a straight back, and hands placed gently in her lap.

"I knew he'd come for me," she said. "Our village's star reader told me the portal would open and a great darkness would come through searching for me." She gave me a wry smile. "I thought it'd be my dear dark brother, but it seems a dark female has come in his stead." Her face lost its humor. "Is he okay?"

I nodded. "Sebastian is supposed to be here, but the Deity pushed me in as the portal closed."

Adriana pressed her lips together and stared at my head. "To get Sebastian to take your crown?"

"No—" I took off the crown but almost dropped it from shock.

It looked terrible. The metal had rusted and warped. The gem had cracks in it. It emitted an abhorrent energy. The magic in the air bent around it. I tossed it on the ground at the far end of the tent as disgust filled me.

"It didn't look like that yesterday," I said.

Adriana stared at the cursed thing. "This planet is made of pure magic. The crown manifested in its true form, unhidden by deceptions and lies."

"So my life force is repulsive?"

Adriana furrowed her brow. "The power is repulsive because it is unnatural. The magic in this world is simpler than yours. Life, nature, alignment, it's all plain to see." She gestured outside the tent. "Every plant and animal, the sun, the moon, and the water are pure magic and all glow with alignment."

She gestured toward my arm.

I gasped. The sparkles I'd seen around Adriana were on my skin too. My sparkles were darker, blues and purples and greens, decorating my skin and shimmering as I twisted my arms all around.

"You glow because your life force is anything but repulsive." She rifled around in a bag and said, "But you get headaches, don't you?"

I nodded, and she handed me a mirror.

My face sparkled, but the shimmering faded as it got to the top of my head. I curled my lip, almost throwing the mirror down. The skin of my forehead was gray like a corpse and flaking...just like the draxis.

"What the hell?"

"I don't know, but I'd wager a guess that the crown is drawing on your power," she said.

"It's a funnel not a siphon," I said, repeating what Karina and Sebastian had told me.

I thought about how Jeremy in his draxis form had been burned by touching the crown as if the crown scalded him.

"That's certainly what whoever has been siphoning the queens of Palagui would want you to think."

"The deities?" I shook my head. "But why?"

Adriana shrugged. "I don't know, but if Kai pushed you into the portal, I bet they're hoping you will come back with more magic for them to pull from."

"They're deities. Why would they want my power? Or the power of a single fae queen..." I trailed off.

The crown was supposedly connecting the queen to the fae people. Supposedly giving them power, but what if it was the opposite and drawing power from us instead?

But that didn't make sense because then why did Palagui almost lose all fae power when Queen Mari was close to death?

And speaking of, did my being here mean Palagui was erupting into natural disasters, being ravaged by the deities' magic even though Kai made it seem like Luna and Saul couldn't come to our world? Was fae power gone in Palagui?

I sighed. There was nothing I could do about that now. I could only hope they weren't feeling the effects of my absence.

Adriana shook her head. "I don't have those answers, but this world is different than yours, perhaps the magic will reveal something during your time here."

"Am I going on a magic forest spirit quest?" I joked.

She laughed. "It's probably best if we stay near camp. There are dangerous creatures out there that I've placed a ward against."

I snapped my finger in faux dismay. "Darn it."

She patted my hand before standing. "Let's eat. You must be hungry."

I followed Adriana out of the tent and sat in front of the fire. She already had a cooking stand set up with a pot in the middle.

While she added ingredients and stirred, I exhaled a relieved breath. So much turmoil led up to this day, but it turned out fine. Adriana was here. She was waiting for Sebastian. She was alive, and she was okay.

"He's going to be so excited to see you," I said, smiling.

Her lips thinned. "I miss Sebastian, and I was excited to see him too, but I'm not going with you back into the portal."

My smile died.

"You have to," I stammered. "He's been looking for you. He would have been here." I pushed my hair away from my face as the wind blew through the forest. "Adriana, you don't understand. He's..."

I took a breath. How did I explain this to her? I didn't want to make her feel guilty because it wasn't her fault that Sebastian was driven to the lengths he was, but I couldn't leave this world without her. I couldn't go back to Palagui empty handed. I couldn't. Sebastian needed the closure.

She sat quietly, watching the emotions play out on my face. "My life is here, Amaya. My children are here."

My eyes widened. "Children?"

She nodded, smiling. "Yes. My partner, my children, my village."

She had said something about a village before. I'd been too overwhelmed to register it.

"This is my life. I wasn't born here, but this is where my soul feels at home." A soft, faraway look filled her face. "The magic that runs through these rivers runs through my veins."

My heart hurt for Sebastian. He'd spent his life repenting and raging and lost...for nothing.

Adriana was happy here.

How was I going to tell him that I found his sister, but she didn't want to come back?

"This is a lot for you to take in," she said.

"Yes."

"Because he means a great deal to you, and you feel his pain as if it were your own."

She *was* a powerful high priestess because I hadn't felt her power nudging my brain to feel my emotions. Nico had said once that Adriana had been able to do that.

There was no hiding anything from her. And there was no reason to.

"He's my mate," I whispered, smiling despite myself. Pride filled my chest from the act of claiming him.

Adriana spooned the stew she was making from the pot into a bowl and handed me a funny shaped utensil. "Now that sounds like a story I'd like to hear."

I stirred the grain stew around, not really sure what I was eating.

"It is a wheat germ and our planet's vegetables," she said.

"Oh," I said. "No animals?"

"No, I can't risk tainting my magic by ingesting animal life force."

I laughed and took a bite. "Yeah, I don't ingest animal life force either."

As I devoured the stew, and the forest darkened, I told her everything from the beginning.

She cringed when I explained my powers were activated by a draxis attack.

"Sebastian created more draxis?" she asked.

"He said you'd know how to heal them. To turn them back into people."

Adriana set aside her bowl. "I'm sorry, but I don't know how to heal the draxis. I lied and told him I did because I didn't want him to keep punishing himself."

My heart plummeted. It was just as Nico had thought.

"I'm sorry," she said. No doubt feeling my devastation. I'd be coming back through the portal without Adriana and without any hope of healing the draxis.

I forced a smile. "It's not your fault. We'll figure something out."

Hopefully.

My phone buzzed in my pocket. Startled, I almost dropped my bowl on the ground.

With fumbling hands, I retrieved it but felt silly when it was only my calendar notification going off. Did I really expect a phone call from across the galaxy?

For some reason my phone was working as if I was on my world. The time showed it was early morning, and I was late for a meeting with Blake.

I swiped the notification away and looked up, smiling at Adriana. "Would you like to see some photos?"

She grinned.

I only had a few—life had been a bit too overwhelming for photo opportunities lately—but Blake had sent me photos of Sebastian and I on stage at the speech during the darkyra-human festival, and Sloane had sent me photos of her and Nico while they were on their Molbridge trip.

Adriana stared at them for a long time.

I swiped to the last one, blushing a little. I'd taken a picture of Sebastian in secret. He'd been sitting at his desk, sleeves rolled up his forearms, void eyes narrowed as he stared off into the distance. His *trying to figure something out* face.

It was a little embarrassing to show his sister since I had only taken it because I thought he looked hot, but it was the only picture I had of him close up.

"Is he happy?" she asked after studying the picture.

It was a complicated question. My first instinct was to say yes, but she would know I was lying.

"We have happy moments," I hedged.

She gave me a tight smile.

I wished I could tell her he was happy. That we hadn't both been waiting for this day, pinning all of our future happiness on its outcome.

But I couldn't, so I distracted her, and myself, by finishing the story of how I got here. Retelling the most important and traumatic events of my life to an empath was as emotional for me as it was for her.

She felt my fear when Sloane was kidnapped. She felt my anger when Xenos rose the dagger to kill Sebastian and when I broke out of the prison.

I skipped the raunchy details, but she felt my love for Sebastian, my confusion when I betrayed him, and my despair when I thought he was dead.

By the time I was done, the forest had shifted into its nighttime soundtrack. The birds were replaced by low hoots and the chime of nocturnal insects. I didn't actually know if this planet had birds or insects or animals, but it's what my brain ascribed to the sounds.

The air had cooled slightly, but it was still muggy. Magic floated and sparkled through the air.

Adriana had me drink more of the tea before we put the fire out and crawled into the tent.

I was too keyed up to sleep, and she indulged me by answering questions about her life. About her village and her children. A few minutes in, I asked if I could record her answers for Sebastian.

She agreed, and even in the harsh cell phone light, Adriana looked beautiful and animated describing her three daughters and her partner.

Sebastian would see how happy she was. He would get this little glimpse into her life since he hadn't been able to see her himself.

"My little girls, well, they aren't little," she was saying. "They're adolescents actually and at the rebellious stage."

I laughed, but my screen flashed the empty battery signal. I saved the video and tucked my phone into my pocket. "Battery died."

Adriana's lips pressed together in disappointment.

I didn't want her to be sad, so I tried to keep the conversation going, keeping my voice teasing and light. "Sebastian told me that the two of you got into your fair share of trouble."

She laughed. "Oh yes. It was more that I got into trouble and he came along to try to stop me."

She leaned back on her hands. "Part of me always knew I didn't belong in that world. I thought I was uncomfortable in my own skin because I wasn't allowed out of the palace, wasn't allowed to explore who I was, wasn't allowed to go to school or have friends my own age. Which was why I didn't listen when Sebastian came to live with us and my mother told me to stay away from him."

Adriana pressed her lips together. "It took me a long time to find the room in the basement that she'd put him in." Her face darkened. "I found him curled up on the bed, holding his knees. He was always taller than me, but that night he seemed so small. Like he was trying to figure out how to take up less space."

She shook her head and sighed. "Well, do you want to see the rest so I don't have to tell it?"

I furrowed my brow. "What do you mean?"

"You're a darkyra, aren't you? You can read thoughts. I'll show you my memories."

"I can't read a fae's mind."

"Well yeah, but if you're Sebastian's mate, you're strong enough to see my memories if I let you in."

I blinked.

"Sebastian hasn't let you see his memories?" she asked.

I shook my head. "He sends me his thoughts, and we have conversations, but I've never, like, been in his head."

And as soon as I said it out loud, I knew he wouldn't have ever wanted me in his head. He was secretive and guarded because he was ashamed of his shadow. He wouldn't have wanted me to see those parts of him.

Adriana frowned. "I assumed since you were mates..."

"We haven't accepted the bond yet."

"Oh."

"He—We wanted to wait until we had the ceremony."

She nodded sagely. "He always wants to do things by the book."

The corner of my mouth quirked up. "Yeah, he does." I loved that he needed control, that he wanted everything to be just right. I loved him with the kind of intensity that made me want to know every piece of him, to consume even other people's memories of him. "So how do I see your memories?"

"I'll relax the magic around my mind. You do whatever you usually do to read a human's thoughts," she said.

I closed my eyes, and focused on the power that dwelled in my core. It was actually easier to tap into on this world.

My shadows trickled out, and I sensed the wall of Adriana's aura as it resisted, but then softened and let me in. It reminded me of when Sebastian had let me draw on his power at the Hollow. He'd let me in as much as he'd been able to.

The memory she wanted me to experience was on the surface. It shifted into solidity, clear enough to watch like a movie.

I felt myself as a little girl, tiptoeing through the palace basement at night, hearing muffled sobs from behind a door and finding a boy. I felt my heart lurch. Mine and Adriana's.

She moved into the room and climbed into his bed, unafraid.

"What are you doing? Who are you?" Sebastian as a boy asked. Dark circles hollowed the skin under his wide fearful eyes.

"Adriana." Her voice was young and dainty, but the memory still held her essence, an inner tenacity and elegance. "I'm your cousin. I've been trying to find you."

He was shaking.

"Are you cold?" she asked.

"No. I'm afraid."

"Of the dark?" It was dark in the room. Not even a window to let in the light of the moon.

His teeth chattered. "The shadows will hurt you if you don't leave. They hurt everyone that gets near me."

"They aren't hurting me now."

"They will. They will kill you."

"But why?"

"Because I'm bad. Something is wrong with me."

"Something is wrong with me too," Adriana said. "I don't think I'm like everyone else. So I don't think your shadows could hurt me."

He shifted toward her. "What's wrong with you?"

She shrugged. "There's something here"—she pressed a hand to her chest—"something that feels off like when there's an itchy tag in your shirt."

He blinked but recognition dawned in his eyes.

"Do you want to know a secret?" she asked.

He nodded, seeming breathless.

"I don't think your shadows could ever kill me because I don't think I'm supposed to be here anyway."

They were both silent a long time, staring at each other with fragile blossoming hope.

"Do you want to come to my room?" Adriana asked. "We can eat the snack cakes I snuck out from the kitchen, and I'll show you my books."

"Are you sure I'm allowed?" he asked.

"I'm sure," she said. She took his hand and led him to her room, where they stayed up all night talking.

Well, Adriana did most of the talking. She sensed that he was nervous, so she kept rambling about anything and everything to make him feel at home.

The Queen and King found out what Adriana had done the next day. They were livid and locked Adriana and Sebastian in their separate rooms, but it didn't deter Adriana.

She asked for him constantly.

The memory sped up, through all of her requests to see him.

When her mother still refused, Adriana stopped going to the library to learn from her governess until Sebastian was invited to learn with her.

After that manipulation worked, she refused to eat until he was invited to dinner with the family.

Xenos teased her, calling her a crybaby, which seemed especially callous given Xenos was a full-grown male and Adriana was a child.

But one morning the Queen finally snapped.

"He's dangerous," she said. "He will hurt you, Adriana. You are the only hope for this country. If you die, our people will die. Take your responsibility seriously."

"Take *your* responsibility seriously!" Adriana stood up. "He's living here. That means you're responsible for him. And you're killing him. He's dying all alone in that room. He needs me. He needs his family. That's your responsibility."

The Queen was stunned by her outburst.

Adriana stormed out of the dining room, refusing to eat dinner for the third night in a row.

That night, Adriana snuck out of her room, finding, for once, it wasn't locked.

Neither was Sebastian's.

She brought him to her room, and they shared the snacks she'd scarfed from the kitchen, and he described what it was like to go to a real school.

The next morning Adriana took him everywhere she went. And though everyone looked on warily, no one stopped them as she tugged him to breakfast, and lunch, and outside to play in the gardens.

She almost couldn't convince him to go to dinner because he was afraid he would enrage Queen Mari, but Adriana promised him that she would fight for him.

Xenos had scoffed when he saw Sebastian sitting next to Adriana at the table. When the Queen and King entered, they didn't get angry, but they didn't acknowledge him either.

The family ate in silence, but Adriana was grinning ear-to-ear.

The palace guards and staff continued to watch Sebastian like he was a bomb, but Adriana was persistent, and eventually, he stopped being the threat they all thought he was.

The Queen complimented his studies when his tutors had said he was excelling quickly for his age, and when the Queen hired trainers to help Adriana hone her powers, she encouraged Sebastian to attend the lessons.

Flashes of memories of them laughing and playing together whirled by.

There was an image of the King's photo displayed next to a casket. Adriana was still young, and though she was sad, there was no deep grief. She must have not been close to her father. I'd never heard Sebastian mention him either, and that must be why. He'd died soon after Sebastian came to the palace.

They grew like vines entangled around one another.

He was her shadow, and she was his. Practically twins, birthdays only separated by nine months. Both of them didn't fit in. Both of them were watched constantly, though for different reasons. Hopes and fears pinned to them that they hadn't asked for.

Adriana switched to a memory of them as teenagers. She was cajoling Sebastian into sifting them to the city. She threatened that if he didn't sift her, she would get their young trainer, Yael, to sift her instead because he'd been flirting with her earlier that week.

"He's too old for you!" Sebastian protested.

Adriana shrugged. "So what? He'll take me to the city. He'll probably only want a kiss."

"Adriana, don't be naïve. Yael is twice your age. He's going to want a lot more than a kiss."

She shrugged again. "It's going to happen eventually. Guess it'll be tonight."

"Fine," Sebastian said, throwing up his hands. "Fine. I'll sift you to the city but promise not to go near him."

"I promise." She smiled in triumph. She didn't tell Sebastian that she wouldn't have asked Yael anyway. Sebastian was too worked up to realize that Yael couldn't have sifted two people all the way to the city. Only Sebastian's powers were strong enough to do that.

That was the first night Adriana threw up from drinking.

Sebastian held her hair.

Two weekends later, she rubbed his back as he threw up in a bush from his own drinking mishap.

She told him, "The only way to stop feeling sick is to keep drinking."

He groaned and half-heartedly slapped her hands away.

She only giggled, but her chuckling stopped when she saw someone crossing the street. "Bash! Get up. Nico is over there. He'll rat us out to Mother if he sees you throwing up."

Sebastian turned around and wiped his mouth clearly disgusted with himself. "Nico has probably already thrown up in this exact bush. He's not going to rat us out."

Sebastian waved and called out to Nico, who was scowling, but his face brightened when he saw them, and he jogged across the street.

Nico grinned wide as if he'd never been happier in his life to see anyone. Adriana's heart raced as his eyes settled on her.

But he smiles like that at everyone, she thought to herself. That was just Nico. Handsome and friendly and kind. She always stared at him from across the table at the council meetings her mother forced her and Sebastian to attend. Nico's father made him go as well.

"What happened to you?" Sebastian asked. "Why is your hand bleeding?"

Nico stepped under the street light, illuminating the fresh bruises that made up the left side of his face. They were red and swollen, but they'd be a deep purple tomorrow if he didn't get them healed.

Nico frowned at his hand and shook it out. Blood splattered the sidewalk. "Got into a little scuffle. No big deal. You should see the other guy."

"I can heal you," Adriana offered.

Nico's sparkling happiness returned. "You'd do that for me?"

She blushed and nodded.

"Healed by the Princess of Palagui," Nico said as Adriana let her light trickle down to knit the broken skin together on his hand. "I'm so lucky."

Adriana swallowed, unable to respond, and moved to heal his face.

The memory faded out of my head, and I was brought back to the tent with Adriana.

I blinked back into my own body. My heart ached from longing for my mate, from pain for the little boy who'd been through so much.

"Will you show me more?" I asked. "Anything you can remember of him? Please."

Maybe it was being a galaxy away from him, or maybe it was the way the mating bond strangled my heart in a chokehold, but I needed, on a visceral level, to see him, even if it was through Adriana's hundred-year-old memories. I wanted to know the boy he'd been. I wanted to know everything.

Adriana beamed.

We closed our eyes, and she indulged my hunger to learn every piece of him.

Chapter Forty-Three

Sebastian

There were a lot of things that I was sorry for. A lot of pain and hurt and death that I'd caused. There were a lot of things I'd done in my life that I regretted doing.

But killing those solisers wasn't one of them.

Killing Hugo hadn't been either.

I'd been right in my instincts when I took the throne. Palaguian citizens had a certain idea in their minds about what having darkyra rulers would mean for them, and while I believed yesterday's attack didn't reflect most people's opinion, it was still egged on by the fear the media had dosed the public with.

They wanted a King of Darkness to be afraid of?

Well, they were going to get him.

There was no way in hell I was going to let the media blame Amaya for what happened to those solisers. There would not be a civil war in Palagui because a violent minority thought they could infect the nation with their hatred.

They'd been so proud of the terror they were causing that they livestreamed their attack, which was how the video survived the first floor's destruction.

I waited for the panic to set in as I rewatched the video on Nico's phone in the bathroom at the research center, waited for the terror that my secret shame had been outed, but I felt nothing except cold precision. A ruthlessness that I'd always attributed to my shadow's devious intents.

I'd been afraid of my shadow my entire life, afraid of the outbursts, the uncontrollable power that pumped in my veins, but that wasn't the only reason.

Fear of my shadow's whispered encouragements for murder only held validity if some part of me had wanted to kill in the first place.

I was afraid of myself. Afraid of what I was capable of. But as I handed Nico's phone back and gathered my shadows to sift us, I realized that being afraid of my power had been what everyone used to weaponize me.

Xenos had let the rumors of my shadow's destruction run rampant among the courtiers because it ensured that no one would dare challenge him. No one would ever suggest that I might be a better ruler.

The Queen had been so terrified of me that she sent me away as a child, then she locked me up, and only after I proved useful as a body guard for Adriana did she accept me.

Kai bargained for my conception as a tool for whatever darkyra domination they had planned for the world.

Everyone around me used my power, and my fear of my power, to get what they wanted.

And I was fucking done.

I'd made a promise to Amaya that I'd rule the country if she wasn't here to do it, so I would. She was coming home tonight to a better Palagui than we had yesterday. I'd make sure of it.

Due to the attack, court wasn't open until the engineers could assess the damage and determine if it was safe, so Amaya and Blake had planned to meet in Leva and Erik's joint office downtown. I sifted Nico to the townhouse, so he could drive to port and pick up Amaya's parents while I went to the office.

Voices filtered down the hall as I walked from the lobby to one of the conference rooms.

Our public relations team was seated around the table with Blake at the head, standing, their face red from yelling. "This is unacceptable—"

The public relations team sat up from their slouched positions when I walked in, and the bored and annoyed looks on their faces melted into a barely veiled anxiety.

Blake's shoulders fell, and they moved out of the way for me.

I let a moment pass, staring at each one of them until I made my way around the table to Blake. "What were you saying was unacceptable?"

They worried their lip. "The way the media is talking about the video."

"I agree. And what have you all come up with to fix it?"

Not a single person spoke or would meet my gaze.

Shadows were pulsing under my skin with anger. I leaned over the table. "You were warned about the draxis rumors. What did you have planned to stop them?"

One of them shook their heads. "Rumors about the draxis we could contradict, but a video—"

"Enough," I interrupted and held up a hand. "You're all fired. If you aren't out of this building in the next two minutes, I will snap your necks just like you saw on that video."

There was a moment of shock before it was replaced by chairs being flung back and people running out of the room. Blake rose, but I put a hand on their shoulder. "Not you. Sit."

I took one of the vacated chairs and turned to Blake. "I wouldn't have actually snapped their necks," I said. "Death for incompetence is a bit much. But it seemed like a good motivator to get them out of my face with minimal bellyaching."

Blake's face contorted from disbelief, to laughter, to confusion. "With all due respect, your majesty—"

"Blake, I've asked you several times to call me Bash," I said. "No need for formalities."

"Bash," Blake said, though they made a funny face like they felt uncomfortable. "You just fired your entire public relations team when you are in the middle of a public relations crisis."

"I know. But I kind of have the feeling I wouldn't be in a crisis if they would have taken their job seriously from the beginning. No one could have predicted a SoCo attack, but the media has been spinning slanderous stories about us from the beginning, and they've been ignoring it, hoping it'd go away or hoping some stupid puff piece would make the nation accept us."

Blake sighed. "I didn't want to say anything because it felt wrong given all the discrimination I face as a human, but a whole team of soliser PR guys for a darkyra queen and king never sat right with me."

I interlaced my fingers. "Agreed. I should have paid more attention, but I was distracted getting us out of one crisis and then another. Now that you're in charge you can hire whoever you want."

Blake nodded and started writing something down on their notepad. Their head whipped up as my statement sunk in. "Wait. Did you say I was in charge?"

I smiled. "Amaya will need a new assistant, but we can get that squared away later. Your salary increase will reflect your new job title. We'll negotiate specifics after all of this is dealt with."

"Are you sure? I mean I've never—"

"Don't argue for your limitations, Blake," I said. "Amaya was going to get you on the PR team when there was an opening, and I've just made several openings. This is what you wanted, wasn't it?"

They nodded eagerly. "Yes."

"Good." I sat back. "So let's brainstorm how to get out of this shitshow."

"Well, I actually have an idea," Blake said. "They shot it down because it's a bit...involved."

I leaned in. "I'm listening."

"When I first saw the video. I hadn't heard the newscaster's lead up. Just saw the video, and what I saw was the Queen of Palagui single-handedly stopping a group of draxis that would have taken three times the number of fae to take down. I saw her as a hero, but that was because I knew about the hostages. The public needs to know about the SoCo threats, and that they were responsible for the attacks. They need the backstory to understand what that video was showing.

"We get reputable media outlets to interview the hostages that are willing to speak. The media was at court yesterday, so there are plenty of videos of you and Amaya saving people that mysteriously haven't been shown."

I pulled out my phone and started drafting an email. "The chief of the security force put everyone on a gag order so as not to get copycat attacks, but I agree. We need to stop the misinformation."

Blake scribbled things down on their notepad. "The other thing is when I watched the video, I didn't see solisers being turned *into* draxis. I saw solisers who'd been *possessed* by draxis, threatening our Queen, and her shadows took them out."

I tilted my head and pressed my lips together. It wasn't the truth, but the truth didn't make for a digestible sound bite like this did.

Blake's eyes glowed as they started talking animatedly. "And it's like, why would a group of *light bringers* ever attack the Queen and take hostages? Well, because they were possessed by draxis, of course. Why would anyone do something so terrible if they weren't possessed?"

A slow smile spread across my face. "And if we play that angle up, we can effectively undercut SoCo recruitment because people are going to be worried if they join, they'll be turned into draxis."

The disgruntled solisers wouldn't go away forever if we disbanded SoCo. They'd form another group eventually, but we'd be more vigilant and proactive this time.

"Exactly!" Blake said. "I'll schedule an interview with Amaya this afternoon. I think it'd be best to hear straight from her what happened."

"No. Me. It has to be me. Amaya won't be available today."

Blake stopped writing and looked up with alarm. "Is she okay?"

"She's okay," I said. The mating bond still ached in my chest and shadows pulsed in my veins. My mate was alive. "Just unavailable. I will do the interviews. Did I fire our speech writer?"

Blake shook their head. "Jamie went to get coffee for everyone."

"Do you like this Jamie?"

Blake blushed and started stammering, "Uh...I mean I—"

I tried to hide my smile. "I meant should I fire Jamie too? We can get the other administrative staff to step in today as you delegate what needs done, but a speech writer is harder to come by on short notice."

Blake scratched their nose. "Right, of course, I knew what you meant. Uh, Jamie is good people."

"Okay. Good. Let's get a speech written up then, but I need to get one part of the story straight."

"What?"

"Amaya didn't kill the solisers," I said. "I did. The video wasn't pointed in the right direction because I was behind the person filming. It was my shadows. It was my kill."

Now that we were touting this as a hero story, it felt arrogant to say I wanted this attributed to me, but if the public didn't buy it, I wanted the truth to be out there.

Blake nodded vigorously. "Yes sir. We were told not much survived the blast, but maybe there's some security footage we could use."

I snapped my fingers. "Yes. I believe our cameras upload directly to the cloud on an off-site server."

"There's something else you should know," Blake said.

"What?"

"Amaya was worried the councilmembers could be targeted, so she had me contact everyone last night after the attack."

The corner of my lip twitched. Of course she did. Because while anyone else would be worried about themselves, Amaya was worried about others getting hurt.

"I warned everyone," Blake continued. "But I couldn't get a hold of Vince or Leva. And I still haven't been able to reach them this morning." Blake paused before finishing, "They always answer their phones."

I leaned back in my chair and rubbed a hand over my mouth.

As a councilmember, Vince would know the security protocols at court. He'd know which guards would be working and whether they'd help him get a group of rioting solisers into a government building.

But Leva? Sweet, quiet, and efficient Leva? It was hard to believe she was involved in this.

"I'll send people to both of their houses and offices to search for information about whether they were part of the attack." I scrolled through my phone and found the contact I was looking for. "If you hear from either of them, let me know immediately. You do whatever you need to today. No need to run things by me. Just get it done."

"I'm on it," Blake said and got up to leave.

"You need a team," I said as the call was dialing. "Get whoever you trust at court. Tell them it's an emergency and tell them I'll pay them double to do whatever you need."

Blake sprinted out of the room and down the hall. Their voice boomed with confidence as they efficiently directed the staff to get what they needed.

The dial tone ended as my call was picked up. "Good morning, your royal darkness," she said. "What can I assist you with today?"

"Cut the shit, Delilah. I need your help."

***

The day passed in a blur of people running around and sorting through the media mess, and despite my mind being fully occupied by damage control maneuvers, I still pressed into the ache of my heart obsessively.

She was alive. She was okay. She was coming back.

The mantra kept me sane enough to move forward.

We contacted a film journalist from a reputable news source to give them the exclusive story on what happened. The chief of the security force was interviewed. He confirmed we'd kept the SoCo threats a secret so as not to worry the public, but that yesterday's attack was considered domestic terrorism. Employees in court described the threats they'd heard over the intercom. The SoCo organization was officially labeled as a hate group, and we asked the public to come forward with information on its members.

We even used the damning footage to our advantage. The lady on the street that said that darkyras couldn't turn people into draxis helped our case when we explained the solisers were possessed by the draxis and that the Queen doesn't have the ability to turn people into draxis.

My interview was a solemn and stern affair. I explained what happened, the disgusting threats I had heard the solisers yelling at my mate, and how I killed the draxis-possessed solisers. Blake tracked down security footage that backed up my story.

By late afternoon, the story changed from the public focusing on bringing down the Queen of Darkness to headlines discussing how amazing it was that the Queen and King of Palagui were mates.

I hadn't realized we'd never gone public about our mating, so I'd inadvertently given everyone a different story to obsess over.

It would never cease to amaze me how hungry people were for gossip, but if they were discussing our mating, they weren't demanding our heads.

Maybe Amaya and I should have done those puff pieces after all.

Nevertheless, we built the narrative that SoCo was the enemy and that the Queen and King of Darkness saved Palagui from possession by shadow creatures.

I kept waiting for the moment Blake would come running to tell me that the media found out about the high priestesses and draxis at the research center. That they found a scientist who would confirm that I created the draxis. Vince knew after all, had seen for himself, that the story we were spinning was a lie.

But that moment never came.

If Vince had been part of the SoCo attacks, why wasn't he telling the rest of the story?

Delilah and a few high priestesses she trusted went to raid Vince's and Leva's houses and offices, but they didn't find anything. Delilah managed to bring in a few boxes of paperwork that Vince left out, but neither of us had any hope there'd be any evidence of what he'd done. The fact that he disappeared was proof enough for me that he was responsible for the attacks.

I still didn't know what to make of Leva's disappearance and just hoped the Vince hadn't somehow kidnapped her or forced her to work with him.

By that afternoon, Blake had gotten most of the media on our side. The only station that continued to show the original video was the soliser conglomeration, which was starting to look more and more like an extension of the SoCo hate group than a legitimate news source.

Nico confirmed he had picked up Amaya's parents and taken them to the townhouse. I was dreading meeting them without being able to say where their daughter currently was, but I'd put it off long enough.

I checked in with Blake before leaving, and then sifted back to the townhouse to find Nico pacing in the kitchen.

"I think I'm going to Delnee," Nico said.

"Why? What happened?"

"Nothing. Nothing. I just..." He sighed. "I miss Sloane. She sent me a text this morning that said they went to a gala last night and she's hungover and sick today, which is why she hasn't called me. But not talking to her is making me crazy. I know she's just sleeping it off, but like—" He grabbed his hair at the scalp and pulled. "I just need to see her."

The sound of the television playing from the living room momentarily distracted me with anxiety. Amaya's parents were here. In my house. And I'd lost their daughter. And they were going to hate me forever.

"My heart hurts like it did before we accepted the bond," Nico said, pulling me back from my impending spiral.

"Like she's in trouble?"

He kept shifting and fidgeting. "No. I don't know. Maybe. I mean, if she's hungover and throwing up, I guess maybe I could be sensing she's sick? I just..." He flung his arms out like he was shaking off water. "I don't know. Maybe it's everything that happened yesterday that has me on edge?"

"Do you want me to sift to Delnee to check on her?"

There was only an hour until dusk. Sifting to Delnee and finding the girls, then sifting back to the Hollow would push me to the limit of my power, but I'd do it. Sloane and Gwen were family. Amaya would want me to find them if Nico thought something was wrong.

"No. You need to go to the portal and get Amaya back." He nodded his head once, staring at the ground, and then more vigorously as a decision settled into place. "I'm going to go to Delnee. Maybe I won't even tell her. I'll check that she's okay, and seeing her will make this antsy feeling go away. I don't want her to think I'm an obsessive, controlling mate who can't even let her visit family for a few days without acting like a lunatic, but I just need to see her."

"You're banned from the country. Do you have time to forge travel permits with a fake ID?"

"I won't need travel permits or a fake ID if I don't take a jet."

I narrowed my eyes. "You're not doing what I think you're doing…"

He blinked, and a ring of orange appeared around his irises. "I need to see Sloane, and I'm not wasting a second on doing things through the proper channels."

I clapped a hand on his shoulder, knowing there would be no talking him out of this, knowing that if I was in his position, and it was Amaya that was sick—even with only a hangover—I would have already given in to being a crazed lunatic of a mate. "Look up the naval patterns in case you need to take a break on one of the boats."

He rubbed his hands together. "I have to go pack."

"And I have to go meet my in-laws."

My shadows flickered under my skin with nerves, but also excitement. In less than an hour, I'd see my mate again. I just had to smile and lie through my teeth to her parents about where she was for the next thirty minutes.

Nico chuckled. "Good luck."

"You too."

Chapter Forty-Four

Amaya

Without Sebastian, the bond sickness returned. I woke next to Adriana and could barely open my eyes. My temples pounded, and even the dimmed light from inside the tent was too bright.

Adriana went into the forest and found herbs that were supposed to ease headaches, and while they helped, it only took off the worst of the pain.

"Are you sure it's the bond sickness?" Adriana asked softly.

My eardrums couldn't handle anything louder than a whisper. We'd been sitting inside the tent together all morning because moving hurt too much.

"It's been a full day on this planet since I touched him," I said. "This happened once before after we went a day without being near one another."

Adriana pursed her lips and tilted her head, thinking.

"What?"

"When that happened, was he as bad as you were?" she asked.

"I think so. We both were tired and had brain fog," I said, trying to remember the exact symptoms. "I don't think he had a headache like me, but I've always been susceptible to migraines."

"It's the crown," Adriana said. "I'm sure the bond sickness isn't exactly helping, but you can barely lift your head. The crown is feeding on your magic, and your high priestess power can't keep up."

I worried my lip before taking another sip of tea. The deities had said I wasn't strong enough to handle the crown. I touched my forehead, and though I couldn't feel the gray flaking skin I'd seen in the mirror yesterday, the horror of it still made me shiver.

"You aren't initiated," Adriana said and inclined her head to my forearms. "As a high priestess."

I stared down at my arms which only had the darkyra tattoos that she wouldn't be able to see. "No. Just as a darkyra."

"Initiation wouldn't increase your power, but it may help your body better utilize them by strengthening your connection to the source. It may help the headaches."

It was a great idea. I didn't know why I hadn't thought of it.

"You're absolutely right. I'll do it the first full moon I get back."

"Why wait?"

I furrowed my brow.

"The portal between our worlds usually only opens once, but we have several moons. Yesterday our moon, Zillon, lined up with your moon and today our other moon, Zallon, will eclipse the sun this afternoon and line up with your moon. That's why the portal is opening twice," Adriana said.

"Your star reader told you this?"

Adriana nodded. "She's a mystic. I'm not entirely sure how she knows things…she just does. The eclipse will start soon, and I can't think of anything more fitting for someone with both darkyra and high priestess powers than to be initiated at the moment the moon shadows the world."

I chuckled lightly, trying not to jostle my head. "True, but don't we have different moon goddesses? The one on my world doesn't rule yours, does she?"

"Initiation has nothing to do with the deities," Adriana said. "You dedicate yourself to the source of your magic. If you went to a world without moons or without darkness, you wouldn't have magic, but we have both here, so an initiation under our moon or any moon will work."

"Fae magic doesn't come from the deities?"

Adriana shook her head. "Our deities on this world grant certain boons and bargains if you are loyal to them, but they don't make fae people. We are born with our magic."

"But the fairy tale said the deities gave the fae their power," I said.

"That fairy tale was probably created by one of the deities to make the fae do as they wanted without having to give them anything in return."

I narrowed my eyes. If that was true, why would Kai want a darkyra queen ruling Palagui, and why would Luna and Saul care who held the crown? They received no benefit from us having or not having magic. Especially if Luna and Saul couldn't come to our world like Kai said.

Adriana scrunched up her forehead. "I have heard of magical beings that can grant powers to humans, but even then, it doesn't turn them fae."

I barely heard what she said. My mind whirled, trying to come up with an explanation for the deities' motivations.

But if fae people's power came from the moon, sun, and darkness, why did we almost lose all of our magic when Queen Mari was dying?

Unless...

Unless the crown wasn't a funnel. Unless it *was* a siphon.

The Queen's life force had been drained, so the crown started draining from the people and the magic in the land. Sebastian had said that the fae people have collectively been losing power in the past century.

I thought about how Nico and Sloane accepted the mating bond before breaking us out of prison because they'd planned to draw power from it since they wouldn't be able to rely on the queen and the crown.

But they couldn't.

Because the crown siphoned it away too. Siphoned it into the deities' hands.

Kai preferred a darkyra on the throne so they could siphon my connection to the darkness and shadows. Luna and Saul must prefer the light magic of high priestesses. That's why they were upset I wasn't strong enough for them.

The moment I put on the crown, a dark foreignness bloomed alive within me. Was that the siphoning magic taking hold?

"How does someone untie something to their life force?" I asked.

She sipped her tea as she thought. The tendrils of heat from the liquid swirled in the air. "Well, magic is about intentions."

I nodded. That's what Sebastian had always told me too.

"We bargain with one another based on intentions," Adriana said. "We accept mating bonds based on intentions. And we can negate our bonds and bargains by indicating our intention to do so. The queen passes on the crown to the next heir by holding the intention for the power to transfer." She shrugged. "How did you tie the crown to your life force in the first place?"

"The deities…" I trailed off because that wasn't right. They hadn't wanted me to have the crown. I stole it, and I'd thought they let me get away with it, but what if they'd hadn't been able to stop me once I had the crown on my head and the intention in my heart?

I shook my head. "I think I just wanted it, and I took it."

Adriana raised her mug. "Well, there you go."

I stood, ignoring the slight dizziness. Excitement temporarily numbed the residual pain. "Do you think I'll have enough time between the solar eclipse and the portal opening to finish initiation?"

The last thing I needed was to miss the portal. Darkyra initiation had taken days within the Hollow, though it had felt like an hour.

Adriana smiled. "If that's your intention. My star reader said that when the eclipse started, I'd know the portal was reopening within the hour."

I blinked. Had my darkyra initiation only taken as long as it did because I walked in there knowing I had to be back for the engagement party?

Gwen's initiation didn't take nearly as long. She left in the evening and was back by the morning in time for her to leave and go on her flight to Palagui.

Still, I hesitated.

"If you're in trance when the portal opens, I'll pull you out. You might have a headache if you don't finish, but you already have that so what do you have to lose?"

I trusted Adriana, and she was right. Maybe this would fix my headaches. I had no doubt Kai was going to be waiting on the other side of the portal when I returned, and if being initiated gave me even a little bit more control of my power, I might need it for whatever they had planned next.

Adriana dug inside her bags and handed me a dagger in its sheath. "Being initiated into something larger than yourself never comes without sacrifice."

Grasping the dagger, I nodded my thanks and exited the tent to sit on the ground near the portal. I situated myself on the bed of leaves Adriana had made as a landing pad and took the dagger out.

Taking a deep breath, I said, "I offer my blood as a symbol of my sacrifice and my intent to be initiated as a high priestess under the power of the moon."

I sliced my hand and squeezed it into a fist, dripping the blood on the ground as the world became darker. The moon moved in front of the sun and cast its shadow over me.

"And I'll be back before the portal opens," I whispered in a rush as my eyelids closed, and I fell over onto the soft bed of moss.

I sifted into the astral field and rematerialized on the infinite staircase from my hallucinations in the prison.

My heart sped up as the memory of old fear became my new reality. Rationally, I knew I was hallucinating.

My body, however, did not.

It only registered the shadows nipping at my heels, and the way my thighs burned from the exertion of climbing. Sickening dread felt heavy in my stomach as I realized I had only two choices.

Continue climbing to the light above, which never got any closer.

Or tumble into the dark expanse below.

Someone who delights in killing isn't welcome into the spiritual tradition of healing and empathy.

The voice was not my own, not my shadow, not any that I'd heard before. It wasn't so much that I heard the words but felt them vibrating through me like a mallet clubbing a bell.

It reminded me of the presence I felt when I died in the lake that brought me to the place between the worlds. It had waited and watched me in the silence. It had judged me as unworthy then too.

My shoulders collapsed as the truth settled inside of me. Gwen had told me to be an initiated high priestess you had to prove you had control of your emotions and powers.

But I couldn't say I did. My emotions ruled my decisions and fueled my powers.

It was love for Sebastian that had me lying to Palagui and the council about the draxis. He could turn everyone in the world into a shadow creature, and I'd still be devoted to him. I'd still protect him.

It was fear and rage that I'd used to kill Silas and the solisers in Delnee.

It was that same anger that I'd used to trick Xenos and kill him when his back had turned. Never feeling a moment of guilt.

It was excitement and revenge that I'd used to kill the guards in the prison. The ones with the SoCo tattoos that may or may not have been truly bad.

I stole the crown because I felt entitled to the power.

I've done terrible things and felt no remorse.

I've done terrible things and reveled in the high of doing them.

Had Kai sufficiently twisted my mind in the prison to make me lose my sense of right and wrong? Had my shadow's power truly corrupted me?

Maybe the voice was right. I didn't deserve to wield the moon's power, to be inducted in the tradition of healing and empathy.

Maybe the darkness of my soul had won.

I looked up at the light shining down from the top of the infinite stairs. I couldn't get to the top because I wasn't a good person. I didn't regret anything I'd done.

Shadows wrapped around my ankles, beckoning me. I stared at my palms as the white high priestess light mixed with the shadows in my blood and turned the air around my hands gray.

I was so tired.

So tired of climbing these stairs. So tired of trying to be good. So tired of worrying about how my decisions would be perceived. Tired of waiting for the day when I'd wake up and finally be perfect and approved of.

Most importantly, I was tired of carrying the societal expectations for female martyrdom and pure morality.

I was done.

Done waiting for a strange voice's acceptance. Done hoping Palagui's citizens would see my decisions favorably. Done fighting and rebelling against forces that I claimed I didn't care about, but anxiously kept track of anyway.

I didn't need a deity's approval. Not on this world or my own. Only here in Adriana's world of pure magic did the truth become clear.

My power expanded from within me. High priestess light intertwined with shadows and filled the stairwell into a gray fog.

I wasn't good. I wasn't bad.

But I was capable of both good and bad.

There was no denying I had instincts and impulses that warred with my logic and reasoning. I had a shadow who was hungry and possessive and fierce.

But I also had a guiding light for justice and an empathy for suffering. The desire to heal people's minds and bodies and spirits.

I'd been so concerned by my lack of guilt that I didn't trust myself to not give in to some evil growing inside me, but that was just a distraction.

Kai wanted me to believe my soul was more dark than light to serve their purposes.

The world wanted me to question my voice and my power and my right to wield it.

Everyone wanted to categorize me as good or bad. Darkyra or high priestess. Dark or light.

But if you added up all my actions, all my motivations, all my intentions...I think the only color you'd come away with is gray.

I didn't need to climb this staircase. Didn't need to descend into its depths.

There was nowhere I had to go. Nothing I needed to do. I didn't need to perform as the queen or define who I was and project my manufactured reality out to make people believe I was good or bad or strong or worthy.

I couldn't see myself clearly because I'd been distracted by trying to find my ideal self.

But I was who I was. Kai couldn't rename me. The media and our PR team couldn't label and define me.

And I didn't need to decide which Amaya I *should* be.

I could just be who I was without needing to choose, without needing to worry about who others saw me as. Their perceptions of me didn't matter. Only what I believed myself to be.

I let the light shine down on me from above and the darkness envelop me from below and transcended my self-limiting beliefs by trusting the power from within, trusting the power that connected every fae, the power of the moon, of the shadows.

The crown on my head shattered. It'd been a false idol. The crown didn't hold my power. The crown didn't hold Palagui's power either.

It was blasphemous, but the fact that I had power on a world that Kai, Luna, and Saul didn't rule over, that I could initiate myself as a high priestess without needing the Moon Goddess's permission, meant Adriana was right.

My power came from within, came from my connection to the magic of the world around me. Channeled through me.

Darkyras' power came from the shadows, not Kai. High priestesses' power came from the moon, not Luna. Solisers' power came from the sun, not Saul.

False idols. Distractions. Fabricated myths the deities had concocted to keep us shackled.

Black sparkles blinded me until I blinked my eyes open.

My forearms prickled to an almost burn. I watched as the seven moon phases tattoos were etched into my skin.

The shadow that the moon had cast disappeared, and the sun shone through the canopy of the trees.

I took a deep breath and sat up, feeling exactly the same, but somehow also different. The pounding in my temples had lessened. My magic eased me as much as it quickened my pulse, excited my motivations, expanded my belief in my own capabilities. I felt none of the erratic energy I had after my darkyra initiation, maybe because my high priestess power was less potent.

Adriana was in front of me. She offered a hand to help me stand. "Are you ready to go home?"

I nodded.

She pointed behind me, and the portal appeared. From this world, the portal wasn't a black pit of darkness. It was a swirling whirlpool of misty rainbows, like when sunlight plays off the droplets at the bottom of a waterfall.

She reached into her pocket and pulled out a folded rough brown paper. "I still write in our language. It's just much easier than this planet's," she said. "Will you give this to him?"

"Of course." I tucked the note in my pocket and wrapped my arms around Adriana. "I'm so glad to have met you."

"Me too," she said, squeezing me. "Take care of my brother. Tell him I love him."

I smiled and pulled back. "I will."

"And Nico too," she added with a watery laugh.

I nodded and waved one last time over my shoulder as I stepped into the portal.

I wasn't even worried about the pain. I'd have walked through hell to get back to Sebastian.

He was my home. My mate. The person the universe bonded me to.

And that was the intention I held in my heart as I careened through the break between our worlds.

Chapter Forty-Five

Amaya

The harsh popping of power grated my skin, and though I'd been bracing for the feeling, it still took the breath from my lungs. I tried to claw my way out, but it was like the portal knew I wasn't supposed to be world jumping, and made it as difficult as it could for me to work my way through.

My chest burned from lack of air. My head spun, but in an instant everything shifted. My heart began to sing, and our bond vibrated with anticipation.

I was greeted by the warm embrace of strong arms.

Crawling up his body, I clung to him, wrapping my arms and legs around him and pressing my face into his chest.

He carried me the rest of the way through the portal and back to our world. *Our world* not home because I'd already come home the moment he'd appeared.

I sucked in a huge breath of the damp humid air of the Hollow but didn't release my death grip around him.

"Amaya." Sebastian breathed into my hair. "Thank the Goddess."

I squeezed my arms around his neck and my legs around his waist, too overcome to speak. The vanilla of his affection flickered in and out amongst the overwhelming pure sugary sweetness of relief.

We remained locked in our position, locked around one another until the portal's magic snapped out of existence.

I lowered my legs to the ground and slid my hands down his chest, pulling back enough to see him. His ice-blue eyes darted along my face, checking if I was okay.

I had so much to tell him I didn't even know where to begin.

"I'm so sorry," he said. "I shouldn't have ever risked it. I shouldn't have put either of us in this situation. I never will again. I swear to you. I was trying to escape my own guilt and grief. It was incredibly stupid to risk losing you or being stuck on a world without you."

"Shhh," I said and put a finger to his lips. "You have nothing to apologize for. I would never blame you for wanting to save your sister."

"It was stupid," he said under my finger.

I shook my head. "It wasn't. You love her. And she loves you."

He furrowed his brows at first, and then realization dawned on him, and he gasped.

I smiled and ran my hands down his chest. "Adriana was there, waiting for you. She knew you'd come back. She was camping out."

He made a strangled noise in the back of his throat.

"She lives in a house by a creek with her partner and three daughters. The village star reader told her the portal would open, and that darkness was looking for her. She knew you'd come. She's happy, Sebastian."

"She's alive? She's okay?"

I nodded. "Alive and okay and happy."

He took an uneven breath and used one hand to cover his eyes as emotion welled up.

"I have a video of her on my phone. It's dead, but she talks for like two hours about her life and her girls, and as soon as I get to a charger, I'll show you. And she gave me this." I dug in my pocket and handed him the note.

His hands shook as he took the page and delicately unfolded it. I pressed the side of my face to his bicep and wrapped my arms around his waist as he read.

"She says she's where she always belonged," he whispered. "That she never blamed me, and it's time for me to forgive myself and move on."

I fisted my fingers into his shirt, wishing I could claw into him, resisting the urge to bite his arm just so I could have my teeth inside of him.

"She said not to come back," he said. "That she won't be there next time, and she doesn't want me to live my life waiting to see her."

I winced. It was harsh, but Adriana knew Sebastian as well as I did. He didn't let go of unfinished things. His need for control didn't allow for dangling threads of uncertainty. If he knew she was alive, maybe in another hundred years he'd try again to see her, but she didn't want him living in the future or risking himself by going through the portal.

I stroked my fingers along the side of his waist under his shirt. "I'm sorry."

"No," he said and folded up the note and tucked it away. "She's right. Nico was too. It was a stupid risk to take, especially since she was okay this whole time."

I didn't tell him that I wasn't sure if she was okay the *whole* time. I noticed last night she avoided talking about what happened after she came through the portal and how she found her village, but I didn't pry. There were some things that Adriana wanted to keep to herself.

Sebastian's sugary relief shifted into bitterness. I peered up at him, and his gaze had gone faraway.

"You okay?"

"She was okay this whole time," he whispered.

Aching sympathy flooded me. He'd spent the last hundred years in agony over what happened to Adriana. He tore himself apart and dedicated himself to finding her, but now it was over. He'd tortured himself for nothing.

I tasted the confusing mix of his emotions. Relief that she was okay. Grief that he would never see her. Regret that he'd spent so much time punishing himself.

The bitterness of his sorrow won out, but there was no heaviness in this emotion, no sense of collapse. It was as pure as sadness could get. No darkness clouding his aura or shutting him down.

Which reminded me of the darkness that hovered around my head.

I took off the crown and stared at it. If I left my eyes unfocused, I could make out a darkness around the edges. Maybe a residual effect from being on Adriana's world.

"There's so much I need to tell you—" I started, but a burst of humid air from inside the Hollow whirled around us.

Kai stepped out of the shadows. "Welcome home, Maya. Did you have a good vacation?"

I glared but didn't bother correcting them on my name. "Adriana is fine if you were wondering. No thanks to you."

They shrugged and looked at their nails. "So nice to hear." Sarcasm dripped from their words. They glanced up and zeroed in on the crown in my hands.

"Better keep that close," Kai said. "I tried to warn you that if you didn't kill your enemies, they'd come after you."

I narrowed my eyes at Kai, and then studied the crown. The darkness that hovered around the crown formed a loose line toward Kai too. Maybe my theories were true. Why else would it be tied to them?

Maybe that was the real reason Kai was so insistent on a darkyra having the crown, because it made it easier for them to feed off the fae darkyra people.

I twisted the crown in my hands, pressing and pulling on the metal.

Kai watched me, eyes going wide. "Whatever you think you're going to do," they said. "Don't."

If tying my life force to this crown had been something like a bargain, I needed to tread carefully. I'd seen the repercussions for a broken bargain in Nico. Except, I hadn't made a bargain with the deities. I'd made the bargain with the crown itself.

I rescind whatever connection there is between us. I don't need a crown to be powerful. I sent the thought in a shadow toward the crown as if it was a living object.

The metal began to warm in my hands. Encouraged, I used my high priestess light to melt it until it bent and the diamonds fell to the ground.

"Stop!" Kai said. They stepped forward with an outstretched hand but didn't move fast enough.

Sebastian summoned his shadows, more shadows than I'd ever seen him control. They came from the depths of the earth, through the cave of the Hollow, and catapulted toward Kai.

Kai struggled as the shadows pressed them into the wall of the cave.

A thin line of shadows hovered between me, Kai, and the diamonds. Shadows and high priestess light welled up from within me, from within my very soul, and flowed into the diamonds, but they withstood the attack and started to drain my energy.

The shrill sound of nails scraping glass filled the cave as my shadows and light hurtled into the gems.

Kai screamed, but it was cut off as Sebastian's shadows spun around their head and snapped their neck. Their body slumped and fell to the ground as the shadows retreated.

Sebastian stood, shocked and frozen for a split second until he turned toward me.

"I have to break them," I said, pushing back my hair as dark wind blew it around my face. Sweat broke out on my forehead as all my muscles tensed in focus. "But I don't have enough—"

"We do," he said and grabbed my hand. "We have enough."

He didn't ask questions. Didn't demand to know what I was doing. He just interlaced his fingers with mine and lifted his hand toward the diamonds.

The dark power that filled me, that intertwined with mine, was so familiar, and yet, I'd never felt anything of this magnitude tunneling from my mate. As if the Sebastian I'd left when I was pushed into the portal was only a hologram of the male that stood beside me.

Power funneled out of us, more and more, shuttling toward the diamonds until they began vibrating and producing the tinny sound of energy meeting a breaking point. The cave shook and pieces of rock started to fall.

Light and shadow merged.

Sebastian and I, together, shattered the diamonds.

Tiny shards sparked outward. I ducked, and Sebastian flung his body over mine to shield me.

The Hollow stopped trembling, and all sound disappeared except for that of our heavy breathing.

Slowly, we straightened and looked around the cave. Nothing remained of the crown or the diamonds, except tiny sparkling shards.

"Why did we break the crown?" Sebastian asked.

"How did you kill Kai?" I asked at the same time.

Sebastian stared at their body slumped in the corner. Kai's head was twisted entirely backward. "I have no idea."

Neither did I, so I answered his question. "On Adriana's world the crown was a repulsive magic. It was feeding off me like I suspected during the healing ritual. When Queen Mari died, Palagui's citizens lost their fae power not because they were getting power from the queen, but because the crown was siphoning it from them without a queen to draw on."

Sebastian's eyes widened. "Why?"

"I think the deities were stealing from us," I said. "I think that's what the crown always was. A way for them to take fae power."

"Wrong," a voice said.

Sebastian and I startled.

We watched as the Darkyra Deity groaned and twisted their head back into the right position. They blinked and smacked their lips before looking around at the shards on the ground.

Then Kai smiled wide.

And my stomach plummeted.

Oh no.

No. No. No.

I'd made a huge mistake. Kai was an immortal and had been standing only a few paces away from me when I started destroying the crown.

If they'd wanted to stop me, they could have done it.

But they didn't.

Kai jumped up and stretched their arms as if waking up from a nap.

Sebastian and I exchanged a look.

The Deity fluffed their clothes and strolled toward the Hollow entrance.

"Where are you going?" I yelled, walking after them.

"Out," they said and strode into the middle of the meadow.

It struck me how weird it was to see them in their deity form outside the Hollow. They'd only ever left if they were possessing someone. Almost like maybe they *couldn't* leave without possessing someone...

Kai waved out their arms and spun in a circle under the moonlight. "I'm free," they said in a sing-song voice.

A sinking dread weighed down my steps.

"You tricked me," I whispered. My mind was spinning, trying to catch up, trying to figure out what had been lies and what had been the truth. "You wanted me to break the crown."

I played right into their hand.

"The crown was tied to you" I said, slowly. "And it was tied to me because it was keeping you here."

I broke the crown and unleashed a monster into the world. That's why it was siphoning my power, Palagui's powers.

It'd take a powerful fae or a country of them to keep a deity bound to one world.

"You needed my power to break the crown," I said. "That's why you wanted me on the throne."

Kai stopped spinning. They smiled condescendingly. "Oh Maya, it wasn't your power you used."

I furrowed my brows.

Kai snorted. "Come on." They waved a dismissive hand. "You think a little pathetic girl from a tiny suburb was somehow born with enough darkyra power to break a bargain between three deities? You think a weakling high priestess would be strong enough to hold the crown for as long as you have?" They lowered their chin and gave me wide eyes. "Really?" They laughed. "You really think you're special?"

I clenched my jaw to fight having any reaction, but my heartbeat ratcheted higher.

"You did!" They laughed and clutched their stomach, laughing hard enough to bend forward. "You thought you were special enough, powerful enough, to activate the mating bond with a fae who was conceived by a deity?"

"I am powerful enough," I said, widening my stance and standing straighter. "I'm the queen. I held the crown. And Sebastian and I broke it because we're mates, and together, we're the most powerful people in this world,"

Kai wasn't going to belittle me, wasn't going to twist reality like they had in the prison. They weren't going to make me believe their lies.

"You're the queen because *I made you* a queen!" Kai said. "I made it possible. You have a mate because I gave you the power to draw one in. You were plucked from obscurity because I needed someone weak enough to mold. You were never a player in this game. You were only my chess piece."

I shook my head, but my movements were becoming too frantic to be convincing. "No. No. You are a liar. Everything you say is a lie."

Kai tilted their head to the side and smiled. "Let me tell you a story. Once upon a time, there was a shadow deity who was tricked into a terrible bargain with the sun and the moon deities. They trapped me on this world, but couldn't stay themselves to keep the bargain in place, so they needed a source of power to bind me here. They spun a story to the fae about responsibility and dignity and honor. They bargained with a country isolated enough from others that they would believe their fairy tales."

Kai shrugged. "I tried to tell the fae. Tried to warn them that the crown was hurting them, but Luna and Saul made sure the world was poisoned against the darkness. No one listened to me.

"The magic of the bargain made sure I couldn't break the crown itself nor could I possess someone to do it. And since I was bound here, my power was only a tiny sliver of what it had been."

Kai sighed. "Luna and Saul knew I'd try to drain fae power from the people, so they cursed my magic. If I tried to take too much power, it'd sever the connection between that person and the source of their power, ensuring I'd never be able to take more than a bit at a time, and never enough to free myself."

My jaw dropped. "That's why the draxis are created. Why only Sebastian and you can make them."

Why the crown had burned Jeremy. If Kai couldn't touch it and destroy it, certainly the magic wouldn't let a creature Kai created destroy it either.

Kai nodded solemnly, then fluttered their fingers in excitement. "I had to get creative. It took a century of bargains to finally possess the right person and get close enough to a human climbing the ranks in Delnee with an interesting prejudice I could exploit. Their civil war was already underway before I came, I just quickened the end. In exchange for the power of six million fae, the humans could rewrite history."

"You turned Delnee's fae people into draxis?" I asked, anger burning through my veins.

Kai sighed, exasperated. "All except a few fae that the humans wanted spared. I siphoned their power, turned them into draxis, and killed them."

"That's genocide. You betrayed your own!"

They rolled their eyes. "I claim no ownership over your world's people. The darkyra shadow power may be sourced from the same place as mine, but don't belittle me by putting me in the same league as your kind. Besides, I didn't kill the children whose powers hadn't activated yet. Don't I get some credit for that?"

I ignored that question and asked, "The Moon Goddess and Sun God didn't know you'd do this? That you could turn everyone into draxis?"

Kai waved a dismissive hand. "Luna and Saul have gotten sloppy and complacent over the last few centuries. They're busy fighting for power on other worlds. They keep an eye on Palagui and Palagui's citizens, but they haven't kept up with this world's advances and how easy it is nowadays for me to travel to another country. They damned me here when the people of Palagui thought they made up the entire world. If I would have tried to turn Palagui's people into draxis, Luna and Saul would have definitely gotten wind of that, but Delnee was the next closest country."

"What did you do with the power you stole from Delnee?" Sebastian asked. His voice became eerily quiet.

I was still reeling from the fact that it was Kai's fault I didn't grow up fae. That an entire country was wiped clean of a people.

"Funny you should ask." He waved a hand to gesture to Sebastian.

Sebastian clenched his fists.

I frowned. "What are you saying?"

Kai put their hands on their hips. "I'm saying, dear Maya, that the power of six million fae resides within your mate."

My thoughts all stuttered to a halt.

"Being my spawn meant he only inherited my cursed magic," Kai said. "I knew he would need a lot more if I wanted him to destroy the crown."

Sebastian shook his head. "You're lying!"

Kai rolled their eyes. "Why would I lie about this? I'm free. I gain nothing by explaining any of this, except the satisfaction of retelling a well-executed plan several centuries in the making."

"Take it back. Give the power back to the people you've taken it from," Sebastian said.

Kai's eyes rolled into the top of their head. "Seriously? You know that's not how it works. For one, all of those people are dead. For two, if you lost your power, you'd lose something else as well."

Kai's eyes cut to me.

Sebastian went silent.

"No powers. No mating bond." Kai clapped their hands together, eagerness effusing. "And I haven't even gotten to the best part of the story."

They looked at me as they walked closer. "One hundred and twenty-nine years ago, I made a bargain with a desperate queen and spawned a darkyra in line for the throne, and thereby ensuring my offspring had both the means to get the crown and the power to destroy it."

Kai raised their hands in flourish and dramatically said, "*But* I'd need him to betray his own people, betray what he was raised to believe, so I began training him, to mold him into the darkyra he was capable of being."

They shook their head in disappointment. "My first plan was to remove his siblings when he came of age, so he'd take the crown for himself. I'd wait until he saw what the crown was doing to his body, and then he would listen to me when I told him to destroy it.

"I possessed one of the courtiers to get close to Adriana during her initiation celebration, and since I had some power saved from Delnee, I started the earthquake and stole her away, trying to force my offspring's hand in the matter."

Kai curled their lip in disgust. "But when I got rid of her, and my progeny fell to pieces, I realized I'd miscalculated. Self-preservation wasn't his strongest motive.

"So I asked myself, why would a darkyra with a high priestess's martyr complex destroy the crown that he thought was keeping his people safe?" Kai tapped their fingers on their chin. "He'd have to have a stronger incentive than it killing his mother because that wasn't working. I'd have to give him a reason that he would risk letting the entire world die..."

My blood ran cold.

Kai smiled wickedly at me. "I'd have to give him a mate."

"No," Sebastian said, shaking his head. "No," he repeated over and over.

"Of course, I couldn't let him ruin my plan by tying himself to another person," Kai continued. "So to unbind his powers I made him bargain that he wouldn't be with another until I could gather enough power to give him a mate." Kai shrugged. "I always intended to break our bargain. The best part was that that person wouldn't need to be as strong as you, just stronger than any other fae in the world for your powers to recognize the match."

Kai blinked their eyes rapidly, still smiling. "Do you want to know how long it takes to siphon little bits of power from darkyra who come to the Hollow for initiation, slow enough that they don't notice, that my siblings wouldn't notice?"

My jaw was shaking, breathing coming faster.

"About 110 years," Kai said. "And 110 years later, I possessed a flight attendant taking the foreign ambassador to Delnee, followed him to the city, found one of the draxis he'd left behind, and waited. Waited and waited. Waited for someone, *anyone*, to walk down that street."

I pressed my tongue to the roof of my mouth, trying to fight the tears.

"Finally"—Kai tilted their head—"A random female walked by. It could have been anyone at all, but I let the draxis attack, and once you were passed out, I gave you enough power to entice a mate." They snapped their fingers. "And just like that I gave him a reason to behave."

"My darkyra power isn't my own?" I asked in a whisper, but I knew the answer, understood now what Kai had been telling me all along.

Kai made me. I was their puppet.

"My darkyra power isn't *my* own," Sebastian said. His voice was angry, and he refused to look at me.

I guess I couldn't blame him. I wasn't his mate.

Not truly. I was just a random person. The only thing we had in common was our stolen power.

The power that I'd relied on. The power that had gotten me through so much wasn't even mine to begin with.

I couldn't have killed the solisers in the apartment, killed Xenos or made it through the torture of the prison. I wouldn't be alive right now if not for my stolen power.

Sebastian wouldn't be my mate.

He wouldn't have looked twice at me.

Sloane had always known. She knew when she sensed my high priestess power that I was weak.

The nagging feeling that I wasn't good enough, the one that I'd only been able to hush when I used my power, when I tapped into what I thought was my true self. I'd thought my magic had always been there, just waiting to be uncovered.

But it was all a lie.

I didn't deserve my power any more than anyone else did.

There was nothing special about me. There was nothing about me that deserved to have Sebastian as a mate.

Kai was still talking. "—I could have never expected this turn of events. I assumed I'd wait another two centuries before the crown would start to break you down, and my spawn would finally relent and break the crown to save his mate from dying, but you saved me so much time by destroying it yourself."

I pressed my fingers into my eyes, willing the tears not to come. I hadn't realized until this moment how much weight I'd put on the bond between us. Finding out I was mated to Sebastian was a shock, trying to kill him and it not working was a shock, but the moment the truth was revealed, it felt like a weight was lifted.

There was a reason. A reason I felt strongly toward him, and more than that, the bond meant that I knew he felt just as strongly toward me.

Without it...What would we be?

I liked it. I wanted it. This magical tie between us, a bargain our powers had made. I'd thought it was fate, or soulmates, or some innate draw, but it was manufactured.

It wasn't real. None of what he felt for me was real.

He's going to leave. There's nothing tying him to us. He's not ours, my shadow cried. I'd never heard her so distraught. My entire body felt like it was quivering from her fear.

I could feel the beginnings of a breakdown. My breathing was getting shallow. My mind was spinning, and my thoughts were just an erratic drum beat of, *He doesn't love you. He doesn't want you. You aren't good enough. You aren't powerful enough.*

Stop, Amaya.

I couldn't. I couldn't handle his voice in my head, knowing he wasn't mine. My heart ached, and it felt worse because it was all fake.

Little warrior, he said. *Look at me.* His voice was soft but held a stern authority that had me obeying on instinct.

What have I always told you about my power? he asked.

That you can't control it?

He shook his head. *That even when my shadows were numbed out with fae nettle, shot up with suppression in the prison, and when I was actively fighting my feelings for you—it was all never enough to stop me from falling for you.* He walked over and cupped my jaw in both hands. *What I feel for you has nothing to do with my powers.*

My eyes fluttered shut as I pressed my hands to his chest, trying to calm my breathing, to feel his heartbeat under my hands and slow my heart's pace to it.

I let his words seep into my brain. I felt their sincerity and could taste his sweet affection on my tongue.

Maybe our powers nudged us, but he was right. Our powers didn't force our feelings, if they did, they would have disappeared in the prison, but they hadn't. And I fell in love with him last fall despite my powers being bound.

"You told Amaya that shadows were dying," Sebastian said. "That a darkyra had to take the crown to restore our place. It was all a lie."

Kai rolled their eyes. "Shadows *were* dying. I had to wait thousands of years, conserving my power so I'd have enough to take from the six million fae. *I* was dying on the inside. You know how it feels to be powerless. And by destroying the crown, your mate did restore my rightful place. I don't deserve to be trapped here."

I shook my head. "What are we supposed to do when Luna and Saul find out that we did this?" Are we going to have two angry deities after us?

"I've told you, Maya," Kai said. "Luna and Saul cannot come here. As long as you don't travel to a world they frequent, you'll be fine."

The dry grass rustled, and Kai quirked their head toward the Hollow. "The portal has reopened, and I'm sure as hell not staying here."

"Where do you think you're going?" I asked as they strode off.

Kai walked backward and smirked, arms outstretched. "I've got big plans, Maya. But don't worry, our bargain still holds. You and your friends have already played your part. I won't be back to this terrible planet to interfere in your dull little lives anymore. I have much better things to do with my time now."

With that, they spun around and disappeared into the shadows.

"Should we stop them?"

Sebastian sighed. "Let them be someone else's problem for a few thousand years."

I snorted a laugh, but it was a little manic.

The fact still shook me. My fae power was not my own.

But did that matter?

I'd persevered through my anxiety when I thought I was human. I'd held strong through my depression when I bound my powers. I'd survived torture in prison when my magic was suppressed.

I hadn't had fae power then.

My true power, my inner strength, may have been enhanced by my fae magic, but it had always been there. I was strong, and I could pull on the strength of my friends, from Gwen and Sloane and Nico. I had Sebastian, whether or not we were mated through a mystical bond.

I was who I was not because of, nor in spite of, but regardless of what Kai had done.

I shook my head, still reeling from all Kai had admitted to doing.

Their magic was cursed, and through them Sebastian's power was too.

They'd said severing a fae's connection to the source of their power is what turned them into draxis.

Which meant...

"Sebastian," I said, my voice quiet as the revelation moved through my body, making my heart beat with excitement. "I know how to heal the draxis."

Chapter Forty-Six

Amaya

We made a pit stop before going to the research center.

In the living room of the townhouse, I had a tearful reunion with my parents. It was bizarre to see them in Palagui, to see them in the same room as Sebastian. Like the colliding of my two worlds.

The last time I'd seen them, almost a year ago now, I was an entirely different person.

Yet, as their arms wrapped me in a hug, I felt their love all the same.

Mercifully, they didn't hammer me with a million questions. Whether that was because Sebastian had answered them or because they sensed that I was in a hurry to get somewhere, I didn't know.

When I pulled back from our hug, they took each of my arms in theirs, and their only question was "Honey, you got tattoos?"

I glanced at Sebastian, who looked like he was suppressing a laugh.

"Yeah," I said. "What do you see?"

"Moons," they both said in unison.

"Who activated their powers?" I asked Sebastian.

He shrugged. "They've been off the suppressants and surrounded by fae power on the ship. It probably wasn't a dramatic activation like yours, just a gradual awakening."

I bit my lip because it most certainly wasn't as dramatic as my activation since I wasn't even supposed to be a darkyra. I blinked and shook my head, forcing a smile for my parents.

"There's a lot we need to catch up on," I said.

I promised them I would spend all day tomorrow with them. We hugged again, and they went upstairs to the room that Sebastian had already set up, claiming they were tired from the long day.

"Good night," my father said, climbing the stairs.

"Night," I said.

My mother smiled warmly and squeezed Sebastian's arm as she walked by. "Night."

Sebastian responded in kind, and we stood in silence in the living room until we heard their door close.

"Your parents are nice," he said just above a whisper.

I nodded, unable to resist stepping closer and pressing my forehead to his chest and wrapping my arms around him.

"They didn't grill you? I asked. "Or say anything embarrassing about me while I was gone?"

"They did not."

"Give it time."

Sebastian laughed softly. "They love you. They missed you." He said it like facts that he'd been told were supposed to be true, but had never seen evidence of in his life.

And I guess he hadn't seen that kind of parental love before.

"I know." I tightened my embrace. "They'll love you too."

It wasn't so much a promise as an inevitability. I didn't think my parents had the capacity to hate anyone. They both probably had empathetic powers like me that had been lying in wait.

"I don't know about that," Sebastian said. "I'm the male that took their daughter to another country and puts her in constant danger."

"Hey!" I said and smacked his arm. "Don't take credit for that last one. I do that all on my own."

He snorted.

"And I basically manipulated you into taking me here, so you don't get credit for that either."

He smiled and raised his eyebrows. "Oh, I was manipulated?"

I nodded solemnly. "Yeah. I'm sorry you had to find out this way. I'd hoped to keep it a secret for the rest of our marriage, but you got took."

He smirked. "I sort of remember someone saying they'd do anything I wanted if I took them to Palagui."

"It was part of the con. I told you I'm a great actress."

He hummed. "You're right. You've had me wrapped around your finger since the moment I laid eyes on you."

We stared at each other with secret little smiles. I wanted to sink my teeth into his lip and claw my nails into his back. I wanted to reunite in ways that would not be possible knowing my parents were under the same roof.

But it was a full moon tonight, just like it'd been on Adriana's world.

Which meant we had to do this now or we wouldn't get to try again for another month.

We sifted, stepping into the astral field, our magic intertwining as we moved through one plane of existence to another.

It was late, and only two scientists at the research center were working. I explained my theory—without divulging where I'd learned the information from—that the draxis still had their power and life force, they'd just been disconnected from the source.

They needed re-initiated. A hybrid healing ritual that would allow their life forces to generate the power to return them to their true selves. I'd brought the binder Sloane had made that outlined the healing rituals she'd watched during her internship and scanned it to get an idea of what we could try.

The scientists were nervous about letting us take a draxis outside, but I convinced them this would only work under the light of the full moon.

Sebastian and I were the strongest fae in Palagui. We could handle a single draxis.

We wouldn't make the same mistake we had with Jeremy. We wouldn't feed them *our* power because that wasn't what they needed.

They were drawn to fae power because that was what they were missing. They fed on it to keep strong, but it wasn't enough to return them to who they were because they needed to generate it for themselves.

We warded the outer edges of the area that surrounded the research center, so even if the draxis woke, they wouldn't be able to escape. I laid out a blanket on the damp, dewy grass, and Sebastian set the first draxis between us.

The healing ritual required having several people the patient trusted to help them. We wouldn't be able to facilitate that, but Sebastian had several of the crystals that he'd tied to the draxis with his shadow. I charged them with the light of the moon and my own high priestess power and placed them in a circle around us so they'd act as additional conduits and reservoirs.

I sat in silence for a moment and closed my eyes, trying to clear my mind of distractions, letting go of the thoughts about the past, about the future, leaving only space and awareness for this moment.

Initiation required sacrifice, but the draxis had already themselves been a sacrifice. Their powers had been the only thing that kept the Queen alive as long as they did.

More than that, without having to discuss it aloud, I knew Sebastian and I both had the sense that the penance was ours to bear.

He'd forced their sacrifice. I'd covered up his crimes against them. We'd both killed and lied and stole. We'd both done terrible things, things we wished we didn't have to do, but our circumstances had demanded action.

We sliced open our palms with a dagger and clasped our bloody hands over the draxis.

Our magic twined together. Shadows and moon light filled the circle the crystals had created. It was here, within the circle, I made the silent vow to carry his sins, and felt an ease fill me as I knew he'd carry mine as well.

"We invoke the power of the moon, the spirit of empathy, the tides of emotion," I said. Sebastian was a darkyra, but our powers hadn't mattered in the healing ritual, only that there was power in community and connection.

A light beam from the moon struck the crystals, lighting them up and creating a line of energy between them, surrounding us and the draxis in pale moonlight.

Our breathing deepened, synchronized, and something like gratitude or a peaceful ecstasy flooded my body.

The delicious spent feeling of an invigorated exhaustion after training with Gwen.

The peace and stillness of sitting with Sloane in meditation.

The bubbling joy of dancing and drinking and singing with my best friends.

The stability and sureness of Nico's love and loyalty.

The giddy lightness of Sebastian's affection.

All of these little fleeting moments spun through my mind.

An almost imperceptible thrumming rose from the ground. The moon's light rained down like a mist.

If it were possible to create a portal from intention alone, I believed we had created one right there. My awareness transcended my conscious reality. We went somewhere beyond time and space. Somewhere that existed outside the realm of our lives.

It was the closest thing to a religious experience I'd ever had.

And there was no worship of the deities. Kai, Luna, and Saul were not involved in this. They were not the source of fae power. It was a greater energy. The one we summoned when we spoke of the Goddess. The power that lived in all of us, that lived in nature. The innate intelligence that turned seeds into saplings and saplings into trees.

A chant rose silently within me. Its origin unknown. Soft at first, until the ground below vibrated with its pure intention.

May we be a vessel for healing.

Over and over, the chant thumped a steady drumbeat in my core. The magic of the moon sprinkled over us like a gentle twinkling.

My hands felt warm, light bursting from them as evidenced by the pink tinge I saw from under my closed eyelids.

I didn't need assurances it was working. I could feel it under my palms, flowing through me like my healing light, but something altogether different, stronger, more potent, more alive, with a consciousness all of its own. The connection between me and Sebastian, between the moon and all the high priestesses of this world and the next.

The power within me lit up, becoming obvious in a way that I'd been blind to before.

All of our emotions were interwoven.

All of our fears. All of our hopes and dreams.

A grounded sort of ecstasy held us, for what simultaneously felt like five minutes and forever. It pulsed through us, magic coursing through our veins like a river, a sieve cleansing and healing and stitching not just the draxis into high priestesses, but every fae in the world, connecting us for even just one second of communal bliss.

We opened our eyes in sync and peered down at the female that laid in front of us. No longer a draxis, but a person once more. Whole and connected to her power and the power of the moon.

We wrapped her in a blanket, and in a deferential silence, Sebastian carried her into the research center.

The scientists were awed, but also somehow felt what we needed from them without anyone speaking a word. Maybe for this moment, we were all connected. One scientist took the healed high priestess and wheeled her into a room, while the other prepared the next draxis for the ritual.

It took all night to heal them.

And though time was moving, Sebastian and I, and even the scientists working that night, seemed to be moving in a trance. There was no boredom, no pain, no fear, no sense of needing to hurry. There was only calm peace and reverence to a greater power.

By the time the moon had crested the horizon, all of the high priestesses had been healed.

The healing ritual had exhausted us, but we weren't done.

After ensuring that the high priestesses were resting and taken care of at the research center, Sebastian carried the last person we needed to heal out of his room, and I sifted the three of us to the Hollow.

Ideally, we would have healed Jeremy at midnight on a new moon when the darkness and shadows were in full force, but unlike the high priestesses, the Hollow held darkyra magic every day of the month.

Our void eyes came out, and we saw through the depths of the darkness within the heart of the Hollow.

Black sparkling shadows shimmered with purity throughout the cave. The magic had rebalanced since Kai had left.

The haze of trance hung thick around us. We needed no words as Sebastian laid Jeremy down and I set up the crystals around us. Though the cuts on our hand had since scabbed over, we clasped our hands over Jeremy's body.

"We invoke the power of darkness, the spirit of shadows, the mysteries held in the depths of the world," Sebastian said.

Shadows rained down on us, through us. Roots sprouted from under our feet and legs. They dug into the rock and spread through the mountain, deep, deep down through the crevices. Darkness rumbled and power swirled in my core. A concentrated energy that was channeled from somewhere in the middle of the world. A darkness that knew no light, that didn't need its opposite to define itself.

This time, I opened my eyes and watched as the dark power ran through the crystals, magnetized through Sebastian and me, and then, funneled into Jeremy. From under our hovered hands, black sparkling light trickled from our fingertips.

The ashen flakes on his face and arms fell away, revealing newly healed skin underneath.

What were tentacles loosened and formed back into fingers and arms. His body inflated with life, with power, with his true essence.

His hair grew back, no longer patchy and thin.

He stirred, though still asleep, and his hands began to twitch.

A calmness fell over me. A surety. I may not have been born with the darkyra power I had, but I could use it to heal the draxis, to heal Palagui, to right the wrongs of the world.

I didn't need to be special or chosen. I could choose myself.

As the shadow power continued to flow, Jeremy's cheekbones became less prominent, and his face regained color. His sleeping expression was soft and peaceful.

The roots, which had grounded us, retreated. Our shadows slowed, trickling out until finally stopping altogether.

We sat in the quiet stillness of the dark cave. There was space between my thoughts. An easeful serenity coated my brain.

With careful and precise movements, Sebastian picked Jeremy up, and we sifted him back to the research center before going home ourselves and falling into a deep, dreamless sleep.

Chapter Forty-Seven

Amaya

Residuals of the energy we generated from the ritual percolated inside of us, so we ended up being wide awake by early afternoon despite having stayed up all night.

Sebastian filled me in on everything I missed while I was in the portal. Blake was handling the press and the aftermath of the SoCo attacks, and Delilah had raided Vince's and Leva's houses and offices.

Delilah texted early that morning to say she found some kind of coded message in Vince's paperwork. She had people working to decipher it, which hopefully meant we would have evidence he was behind the attacks.

Nico had gone to Delnee because his bond was feeling antsy from not being near Sloane. I had a visceral understanding of that pain, and I'd only been away from Sebastian for what my body registered as a day and a half.

In the last message I'd sent on our encrypted server to Sloane and Gwen, I'd told them about the SoCo attacks—but only in so many words—not wanting them to rush home and potentially get caught up in another attack. I was just glad it seemed they took my suggestion to extend their stay.

The security force was being extra vigilant in airports, train stations, and other public venues, and so far, we haven't heard of any problems.

"Did you hear from Nico yet?" I asked while pouring myself tea. It was some fancy brand that Gwen had bought at the tea shoppe downtown.

"No," Sebastian said after checking his phone. "But that isn't unusual. He probably won't land for another few hours."

I narrowed my eyes. "You said he left last night. A flight to Delnee isn't that long."

He lifted the lid to a box of pastries that was on the counter. My parents must have gone to the bakery down the street. I hadn't seen them yet, but they had left a note on the counter that they went for a walk around the neighborhood.

With a smile, Sebastian said, "He didn't take a plane."

I put the tea kettle down and turned to face him, tilting my head. "Then how..."

His grin just widened.

"No!"

Sebastian chuckled and nodded, biting into a pastry.

"Wait. Wait. Wait. No way!"

Sebastian shrugged. "He probably took a break on one of the ships in the middle of the ocean last night."

"But...I thought it was a joke,' I said. "Nico is actually a dragon?"

"All solisers have a true form, and though it's rare, some retained the ability to shift," Sebastian said. "It's supposed to be a super guarded secret, but well, you know Nico..."

"But wait. How did Gwen know before me?" I whined.

Sebastian poured himself a mug of tea. "I'm guessing it must be her high priestess empathy that allows her to know *just* how to insult people to cut into their vulnerabilities. She probably doesn't actually know for sure. I doubt Sloane would have told her and not you."

The front door opened, and I peeked around the corner to see my parents in the entryway.

"You kids are finally awake!" My father said, good-naturedly.

"Yep," I said. "Thanks for the pastries."

"No problem," my mother said as they both walked into the kitchen. "We were exploring. The bakery down the street is the cutest thing."

"Where else did you go? I don't know if it's a good idea for you to go too far…"

I looked at Sebastian. SoCo didn't know we lived in the townhouse, but if they tried, they could find the information. My parents would be safe within the wards but not outside of them.

"Oh, don't worry," my father said. "Your mother and I are more than capable of taking care of ourselves."

I bit my lip.

The guards have been keeping a close eye on the heat maps. If a large group of solisers is gathering in the city, we'll know, Sebastian said.

I nodded.

"We're actually going to do some more exploring today. We only came back so I could change into my walking shoes," my mother said. Her smile was almost conspiratorial.

"Uh…Okay," I said. "I thought we were going to hang out. I figured you'd have questions and—"

My mother waved a dismissive hand. "We've got plenty of time for that. We've been cooped up on a ship for days and want to stretch our legs."

"Okay. I can come with you," I said, setting my mug down.

"Maybe next time."

I furrowed my brow.

"We just want to explore, Amaya," my mother said. "How about the four of us meet at seven tonight and we'll all get a fancy dinner, huh? Our treat."

This was all very odd. "You don't have Palaguian money…"

"We have some, but yes, that's another thing your father and I will need to do. Exchange our currency at the bank."

"Mother, I brought you here. We have money to—"

She patted my hand. "Don't you have queenly duties to do or something?"

I looked at Sebastian, who was smiling, but he quickly hid the expression by drinking from his mug. He wasn't hiding his emotions from me, but I saw the flash of shadows in his eyes that told me he'd changed them. He only had a faint vanilla affection.

As for my parents, they were just...happy.

Like really happy. A happy that was so sickeningly sweet it rivaled the pastries.

I mean, okay...whatever. At least they weren't upset about having to disappear in the middle of the night and leave everything they'd ever known. If they wanted to explore the city by themselves, who was I to tell them no?

I shrugged. "Okay, but text me every so often so I know where you are."

Sebastian and Nico had already set my parents up with new cell phones while I'd been gone.

"Okay, honey. We'll see you tonight," she said.

My mother smiled at Sebastian as she left the kitchen. My father clapped a hand on his shoulder as he followed her out. The front door opened and shut as they left.

"That was weird..." I squinted my eyes. "What are you hiding?"

Sebastian sighed in a faux exasperation, the corners of his mouth curving up. He put his mug down and crossed the kitchen to stand in front of me.

Curling a piece of my hair around my ear, he said, "They're just trying to give us space."

"Why?" Suspicion elongated the word.

Sebastian's hands came to my waist. "Because yesterday, while you were in the portal, I explained to them that our marriage was a hasty thing and that I wanted to ask you to marry me for real. That I was hoping they'd give us their blessing."

"You did?" My voice pitched higher.

"Mmhmm," he said, fingers tracing down the side of my face. "Felt guilty doing it too after just having gotten done lying to them about where you were. But I figured you could decide how much of that story you wanted to tell."

I tapped my hands on his chest impatiently. "And what'd they say?"

He grinned. "They said if I promised to take care of you and love you, I had their blessing."

I smiled so big it hurt my cheeks. I didn't expect anything less, but for some reason, my heart was racing with anticipation. "And what'd you say?"

He cupped my jaw, thumbs stroking my cheekbones. "I told them that was an easy promise to make because I already intended on doing both in this lifetime and the next."

My stomach flipped. I didn't think hearing his declarations of love would ever get old. "I bet that won my mother over."

"I think so," he said. "She hugged me and told me even though she didn't know me well, she's always had a gut instinct about people and I..." He released an uneven breath, glancing away and blinking several times before his gaze met mine again. He took a steadying breath. "She said that she just knew I was one of the good ones."

My eyes filled with tears, and I nodded through them. My mother was a high priestess, and if I had to bet, an empath. It'd made those times she'd given me advice based on her *motherly intuition* suddenly make sense.

"You are, Sebastian. You're a good one," I said and leaned on my tiptoes to kiss him. He returned the quick peck. "And what'd my father say? How'd you win him over?"

Sebastian shrugged. "Oh, I think he warmed up to me later when he asked me what the sports teams were like in Palagui and I told him Nico and I had season tickets to the ball field. Not that we've gotten to use them in the last year. What with everything going on."

I snorted. That tracked.

My father was quiet and thoughtful, but one-on-one he always knew just how to motivate me, attuned to the moments I needed pushed and the ones I needed encouraged. I'm not sure if that made him an empath or maybe he'd develop powers like Sloane.

"So you got their blessing," I said and leaned my head against his chest, wrapping my arms around his torso. I hadn't been worried about introducing them to Sebastian at all. I knew they'd welcome him into our family.

His fingers traced up and down my back as he rested his chin on the top of my head. "Yes. Right away your mother asked when I was going to do it, and after all the turmoil of the portal, I blurted out that I'd do it today. I wanted to plan something more romantic than standing in our kitchen...But I..." He took a deep breath, his chest expanding under my cheek, and let it out slow. "There were moments yesterday that I thought I'd never see you again...and having to wait a second longer than I needed to, I just couldn't do it."

He leaned back and looked down at me. "I don't want to save things for later. I want you to know now. Today. How much you mean to me. How honored I am to be your mate. How much I love you, and how much I want to be tied to you in every way possible. Officially. Without any bargains or deities to influence our decisions."

My jaw was quivering, and tears blurred my vision as I nodded. He squeezed my arms and stepped backward. My body swayed, trying to close the distance that he was putting between us until I realized what he was doing.

He fell to one knee and held both of my hands in his. I had to hurry and blink away my tears else I'd miss all of this with my blubbering.

Sebastian looked up at me with his ice-blue eyes, shadows dancing in the irises. "I meant everything I said when I proposed to you at court, even though I couldn't find the words to admit it then. I wanted you to know, to hear, to feel, how nothing about our relationship had ever been pretend to me. My entire world shifted when I first saw you. And every day since, I've fallen more in love with the ferocity of your spirit, the depth of your loyalty, and the kindness of your heart. Your shadows sparkle with enough light for me to see that I don't have to be afraid of the dark." He smiled shyly as if he didn't already know my answer as he asked, "Will you marry me? Stand by my side when we face the void?"

I choked out a sobbing, "Yes."

Before he could stand, I fell to my knees too and wrapped my arms around his neck. My shadows trickled out around us. My emotions were too intense for me to have any control of them.

A racing euphoria, floating and easeful as much as it was energizing, merged into vanilla affection, and a symphony of feelings combined into one. Our unconditional love was woven in our shadows, which were seeping out from both of us and filling the kitchen.

I pulled back and sniffed a little. "But are you sure?" I whispered. "It doesn't bother you that I'm only your mate because I got lost and walked down the wrong street at the wrong time?"

"Amaya," he said my name gentle, but a touch admonishingly. "It wasn't the wrong street or the wrong time. We were always meant to happen. We were always going to happen, one way or another."

His words were sweet, even if the sentiment was false. Kai made it clear I could have been anyone. And I would always wonder if I had just gotten lucky. If Sebastian would have had these feelings for anyone he was mated to.

I swallowed and nodded once, pressing my lips to his for a brutal kiss. If this was just luck, if falling in love with the most perfect male and having him love me back was all cosmic chance, well then, I wasn't going to waste the fate the Goddess had gifted me.

Sebastian was *mine*.

I pulled back and placed my hands on either side of his face. "I am so sorry for ever spending a second of my life doubting that you weren't the kindest, most selfless person I'd ever met. You and your shadow, and all the other parts and pieces of you, I love them all. I just love you. I promise you I'll spend the rest of my life trying to love you the way you deserve. I'll love you every day for the rest of our lives. And, for as long as my soul is in existence, it will love yours."

I took a deep breath because I felt it now, the vulnerability of what I was about to ask, putting myself out there and risking rejection. "Will you accept the mating bond with me?"

He smiled, and his hands gripped my hips tight. "Yes."

"Today," I clarified. "Right now."

His smile froze, and he blinked once.

My stomach sank.

Chapter Forty-Eight

Amaya

"I still want to do the ceremony and celebrate in the winter," I said in a rush. "Blake would kill me if I canceled anyway. But I don't want to wait anymore. I love you so much, and I want to be tied to you in every way too—"

His mouth slammed onto mine, silencing me. "Yes. Yes," he said, pulling back just enough to breathe the words on top of my lips. "I don't want to wait another second."

Relief and excitement rushed through me, and I wrapped my arms around his neck as he grabbed my thighs and hiked me up his body. Shadows gathered and swept in to take us to our bedroom.

The ache in my chest tingled with awareness. Even the shadows could feel the frantic energy that had taken over.

He sat on the bed, and my legs came to either side of his lap, our mouths never leaving one another as I straddled him. It was teeth and tongues and lips, all hot and needy and desperate.

The shadows had followed us from the kitchen and thickened in the room, blocking out the light from the windows.

His hands slid up my bare thighs underneath my loose gym shorts and palmed the flesh of my ass.

With shaking hands, I worked to unbutton his collared shirt, annoyed he was already dressed for the day while I was in easily removable sleep clothes.

I made a frustrated noise in the back of my throat. I could feel his smile under my lips. He took mercy on me and helped with the buttons. When I could finally push the shirt off his shoulders, I felt the crinkling of paper in the breast pocket.

He must have wanted to keep Adriana's letter with him today.

The sweetness of that made my frantic energy fraction down. I didn't want him to lose the letter or have it get ripped in my hastiness to get him naked.

I took a breath, and as he removed his arms from the shirt and set it aside, grabbing for me again, I tilted my body back and reached inside the pocket to set the folded page on the nightstand. "I don't want you to lose this—"

He froze under me.

I pulled the note from the shirt pocket, but it wasn't the strange brown paper that Adriana had written on.

He grabbed my wrist and plucked the paper from my hand.

I furrowed my brow. "What is that?" I asked, concern in my voice given his abrupt reaction.

"Nothing," he said far too quickly and tossed the note on the nightstand, and his shirt over top of it.

"Sebastian," I said.

He cringed. The thick cinnamon of lust had veered into sour anxiety.

I leaned over to the nightstand, keeping one eye on him as he watched me grab the folded page.

The edges were worn down, the paper soft as if it'd been opened and refolded several times over, possibly crinkled up at one point.

I sucked in a breath as I scanned the words.

My blue-eyed and void-eyed comparison sheet.

"Why do you have this?" I asked.

He pressed his lips together and shrugged. His eyes didn't meet mine. "I found it...And I thought if I knew what you needed from me, I could be that person for you. The one you wanted."

My heart was breaking, and I exhaled, shoulder sagging. I put both of my hands on his jaw, tilting his head so he was forced to look at me. "I threw this away. You weren't supposed to see it."

"I know." His brows pulled inward in consternation. "I'm sorry."

"No, you don't get it. I threw it away because I didn't need it."

I sat back and ripped the paper in half and then quarters and threw it on the ground. "I wrote that list because I didn't understand how you could be two people, but it was because you aren't. I didn't even need to finish the list. It didn't matter what color your eyes were. It doesn't matter. You are the person I need. You are the person I want. It doesn't matter what part of you is in control. There's no trying to be what I want because you already are."

He searched my eyes.

"I didn't need a list to remember why I loved you," I said. "You showed me every single day."

He inhaled deeply and put both of my hands over his heart. "When you went through the portal, when it snapped close on me as I tried to follow you, I could feel the threads of our bond fraying. I thought the unfulfilled bond was painful, but being worlds away from you, not knowing if you were alive or coming back, was such a deep agony. And I realized that this was what you were going to feel if I would have gone into the portal. I shouldn't have ever suggested it. This relationship"—He squeezed my hands over his heart—"*You are the most important thing to me.*"

"Sebastian," I said, tears in my eyes. "I knew you had to do it. Had to find her. I never wanted you to be in pain."

He shook his head. "It's okay because that pain was the only way I knew you were alive. And I wouldn't have wished it away for a single day for another hundred years just so I could follow it back to you."

He brushed my tears away with his thumbs. I pressed my lips to his, trying to show him through my kiss how important he was to me, how much I loved exactly who he was.

"I love every part of you. I want to accept the bond," I said when I pulled back and leaned my forehead against his.

"Me too," he said, smiling.

Our next kiss was gentle, just the quick brush of lips before sudden nerves fluttered in my belly.

"So how do we...you know, *do* it?" I whispered.

Sebastian smirked. A finger trailed along my arm. "Well, first I'm going to lick your pussy until you're screaming my name loud enough for all of Palagui to hear, then I'm going to put my—"

"Sebastian!" I said and hit him lightly on the chest. "That is *not* what I meant."

He kissed my palm, sweet and tender. "Everything I've read said that the bond is about intentions. It can never be forced or manipulated. The bond makes us want each other, makes us hunger, but we have to both want it and be completely open to it. That's why orgasms are involved because of the vulnerability, but there are no accidents. We have to intend to accept it."

"I should have asked Sloane for more specifics."

"It's probably different for everyone."

I pursed my lips. "What if it doesn't work, does that mean one of us doesn't want it enough?"

He ran his lips over my knuckles. "There's no pressure. I want you forever. I want the bond between us, but if we have to try several times to get it to take..." He shrugged and grinned. "I won't mind that either."

I smiled back and nodded. "I want to be your mate."

His eyes darkened, becoming feral. "You're mine," he said, his voice low and gravelly. "All fucking mine. I'm going to claim you."

A rush of heat and arousal pooled low between my legs at the thought of being claimed.

With one arm curled around me, he moved me to the middle of the bed, hovering over me and coming in for a searing kiss.

My hands traveled along his chest and stomach, reveling in the feel of the sinewy muscles of his torso. I kneaded my fingers into his pecs, wanting to squeeze and touch every inch of his body.

At the same time, I reached down to push off his pants and he tried to tug my shirt off. We broke apart only long enough to remove the fabric between us with a clumsy wiggle of hips and tossing of elbows.

We became a blur of hands and lips and shadows skating along skin as our breath mingled, and his hard naked body covered mine.

Was it the culmination of the days I spent missing him, or was it his fear that I wouldn't come back that made us move like if we didn't hurry, we'd disappear.

Or was it the bond and our shadows knowing that we were finally ready that made my mind narrow in on one thought only: I need him inside me *now*.

Our kisses shifted from sweet to pure need, hungry tongues and rough hands, grasping and squeezing. The cinnamon of his lust filled my mouth with a heady spice. The bond ached with a renewed pain under my collar bone. A tugging from under my ribs.

"Fuck," I said as his lips connected with my jaw, my neck, the swell of my breasts. I was on fire with need. Heat was liquifying my insides, demanding more, more, more.

"I know," he said, out of breath as if we'd just ran a marathon. "It's intense."

It wasn't just desire. It wasn't even about sex. My body hummed, vibrated with a need to simultaneously compress and expand. I wanted to break into nothingness, to fold inside of him, and be surrounded by him forever.

I ran my hands along his biceps and the hard muscles of his shoulders. I had the inexplicable urge to claw him until half-moon crescent shapes appeared on his skin. To mark him as mine.

I kissed his collarbone, soft, short pecks at first, until I got to the edge of his shoulder and bit down. The groan that rumbled from his chest only encouraged me to suck and sink my teeth in deeper.

I angled my hips up toward his. His hard cock pressed and rubbed on the top of my mound and coaxed my body to respond.

The stretch on my inner thighs was delicious as I spread my legs wider, wanting more, wanting to feel completely bared, open, vulnerable.

"I want to savor you. I want to take my time with you," he said, but in contrast to his words, his thumb found my clit and his fingers pressed into me, sliding in easily as my body had been slick and wanting since the moment he declared he was going to claim me.

"Savor later. Fuck me now," I gasped out as the pleasure tingled low in my stomach, mixing with the ache of the bond and making my body just one giant needy mess.

He complied with my demanding, replacing his fingers with his cock in one swift move, and we both sucked in a breath as he entered me. His head dropped to my shoulder, and his body trembled as he thrust into me, bringing me to the pinnacle faster than I ever thought possible.

My hands were blinking with light. My high priestess power stuttering in and out along my darkyra tattoos.

"More," I said. Maybe it was me. Or maybe it was my shadow because my voice had become hoarse.

I moved my hips, angling up to meet him thrust for thrust. My body gripped him, clenching tighter as if that alone would keep him from disappearing.

Both our movements became frazzled, hurried, sprinting toward the edge of the cliff without abandon.

His face creased, eyes fluttering shut. "Fuck. Fuck," he panted. "I'm sorry. I can't—"

But he didn't need to, because as his shadow swirled around my clit, I dug my fingers into his back and came with a loud moan that was followed by his groan of release.

My body shook to the point of pain. My calves cramped, and the bottom of my feet hurt from how hard they curled. My abs hurt from the spasming.

He flattened me with his weight, crushing me to the point it was hard to breathe, and I found myself needing it. Some weird desire to be suffocated by him.

He took a deep breath and pulled back to look at me.

Our eyes were darting around, as if waiting to see if magical bells would start ringing or an explosion of mystical energy would happen from accepting the bond.

"Did it work?" I whispered. My muscles ached, and my power vibrated, a live wire in my core.

"I don't know." He furrowed his eyebrows. "I don't feel any different."

"Me either."

We laughed at the ridiculousness of it all.

"Honestly," he said. "That was a little pathetic. I was too keyed up to even enjoy it. Don't get me wrong. It was good. It's always good with you, but it was like…" He tilted his head left and right, trying to find the words.

I scrunched up my nose. I didn't know how to describe it either. The orgasm was almost painful in intensity, and yet, lacked the complete satisfaction of release. It was hard to explain. "No. I know exactly what you mean."

"I think we could do much better if we try again," he said, nuzzling his nose along my jaw. "And again. And again if we have to."

I giggled. "And again. And again. And again."

There was a smile in his voice as he said, "Your parents don't expect us until seven tonight. And other than checking on the high priestesses and Jeremy later, we have the whole day to ourselves. I told Blake we'd need the day off."

I tangled my fingers in the longer portion of his hair and sighed. We hadn't had a day to ourselves in a long time. A day without any emotional turmoil or dealing with the chaos of running a country.

"That sounds perfect."

He kissed my neck and down to my collarbone. I knew he was tracing my faint scars with his lips. He always did that in the blissful afterglow of our orgasms. There wasn't the guilt and shame that had accompanied those actions at the beginning, just a sweet tenderness, an acknowledgement.

Usually, his worshipful kisses lulled me into sleep, but today they were stoking the heat that hadn't been quelled.

He was right. If we had to do this all day, I didn't think I would mind one bit.

"Oh wait!" I wiggled out from under him and hopped up beside the bed. "I have an idea."

I reached down and put on his button-up shirt because I felt awkward standing completely naked.

He raised an eyebrow. "So far, I'm not a fan of this idea. I liked you without clothes."

"That's not the idea." I couldn't stifle my grin as I opened his nightstand drawer and shuffled the things in the front so I could pull out the goodies I knew were hidden in the back. I pulled out the box and set it on the bed.

"We can use..." I smiled triumphantly and opened the box and grabbed the first thing my hands landed on. I squinted my eyes at the object. "Whatever this thing is."

His face was neutral. "How did you know that was in there?"

"Uh," I said. He had no emotion, nothing for me to read on his face or taste in my mouth. "I found it..."

"You found it?"

"Yeah. I found it while snooping in your stuff when you were in Merbany before..." I waved a hand. "When I thought..."

"When you thought I was evil?"

"When I thought you *might* be evil," I corrected.

He plucked the object from my hand and looked at it hard. He pressed something on one end and it telescoped out with an ominous *click, click, click.*

"This, Amaya, is a riding crop." His eyes found mine, and he snapped the leather piece on the palm of his hand. The sound echoed in the room. My heart started racing, and heat pooled in my stomach.

"And what's it for?" I asked, already breathless. I knew what it was for. We both knew I knew what it was for, but I wanted him to say it.

He hit his palm again and smiled with a dangerous gleam. Shadows swirled in his eyes. "This is what I'm going to use to punish you for snooping in my things."

I swallowed and stared at the leather piece on his palm, and then looked back at him. I crossed my arms over my chest. "No."

"Oh, yes."

"You can't," I said.

"And why not?"

I planted both palms on either side of him on the bed and leaned over until my mouth was at his ear. "You'd have to catch me first," I whispered, and before he could react, I sifted.

I sifted to the beach house. One, because I didn't want my parents to come home and accidentally hear us, and two, because there was something about it being far away that made the chase all the more exciting.

I had about thirty seconds to hide before he would catch up to where I'd gone, less if he followed my magic as I sifted. I darted around the living room and through the dining room, but there was no place to hide.

My breathing was coming heavier, but I couldn't stop smiling. There was a closet near the entrance, and with the feeling that time was running out, I sprinted to it, flung myself in, and closed the door.

The game was a little unfair because I felt it in my bones, in the tug of the bond, when he sifted into the house. My magic called to him as his did to me. It didn't care about the game we were playing, but still he walked slowly around the house, dragging out the anticipation.

"Where are you, little warrior?" he taunted. "Come out and I'll make your punishment quick."

The thump of my heart sounded too loud, like it was echoing in the tiny closet, and my breathing was so ragged that he probably didn't even need our bond to figure out where I was hiding.

"If I have to find you, it's only going to make it worse for you," he said.

I swallowed, and my whole body tensed with excitement from his threats. I didn't know why I liked this. Liked him chasing me, liked him punishing and praising me. I'd never been this way with anyone else. He brought out parts of me that went wild with need. Our relationship had started off with a mixture of threats and flirtation.

This was who we were.

And I loved it.

His footsteps fell louder as he came closer. He was on the other side of the door; I could feel his presence, but he slowly turned the door knob, and my heart stuttered.

He opened the door in a swift pull and smiled. "Gotcha."

I knew he was there, but I still squeaked from the jump scare.

I tried to skate past him. No way in hell I was going down without a fight, but he lunged for me and wrapped an arm around my waist and lifted me up.

"Oh no, uh uh," he said. "You aren't going anywhere."

I kicked my legs and squeezed the arm that was holding my waist.

"No. Let me go," I play-yelled and wiggled around in his arms.

"You're mine now," he said, holding me tighter. His lips were at my ear, breath hot along my neck as he said, "There's no escape for you, little warrior. There's no where you can go that I won't find you."

The threat shouldn't have been romantic. It shouldn't have made my eyelids flutter and feelings of peace and safety cascade through me.

But he would. He would always find me. He would have waited a hundred years if I'd been lost in the portal. He'd have stopped at nothing to get me back.

I'd have done the same. I'd have waited a thousand years for him.

He lowered me to my feet in the dining room and spun me around, grabbing my jaw with one hand and dragging me to him. His mouth devoured mine, tongue plunging in, taking and dominating, and I let him. My body sagged from the intensity, and a low moan was ripped from my chest. He swallowed my sounds. His tongue flicking inside my mouth, greedy for more.

When he yanked himself away, his hooded eyes darted along my face. "I'm going to bend you over this table, and if you're a good girl and take your punishment, I'll make you come so hard you'll see stars."

My core throbbed in response. The grip of his hand on my jaw tightened while his thumb swiped left and right over my lips.

"Are you going to be good?" he asked.

I nodded but could feel the defiance of my shadow swirling through me and knew he saw it in my eyes. I took his thumb into my mouth and sucked while keeping my gaze on him.

His nostrils flared, and his breathing increased. He stepped closer.

He'd pulled on sweatpants before sifting to chase me, but they were doing nothing to hide his erection pressing into me, pinning me with the table at my back.

He removed his thumb from my mouth with a *pop*, and he took off the shirt of his I was wearing.

It fell to the ground, and he spun me around and pressed on my shoulder blades until I laid my forearms over the table.

He reached into his pocket and set the collapsable riding crop next to me.

I shivered as he traced his fingertips down my back with a feather-light touch. His lips followed the trail his fingers made, kissing soft and gentle down each ridge of my spine.

He went impossibly slow. My legs shook with anticipation.

"I thought you were going to punish me," I whined.

He growled. "I'll take all the time I want with you."

Grabbing one of my wrists and then the other, he took my support out from under me and pressed my chest to the table. He gathered both of my wrists at the small of my back with one hand.

I turned my head, blowing hair from my face. Shadows came and aided the effort so I could see the outline of him in my peripheral.

"You're mine now," he said. "I'll do whatever I want to you. Whenever I want to. And you'll just take it, won't you? You'll be so good and take what I give you."

"Yes," I whispered. With those words, some part of my mind turned off. All I had to do was listen. All I had to do was feel. He'd take care of me. He'd protect me. He'd stop if I asked him to because I was completely and utterly safe with him.

One hand tightened around my wrists while the other trailed up my leg, over my ass, and along my spine, before going back down again.

"So pretty. So perfect," he said, running a hand along my thigh, playing with the crease of my ass until his fingers spread me and ran along my wet slit. "So wet," he said on a groan. "You like this? You want to be punished, don't you, my little brat?"

"Yes."

He kicked one foot to nudge the inner side of my ankles and spread my legs wider. "Stay just like that."

I held the position, though it was harder with my legs spread. All my focus was overtaken by the *click* of the telescoped handle of the riding crop.

"What do you say if you want to end this?" he asked.

"Stop," I answered in a rush, remembering our safe word from the last time we played.

"Good girl."

He let the leather piece caress my skin. I tensed, waiting for the first hit, but it didn't come. The crop brushed over my entrance and tapped my clit with the lightest pressure.

I sucked in a breath. "Please, Sebastian."

The crop left my skin and hit the back of my thigh with a loud *thwack*, but it sounded worse than it felt. It was softer than the sting of his hand.

He did it once more, and then again, but it wasn't enough.

"Harder."

He complied, and the next smack made my leg muscles jump. An electric sensation twirled down my spine, and I moaned.

The next several slaps were harder, each one edging up in intensity, each one unraveling something inside me, a freedom, a release of control.

"More," I said. My moans had turned into gasps.

The crop moved closer and closer toward my core, hitting the more sensitive skin of my inner thighs before rubbing across my clit. Ripples of pleasure cascaded through me.

There was only a brief moment of cold air until the next strike landed on my slick core. The next closer, then closer, until the last hit jolted my throbbing and aching clit. I couldn't hold back the moan. My hips bucked, wanting more friction.

"Why am I doing this?" he asked.

"Uh." My brain was muddled. The stinging tingle on my lower body and the heat in my core was all I could think about. The crop was a faint barely there touch, teasing my clit, back and forth, back and forth. My eyelids fluttered, and my breath came in heavy pants.

He smacked me again, and I jolted.

"Uh, because I..." Lightheaded and spacey, I couldn't think, couldn't even begin to follow what he was saying or asking, couldn't find words or meaning. The crop parted the wet lips of my core, spreading my arousal up and down.

I lost focus again and *smack*. "Because you?" he repeated.

I swallowed and tried to take a deep breath, but it was uneven. What had he asked? Oh, right.

"Because I snooped in your stuff," I said, finally remembering the game I was playing, finally remembering my role.

"That's right," he said, planting three consecutive smacks at the junction of my legs and ass. The skin burned, but it was a pleasant pain. "Because you were a very bad girl who snooped in my stuff."

In contrast to his words, his fingers scraped along my scalp, carding through my hair. My body became limp as the simple touch erased all the tension that had built up.

"But you're taking your punishment so beautifully," he said.

"I'm sorry. I shouldn't have looked in your stuff," I said, breathless. "I'll make it up to you."

"Oh yeah?" He lightly caressed the hot flesh of my backside. His fingers so cold in comparison. "How are you going to do that?"

At some point he'd released my wrists, but I hadn't moved them from their position at my back. Without him holding me anymore, I was able to push myself up off the table and sink to the floor on my knees before him.

The ceramic tile was not comfortable, but it was so worth it when his eyes hooded as he stared down at me, and a breath whooshed from him.

I put my hands on his thighs and moved in closer to nuzzle my face along the hard length of him hidden under his sweatpants. Looking up at him with the best impression of wide, innocent eyes I could muster, I reached toward his waistband, but he caught my hand.

"Amaya," he said, anguished but soft. "You don't have to make anything up to me."

"I want to do this," I said and tried to convey with my eyes how much longing I felt for him. That it wasn't about making anything up to him. I wanted to be his undoing. "I want you to come in my mouth."

He exhaled sharply, and his eyes rolled into the back of his head. "Yeah?"

"Yeah." I tried to grab at his waistband again, but he stopped me.

"Wait." He took a few steps backward toward the living room until he leaned on the back of the couch. "Over here."

I followed and realized why we moved when my knees stopped aching as they met the soft carpet.

"Better?" he asked.

I smiled, pulling down his sweatpants. "Much better."

I grabbed the base of him and licked off a bead of precome on the tip and swirled my tongue around the head.

He gathered my hair away from my face with one hand as I sucked and stroked him in time.

He held the back of my head with a firm grip, but let me set the pace, giving me only what I could take. My tongue teased him as my hands twisted up and down his length.

A sharp hiss of pleasure escaped his lips as I took him deeper, but I didn't speed up. I lavished my tongue along his shaft, trying to take my time, intoxicated by the taste of him, by the sounds I could make him produce, by the sweet praise he mumbled in between moans. I could feel the *ah, fuck* and the *you're so perfect* as if they were pinging through my body, settling low in my core as a throbbing pulse.

I sucked harder and faster, almost beyond my control as I lost myself in the wash of his words cascading over me.

He watched me with a hooded gaze "You're so good at that. So perfect. You're all mine, aren't you?"

I hummed my affirmation, and his eyes practically went cross.

Shadows replaced his hands holding back my hair as he reached behind him to grip the back of the couch.

I tried relaxing my throat, holding my breath, and taking him as deep as I could. I gagged a little as he hit the back of my throat, but when whatever words he was going to say stuttered out incomprehensibly, I was encouraged to try again.

I took a deeper breath and relaxed, swallowing him down until I'd successfully made him lose all coherence. He groaned, losing his train of thought. His words turned into broken murmurs of affirmations and swearing, and his knuckles started turning white.

My clit throbbed each time he praised me. I was slick and wet, so turned on from how turned on I could make him.

His legs started shaking. His abs quivered. I looked up at him as his mouth fell open and his eyebrows pulled inward.

"Okay. Okay. I'm going to—" His eyes scrunched shut, and he tilted his head back.

I pulled back to suck the head and used my hand on the rest of his length until the salty taste of him filled my mouth. His orgasm shuttered through him, and then the echo of it shuttered through me too. The press of his shadow's pleasure flickered along my arms.

I swallowed everything he gave me and pulled back to lick him clean until he was spasming from oversensitivity.

His breath came ragged, chest heaving as he looked down at me with an awed reverence.

"You made my legs weak," he said, still gripping the couch to hold himself up.

I grinned, wildly proud of myself, and rested the side of my face on his thigh. His fingers threaded through my hair, scraping along my scalp, stroking me while he recovered.

When his breathing became steadier, he offered me a hand and helped me to stand, before holding my hips and lifting me onto the back of the couch so I was perfectly level with him. I pulled his shoulders toward me and wrapped my legs around his waist.

There was still the drumbeat of need in the background, but something about having his skin on my skin, having my hands on him, settled the worst of the need.

His lips found mine, sweet and soft, while the backs of his fingers stroked my arms, eliciting goosebumps. His kisses turned more fervent, alternating between sucking on my bottom lip and sliding his tongue through my mouth with a possessive hunger.

I was vibrating in his arms. His hands slid along my thighs, in between our bodies, and brushed against my clit, causing a jolt of electricity to spasm through me.

His lips trailed along my neck, sucking on the skin just enough to leave a mark, repeating the pattern down my breasts. "I owe you an orgasm, but this isn't where I want to do it."

Before I could say anything, he sifted us. The shadows didn't need to dissipate for me to know we were in the bedroom as I landed on the soft blankets. The scent of him, the feel of his power, enveloped me.

He laid on his back. "Get over here."

I threw my leg over his waist and straddled him.

He shook his head. "Higher."

I scooted up, but it wasn't enough because he yanked at my thighs. "Higher. Sit on my face."

"Uh. What?"

"Put your thighs by my ears and ride my face."

"Are you sure?"

"Uh huh," he said, his fingers sinking into my thighs and pulling me up his body. "Very sure."

"Okay," I said tentatively and held on to the bed frame for support as I put my knees on either side of his face.

He wrapped his arms around my thighs and pulled them in close as I hovered over top of him. "Sit, Amaya. Give me your weight."

"I'll hurt you. I'll suffocate you if I do that."

I could hear the eye-roll in his words. "I want it. I want your pussy suffocating me. Just trust me. I'll tap your thigh if I want to stop, okay?"

I worried my lip, but said, "Okay."

Settling my full weight on him, he squeezed my thighs even tighter as his tongue found my clit and languidly licked me.

A heartbeat of need throbbed between my legs. I was still a little nervous about hurting him, but the more he teased, the faster my need built until my hips were jerking and grinding in little movements on his face, trying to get more.

While his tongue played with my clit, the cool caress of his shadow tickled along my feet, running along the arch of my foot, twirling along my ankle and tickling my inner thighs until it found the hot heat of my core and plunged inside of me.

I grabbed the headboard tighter and moaned as the shadow thickened and pulsed and vibrated, plucking the pleasure point of my inner walls.

His lips latched on to my clit, sucking, devouring me. I rocked my hips, losing all fears of suffocating him and giving in to the pleasure peaking inside me.

I felt the impending orgasm. The intensity of it lingered on the edges. I could barely contain my body's shaking, like it was breaking me down, breaking me apart, reaching and reaching for something it couldn't find.

I didn't know how he knew what I needed because the deep voice of his shadow spoke in my head. *You're mine*, he said with the rumble of a deep growl. *I claim you as my mate.*

Something squeezed inside my chest like a fist around my heart. The tightness eased the quivering fear that I hadn't realized had taken over, and all that was left was floaty bliss.

I looked at him between my legs. His eyelids fluttered as he watched my body tremble under his touch.

One of his hands unhooked from around my thighs and palmed my breast, fingers pinching and teasing the nipple.

I moaned his name on a choked breath, and the orgasm flooded me. Bright, blinding light warred with the darkness of the shadows. I tensed, and then relaxed. The shadows held me and kept me from collapsing as the pleasure raced through my body.

Trembling, I laid my forehead against the headboard for a second until the orgasm faded enough for me to roll off of him.

My muscles sagged from how hard they'd tightened.

It wasn't unexpected, but somehow, I wasn't prepared to feel so untethered and unmoored, floating like our shadows.

Sebastian climbed between my legs and leaned over me, showering me with soft kisses on my face, my collarbones, my breasts, my ribs, grounding me, bringing me back from the ether.

His mouth found my ear, and I tilted my head, enjoying the tingles from his tongue on my earlobe.

How could I still want more after that? The mating bond was a ruthless thing.

He kissed my neck and shifted so I felt the hard press of him in between my thighs.

"How are you hard again?" I asked in disbelief and appreciation.

He chuckled. "The bond demands fulfillment." With a smirk, he added, "Plus my mate *was* grinding on my face."

The head of his cock rubbed against me. I skated my hand between us and guided him up and down my slit, spreading my arousal, teasing us. As he watched, his hands glided along my thighs and over my hipbones. I notched him at my entrance, and he thrust forward impossibly slow.

We both stared, transfixed at the length of him disappearing inside of me. Deeper and deeper each time, he slid back and pumped in again.

"Look how good you take me," he said as he picked up the pace. His fingers found the throbbing bundle of nerves at the apex of my thighs, and he rubbed me in slow circles.

"Ahh," I said. "You feel so good inside of me. I need more."

Power was surging through my veins, his and mine, and I was getting high on it. I rolled my hips, and he leaned over me, cocooning me in his arms.

His chest rubbed against my hardened nipples as his hips snapped back harder and faster. His shadow took over teasing my clit. The touch even colder against my hot sensitive skin.

My fingernails dug into his back as a stuttering moan escaped. Sebastian kissed me, inhaling my sounds of pleasure.

My shadow vibrated with excitement as his lips caressed mine. All of the kisses we had before this one couldn't compare. As if some part of us had always been worried that the next kiss would never come or if we slowed down the feelings between us would vanish.

But this kiss was different. There was no fear. No other emotions to taint the feeling of his sweet love, of his cinnamon lust. There was just a peace, a knowing: he was mine forever.

It was the first kiss of a million that would stretch between us. Because he was my mate. And I was his. And when his lips claimed mine, it felt like warmth and bliss and safety and home.

The world rippled around us, becoming out of focus.

I clenched around his throbbing cock as bolts of sensation pulsed throughout my body.

His strokes increased, finding the perfect rhythm, chasing the feeling that was just ahead for both of us. The only sound was the slapping of flesh and our heavy breathing as the pleasure hitched higher.

He gazed into my eyes. "I love you," he said. "My pretty, perfect mate." The words came out staggered between pants of breath.

"I love you too." I forced my eyes to stay open, to return his gaze, but blinding pleasure was zapping up my spine. "My mate," I said. "My Sebastian."

I got to see the moment. The way his mouth fell open and his forehead scrunched up. The moment he came and his power was linked to me. There wasn't a taste or a color because I wasn't interpreting his feelings. There was just him.

His orgasm rocketed through me, inducing my own. I cried out as my body shook, tightening and clenching.

I was shattered completely. Broken into pieces and joined with his to be molded into something new. A disorienting and exhilarating sensation of bliss swept in.

The mating bond thrummed below my collarbone and resonated through both of our shadows. Pressure built before I was careening into a sacred darkness. Our shadows sifted us to the astral field where we disintegrated into particles, frozen and floating for only a moment before merging into an expansive eternity. Our energy attuned. New depths of power settled within us.

The bond snapped into place.

And took us home.

Magic spiraled up both my arms and settled within my heart. It was like being able to take a deep breath, the ease that filled me.

The first time I saw him my entire being seemed to shift. My blood moved in an opposite direction as if my body started changing, energy attuning to him in that very instant. Recognizing what he was long before I had the words to explain it.

Even now words didn't describe what it was like to be in sync. For my heart to beat to the same rhythm of his.

When I opened my eyes, I was in our bed. My body held tight to his. I wrapped my arms around his neck and my legs around his waist. His nose pressed into my neck as he released a shuttering breath from the magnitude of the moment.

Mine. Mine. Mine, his shadow chanted. Or perhaps it was my shadow.

All I could feel was him. His body on mine. His shadow against my skin. All of him surrounding me. Our shadows intermixed until there was no separation between them. No separation between us.

It was a primal sort of transcendence to give in to an instinct that we'd ignored and suppressed for so long. The sweet relief of letting go of resistance. Of my shadow, my heart, finally relaxing because we were exactly where we were supposed to be.

In my mate's arms. Cocooned by our shadows. Our powers vibrating within us to new heights.

In that moment, I was home. From within the hallowed darkness, our shadows had tied us together for eternity.

Chapter Forty-Nine

Sebastian

My shadow had stretched, grasping, reaching for the thread between us until we found each other, and her shadow coiled around us like a snake and squeezed.

She tied our souls together, and we dissolved into one.

The happiness and safety of it was overwhelming.

We fell into each other's arms on the bed. My beautiful mate was within me now. Her shadow filled in the cracks and made my broken pieces whole.

Tears dampened her cheeks, but I kissed them away, cupping her jaw. I didn't need to ask why she was crying.

"I know, baby," I said. "I feel it too."

Our powers had merged. Our auras had aligned, and with that, an awareness of one another settled in. I knew her and she knew me.

I felt the pure unconditional love that she'd given me a taste of within her shadowed memory. It acted as the glue that solidified all the frayed threads of our bond.

I rolled us, pulling her on top of me and placing a soft peck on her lips before tucking her head under my chin, holding her to me so all of her body was against all of mine. A tremor ran through her, ran through me.

We were one. Shadows and bodies and emotions and hearts.

I was hers and she was mine.

She nuzzled her face into my neck and pressed into me.

The only sound in the room was our heartbeats thumping in time, communicating in a way neither Amaya nor I could control. A language only our shadows spoke.

Th-thump. *Love.*

Th-thump. *Mate.*

Th-thump. *Mine.*

Chapter Fifty

Nico

If I hadn't destroyed my ability to shift without excruciating pain, I would be in my dragon form every day.

When I banked left toward the patch of green up ahead, the wind howled and whistled in my ears. The cold air cut across my wings. If it weren't for my thick-scaled skin, I would have been freezing this far up in the air, even with my naturally higher body temperature as a soliser.

Shifting had always been uncomfortable. It wasn't natural for the fae body to lengthen bones, rearrange muscle, grow scaled skin tissue and vertebrae to form wings. The ability was a relic from a time when solisers lived in the air, when all fae were more animal than person.

But after the military pumped me full of experimental steroids for decades and left me to deteriorate in our enemies' dank prison cell on the edge of the world for years, well, my shifting power had never really recovered.

I had barely recovered.

But those memories were distant and detached when I was in the air. Flying was both exhilarating and peaceful. I remembered being a child and my dad taking me to our cabin, which was far enough away from people that he would allow me to shift. There were moments when I was sure that I'd never shift back. That what was actually unnatural was my fae body. That my dragon form was who I was meant to be.

All of my thoughts and feelings faded away. Everything was so simple and glorious. It was just the wind under my wings and the feeling that I could touch the sky.

There was a slight ache in my left wing that twinged as I leaned to cut up above the clouds to keep myself from being spotted. The ache wasn't a surprise. My left shoulder had given me trouble since I was sixteen and dislocated it in the boxing ring.

I had hoped landing on a cargo ship last night to rest would have eased the strain, but it'd been so long since I'd used my back muscles in this way that pain was inevitable.

I didn't mind pain. In fact, I liked it. It kept my mind focused on the task at hand so I didn't slip completely into my dragon instincts.

When the sky had darkened last night, I swooped down low enough to spot one of our cargo ships. I landed on the end furthest from the engine room and tucked myself between two metal shipping containers. I was up in the sky at dawn before the crew could realize there was a dragon in their midst.

My shoulder needed the rest, but I didn't. I could have flown all through the night, except I didn't want to get to Delnee until morning. I planned on waiting outside Sloane's apartment until she left for the day. I would see that she was okay, and then I'd go home.

Yeah, it was a little stalker-y, but it was better than just showing up unannounced because I missed her and the bond hurt.

If she wanted to come home, she would.

If her side of the bond hurt, she would have told me.

But she didn't. And she hadn't. So, I was just going to discreetly check on her, and she would never have to know.

I flapped my wings harder toward the forest that was coming into view, pushing my muscles to the limit in hopes I'd shake off the deep sinking feeling in my gut that was telling me to turn around and go back to Palagui.

I was just scared Sloane would spot me, I reasoned. That I'd be so desperate for the sight of her pretty green eyes that I'd get too close, and she would see me and realize I was a crazed, obsessed male. It would make her want to break the bond and never see me again.

I held on to that rationalization, even as my overprotective dragon instincts—which usually blunted my analytical reasoning—tried to break free. They demanded I find Sloane, scoop her up, hoard her somewhere safe, and never let her out of my sight again.

That was crazy though. Over the top. Too much.

When I landed on the coastline near a thick forest in northern Delnee, I had to suppress the roar that was rumbling from somewhere deep inside. That possessiveness was flaring to life no matter how much I tried to quell it.

My claws dug into the ground, and I circled the area once, twice, a third time, agitation making my skin crawl. I sniffed the air, searching for a threat, but there was none.

Without the distraction of the pain from flying, I could no longer hold back the animalistic part of me. I finally gave in to the heartache from the bond, letting it sink in, and letting my dragon instinct take over and shut off every logical explanation my brain offered for why I felt this way.

Sloane, my body chanted.

Sloane, my mind sung.

Sloane, my heart cried.

I tuned in, and the rest of the world fell silent as her name, her memory, the ghost of her soul, vibrated through my body. It coursed through my veins.

Every part of me was screaming to fly home, fly to Palagui.

Clarity shot through me like a sharp stab to the gut.

Sloane wasn't here. She was in Palagui, and she was in trouble. My mate was in trouble.

I stomped, and angry fire snorted from my nose. It scorched a patch of grass, but I couldn't control the rage driving me now.

I launched into the air and flew harder than I had in my entire life. Up to this point, I'd been coasting, only flapping my wings enough to keep up my momentum, but now I could see the vibrations in the water from the force of my wings.

My shoulder ached, and my muscles screamed in agony, but I used the pain as my motivator. If I was in pain, I was alive. If I was in pain, I was one moment closer to her.

My mind focused and narrowed, latching on to the mantra of Sloane's name.

I was going to save my mate.

And I'd burn down anything and anyone that got in my way.

***

I flew for six hours straight. This was on top of the two hours I'd flown this morning to get to Delnee. I should have been exhausted, should have been at the last of my energy reserves, but something primordial was in control now.

That inner beckoning had called me toward the northern portion of the west coast of Palagui, south of the fae prison, and about fifty miles from the research center.

A large commercial fishing boat was docked at the mostly abandoned port and, even stranger, was the groups of people—like ants from my vantage point—disembarking and standing on the dock.

I angled my wings to the right, not wanting to draw attention, and made a wide loop into the forest, landing in the first open area I could find.

I tucked my wings to my sides and slithered through the forest, peering out from the coastal fringe.

I zeroed in on her, and despite the strange situation keeping my whiskers around my nose pinned back, I sighed in relief.

Sloane stood on the boat, her short blonde hair blowing in the wind. Her face was twisted and tight. Her posture exuded anger, but she was whole. She was okay.

Her gaze whipped to the forest, scanning the trees until her eyes landed on me.

I didn't know what a dragon looked like when they smiled, but I couldn't not smile at her.

She drew in a deep breath, and her shoulders relaxed. She scrunched up her face like she did when she was trying not to cry, but a small smile crossed her face at the same time.

The text about her being hungover had been a lie. She'd been taken, and someone wanted me to think the ache in our bond had been because she was sick, not because she was in trouble.

There was a shout, and Sloane trained her gaze away from me.

I took in the rest of the scene.

Something like fifty high priestesses in their uniforms filed down the ramp from the boat onto the dock.

I clenched my claws into fists and fought the urge to breathe fire as Caroline pushed Sloane off the ship. An older high priestess with the same dark skin and high cheekbones as Gwen held her upper arm and steered her off the ship beside Caroline.

They marched down the dock, halting at the end. From my angle, I couldn't see what they were doing. With precise steps, I tiptoed through the forest to get closer.

The animal instinct in me knew exactly where to place my feet so as not to disturb the vegetation and make noise. I halted as close as I could get without risking the wind taking my scent and giving away my position.

Sloane didn't look at me again, but the bond no longer ached like it had, just a faint pulse of nerves. I tried to blanket it with peace and safety. I'd save her. I'd protect her. She was going to be okay.

I needed a plan.

Caroline, and the female I was assuming was Gwen's mother, Evelynne, stopped in front of a group of males. From their build, I'd guess solisers. The group parted, and Vince strolled out.

That asshole was going to die.

I was going to sink my teeth into his torso, into Caroline's torso, and rip them apart. Blistering rage blinded me. Smoke emanated from my nostrils, and I had almost lost control when Sloane's eyes found mine.

She gave me a single minute shake of her head.

Calm down, her eyes said.

My body twitched, but I tried to slow my racing heart.

Vince and Caroline started talking. From this far away, I wouldn't have been able to hear them in my fae form.

But my senses were heightened as a dragon. I closed my eyes and tuned into their voices, letting the sounds of the ocean waves, the sea gulls, and the water lapping against the boat, all drop away.

"I trust your journey was smooth," Vince said.

"It took longer than you promised it would," Caroline said.

There was a scuffling noise, and I opened my eyes to watch Caroline hand Sloane off to another high priestess. Sloane yanked her arm back. Sunlight hit the silver of the fae cuffs around her wrists.

Vince sighed. "This was the only boat the members of SoCo had that was large enough for your army, but small enough not to draw attention when the captain claimed engine failures and docked here."

The wind took that moment to howl a loud piercing noise, rustling the trees in the forest and drowning out what they'd said next.

By the time it died down, Vince asked, "Where's Harrison's army?"

"I didn't want a bunch of powerless humans," Caroline said. "I brought the legacy high priestesses. That's all we'll need."

"He wouldn't give them to you."

When someone else answered, I peeked my eyes open. Evelynne said, "Harrison backed out after I told him they mind controlled him. He said he'd put his neck out on the line enough by hiding Caroline, and until we secured the crown, he didn't want to get involved."

Amaya and Sebastian thought they'd stopped a war with Delnee. But moving troops and buying suppression chemicals hadn't been Harrison's biggest secret. It was Caroline. Why would he put his people at risk when he could watch fae fight fae until there was nothing left of us?

"But I have Harrison's son as leverage," Caroline said with a smile in her voice. "Rien will make sure his father doesn't go back on his promises again. We might need his army if the council doesn't accept her claim to the throne."

"They will," Vince said. "They'll have to."

"Where is she?" Caroline asked.

I guess Caroline gave up on the idea of forcing Gwen to take the crown, but who did they have in mind instead?

"Meeting us at the research center."

"Why? I thought we were cornering them at the palace?"

Vince shook his head. "A soliser guard at the research center said they both came in about ten minutes ago. It's closer than the palace and less warded."

"Without wards what are we going to use to protect ourselves?" Evelynne asked.

Blue flames erupted around the group of high priestesses. They didn't scream, but they jumped, only to realize the fire wasn't harming them.

"My fire will act as a barrier. It'll protect the people I want it to," Vince said.

He was a fire warder.

He'd never spoken about his power before, and it wasn't like a councilmember and politician would need a defensive move like that on the campaign trail.

The plan I'd been concocting in the back of my head went up in smoke. Even if I managed to fly in and land long enough for Sloane, Gwen, and Rien to climb on my back and managed to protect them from fire balls and high priestess light, I wouldn't be able to get close unless I broke his ward.

It wasn't impossible. I was most certainly a hell of a lot more determined than Vince, but he'd feel the moment I started breaking through and that would take away my element of surprise.

I'd have to wait until he was distracted.

Sloane's eyes locked on mine. They went toward the forest, toward the research center, harsh and intent, and then darted back to me.

I knew what she was saying. She wanted me to warn Bash and Amaya. She wanted me to think and plan.

I wanted to snap Vince in half with my jaw. I wanted to rip Caroline to shreds with my claws. I wanted to burn everyone who stood on that beach and kept my mate away from me.

But I couldn't. Sloane needed me to be strategic and not give in to the rage.

She gave me a final soft, longing look, nodded once, and let herself be ushered away.

It ripped me apart, but I stayed where I was long enough for the group to disappear into the vehicles that revved their engines in the distance.

I stepped onto the beach, flapped my wings, and flew into the air, keeping myself far away from the road that cut through the forest toward the research center.

The mating bond thrummed as if Sloane had run her fingertips over it in a soft caress.

A burst of flames escaped from my mouth, and I flew even harder.

The blood in my veins chanted its steady mantra.

Sloane. Sloane. Sloane.

Chapter Fifty-One

Sebastian

From a scientific perspective, when the mating bond is accepted, there is a surge of fae magic growth hormones, and auric field boundaries dissolve and merge. Essentially, both partners' entire bodies change to allow for the power of the other to be absorbed.

Brain chemistry changes. Mirror neurons become enhanced and attuned to their partner. It's not sensing feelings like an empath or even reading and sending thoughts like a darkyra. It's a knowing. The synchronicity between mates extends to emotional states, movement, and intentions. Each person still has boundaries and autonomy, but body, mind, and soul resonate with their partner.

From an anecdotal perspective, being bonded was the deepest sense of calm I'd ever experienced.

It was strange for my chest to no longer ache. That pain had been replaced by a brilliance that had no words to describe it in its totality.

Ease. Safety. Home. Belonging. A feeling that my soul could finally relax.

We'd spent the rest of the day tangled around one another, drunk on the afterglow, and we might have stayed in that liminal space for days, weeks, months even, if it hadn't been for the plans we'd made with Amaya's parents.

They texted us the address of the restaurant they had gotten a reservation at and—with great reluctance to leave our blissed-out bubble—we'd gotten dressed and confirmed our plans. An hour before our dinner reservation, we sifted to the research center to check on Jeremy and the high priestesses.

The scientists were running around the center with a buoyant energy. Healing the draxis was a scientific discovery they were eager to research on a biological level.

I didn't really care about the science behind it. I was just glad it was over.

Well, almost over. I needed to face the high priestesses I'd hurt and explain and apologize. Nico had been right about needing to practice while they were draxis, but I was still nervous.

I held no illusions that they'd forgive me. I would be glared at and hated at best, spit on or attacked at worst, but they needed to know what happened to them and why. The hardest part of coming to terms with my own trauma had been not having the full memories of what happened. I blamed myself for the pain that only my body and shadow could remember.

Still, I was a coward, so I decided to go see Jeremy first.

Amaya and I walked into the hospital room on the first floor of the research center. Jeremy had a room to himself as he was the only darkyra turned draxis.

He took a deep breath and pushed himself into a seated position when we walked in. "I wondered if you'd come see me," he said as a greeting.

"Maybe I should let you two catch up," Amaya said, making to leave.

"Wait," Jeremy said.

She paused and turned to him.

"I'm sorry, Amaya. For trying to kill you. For...making that bargain and doing what I did. You'll never know how sorry I am," he said.

She gave him a sad smile. "I know, Jeremy. I forgive you. I know it wasn't you. I'm sorry we sent you to that prison and didn't try to find out what really happened."

"No. I...I deserved it. I'm sorry for how I treated you before. I was cruel and I shouldn't have..." He looked at his hands. "I'm sorry."

"It's okay," Amaya said. "I've been tricked into several terrible bargains. I know how much it sucks."

Jeremy forced an awkward smile. "Thanks for turning me back though. Being a draxis was dreadful," he said jokingly.

"You remember it?" Amaya asked, walking into the room. We stood at the end of his bed.

Jeremy nodded. "Well, some of it. I think the prison suppression might have messed me up for a bit, but I remember the two of you trying to heal me in that room in the basement. I remember waking up and being hungry. I have memories, but I didn't have the ability to make decisions or understand. I was just starving."

My stomach lurched because I'd been hoping the high priestesses wouldn't have memories of their time as a draxis. Wouldn't have to deal with their past haunting them.

"There's a program in Molbridge we'll get you and the high priestesses into," I said. "To help you deal with what happened on a psychological level, once the scientists clear you for release."

Jeremy shrugged. "They've already cleared me. I'm fine physically. My muscles are a little atrophied from disuse, but after some physical therapy, I'll be good as new."

"Wow," Amaya said. "That's incredible."

"There's no long-term damage?" I asked.

Jeremy shook his head and opened his mouth to respond, but a scientist ran in with a wild look in his eyes. "Your majesties."

"What?" I asked, already heading to the door.

"There's a naked male running up and down the halls demanding to see you, and I can't find any of our guards," the scientist said, wringing his hands.

I furrowed my brow, until I heard Nico's voice, and ran out of the room.

Nico was bent over the wall, huffing and puffing, but relief sagged his features when he saw us. "We've got trouble."

Someone handed Nico a medical gown, which he didn't bother to put on, and he summarized what he'd seen on the northern shores.

My heart raced, and Amaya's face became pale.

Nico confirmed that the missing guards at the research center were no coincidence. They'd been warned of what was to come.

"We've got, what? An hour before they get here?" Amaya asked.

Nico nodded. "I need to shift back," he said, but he was cringing as we followed him to the lobby door.

"Are you sure you can?" I asked.

He huffed dismissively rather than respond to the question. "I'll set up wards around the perimeter."

"Okay," I said. There was no use fighting him. Not when his mate was in trouble. "But don't activate the wards. Amaya and I will sift the scientists and high priestesses out to safety."

Nico threw the medical gown to the floor and ran out the door. A crackle of fire snapped and popped from outside, and an orange scaled dragon flew by the window.

We hadn't been very discreet, and the commotion brought most of the scientists and high priestesses out from their rooms.

Amaya and I urged everyone to prepare to be sifted out. Most of the scientists acquiesced to our insistence they needed to leave. The high priestesses however...

"Tell us what's going on," one of them said with her hands on her hips. Her eyes held a confidence and defiance that you wouldn't think someone who'd just been healed from being a draxis less than twelve hours ago would have. She seemed to have made herself the leader of the high priestess group. They all stood behind her in solidarity. "Don't you think we've been kept in the dark enough?"

I cringed as guilt hit me in the gut. She was right, so I answered, "Two ex-councilmembers are bringing an army of high priestesses and solisers here to get the Queen to give up her crown."

"Which councilmembers?" Another high priestess asked. This one was much younger than their leader, but her voice was just as strong.

I licked my lips. They would recognize Caroline as their representative.

But still, I couldn't lie. "Caroline Nueblots and Vince Kane, but I'm telling you Caroline has gone rogue in the last few months. She has a vendetta, and she's willing to go to any lengths to—"

"We believe you," the first high priestess said.

My eyes widened. "You do?

They must not know what I did. That was the only way they would ever believe anything I ever said. It wasn't a great time to get into that discussion when there was an army on the way.

The high priestess leader nodded. "We all…" She looked around at the group. "We all heard your apology. We heard your explanations. The empaths felt your sincerity and your pain. We believe you."

I swallowed the emotion threatening to rise. It was more than I deserved, more than I could have ever hoped to get.

"And I won't speak for everyone here," the leader said. "But I'm old enough to know how a grudge can rot someone from the inside, and I've felt hollow enough. I'm not starting my new life holding on to anger and resentment." She looked me square in the eye. "I forgive you. I don't want to be your friend, and I don't want to ever see you or your shadow again, but I forgive you for what you did to keep our country from falling apart."

Inhaling a ragged breath, I nodded once. "Thank you. I didn't know you could hear me while you were draxis. I planned on apologizing to each of you today and telling you that I've set up trusts in each of your names and funded them myself. You'll have enough to start a new life if that's what you choose or to take care of yourselves and your families after you leave here. I know it'll never make up for what happened, but I hope it can help you live the rest of your life in comfort."

"But you need to be alive to get to do that," Amaya said. "So we need to start sifting you out of here."

The lead high priestess shook her head. "If they have an army, you're going to need back up. I didn't suffer as a draxis just for the country to be turned back over to the solisers. I've felt enough of your emotions to trust you have our best interests at heart."

I looked at Amaya. She shrugged.

"I'll stand with you," another high priestess said. And a chorus of voices repeated the words.

I shook my head. "I can't ask you—"

"You aren't asking," the lead high priestess said. "We're volunteering. Tell us the plan."

Amaya smiled and stepped forward, outlining the plan we'd gone over in our heads while we'd been sifting the scientists out.

There were several high priestesses who hadn't been cleared, so I sifted them to the hospital in the city while Amaya sifted her parents to Nico's cabin just in case Vince decided to attack the townhouse.

I tried to convince Jeremy to leave, but he refused when he saw the others staying behind.

Amaya, Nico, and I would have thirty high priestesses and one darkyra to stand with us against the hundreds of legacy high priestesses and solisers that made up Caroline and Vince's army.

We were outnumbered, but if things went as planned, we wouldn't need to resort to a battle.

Amaya came back from sifting her parents with an annoyed furrow to her brows. I finished handing out the daggers I'd raided from Gwen's supply at the townhouse. She'd had enough to give each high priestess two. I'd have to ask her where the hell she was getting her weaponry from and why she was stockpiling it when we got her back.

What's wrong? I asked Amaya.

She rolled her eyes. *My parents wanted to help.*

I smiled. *So you're saying the run-into-danger trait is genetic?*

She put a hand on her hip and pursed her lips, giving me a sassy look. *I have no idea what you're talking about.*

Uh huh. Okay.

She tugged on my hand, and we walked down an empty hall. Everyone was prepared and ready to act as soon as Caroline and Vince showed up. This would be our last quiet moment together before chaos broke loose.

"You know, I would have thought you were used to the females in your life getting into trouble. Adriana showed me her memories of you playing the hero," Amaya said teasingly.

"She showed you memories of me?"

She chewed on her lip and nodded, leaning against a wall and taking both of my hands in hers. "Yeah. Does that upset you?"

I released a deep breath, pulling her into my arms. "No. They were her memories to share."

She squeezed her arms around my waist. "You never told me darkyra could read fae memories. Did you not want me to know because you were afraid I'd ask you to share yours with me?"

My only response was to shrug. I'm not sure if I'd had that conscious thought. For so long I couldn't even face my own memories, let alone consider sharing them with someone else.

She ran her hands up my chest and continued, "Because I'd never demand that from you, Sebastian. The only memories I want you to share with me are the ones we're going to make together."

Goddess, she really was the most perfect mate.

"Thank you for saying that," I whispered. I cupped her jaw and leaned down to kiss her. Our mouths slotted together, and I ran my hands over the swell of her hips as she pressed her chest to mine.

There was heat and passion and promise in the kiss. A promise that we'd make a million amazing memories together. A vow that I'd cherish the mundane and the magical parts of our lives equally.

I threaded my fingers through her hair and held her close. Shadows hovered around us, darkening the space. She melted into me with a soft sigh as my tongue swept through her mouth.

I had the profound realization hit me when her shadows curled around mine.

It'd always be this way. For the rest of our lives.

The pieces of her soul would dwell within me every day, for every happiness, every sadness, every frustration, and every pain.

Through it all, we'd be together.

"I love you," I whispered on her lips, leaning my forehead on hers.

Her fingers brushed along the side of my face. "I love you too."

Orange flickering drew both of our gazes to the window. Fire ignited the forest surrounding the research center. The inferno encircled us, sending us into a ring of hell I hadn't known existed.

With it, anger burned in my chest. After everything we'd gone through, after all the trials, all the pain, all the grief—that anyone dared to threaten me and my mate only proved how little they knew about my capacity for vengeance.

I hadn't come this far just to lose the only person that made all my suffering worth enduring.

Chapter Fifty-Two

Amaya

We watched from the window as Caroline, Vince, and Evelynne led their army through the forest and into the open area to the left of the research center.

Fire blazed around the edges of the forest, making escape impossible for anyone who couldn't sift. Sebastian and I could save ourselves. Jeremy, himself, but none of us would have left the high priestesses to die.

And we weren't running from this. I was ending it tonight.

The army halted, and two high priestesses brought Gwen and Sloane to the front next to Caroline. Their arms tied together with rope, silver fae cuffs on each wrist.

"Where's Rien?" I whispered.

Sebastian shook his head. "Would Caroline have left him in the ship? Nico said Rien was her insurance policy for Harrison. She wouldn't want to risk a human in a fae fight if she needed him alive after it was done."

Our high priestesses would be safe within the ward around the building of the research center, and wanting to keep their presence a secret for as long as we could—and hoping to avoid a fight altogether—they would wait inside until we gave the signal.

Thick black smoke filled the air from the fire ravaging the outskirts of the research center. The intensity of the heat could be felt even from inside the cement walls. There was no doubt of Caroline and Vince's message: We're here and you are surrounded.

My mate and I walked out of the research center and into the open field. Our shadows led the way, rolling like fog around our feet.

Nico said that Vince was a fire warder, and sure enough, a low blue flame wrapped around the edges of their group. He must have been pretty powerful too for the ward to encompass everyone.

Our plan was to exchange the powerless crown for Gwen and Sloane, and when Caroline and Vince were distracted, we would focus all of our power on one spot to break the ward. If we tried to break it now, we risked hurting Gwen and Sloane if it exploded from the amount of power pummeling toward it.

But as the dwindling light of sunset shimmered against Sloane, I noticed something else that might complicate our plan if Caroline didn't come for a trade.

Sloane and Gwen have separate wards around them, I said to Sebastian. I scanned the group and saw them. Two high priestess fae warders were standing directly behind them.

They aren't the only ones. It wouldn't be smart to only use two. They probably have more hidden in the forest somewhere, Sebastian said. *I'll get Nico on it.*

We halted a few paces away from Caroline. Sebastian wasn't a warder, but his shadows hovered between us, creating a barrier that would spring up and attack if provoked.

"Let Gwen and Sloane go," I said to Caroline in the deeper voice of my shadow. I didn't want her to know that I knew about Rien being hidden on her ship.

The threat of danger and violence loomed as the flames encircling the field crackled.

"Pass on the crown and they won't be hurt," Caroline said.

"Release them," I countered. "And we won't kill you."

Caroline snorted. "You have no leverage here. You won't be making the demands." The high priestesses' hands glowed and the solisers' palms blazed.

I scoffed. "We can take out your entire army with our eyes closed."

Sebastian had taken out the solisers at court. The two of us together could obliterate everyone in this field if the ward went down.

"The second you attempt to break our ward is the moment I'll slit their throats," Caroline said.

I shook my head and changed tactics. "You expect me to believe you'll actually hurt your niece? Or Sloane, a high priestess, someone you claim you're doing all this to save?"

Caroline's eyes deadened. "I'll do whatever it takes to save my people. I would think as queen you'd understand the concept of sacrificing a few to save the whole."

Her words landed a little too close to home, but I tried to hide my expression. In fact, it was the opposite. I wasn't a good queen because I would sacrifice everyone in the world for my mate, for my best friends, for my family.

Caroline sneered.

But she knew that, knew exactly what she would have to do to get me to give up my crown and power.

I was just as ruthless as Caroline. The only difference between us was who we were fighting for.

My gaze landed on Evelynne. She didn't look at her daughter and trained her gaze on the distance behind me. Caroline might be willing to kill her niece for the crown, but Evelynne…

Caroline would have told her that she'd bluff about killing Gwen and Sloane. It'd be a gamble, but we needed to call Caroline's bluff without actually getting them killed and flip Evelynne to our side. She'd be able to call off her high priestesses who were warding them, and hopefully we could avoid a battle altogether.

I lifted my chin. "I don't believe you. You won't hurt them, and I won't give you the crown. If you stand down, I won't kill you. And—"

Caroline yanked Gwen's arm so she stumbled forward. The high priestesses holding her on either side had already untied the ropes around her arms. Caroline unsheathed her dagger and sliced up Gwen's forearm from her inner wrist to elbow.

Sloane screamed Gwen's name. Instinctively, I started to run, but Sebastian grabbed me before the thought had even settled in my mind and kept me from tossing myself into the blue blaze of Vince's ward.

The high priestess nearest Sloane made an identical slash on her arm, but Sloane didn't scream. Her chest started heaving, and her eyes screwed shut, trying to press down the pain.

The trees in the forest rumbled and shook. No, not the trees, I realized when Sloane's eyes darted toward the sound.

I held my breath, hoping Nico could fight the urge to attack the people hurting his mate.

Sloane stared with intensity into the forest and shook her head once.

No one else seemed to register who lurked from afar.

"The Queen of Darkness has made her decision about what's most important to her," Caroline said.

Gwen and Sloane gritted their teeth and didn't make a single sound as blood gushed from their arms. The fae cuffs negated their healing abilities.

Vince's eyes darted from me to Caroline and back again. Evelynne continued to stare unseeingly at the tree line, but her hands were tightening into fists.

"You're going to let your sister kill me, Mother?" Gwen said. "Your new concern for me was all just a ruse, wasn't it? You never loved me." Gwen laughed hysterically. "Fuck you too, Mom."

Evelynne's jaw trembled, but she didn't move.

I could feel Caroline's gaze on me, waiting for the moment I'd break. I kept my face as neutral as possible, but I could smell the copper of their blood from where I stood.

"Caroline," Evelynne hissed under her breath.

Gwen blinked several times. Her head bobbed a bit from wooziness, and she leaned on the high priestesses holding her. She was losing too much blood.

"Caroline!" Evelynne yelled when she hadn't gotten a response. She made to move toward Gwen, but two solisers grabbed her. Panic entered her eyes. "What are you doing?"

"What needs to be done," Caroline said.

Evelynne jerked left and right, trying to get out of their hold. "Caroline! You're going too far. You said you wouldn't hurt her."

The high priestesses looked at one another, trying to gauge who they were supposed to follow, but none moved to help their captain as the solisers cuffed Evelynne and weaved rope around her arms.

"I told you we would have to make sacrifices," Caroline said. "I told you I wouldn't lose anyone without reason. Direct your anger toward the cause of your daughter's pain. Because until the Queen of Darkness hands over the crown, we will all watch as Gwen and Sloane die."

The cuts were deep enough that they would only have a few minutes before they bled out and no high priestess healing would save them.

"Fine!" I said and put my hands up in surrender. "Fine. Just…Just heal them okay. Heal them first and I'll give you the crown."

I stepped forward and took the crown off my head holding it in front of my torso.

Caroline inclined her head to the high priestesses, and they healed Gwen and Sloane. Light flashed, and the skin was knitted back together. Their arms were bent behind their backs and retied with ropes.

Vince sighed in relief. "Are we done with the dramatics now?"

He waved a hand, and the solisers parted, allowing a female to walk through.

My jaw dropped. I felt Sebastian's shock flash like static through me accompanied by a burnt taste.

Leva didn't smile. She clasped her hands in front of her as she stood next to Vince.

"Leva will take the crown," he said.

Leva's ankle-length dress billowed around her legs as she walked through the blue flame of the ward. Another smaller ward traveled with her until she halted halfway to us.

"She's not a high priestess. The crown will destroy her," I said.

Caroline rolled her eyes.

"My deal with Caroline includes making Leva the queen," Vince said. "She can handle the crown. Can't you, my dear?"

Leva nodded solemnly, not meeting my gaze.

"And what does that make you?" I asked.

Vince grinned and raised an eyebrow.

I threw out an arm, looking to Caroline. "This is what you want? You hate darkyra so much that you'd rather have a soliser queen and king? You wanted to kill Xenos!"

I felt sick. Vince would marry Leva, and both Caroline and Vince would use her while the crown ate away at her body. They didn't care if it was only a few decades or a few years. They'd just find another person to use and abuse when she died. And poor Leva must be too scared to stand up to them.

Caroline sighed. "Xenos was an incompetent waste of space. Leva will be queen and Vince will be king and I will be their right hand. Because as you so astutely pointed out, Leva isn't a high priestess, so she'll need me and my high priestesses to heal her each day to make sure the crown doesn't take her prematurely. A mutually beneficial relationship."

Or mutual destruction. If Vince and Leva didn't listen to Caroline, she would make sure there were no high priestesses around to heal her. Leva would die, and Caroline would put someone else she could control on the throne.

I stepped into the middle of the field. "After I put this on her head, you'll let Sloane and Gwen go. You'll let all of us leave alive. We won't fight you." I glanced at Evelynne, then Vince, and finally Caroline. "My friends are more important to me than power."

While I was holding the crown, it was the only leverage I had to keep us all alive. They couldn't steal it. I had to pass it on. Or they had to kill me, but if they did that, they would risk fae power dying.

Or so they thought.

"Pass on the crown to Leva and I will free Sloane and Gwen," Caroline commanded.

I needed to make this believable, but I couldn't recall what Queen Mari had said to me to pass on the crown. My mind was mush from the adrenaline.

Clearing my throat, I said, "Leva Lussier, I pass on the Palaguian crown to you. The citizens are your children, your responsibility. The magic of the crown is yours to wield with Palagui in your heart."

Leva was shorter than me, but she bowed as I placed the crown on her head.

No one knew the crown was fake, and no one except the five of us who'd been in the Queen's chamber knew that the real crown had made me pass out and sent me to another realm.

Leva straightened. The flames behind us gleamed in the reflection of the metal of the crown.

She stared at her hands as blue flame seemed to light her from within. A pulse of power flickered through her, as if...as if the crown actually had power.

But I knew for a fact that it didn't.

She was acting.

I schooled my expression, but what the hell? Why was she pretending? Maybe she assumed I wouldn't really give her the crown. Maybe she was hoping to buy us time.

Maybe Leva wasn't being manipulated at all. She was conning *them*.

Leva's eyes finally met mine. She nodded once as if hearing the question, and she stoically walked back to Vince's side, the blue flame of her pretend crown's power continuing to light her entire body.

Leva may be quiet. She may be shy and unassuming and have the ability to slip into the background, but she used everyone's underestimation of her to her advantage.

Caroline smiled in triumph. "Take her to the ship."

A few high priestesses came toward Leva, but Vince snapped, "No. My people will take her."

"Mateo, take Leva to my safe house," Vince said.

"Yes sir." A heavily scarred soliser stepped out and escorted Leva back into the forest.

"There. You have your queen. Let them go," I said.

I was entirely unsurprised when Caroline said, "I'll free Gwen and Sloane. Free them from the darkness and shadows that are hooked in their brains."

She stepped forward, high priestess light in her palm. "You and your mate can fight, but Gwen and Sloane are not leaving this meadow with your shadows inside them. Either they will die or you will. It's that simple."

"Caroline!" Evelynne renewed her fight against the solisers, but two more had joined in holding her back.

"She's not your daughter anymore," Caroline called out, never taking her eyes from me. "She's a shadow puppet, and either they release her or she's better off dead anyway."

Vince took over holding Gwen with one hand tight around her upper arm and the other positioning a dagger at her neck. The high priestess who cut Sloane held her in the same position.

We had one more trick up our sleeve. Nico had been able to place a ward around the outskirts that would negate fae power, but he didn't have time to tie it to each of us, which meant it would negate everyone's power in this field except his.

And our mating bond.

But we couldn't be sure that would be enough to take on an entire army by ourselves.

Given Jeremy had no experience in hand-to-hand combat, we'd commanded him to stay in the forest and wait for our signal to activate the ward.

A strange howl filled the air that could have been mistaken for a gust of wind, but the way Sloane's eyes widened slightly, I knew it was Nico.

Nico is signaling he found Gwen's and Sloane's warders in the forest, Sebastian said.

A little blossom of hope sprung up, only to wither when Sebastian said, "It's my shadows controlling them." He stepped to the edge of Vince's ward. "Not Amaya's."

The shock on my face was not an act.

What are you doing? I asked.

If we're going to end this, I need to get close to Caroline. Jeremy will activate the ward, and I'll pull on our bond to kill her. You run to Gwen. Nico will get to Sloane. The four of you get the hell out of here.

I'm not leaving you!

When Caroline is dead, Jeremy will deactivate the ward, and I'll sift.

I swallowed.

"Kill me first and you'll see," Sebastian said to Caroline. "Gwen and Sloane will go back to normal. Amaya will too. I've been controlling them all."

Vince shrugged. "Killing him would end the Laurent line. Without a claim to the throne, no one would ever prefer a foreigner darkyra as our queen over a soliser citizen. Amaya's high priestess power is weak, and without her mate, her powers would dwindle. She wouldn't be a threat."

I never thought I'd see the day that Vince would argue to spare my life.

Caroline looked between me and Sebastian. She turned to someone behind her, and they tossed something through the ward and across the field.

Two fae cuffs came tumbling over.

Silver fae cuffs with black numbers etched on the side.

Caroline *did* take the fae cuffs we'd switched out for the deal with Harrison.

It didn't surprise me since they'd vanished along with her, but their reappearance tickled something in the back of my head.

Harrison had made a deal with Xenos for these cuffs.

Xenos, who never bothered himself with international politics. And Harrison, who just dropped the matter completely when the fae cuffs Rien brought back weren't the right ones.

Something never sat right about that, but I couldn't put my finger on what.

"Put those on," she said. "When I'm sure your shadows have released them and they surrender, you have my word that no one will get hurt."

Sebastian retrieved the cuffs. He undid each of the clasps with slow precision.

My heart started racing. As soon as the cuffs snapped on, he wouldn't be able to send me his thoughts.

Stick to the plan, he said. *No matter what happens. Get Gwen and run.*

I love you, I said instead of making a promise I knew I couldn't keep.

I heard his sigh in my head. *I love you too.*

Sebastian snapped one cuff on and then the other, cutting me off from his thoughts.

He walked across the field, his wrists cuffed, and arms up in surrender.

My breathing got heavier the closer he walked to their ward. I tried to focus on the imprint of his heartbeat that resided within my body, but it was muffled.

Four high priestesses stepped outside the ward and met Sebastian halfway. The globes of light in their palms winked out when they saw he wasn't running or fighting. They each grabbed his arm and pulled him through Vince's ward.

I couldn't hide my wince as he walked through, but the blue flames didn't hurt him.

The high priestesses brought him in front of Caroline and pushed on his shoulders, forcing him to kneel.

My hands curled into fists. No one makes him kneel. No one has power over him like that. I was going to rip off Caroline's head. Then Vince's. I was going to destroy everyone in this field.

But something like faint tapping on the bond's threads pulled me back from my murderous imaginings. I forced myself to look away from Sebastian and calculated the space between Vince's dagger and Gwen's throat.

When Jeremy activated the ward, it would damage Vince's power and distract him so I could make it to her before his blade did.

Caroline raised her dagger over her head. Every fiber of my being was screaming at me to run, to fight, to protect my mate, but strangely enough, it was my shadow who whispered, *There's something off about Vince.*

I wanted to rage at her. There had always been something off-kilter about him, and now wasn't the time for psychological musings over a deranged bully, but my gaze met his across the field.

Vince wasn't staring at Sebastian. He was looking at me. He smiled, mouthing something...something like, *Ready?*

Vince tightened his grip on the dagger at Gwen's neck, pressing it close to her skin. She winced as he sliced her neck, and a trickle of blood ran down.

His mouth moved beside her ear, but his devious eyes stayed on me. Her face slackened from whatever he whispered.

He was planning on killing her anyway. That was what he was saying. He didn't actually care about Sloane's and Gwen's lives. He didn't care about mine. He was going to kill Gwen the second Caroline killed Sebastian.

He was going to kill the people I loved simply because he could. He was going to destroy Palagui.

No. I wouldn't let him.

He was going to *die.*

Sebastian whistled our signal, and a heavy blanket of magic fell over the field.

The lobby door of the research center was thrown open, and the fire at the edge of the forest was snuffed out as Jeremy activated our ward. Vince's blue-flamed ward extinguished, and like dominos, everyone slowly realized their powers had disappeared, but I was already sprinting.

The two warders who'd been casting around Gwen and Sloane fell to their knees, screaming as blood trickled out of their eyes from using their power as our ward was activated.

My mind was split. Somehow the consciousness of our bond had me feeling both my own actions and the ghost of Sebastian's at the same time.

He pulled on the mating bond, funneling the power into his shadows to slam the high priestesses holding him to the ground.

I was focused on my target.

But Vince didn't fall to his knees screaming. Blood wasn't trickling from his eyes.

I pumped my arms and legs harder to get across the field.

He hadn't been affected by our ward's activation. Almost like he'd dropped his power the second before the ward fell over us.

Pure fury fueled my dash. I had only heartbeats to get to him.

Sebastian lunged at Caroline.

"Kill them," Caroline screamed. Her words were choked out as Sebastian's hands wrapped around her throat.

"No!" My legs weren't moving quick enough. I couldn't get to Gwen in time.

"Now," Vince hollered.

My vision blurred, narrowing in on the blood at Gwen's neck. Every other sound fell away. All I could hear was the slice of a dagger as it met resistance.

Chapter Fifty-Three

Amaya

"Now!" Vince yelled as he moved the dagger across Gwen's throat and to her back.

She didn't fall.

He sliced through the ropes binding her arms. He'd already removed the cuffs around her wrists. Gwen held Vince's dagger in her right hand and threw herself on top of the high priestess holding Sloane.

The dagger lodged in the high priestess's windpipe before she could even realize what had happened.

I made it to them as Gwen started cutting Sloane's ropes. A dragon shaped shadow fell over us, and screaming began as a burst of fire caught half of the SoCo army aflame.

The shadow disappeared as Nico landed and curled his scaled body around to protect us. Gwen unlocked Sloane's cuffs.

"Where did you get that key?" I asked at the same time Gwen asked, "You have backup coming?"

I nodded. She must have meant the high priestesses in the research center. The sounds of battle, the *snap* of bones and *thump* of falling bodies, echoed in the field as the SoCo army began to fight the few high priestesses we had on our side.

I needed Gwen and Sloane out of here.

Gwen interlaced her hands, leaned down, and made a step for Sloane's foot. Sloane hiked herself up onto Nico's back.

I did the same for Gwen. The girls both offered their hands to pull me up, but I refused.

"Sebastian," I said.

My friends didn't fight me, understanding I couldn't leave my mate to fight alone. Gwen slipped the key to the cuffs and the dagger into my hand, and Nico launched into the air with the girls hanging on his back.

The prickle of my magic returned as the ward deactivated and it felt like I could breathe again.

All at once, the field lit up with fire and light as power returned.

Which was when chaos erupted.

People ran from the edges of the forest, yelling a war cry. They surrounded us from every angle. Hundreds and hundreds of them, running from what seemed like nowhere, from the darkness. A never-ending stream of them raced toward us.

And I knew we were done. We were all going to die.

We'd already been outnumbered, but even Sebastian and I couldn't take on this many fae. They'd been hiding in the forest, waiting for the moment to kill us.

We had never stood a chance.

Except...the people flooding the field from the forest weren't attacking me nor the high priestesses from the research center.

They wore black armbands, and as shadows and fire and light catapulted into one another, I realized they were fighting for *us*.

Darkyra, soliser, and high priestess surrounded the SoCo army and the legacy high priestesses, taking them on three to one.

Shadows and fire and light fought, entangled in one another. Yells and chants and grunts filled the space.

I didn't have time to figure out where they'd come from or why they were helping us because an icy sizzling sensation ripped through my chest, almost bringing me to my knees.

I gasped, but it wasn't *my* pain I was feeling.

The bond pulled taut, dragging me toward him like hooks had been pierced into my heart.

My shadows gathered, and I sifted through the sounds of fighting, through the mass of bodies, to rematerialize next to my partially collapsed mate.

He'd managed to fight the high priestesses off with the mating bond powering his shadows, but the cuffs on his wrists made sure he wouldn't be able to use his full strength.

I wanted to erupt with power, to kill everyone that dared to threaten my friends and my mate, but the downside of having backup was that if Sebastian and I detonated, we'd kill everyone in this field, including our allies.

I had to be careful and precise.

My shadow didn't need my commands, she unleashed into the field in a slither, cutting down the high priestesses whose light blazed toward my mate.

I lunged to cover Sebastian as the lash of my shadow whipped and felled one high priestess, then two, and a third.

I handed him the key to the fae cuffs, and tried to hold back our attackers while healing him with my light.

His void eyes met my own. "Why don't you ever do as I say?" he asked as he unlatched his cuffs.

"Because I'm a brat," I quipped. "You can punish me later."

He snorted, and his cuffs fell to the ground.

Flames and light punched holes into my shadows—it felt like every high priestess and soliser was on us—but the shadows replenished when Sebastian's power whirled through the mating bond.

"Should we show them what our shadows can really do?" he asked.

My eyebrows lowered as a wicked smile spread across my face. "Let's give them a show," I said, my shadow said. Her fury vibrated under my skin, making the hair on my arms stand. Blood lust pounded in my temples. The dark vicious part of me came alive.

I sunk into a defensive posture, and we fought through the high priestesses and solisers who were charging toward us.

Fierce anger and a violence that had no end erupted through me, through my shadows. They squeezed and murdered everyone who dared to come close to us, though careful to avoid the high priestesses from the research center and the fae with black armbands.

The legacy high priestesses' roars of anger were turned into agonized screams.

The solisers' demands for vengeance were cut off by the sounds of twisting necks.

The piles of bodies around the two of us became a better deterrent than the threat of our shadows did.

As we continued to take out our dwindling combatants, I scanned the field and spotted our true target.

A group of high priestesses were racing toward the edge of the forest, Caroline in the middle of the pack.

I didn't have to speak to Sebastian; he felt my intention through the bond, and we sifted together to the edge of the field.

A savage rage filled me, and my shadows created total darkness, blinding the escaping group.

Nico, Gwen, and Sloane provided the means for our aerial attack. From above, fire rain down in tiny, concentrated spurts. They made sure to keep a ring of fire at our backs, reinforcing it each time a soliser tried to come at us from behind.

The high priestesses threw out their light and encircled Caroline in protection. Our shadows were everywhere though, they couldn't be stopped, couldn't be halted.

Caroline had been right to fear us.

Together, we were unstoppable.

Caroline's light flung out in different directions but didn't come near us, like she was fighting with a blindfold on.

My shadows faded from around Caroline just enough so we could watch her eyes widened in fear at what was coming for her.

Sebastian grabbed my hand, and raising our palms, our shadows intermixed and funneled into the female that betrayed us, who had gotten us locked up and tortured in prison, who would have killed her own niece to get power.

The shadows congregated toward her chest at first, where the protection ruby no doubt hid under her clothes.

It didn't matter. There was nothing strong enough to stop us. To stop our power. To stop us from taking our revenge.

At first, the high priestesses pressed in tightly toward Caroline, not quite blocking her, but maybe hoping the ruby she wore afforded them protection too.

The sound of shattering crystal pierced the air. The screams of high priestesses falling, impaled from the shards, rung in my ears.

Caroline fell to her hands and knees and looked up at us.

Sebastian grabbed her, hauled her to her feet, and held her arms behind her back, just as she'd held Gwen.

I curled my lip in disgust and held my dagger at her throat. "Killing you would be too kind after all the hell you put us through," I said. "But I guess you won't be able to say the Queen of Darkness never did anything kind for you, because I don't want to wake up tomorrow knowing you're still breathing."

My shadows turned into knifes, and just as they were about to slice into her stomach, a voice yelled out, "Let her go or your darkyra friend joins her in the afterlife."

Evelynne walked through the darkness, her steps sure and confident, as she held Jeremy with a dagger at his neck. His void eyes weren't out. Two silver fae cuffs were clasped around his wrists.

"Found who activated your ward," Evelynne said. "He must be pretty important to you if you got him to stay out of the fight."

"I'm sorry," Jeremy said. "I didn't see her coming. She attacked me from behind."

No one moved. The crackle of fire and guttural clash of battle continued around us. We needed to end this or more people were going to die.

Our shadows could kill Evelynne in a blink of an eye, but she could kill Jeremy just as fast.

"She was going to kill your daughter!" I said. "Why are you saving her?"

"She was bluffing," Evelynne said. "We had to make it look real. Had to make it look like I was worried to make you believe it."

"Bullshit," I said. "She would have killed them both and you know it. This isn't the first time she's betrayed you. She was going to force Gwen to take the crown. She didn't care if it would kill her."

The sound of a female screaming in agony filled the air, and Evelynne's eyes darted around like she recognized the voice. She turned back and shook her head, less convincingly now. "She was buying time while she tried to find a substitute..."

"Caroline has been planning to betray you from the beginning," I said.

Something about saying those words out loud made a realization click in my head. All the stuff she said to Gwen about Delnee not trusting her when she claimed darkness had taken their fae powers. She had been right: Kai *had* taken their powers. But she hadn't been right about who was to blame.

She'd been trying to find a way to make the Delnee high priestesses believe her for the last hundred years.

It had never made sense why Xenos would make a deal with Harrison for the fae cuffs. He couldn't be bothered with secrets and politics if it didn't directly benefit his lifestyle.

Because it wasn't Xenos.

"Ask her who actually made the deal with Harrison to get the fae cuffs to lock up the legacy high priestesses," I said.

Caroline impersonated Xenos. She wanted the high priestesses in Delnee to believe that they were in trouble.

Even if she had to put them in trouble herself.

Evelynne's eyes darted to Caroline, who was shaking her head.

Caroline sputtered. "She's twisting everything. You weren't safe in Delnee! Our people needed a reason to rally! The humans, the darkyra, even the solisers—they would all destroy us if they could. We needed to be united. You didn't believe me a hundred years ago. No one did. You needed to see what Harrison would do if given the chance. What the shadows were capable of."

"Evelynne," I said. "If Sebastian and I could control fae minds, why wouldn't we have controlled Caroline or you? She's been lying to you, spreading false narratives to get you to turn against us."

"You saw how Harrison acted when we compelled him," Sebastian said. "Did Gwen ever act like that? Dead behind the eyes?"

Understanding sank Evelynne's shoulders. I knew it wasn't only our reasoning that convinced her. She'd already had doubts. I could see it in her eyes. The way she couldn't look at Gwen while Caroline cut her. She knew somewhere deep down that she didn't trust Caroline. But loyalty to the high priestess faction kept her blind.

Evelynne's hands dropped from Jeremy, and he scrambled away from her. She brought her fingers to her mouth and whistled. "Stand down!"

"No!" Caroline cried out, and she yanked herself forward, ripping out of Sebastian's grip.

But she wouldn't have been strong enough for that.

He'd let her go.

Your kill, my beautiful darkness, he crooned in my head.

I smiled as my wickedness rose. My shadow vibrated underneath my skin. My heart pounded with adrenaline and excitement.

Caroline stumbled, and high priestess light brightened in her palms, but before she could gather the strength to protect herself, my power burst.

Black sparkling light crashed into her.

It destroyed her bones. Released her life force. And left only a spiral of smoke where she'd stood.

The fighting ceased. Shouting and explosions of fae power were replaced by calls from the wounded for help.

"We surrender," Evelynne said and put her hands up, falling to her knees. "I beg for your mercy on behalf of my high priestesses."

The solisers that made up the SoCo army looked around the field in a panic but extinguished their flames when Vince never emerged to tell them what to do. They were outnumbered and surrounded. There was nowhere to run or retreat.

The field was filled with confused looks, heavy breathing, and the flapping of dragon wings in the air.

Nico landed near us. Gwen and Sloane slipped off his back and ran to me.

The three of us wrapped our arms around one another. They were okay.

We were all okay.

Evelynne didn't fight as she was cuffed. "I'm sorry, Gwen," she said. "I thought I was protecting you."

Gwen refused to look at her mother.

What should we do with her? I asked Gwen in her head.

She answered aloud, "Slit her throat. She would have let her sister slit mine."

Evelynne sobbed. "No, Gwen, I would never—"

Gwen might not be in the best headspace to make decisions right now.

"No executions," I said. "We'll take them to the prison until we figure out what to do."

Caroline had made her bed, but it didn't feel right killing Evelynne after she surrendered and begged for mercy. I might not be a good person, but I wasn't a monster either.

A commotion drew our attention away. One of the solisers broke free and tried to sprint to the forest. A darkyra shadow appeared in front of them, and a leg was thrown out, tripping the soliser.

The darkyra bent over to cuff the soliser. Something about them looked kind of familiar.

"Oh my Goddess," Gwen whispered.

The shadows cleared, and the darkyra in question turned. Her eyes met Gwen's as two people with black armbands took over for her and grabbed the soliser lying on the ground.

Daria wiped her hair from her face and tentatively smiled as she walked toward us.

She halted in front of Gwen, who was just staring slack-jawed. Daria's smile died, and she took a deep breath. "Figured I'd need a pretty grand gesture to get you to forgive me for kidnapping you and getting your friends thrown in prison." She put both her palms out and gestured around the field. "So I built you an army."

Daria sucked her bottom lip into her mouth, waiting for Gwen to react. Everyone's eyes were glued on them.

Gwen blinked and blinked for a few moments.

Then she stepped toward Daria and pushed her shoulder. "You."

She pushed her again, forcing Daria to step back or she'd lose her balance. "Are."

Another push. Daria just took her assaults. "Fucking."

Gwen's fingers curled into fistfuls of Daria's shirt, and she dragged her close.

"Crazy," she said on an exhale, and before Daria could react, Gwen pressed up on her toes and kissed her.

Daria froze for only an instant, then her hands found Gwen's waist, and she kissed her back, pulling her in. Gwen's fingers twisted into her hair at the nape of her neck. Their kiss was brutal and angry, like Gwen was trying to maul her out of her system.

Daria pulled back, laughing. "Does this mean you forgive me?"

Gwen pressed her lips together, shaking her head in disbelief. "We wouldn't be alive if it weren't for you," she said and kissed Daria again.

A throat cleared, and they pulled away from each other. Vince walked out from the forest.

"Arrest him," I said.

No one moved. A small blue flame ward encircled him. He crossed his arms over his chest, smirking.

Sebastian and I reacted in sync, gathering our shadows as Vince said, "Must I say the silly little code?" He rolled his eyes. "The darkness conceals even those who hide in plain sight."

Our shadows stuttered, surprise rippling through us.

Vince held out his arms to either side. "Well, sister, are you going to tell them who helped you with your army? Or shall I?"

Chapter Fifty-Four

Amaya

Spring had arrived. Pops of color were sprinkled throughout the cemetery from the blooming flowers. Death and life meshed into one.

I squeezed Sebastian's hand as we stood in front of his family's mausoleum where all of the queens had been laid to rest.

We'd been standing at the threshold for the past few minutes as he gathered the fortitude to go inside.

It'd been his shadow that had endured the funeral for his mother, and while I'm sure he had access to those memories, in a way, this was the first time he was facing his loss and the accompanying grief as an integrated person.

Sebastian took a deep breath, and we stepped inside. We walked straight, took a right, then a left.

My eyes could barely keep up with the pictures of the queens and their plaques. We passed thousands of years of royalty in a few short paces.

We stopped and looked up at a portrait.

But it wasn't his mother we stood in front of.

Adriana's smiling face stared out at us, so different from all the other photos, which depicted a queen in full regal attire with their stern and proud expressions. Adriana's picture looked more like a high school class photo. She was beaming. Her face round with youth and her eyes innocent and joyful.

"It always felt wrong to me that they'd hung her picture here," Sebastian whispered. "They didn't know I'd lost her to the portal. They all believed she was dead, but I couldn't let myself accept that."

"We can take it down if you want."

He pressed his lips together and continued to stare up at Adriana.

"I know she said not to, but we could try to visit her in another hundred years," I said. "Dr. Henderson can figure out if there's another solar eclipse—"

"No," he said, shaking his head. "It's time to move on. Time to let the past go."

My eyebrows pulled together in sympathy. His bitter sadness filled me, but it wasn't overwhelming or all-consuming. A clean grief that would hopefully lessen over time, though it would likely never disappear.

"As far as this world is concerned, Adriana did die. And I've been lucky enough to get proof that she went to another world and is happy and healthy. That's more than most people get when they lose someone," he said.

"It is," I said. "But that doesn't mean it's going to hurt any less."

He pressed his tongue into his upper lip and nodded. He dropped my hand, glanced left and right as if checking no one was watching, and reached up to wiggle the picture down from the wall. "She's not dead yet. She's gone. But she's not dead. Her picture can be hung up when..." He shrugged. "When I die, I guess."

I nodded. "Okay."

He exhaled and tucked the photo under his arm.

The next words were out of my mouth before I thought about them. "Are you..." I cleared my throat. "Uh, do you..."

He looked down at me, waiting.

I cringed. "Sorry, this is a morbid question."

"Seems the appropriate setting for one," he said, a small smirk tugging on his lips.

"Do you want to be buried here?"

He shook his head. "Queens only. I won't be here."

I bit my lip.

"You'll be here then," he said.

I squeezed his hand. "I don't want to be here. I want to be wherever you are."

He kissed my forehead. "You and I have lots of time to decide on our death wishes."

I leaned against his shoulder. "As long as Kai doesn't come back with some darkyra army. Or Luna and Saul."

"Kai won't come back to this world in our lifetime. They created a centuries-long plan just to get off this planet." Sebastian wrapped an arm around my waist and pulled me into his side. "And if Luna and Saul could come here, they would have already. I think, for once, Kai was telling the truth about their inability to travel to our world. Even if they do find their way here, there's no army or deity that I'd let take you away from me."

We stood there, letting time slip past us, enjoying a moment to breathe because for once we weren't in a rush to save and fix and go and do. We had a lot of decisions to make in the coming weeks, but we had time to mull them over.

Love radiated down the mating bond, and my eyes closed for a minute as I let the bliss of my mate's presence fill me.

It was an odd place to find peace, amongst the dead, but something about being surrounded by centuries of queens gave me a quiet strength, a gratitude for my life.

Sebastian and I took a couple steps to the left and stood in front of the next photo. It must have been taken decades ago because Queen Mari looked healthy and full of life. She had the same flat line of her mouth that the other queens had, but her eyes sparkled with a humor and zest that I'd seen in Adriana.

I didn't know what I should feel staring up at my mate's mother. The female who'd at one point seemed to love her son deeply, and at another seemed to only see him as a tool. Adriana's memories of their mother only added to the rage that flickered alive when I thought about her.

He'd told me the Queen knew about the draxis. Knew that her son took high priestesses' powers to keep her alive, though they never discussed it out right.

I'd only had two interactions with her and had conflicting feelings. And having heard Sebastian's shadow's opinion, as well as knowing his own, I knew I wasn't the only one who didn't know how to feel.

After our second healing ritual, he'd told me about the memory that had triggered his flashbacks. He said he had finally gotten to a place that he could verbalize the memory without reliving it.

To have so brutally lost both of his parents—the only adults who had ever treated him with love and acceptance—was horrific. It was no wonder Sebastian grew up trying desperately to atone for his perceived sins, trying to get his mother's love.

But Palagui always came first for her. The country was more important than the high priestesses' powers. More important than her darkyra son who had to deal with the trauma of taking them. More important than her high priestess daughter whose life would have been siphoned by the crown she'd inherit.

As if echoing my thoughts, Sebastian said, "She wasn't a great mother." He pursed his lips. "But in her day, she was a great queen."

The words hung in the air between us.

I thought about all the decisions I'd made as queen so far. I wanted Palagui to prosper, wanted people who were struggling to find safety and hope. I wanted to change the world for the better, but...

I peeked up at Sebastian. I would always choose to protect him, protect my friends, my family.

And I wouldn't regret that choice.

I would always do my best for the citizens of Palagui. To be fair and to help those who needed it. To work hard to find solutions and keep an open mind about issues.

But I wouldn't be in this mausoleum. I didn't want to be remembered as a great queen.

I wanted to be remembered as a devoted mate, a loving daughter, a loyal best friend, and the best auntie ever to my friends' children.

That was what was most important to me. And I didn't give a damn what anyone else thought about it.

Sebastian exhaled a heavy sigh. His bitter sadness shifted as he took the first step toward closure.

Hand-in-hand, we started toward the door, and as we left, I realized what the next steps for Palagui would need to be.

***

I rubbed my eyes and pinched the bridge of my nose. A non-crown induced headache was forming. The same way all of my non-crown induced headaches formed nowadays.

"What now, Vince?"

"I have a proposal I'd like to bring forward," he said.

We could still kill him, my shadow offered.

I sucked my lips into my mouth to hide my smile. I knew shadows had flashed in my eyes when Sebastian's gaze narrowed in on me. We'd gone back to sitting across from one another in council meetings since we didn't have to worry about bond sickness anymore.

I know that look, he said in my head. *Either you're thinking about killing or fucking. Which is it?*

I smiled. *Both now.*

He smirked.

Will you back me up if I strangle Vince with my shadows? I asked.

Always, he said. *You could murder everyone in this room and I'd back you up.*

My mate and I were not heroes, but despite our shadows' desire for destruction and killing, we managed to do our best to run the country.

I exhaled dramatically, turning to the soliser who'd held a dagger to my best friend's throat, who'd been a pain in my ass since day one, who'd went undercover as a double agent to infiltrate SoCo and was one of the people we had to thank for finally bringing Caroline and the terrorist group down.

"Let me guess," I said. "You'd like to propose knocking down public schools, religious facilities, and parks to make way for luxury high-rise condominiums?"

He squinted his eyes and gave me an annoyed look. "I would never suggest that."

"Uh huh."

"Everyone knows people buying condominiums will pay more if they are near public parks," he said, rolling his eyes. "I have a few developers in Merbany who would like to knock down the decrepit buildings along Oak and Schuster. They proposed condos, but if you'd rather have apartments, I'm sure they would be amendable."

I narrowed my eyes. "Oak and Schuster..." I racked my brain. "Aren't those the affordable housing apartments?"

Vince worked his jaw. "Yes...But I think we can get them to put in at least ten units at fifty percent area median income."

"No," I said.

"Okay, fifteen units," Vince said, sighing as if put out.

"No."

"Maybe before denying it outright, like you do every proposal I bring forward, you should think about the new development and how it will generate tax dollars for Palagui since I know we are sorely lacking—"

I tuned Vince out.

Part of me wished I could have gotten rid of him, that he was working with SoCo and I could have arrested him too.

But unfortunately, that wasn't what happened.

"You're related?" I had all but screeched at Daria in the field outside the research center. Then I'd immediately scrunched up my face in repulsion. Vince had made a lot of sexual innuendos toward Daria.

Daria sighed. "My *foster* brother and I didn't grow up together. We only met when we were sixteen and were sent to the same group home."

"We don't share blood," Vince said and shrugged. "Or any other bodily fluids for that matter." He smirked. "At least not anymore."

"You're disgusting," Daria deadpanned. "And I hate you."

He curled his lip. "I hate you too."

"Vince was your connection to the council?" Gwen said, aghast. She mumbled something like "Annabelle said..." But I couldn't quite make it out. She'd never mentioned an Annabelle before. Maybe I misheard her.

"Someone explain," Sebastian said. "Or I reserve the right to twist his neck."

So Daria did.

Vince had been calling Daria every week since she'd disappeared. He left her long detailed messages about what was happening at the council meetings and about SoCo. He knew that even if she wasn't answering, she was planning something behind the scenes. For all their antagonism, apparently Daria and Vince had an alliance when it came down to it. That was why he was so concerned about Daria's whereabouts during the first council meeting.

I couldn't exactly parse the intricacies of their relationship. Something like a mix between sibling rivalry and exes who hated each other but worked together?

Vince needed things from Daria that he couldn't get without getting his hands dirty. Daria needed Vince's connections to Xenos's inner circle.

Daria's vigilante bar was also the meeting place for her secret resistance group. Darkyras, high priestesses, and even solisers who fought for human and darkyra rights, who helped Daria enact her vigilante justice, all met there.

After the hurricane, Daria didn't plan on coming back to the council, even after Vince assured her that we'd forgiven her for her part in getting us into prison. Her efforts—helping get people out of the city before the hurricane—had reminded her that working on the ground floor had always been her calling, not politics.

She didn't say as much, but the way her eyes kept darting to Gwen, I think she was also scared to face her.

But when Vince told her about SoCo's threats, she started digging into it, and they figured out the group was being funded by wealthy solisers in Merbany. Vince and Leva went undercover into the group.

"Why the hell didn't you just tell us?" I asked, exasperated.

"Would you have believed me?" Vince asked.

No. I thought about the bargain of loyalty he'd made to us. About his threats to endure the pain of the bargain to betray us.

I pressed my lips together. "I'd have believed Leva or Daria."

"Leva didn't get involved until the end when SoCo got into contact with Caroline," Vince said. "And as for Daria..." He looked at his foster sister.

Daria winced. "I'm sorry. It's my fault he didn't tell you. I couldn't..." She shifted on her feet. "I thought if I took care of everything in the background, no one would ever need to know."

"And the attack at court? On the palace?" Sebastian asked, glaring at Vince.

He sighed. "I asked you if you'd be at court that day. You told me you'd be at the festival. If I'd wanted to actually hurt you, I could have sent the group to your house, but I knew you weren't staying at the palace."

"SoCo didn't trust him," Daria said. "They wanted Vince to prove he was on their side. He had to give them something."

Vince planned the attacks, but he knew the wards at the palace would hold SoCo off, and he was the one that went into court and started the active shooter warning, hoping to keep everyone safe.

I thought about how insistent he'd been when he asked if Sebastian and I would be in court on the day of the festival. How he kept asking if we would be there all day. He hadn't just been trying to be annoying. He'd been trying to make sure we wouldn't be caught in the crossfire.

"Except they all went awol,' Vince said. "Taking hostages and burning everything, and I certainly didn't know they were planning on livestreaming the whole thing. It was supposed to be a protest to scare you. I had no idea they were going to actually hurt people."

"We were going to come clean after that clusterfuck," Daria said. "But then one of the SoCo leaders said Caroline had been in contact with him. Apparently, they had a relationship of some sort in the past. Caroline needed a way to get into Palagui undetected to corner you and take the crown, but everything happened so fast."

"I knew shit was going south," Vince said. "There was no way it couldn't after the attacks. That's why I left the coded messages."

Sebastian sighed. "Delilah mentioned those, but I haven't seen her today." He took out his phone and showed me the screen. Thirty missed calls from Delilah and dozens of texts.

Vince is working undercover with SoCo. Call me was the preview of the first text.

"See?" Vince said, casually putting his hands in his pockets. "I'm a good guy."

I gave him an incredulous look.

"Vince was going to lead Caroline and the rest of SoCo to the palace, and I was going to meet them there with my army," Daria said. "We were going to finish this. And then I could come to you, hoping to have earned your forgiveness by killing your enemies, hoping that would make up for getting the two of you tortured in prison."

"Oh Daria," Sebastian said, shaking his head. His shoulders slumped.

Daria stared at her feet and shrugged.

If anyone could understand Daria's need to earn forgiveness, it was going to be Sebastian.

"Hoping it'd make up for keeping you locked in my basement," she added, glancing at Gwen, who pressed her lips together and broke eye contact.

Daria took a deep breath. "Then Vince changed the plan, and my darkyras had to sift the high priestesses and solisers here. It took a while to move this many people."

"It was going to be safer to battle here than at the palace," Vince said. "There'd be no innocent people involved. I learned my lesson from the disaster at court."

"The scientists? The high priestesses? You were going to let them die?" I asked.

"I knew the wards around the research center would protect them," Vince said. "And the research center is more remote than the palace. There was no chance of any bystanders this time."

Which was how despite Vince being the needle in my side and the villain I'd pinned everything on in my head, he was sitting next to me at the council meeting, trying to convince me to displace people from their homes so his already wealthy constituents could make more money.

"You aren't going to win this one," Sebastian said. Vince opened his mouth to protest, but Sebastian flicked out a shadow to zip his lips. "Your voice is grating my last nerve."

Vince crossed his arms and slumped down. Sebastian hadn't closed his nose, so he should just be happy my mate is nicer than I am.

"Uhm, actually," Leva said, straightening in her seat. "Vince and I have been in discussions with a startup in the city. We were going to suggest a joint venture between the Merbany developers and a Palagui City nonprofit. I think together they could make a return on their investment and also increase the number of affordable housing units."

A few weeks ago, hearing Leva say she was working on a proposal with Vince would have made me suspicious that he was going to take advantage of her, but just because she was shy didn't mean she was a pushover. She'd already proved as much.

Sebastian released Vince's mouth.

Vince scoffed. "If you would have let me finish, I was going to say that. I was just priming the negotiation."

Aurelio snorted. "Priming the negotiation? You know, for a soliser, you sure are shady."

Vince scowled, but he didn't look at the human representative across from him.

Gwen snickered. "Yeah, Vince. You wanna shine a little *sun*light on what you're actually up to this time?"

I ignored their goading and inclined my head to Leva. "Would you mind getting us their business plan and official proposal? We'll review it for next week's meeting."

She nodded eagerly, writing in her notepad.

Vince mumbled something under his breath, but we all ignored him as Gerald said, "James Endlouer, the soliser who protected the hostages from the attack on court got out of the hospital today. If your schedules allow, I think we should hold the ceremony to award his medal of bravery next month?"

"That sounds good," I said. "My new assistant will make sure everything is planned."

"Harrison reached out to me," Sebastian said. "He claims Delnee had nothing to do with the coup and they didn't even know Caroline was in the country. They want a diplomatic meeting with us. Want Rien to come home."

Rien had stayed in Palagui for the last few weeks. He told his father he wasn't being held hostage, but I wondered if he believed him.

"Rien is ready to go back," Delilah said. "And I'd like to propose that I go with him."

I furrowed my brow. "Why?" Since when were they talking to one another?

"I've spoken to the Society," she said. "We're concerned about the legacy high priestesses in Delnee. The only ones left in their country are the elderly or the ones who aren't equipped to lead their military. We agreed it would be best to send one of ours to lead their Society."

"Harrison would never go for that," Sebastian said.

Delilah shrugged. "No probably not, but Harrison knows we know that he betrayed us. If you make it a condition of your peace talks, he will have to go for it. Delnee needs Palagui as an ally. Even more now that their fae military has just been gutted."

It would be good to have someone over there. Someone to keep an eye on things and to keep Rien safe too.

"You've been voted as rep. You want to leave?" Sebastian said.

"Gwen and I have worked out an agreement," Delilah said, staring at Gwen, who nodded. "We're going to be co-reps. She was already going to be my second. She knows what needs to be done. And the Society's board already agreed this was in the best interest of the high priestesses. We stick together, no matter what country we belong to."

Our compulsion over Harrison might have delayed Delnee's plans against us, but none of us believed that would deter them forever. We were under no illusions that Delnee was a true ally, and if we had

Delilah and Rien over there to keep an eye on things, maybe it could buy us a few years of peace until we shored up our defenses and proved to them it would be stupid to start a war they couldn't win.

"Gwen and Rien have been getting me up to speed on the happenings in Delnee," Delilah said. "I only need the approval of my queen and king."

I think it's a good idea, I said to Sebastian.

He nodded.

"Okay. You have our approval," I said. "We'll discuss it with Harrison next week."

"Speaking of," Gwen said. "The Society is asking you for leniency on behalf of the legacy high priestesses involved in the attack."

"And what do you think?" I asked.

Gwen sighed. She'd been to the prison once to see her mother but refused to talk about it. I think she was still processing the whiplash of her mother's behavior. She'd started to let her guard down and open up to her mother's affections, only to be betrayed, and then was told she did it all to protect her.

In a lot of ways, Gwen's mother and Daria had done the same thing to her, which I think is why she's having trouble talking to either of them.

As it stood, Evelynne, the legacy high priestesses, and the solisers involved in the attack were all being held in prison and awaiting sentencing.

"Loyalty is the basis for being a high priestess," Gwen started slowly. "They went into battle thinking they were protecting their sisters from evil. It's not their fault they didn't have all the facts right."

I drummed my fingers on the table. We were intimately aware of the consequences of trusting the wrong person, of trusting Caroline in particular. "Maybe we could come to some sort of arrangement.

If they are willing to follow Delilah, maybe we send them back to Delnee with some conditions in place. Maybe a fealty bargain?"

Gwen nodded.

"And the solisers of SoCo?" Gerald asked.

SoCo was a completely different situation. Those people weren't forced into the military by their government. Yes, they believed they were saving people from evil, but they chose which facts to believe in. The high priestesses didn't.

Still…wasn't mercy and second chances what a good queen should offer?

"I'll consult with some experts to see if they are capable of reforming their views," I said. "But I can't promise anything. The solisers in Palagui need to see that we won't tolerate their faction discrimination and violence."

Gerald wasn't going to push it and only brought anything up at all because he had a duty as the soliser representative.

"We just better hope there isn't another prison break before your reforms take place," Jeremy said. He'd joined Blake's public relations team after he'd finished physical therapy. Fortunately, all the former draxis had recovered quickly.

"Yes," I said. "Well, that won't be a problem."

No one besides us knew that the crown had been destroyed or that it had never actually given the citizens their power to begin with.

In fact, without the crown, Palagui's people have had an increase in power since there was no longer a siphon resting on my head. Which, on top of Blake's campaigning on my behalf, had all but made the Queen of Darkness hatred go away.

Even reluctant solisers and their media couldn't deny that my queendom wasn't benefiting them.

The citizens had more power than their parents, grandparents, and great grandparents ever had. They attributed their increase in power to me. If there was anything that was going to win the fae people over, it was giving them more power.

Which, okay, yeah, I kind of did make their powers increase, but not in the way they thought.

Everyone assumed that it took a few months for the effect of a new queen to take hold. Sloane explained that Karina told her, an increase in power also increases endorphins and happy hormones, which explained why everyone in Palagui was better off than they had been.

I just hoped it stuck.

We talked about how we would tell people that the crown and the queen weren't the cause, but we hadn't come up with a solution that wouldn't incite a rebellion or another call for my head.

We needed to slowly introduce that the citizens were responsible for their own power and could generate it through rituals and community gatherings. It'd likely take years, maybe decades, to get the traditionalist fae of Palagui to start to see a new way of life.

But I didn't plan to be queen for the rest of my life. And I wasn't going to have a child to pass the power to, so we needed to figure out how to transition Palagui from a monarchy to…something else.

Granted, we might need to find a solution faster than we'd hoped.

The council meeting ended, and everyone filed out except Sebastian, Gwen, and me.

"I heard back from the biggest nation in the east," Sebastian said as he collected his papers in front of him. "They want to give us aid money to help modernize our infrastructure and offered to sponsor our permits with the International Aviation Org for an aerial military."

It was something we needed. For the last hundred years as Queen Mari deteriorated, Palagui's infrastructure had aged. Along with the destruction from the hurricane, we were severely in need of upgrades to keep the country safe.

"Why do they want to help us now?" I asked.

He sighed. "I've been in talks with them for years, but when they heard about us pushing back Delnee…It got them interested."

"And the fact they want to improve our military isn't a coincidence?" Gwen asked.

Sebastian shook his head. "They want to help us because they want us to *convince* Delnee to give power back to the fae."

"They want us to go to war," I deadpanned.

"We might already be in war," Sebastian said. "It's not like it was a hundred years ago. We don't march in lines and fight until one side gives up. Entire countries have been invaded and occupied without an official declaration. It's economic and political manipulations that dominate modern warfare."

I rubbed my temples. "Can we figure out how to be friends with them without committing to leading the charge against Delnee?"

Sebastian shrugged. "Maybe, but that's not their only condition."

"What else do they want? My first born?" I joked.

Sebastian didn't laugh. "They want Palagui to be a democracy. We'd have to step down."

"Why?" I asked. "We have democracy at every level. We're just like presidents."

"Unelected presidents," Gwen said.

It was already our plan to move in that direction, but we needed time. We needed to get Palagui to stability. Needed to change the cultural stigma against humans and darkyras and make sure that the president they elected wasn't a soliser factionist.

Although…wasn't that the point of democracy?

Maybe this was exactly why leaders became dictators. Everyone thought they knew what was best. Would I continue to put off stepping down because Palagui wasn't *ready*?

"We can't afford to lose their friendship," I said. "Not with how strained our relationship with Delnee is. I don't want Palagui to be stuck in another position of having no help when we need it. Let's talk to them. If they see we are willing to play ball, maybe they'll be more inclined to keep us in power until after they get what they want from Delnee."

I hadn't wanted to be queen…but now that I was, I didn't want to give up the political power.

The hypocrisy clawed inside my chest. My darkyra power was stolen and given to me by chance. I'd stolen the crown's power and only held on to it by chance too.

How could I feel entitled to something I didn't earn? Something I shouldn't have had to begin with?

But maybe that was life.

We were all given some level of privilege that we hadn't earned. Luck and fate intertwined to give some people more opportunity than others. All that mattered is what we did with it.

There'd always be people who didn't agree with my decisions. People who hated me and what I stood for. But I could use my position for good while I had it.

I didn't need to worry about becoming a dictator because I still had—I'd always had—discernment. My shadow was ruthless and vengeful, but I wasn't only my shadow. I was my healing high priestess light too.

And I had the inner strength to decide which power I needed to step into at any given moment. I knew what mattered. I valued family and friends and making the world a better place for everyone. It was remembering my friends and Sebastian that had given me the strength to break Kai's illusions while I was in the prison. It was holding to my values of equity, fairness, and protecting those who couldn't protect themselves that guided my decisions as queen so far.

And it was those values I would continue to lead with. Those values that I'd use to make decisions. And when the time came for us to step down, we wouldn't resist.

We knew what was really important in life.

Chapter Fifty-Five

Amaya

"It's honestly so ugly," Sloane said.

"Really tacky," Gwen added. "We should smash it to pieces."

I sighed. "But isn't it a historical relic? Should we be smashing historic relics?"

"But it'd be so much fun," Gwen said.

Gwen tilted her head, sizing up the piece in front of us. She'd been a little...worked up in the last few weeks. After seeing her mother in prison, Sloane had dragged Gwen into my bedroom, and we'd spent the weekend in bed watching Palagui's version of reality tv.

We'd hoped she would open up about her mother or about why she was avoiding Daria after their passionate kiss on the battlefield.

Like she always did, she shut us down. She didn't want to talk about her feelings and said she couldn't be blamed for her actions after almost being killed by her aunt while her mother watched.

She forgave Daria, but that didn't mean she wanted to be with her. She said she didn't need to be in a relationship to be happy, and she would appreciate it if her best friends didn't question her relationship status every time they saw her.

Sloane and I apologized and promised we would stop asking.

That didn't mean Sloane and I didn't meet each other's eye every time Gwen and Daria had an awkward yet cordial conversation.

Gwen buzzed with pent-up energy that I wouldn't call sexual tension…but I wouldn't *not* call it that either.

Sloane smiled mischievously as she brought high priestess light to her palms. She and Nico moved out of the apartment above the garage to Molbridge. Sloane started working at the healing center but was still deciding if she wanted to go back to school. For now, she was just trying it out. She'd even managed to get her grandmother to move to Palagui. With everything that happened, it was easy to convince her she would be safer here.

Nico got a job at the youth center in Molbridge, and they were buying a house near the coast. Gwen and I were sad that she was moving so far away, but I could sift us to her, or her to us, whenever we wanted. We spent most weekends together.

Ironically, Gwen moved into the apartment over the garage.

A point that Nico made sure to bring up in every conversation.

"Do you plan to mooch off your friend forever?" he would tease her.

To which she would ignore, and Sloane would playfully scold Nico.

It was dusk, and the setting sun made the top floor of court look eerily like it had the first time I'd been here. The ground was sticky with spilt alcohol, and the air still held the faint whiff of desperation. The difference being there were no naked females dancing, or drugs being passed around on trays, or giant lizard creatures eating humans.

Still, the memories made my skin crawl.

Needless to say, maybe we all had a little pent-up aggression we needed to take out on something.

"Alright," I said. "Fuck it."

I held up my palms, and white light gathered in my hands. Sloane squealed, and Gwen made an excited growling noise in the back of her throat as she followed suit.

The three of us focused our light on the golden fire throne. Power thrummed between us, brightening the otherwise dark space.

No one had been up here since Xenos died. One of the janitors had asked if I wanted to redecorate to prepare for all the galas I was supposed to hold here.

I'd shaken my head and told them to sell everything.

But I had second thoughts this evening because what if I'd just told them to sell some thousand-year-old family heirloom?

I dragged Sloane and Gwen upstairs with me and texted Sebastian and Nico to meet us here when they had a chance.

If the throne did turn out to be a historic relic, it represented the solisers dominion over everyone, and maybe it was wrong, but it sure felt good to destroy.

Our power heated the throne, melting the gold, until the decorative fire cracked, and tiny fissures turned into one large split up the middle.

We lowered our hands. Our mouths hung agape at what was hidden underneath.

The gold fell in pieces, leaving a perfectly preserved black opal structure in its place. Golden spirals over took the legs and arms. The seven phases of the moon were silver adornments at the top of the seat.

I smiled. "I don't want to smash that."

"No definitely not," Sloane said, with an appreciative lilt to her voice.

We silently admire the throne, until...

"First one on the throne gets to be queen for the day!" Gwen said and sprinted forward.

"I'm queen every day!" I said but ran after her.

Gwen jogged backward "Oh, did I forget to mention? Queen gets to pick the show we watch when we get home."

Sloane and I picked up the pace to catch up with her.

Giggling, we fought and pushed each other to sit on the throne. I took an elbow to the face, and I'm pretty sure I was squishing Sloane's thigh by sitting on her and trying to get her to move with my hip. Gwen shimmied her way on the other side, and all three of us managed to fit together, sort of, just barely.

"Huh, here I thought the queen was supposed to be noble and regal," Nico called out as he and Sebastian walked in from the hall. He pretended to look around the room. "Don't see that anywhere."

"How dare you!" I said.

"No insulting the queens!" Gwen exclaimed.

"Off with his head!" Sloane commanded in a haughty tone.

Our laughter echoed through the room. My stomach pinched from giggling so hard.

My heart was so full, the sweet unyielding love of my friends filled me with an effervescence that lifted my spirits and reassured my fears. No matter what happened to Palagui, my friends would be beside me through it all.

Sebastian leaned against one of the booths across the way, his arms crossed over his chest, watching us with a smile on his face.

I curled my finger and beckoned him over.

He pushed off the booth and strode toward me, hands in his pockets. I reached up and pulled his face down to mine, kissing him long and deep until I was breathless.

"This is making me very uncomfortable," Gwen said with her usual faux disgust.

"I think it's hot," Sloane said and waved Nico over.

He ran to her like his life depended on it.

"Ew." Gwen pushed me. "Go do that somewhere else."

I grinned and rolled my eyes, hopping off the throne and grabbing Sebastian's hand to drag him to the outer edge of the top floor.

"Wait, who won? Who picks what we watch tonight?" Sloane asked.

"I do," Gwen said.

"Fine," Sloane said.

Nico made a groaning noise.

I shook my head at them and left them to their needling.

Sebastian and I looked out the floor-to-ceiling windows. The view was spectacular. I could see why Xenos didn't want it to be blocked. The skyscrapers dotted the landscape, but I could see the ocean in the distance. The sun had set, and streetlights and cars blinked in the darkness.

The immensity of the city didn't overwhelm me or make me feel trapped like it had when I first arrived. The insecurity I'd tried to outrun by escaping to Pointedelle a year ago hadn't completely gone away. There were days when I questioned myself and my competence, but I didn't let those feelings overtake me. I reminded myself how much I'd conquered, and how that strength—that power—had always been inside me.

I felt Sebastian's eyes on the side of my face and glanced at him.

"What?" I said, blushing from the heat in his gaze.

"I'm just thinking about the first time I saw you."

"When I was passed out on the sidewalk from the draxis?" I scoffed. "Real attractive."

He smiled and shook his head. "Before that."

I furrowed my brow. "What?"

Sebastian put his hands on my hips and pulled me in. I put my hands on his forearms. "The first time I saw you, my shadow was in control. I didn't have the memory until we integrated."

My lips parted in shock.

"I'd come to Delnee after having just taken a bunch of high priestesses' powers. My shadow fought me for control, and I was too weak to stop him." He smiled ruefully. "My shadow walked us to a bar in the business district, huddled us away in a booth in the back, wearing sunglasses indoors to hide our void eyes."

I laughed softly picturing it.

"He was annoyed that the bar was so empty and there was no havoc to create." He rolled his eyes. "But just as he got up to leave, a beautiful girl walked in with her suitcase."

My face slackened.

"She looked a little frazzled and nervous," he said and curled a piece of my hair behind my ear. 'But it was like my whole world had rearranged itself. I watched you looking around the bar and begged for your eyes to land on me, but they skated by. I decided I was going to talk to you, but my shadows started rebelling, seeping out of my fingertips. There was a horrible pounding in my head as the other half of me used the distraction to start fighting to regain control."

He shook his head. "I left through the back, too afraid that if I walked past you to get to the door, if I smelled your scent, or heard your voice, I'd lose it completely."

A chill went up my spine.

"I walked around the city in a daze, and finally wrestled control of my body back from my shadow. I felt this terrible ache in my heart and reacted without thought, sifting to find you lying in that alley. I'd thought that was the first time I'd seen you, but it was only the first time that part of me had seen you."

"Are you..." I said, swallowing. "This really happened?" Tears welled in my eyes because if this was true, that would mean that Sebastian had noticed me—his shadow noticed me—before Kai had given me powers to force the mating bond, before my high priestess powers had even activated.

His fingers trailed along my face as he nodded. "Would you like to see the memory?"

Epilogue

Sebastian – Six months later

The echo of laughter bounced off the sand dunes from the patio below the balcony, but I couldn't take my eyes off the waves in the distance. They crashed violently onto the beach.

They weren't warning of another natural disaster. It was just the changing of tides that came with the start of the fall season.

And still, an anxious energy kept my shadows on edge. I couldn't stop myself from wondering if this perfectly normal weather pattern was some kind of bad omen.

SoCo would rise again. Kai would come back. Harrison would attack and destroy Palagui.

I'd lose Amaya. I'd lose my friends. I'd lose everything.

A door shut from inside the bedroom. Amaya's footsteps came closer.

"My parents will be here soon," she said, opening a drawer and rummaging around. "They insisted on driving instead of letting me sift them. Said they wanted to take the scenic route." I could hear the shrug in her voice. "I guess I understand. There's so much of the country I haven't seen either, and it's good that they are adjusting..."

I felt her step out onto the balcony without needing to turn. Her arms wrapped around my waist from behind, and she rested her head on my back.

"We could take the scenic route next time," I said, trying and failing to take my eyes off the ocean. "I'll show you the country."

She didn't respond right away.

I was glad Amaya's parents were settling into Palagui with such ease. They'd stayed with us in the townhouse for a few months, but after they'd developed empathic powers, it made things a little uncomfortable for everyone.

Turns out it was harder to hide our bond's feelings than it was our own. We tried to shield it, but it wasn't a regular emotion that could be boxed up and pushed away. There was no fortress we could build around it because it lived outside of both of us, in our auras, in the ether between us.

They purchased a home in Molbridge because the suburban setting reminded them of Bellstead. Their house wasn't far from Sloane and Nico's actually.

"What's wrong?" Amaya's voice was soft and concerned.

I tapped her hands, which were resting over my heart. "Nothing," I said automatically, and then sighed, knowing she'd sense my lie.

She waited while I tried to gather my thoughts.

"I feel like things are too…" An especially brutal wave crashed on the shoreline, and more laughter from below melded into the soundscape. "Good."

It was ridiculous. I didn't want things to be bad. I didn't want to deal with natural disasters, and terrorism, and torture.

But without an impending crisis, I felt like I was living in limbo, bracing myself for the next terrible thing to happen.

There were issues I could focus on like what was going to happen with Delnee or whether we should get into a deal with the countries in the east, but none of those were pressing or demanding at the moment.

When the adrenaline died off, I'd been exhausted. I'd thought I needed to rest and recover, but I didn't feel refreshed…I just felt uneasy.

Amaya nodded against my back. "It's like when you're trying to fall asleep and you jerk yourself awake. You were almost there, but *bam* you're hit with sudden dread, and even though your conscious mind didn't want to, it shook you awake."

"Yes," I sighed. "Exactly."

Amaya released me long enough to shimmy her way between me and the railing. With her hands on my face, she dragged my eyes off the ocean and onto her.

"I don't know if you and I will ever be able to let go of the pieces of us that are always a bit afraid of not being good enough or that feel we need to stay alert for the next bad thing to happen," she said.

I narrowed my eyes playfully. "This is the worst pep talk I've ever heard."

She pinched my side. "Hold on. I'm not done."

I chuckled.

"The only way we can enjoy the moments of happiness that we do have is by not getting upset when the rolling sense of dread or spike of anxiety comes in." She shrugged. "When I jerk myself awake, instead of staring at the ceiling and wishing I could just stop being so anxious...I try to take a few deep breaths and realize that my brain or my shadow is just trying to keep me safe."

I took a deep breath and exhaled it out. This pep talk was sounding similar to the one I'd given her in the meadow when her depression from binding her powers had reappeared.

I'd have to let the emotion happen without resisting it.

"We're never going to stop our instinct to scan the horizon and look for the next problem that's coming our way," she continued. "But we can catch ourselves doing it and choose to look for something good instead."

I put my arm around her and tucked her head under my chin. "That was a pretty good pep talk," I conceded.

She giggled and squeezed me. "I told you."

The ocean crashed against the shore, but I didn't let it catch my gaze. I leaned back and looked into Amaya's eyes. "You," I said. "You are my good thing."

She smiled and reached up on her tiptoes to kiss me. "You're *my* good thing."

Our kiss deepened, and the bond thrummed between us, hungry and eager for a physical expression of our love, but a car door slammed and voices filtered up.

We would have probably ignored them, ignored our friends drinking and eating on the patio below us, if it weren't for Amaya's father's voice echoing from the side yard. "Where are the kids?"

"Can't you feel that?" her mother said. "They're upstairs."

"Oh." Her father's voice went flat. "Yeah."

We pulled apart. I chuckled at the blush on Amaya's cheeks.

"Come on," she said. "Let's go downstairs."

We'd invited everyone over to the beach house for one last outdoor get-together before it got too cold.

"Want me to start grilling?" Amaya's father asked as he handed me a bottle of wine.

"Sure. I'll get the stuff from inside," I said.

"No need," Amaya's mother said and grabbed my arm, pulling me down so she could kiss my cheek in greeting. "I've got it. You go relax." She refused my offer of help and hauled two armfuls of groceries into the kitchen.

Amaya took the fruit platter from her father and went to the patio table.

I went back out to their car, knowing that they'd have at least one more load of pre-made goodies to bring in. Amaya's parents always came with enough food to feed us for a week.

It was odd to me, given I don't think my mother had ever cooked anything in her life, but I liked it.

They'd truly accepted me into their family, despite everything I put their daughter through. Not just me either. All of us were their "kids" now. Even though Nico and I were decades older than them, we'd all been unofficially adopted.

I grabbed the last of the containers from the backseat and brought them inside.

Amaya's mother was already pulling the cutting board out of the cupboard.

"Oh, you didn't have to do that!" she said as I put the bags on the counter.

"It's fine, really," I said.

She smiled. "How are you doing?"

"Good."

She stared at me expectantly.

I sighed. Empaths were really the worst. I glanced out the kitchen window. Amaya's back was to us, but she was talking exuberantly with her hands to Nico.

"I'm good," I said, turning back to help wash the vegetables. "Really."

Amaya's mother patted my shoulder. "Good." She glanced out the window and squinted her eyes. "What are they doing?"

Amaya had turned toward us. Her face was bright red and scrunched up. Tears streaked down her face.

Panic jolted through me, and I sifted outside.

Sloane and Gwen were chanting Amaya's name, while Nico was lounging in the patio chair, popping hot peppers into his mouth like they were candy.

Amaya was blinking away tears and chewing with an open mouth, looking like she was in physical pain.

She made a distressed noise and went to the bushes and spit.

"You win," she choked out.

Nico stood, his chair scraping along the cement. He threw his fists up in triumph.

"Nico," I growled. "Want to tell me why you're making my mate cry?"

"Can't help that your mate has the palate of a baby straight from the womb," he said.

"We were bonding," Amaya said between gulps of water.

"And determining the order of our brackets," Nico said as he shuffled a deck of cards. "You want in? If you want a chance to play, you have to eat at least five hot peppers. Thems the rules."

"No thanks," I said.

Nico shrugged. "Suit yourself."

Gwen sat down across from Nico and cracked her knuckles. "Ready to lose again fire breather?"

"Maybe I should let you win," Nico said. "Since you're so hard up on cash that you have to mooch off your friends by living in their garage apartment."

I went back into the kitchen, tuning out Nico and Gwen's smack talk. I spent the rest of the afternoon inside with Amaya's mother, discussing Molbridge and their new home.

Sure enough, by the time I came back out, Gwen was flinging her cards on the table.

"Ha!" she said.

Nico narrowed his eyes, but his features fell as he saw what she had. "You're a fucking cheater," he mumbled.

"It's okay, babe," Sloane cooed, patting Nico's shoulder.

Gwen smirked.

"Best three out of five," Nico said.

Gwen raised an eyebrow. "No way. I won. Pay up."

"What happened to the bracket?" I asked, sitting beside Amaya.

"No more bracket," Amaya whispered. "When Gwen loses, she demands a rematch. When Nico loses, he does the same."

"We could be here all night," Sloane added.

"No," Gwen said. "We aren't because I won. Pay up." She held out her hand.

Nico sighed and unclasped the gold cuffs on each of his wrists and slid them over to Gwen.

"Aren't those family heirlooms?" I asked.

"Yes," Nico mumbled. "You better not hock them at a pawn shop or something."

"These are all mine now. I can do whatever I want with them," Gwen said.

"What did Gwen wager?" I asked.

"The earrings her mother gave her." Sloane shrugged. "They were her great-great grandmothers."

I wondered if Gwen was willing to wager them because she didn't want ties to her family anymore.

"So," Gwen said, weighing the cuffs in her hand as if trying to determine their worth. Nico glared at her. "I invited Daria," she said in a rushed whisper.

It took a second for the girls to react

"Oh, you did, did you?" Sloane said.

"Well, that's nice," Amaya said, grinning at her.

"Don't start," Gwen said, not looking at them. "It's not what you think."

Amaya and Sloane shared a look.

"Okay," Amaya said. "I swear we won't say another word, but..."

Gwen glanced at her.

"Maybe you should let my father borrow those cuffs for the night," Amaya said with a careful tone. "So he doesn't have to feel the *tension* between you two."

Gwen's face pinched as she pushed her tongue into her upper lip, thinking for a moment. Then, she got out of her chair and grabbed the cuffs.

We all watched as she walked over to the grill and said something to Amaya's father. He furrowed his brows but nodded.

Everyone started laughing, and Gwen gave us the middle finger behind her back as she walked inside.

From where we sat, the sound of the waves was muffled by the dunes that surrounded us and drowned out by the laughter and music playing in the background.

As Amaya's father put on the cuffs, I pulled my mate onto my lap.

She threw her arms around my neck, leaning against me. I kissed her shoulder and let her feed me a grape from the food platter in the middle of the table.

"I love you," I whispered into her neck, tightening my grip around her waist.

She kissed me and rested her forehead on mine. "I love you too."

As the sky darkened, we ate and drank and laughed, passing the time enjoying each other's company and being doted on by Amaya's parents.

My mate. My friends. And my new family.

Those were the good things I chose to focus on that night.

The good things I'd always choose to focus on when the waves came crashing in.

Epilogue

Amaya

It snowed on the day of our mating ceremony. The fluffy flakes melted on contact when they hit the top of my head and threatened to undo all the work my hairstylist had done curling my hair into a soft bounce that tumbled around my shoulders.

I forgot to be concerned when I met Sebastian's gaze. The awe and wonder and reverence in his eyes erased all my fears and insecurities.

We'd asked Nico to be our officiant, and I'm sure he did a great job, but I couldn't remember a single word he'd said that day.

I couldn't even remember my vows after they'd left my mouth. I'd memorized them only long enough to recite them, but with the adrenaline of standing in front of a hundred people (and hundreds of thousands who were watching on tv), I'd blacked out most of the ceremony, leaving only the impression of Sebastian's feelings.

I focused on his unconditional love flowing through my veins. On the feel of his fingers clasping the mating cuffs around my wrists. On the way my fourth finger tingled with magic under the ink of our marriage binding tattoo. On the sentence from his own vows that gave me the most hope for our future.

"My world is filled with darkness," he said. "But your love has shown me that I don't have to fear the shadows."

We were two darkyra ruling a country divided, navigating the threat posed by their ally nation, and faking friendships with countries across the world. There would always be things to worry over.

But neither of us needed to hide anymore. Neither of us had to mask our feelings, our fears, our pain. We would get through whatever came next together.

After we'd recited our personal vows, Nico led us through the traditional darkyra vows.

We promised to face the void together and sealed our devotion with a kiss.

As Sebastian's lips landed on mine, I felt the voice of his shadow rumbling from somewhere deep within. His words were an echo of the ones my heart chanted.

Love. Mate. Mine.

THE END

Author Note

Amaya and Sebastian's adventure is over, but the story continues. Read Sloane & Nico's novella, *My Fire My Heart*. Sign up for my author newsletter to be the first to hear about the next release at AlexandraLarson.com.

See where it all began: Read an **exclusive bonus scene** from *Ascend from the Shadows* in Sebastian's point of view, available through my newsletter. Download here: AlexandraLarson.com/Ascend

YouTube and Spotify playlists are available on my website.

Reviews on Amazon really help indie authors. If you'd like to support my work, please consider leaving a review!

Character List

Types of Magical Beings:

Darkyra (dar-kai-ra)—shadow wielders

High Priestess (hi pre-st-euh-st)—healing & emotional powers

Soliser (so-less-er)—fire wielders

Draxis (dr-ax-sis)—shadow demon creatures, humanoid husks that suck up electrical energy, life force, and fae power

Locations:

Palagui (Pal-auh-gwa-i)—The fae country Sebastian & Nico are from

Palagui City (Pal-auh-gwa-i City)—capital city in Palagui

Molbridge (Mol-bridge)—northern town in Palagui

Merbany (Mer-bau-nee)—wealthy southern beach town in Palagui

Delnee (Del-nee)—Amaya, Gwen, & Sloane's home country, human ruled

Pointedelle (Point-dell)—capital city of Delnee

Bellstead (Bell-stead)—Amaya's suburban hometown in Delnee

Characters:

Amaya Mevson (Auh-my-auh Mev-son)—high priestess & darkyra—Gwen & Sloane's best friend, Sebastian's mate

Gwen Nueblots (Gwehn New-blots)—high priestess—Amaya & Sloane's best friend

Sloane Knight (S-loan Night)—high priestess—Amaya & Gwen's best friend, Nico's mate

Sebastian (Bash) Renwick (Suh-bash-ton Ren-wick)—darkyra—Amaya's mate, Nico's best friend

Nico Manguina (Knee-co Man-gwin-auh)—soliser—Sloane's mate, Sebastian's best friend

Rien Astora (Ryan As-tor-auh)—human—Amaya's former lover

Daria Reeves (Dar-e-auh Ree-vu-s)—darkyra—council representative for the darkyras of Palagui

Adriana Laurent (Auh-dree-on-auh Lor-raunt)—high priestess—Sebastian's sister, lost to the portal
Delilah Pembroke (Dee-lye-la Pem-brook)—high priestess—Sebastian's former lover
Jeremy Manaudou (Jer-auh-me Man-auh-do)—darkyra—Sebastian's former boyfriend
Caroline Nueblots (Care-o-line New-blots)—high priestess—Gwen's aunt, council representative for the High Priestess Society of Palagui
Evelynne Nueblots (Ev-auh-lyn New-blots)—high priestess—Gwen's mother, captain of Delnee High Priestess Society and Delnee's military
Harrison Astora (Hair-uh-son As-tor-auh)—human—mayor of Pointedelle turned vice president of Delnee
Silas Thorn (Sigh-las Th-orn)—human—real estate developer in Delnee (Amaya & Sebastian murdered in book 1)
Xenos Laurent (Zen-o-s – lor-raunt)—soliser—Sebastian & Adriana's brother, former Prince of Palagui (Amaya murdered in book 2)
Gerald Manguina (Jer-auh-ld Man-gwin-auh)—soliser—Nico's father, council representative for the solisers of Palagui

Spoiler Warning: The next page starts new characters in book 3. Do not read until the end of Chapter 15.

Darkyra Deity (Kai) (Kuh-eye)—One of the three fae deities; shadow powers

Moon Goddess (Luna) (Lou-na)—One of the three fae deities; healing/emotional powers

Sun God (Saul) (S-all)—One of the three fae deities; fire powers

Vince Kane (Vins K-ay-n)—soliser—council representative of Merbany

Micah Bensen (My-cauh Ben-sen)—high priest—council representative of Molbridge

Erik Barbeau (Air-rick Bar-Bow)—soliser—council representative of Palagui City Region 1

Hugo Bayen (Hugh-go Bay-en)—soliser—former council representative of Palagui City Region 2 (Sebastian killed in book 3)

Leva Lussier (L-euh-va L-auh-see-a)—soliser—council representative of Palagui City Region 2 (replaced Hugo Bayen)

Blake Fletcher (Bl-ay-kuh Fl-euh-tuh-cher)—human—secretary turned administrative assistant for Amaya at court

Aurelio Gustav (Or-elle-ee-oh Gus-tauhv)—human—council representative for the humans of Palagui (introduced in Chapter 32)

Acknowledgements

First and foremost, I want to thank you for reading. Thank you. Thank you. Thank you. Thank you to all of the readers for picking up my books and giving them a shot. I'm so deeply moved and honored that you've chosen to spend time reading this series.

Thank you to Sierra for listening to me complain, encouraging me when I'm at my wits end with self-publishing, and debating romance philosophy and feminist theory with me.

Thank you to Jess and Alex for being such amazing and bright sources of love and encouragement. For being my hype team. For loving Sebastian as much as I do. I hope you feel like all of the cliffhangers paid off and were worth the year of torture I put you through!

Thank you to my family for supporting me! To Momma for proofreading and letting me go on for hours talking about writing. To Jared for listening intently as I read aloud my favorite sections.

Thank you to my cover designer, Stefanie, for once again understanding my vision and executing it beyond what I thought was possible. Thank you to all of my beta readers for soldiering through the early drafts and making the book better with your comments.

My favorite part of writing about magic is making the fantasy mechanisms as true and close to reality as possible. For that I've read several nonfiction books to help shape the narrative. The hurricane aftermath portrayal was based on *A Paradise Built in Hell* (Rebecca Solnit) as well as internet research on Hurricane Katrina. The details about the economics and the international politics of running a small country in modern times were based on several books: *What It Is Like To Go To War* (Karl Marlantes), *Doppelganger: A Trip into the Mirror World* (Naomi Klein) and *The Shock Doctrine* (Naomi Klein), along with the BBC's Five Steps to Tyranny (2001) documentary. The healing Sebastian received in Molbridge, as well as his experience of dissociation, repressed trauma, and complex PTSD were based on *The Body Keeps the Score* (Bessel van der Kolk). The spiritual healing techniques and the details of how fae power works were inspired by *Energy Medicine* (Jill Blakeway) and *The Spiral Dance* (Starhawk).

The Dark Perceptions series is based on my own experience with mental health struggles. I wanted Amaya to go through a journey of finding herself in a way that closely mirrored my own (minus the tatted shadow wielder & magic! Boo!). Ascend (Anxiety), Descend (Depression), and Seize (Inner Strength) were written in order to process and reflect, but also integrate everything that I've learned while in Kara Loewentheil's program: The Feminist Self-Help Society. I wouldn't be the person I am today without it.

If you identified with Amaya's mental health struggles, know that you aren't alone. The more upfront and honest I am about my experiences, the more I realize that there are people out there with the same fears, shame, and pain. But we all deserve to be happy and whole, no matter what anxiety, depression, or society tells us. As Sebastian says throughout the series: you don't have to hide your feelings and you don't have to apologize for having them. Reach out and share your story—normalizing our struggles is the first step to confronting them.

About the Author

Alexandra Larson is a business woman by day and romance author by night. When she's not writing or reading, she's trying to soak up the limited amount of sun the Northern Hemisphere provides.

Sign up for her author newsletter to be the first to know about new releases at AlexandraLarson.com.

www.ingramcontent.com/pod-product-compliance
Lightning Source LLC
Chambersburg PA
CBHW031148310726
48969CB00001B/9